Minette Walters lives in Hampshire with her husband and two children. She has worked as a magazine editor but is now a full-time writer.

With her debut, *The Ice House*, she won the Crime Writers' Association John Creasey Award for the best first crime novel of 1992. Rapidly establishing a reputation as one of the most exciting crime novelists writing today, her second novel, *The Sculptress*, was acclaimed by critics as one of the most compelling and powerful novels of the year and won the Edgar Allan Poe Award for the best crime novel published in America in 1993.

In 1994 Minette Walters achieved a unique triple when *The Scold's Bridle* was awarded the CWA Gold Dagger for best crime novel of the year. Her following novels, *The Dark Room*, *The Echo* and *The Breaker*, were also published to further critical acclaim.

BBC TV has adapted all five novels with huge success, most recently *The Dark Room* starring Dervla Kirwan and James Wilby.

By the same author

The Dark Room

The Echo

The Breaker

The Shape of Snakes

Acid Row

Fox Evil

Disordered Minds

MINETTE WALTERS

THE Ice House & THE Sculptress

PAN BOOKS

The Ice House first published 1992 by Macmillan.
First published in paperback 1993 by Pan Books and reissued 1998.
The Sculptress first published 1993 by Macmillan.
First published in paperback 1996 by Pan Books.

This omnibus first published 2006 by Pan Books
an imprint of Pan Macmillan Ltd
Pan Macmillan, 20 New Wharf Road, London N1 9RR
Basingstoke and Oxford
Associated companies throughout the world
www.panmacmillan.com

ISBN-13: 978-0-330-44683-9
ISBN-10: 0-330-44683-5

Grateful acknowledgement is made to Encyclopaedia Britannica, Inc.,
for permission to quote from ***Encyclopaedia Britannica***,
15th edition (1992), 12:535

1 3 5 7 9 8 6 4 2

A CIP catalogue record for this book is available from
the British Library.

Printed and bound in Great Britain by
Mackays of Chatham plc, Chatham, Kent

THE
Ice House

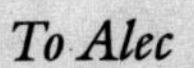
To Alec

'Revenge is a kind of wild justice, which the more man's nature runs to, the more ought law to weed it out.'

FRANCIS BACON

'O wad some Pow'r the giftie gie us
To see oursels as others see us!
It wad frae mony a blunder free us,
And foolish notion.'

ROBERT BURNS, *'To a Louse'*

Southern Evening Herald – 23rd March

Growing Police Anxiety

Following intensive questioning at airports, docks and ferry companies in the search for missing businessman David Maybury, police have [illegible] It is now [illegible] days since he was last seen [illegible] detective in charge of the investigation, [illegible] the possibility of foul play. Police efforts are [illegible] on a thorough search of Streech Grange Estate and the surrounding farmland.

There have been numerous reported sightings of the missing man over the past week, but none that could be substantiated. David Maybury, 44, was wearing [illegible] the night he [illegible] and [illegible] a financial [illegible]

[illegible]

[illegible] – 15th April

To The Manor Buried

M[illegible] Many [illegible] being dug up [illegible] Maybury [illegible] 'This house has been in my family for [illegible] years and the garden is the resting place of several generations. The police have no business [illegible]'

[illegible] say that David Maybury, 44, [illegible] difficulties shortly before he disappeared. His wine business, [illegible] by his wife and run from the cellars of their home, was virtually bankrupt. Friends talk of constant rows between the couple. Police are treating his disappearance as murder.

Southern Evening Herald – 23rd March

Growing Police Anxiety

Following intensive questioning at airports, docks and ferry terminals in the search for the missing businessman, David Maybury, police have expressed concern for his welfare. 'It is now ten days since he vanished,' said Inspector Walsh, the detective in charge of the investigation, 'and we cannot rule out the possibility of foul play.' Police efforts are being concentrated on a thorough search of Streech Grange Estate and the surrounding farmland.

There have been numerous reported sightings of the missing man over the past week, but none that could be substantiated. David Maybury, 44, was wearing a charcoal-grey pinstripe suit on the night he vanished. He is 5′10″ tall, of average build, with dark hair and eyes.

Sun – 15th April

To The Manor Buried

Mrs Phoebe Maybury, 27, beautiful red-haired wife of missing businessman David Maybury, looked on in fury as police dug up her garden in their search for her husband. Mrs Maybury, an avid gardener herself, declared: 'This house has been in my family for years and the garden is the product of several generations. The police have no business to destroy it.'

Reliable sources say that David Maybury, 44, was in financial difficulties shortly before he disappeared. His wine business, funded by his wife and run from the cellars of their house, was virtually bankrupt. Friends talk of constant rows between the couple. Police are treating his disappearance as murder.

Daily Telegraph – 9th August

Police Team Disbanded

Police admitted last night to being baffled over the disappearance of Hampshire man, David Maybury. In spite of a long and thorough investigation, no trace of him has been found, and the team involved in the enquiry has been disbanded. The file will remain open, according to police sources, but there is little confidence in solving the mystery. 'The public has been very helpful,' said a police spokesman. 'We have built a clear picture of what happened the night he vanished, but until we find his body, there's little more we can do.'

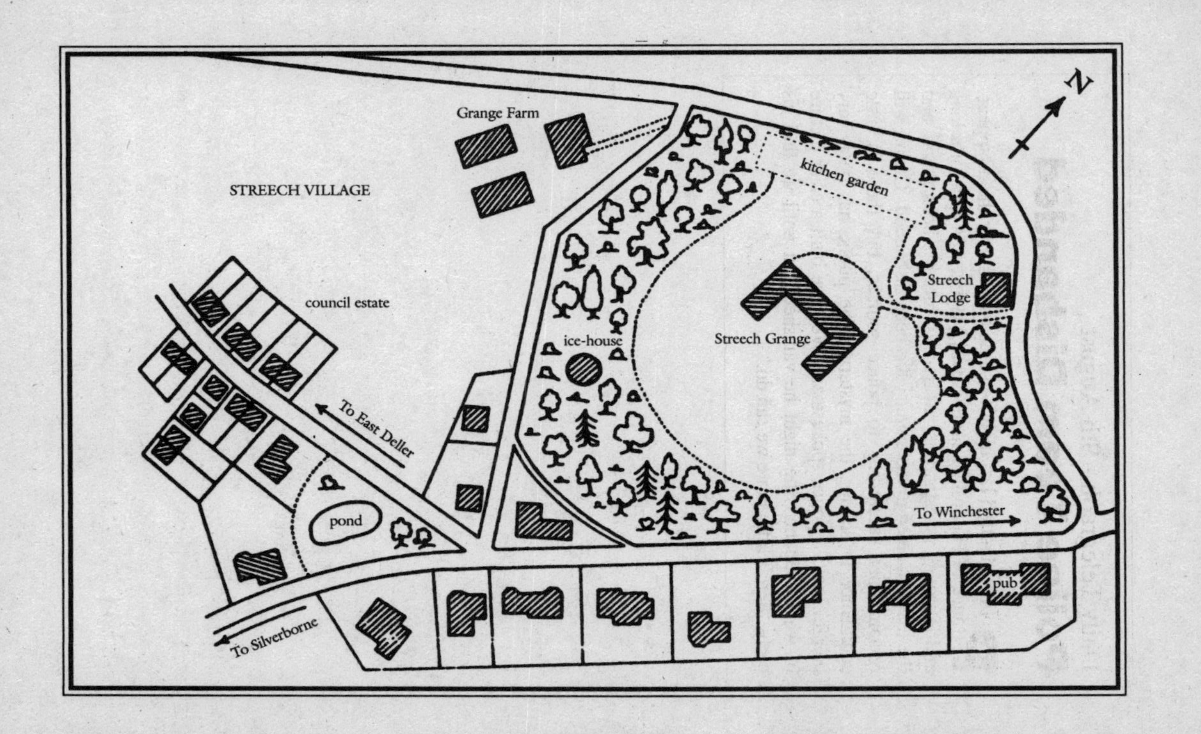
N
Grange Farm
STREECH VILLAGE
kitchen garden
Streech Lodge
council estate
ice-house
Streech Grange
To East Deller
pond
To Winchester
pub
To Silverborne

One

'FRED PHILLIPS IS *running*.' Anne Cattrell's remark burst upon the silence of that August afternoon like a fart at a vicar's tea-party.

Startled, her two companions looked up, Diana from her sketch-pad, Phoebe from her gardening book, their eyes watering at this abrupt transition from the printed page to brilliant sunlight. They had sat in contented stillness for an hour, grouped about a wrought-iron table on the terrace of their house where the wreckage of a lazy tea jostled with the flotsam of their professional lives: a pair of secateurs, an open paint-box, pages of manuscript, one with a circular tea stain where Anne had dumped a cup without thinking.

Phoebe was perched on an upright chair at right angles to the table, crossed ankles tucked neatly beneath her, red hair corkscrewing in flaming whorls about her shoulders. Her position was hardly changed from half an hour previously when she had finished her tea and guiltily buried her nose in her book instead of returning to the greenhouse to finish off a bulk order for five hundred Ivyleaf Pelargonium cuttings. Diana, unashamedly glistening with Ambre Solaire, reclined on a sun-lounger, the pleated skirt of her printed cotton dress spilling over the sides and brushing the flagstones. One elegant hand toyed with the underbelly of the Labrador lying beside her, the other drew swirling doodles in the margin of her sketch-pad which should have been filled – but was not – with commissioned designs for a cottage interior in Fowey. Anne, who had been struggling between intermittent dozes to conjure up a thousand words on 'Vaginal Orgasm – Fact or Fiction' for an obscure magazine, was drawn up tight against the table, chin on hands, dark eyes staring down the long vista of landscaped garden in front of her.

Phoebe glanced at her briefly then turned to follow her gaze, peering over her spectacles across the wide expanse of lawn. 'Good lord!' she exclaimed.

Her gardener, a man of massive proportions, was pounding across the grass, naked to the waist, his huge belly lapping at his trousers like some monstrous tidal wave. The semi-nudity was surprising enough, for Fred held strong views about his position at Streech Grange. Among other things, this required Phoebe to whistle a warning of her approach in the garden so that he might clothe himself suitably for what he referred to as a parley-vous, even in the heat of summer.

'Perhaps he's won the pools,' suggested Diana, but without conviction, as the three women watched his rapidly slowing advance.

'Highly unlikely,' countered Anne, pushing her chair away from the table. 'Fred's inertia would demand a more powerful stimulus than filthy lucre to prompt this bout of activity.'

They watched the rest of Fred's approach in silence. He was walking by the time he reached the terrace. He paused for a moment, leaning one hand heavily on the low wall bordering the flagstones, catching his breath. There was a tinge of grey to the weathered cheeks, a rasp in his throat. Concerned, Phoebe gestured to Diana to pull forward a vacant chair, then she stood up, took Fred's arm and helped him into it.

'Whatever's happened?' she asked anxiously.

'Oh, madam, something awful.' He was sweating profusely, unable to get the words out quickly. Perspiration ran in streams over his fat brown breasts, soft and round like a woman's, and the smell was all-pervading, consuming the sweet scent of the roses which nodded in beds at the edge of the terrace. Aware of this and of his nakedness, he wrung his hands in embarrassment. 'I'm so sorry, madam.'

Diana swung her legs off the lounger and sat up, twitching a rug off the back of her chair and placing it neatly across his shoulders. 'You should keep yourself warm after a run like that, Fred.'

He wrapped the rug around him, nodding his

appreciation. 'What's happened, Fred?' Phoebe asked again.

'I don't rightly know how to say it' – she thought she saw compassion in his eyes – 'but it's got to be told.'

'Then tell me,' she prompted gently. 'I'm sure it can't be that bad.' She glanced at Benson, the yellow Labrador, still lying placidly by Diana's chair. 'Has Hedges been run over?'

He reached out a rough, mud-caked hand from between the folds of the rug and with a familiarity that was quite out of character placed it on hers and squeezed gently. The gesture was as brief as it was unexpected. 'There's a body in the old ice house, madam.'

There was a moment's silence. 'A body?' echoed Phoebe. 'What sort of body?' Her voice was unemotional, steady.

Anne flicked a glance in her direction. There were times, she thought, when her friend's composure frightened her.

'To tell you the truth, madam, I didn't look too close. It was a shock, coming on it the way I did.' He stared unhappily at his feet. 'Stepped on it, like, before I saw it. There was a bit of a smell afterwards.' They all looked in fascination at his gardening boots and he, regretting his impulsive statement, shuffled them awkwardly out of sight under the rug. 'It's all right, madam,' he said, 'wiped them on the grass soon as I could.'

The cup and saucer in Phoebe's hand rattled and she put them carefully on the table beside her secateurs. 'Of course you did, Fred. How thoughtful of you. Would you like some tea? A cake perhaps?' she asked him.

'No, thank you, madam.'

Diana turned away, suppressing an awful desire to laugh. Only Phoebe, she thought, of all the women she knew would offer cake in such circumstances. In its way it was admirable, for Phoebe, more than any of them, would be affected by Fred's shocking revelation.

Anne scrabbled among the pages of her manuscript in search of her cigarettes. With an abrupt movement she flicked the box open and offered it to Fred. He glanced at Phoebe for a permission he didn't need and she nodded gravely. 'Thank you kindly, Miss Cattrell. My nerves are that shook up.'

Anne lit it for him, holding his hand steady with hers. 'Let's get this straight, Fred,' she said, her dark eyes searching his. 'It's a person's dead body. Is that right?'

'That's right, Miss Cattrell.'

'Do you know who it is?'

'I can't say I do, miss.' He spoke with reluctance. 'I can't say anyone will know who it is.' He drew deeply on his cigarette, the sweat of suppressed nausea breaking out on his forehead. 'The truth is, from the quick look I had, there's not much of it left. It must have been there a while.'

The three women looked at him aghast. 'But surely it's got clothes on, Fred?' Diana asked nervously. 'At least you know if it's a man or woman.'

'No clothes that I could see, Mrs Goode.'

'You'd better show me.' Phoebe stood up with sudden decision and Fred rose awkwardly to his feet. 'I'd rather not, madam. You shouldn't see it. I don't want to take you down there.'

'Then I'll go on my own.' She smiled suddenly and laid a hand on his arm. 'I'm sorry but I have to see it. You do understand that, don't you, Fred?'

He stubbed out his cigarette and pulled the rug tighter about his shoulders. 'If you're that intent on going, I'll come with you. It's not something you should see alone.'

'Thank you.' She turned to Diana. 'Will you phone the police for me?'

'Of course.'

Anne pushed her chair back. 'I'll come with you,' she told Phoebe. Then she called after Diana as she followed the other two across the grass. 'You might lay on some brandy, I'll be needing some, even if no one else does.'

*

They grouped themselves in a nervous huddle a few yards from the entrance to the ice house. It was an unusual structure, designed and built in the eighteenth century to resemble a small hillock. Its function as an ice-store had ceased years ago with the advent of the refrigerator, and Nature had reasserted her dominion over it so that ranks of nettles marched in their hundreds around the base, making a natural fusion between the man-made dome and the solid earth. The only entrance, a wide low doorway, was set into the ice-house wall at the end of an overgrown pathway. The doorway, too, had long since lost itself in a mass of tangled brambles which grew over it in a thorny curtain from above and below. It was revealed now only because Fred had hacked and trampled the curtain aside to reach it.

A lighted torch lay abandoned on the ground at their feet. Phoebe picked it up. 'What made you go in there?' she asked Fred. 'We haven't used it for years.'

He pulled a face. 'I wish I hadn't, madam, God knows. What the eye doesn't see, the heart doesn't grieve over and that's a fact. I've been repairing the kitchen garden wall, where it collapsed a week ago. Half the bricks are unusable – I understood, when I saw the state of them, why the wall collapsed. Handful of dust, some of them. Anyway, I thought of the bricks we stored in here some years back, the ones from the outhouse we demolished. You said: "Hang on to the good ones, Fred, you never know when we might need them for repairs."'

'I remember.'

'So I wanted to use them for the wall.'

'Of course. You had to cut the brambles away?'

He nodded. 'I couldn't see the door, it was overgrown.' He pointed to a scythe lying to one side of the ice house. 'I used that and my boots to reach it.'

'Come on,' said Anne suddenly. 'Let's get it over with. Talking isn't going to make it any easier.'

'Yes,' said Phoebe quietly. 'Does the door open any wider, Fred?'

'It does, madam. I had it full open before I stepped on what's in there. Pulled it to as far as I could when I left in case anyone came by.' He pursed his lips. 'To tell you the truth, it's wider now than when I left it.'

He walked forward reluctantly and, with a sudden movement, kicked the door. It swung open on creaking hinges. Phoebe crouched and shone the torch into the interior, bathing the contents with warm golden light. It wasn't so much the blackened and eyeless corpse that caused her to vomit, as the sight of Hedges rolling quietly and purposefully in the decomposing remains of the bowels. He came out with his tail between his legs and lay on the grass watching her, head between paws, as she heaved her tea on to the grass.

Two

SILVERBORNE POLICE STATION, a modern triumph of polished chrome features and sealed tinted windows, baked in the sun amid its more traditional neighbours. Inside, the air-conditioning had broken down again and as the hours passed and the atmosphere overheated so did the policemen. They grew sticky and squabbled amongst themselves like young children. Those who could, got out; those who couldn't, jealously guarded their electric fans and prayed for a quick end to their shift. For Detective Chief Inspector Walsh, sweating profusely over some paperwork in his office, the order to take a team to Streech Grange came like a miraculous breath of air through the sealed windows. He whistled happily to himself as he made his way to the briefing room. But for Detective Sergeant McLoughlin, detailed to assist him, the knowledge that he was going to miss opening time and the cold lager he'd promised himself was the last straw.

*

Diana heard the approaching cars before the others. She finished her brandy and put the glass on the sideboard. 'Fingers out, girls. Here they come.'

Phoebe walked over to the mantelpiece, her face abnormally white against the vivid red hair. She was a tall woman who was rarely seen out of checked shirts and old Levis. But on her return from the ice house she had taken the trouble to change into a long-sleeved, high-collared silk dress. There was no doubting she looked at home in the elegant room with its pastel shades and draped velvet curtains but, to Anne at least, she had the air of a stranger. She smiled distantly at her two friends. 'I'm terribly sorry about this.'

Anne, as usual, was chain-smoking. She blew a stream of grey into the air above her where she sat on the sofa, head resting against the back. 'Don't be a fool,' she said bluntly. 'No one's going to hold you responsible because some idiot chooses to die on your property. There'll be a simple explanation: a tramp took shelter and had a heart attack.'

'My thoughts precisely,' said Diana, walking to the sofa. 'Give me a cigarette, there's a dear. My nerves are like piano wires, waiting for a Rachmaninov concerto to hit them.'

Anne chuckled and handed over the packet. 'Do you want one, Pheeb?'

She shook her head and started to polish her spectacles on her skirt hem, absent-mindedly lifting it to waist level and revealing her lack of knickers. Anne found the vagueness of the gesture reassuring.

'There won't be any glass left if you go on doing that,' she pointed out gently.

Phoebe sighed, dropped her skirt and put the spectacles back on. 'Tramps don't have heart attacks on other people's property in the nude,' she said.

The doorbell rang. They heard Molly Phillips, Fred's wife, walk to the front door and without a word, indeed quite by instinct, Anne and Diana positioned themselves on either side of the mantelpiece, flanking Phoebe. As the door opened it occurred to Diana that this might not have been a wise move. To the police mind, she feared, they would seem not so much to be supporting her – the intention – as guarding her.

Molly ushered in two men. 'Chief Inspector Walsh and Detective Sergeant McLoughlin, madam. There's a whole lot more outside. Shall I ask Fred to keep an eye on them?'

'No, that's all right, Molly. I'm sure they'll behave themselves.'

'If you say so, madam. Me, I'm not so sure. They've already scuffed their great clumsy feet over the gravel where Fred raked it so careful this morning.' She glared accusingly at the two men.

'Thank you, Molly. Perhaps you could make tea for everyone. I'm sure it will be welcome.'

'Right you are, madam.' The housekeeper closed

the door behind her and stomped off down the corridor towards the kitchen.

George Walsh listened till her footsteps died away, then he came forward and held out his hand. He was a thin stooping man who had a bizarre habit of jerking his head from side to side, like a sufferer from Parkinson's disease. It gave him an appearance of vulnerability that was deceptive.

'Good afternoon, Mrs Maybury. We've met before, if you remember.' He could recall her vividly as she had been that first time, standing where she was now. Ten years, he thought, and she had hardly changed, still the lady of the manor, remote and aloof in the security of her position. The dramas of those years might never have been. There was certainly no evidence in the calm, unlined face which smiled at him now. There was a quality of stillness about her that was unnatural. The village called her a witch, and he had always understood why.

Phoebe shook his hand. 'Yes, I do remember. It was your first big case.' Her voice was low-pitched, attractive. 'You had just been made Detective Inspector, I think. I don't believe you've met my friends, Miss Cattrell and Mrs Goode.' She gestured to Anne and Diana who shook hands solemnly in turn with the Chief Inspector. 'They live here now.'

Walsh studied the two women with interest. 'Permanently?' he asked.

'Most of the time,' said Diana, 'when our work

doesn't take us away. We're both self-employed. I'm an interior designer, Anne's a freelance journalist.'

Walsh nodded, but Anne could see that Diana had told him nothing he didn't already know. 'I envy you.' He spoke the truth. He had coveted Streech Grange since the first time he had seen it.

Phoebe put out her hand to the other man. 'Good afternoon, Sergeant McLoughlin. May I introduce Mrs Goode and Miss Cattrell.'

He was in his mid-thirties, of an age with the women, a dark, brooding man with cold eyes. In the twist of his lips, he had brought with him the irritability of the Police Station, concentrated, malignant. He regarded Phoebe and her friends with weary contempt and paid lip-service to etiquette by brushing their fingers with his in the briefest of exchanges. His dislike, uncalled-for, slapped against their unprotected cheeks.

To the consternation of her friends, who could feel the vibrations of her anger, Anne rose recklessly to the challenge. 'My, my, Sergeant, what *have* you been hearing about us?' She lifted a sardonic eyebrow then deliberately wiped her fingers down her Levis. 'You're scarcely off your mother's breast, so won't have been around the last time the Grange was the centre of police attention. Let me guess now. Our reputation – ' she indicated herself and the other two women – 'has preceded us. Which of our widely talked-about activities upsets you the most, I wonder? Child abuse, witchcraft or lesbianism?' She searched his face with scornful eyes. 'Lesbianism,' she murmured. 'Yes, you would find that the most threatening but, then, it's the only one that's true, isn't it?'

McLoughlin's temper, already fired by the heat of the day, nearly erupted. He breathed deeply. 'I've nothing against dykes, Miss Cattrell,' he said evenly. 'I just wouldn't stick my finger in one, that's all.'

Diana stubbed out her cigarette with rather more violence than was necessary. 'Don't tease the poor man, Anne,' she said dryly. 'He's going to need all his wits to sort out the mess in the ice house.'

Stiffly, Phoebe took the seat nearest her and gestured the others to sit down. Walsh sat in the chair opposite her, Anne and Diana on the sofa, leaving McLoughlin to perch on a delicate tapestry stool. His discomfort, as he folded his long legs awkwardly beneath him, was obvious to all.

'Take care you don't break that, Sergeant,' snapped Walsh. 'I don't like clumsiness any more than the housekeeper does. Well now, Mrs Maybury, perhaps you'd like to tell us why you called us out.'

'I thought Mrs Goode explained it on the telephone.'

He fished a piece of paper from his pocket. '"Body in ice house, Streech Grange. Discovered at 4.35 p.m." Not much of an explanation, is it? Tell me what happened.'

'That's it, really. Fred Phillips, my gardener, found the body about that time and came and told us. Diana phoned you while Fred took Anne and me to look at it.'

'So you've seen it?'

'Yes.'

'Who is it? Do you know?'

'The body's unrecognisable.'

With an abrupt movement, Anne lit another cigarette. 'It's putrid, Inspector, black, disgusting. *No one* would know who it was.' She spoke impatiently, her deep voice clipping the words short.

Walsh nodded. 'I see. Did your gardener suggest you look at the body?'

Phoebe shook her head. 'No, he suggested I shouldn't. I insisted on going.'

'Why?'

She shrugged. 'Natural curiosity, I suppose. Wouldn't you have gone?'

He was silent for a moment. '*Is* it your husband, Mrs Maybury?'

'I've already told you the body is unrecognisable.'

'Did you insist on going because you thought it *might* be your husband?'

'Of course. But I've realised since it couldn't possibly be.'

'Why is that?'

'It was something Fred said. He reminded me that

we stored some bricks in the ice house about six years ago when we demolished an outhouse. David had been gone four years by that time.'

'His body was never found. We never traced him,' Walsh reminded her. 'Perhaps he came back.'

Diana laughed nervously. 'He couldn't come back, Inspector. He's dead. Murdered.'

'How do you know, Mrs Goode?'

'Because he'd have been back long before this if he wasn't. David always knew which side his bread was buttered.'

Walsh crossed his legs and smiled. 'The case is still open. *We've* never been able to prove he was murdered.'

Diana's face was suddenly grim. 'Because you concentrated all your energies on trying to pin the murder on Phoebe. You gave up when you couldn't prove it. You never made any attempt to ask me for a list of suspects. I could have given you a hundred likely names; Anne could have given you another hundred. David Maybury was the most out-and-out bastard who ever lived. He deserved to die.' She wondered if she had overdone it and glanced briefly at Phoebe. 'Sorry, love, but if more people had said it ten years ago, things might have been less hard for you.'

Anne nodded agreement. 'You'll waste a lot of time if you think that thing out there is David Maybury.' She stood up and walked over to sit on the arm of Phoebe's chair. 'For the record, Inspector, both Diana and I helped clear years of accumulated rubbish out the ice house before Fred stacked the bricks in it. There were no corpses in there six years ago. Isn't that right, Di?'

Diana looked amused and inclined her head. 'It wouldn't have been the place to look for him, anyway. He's at the bottom of the sea somewhere, food for crabs and lobsters.' She looked at McLoughlin. 'Are you partial to crabs, Sergeant?'

Walsh intervened before McLoughlin could say anything. 'We followed up every known contact or associate Mr Maybury had. There was no evidence to connect any of them with his disappearance.'

Anne tossed her cigarette into the fireplace. 'Balls!' she exclaimed amiably. 'I'll tell you something, you never questioned me either and in my list of a hundred possible suspects *I* should have featured in the top ten.'

'You're quite mistaken, Miss Cattrell.' Inspector Walsh was unruffled. 'We went into your background very thoroughly. At the time of Mr Maybury's disappearance, in fact throughout most of our investigation, you were camped with your lady friends on Greenham Common under the eyes not only of the guards at the American Airforce base but also of the Newbury police and assorted television cameras. It was quite an alibi.'

'You're right. I'd forgotten. Touché, Inspector.' She chuckled. 'I was researching a feature for one of the colour supplements.' Out of the corner of her eye, she saw McLoughlin's lips thin to a disapproving line. 'But, hell, it was fun,' she went on in a dreamy voice. 'That camp is the best thing that's ever happened to me.'

Frowning, Phoebe laid a restraining hand on her arm and stood up. 'This is all irrelevant. Until you've examined the body, it seems to me quite pointless to speculate on whether or not it's David's. If you care to come with me, gentlemen, I will show you where it is.'

'Let Fred do it,' Diana protested.

'No. He's had enough shocks for one day. I'm all right. Could you make sure Molly's organising the tea?'

She opened the French windows and led the way on to the terrace. Benson and Hedges roused themselves from the warm flagstones and pushed their noses into her hand. Hedges's fur was still fluffy from his bath. She paused to stroke his head gently and pull his ears. 'There's one thing I really ought to tell you, Inspector,' she said.

Anne, watching from inside the drawing-room, gave a gurgle of laughter. 'Phoebe's confessing to Hedges's little peccadillo and the Sergeant's turned green around the gills.'

Diana pushed herself out of the sofa and walked towards her. 'Don't underestimate him, Anne,' she said. 'You're such a fool sometimes. Why do you always have to antagonise people?'

'I don't. I simply refuse to kowtow to their small-minded conventions. If they feel antagonised that's their problem. Principles should never be compromised. The minute they are, they cease to be principles.'

'Maybe, but you don't have to shove them down reluctant throats. A little common sense wouldn't come amiss at the moment. We do have a dead body on the premises. Or had you forgotten?' Her voice was more anxious than ironic.

Anne turned away from the window. 'You're probably right,' she agreed meekly.

'So you'll be careful?'

'I'll be careful.'

Diana frowned. 'I do wish I understood you. I never have, you know.'

Affection surged in Anne as she studied her friend's worried face. Poor old Di, she thought, how she hated all this. She should never have come to Streech. Her natural environment was an ivory tower where visitors were vetted and unpleasantness unheard of. 'You have no problem understanding me,' she pointed out lightly, 'you have a problem *agreeing* with me. My petty anarchies offend your sensibilities. I often wonder why you go along with them.'

Diana walked to the door. 'Which reminds me, next time you want me to lie for you, warn me first, will you? I'm not as good at controlling my facial muscles as you are.'

'Nonsense,' said Anne, dropping into an armchair. 'You're the most accomplished liar I know.'

Diana paused with her hand on the doorknob. 'Why do you say that?' she asked sharply.

'Because,' Anne teased her rigid back, 'I was there when you told Lady Weevil that her choice of colours for her drawing-room was sophisticated. Anyone who could do that with a straight face must have unlimited muscle control.'

'Lady *Keevil*,' corrected Diana, looking round with a smile. 'I should never have let you come with me. That contract was worth a fortune.'

Anne was unrepentant. 'I needed the lift and you can hardly blame me if I got her name wrong. Everything she said sounded as if it had been squeezed through a wet flannel. Anyway, I did you a favour. Cherry-red carpets and lime-green curtains, for God's sake! Think of your reputation.'

'You know her father was a fruit wholesaler.'

'You *do* surprise me,' said Anne dryly.

Three

INSIDE THE ICE house Chief Inspector Walsh firmly suppressed a slight movement in his bowels. Sergeant McLoughlin showed less control. He ran out of the building and was sick in the nettles alongside it. Unaware that she would have sympathised, he was thankful that Phoebe Maybury had returned to the Grange and was not there to see him.

'Not very nice, is it?' remarked Walsh when the Sergeant came back. 'Careful where you're stepping. There are bits all over the place. Must have been where the dog disturbed it.'

McLoughlin held a handkerchief to his mouth and retched violently. There was a strong smell of beer about him, and the Inspector eyed him with disfavour. A man of moods himself, he found inconsistency in others unendurable. He knew McLoughlin as well as any of the men he worked with, thought of him as a conscientious type, honest, intelligent, dependable. He even liked the man – he was one of the few who could cope with the notorious pendulum-swings of Walsh's temperament – but to see McLoughlin's weaknesses, disclosed like guilty secrets, irritated Walsh. 'What the hell's the matter with you?' he demanded. 'Five minutes ago you couldn't even be civil, now you're puking like a bloody baby.'

'Nothing, sir.'

'Nothing, sir,' mimicked Walsh savagely. He would have said more but there was an anger about the younger man that stilled his waspish tongue. With a sigh he took McLoughlin's arm and pushed him outside. 'Get me a photographer and some decent lights – it's impossible to see properly. And tell Dr Webster to get down here as fast as he can. I left a message for him so he should be at the Station by now.' He patted the Sergeant's arm clumsily, remembering perhaps that McLoughlin was more often his supporter than his detractor. 'If it's any consolation, Andy, I've never seen anything as nasty as this.'

As McLoughlin returned thankfully to the house, Inspector Walsh took a pipe from his pocket, filled it and lit it thoughtfully, then began a careful examination of the ground and the brambles around the door and pathway. The ground itself told him little. The summer had been an exceptional one and the last four weeks of almost perpetual sunshine had baked it hard. The only visible tracks were where feet, probably Fred's, had trampled the weeds and grass in front of the brambles. Previous tracks, if any, had long since been obliterated. The brambles might prove more interesting. It was evident, if there were no other entrance to the ice house, that the body had at some point traversed this thorny barrier, either alive on its own two legs or dead on the back of someone else's. The big question was, how long ago? How long had that nightmare been in there?

He walked slowly round the hillock. It would, of course, have been easier to satisfy himself that the door was the only entrance from inside the structure. He excused his reluctance to do this on the basis of not wishing to disturb the evidence more than was necessary but, being honest, he knew it was an excuse. The grisly tomb held no attractions for a man alone, even for a policeman intent on discovering the truth.

He spent some time investigating round the base of an untamed laurel which grew at the back of the ice house, using a discarded bamboo stake to stir up the leaf mould which had collected there. His efforts uncovered only solid brickwork, which looked strong enough to withstand another two hundred years of probing roots. In those days, he thought, they built to last.

He sat back on his heels for a moment, puffing on his pipe, then resumed his search, poking his stick at intervals into the nettles at the base of the ice-house roof but finding no other obvious points of weakness. He returned to the door and a closer examination of the brambles.

He was no gardener, he relied on his wife to tend their small patio garden where everything grew neatly in tubs, but even to his uneducated eye the brambles had a look of permanence. He spent some moments peering thoughtfully at the clods of earth and grass above the doorway, where roots had been torn free in handfuls, then, careful to avoid the grass which had been trodden on, he squatted beside the area of brambles which had been scythed and trampled flat. The broken stems were green with sap, most of the fruit was still unripe but the odd blackberry, more mature than its fellows, showed black and juicy amidst the ruins of its parent. With the end of the bamboo he carefully lifted the flattened mass of vegetation nearest to him and peered beneath it.

'Found anything, sir?' McLoughlin had returned.

'Look under here, Andy, and tell me what you see.'

McLoughlin knelt obligingly beside his superior and stared where Walsh was pointing. 'What am I looking for?'

'Stems with old breaks in them. We are safe in assuming our body didn't pole vault over this little lot.'

McLoughlin shook his head. 'We'd have to take the brambles apart for that, bit by bit, and I doubt we'd have much joy even then. Whoever flattened them did a thorough job.'

Walsh lowered the vegetation and removed the bamboo. 'The gardener, according to Mrs Maybury.'

'Looks as if he's put a steam-roller over it.'

'It's interesting, isn't it?' Walsh stood up. 'Did you get hold of Webster?'

'He's on his way, should be here in ten minutes. I've told the others to wait for him. Nick Robinson's already laid on the lights and the camera, so the gardener's showing them all down here once Webster arrives. Except young Williams. I've left him in the house to take background statements and keep his eyes open. He's a sharp lad. If there's anything to see, he'll see it.'

'Good. The mortuary van?'

'On stand-by at the station.'

Walsh moved a few yards away and sat down on the grass. 'We'll wait. There's nothing to be done until the photographs have been taken.' He blew a cloud of smoke out of the side of his mouth and squinted through it at McLoughlin. 'What is a nude corpse doing in Mrs Maybury's ice house, Sergeant? And what or, perhaps, who, has been eating it?'

With a groan, McLoughlin reached for his handkerchief.

PC Williams had taken statements from Mrs Maybury, Mrs Goode and Miss Cattrell and was now with Molly

Phillips in the kitchen. For some reason that he couldn't understand, she was being deliberately obstructive and he thought with irritation that his colleagues had a knack of landing themselves the decent jobs. With ill-disguised satisfaction they had set off down the garden with Fred Phillips and the new arrivals and their assorted paraphernalia. Williams, who had seen Andy McLoughlin's face when he came up from the ice house, was consumed with curiosity as to what was down there. McLoughlin's nerves were sprung with Scottish steel, and he had looked as sick as a dog.

Reluctantly Constable Williams returned to the job in hand. 'So the first you knew about this body was when Mrs Goode came in to telephone?'

'What if it was?'

He looked at her in exasperation. 'Do you always answer questions with questions?'

'Maybe, maybe not. That's my business.'

He was only a lad, the sort that people looked at and said: Policemen are getting younger. He tried a wheedling approach that had worked for him on a couple of occasions in the past. 'Listen, Ma – '

'Don't you "Ma" me,' she spat at him viciously. 'You're no son of mine. I don't have kids.' She turned her back on him and busied herself slicing carrots into a saucepan. 'You should be ashamed of yourself. What would your mother say? She's the only one you've a right to call Ma like that.'

Frustrated old cow, he thought. He looked at the thin, drooping shoulders and reckoned her problem was that her old man had never given her a proper working over. 'I don't even know who she is.'

She was still for a moment, knife poised in mid-air, then went on with her slicing. She said nothing.

Williams tried another tack. 'All I'm doing, Mrs Phillips, is getting some background details on the discovery of the body. Mrs Goode has told me she came into the house to make the telephone call to us. She said you were in the hall when she made it and that afterwards she went down to the cellar to get some brandy because there was none left on the sideboard. Is that right?'

'If Mrs Goode says it is, that's enough for you. There's no need to come sneaking round here behind her back trying to find out if she's telling lies.'

He looked at her sharply. '*Is* she telling lies?'

'No, she's not. The very idea.'

'Then what's all the mystery?' he asked her angry back. 'What are you being so secretive about?'

She rounded on him. 'Don't you take that tone with me. I know your sort. None better. You'll not browbeat me.' She whisked the teacup from under his nose where he sat at the table and dumped it unceremoniously in her washing-up bowl. He could have sworn there were tears in her eyes.

*

The police photographer picked his way gingerly out of the doorway and lifted the camera strap over his neck. 'Finished, sir,' he told Walsh.

The Chief Inspector placed a hand on his shoulder. 'Good man. Back to the Station with you then and get that film developed.' He turned to the pathologist. 'Shall we go in, Webster?'

Dr Webster smiled grimly. 'Do I have a choice?'

'After you,' said Walsh maliciously.

The scene was lit now with battery-run arc-lights, every detail showing with stark clarity, no shadows to soften the shocking impact. Walsh gazed dispassionately on the body. It was true, he thought, that exposure to violence desensitised a man. He could barely recall his earlier repugnance, though perhaps the lights had something to do with this. As a child the dark had held terrors for him, with nightmare creations of his imagining lurking in the corners of his bedroom. His father, in other respects a kind man but fearing the embarrassment of an effeminate son, was unsympathetic and had closed his ears to the muffled weeping inside a bedroom from which all the light bulbs had been removed.

'Good God,' said Webster, surveying the ice-house floor with marked distaste. He picked his way carefully towards the centre of it, avoiding tattered pieces of hardened entrail which lay on the flagstones. He looked at the head. 'Good God,' he said again.

The head, still tethered to the upper torso by

blackened sinew, was wedged in a gap in the top row of a neat stack of bricks. Dull grey hair, long enough to be a woman's, spilled out of the gap. Eyeless sockets, showing bone underneath, and exposed upper and lower jaw bones gleamed white against the blackened musculature of the face. The chest area, anchored by the head against the vertical face of bricks, looked as if it had been skilfully filleted. The lower half of the body lay unnaturally askew of its top half in a position that no living person, however supple, could have achieved. The abdominal region had all but disappeared though shreds of it lay about as mute witnesses that it had once existed. There were no genitals. The lower half of the left arm, propped on a smaller pile of bricks, was some four feet from the body, much of the flesh stripped away, but some sinews remaining to show it had been wrenched from its elbow. The right arm, pressed against the torso, had the same blackened quality as the head with patches of white bone showing through. Of the legs, only the calves and feet were immediately recognisable, but at a distance from each other in a grotesque parody of the splits and twisted upside down so that soles pointed at the ice-house roof. Of the thighs, only splintered bones remained.

'Well?' said Walsh after some minutes during which the pathologist took temperature readings and made a rough sketch of the lie of the body.

'What do you want to know?'

'Man or woman?'

Webster pointed to the feet. 'From the size, I'd guess a man. We can't be sure until we've done some measurements, of course, but it looks like it. If it's not a man, it was a big woman and a mannish one.'

'The hair's on the long side for a man. Unless it grew significantly after death.'

'Where have you been living, George? Even if it were down to the waist, it wouldn't tell you anything about the sex. And hair growth after death is minimal. No,' continued Webster, 'all things considered, I'd say we're dealing with a man, subject to confirmation, of course.'

'Any idea of age?'

'None, except that he's probably over twenty-one and even that's not certain. Some people go grey in their teens. I'll have to X-ray the skull for fusion between the plates.'

'How long has he been dead?'

Webster pursed his lips. 'That's going to be a bugger to decide. Old Fred out there said there was a bit of a stink when he stepped on it which would indicate a comparatively recent demise.' He sucked his teeth thoughtfully for some minutes, then shook his head and examined the floor carefully, using a spatula to loosen some dark material near the door. He sniffed the spatula. 'Excreta,' he announced, 'fairly recent, probably animal. You'd better take a cast of that to see if it's got Fred's boot prints. How long's he been dead?' He shivered suddenly. 'This is an ice house and several degrees cooler than it is outside. No obvious maggot infestation which implies the blowflies weren't attracted. If they had been, there'd be even less of it left. Frankly, George, your guess is as good as mine how long dead flesh would keep in this temperature. There is also the small matter of decomposition being hastened by consumption. We could be talking weeks, we could be talking months. I just don't know. I'll need to consult on this one.'

'Years?'

'No,' Webster said firmly. 'You'd be looking at a skeleton.'

'Supposing he was frozen when he came in. Would that make a difference?'

The pathologist snorted. 'You mean frozen as in fish fingers?' Walsh nodded. 'That's really too fantastic, George. You'd need a commercial freezer to freeze a man this size, and how would you transport him here? And why freeze him in the first place?' Webster frowned. 'It wouldn't make much difference as far as your investigation goes either. An ice house only keeps things frozen when it's full of ice. A frozen man would defrost in here just like a turkey in a larder. No, that's got to be out of the question.'

Walsh was staring thoughtfully at the severed arm. 'Has it? Odder things have happened. Perhaps he's been in cold storage for ten years and was left here recently for someone to find.'

Webster whistled. 'David Maybury?'

'It's a possibility.' He squatted down and gestured to the distorted and tattered hand. 'What do you make of this? Looks to me as if the last two fingers are missing.'

Webster joined him. 'It's difficult to say,' he said doubtfully. 'Something's had a damn good go at it.' He glanced about the floor. 'You'll have to sweep up very thoroughly, make sure you don't miss anything. It's certainly odd. Could be coincidence, I suppose.'

Walsh stood up. 'I don't believe in coincidences. Any idea what he died of?'

'A first guess, George. Massive bleeding from a wound or wounds in his abdomen.'

Walsh glanced at him in surprise. 'You're very positive.'

'A guess, I said. You'll have to find his clothes to be sure. But look at him. The area from the abdomen down has been completely devoured, except for the lower halves of the legs. Imagine him sitting up, legs out in front of him, with blood pouring out of his belly. It would be seeping over precisely those parts which have been eaten.'

Inspector Walsh felt suddenly faint. 'Are you saying whatever it was ate him while he was still alive?'

'Well, don't have nightmares about it, old chap. If he was alive, he'd have been in a coma and wouldn't have known anything about it, otherwise he'd have scared the scavengers off. Stands to reason. Of course,' he continued thoughtfully, 'if he was defrosting slowly, the blood and water would liquefy to achieve the same result.'

Walsh performed the laborious ritual of lighting his pipe again, billowing clouds of blue smoke from the side of his mouth. Webster's mention of smell had made him aware of an underlying odour which he hadn't previously noticed. For some minutes he watched the doctor making a close examination of the head and chest, at one point taking some measurements. 'What sort of scavengers are we talking about? Foxes, rats?'

'Difficult to say.' He peered closely at one of the eye sockets, before indicating the fractured thigh bones. 'Something with strong jaws, I would guess. One thing's for certain, two of them have had a fight over him. Look at the way the legs are lying and that arm, pulled apart at the elbow. I'd say there's been a tug-of-war here.' He pursed his lips again. 'Badgers possibly. More likely dogs.'

Walsh thought of the yellow Labradors lying on the warm flagstones, remembered how one of them had nuzzled the palm of his hand. With an abrupt movement, he wiped the hand down his trouser leg. He puffed smoke relentlessly into the atmosphere. 'I follow your reasoning about why the animals should have gone for the abdomen and thighs, but they seem to have done a pretty good job on the top half as well. Why is that? Is it normal?'

Webster stood up and wiped his forehead with the

sleeve of his shirt. 'God knows, George. About the only thing I'm sure of is that this whole thing is abnormal. I'll hazard a guess that the poor sod pressed his left hand to his belly to try to stop the blood running out or hold his guts in, whichever you prefer, then did what I just did – wiped the sweat off his face and smeared himself with blood. That would have attracted rats or whatever to his left hand and arm and the upper half of his body.'

'You said he'd have been in a coma.' Walsh's tone was accusing.

'Maybe he was, maybe he wasn't. How the hell should I know? Anyway, people move in comas.'

Walsh took his pipe out of his mouth and used its stem to point at the chest. 'Shall I tell you what that looks like to me?'

'Go on.'

'The bones on a breast of lamb after my wife's skinned the meat off it with a sharp knife.'

Webster looked tired. 'I know. I'm hoping it's deceptive. If it's not – well, you don't need me to spell out what it means.'

'The villagers say the women here are witches.'

Webster peeled off his gloves. 'Let's get out of here – unless there's anything else you think I can tell you. My own view is I'll find out more when I've got him on the slab.'

'Just one thing. Do you reckon he got his abdominal wound here or somewhere else?'

Webster picked up his case and led the way out. 'Don't ask me, George. The only thing I'm sure of is that he was alive when he got here. Whether he was *already* bleeding, I wouldn't know.' He paused in the doorway. 'Unless there's anything in this freezer theory, of course. Then he'd have been good and dead.'

Four

THREE HOURS LATER, after the remains had been painstakingly removed under the direction of Dr Webster, and a laborious investigation of the ice-house interior had revealed little of note beyond a pile of dead bracken in one corner, the door was sealed and Walsh and McLoughlin returned to Streech Grange. Phoebe offered them the library to work in and, with a remarkable lack of curiosity, left them to their deliberations.

A team of policemen remained behind to comb the area in expanding circles round the ice house. Privately, Walsh thought this a wasted exercise – if too much time had elapsed between the body's arrival and its discovery, the surrounding area would tell them nothing. However, routine work had produced unlikely evidence before, and now various samples from the ice house were awaiting dispatch to the forensic labs. These included brick dust, tufts of fur, some discoloured mud off the floor and what Dr

Webster asserted were the splintered remains of a lamb bone which McLoughlin had found amongst the brambles outside the door. Young Constable Williams, still ignorant of exactly what had been in the ice house, was summoned to the library.

He found Walsh and McLoughlin sitting side by side behind a mahogany desk of heroic proportions, the photographic evidence, developed at speed, spread fan-like in front of them. An ancient Anglepoise lamp with a green shade was the only lighting in the rapidly darkening room and, as Williams entered, Walsh bent the light away to soften the brightness of its glare. For the young PC, viewing the pictures upside down and in semi-darkness, it was a tantalising glimpse of the horrors he had so far only imagined. He read his small collection of statements with half an eye on McLoughlin's face, where black hollows were etched deep by the shadowy light. Jesus, but the bastard looked ill. He wondered if the whispers he'd heard were true.

'Their statements about the finding of the body are all consistent, sir. Nothing untoward in that direction.' He looked suddenly smug. 'But I reckon I've got a lead in another direction.'

'You do, do you?'

'Yes, sir. I'm betting Mr and Mrs Phillips were inside before they came to work here.' He consulted his neat and tiny script. 'Mrs Phillips was very peculiar, wouldn't answer any of my questions, kept accusing me of browbeating her, which I wasn't, and saying: "That's for me to know and you to find out." When I told her I'd have to take it up with Mrs Maybury, she damn near bit my head off. "Don't you go worrying madam," she said, "Fred and me's kept our noses clean since we've been out and that's all you need to know."' He looked up triumphantly.

Walsh made a note on a piece of paper. 'All right, Constable, we'll look into it.'

McLoughlin saw the boy's disappointment and stirred himself. 'Good work, Williams,' he murmured. 'I think we should lay on sandwiches, sir. No one's had anything to eat since midday.' He thought of the liquid lunch he'd lost into the brambles. He'd have given his right arm for a beer. 'There's a pub at the bottom of the hill. Could Gavin get something made up for the lads?'

Testily, Walsh fished two tenners out of his jacket pocket. 'Sandwiches,' he ordered. 'Nothing too expensive. Leave some with us and take the rest to the ice house. You can stay and help the search down there.' He glanced behind him out of the window. 'They've got the arc-lights. Tell them to keep going as long as they can. We'll be down later. And don't forget my change.'

'Sir.' Williams left in a hurry before the Inspector could change his mind.

'He wouldn't be so bloody keen if he'd seen what was there,' remarked Walsh acidly, poking the photographs with a skinny finger. 'I wonder if he's right about the Phillips couple. Does the name ring a bell with you?'

'No.'

'Nor with me. Let's run through what we've got.' He took out his pipe and stuffed tobacco absent-mindedly into the bowl. Aloud, he sifted fussily through what facts they had, picking at them like chicken bones.

McLoughlin listened but didn't hear. His head hurt where a blood vessel, engorged and fat, was threatening to burst. Its roaring deafened him.

He picked a pencil off the desk and balanced it between his fingers. The ends trembled violently and he let it fall with a clatter. He forced himself to concentrate.

'So where do we start, Andy?'

'The ice house and who knew it was there. It has to be the key.' He isolated an exterior shot from the photographs on the desk and held it to the lamplight with shaking fingers. 'It looks like a hill,' he muttered. 'How would a stranger know it was hollow?'

Walsh clamped the pipe between his teeth and lit it. He didn't answer but took the photograph and studied it intently, smoking for a minute or two in silence.

Unemotionally, McLoughlin gazed on the pictures of the body. 'Is it Maybury?'

'Too early to say. Webster's gone back to check the dental and medical records. The bugger is we can't compare fingerprints. We weren't able to lift any from the house at the time of his disappearance. Not that we'd get a match. Both hands out there were in ribbons.' He tamped the burning tobacco with the end of his thumb. 'David Maybury had a very distinctive characteristic,' he continued after a moment. 'The last two fingers of his left hand were missing. He lost them in a shooting accident.'

McLoughlin felt the first flutterings of awakening interest. 'So it *is* him.'

'Could be.'

'That body hasn't been there ten years, sir. Dr Webster was talking in terms of months.'

'Maybe, maybe. I'll reserve judgement till I've seen the post-mortem report.'

'What was he like? Mrs Goode called him an out-and-out bastard.'

'I'd say that's a fair assessment. You can read up about him. It's all on file. I had a psychologist go through the evidence we took from the people who knew him. His unofficial verdict, bearing in mind he never met the man, was that Maybury showed marked psychopathic tendencies, particularly when drunk. He had a habit of beating people up, women as well as men.' Walsh puffed a spurt of smoke from the side of his mouth and eyed his subordinate. 'He put himself about a bit. We turned up at least three little tarts who kept warm beds for him in London.'

'Did she know?' He nodded towards the hall.

Walsh shrugged. 'Claimed she didn't.'

'Did he beat her up?'

'Undoubtedly, I should think, except she denied it. She had a bruise the size of a football on her face when she reported him missing and we found out she was twice admitted to hospital when he was alive, once with a fractured wrist and once with cracked ribs and a broken collar-bone. She told doctors she was accident-prone.' He gave a harsh laugh. 'They didn't believe her any more than I did. He used her as his personal punch bag whenever he was drunk.'

'So why didn't she leave? Or perhaps she enjoyed the attention?'

Walsh considered him thoughtfully for a moment. He started to say something, then thought better of it. 'Streech Grange has been in her family for years. He lived here on sufferance and used her capital to run a small wine business from the house. Presumably most of the stock's still here if she hasn't drunk or sold it. No, she wouldn't leave. In fact I can't imagine any circumstances at all, not even fire, which would make her abandon her precious Streech Grange. She's a very tough lady.'

'And, I suppose, as he was in clover, he wouldn't go either.'

'That's about the size of it.'

'So she got rid of him.'

Walsh nodded.

'But you couldn't prove it.'

'No.'

McLoughlin's bleak face cracked into a semblance of a grin. 'She must have come up with one hell of a story.'

'Matter of fact, it was bloody awful. She told us he walked out one night and never returned.' Walsh wiped a dribble of tar and saliva off the end of his pipe with his sleeve. 'It was three days before she reported him missing, and she only did that because people had started to ask where he was. In that time she packed up all his clothes and sent them off to some charity whose name she couldn't remember, she burnt all his photos and went through this house with a vacuum cleaner and a cloth soaked with bleach to remove every last trace of him. In other words she behaved exactly like someone who had just murdered her husband and was trying to get rid of the evidence. We salvaged some hair that she'd missed in a brush, a current passport and photo that she'd overlooked at the back of a desk drawer, and an old blood donor card. And that was it. We turned this house and garden upside down, called in forensic to do a microscopic search and it was a waste of time. We scoured the countryside for him, showed his photo at all the ports and airports in case he'd somehow got through without a passport, alerted Interpol to look for him on the Continent, dredged lakes and rivers, released his photo to the national newspapers. Nothing. He simply vanished into thin air.'

'So how did she explain the bruise on her face?'

The Inspector chuckled. 'A door. What else? I tried to help her, suggested she killed her husband in self-defence. But no, he never touched her.' He shook his head, remembering. 'Extraordinary woman. She never made it easy for herself. She could have manufactured any number of stories to convince us he'd planned his disappearance – money troubles, for a start. He left her well-nigh penniless. But she did the reverse – she kept stolidly repeating that one night and for no reason he simply walked out and never came back. Only dead men disappear as completely as that.'

'Clever,' said McLoughlin reluctantly. 'She kept it simple, gave you nothing to pick holes in. So why didn't you charge her? Prosecutions have been brought without bodies before.'

The memories of ten years ago flooded back to try Walsh's patience. 'We couldn't put a case together,' he snapped. 'There wasn't one shred of evidence to dispute her bloody stupid story that he'd upped and left. We needed the body. We dug up half Hampshire looking for the blasted thing.' He fell silent for a moment, then tapped the photograph of the ice house which lay on the desk in front of him. 'You were right about this.'

'In what way?'

'It is the key. We searched Streech gardens from end to end ten years ago and none of us looked in here. I'd never seen an ice house in my life, never even heard of such a thing. So of course I didn't know the bloody hill was hollow. How the hell could I? No one told me. I remember standing on it at one point to get my bearings. I even remember telling one of my chaps to delve deep into those brambles. It was like a jungle.' He wiped the stem of his pipe on his sleeve again before putting it back in his mouth. Dried tar criss-crossed the tweed like black threads. 'I'll lay you any money you like, Andy, Maybury's body was in there all the time.'

There was a knock at the door and Phoebe came in carrying a tray of sandwiches. 'Constable Williams told me you were hungry, Inspector. I asked Molly to make these up for you.'

'Why thank you, Mrs Maybury. Come and sit down.' Phoebe put the tray of sandwiches on the desk, then seated herself in a leather armchair slightly to one side of it. The lamp on the desk shed a pool of light, embracing the three figures in a reluctant intimacy. The smoke from Walsh's pipe hung above them, floating in the air like curling tendrils of cirrus clouds. For one long moment there was complete silence, before the chiming mechanism of a grandfather clock whirred into action and struck the hour, nine o'clock.

Walsh, as if on cue, leant forward and addressed the

woman. 'Why didn't you tell us about the ice house ten years ago, Mrs Maybury?'

For a moment he thought she looked surprised, even a little relieved, then the expression vanished. Afterwards, he couldn't be sure it had been there at all. 'I don't understand,' she said.

Inspector Walsh gestured to McLoughlin to switch on the overhead lights. The muted lamplight disguised, deceived when he wanted to see every nuance of the extraordinarily impassive face. 'It's quite simple,' he murmured, after McLoughlin had flooded the room with brilliant white light, 'in our search for your husband, we never looked in the ice house. We didn't know it was there.' He studied her thoughtfully. 'And you didn't tell us.'

'I don't remember,' she said simply. 'If I didn't tell you, it was because I had forgotten about it. Did you not find it yourselves?'

'No.'

She gave a tiny shrug. 'Does it really matter, Inspector, after all this time?'

He ignored the question. 'Do you recall when the ice house was last used prior to your husband's disappearance?'

She leant her head tiredly against the back of her chair, her red hair splayed out around her pale face. Behind her glasses her eyes looked huge. Walsh knew her to be in her mid-thirties, yet she looked younger than his own daughter. He felt McLoughlin stir in the seat beside him as if her fragility had touched him in some way. Damn the woman, he thought with irritation, remembering the emotions she had once stirred in him. That appearance of vulnerability was a thin cloak for the sharp mind beneath.

'You'll have to let me think about it,' she said. 'At the moment, I honestly can't remember if we ever used it when David was alive. I have no recollection of it.' She paused briefly. 'I *do* recall my father using it as a darkroom one winter when I was on holiday from school. He didn't do it for very long.' She smiled. 'He said it was a confounded bore slogging all the way down there in the cold.' She gave a low ripple of laughter as if memories of her father made her happy. 'He took the films to a professional in Silverborne instead. My mother said it was because he enjoyed blaming someone else when the prints were disappointing, which they often were. He wasn't a very good photographer.' She looked steadily at the Inspector. 'I can't remember its being used after that, not until we decided to stack the bricks in there. The children might know. I suppose I could ask them.'

Walsh remembered her children, a gangling ten-year-old boy, arriving home from his boarding prep-school in the middle of the investigation, his eyes the same clear blue as his mother's, and an eight-year-old daughter with a bush of curling dark hair. They had protected her, he recalled, with the same fierce quality that her two friends had shown earlier in the drawing-room. 'Jonathan and Jane,' he said. 'Do they still live at home, Mrs Maybury?'

'Not really. Jonathan rents a flat in London. He's a medical student at Guy's. Jane is studying politics and philosophy at Oxford. They spend the odd weekend and holidays here. That's all.'

'They've done well. You must be pleased.' He thought sourly of his own daughter who had got herself pregnant at sixteen and who now, at the age of twenty-five, was divorced with four children, and had nothing to look forward to except life in a tatty council flat. He consulted his notes. 'You seem to have acquired a profession since I last saw you, Mrs Maybury. Constable Williams tells me you're a market gardener.'

Phoebe seemed puzzled by his change of direction. 'Fred's helped me build up a small Pelargonium nursery.' She spoke warily. 'We specialise in the Ivyleaf varieties.'

'Who buys them?'

'We have two main customers in this country, one's a supermarket chain and the other's a garden-supplies outlet in Devon and Cornwall. We've also had a few bulk orders from the States which we've air-freighted out.' She was intensely suspicious of him. 'Why do you want to know?'

'No particular reason,' he assured her. He sucked noisily on his pipe. 'I expect you get a lot of customers from the village.'

'None,' she said shortly. 'We don't sell direct to the

public and, anyway, they wouldn't come here if we did.'

'You're not very popular in Streech, are you, Mrs Maybury?'

'So it would seem, Inspector.'

'You worked as a receptionist in the doctor's surgery ten years ago. Didn't you like that job?'

A flicker of amusement lifted the corners of her mouth. 'I was asked to leave. The patients felt uncomfortable with a murderess.'

'Did your husband know about the ice house?' He shot the question at her suddenly, unnerving her.

'That it was there, you mean?'

He nodded.

'I'm sure he must have done, though, as I say, I don't remember him ever going in there.'

Walsh made a note. 'We'll follow that up. The children may remember something. Will they be here this weekend, Mrs Maybury?'

She felt cold. 'I suppose if they don't come down, you'll send a policeman to them.'

'It's important.'

There was a tremor in her voice. 'Is it, Inspector? You have our word there was no body in there six years ago. What possible connection can that – that thing have with David's disappearance?' She took off her glasses and pressed her fingertips against her eyelids. 'I don't want the children harassed. They suffered enough when David went missing. To have the whole ghastly trauma played out a second time and for no obvious reason would be intolerable.'

Walsh smiled indulgently. 'Routine questions, Mrs Maybury. Hardly very traumatic, surely?'

She put her glasses on again, angered by his response. 'You were extraordinarily stupid ten years ago, of course. Why I ever assumed the passage of time would make you any brighter, I can't think. You sent us to hell and you call it "hardly traumatic". Do you know what hell is? Hell is what a little girl of eight goes through when the police dig up all the flowerbeds and question her mother for hours on end in a closed room. Hell is what is in your young son's eyes when his father deserts him without a word of explanation and his mother is accused of murder. Hell is seeing your children hurting and not being able to do a damn thing to stop it. You asked me if I was pleased with their achievements.' She leaned forward, her face twisted. 'Surely even you could have come up with something a little more imaginative? They have lived through the mysterious disappearance of their father, their mother being branded a murderess, their home being turned into a tourist attraction for the ghoulish and they have survived it relatively unscathed. I think "ecstatic" might be a better description of how I feel about the way they've turned out.'

'We suggested at the time you should send the

children away, Mrs Maybury.' Walsh kept his voice carefully neutral. 'You chose to keep them here against our advice.'

Phoebe stood up. It was only the second time he had ever seen any violent emotion on that face. 'My God, I hate you.' She put her hands on the desk and he saw that the fingers trembled uncontrollably. 'Where was I to send them? My parents were dead, I had no brothers or sisters, neither Anne nor Diana was in a position to care for them. Was I supposed to entrust them to strangers when their own secure world was turning upside down?' She thought of her only relation, her father's unmarried sister, who had fallen out with the family years before. The old lady had read between every line of every newspaper with voracious delight and had penned her own small piece of poison to Phoebe on the subject of the sins of the parents. What her intentions were in writing the letter was anyone's guess but, in a strange way, her warped predictions for Jonathan and Jane had been a liberation for Phoebe. She had seen clearly then – and for the first time – that the past was dead and buried and that regrets would achieve her nothing.

'How dare you speak to me of choice! My only choice was to smile while you shat on me and never once let the children know how frightened and alone I felt.' Her fingers gripped the edge of the desk. 'I will not go through all that again. I will not allow you to stick your dirty fingers into my children's lives. You've spread your filthy muck here once. You're bloody well not going to do it again.' She turned away and walked to the door.

'I've some more questions for you, Mrs Maybury. Please don't go.'

She looked round briefly as she opened the door. 'Fuck off, Inspector.' The door slammed behind her.

McLoughlin had listened to their exchange with rapt attention. 'Bit of a sea-change from this afternoon. Is she always as volatile?'

'Quite the reverse. Ten years ago we never rattled her composure once.' He sucked thoughtfully on his filthy briar.

'It's those two dykes she's shacked up with. They've turned her against men.'

Walsh was amused. 'I should think David Maybury did that years ago. Let's talk to Mrs Goode. Will you go and find her?'

McLoughlin reached for a sandwich and crammed it into his mouth before standing up. 'What about the other one? Shall I line her up too?'

The Chief Inspector thought for a moment. 'No. She's a dark horse, that one. I'll let her stew till I've checked up on her.'

From where he was standing, McLoughlin could see pink scalp shining through Walsh's thinning hair. He felt a sudden tenderness for the older man, as if Phoebe's hostility had exorcised his own and reminded him where his loyalties lay. 'She's your most likely suspect, sir. She'd have enjoyed cutting that poor sod's balls off. The other two would have hated it.'

'You're probably right, lad, but I'm betting he was dead when she did it.'

Five

STREECH GRANGE WAS a fine old Jacobean mansion built of grey stone, with mullioned, leaded windows and steep slate roofs. Two wings, later additions, extended out at either end of the main body of the house, embracing the sides of the flagged terrace where the women had taken their tea. Stud partitions inside made each of these wings self-contained, with unlocked doors on the ground floor giving access to and from them. Sergeant McLoughlin, after a fruitless search of the drawing-room and the kitchen which were both empty, came to the communicating door with the east wing. He tapped lightly but, getting no response, turned the handle and walked down the corridor in front of him.

A door stood ajar at the end. He could hear a deep voice – unmistakably Anne Cattrell's – coming from inside the room. He listened.

'. . . stick to your guns and don't let the bastards intimidate you. God knows, I've had more experience of them than most. Whatever happens, Jane must be kept out of the way. You agree?' There was a murmur of assent. 'And, old love, if you can wipe the smirk off that Sergeant's face, you'll have my lifelong admiration.'

'I suppose it's occurred to you' – the lighter amused voice was Diana's – 'that he might have been born with that smirk. Perhaps it's a disability he's had to learn to cope with, like a withered arm. You'd be quite sympathetic if that were the case.'

Anne gave her throaty laugh. 'The only disabilities that idiot has are both in his trousers.'

'Namely?'

'He's a prick and an arsehole.'

Diana crowed with laughter and McLoughlin felt a dull flush creep up his neck. He trod softly to the communicating door, closed it behind him and knocked again, this time more loudly. When, after some moments, Anne opened the door, he was ready with his most sardonic smile.

'Yes, Sergeant?'

'I'm looking for Mrs Goode. Inspector Walsh would like a word with her.'

'This is my wing. She's not here.'

The lie was so blatant that he looked at her in astonishment. 'But – ' He paused.

'But what, Sergeant?'

'Where will I find her?'

'I've no idea. Perhaps the Inspector would like to speak to me instead?'

McLoughlin pushed past her impatiently and walked down the corridor and into the room. There was no one in there. He frowned. The room was a large one with a desk at one end and a sofa and armchairs grouped about a wide fireplace at the other. Pot plants grew in profusion everywhere, cascading like green waterfalls from the mantelpiece, climbing up lattice-work on one of the walls, dappling the light from the lamps on low occasional tables. Floor to ceiling curtains in a herring-bone pattern of pale pinks, greys and blues were drawn along the length of the two outside walls, a royal blue carpet covered the floor, bright abstract paintings laughed merrily from the picture rails. Books in bookcases stood as straight as soldiers wherever there was a space. It was a delightful room, not one that McLoughlin would ever have associated with the tiny muscular woman who had followed him in and was now leaning her cropped, dark head against the door-jamb, waiting.

'Do you make a habit of forcing your way into people's private apartments, Sergeant? I have no recollection of inviting you in.'

'We have Mrs Maybury's permission to come and go as we please,' he said dismissively.

She walked over to one of the armchairs and slumped into it, taking a cigarette from a packet on the arm. 'Of course, in her house,' she agreed, lighting the cigarette. 'But this wing is mine. You have no authority to enter here except by permission or with a warrant.'

'I'm sorry,' he said stiffly. He felt suddenly uncomfortable, towering over her, conspicuously ill-at-ease while she, by contrast, was relaxed. 'I was not aware you owned this part of the house.'

'I don't own it, I rent it, but the legal position with regard to police entry is the same.' She smiled thinly. 'As a matter of interest, what possible reason had you for thinking Mrs Goode might be in here?'

He saw one of the curtain edges lift as a gentle breeze caught it, and realised Diana must have left by a French window. He cursed himself silently for allowing this woman to make a mockery of him. 'I couldn't find her anywhere else,' he said brusquely, 'and Inspector Walsh wants to speak to her. Does she live in the other wing?'

'She rents the other wing. As to living in it – surely you've guessed we all three rather muck in together. It's what's known as a ménage à trois, though in our case, rather loosely. The average threesome includes both sexes. We, I'm afraid, are more exclusive, preferring, as we do, our peculiarly – how shall I describe it? – spicy female sex. Three makes for more exciting encounters than two, don't you think. Or have you never tried?'

His dislike of her was irrational and intense. He

jerked his head in the direction of the main part of the house. 'Have you corrupted her children the way you've corrupted her?'

She laughed softly and stood up. 'You'll find Mrs Goode in her sitting-room, I expect. I'll show you out.' She led the way along her corridor and opened the door. 'Walk straight through the main body of the house until you reach the west wing. It's a mirror image of this. You'll find a similar door to mine leading into it.' She pointed to a bell on the wall which he hadn't previously noticed. 'I should ring that if I were you. At the very least, it would be polite.' She stood watching him as he walked away, a scornful smile distorting her lips.

Andy McLoughlin had to pass the library door to reach the west wing so he looked in to tell Walsh it would be a few minutes yet before he returned with Diana Goode. To his surprise, she was in there already, sitting in the chair Phoebe had sat in. She and the Inspector turned their heads as the door opened. They were laughing together like people sharing a private joke.

'There you are, Sergeant. We've been waiting for you.'

He took his seat again and viewed Diana with suspicion. 'How did you know the Inspector wanted to talk to you?' He pictured her outside the French windows listening to Anne Cattrell making a fool of him.

'I didn't, Sergeant. I popped my head in to see if you wanted a cup of coffee.' She smiled good-humouredly and crossed one elegant leg over the other. 'What did you want to talk to me about, Inspector?'

There was an appreciative gleam in George Walsh's eye. 'How long have you known Mrs Maybury?' he asked her.

'Twenty-five years. Since we were twelve. We were at boarding school together. Anne, too.'

'A long time.'

'Yes. We've known her longer than anyone else, I suppose, longer even than her parents did. They died when she was in her early twenties.' She came to a halt. 'But you know all about that from last time,' she finished awkwardly.

'Remind us,' Walsh encouraged.

Diana lowered her eyes to hide their expression. It was all very well for Anne to say don't let the bastards intimidate you. Knowledge itself was intimidating. With one casual reference, the sort she might make to anyone, she had rekindled the sparks of an old suspicion. No smoke without fire, everyone had said when David disappeared.

'They died in a car crash, didn't they?' Walsh prompted.

She nodded. 'The brakes failed. They were dead

when they were cut out of the wreckage.' There was a long silence.

'If I remember correctly,' said Walsh to McLoughlin when Diana didn't go on, 'there were rumours of sabotage. Am I right, Mrs Goode? The village seemed to think Mrs Maybury caused the accident to get her hands prematurely on her inheritance. People have long memories. The story was resurrected at the time of Mr Maybury's disappearance.'

McLoughlin studied Diana's bent head. 'Why should they think that?' he asked.

'Because they're stupid,' she said fiercely. 'There was no truth in it. The Coroner's verdict couldn't have been clearer – the brakes failed because fluid had leaked from a corroded hose. The car was supposed to have been serviced three weeks before by a man called Casey who owned the garage in the village. He was just a bloody little crook. He took the money and didn't do the job.' She frowned. 'There was talk of a prosecution but it never came to anything. Not enough evidence, apparently. Anyway, it was Casey who started rumours that Phoebe had sabotaged the car to get her hands on Streech Grange. He didn't want to lose his customers.'

McLoughlin looked her up and down, but there was no appreciative gleam in his eyes. His indifference was complete and, to a woman like Diana who used flirtation to manipulate both sexes, it was daunting.

Charm was powerless against a stone wall. 'There must have been more to it than that,' he suggested dryly. 'People aren't usually so gullible.'

She played with the hem of her jacket. 'It was David's fault. Phoebe's parents had given them a little house in Pimlico as a wedding present which David used as collateral for a loan. He lost the lot on some stock market gamble, couldn't make the repayments and they were in the throes of foreclosure at the time of the accident, with two small children, no money and nowhere to go.' She shook her head. 'God knows how, but that became public knowledge. The locals lapped up what Casey was saying, put two and two together and made five. From the moment Phoebe took over this house, she was damned. David's disappearance a few years later simply confirmed all their prejudices.' She sighed. 'The sickening thing is, they didn't believe Casey either. He went bankrupt ten months later when all his customers deserted him. He had to sell up and move away, so there was some justice,' she said spitefully. 'Not that it did Phoebe any good. They were too damn stupid to see that if he was lying, she was innocent.'

McLoughlin leaned back in his chair, splaying strong fingers against the desk-top. He flicked her an unexpectedly boyish smile. 'It must have been awful for her.'

She responded guardedly. 'It was. She was so young and she had to cope with it alone. David either took himself off for weeks at a time or made matters worse by getting into rows with people.'

His eyes softened, as if he understood loneliness and could sympathise with it. 'And I suppose her friends here deserted her because of him?'

Diana thawed. 'She never really had any, that was half the trouble. If she had, it would have made all the difference. She went away to boarding school at the age of twelve, married at seventeen and only came back when her parents were dead. She's never had any friends in Streech.'

McLoughlin drummed his fingers softly on the mahogany. '"The worst solitude is to be destitute of sincere friendship." Francis Bacon said that four hundred years ago.'

She was quite taken aback. Anne used Francis Bacon quotes as a matter of course but they tended to be flippant, throw-away lines, tossed into a conversation for careless effect. McLoughlin's dark voice lingered over the words, rolling them on his tongue, giving them weight. She was as surprised by their aptness as by the fact that he knew them. She regarded him thoughtfully.

'But he also said, "The mould of a man's fortune is in his own hands."' His lips twisted cruelly. 'It's odd, isn't it, how Mrs Maybury brings out the worst in people? What's her secret, I wonder?' He stirred the photographs of crude death with the end of his pencil, turning them slowly so that Diana could see them.

'Why didn't she sell the Grange and move away, once she'd got rid of her husband?'

For all her surface sophistication, Diana was naive. Brutality shocked her because she never saw it coming. 'She couldn't,' she snapped angrily. 'It's not Phoebe's to sell. After a year of marriage to that bastard, she persuaded her father to change his Will and leave the house to her children. We three rent it from them.'

'Then why haven't her children sold it? Have they no sympathy for their mother?' He caught her eye. 'Or perhaps they don't like her? It seems to be a common problem for Mrs Maybury.'

Anger threatened to overwhelm Diana. She forced herself to stay calm. 'The idea, Sergeant, was to prevent David turning the house into ready cash and leaving Phoebe and the children homeless the minute the Gallaghers died. He'd have done it, too, given half a chance. He went through the money she inherited in record time. Colonel Gallagher, Phoebe's father, left instructions that the house could not be sold or mortgaged except under the most exceptional circumstances before Jane's twenty-first birthday. The responsibility for deciding whether those circumstances – principally financial distress on the part of Phoebe and her children – ever materialise was left to two trustees. In the view of the trustees, things have never got so bad that the sale of the Grange was the only option.'

'Was no other distress taken into account?'

'Of course not,' she said with heavy sarcasm. 'How could it have been? Colonel Gallagher wasn't clairvoyant. He did give discretion to the trustees but they have chosen to stick to the precise terms of the Will. In view of the uncertainty over David, whether he's dead or alive, it seemed the safest thing to do, even if Phoebe did suffer.' She glanced at Walsh to draw him back into the discussion. McLoughlin frightened her. 'The trustees have always put the children first, as they were instructed to do under the terms of the Will.'

McLoughlin's amusement was genuine. 'I'm beginning to feel quite sorry for Mrs Maybury. Does she dislike these trustees as much as they seem to dislike her?'

'I wouldn't know, Sergeant. I've never asked her.'

'Who are they?'

Chief Inspector Walsh chuckled. The lad had just hanged himself. 'Miss Anne Cattrell and Mrs Diana Goode. It was some Will, gave you two ladies a deal of responsibility when you were barely in your twenties. We've a copy on file,' he told the Sergeant. 'Colonel Gallagher must have thought very highly of you both to entrust you with his grandchildren's future.'

Diana smiled. She must remember to tell Anne how she'd wiped the smirk off McLoughlin's face. 'He did,' she said. 'Why should that surprise you?'

Walsh pursed his lips. 'I found it surprising ten years ago, but then I had never met you and Miss

Cattrell. You were abroad at that time, I think, Mrs Goode.' He smiled and dropped one eyelid in what looked remarkably like a wink. 'I do not find it surprising now.'

She inclined her head. 'Thank you. My ex-husband is American. I was with him in the States when David vanished. I returned a year later after my divorce.'

She continued to look at Walsh but the hairs on her neck bristled under the weight of McLoughlin's gaze. She didn't want to catch his eye again. 'Did Colonel Gallagher know about the relationship you and Miss Cattrell had with his daughter?' he asked softly.

'That we were friends, you mean?' She kept her eyes on the Inspector.

'I was thinking more in terms of the bedroom, Mrs Goode, and the effect your fun and games might have on his grandchildren. Or didn't he know about that?'

Diana stared at her hands. She found people's contempt so difficult to handle and she wished she had one half of Anne's indifference to it. 'Not that it's any of your business, Sergeant,' she said at last, 'but Gerald Gallagher knew everything there was to know about us. He was not a man you had to hide things from.'

Walsh had been busily replenishing his pipe with tobacco. He put it into his mouth and lit it, belching more smoke into the already fuggy atmosphere. 'After they came back to the house, did either Mrs Maybury or Miss Cattrell suggest that they thought the body in the ice house was David Maybury's?'

'No.'

'Did either of them say who they thought it might be?'

'Anne said it was probably a tramp who had had a heart attack.'

'Mrs Maybury?'

Diana thought for a moment. 'Her only comment was that tramps don't die of heart attacks in the nude.'

'What's your view, Mrs Goode?'

'I don't have a view, Inspector, except that it isn't David. You've already had my reasons for that.'

'Why do you and Miss Cattrell want Jane Maybury kept out of the way?' McLoughlin asked suddenly.

There was no hesitation in her answer though she glanced at him curiously as she spoke. 'Jane was anorexic until eighteen months ago. She took a place at Oxford last September with her consultant's blessing, but he warned her not to put herself under unnecessary pressure. As trustees, we endorse Phoebe's view that Jane should be protected from this. She's still painfully thin. Undue anxiety would use up her reserves of energy. Do you consider that unreasonable, Sergeant?'

'Not at all,' he answered mildly.

'I wonder why Mrs Maybury didn't explain her daughter's condition to us,' asked Walsh. 'Has she a particular reason for keeping quiet about it?'

'None that I know of, but perhaps experience has taught her to be circumspect where the police are concerned.'

'How so?' He was affable.

'It's in your nature to go for the weak link. We all know that Jane can tell you nothing about that body, but Phoebe's probably afraid you'll question her until she cracks. And only when you've broken her will you be satisfied that she knew nothing in the first place.'

'You've a very twisted view of us, Mrs Goode.'

Diana forced a light laugh. 'Surely not, Inspector. Of the three of us, I'm the only one who retains some confidence in you. It is I, after all, who is giving you information.' She uncrossed her legs and drew them up on to the chair, covering them entirely with her knitted jacket. Her eyes rested briefly on the photographs. 'Is it a man's body? Anne and Phoebe couldn't tell.'

'At the moment we think so.'

'Murdered?'

'Probably.'

'Then take my advice and look in this village or the surrounding ones for your victim and your murderer. Phoebe is such an obvious scapegoat for someone else's crime. Shove the body on to her property and leave her to carry the can, that will have been the thinking behind this.'

Walsh nodded appreciatively as he pencilled a note

on his pad. 'It's a possibility, Mrs Goode, a definite possibility. You're interested in psychology?'

He's quite a poppet after all, thought Diana, unleashing one of the calculatedly charming smiles she reserved for her more biddable customers. 'I use it all the time in my work,' she told him, 'though I don't suppose a clinician would call what I use psychology.'

He beamed back at her. 'So what would *he* call it?'

'Hidden persuasion, I should think.' She thought of Lady Keevil and her lime-green curtains. Lies, Anne would call it.

'Do your clients come here to consult you?'

She shook her head. 'No. It's their interiors they want designing, not mine. I go to them.'

'But you're an attractive woman, Mrs Goode.' His admiration for her was blatant. 'You must have a lot of friends who come visiting, people from the village, people you've met over the years.'

She wondered if he guessed how tender this particular nerve was, how deeply she felt the isolation of their lives. At first, bruised and battered from the break-up of her marriage, it had hardly mattered. She had withdrawn inside the walls of Streech Grange to lick her wounds in peace, grateful for the absence of well-meaning friends and their embarrassing commiserations. The shock of discovery, as her scars healed and she tendered for one or two small design contracts, that Phoebe's exclusion had been imposed and not chosen had been a real one. She had learnt what it was to be a pariah; she had watched Phoebe nurture her hate; she had watched Anne's tolerance turn to cynical indifference; she had heard her own voice grow brittle. 'No,' she corrected him. 'We have very few visitors, certainly never from the village.'

His eyes were encouraging. 'Then tell me, assuming you're right and our victim and murderer are local, how could they know about the ice house and, if they did know about it, how did they find it? I think you'll agree it's well disguised.'

'Anyone could know about it,' she said dismissively. 'Fred may have mentioned it in the pub after he stacked the bricks in there. Phoebe's parents may have told people about it. I don't see that as a mystery.'

'All right. Now tell me how you find it if you haven't been shown where it is? Presumably none of you has noticed an intruder searching the grounds or you'd have mentioned it. And another thing, why was it necessary to put the body in there at all?'

She shrugged. 'It's a good hiding place.'

'How did the murderer know that? How did he or she know the ice house wasn't in regular use? And what was the point of hiding the body if the idea was to make Phoebe Maybury the scapegoat? You see, Mrs Goode, the picture is rather unclear.'

She thought for a moment. 'You can't rule out pure chance. Someone committed a murder, decided to get rid of the body in the Grange grounds in the hopes that, if it was discovered, the police would concentrate their efforts on Phoebe, and stumbled on the ice house by accident while looking for somewhere to put the body.'

'But the ice house is half a mile from the gates,' Walsh objected. 'Do you seriously believe that a murderer staggered past the Lodge House and all the way down your drive and across your lawn in pitch darkness with a body on his shoulders? We can assume, I think, that no one would have been mad enough to do it during the daytime. Why didn't he simply bury the body in the wood near the gates?'

She looked uncomfortable. 'Perhaps he came over the wall at the back and approached the ice house from that direction.'

'Wouldn't that have meant negotiating his way through Grange Farm, which if I remember correctly adjoins the Grange at the back?' She nodded reluctantly. 'Why run that danger? And why, having run it, not bury the body quickly, in the woodland there? Why was it so important to put him in the ice house?'

Diana shivered suddenly. She understood perfectly that he was trying to box her in, force her on to the defensive and admit that knowledge of the ice house and its whereabouts was a crucial element. 'It seems to me, Inspector,' she continued coolly, 'that you have made a number of assumptions which – correct me if I'm wrong – have yet to be substantiated. First, you are assuming the body was taken there. Perhaps whoever it was went under his – or her – own steam and met the murderer there.'

'Of course we've considered that possibility, Mrs Goode. It doesn't alter our thinking at all. We must still ask: Why the ice house and how did they know where to find it unless they had been there before?'

'Well, then,' she said, 'work on the assumption that people have been there and find out who they are. Off the top of my head, I could make several suggestions. Friends of Colonel Gallagher and his wife, for example.'

'Who would be in their seventies or eighties by now. Of course it's possible that an elderly person was responsible but statistically unlikely.'

'People to whom Phoebe or David pointed it out.'

McLoughlin moved on his chair. 'Mrs Maybury has already told us she'd forgotten all about it, so much so that she omitted to tell the police it was there when they were searching the grounds for her husband. It seems unlikely, if she had forgotten it to that extent, that she would have remembered to point it out to casual visitors who, from what you yourself have said, don't come here anyway.'

'David then.'

'Now you have it, Mrs Goode,' said the Inspector. 'David Maybury may well have shown the ice house to someone, to several people even, but Mrs Maybury has no recollection of it. Indeed, she cannot recall *him* ever using it though she did agree that he was probably aware of its existence. Frankly, Mrs Goode, at the moment I don't see how we can proceed in that direction unless Mrs Maybury or the children can remember occasions or names that might give us a lead.'

'The children,' said Diana, leaning forward. 'I should have thought of it before. They will have taken their friends there when they were younger. You know how inquisitive children are, there can't be an inch of this estate they won't have explored with their gang.' She sank back with sudden relief. 'That's it, of course. It'll be one of the village children who grew up with them, hardly a child now, though – someone in his early twenties.' She noticed the smirk was back on McLoughlin's face.

Walsh spoke gently. 'I agree entirely that that is a possibility. Which is why it's so important for us to question Jonathan *and* Jane. It can't be avoided, you know, however much you and her mother may dislike the idea. Jane may be the only one who can lead us to a murderer.' He reached for another sandwich. 'The police are not barbarians, Mrs Goode. I can assure you we will be sympathetic and tactful in our dealings with her. I hope you will persuade Mrs Maybury of that.'

Diana uncurled her legs and stood up. Quite unaware of it, she leant on the desk in just the way Phoebe had done, as if close proximity had taught the women to adopt each other's mannerisms. 'I can't promise anything, Inspector. Phoebe has a mind of her own.'

'She has no choice in the matter,' he said flatly, 'except to influence her daughter over whether we question her here or in Oxford. Under the circumstances, I imagine Mrs Maybury would prefer it to be here.'

Diana straightened. 'Is there anything else you want to ask me?'

'Only two more things tonight. Tomorrow Sergeant McLoughlin will question you in more detail.' He looked up at her. 'How did Mrs Maybury come to employ the Phillipses? Did she advertise or did she apply to an agency?'

Diana's hands were fluttering. She thrust them into the pockets of her jacket. 'I believe Anne arranged it,' she said. 'You'll have to ask her.'

'Thank you. Now, just one more thing. When you helped clear the rubbish from the ice house what exactly was in there and what did you do with it?'

'It was ages ago,' she said uncomfortably. 'I can't remember. Nothing out of the way, just rubbish.'

Walsh looked at her thoughtfully. 'Describe the inside of the ice house to me, Mrs Goode.' He watched her eyes search rapidly amongst the photographs on the desk, but he had turned over all the general shots when she first came in. 'How big is it? What shape is the doorway? What's the floor made of?'

'I can't remember.'

He smiled a slow, satisfied smile and she was reminded of a stuffed timber wolf she had once seen with bared teeth and staring glass eyes. 'Thank you,' he said. She was dismissed.

Six

DIANA FOUND PHOEBE watching the ten o'clock news in the television room. The flickering colours from the set provided the only light and they played across Phoebe's glasses, hiding her eyes and giving her the look of a blind woman. Diana snapped on the table lamp.

'You'll get a headache,' she said, flopping into the seat beside Phoebe, reaching out to stroke the softly tanned forearm.

Phoebe muted the sound of the television with the remote control on her lap, but left the picture running. 'I've got one already,' she admitted tiredly. She took off her glasses and held a handkerchief to her red-rimmed eyes. 'Sorry,' she said.

'What about?'

'Blubbing. I thought I'd grown out of it.'

Diana pulled a footstool forward with her toes and settled her feet on it comfortably. 'A good blub is one of my few remaining pleasures.'

Phoebe smiled. 'But not very helpful.' She tucked the handkerchief into her sleeve and replaced her glasses.

'Have you had anything to eat?'

'I'm not hungry. Molly left a casserole in the Aga if you are.'

'Mm, she told me before she left. I'm not hungry either.'

They lapsed into silence.

'It's a bloody mess, isn't it?' said Phoebe after a while.

'I'm afraid so.' Diana pushed her sandals off her feet and let them drop to the floor. 'The Inspector's no fool.' She kept her voice deliberately light.

Phoebe spoke harshly. 'I hate him. How old would you say he is?'

'Late fifties.'

'He hasn't aged much. He looked like a genial professor ten years ago.' She considered for a moment. 'But that's not his character. He's anything but genial. He's dangerous, Di. For God's sake don't forget it.'

The other woman nodded. 'And his incubus, Jock-the-Ripper? What did you make of him?'

Phoebe looked surprised as if the other woman had mentioned an irrelevance. 'The Sergeant? He didn't say much. Why do you ask?'

With rhythmical movements, as if she were stroking a cat, Diana smoothed the woollen pile on the front of her jacket. 'Anne's spoiling for a fight with him and

I'm not sure why.' She glanced speculatively at Phoebe, who shrugged. 'She's making a mistake. She took one look at him in the drawing-room, labelled him "Pig-ignorant" and made up her mind to walk all over him. Damn!' she said with feeling. 'Why can't she learn to compromise occasionally? She'll have us up to our necks in shit if she's not careful.'

'Have they spoken to her yet?'

'No, they've told her they'll talk to her tomorrow. They seem very relaxed about it all. We have their official permission to go to bed.'

Phoebe closed her eyes and pressed long fingers against her temples. 'What did they ask you?'

Diana twisted in her chair to look at her friend. 'From what they implied, exactly what they asked you.'

'Except that I walked out and refused to answer their questions.' She opened her eyes and looked ruefully at the other woman. 'I know,' she said. 'It was very silly of me but they made me so angry. Strange, isn't it? I stood up to hours of interrogation when David went. This time, I lasted five minutes. I found myself hating that man so much, I wanted to claw his eyes out. I could have done it, too.'

Diana reached out again and briefly touched her arm. 'I don't think it's strange – any psychiatrist would tell you that anger is a normal reaction to stress – but it's probably unwise.' She pulled a face. 'Anne will say I've bottled out, of course, but my view is we should give them all the co-operation we can. The sooner they sort it out and leave us alone, the better.'

'They want to question the children.'

'I know and I don't think we can prevent it.'

'I could ask Jane's psychiatrist to write a report advising against it. Would that stop them?'

'For a day or two perhaps before they secured an order for a second opinion. That would declare her competent to answer questions. You know yourself, her own psychiatrist pronounced her fit eighteen months ago.'

'Not for this.' Phoebe massaged her temples vigorously. 'I'm frightened, Di. I really think she's managed to blot it all out. If they make her remember now, God knows what will happen.'

'Talk to Anne,' Diana said. 'She can be more objective than you. You may find that you're underestimating Jane's strengths. She is your daughter, after all.'

'Meaning that I am less able to be objective?'

Go easy, Diana told herself. 'Meaning that she will have inherited the rigid Gallagher backbone, you oaf.'

'You're forgetting her father. However much I might like to pretend otherwise, there is some of David in each of them.'

'He wasn't all bad, Pheeb.'

Tears welled uncontrollably in Phoebe's eyes. She blinked them away angrily. 'But he was, and you know it as well as I do. You told the Inspector so this afternoon and you were right. He was rotten to the core. In time, if we hadn't got shot of him, he'd have turned me and the children rotten too. He had a damn good try in all conscience.' She was silent for a moment. 'It's the only thing I hold against my parents. If they hadn't been so conventional I need never have married him. I could have had Jonny and brought him up on my own.'

'It was difficult for them.' But I agree with her, thought Diana. There was no excuse for what her parents did, so why am I defending them? 'They did what they thought was right.'

'I was seventeen, for Christ's sake – ' Phoebe's nails bit deep into her palms – 'younger than Jane is now. I allowed myself to be married off to a bastard twice my age simply because he'd seduced me, and then I just stood by and watched him rewarded for it. Christ,' she spat, 'it makes me sick to think of the money he bled from my father.'

Then don't think about it, Diana wanted to say. You've tried to forget them, but there *were* good times, times at the beginning when Anne and I envied you because you were a woman and we were still gangling schoolgirls. One weekend in particular, it was still vivid in her memory, when David on some mad whim had taken the three of them on a business trip to Paris. She forgot which company he was working for, there had been so many, but the weekend she would never forget. David, so assured, so deft in his choice of where to go and what to do, so unaffected by the foreignness of it all; Phoebe, four months pregnant, lovely face framed in a glorious picture hat, so delighted with herself and with David; and Anne and Diana, out for half-term, in a fantasy of beautiful people in beautiful places. And it was fantasy, of course, for the reality of David Maybury was brutish, ugly – Diana had discovered that for herself – yet once, in Paris, they had known enchantment.

Phoebe stood abruptly, walked over to the television set and switched it off. She spoke with her back to Diana. 'Do you know what kept me going through all those hours of police questioning last time? How it was I managed to stay so calm in spite of what they were accusing me of?' She turned round and Diana saw that the tears had stopped as suddenly as they had started. 'It was relief, sheer bloody relief that I had got rid of the bastard so easily.'

Diana glanced at the curtains. It was cold for a night in August, she thought, and Phoebe must have left the window open. 'You're talking rubbish,' she said firmly. 'The last ten years have addled your brain. There was nothing easy about getting rid of David. Good God, woman, he'd been an albatross round your neck since the day you married him, still is.' She pulled her jacket tighter about her. 'If only they'd found a body somewhere that you could have identified.'

'If pigs could fly,' reflected Phoebe as she tidied the

room and punched the cushions ferociously into airy plumpness.

Diana picked up an empty coffee cup and walked through into the kitchen. 'They're concentrating their efforts on the ice house,' she announced over her shoulder. She ran the tap and washed the cup. 'They're working on the assumption that no one knows where it is.' She heard the sound of the window being closed in the televison room. 'If I were you, I'd make a list of anyone you, David or the children have ever shown it to. I'm sure there'll be a lot of names.'

Phoebe laughed bitterly and drew a scrap of paper from her pocket. 'I've been racking my brains ever since I left the library. Result: Peter and Emma Barnes, and I can't swear to them.'

'You mean the awful Dilys's children?'

'Yes. They used to roam about the garden during one school holidays, looking for Jonathan and Jane. I'm sure Dilys put them up to it as a way of getting in with us.'

'But there must have been other children, Pheeb, in the early days.'

'No, not even schoolfriends. Jon was boarding, remember, and never wanted friends to stay, and Jane never wanted friends full stop. It was my fault. I should have encouraged them but things were just so difficult that I was really glad they were antisocial.'

'So what happened with Peter and Emma?'

'It all became rather unpleasant. Emma kept taking

her knickers down in front of Jonathan.' She shook her head. 'I drew the line when he started taking his down, too. He was nine.' She sighed. 'Anyway, like a fool, I told David. So he promptly phoned Dilys and gave her an earful. He called her a vulgar bitch and said "like mother, like daughter". After that, they never came up here again, but I suppose Jon might have shown them the ice house before they were banned.'

Diana gave a guilty giggle. 'For once David was probably right. Emma hasn't improved much with the passing years, let's face it.'

'He had no business to speak to anyone like that,' said Phoebe coldly. 'God knows, I can't stand the woman, but Jon was behaving as badly as Emma. David never even told him off for it. He thought it was a great joke, talking about Jon becoming a man. I could have killed him for that. If anyone was vulgar, David was.'

Diana was disturbed by Phoebe's mood. She had known her to be bitter before but never with such a depth of feeling over something so petty. It was as if the events of the afternoon had caused a breach in her long-held defences, releasing the pent-up emotions of years. She saw the dangers of it only too clearly. She and Anne had thought of Jane as the weak link. Were they wrong? Was it not Phoebe, after all, who was the more vulnerable?

'You're tired, old thing,' she said calmly, putting

her arm through the other woman's. 'Let's go to bed and sleep on it.'

Phoebe's head drooped wearily. 'I've got such a bloody awful headache.'

'Hardly surprising in the circumstances. Take some aspirin. You'll be a new woman in the morning.'

They walked arm in arm down the corridor. 'Did they ask you about Fred and Molly?' queried Phoebe suddenly.

'A bit.'

'Oh, lord.'

'Don't worry about it.' They had reached the stairs. Diana gave her a kiss and released her. 'Walsh also asked me to describe the ice house,' she said with reluctance.

'I told you he was dangerous,' said Phoebe, walking up the stairs.

Diana's footsteps were loud in the silence. The phrase 'quiet as the grave' came to haunt her as she took off her shoes and tip-toed along the corridor. She eased Anne's door open and looked round it. Anne was at the desk, working at her word-processor. Diana whistled quietly to attract her attention, then pointed at the ceiling. Together they crept up the stairs to Anne's bedroom.

Anne followed her in, eyes alight with mischief and laughter. 'My God, Di, this is so unlike you. You're always such a stickler for appearances. You do realise the place is still crawling with filth?'

'Don't be an idiot. It's not a game this time, so just shut up and listen.'

She pushed Anne on to the bed and perched, cross-legged, beside her. As she spoke, her hands worked nervously, kneading and pummelling the softness of the duvet.

Seven

THE CURTAIN WAS drawn aside and Phoebe Maybury appeared at the window. She stared out for a moment, her hair a fiery red where the lamplight caught it from behind, her eyes huge in her strained white face. Looking at her, George Walsh wondered what emotions had stirred her. Fear? Guilt? Madness even? There was something amiss in those staring eyes. She was so close he could have touched her. He held his breath. She reached out, caught the handle and pulled the window to. The curtain fell back into place and moments later the light was switched off. The murmur of Phoebe's and Diana's voices continued in the kitchen, but their words were no longer audible.

Walsh beckoned to McLoughlin, whom he could dimly see, and led the way on soft feet across the terrace and on to the grass. He had been keeping a wary eye on the lighted windows of Anne's wing where her silhouette, seated at her desk, showed up strongly against the curtains. She had changed position frequently in the last half hour, but had not moved from her seat. Walsh was as sure as he could be that his and McLoughlin's short spell of eavesdropping had been unobserved.

They set off silently in the direction of the ice house, McLoughlin lighting their way with a torch which he kept shaded with one hand. When Walsh judged them far enough away from the house to be unheard, he stopped and turned to his colleague.

'What did you make of that, Andy?'

'I'd say we just heard the clearest admission of guilt we're ever likely to hear,' the other threw out.

'Hm.' Walsh chewed thoughtfully on his lower lip. 'I wonder. What was it she said?'

'She admitted to relief at having got rid of her husband so easily.' He shrugged. 'Seems clear enough to me.'

Walsh started to walk again. 'It wouldn't stand up in a court of law for a minute,' he mused. 'But it's interesting, definitely interesting.' He came to an abrupt halt. 'I think she's cracking at long last. I got the impression that Mrs Goode certainly thinks so. What's her part in this? She can't have been involved in Maybury's disappearance. We had her thoroughly checked and there's no doubt she was in America at the time.'

'Accessory after the fact? She and the Cattrell woman have known Mrs Maybury did it but have kept quiet for the sake of the children.' He shrugged again.

'Bar that, she seems straight enough. She doesn't know much about the ice house, that's for sure.'

'Unless she's bluffing.' He pondered for a few minutes. 'Doesn't it seem odd to you that she can have lived here for eight years and not have seen inside that place?'

The moon came out from behind a cloud and lit their way with a cold grey lustre. McLoughlin switched off the torch. 'Perhaps she didn't fancy it,' he observed with grim humour. 'Perhaps she knew what was in there.'

This remark brought Walsh up short again. 'Well, well,' he murmured, 'I wonder if that's it. It makes sense. No one's going to poke around in a place where they know there's a dead body. They're a hard-bitten trio. I can't see any of them going out of her way to do what's morally right. They'd harbour a corpse quite happily, provided it was out of sight. What do you think?'

His Sergeant scowled. 'Women are a closed book to me, sir. I wouldn't even pretend to understand them.'

Walsh chuckled. 'Kelly been playing you up again?'

The laugh pierced McLoughlin's brain, scintillating and sharp as a needle. He turned away and thrust his hands and the torch deep into the pockets of his bomber jacket. Tempt me, he thought, just tempt me. 'We've had a row. Nothing serious.'

Walsh, who knew enough of McLoughlin's prolonged marital problems to be sympathetic, grunted. 'Funnily enough, I saw her a couple of days ago with Jack Booth. She was swinging along without a care in the world, never seen her so cheerful. She's not pregnant, I suppose? She had a real bloom on her.'

The bastard should have hit him. It would have hurt less. 'That's probably because she's gone to live with Jack,' he said casually. 'She left last week.' Now laugh, you sod, laugh, laugh, laugh, and give me an excuse to smash your face in.

Walsh, at a loss, gave McLoughlin's arm an awkward pat. He understood now why the lad had been so touchy the last few days. To lose your wife was bad enough, to lose her to your closest friend was a belter. My God! Jack Booth, of all people! He'd been best man at their wedding. Well, well. It explained a good deal. Why McLoughlin walked alone these days. Why Jack had suddenly decided to leave the force to work for a security firm in Southampton. 'I had no idea. I'm sorry.'

'It's no big deal, sir. It was all very amicable. No hard feelings on either side.'

He was very cool about it. 'Perhaps it's a temporary infatuation,' Walsh suggested lamely. 'Perhaps she'll come back when she's got over it.'

McLoughlin's teeth gleamed white inside his grin, but the night hid the black rage in his eyes. 'Do me a favour, sir, that's about the last thing I want to hear. God knows we never had much to say to each other before she went. What the hell would we talk about if she came back?' Jesus, he wanted to hit someone. Did they all know? Were they all laughing? He would kill the first person who laughed.

He quickened his pace. 'Thank God we didn't have children. This way, no one loses.'

Walsh, following a few steps behind, pondered the capriciousness of human nature. He could recall a conversation he had had with McLoughlin only months before when the younger man had blamed his marital problems on the fact that he and Kelly had no children. She was bored, he claimed, found her job as a secretary unsatisfying, needed a baby to keep her occupied. Walsh had wisely kept silent, knowing from experience with his daughter that advice on domestic disputes was rarely appreciated, but he had hoped quite fervently that Fate would intervene to prevent some wretched baby being born to keep this ill-matched couple occupied. His own daughter's first pregnancy at the age of sixteen when she was still at school and unmarried had been a shock to him, but the greater shock was to discover that his wife and daughter had never really liked each other. His daughter blamed two disastrous marriages and four children on her restless seeking after love; while his wife blamed their daughter for her wasted opportunities and lack of self-esteem. George tried to make up for past failings by taking an interest in his grandchildren, but he found it difficult. His interest tended to be critical.

He thought them wild and undisciplined and blamed this on his daughter's leniency and their lack of a father-figure.

Walsh's recurring nightmare was that with the careless conception of his daughter he had sown seeds of unhappiness which would grow and mature with every succeeding generation.

He caught up with McLoughlin. 'Life's a puzzle, Andy. You'll look back at the end and see where all the pieces fitted, even if you can't see it now. Things will work out for the best. They always do.'

'Of course they will, sir. "All is for the best in the best of all possible worlds." You believe that crap, do you?'

Walsh was crushed. 'Yes, as a matter of fact.'

They were approaching the ice house which stood silhouetted against the arc-lights on the far side. McLoughlin jerked his head at the open doorway and the blackness inside. 'I can guess where he would have told you to stick your little aphorism. He wouldn't agree with it.'

'But his murderer might.' And so might your wife, Walsh thought acidly, tucked up in bed with a little warm and jovial humanity in the shape of Jack Booth. He raised a hand in greeting to DC Jones as they rounded the building. 'Found anything?'

Jones pointed to a piece of canvas on the ground. 'That's it, sir. We've worked a fifty-metre radius round the ice house. I've told the lads to leave the woodland along the back wall until tomorrow. The lights throw too many shadows to see properly.'

Walsh squatted on his haunches and used a pencil to sort and turn the collection of empty crisp packets, sweet wrappers, two thread-bare tennis balls and other odds and ends. He isolated three used condoms, a pair of faded bikini underpants and several spent cartridges. 'We'll follow these up. I don't think the rest is going to tell us anything.' He pushed himself to his feet. 'Right, I think we'll call it a day. Jones, I want you to continue searching the grounds tomorrow. Concentrate on the areas of woodland, along the back wall and up by the front gates. Get a team together to help you. Andy, you carry on with the questioning until I join you. Ask Fred Phillips if he's used a shotgun recently. We'll check at the station to see whether he or anyone else here is licensed to use one. Sergeant Robinson and the PCs can go door to door in the village.' He indicated the condoms and the knickers. 'They seem unlikely objects for anyone in the Grange to have abandoned in the garden though you' – he looked at McLoughlin – 'might ask tactfully.' He turned to Jones. 'Were they together in the same place?'

'Scattered about, sir. We marked the positions.'

'Good man. It looks as if a local Lothario is in the habit of bringing his girlfriends up here. If so, he may be able to give us some information. I'll have Nick Robinson concentrate on that.'

There was a sour look on McLoughlin's face. He didn't relish the prospect of discussing used condoms with the women at the Grange. 'And you, sir?' he asked.

'Me? I'm going to check back through one or two files, particularly our friend Ms Cattrell's. That's a tough nut. I don't fancy it, not one little bit.' He pursed his lips and tugged at them with a finger and thumb.

'There's a Special Branch file on her as long as your arm, dating back to when she was a student. I had access to bits of it when Maybury went missing. It's how I knew she was at Greenham Common. She's thrown a few spanners in the works over the years. Do you remember the furore a couple of years ago over creative accounting in the Defence Ministry? Someone added a nought to a three million pound tender and the Ministry paid out ten times what the contract was worth. That was an Anne Cattrell scoop. Heads rolled. She's a dab hand at getting heads to roll.' He fingered his jaw thoughtfully. 'I suggest you remember that, Andy.'

'You're coming it a bit strong, aren't you, sir? If she's that good what the hell's she doing stuck out here in the wilds of Hampshire? She should be in London on one of the big nationals.' Walsh's tones of amused admiration had needled him.

'Oh, she's good,' said Walsh waspishly, 'and she did work on a London national before she chucked it all up to come down here and turn freelance. Don't make the mistake of underestimating her. I've seen some of the comments on her file. She's a gutsy little bitch, not the sort to cross swords with lightly. She has a history of left-wing involvement and she knows everything there is to know about civil rights and police powers. She's been a press officer with CND, she's an outspoken feminist, active trade unionist, she's been linked with the Militant Tendency and at one time she was a member of the British Communist Party – '

'Jesus Christ!' McLoughlin broke in angrily. 'What the hell's she doing living in a bloody mansion? Damn it all, sir, they've got a couple of servants working for them.'

'Fascinating, isn't it? What made her jack in her job *and* her principles? I suggest you ask her tomorrow. It's the first damn chance we've had to find out.'

The old man reeked of whisky. He sat like a lumpy Guy Fawkes in the doorway of a tobacconist in Southampton, his legs encased in incongruously bright pink trousers, his ancient hat awry on his bald head, a jolly song on his lips. It was nearly midnight. As drunks will, he called out to passers-by between snatches of song; they, with sidelong glances, crossed the road or scurried by with quickened pace.

A policeman approached and stood in front of him,

wondering what to do with the silly old fool. 'You're a pain in the flaming arse,' he said amiably.

The tramp glared at him. 'A blooming bluebottle,' he said, showing his age, before a gleam of recognition crept into the rheumy eyes. 'Gawd love me, it's Sergeant Jordan,' he cackled. He fished a brown-paper-covered bottle from the recesses of his coat, pulled the cork out with brown teeth and offered it to the bobby. 'Have a drink, me old mate.'

Sergeant Jordan shook his head. 'Not tonight, Josephine.'

The old man tipped up the bottle and emptied the contents into his mouth. His hat fell off and rolled across the doorstep. The Sergeant bent down and retrieved it, clapping it firmly on the tramp's head. 'Come on, you old fool.' He put his hand under an unsavoury arm and heaved the filthy object to its feet.

'You nicking me?'

'Is that what you want?'

'Wouldn't mind, son,' he whined. 'I'm tired. Could just do wiv a decent kip.'

'And I can just do without fumigating the cell after you've been in it,' the policeman muttered, pulling a card out of his pocket and reading the address on it. 'I'm going to do you a favour, probably the first one you've had in years that didn't involve free booze. Come on, you're going to sleep in the Hilton tonight.'

*

George Walsh dropped Sergeants Robinson and McLoughlin at the Lamb and Flag in Winchester Road for a quick pint before closing time, then drove to Silverborne Police Station. His route took him along the High Street past the war memorial and the old cornmarket, now a bank, and between the two rows of darkened shops. Beyond its rapid expansion, Silverborne's only claim to fame in the last ten years had been its physical proximity to Streech Grange and the mystery surrounding David Maybury's disappearance. That Streech should again be the centre of police attention was no coincidence in Walsh's view. There was an inexorability about murder investigations, he believed, with comparatively few remaining unsolved. Certainly lightning like this never struck twice. He was whistling tunelessly as he pushed through the front doors.

Bob Rogers was on duty behind the desk. He looked up as Walsh came in. 'Evening, sir.'

'Bob.'

'The word is you've found Maybury.'

Walsh leant an arm on the desk. 'I'm not taking anything for granted,' he growled. 'The bastard's eluded me for ten years. I can wait another twenty-four hours before I pop the champagne. Any word from Webster?'

Rogers shook his head.

'Busy tonight?'

'Not so you'd notice.'

'Do me a favour then. Get me a list of all persons, men and women, reported missing in our area in, say, the last six months. I'll be in my office.'

Walsh went upstairs, his feet echoing loudly in the deserted corridor. He liked the place at night, empty, silent, with no ringing telephones and no inane chatter outside his door to intrude on his thoughts. He went into his office and snapped on the light. His wife had bought him a painting two Christmases ago to lend a personal touch to his bleak white walls. It hung on the wall opposite the door and greeted him every time he entered the room. He loathed it. It was a symbol of her taste, not his, a herd of glossy black horses with flowing manes galloping through an autumnal forest. He would have preferred some Van Gogh prints for the same price but his wife had laughed at the suggestion. Darling, she had said, anyone can have a print; surely you'd rather have an original? He glared at the pretty picture and wondered, not for the first time, why he found it so hard to say no to his wife.

He went to his filing cabinet and sorted through the C's. 'Cairns', 'Callaghan', 'Calvert', 'Cambridge', 'Cattrell'. He gave an exclamation of satisfaction, withdrew the file from the drawer and took it over to his desk. He opened it and settled into his chair, loosening his tie and kicking off his shoes.

The information was set out in the form of a CV, giving details of Anne Cattrell's history as far as it was known to the Silverborne police at the time of Maybury's disappearance. Additional, more recent information had been added from time to time on the last page. Walsh fingered his lips thoughtfully as he read. It was disappointing on the whole. He had hoped to find a chink in her armour, some small point of leverage he could use to his advantage. But there was nothing. Unless the fact that the last nine years of her life was contained on one page, while the previous ten years covered several, was worth consideration. Why *had* she given up a promising career? If she'd stayed in London she'd have been a top name by now. But in nine years her biggest success had been the Defence Ministry scoop and that, published in a monthly magazine, had been hijacked by staff reporters on the nationals. She had got little credit for it. Indeed, Walsh had only known it was her story because the name had registered in connection with Maybury. If she'd got hitched, her sudden drop in profile would have made sense, but – his face creased into a deep scowl. Was it that simple? Had she and those women entered into some sort of perverted marriage the minute they were all free? He found the idea oddly reassuring. If Mrs Maybury had always been a lesbian, it explained so much. He was gathering the file together when Bob Rogers came in.

'I've got those names for you, sir, and a cup of tea.'

'Good man.' He took the cup gratefully. 'How many?'

Sergeant Rogers consulted his list. 'Five. Two women and three men. The women are pretty obvious runaways – both adolescent or late adolescent, both left home after rows with parents and haven't been seen since. The youngest was fourteen, Mary Lucinda Phelps, known as Lucy. We mounted quite a search for her, if you remember, but never found anything.'

'Yes, I do remember. Looked about twenty-five from her photograph.'

'That's the one. Parents swore she was a virgin, but it turned out she'd had an abortion at the age of thirteen. Poor kid's probably on the streets in London by now. The other one's Suzie Miller, aged eighteen, last seen in early May hitching on the A31 with an older man. We have a witness to that who said she was all over him. Her parents wanted us to treat it as a murder, but there was nothing to suggest anything untoward had happened and we've certainly never found a body. Of the three men, one's a probable suicide, though again we've not found a body, one's semi-senile and gone walkabout, and the other's bolted. That's a young Asian lad of twenty-one, with a history of depression, Mohammed Mirahmadi, five previous suicide attempts, all attempted drownings. Left home three months ago. We dragged some nearby quarry pits but without success. The second on the list's an old man, Keith Chapel, who wandered out of sheltered accommodation in the middle of March, that's nearly five months, and hasn't come back. Mind you, it's odd no one's spotted him. It says here he was wearing bright pink trousers. And finally, a Daniel Clive Thompson, fifty-two, reported missing by his wife nine, ten weeks ago. Inspector Staley looked into that one quite thoroughly. The man's business had gone bust and left a lot of people hopping mad, including most of the employees. The Inspector's view is that he's done a bunk to London. He was last seen getting off a train on Waterloo station.' He looked up.

'Any of them live near Streech?'

'One of the men, Daniel Thompson. Address: Larkfield, East Deller. That's the neighbouring village, isn't it?'

'What's the description?'

'Five feet eleven, grey hair, hazel eyes, well-built, wearing a brown suit, forty-four-inch chest and brown shoes, size eight. Other information: blood group O, appendectomy scar, full set of dentures, tattoos on both forearms. Last sighting, May 25th, at Waterloo. Last seen by his wife on same day when she dropped him at Winchester station. That's all I've got here, but Inspector Staley's got quite a file on him. Shall I look it out for you?'

'No,' Walsh growled angrily. 'It's Maybury.' He watched Bob Rogers walk to the door. 'Damn and blast it! It's like leaving your umbrella behind on a fine day. It always rains. Leave me the list. If I hang on to it, it's bound to be Maybury.' He waited till the door closed, then stared glumly at the description of Daniel Thompson. His face looked ten years older.

Eight

WHEN ANNE ENTERED the library the following morning she found McLoughlin standing by the window, gazing broodingly out over the gravel drive. He turned as she came in and she noticed the black rings of a sleepless night round his eyes and the tell-tale nicks of a clumsy shave on his neck and chin. He smelled of anger and frustration and yesterday's beer. He gestured for her to sit down, waited until she had done so, then settled himself in the chair behind the desk. Particles of dust shimmered and danced in the sunlight that shafted between them. They eyed each other with open dislike.

'I won't keep you long, Miss Cattrell. Chief Inspector Walsh will be here later and I know he has some questions to ask you. For the moment, I'd like to concentrate on the finding of the body and one or two related matters. Perhaps you could start by running through the events of yesterday afternoon, beginning with the arrival of the gardener.'

Anne did as she was asked, knowing it would be a waste of time to point out that she had already done this the previous afternoon for PC Williams. From time to time she glanced at McLoughlin but looked away again when he refused to drop his gaze. There was a new awareness in his eyes which meant he was better informed about her. And how tiresome that was, she thought. Yesterday, he had despised her; today, he saw her as a challenge. With an inward sigh she began to prepare her defences.

'You don't know who he was, how he got there, or when. Had you seen inside the ice house before yesterday?'

'No.'

'Then why did you tell us that you and Mrs Goode had cleared the rubbish out of it six years ago?'

Anne had been well prepared for this by Diana. 'Because it seemed like a good idea at the time.' She fished a cigarette out of her pocket and lit it. 'I wanted to save you time and trouble. You should be looking outside the Grange for your victim and your suspects. It's nothing to do with anyone here.'

He was unimpressed. 'It's never a good idea to tell lies to the police. With your experience you should know that.'

'My experience?' she queried silkily.

'If you don't mind, we'll dispense with the word games, Miss Cattrell. It'll save a lot of time.'

'You're quite right, of course,' she agreed mildly. What a prig the man was!

His eyes narrowed. 'Did you lie because you understood the significance of the ice house and the importance of knowing where it was?'

She was silent for a moment. 'I certainly understood that *you* would consider it significant. You have yet to persuade me that it is. I share Mrs Goode's view that its location is probably known to a number of people, or that chance played a part in the body's being there.'

'We have found some used condoms in the area round the ice house,' McLoughlin said, abruptly changing the subject. 'Have you any idea who would have left them there?'

Anne grinned. 'Well, it isn't me, Sergeant. I don't use them.'

He showed his irritation. 'Have you had intercourse there with someone who does, Miss Cattrell?'

'What, with a *man*?' She gave her throaty chuckle. 'Is that a very sensible question to ask a lesbian?'

He gripped his knees tightly with trembling fingers as a sudden black rage hammered in his head. He felt terrible, his eyes smarting from lack of sleep, his mouth tasting foul. What a loathsome bloody bitch she was, he thought. He took a few shallow breaths and eased his hands on to the desk. They shook with a life of their own. 'Have you?' he asked again.

She watched him closely. 'No, I haven't,' she

answered calmly. 'Nor, as far as I know, has anyone else in the house.' She leaned forward and tapped the end of her cigarette against the side of an ashtray. He moved his hands to his lap.

'Perhaps you could clear up something that puzzles both Chief Inspector Walsh and myself,' he continued. 'We understand you and Mrs Goode have been living here for several years. How is it neither of you has seen inside the ice house?'

'In the same way that most Londoners have never seen inside the Tower. One doesn't tend to explore things on one's own doorstep.'

'Did you know of its existence?'

'I suppose so.' She thought for a moment. 'I must have done. I don't remember being surprised at Fred mentioning it.'

'Did you know where it was?'

'No.'

'What did you think the hillock was?'

'I can only recall walking right round these gardens once and that was when I first came here. I expect I thought the hillock was a hillock.'

McLoughlin didn't believe her. 'Don't you go for walks? With the dogs, with your friends?'

She turned her cigarette in her fingers. 'Do I look like someone who takes exercise, Sergeant?'

He studied her briefly. 'As a matter of fact you do. You're very slim.'

'I eat very little, drink only neat spirits and smoke like a chimney. It does wonders for the figure but leaves me gasping for breath halfway up the stairs.'

'Don't you help with the gardening?'

She raised an eyebrow. 'I'd be a liability. I couldn't tell the difference between a rose-bay willow-herb and a Michaelmas daisy. In any case, when would I find the time? I'm a professional woman. I work all day. We leave the gardening arrangements to Phoebe, that's her province.'

He thought of the pot plants in her room. Was she lying again? But why lie about gardening, for Christ's sake? His hand wandered to the uneven stubble on his jaw, touching, testing, fingering. Without warning, a shutter of panic snapped shut in his brain, blanking his memory. Had he shaved? Where had he slept? Had he had breakfast? His eyes glazed and he looked straight through Anne into a darkness beyond her, as if she was in a dimension outside his narrow line of vision.

Her voice was remote. 'Are you all right?'

The shutter opened again and left him with the nausea of relief. 'Why are you living here, Miss Cattrell?'

'Probably for exactly the same reason you're living in your house. It's as nice a roof over my head as I could find.'

'That's hardly an answer. How do you square Streech Grange and its two servants with your conscience? Isn't it rather too – privileged for your taste?' His voice grated with derision.

Anne stubbed out her cigarette. 'I simply can't answer that question. It's based on so many false premisses that it's entirely hypothetical. Nor, frankly, do I see its relevance.'

'Who suggested you come here? Mrs Maybury?'

'No one. It was my suggestion.'

'Why?'

'Because,' she repeated patiently, 'I thought it would be a nice place to live.'

'That's crap,' he said angrily.

She smiled. 'You're forgetting the sort of woman I am, Sergeant. I have to take my pleasures where I find them. Phoebe wouldn't – couldn't – leave this house to come to London, so I had to come here. It's very simple really.'

There was a long silence. 'Pleasures don't last,' he said softly. The shutter flickered horribly in his brain. '"Pleasures are like poppies spread, You seize the flower, its bloom is shed; Or like the snow falls in the river, A moment white – then melts for ever."' He spoke the words to himself. There was another silence. 'In your case, Miss Cattrell, the price of pleasure would seem to be hypocrisy. That's a high price to pay. Was Mrs Maybury worth it?'

If he'd turned a knife in her gut, he couldn't have hurt her more. She took refuge in anger. 'Let me give you a brief résumé of what led up to this line of questioning. Someone, probably Walsh, told you: she's a feminist, a lefty, a member of CND, an ex-Commie, and God knows what other rubbish besides. And you, exulting in your superiority because you're male and heterosexual, leapt at the chance of having a go at me on matters of principle. You're not interested in truth, McLoughlin. The only issue here is whether you and your inflated ego can make a dent in mine and, Jesus,' she spat at him, 'you're hardly original in that.'

He, too, leant forward so that they were facing each other across the desk. 'Who are Fred and Molly Phillips?'

She was unprepared, as he had known she would be, and she couldn't hide the flash of concern in her eyes. She sat back in her chair and reached for another cigarette.

'They work for Phoebe as housekeeper and gardener.'

'Mrs Goode told us you arranged their employment here. How did you find them?'

'I was introduced to them.'

'Through your work, through your political contacts? Perhaps penal reform is one of your interests?'

Damn him to hell and back, she thought, he wasn't a complete clod after all. 'I'm on the committee of a London-based group for the rehabilitation of ex-prisoners. I met them through that.'

She expected triumph and gave him reluctant credit when he didn't show it. 'Have they always been called Phillips?'

'No.'

'What was their surname?'

'I think you should ask them that.'

He passed a weary hand across his face. 'Well, of course, I can, Miss Cattrell, and that will simply drag out the agony for everybody. We will find out one way or the other.'

She looked out of the window, over his shoulder, to where Phoebe was pinching the dead-heads off the roses bordering the drive. She had lost her tension of the previous evening and squatted contentedly in the sun, tongues of flame curling in her shining hair, nimble fingers snapping through the flower stems. Benson sat hotly beside her, Hedges lay panting in the shade of a dwarf rhododendron. The sun's heat, still far from its peak, shimmered above the warm gravel.

'Jefferson,' said Anne.

The Sergeant made the connection immediately. 'Five years each for the murder of their lodger, Ian Donaghue.'

Anne nodded. 'Do you know why the sentences were so lenient?'

'Yes, I do. Donaghue buggered and killed their twelve-year-old son. They found him before the police did and hanged him.'

She nodded.

'Do you approve of personal vengeance, Miss Cattrell?'

'I sympathise with it.'

He smiled suddenly and for a brief moment she thought he looked quite human. 'Then at last we've found something we can agree on.' He tapped his pencil on the desk. 'How well do the Phillipses get on with Mrs Maybury?'

'Extremely well.' Surprisingly, she giggled. 'Fred treats her like royalty and Molly treats her like muck. It's a stunning combination.'

'I expect they're grateful to her.'

'The reverse. I'd say Phoebe is more grateful to them.'

'Why? She's given them a new home and employment.'

'You see the Grange as it is now but when I moved in nine years ago, Phoebe had been managing on her own for a year. She was shunned by everybody. No one from the village or even Silverborne would work for her. She had to do the gardening, the housework and house maintenance herself and the place was like a tip.' A stone lurched sickeningly in her mind as memories struggled to get out. It was the stench of urine, she thought. Everywhere. On the walls, the carpets, the curtains. She would never forget the terrible stench of urine. 'Fred and Molly's arrival a couple of months after us changed her life.'

McLoughlin stared about the library. There was a

good deal that was original, the carved oak bookcases, moulded plaster cornices, the panelled fireplace, but there were other things that were new, the paintwork, a radiator under the window, secondary glazing in white stove-enamel frames, all certainly under ten years old.

'Have the local people changed their attitude to Mrs Maybury now?'

She followed his gaze. 'Not at all. They still won't do any work for her.' She flicked ash from her cigarette. 'She tries from time to time without success. Silverborne's a dead duck. She's been as far as Winchester and Southampton with the same result. Streech Grange is notorious, Sergeant, but then you already know that, don't you?' She smiled cynically. 'They all seem to think they're going to be murdered the minute they set foot in the place. With some justification, it would seem, after yesterday's little discovery.'

He jerked his head at the window. 'Then who put in the central heating and the double glazing? Fred?'

'Phoebe.'

He laughed with genuine amusement. 'Oh, for God's sake! Look, I know you're on some personal crusade to prove that women are the be-all and end-all, but you can't expect me to swallow *that*.' He got up and strode across to the window. 'Have you any idea how much glass like this weighs?' He tapped a pane of the double-glazing and drew the unwelcome attention of Phoebe outside. She looked at him curiously for a moment then, seeing him turn away, resumed her gardening. He came back to his chair. 'She couldn't begin to lift it, let alone set it professionally in its frame. It would need at least two men, if not three.'

'Or three women,' said Anne, unmoved by his outburst. 'We all lend a hand with the lifting. There are five of us after all, eight on the week-ends when the children come home.'

'Eight?' he queried sharply. 'I thought there were only two children.'

'Three. There's Elizabeth, Diana's daughter, as well.'

McLoughlin ruffled his fingers through his hair, leaving a dark crest pointing towards the ceiling. 'She never mentioned a daughter,' he said sourly, wondering what other surprises lay in store.

'You probably didn't ask her.'

He ignored this. 'You said Mrs Maybury also did the central heating. How?'

'The same way plumbers do it, presumably. I remember she favoured capillary joints so there was a lot of wire wool involved and flux and soldering equipment. There were also numerous lengths of fifteen- and twenty-two-millimetre copper piping lying around. She hired a pipe-bending machine for several weeks with different sized pre-formers to make S-bends and right angles. I got a damned good article on women and DIY out of it.'

He shook his head. 'Who showed her how to do it? Who connected up the boiler?'

'She did.' She was amused by his expression. 'She got a book from the library. It told her exactly what to do.'

Andy McLoughlin was intensely sceptical. In his experience, a woman who could connect a central-heating boiler simply didn't exist. His mother, who held unenlightened ideas about a woman's place in the home, rooted herself firmly in the kitchen, scrubbed and cleaned, washed and cooked and refused adamantly even to learn how to change an electric plug, maintaining it was man's work. His wife, who by contrast had claimed enlightened ideas, had enrolled as a temporary secretary and called herself a career woman. In reality she had idled her days away, painting her nails, playing with her hair, complaining constantly of boredom but doing nothing about it. She had reserved her energies for when her husband came home, unleashing them in a fury of recriminations over his long hours of work, his neglect of her, his failure to notice her appearance, his inability to be the admiring prop her insecure personality demanded. The irony was that he had been attracted to her in the first place because his mother's kitchen mentality appalled him and yet, of the two of them, his mother had the brightest intellect. He had come away from both relationships with a sense, not of his own inadequacy, but of theirs. He had looked for equality and found only an irritating dependence.

'What else has she done?' he demanded curtly, eyeing the professional finish on the rag-rolled emulsion. 'The decorating?'

'No, that's mostly Diana's work, though we've all lent a hand. Di's also done the upholstery and curtaining. What else has Phoebe done?' She thought for a moment. 'She's rewired the house, made two extra bathrooms and put up the stud partitions between our wings and the main body. At the moment, she and Fred are working out how best to tackle a complete overhaul of the roof.' She felt the weight of his scepticism and shrugged. 'She's not trying to prove anything, Sergeant, nor am I by telling you. Phoebe's done what everyone else does and has adapted herself to the situation she finds herself in. She's a fighter. She's not the type to throw in her hand when the cards go against her.'

He thought of his own circumstances. Loneliness frightened him.

'Were you and Mrs Goode worried about Mrs Maybury's mental condition after twelve months alone in this house? Was that your real reason for moving here?'

Could reality be quantified, Anne wondered, any more than truth? To say yes to such a question from such a man would be a betrayal. His capacity for understanding was confined by his prejudices. 'No, Sergeant,' she lied. 'Diana and I have never had a moment's concern over Phoebe's mental condition, as you put it. She's a good deal more stable than you are, for example.'

His eyes narrowed angrily. 'You're a psychiatrist, are you, Miss Cattrell?'

'Put it this way,' she said, leaning forward and studying him coolly. 'I can always recognise a chronic drink problem when I see one.'

The speed with which his hand shot out and gripped her throat was staggering. He pulled her relentlessly towards him across the desk, his fingers biting into her flesh, a tumult of confused emotions governing his actions. The kiss, if the brutal penetration of another's mouth can be called a kiss, was as unplanned as the assault. He released her abruptly and stared at the red weals on her neck. A cold sweat drenched his back as he realised how vulnerable he had made himself. 'I don't know why I did that,' he said. 'I'm sorry.' But he knew that under the same circumstances he would do it again. At last he felt revenged.

She wiped his saliva from her mouth and pulled her shirt collar up round her neck. 'Did you want to ask me anything else?' She spoke as if nothing had happened.

He shook his head. 'Not at the present.' He

watched her stand up. 'You can report me for that, Miss Cattrell.'

'Of course.'

'I don't know why I did it,' he said again.

'I do,' she said. 'Because you're an inadequate little shit.'

Nine

SERGEANT NICK ROBINSON looked up and saw with relief that he had only two more houses to do before he reached the pub. Off to his right rose the hill which passed Streech Grange gates; behind him, some miles distant, lay Winchester; ahead of him, the brick wall which surrounded the southern flank of the Grange Estate hugged the road to East Deller. He checked his watch. It was ten minutes to opening time and he could murder a pint. If there was one thing he loathed, it was door-to-door questioning. With a lighter step he walked up the short drive to Clementine Cottage and – he checked his list – Mrs Amy Ledbetter. He rang the bell.

After some minutes and the laborious rattle of an anti-burglar chain, the door opened six inches. A pair of bright eyes examined him. 'Yes?'

He held out his identification. 'Police, Mrs Ledbetter.'

The card was taken by an arthritically deformed

hand and disappeared inside. 'Wait there, please,' said her voice. 'I intend to phone the Police Station and make sure you are who you say you are.'

'Very well.' He leaned against the side of her porch and lit a cigarette. This was the third telephoned check on him in two hours. He wondered if the uniformed constables were having as much trouble as he was.

Three minutes later the door opened wide and Mrs Ledbetter gestured him into the living-room. She was well into her seventies with a leathery skin and a no-nonsense look about her. She returned his warrant and told him to take a seat. 'There's an ashtray on the table. Well, Sergeant, what can I do for you?'

No need to beat about the bush with this old bat, he thought. Not like her twee little neighbour who claimed that to hear about murder on the television gave her palpitations. 'The remains of a murdered man were discovered in the garden of the Grange yesterday afternoon,' he said baldly. 'We're making enquiries to see if anyone in the village knows anything about it.'

'Oh, no,' said Amy Ledbetter. 'Poor Phoebe.'

DS Robinson looked at her with interest. This was a reaction he hadn't met with before. The mood of the other villagers he had spoken to had been one of vituperative satisfaction.

'Would it surprise you,' he asked the old lady, 'if I said you're the only person so far who's expressed any sympathy for Mrs Maybury?'

She wrinkled her lips into a moue of disgust. 'Of course it wouldn't. The lack of intelligence in this community is staggering. I'd have moved away years ago if I wasn't so fond of my garden. I suppose it's David's body?'

'We don't know yet.'

'I see.' She considered him thoughtfully. 'Well, fire away. What do you want to ask me?'

'Do you know Mrs Maybury well?'

'I've known her all her life. Gerald Gallagher, Phoebe's father, and my husband were old friends. I used to see a lot of her when she was younger and my husband was still alive.'

'And now?'

She frowned. 'No, I see very little of her now. My fault.' She raised one of her gnarled hands. 'Arthritis is the devil. It's more comfortable to stay at home and potter than go out paying calls and it makes you irritable. I was very short with her last time she came to see me and she hasn't been back since. That was about twelve months ago. My fault,' she said again.

Game old bird, he thought, and probably more reliable than the others he'd talked to who had dealt in innuendo and gossip. 'Do you know anything about her two friends, Mrs Goode and Miss Cattrell?'

'I've met them, knew them quite well at one time. Phoebe used to bring them home from school. Nice girls, interesting, full of character.'

Robinson consulted his notebook. 'One of the villagers told me – ' he looked up briefly – 'and I quote: "Those women are dangerous. They have made several attempts to seduce girls in the village, they even tried to get my daughter to join one of their lesbian orgies."' He looked up again. 'Do you know anything about that?'

She brushed a stray hair from her forehead with the back of her curled hand. 'Dilys Barnes, I suppose. She won't thank you for describing her as a villager. She's a shocking snob, likes to think she's one of us.'

He was intrigued. 'How did you know?'

'That it was Dilys? Because she's a very silly woman who tells lies. It's lack of breeding, of course. That type will do anything to avoid being laughed at. They've ruined their children with all their snobbish ideas. They sent the boy off to public school, and he's come back with a chip on his shoulder the size of a mountain. And the daughter, Emma,' she pulled a wry face. 'I'm afraid poor little Emma has become very loose. I think it's her way of getting back at her mother.'

'I see,' he said, completely lost.

She chuckled at his expression. 'She copulates in the woods at Streech Grange,' she explained. 'It's a favourite spot for it.' She chuckled again as the Sergeant's mouth dropped open. 'Emma was seen sneaking out of the grounds late one night and the story her mother put about the next day was that absurd one she's repeated to you.' She shook her head. 'It's nonsense, of course, and no one really believes it, but they pay lip-service to it because they don't like Phoebe. And she's her own worst enemy. She will let them see how much she despises them. That's always a mistake. Anyway, ask Emma. She's not a bad girl. If you keep what she says confidential, she'll tell you the truth I expect.'

He made a note. 'Thank you, I will. You say the woods are a favourite spot for – er – copulation.'

'Very much so,' she said firmly. 'Reggie and I used them a lot before we were married. They're particularly nice in the spring. Bluebell woods, you know. Very pretty.'

He boggled at her.

'Well, well,' she said calmly, 'that surprises you, I see, but the young are really very ignorant about sex. People were no more able to control their desire for it in my day than they are now and, thanks to Marie Stopes, we were not unprotected.' She smiled. 'When you're as old as I am, young man, you'll know that where human nature is concerned, very little changes. Life, for most of us, is the pursuit of pleasure.'

Well, that's true, he thought, thinking of his pint. He abandoned his inhibitions. 'We've found some used condoms on the Grange Estate which ties in with what you've been saying, Mrs Ledbetter. Apart from Emma Barnes, do you know of anyone else who might have been making love up there?'

'Precise knowledge, no. Guesses, yes. If you promise to be tactful in approaching the people concerned, I'll give you two more names.'

He nodded. 'I promise.'

'Paddy Clarke, the landlord at the pub. He's married to a harridan who has no idea how highly sexed he is. She thinks he takes the dog for a walk after closing time while she clears up inside, but I've seen the dog running loose in the moonlight too often to believe that. I don't sleep well,' she added, by way of explanation.

'And the other?'

'Eddie Staines, one of the farmhands up at Bywater Farm. A good-looking young devil, out with a different girlfriend every month. I've seen him set off up that hill a few times.' She nodded in the direction of the Grange.

'That's very helpful,' he said.

'Anything else?'

'Yes.' He looked a little sheepish. 'Have you noticed any strangers about? In the last six months, say?' This question had been greeted with universal amusement.

Mrs Ledbetter cackled. 'Twenty-five years ago I might have been able to give you a sensible answer to a question like that. Nowadays, impossible.' She shrugged. 'There are always strangers about, especially in the summer. Tourists, people driving through and stopping at the pub for lunch, campers from the site at East Deller. We've had a few caravans get stuck in the ditch on the corner, usually French ones, such bad drivers they are. Ask Paddy. He pulls them out with his jeep. No, I can't help you there, I'm afraid.'

'Sure?' he prompted. 'Someone on foot perhaps, someone you remember from years ago?'

She gave an amused snort. 'David Maybury, you mean? I certainly haven't seen him in the last few months. I'd have reported that. The last time I saw David was a week before he disappeared. It was in Winchester in the days when I could still drive and I came across him in Woolworths buying a teddy-bear for Jane. He was a strange character. Vile one day, charming the next, what my husband would have called a cad, the sort of man that women are invariably attracted to.' She lapsed into silence for a moment. 'There was the tramp, of course,' she said.

'What tramp?'

'He came through the village some weeks back. Funny old man with a brown trilby hanging off the back of his head. He was singing "Molly Malone", I remember. Quite beautifully. Ask Paddy. I'm sure he went into the pub.' Her head sank wearily against the back of her chair. 'I'm tired. I can't help you any more. Show yourself out, young man, and don't forget to shut the gate.' She closed her eyes.

DS Robinson rose smartly to his feet. 'Thank you for giving me so much of your time, Mrs Ledbetter.'

She was snoring quietly as he tip-toed out.

Inspector Walsh replaced the telephone receiver and stared thoughtfully into the middle distance. Dr Webster had been irritatingly unhelpful.

'Can't prove it is Maybury, can't prove it isn't,' he had said cheerfully along the wire, 'but my professional guess is it isn't.'

'Why, for God's sake?'

'Too many discrepancies. I can't make a match on the hair for a kick-off, though I'm not saying that's the end of it. I've sent samples off to a friend of mine who claims to be an expert in these things but don't get your hopes up. He warned me that the sample you got off Maybury's hairbrush may have deteriorated too far. Certainly I couldn't do anything with it.'

'What else?'

'Teeth. Did you notice our corpse was toothless? Not an incisor or molar in sight. Indications that he had dentures, but there were none with him. Looks like something or someone removed them. Now, Maybury on the other hand had all his teeth ten years ago and his records show they were in pretty good shape, only four fillings between them. That's a very different picture, George. He'd have to have suffered appalling gum disease to necessitate having all his teeth out within ten years.'

Walsh pondered for a moment. 'Let's say, for whatever reason, he wanted to lose his old identity. He could have had them taken out on purpose.'

Webster chuckled good-humouredly. 'Far-fetched though not impossible. But why would Mrs Maybury remove his dentures in that case, assuming she's our murderer? She, of all people, would know they couldn't identify him. To be honest, George, I'd say it's the other way round. Whoever murdered our chap in the ice house removed anything that would show he *wasn't* Maybury. He's had all his toes and fingertips mauled, for example, as if someone wanted to prevent us taking prints. Yet everyone at that house knows you didn't manage to lift a single workable print ten years ago.'

'God damn it,' exploded Walsh. 'I thought I had the bastard at last. Are you sure, Jim? What about the missing fingers?'

'Well, they're certainly missing, but it looks as though they've been chopped off with a meat cleaver. I've compared them with the records of Maybury's amputations and they're nothing like. Maybury had lost the top two joints of both fingers. Our corpse has had his severed at the base of each finger.'

'Doesn't prove it's not Maybury.'

'I agree, but it does look as if someone who knew

only that he'd lost his last two fingers has tried to make us think it's Maybury. To be honest, George, I'm not even positive at the moment that a human agency is involved. It is quite conceivable, if a little bizarre, that very sharp teeth have mutilated him in the way I've described. Take that filleting you pointed out. I've taken some close-ups of some furrows on the ribs and it's damned hard to say what they are. I can't rule out tooth marks.'

'Blood group?'

'Yup, you've got a match there all right. Both O positive, just like fifty per cent of the population. And, talking of blood, you must find his clothes. There's very little in that mud we scraped off the floor.'

'Great,' Walsh had growled, 'so what good news have you got for me?'

'I'm getting the report typed now, but I'll give you the gist. Male, white, five feet ten inches – give or take an inch on either side, both femurs have been well and truly smashed so I wouldn't be too dogmatic on that one – broad build probably running to fat, hair on chest and shoulder blades, indication of tattoo discolouration on right forearm, size eight shoe. No idea of hair colour but hair was probably dark brown before it went grey. Age, over fifty.'

'Oh, for God's sake, Jim. Can't you be more precise?'

'It's not a precise science as people get older, George, and a few teeth would have helped. It's all a question of fusion between the skull plates, but somewhere between fifty and sixty is my guess at the moment. I'll come back to you when I've done some more homework.'

'All right,' said Walsh grudgingly. 'When did he die?'

'I've taken some advice on this one. The consensus is, weighing the heat of the summer against the cool of the ice house – bearing in mind that the ambient temperature in the ice house may have been quite high if the door was open – and balancing that against the acceleration in decomposition after the scavengers had pulled him open and devoured him, plus possible mutilation by human agency but minus severe maggot infestation because the blowflies didn't lay in numbers, though I've sent some larvae off for further examination – '

'All right, all right, I didn't ask for a bloody biology lesson. How long's he been dead?'

'Eight to twelve weeks or two to three months, whichever you prefer.'

'I don't prefer either of them. They're too vague. There's a month's difference. Which do you favour, eight or twelve?'

'Probably somewhere in the middle, but don't quote me.'

'You'll be lucky,' was Walsh's parting shot. He slammed the phone down crossly, then buzzed his secretary on the intercom. 'Mary, love, could you get me all the details on a man who was reported missing about two months ago? Name: Daniel Thompson, address: somewhere in East Deller. I think you'll find Inspector Staley covered it. If he's free, ask him to give me five minutes, will you?'

'Sure thing,' she breezed back.

His eyes strayed to the huge file on David Maybury which he'd resurrected from the archives that morning, and which, refurbished and glossy in its pristine new folder, sat now on the edge of his desk like a promise of spring. 'You bastard!' said Chief Inspector Walsh.

Ten

SUMMONED BY URGENT telephone calls, Jonathan Maybury and Elizabeth Goode arrived early that afternoon in Jonathan's battered red Mini. As he drove it in through the gates and past the Lodge, Elizabeth turned to him with a worried frown. 'You won't tell anyone, will you?'

'Tell anyone what?'

'You know perfectly well. Promise me, Jon.'

He shrugged. 'OK, but I think you're mad. Much better to come clean now.'

'No,' she said firmly. 'I know what I'm doing.'

He glanced out of the window at the azaleas and rhododendrons, long past their best, which hedged the length of the driveway. 'I wonder if you do. From where I stand, there's very little difference between your paranoia on the subject and your mother's. You'll have to find the guts to speak out sooner or later, Lizzie.'

'Don't be an idiot,' she snapped.

He slowed as the wide sweep of gravel in front of the house opened up before them. Two cars were already parked there. 'Plain-clothes police cars,' he said with grim humour, drawing the Mini alongside one of them. 'I hope you're ready for the thumbscrews.'

'Oh, for God's sake grow up,' she exploded angrily, her worry and her uncertain temper getting the better of her. 'There are times when I could quite happily murder you, Jon.'

'We've found a pair of shoes, sir.' DC Jones placed a transparent plastic bag on the ground at Walsh's feet.

Walsh, who was sitting on a tree stump at the edge of the woodland surrounding the ice house, leaned forward to peer at the bag's contents. The shoes were good quality brown leather with irregular cloudy patches on the surface where damp had penetrated and then dried. One shoe had a brown lace, the other a black lace. Walsh turned the bag over and looked at the soles.

'Interesting,' he said. 'New heels with metal studs. There's hardly a mark on them. What size are they?'

'Eights, sir.' Jones pointed to the shoe with the brown lace. 'You can just make it out on that one.'

Walsh nodded. 'Tell one of your men to go up to the house and find out what size shoes Fred Phillips and Jonathan Maybury wear, then on down to the village to see how Robinson and his chaps are getting on. If they've finished, I want them up here.'

'Righto,' said Jones irreverently.

Walsh stood up. 'I'll be at the ice house with Sergeant McLoughlin.'

DS Robinson returned to the pub as the last customer left.

'Sorry, mate,' said the landlord amiably, recognising him from the pint he had bought earlier. 'Too late. Can't serve you now.'

Robinson proffered his identification. 'DS Robinson, Mr Clarke. I'm asking questions around the village. You're my last port of call.'

Paddy Clarke leaned his elbows on the bar and chuckled. 'The body at the Grange, I suppose. There's been talk of nothing else all lunchtime. Sod all I can tell you about it.'

Nick Robinson perched himself on a bar stool and offered Paddy a cigarette before taking one himself. 'You'd be surprised. People often know more than they think they do.'

He assessed his man rapidly and decided here was another where a straightforward approach would pay. Paddy was a big, bluff man with a ready smile and a shrewd eye. But not a person to cross, Robinson thought. His hands were the size of meat plates.

'We're interested in any strangers who may have

been through Streech in the last few months, Mr Clarke.'

Paddy guffawed with laughter. 'Give me a break. I get strangers in here every day, people taking the back roads down to the West Country, stopping off for a quick lunch. Can't help you there.'

'Fair enough, but someone mentioned seeing an old tramp a while back, thought he may have come in here. Does that ring a bell?'

Paddy squinted through the smoke from his cigarette. 'Funny. I wouldn't have remembered him myself, but now you mention it, we did have one in here, said he'd walked from Winchester. Looked like a bundle of old rags, sat in the corner over there.' He nodded to a corner by the fireplace. 'The wife wanted me to turn him away, but I'd no reason to. He had money and he behaved himself, made a couple of pints last through to closing time then shambled off along the Grange wall. You think he's involved?'

'Not necessarily. We're just looking for leads at the moment. When was this? Can you remember?'

The big man thought for a moment. 'It was pissing down outside. Reckon he came in to dry off. The wife might remember when. I'll ask her and give you a ring if you like.'

'She's not here then?'

'Gone to the Cash and Carry. She'll be back soon.'

Nick Robinson checked his notebook. 'I gather you also do a Good Samaritan act with stranded caravans.'

'About twice a year when idiots cut the corner. It's good for business, mind. They usually feel obliged to come in and eat something.' He nodded towards the window. 'It's the Council's fault. They've stuck a bloody great sign for the East Deller campsite at the top of the hill. I've complained about it but nobody takes any notice.'

'Anything strike you about the people you've rescued, anything unusual?'

'There was a one-legged German midget once with a wife like Raquel Welch. That struck me as unusual.'

Nick Robinson smiled as he made a note. 'Nothing unusual.'

'You don't have much to go on, do you?'

'That depends on you.' Unconsciously, the policeman lowered his voice. 'Is anyone else here?'

Paddy's eyes narrowed slightly. 'No one. What are you after?'

'A confidential chat, sir, preferably with no eavesdroppers,' said Robinson, eyeing the large hands.

Paddy squeezed the glowing end of his cigarette into an ashtray with fingers the size of sausages. 'Go ahead.' His tone was not inviting.

'The body was found in the ice house at the Grange. Do you know the ice house?'

'I know there is one. I couldn't lead you to it.'

'Who told you about it?'

'Probably the same person who told me there's a two-hundred-year-old oak in the woods,' said Paddy with a shrug. 'Maybe I got it from David Maybury's booklet. I couldn't say.'

'What booklet?'

'I've some copies somewhere. David had this idea of fleecing the tourists, wanted to turn the Grange into another Stourhead. He produced a map of the grounds with a short history of the house and had a hundred or so copies printed. It was a dead duck from the word go. He wouldn't spend any money on advertising and who the hell's ever heard of Streech Grange?' Paddy gave a derogatory snort. 'Stupid bastard. He was a cheapskate, always expected something for nothing.'

Robinson's eyes were alight with interest. 'Do you know who else has this booklet?'

'We're talking twelve to thirteen years, Sergeant. As far as I remember, David handed them out to anyone who would pass them on to tourists. Testing the water, he said. Whether anyone else's still got a copy I wouldn't know.'

'Can you look yours out?'

The other man was doubtful. 'Christ knows where they are, but I'll have a go. The wife might know.'

'Thanks. I gather you knew Maybury quite well.'

'As well as I wanted to.'

'What sort of man was he? What was his background?'

Paddy stared thoughtfully at the ceiling, dredging up memories. 'Upper-middle-class, I'd say. He was the son of an Army major who was killed during the war. I don't think David ever really knew his father but old Colonel Gallagher certainly did. I imagine that's why he let Phoebe's marriage go ahead, he thought the son would take after his father.' His lips twisted into a cynical smile. 'Fat chance. David was a bastard through and through. The story goes that when his mother died he had the choice of going to her funeral or going to the Derby. He chose the Derby because he had a fortune riding on the favourite.'

'You didn't like him?'

Paddy accepted another cigarette. 'He was a shit – the kind who enjoys putting people down – but he kept me supplied with fairly decent plonk, plus he was one of my best customers. Bought all his beer from me and drank in here most nights.' He took a deep inhalation of smoke. 'Nobody regretted his disappearance, except me. He left owing me over a hundred quid. I wouldn't have minded so much if I hadn't just settled my wine account with his blasted company.'

'You say "he left". You don't think he was murdered?'

'I've no view on it. Left, murdered, same result. It doubled our trade overnight. With all the media coverage, Streech became quite famous. The ghouls dropped in here for local colour before setting off up the hill to gawp through the Grange gates.' He saw a look of distaste on the Constable's face and shrugged. 'I'm a businessman. The same thing'll happen this time which is why the wife's gone to the Cash and Carry. Take my word for it, there'll be a horde of pressmen in here tonight. I pity those wretched women. They'll not be able to set foot outside their gates without being hounded.'

'How well do you know them?'

A guarded expression came over the big man's face. 'Well enough.'

'Do you know anything about their lesbian activities?'

Paddy Clarke chuckled. 'Who's been winding you up?' he asked.

'Several people have mentioned it,' said Robinson mildly. 'There's no truth in it then?'

'They've got minds like sewers,' said Paddy with disgust. 'Three women living together, keeping themselves to themselves, minding their own business and tongues start to wag.' He gave his derogatory snort again. 'Two of them have kids. That hardly ties in with lesbianism.'

'Anne Cattrell hasn't any and she admitted being a lesbian to a colleague of mine.'

Paddy gave such a shout of laughter that he choked on the smoke from his cigarette. 'For your information,' he said with watering eyes, 'Anne could give Fiona Richmond lessons on sex. 'Struth, man, she's had more lovers than you've had hot dinners. What's your colleague like? A pompous jerk, I'll bet. Anne would enjoy taking the piss out of someone like that.'

DS Robinson refused to be drawn on the subject of Andy McLoughlin. 'How come no one's mentioned this? Surely the people here would find promiscuity as titillating as lesbianism.'

'Because she's discreet, for crying out loud. Do you crap on your doorstep? Anyway, there's no one in this dump she'd give house-room to.' He spoke scathingly. 'She prefers her men with brain as well as brawn.'

'How do you know all this, Mr Clarke?'

Paddy glared at him. 'Never mind how I know. Confidential, you said, and confidential it is. I'm setting the record straight. There's enough bullshit been talked about those women to fill a midden. You'll be telling me next they run a witches' coven. That's another favourite, with poor old Fred cast in the rôle of satanic stallion because of his prison record.'

'Confidentially, sir,' said Robinson after a brief hesitation while he contemplated Fred Phillips in the rôle of satanic stallion, 'I've heard from a number of sources that you might know something about several used condoms we've found near the ice house at the Grange.'

Clarke, he thought, looked positively murderous. 'What sources?'

'A number,' said Robinson firmly, 'but I'm not going to divulge them, just as I won't divulge anything you say to me without your permission. We're in the dark, sir. We need information.'

'To hell with information,' said Paddy aggressively, thrusting his face close to Robinson's. 'I'm a publican, not a bloody policeman. You're the one who's being paid. You do your own dirty work.'

Ten years on the force had given Nick Robinson a certain wiliness. He tucked his pen into his jacket and got off the barstool. 'That's your privilege, sir, but as things stand at the moment the finger's pointing at Mrs Maybury and her friends. They seem to be the only ones with enough knowledge of the grounds to have hidden the body in the ice house. I'll guarantee that if we don't get more information, the three of them will be charged with conspiracy.'

There was a long silence while the publican stared at the policeman. Robinson felt he ought to disapprove of Clarke – if Amy Ledbetter was right, the man was a highly sexed stud – but instead he found himself liking him. Whatever his sexual morality, the man looked you in the eye when he spoke to you.

'God damn it!' said Paddy suddenly, slamming a massive fist on to the bar. 'Sit down, man. I'll get you a beer, but if you ever breathe a word of this to my wife I'll string you up by your balls.'

McLoughlin was waiting at the entrance to the ice house when Walsh arrived with the plastic bag containing the shoes. 'I was told you wanted to see me, sir.'

Walsh removed his jacket and lowered himself on to the sun-baked ground, folding the jacket neatly beside him. 'Sit down, Andy. I'm after a few quiet words away from the house. This whole damned thing's getting more complicated by the minute and I don't want any flapping ears around.' He studied the Sergeant's drawn face with sudden irritability. 'What's the matter with you?' he snapped. 'You look terrible.'

McLoughlin transferred his wallet and loose change from his rear trouser pockets and sat down at a short distance from his boss. 'Nothing,' he said, trying without success to find a comfortable position for his legs. He regarded the other man through half-closed lids. He could never decide whether he liked or disliked Walsh. The Inspector, for all his irascibility, could surprise with a kindness. But not today.

He looked across at Walsh and saw only an insignificant, skinny man, playing tough because the system allowed it. He was tempted to make the Inspector a free gift of his assault on Anne Cattrell that morning just to see his reaction. Would he bark? Or would he bite? Bark, McLoughlin thought with amused contempt. Walsh was no more able to face an unpleasantness than the next man. It would be different, of course, when she put in her written complaint. Then, the machinery of justice would roll and action would be as mechanical as it was inevitable. His certainty that this would happen lifted rather than depressed him. The cut would be clean and final, so much cleaner and so much more final than if he administered it himself. He even felt a stirring of anger against the woman that she hadn't delivered the blow already.

Walsh finished summarising the pathologist's report. 'Well?' he demanded.

The shutter clicked maddeningly in McLoughlin's brain. He stared at Walsh with vacant eyes for a moment, then shook his head. 'You say he's exploring the possibility of mutilation. He's not sure yet?'

Walsh snarled sarcastically. 'Won't commit himself. Claims he hasn't enough experience of eaten bodies. But it's a damned odd rat that chews selectively on the only two fingers Maybury had missing.'

'You'll have to tie Webster down on that,' McLoughlin pointed out thoughtfully. 'It makes a hell of a difference to the case if there was no mutilation.' Dreadful black-and-white footage of Mussolini's corpse, strung by its feet from a lamppost after an angry mob had emasculated it, floated into his mind. Violent, angry, hating faces, jeering their revenge. 'A hell of a difference,' he said quietly.

'Why?'

'It's less likely to be Maybury.'

'You're as bad as Webster,' growled Walsh. 'Jumping to bloody conclusions. Let me tell you, Andy, that body is *more* likely to be Maybury's than anyone else's. It is a statistical improbability that this house should be the centre of two unconnected police investigations in ten years, and it is a statistical *probability*, as I've said all along, that his wife murdered him.'

'Even she couldn't murder him twice, sir. If she did it ten years ago, then it wasn't him in the ice house. If it was him in the ice house, then, by God, she's had a raw deal.'

'She brought it on herself,' said Walsh coldly.

'Maybe, but you've let Maybury grow into an obsession with you, and you can't expect the rest of us to chase red herrings just to prove a point.'

Walsh poked around amongst the folds of his jacket for his pipe. He stuffed it in thoughtful silence. 'I've got this gut feeling, Andy,' he said at last, holding his lighter flame to the tobacco and puffing. 'The moment I saw that mess yesterday, I knew. Found you, you bastard, I said to myself.' He looked up and caught McLoughlin's eye. 'OK, OK, lad, I'm not a fool. I'm not about to tie you all down because of my gut feeling, but the fact remains that the blasted body is unidentifiable. And why? Because someone, somewhere, doesn't want it identified, that's why. Who took the clothes? Where are the dentures? Why no fingerprints? Oh, it's been mutilated all right, and it was as likely to be mutilated because it *was* Maybury as because it wasn't.'

'So where do we go from here? Missing persons?'

'Checked. Our area, anyway. We'll go further afield if necessary, but on the evidence so far a local connection seems probable. We've one likely candidate. A Daniel Thompson from East Deller. The description matches very closely and he went missing around the time Webster thinks our man was killed.' He nodded to the shoes in the plastic bag. 'When he disappeared, he was wearing brown lace-ups. Jones found these in the woods adjoining the farm.'

McLoughlin whistled through his teeth. 'If they're his, is there anyone who can identify them?'

'A wife.' Walsh watched McLoughlin push himself awkwardly to his feet. 'Not so fast,' he snapped petulantly. 'Let's hear how you got on. You spoke to Miss Cattrell? Learn anything?'

McLoughlin plucked at the grass beside him. 'The Phillipses' real name is Jefferson. They were sentenced to five years each for the murder of their lodger Ian Donaghue who buggered and killed their son. He was an only child, twelve years old, born when Mrs Jefferson was forty. Miss Cattrell arranged their employment here.' He looked up. 'They're a possibility, sir. What they've done once, they might do again.'

'Different MO. As far as I remember, they made no secret of Donaghue's execution, even carried out a mock trial in front of his girlfriend and hanged him when he confessed. She was a star witness in their defence, wasn't she? It doesn't square with this murder.'

'Maybe,' said McLoughlin, 'but they've proved

they're capable of murdering for revenge and they're pretty attached to Mrs Maybury. We can't ignore it.'

'Have you questioned them yet?'

McLoughlin winced. 'Up to a point. I had her in after Miss Cattrell. It was like trying to prise information out of an oyster. She's a cantankerous old biddy.' He pulled his notebook out of his shirt pocket and riffled through the pages. 'She let slip one thing which struck me as interesting. I asked her if she was happy here. She said: "The only difference between a fortress and a prison is that in a fortress the doors are locked on the inside."'

'What's interesting about that?'

'Would you describe your house as a fortress?'

'She's senile.' Walsh waved him on impatiently. 'Any more?'

'Diana Goode has a daughter, Elizabeth, who spends odd weekends here. Aged nineteen, has a flat in London which was given her by her father, works as a croupier in one of the big West End casinos. She's a bit wild, or that's the impression her mother gave.'

Walsh grunted.

'Phoebe Maybury has a licensed shotgun,' McLoughlin continued, reading down his notes. 'She's responsible for the spent cartridges. According to Fred, there's a colony of feral cats in and around Grange Farm which use his kitchen garden as their private bog. Mrs Maybury scares them off with a blast from the shotgun but Fred claims she's rather lost interest lately, says it's like trying to hold back the tide.'

'Anyone know anything about the condoms?'

McLoughlin raised a sardonic eyebrow. 'No,' he said with feeling. 'But they all found it very amusing, at my expense. Fred said he's raked up quite a few in the past. I questioned him again about finding the body. His story's the same, no discrepancies.' He ran through the sequence for Walsh's benefit.

When Fred arrived at the ice house, the door was completely obscured by the brambles. He returned to his shed to fetch a torch and a scythe, and trampled the brambles so thoroughly because he had intended to take a wheelbarrow in to remove the bricks and had wanted a clear path. The door had been half-open when he finally came to it. There had been no indication that anyone had been that way recently. After he had found the body, he had paused long enough to swing the door to as far as it would go, then he had taken to his heels.

'Did you press him hard?' Walsh asked.

'I went over it with him three or four times, but he's like his wife. He's single-minded and he doesn't volunteer information. That's the story and he's sticking to it. If he did flatten the brambles after he found the body, he's not going to admit to it.'

'What's your guess, Andy?'

'I'm with you, sir. I'd say it's odds on he found plenty of evidence to show there'd been traffic that way and did his utmost to obliterate it after he found the body.' McLoughlin glanced at the mass of torn vegetation on either side of the doorway. 'He did a good job, too. There's no way of knowing now how many people went in there or when.'

Elizabeth and Jonathan found their mothers and Anne drinking coffee in the drawing-room. Benson and Hedges roused themselves from the carpet to greet the newcomers, sniffing hands, rubbing delightedly against legs, rolling over in an ecstasy of joyful welcome. By contrast the three women were positively diffident. Phoebe held out a hand to her son. Diana patted the seat beside her in tentative invitation. Anne nodded.

Phoebe spoke first. 'Hello, darling. Journey down all right?'

Jonathan perched on the arm of her chair and bent down to peck her cheek. 'Fine. Lizzie persuaded her boss to give her the night off and met me at the hospital. I've skipped an afternoon's lectures. We were on the M3 by midday. We haven't eaten yet,' he added as an afterthought.

Diana stood up. 'I'll get you something.'

'Not yet,' said Elizabeth, catching her hand and pulling her on to the sofa again. 'A few minutes won't make any difference. Tell us what's been happening. We had a quick word with Molly in the kitchen but she didn't exactly lavish us with detail. Do the police know whose body it is? Have they said anything about how it was done?' She blurted the questions, insensitive to feelings, eyes overbright.

Her questions were greeted with surprised silence. In twenty-four hours, the women had unconsciously adjusted themselves to a climate of suspicion. A question must be thought about; answers carefully considered.

Predictably, it was Anne who broke the silence. 'It's really quite frightening, isn't it? Your judgement becomes impaired.' She flicked ash into the fireplace. 'Imagine what it must be like in a police state. You wouldn't dare trust anybody.'

Diana threw her a grateful glance. 'You tell them. I'm not trained for this sort of thing. My forte is amusing anecdotes with a punchline. When this is over, I'll polish it up, exaggerate the more titillating bits and give everyone something to laugh about over dinner.' She shook her head. 'But not now. At the moment, it's not very funny.'

'Oh, I don't know,' said Phoebe surprisingly. 'I had a good laugh this morning when Molly caught Sergeant McLoughlin in the downstairs cupboard. She chased him out with a broom. The poor man looked absolutely terrified. Apparently he was trying to find the bog.'

Elizabeth giggled nervously. 'What's he like?'

'Confused,' said Anne dryly, catching the points of

her shirt collar and holding them together. 'Now, Lizzie, what was it you asked? Do they know whose body it is? No. Have they said anything about how it was done? No.' She leant forward and held up her fingers to tick off points. 'The situation, as far as we know it, is this.' Slowly and lucidly she ran through the details of the finding of the body, its removal, the police examination of the ice house and grounds and their subsequent questioning. 'The next step, I think, will be a search warrant.' She turned to Phoebe. 'It would be logical. They'll want to go through the house with a fine-tooth comb.'

'I don't understand why they didn't do it last night.'

Anne frowned. 'I've been wondering about that but I suspect they've been waiting for the results of the post-mortem. They'll want to know what they're looking for. In some ways it makes it worse.'

Jonathan turned to his mother. 'You said on the phone they wanted to question us. What about?'

Phoebe took off her glasses and polished them on her shirt hem. 'They want the names of anyone you showed the ice house to.' She looked up at him and he wondered, not for the first time, why she wore glasses. Without them she was beautiful; with them she was ordinary. Once, when he was a child, he had looked through them. It had been a kind of betrayal to discover the lenses were clear glass.

'What about Jane?' he said immediately. 'Are they going to question her too?'

'Yes.'

'You mustn't let them,' he said urgently.

She took his hand and held it between hers. 'We don't think we can stop them, darling, and if we try we may make it worse. She'll be home tomorrow. Anne says we should trust her.'

Jonathan stood up angrily. 'You're mad, Anne. She'll destroy herself and Mum.'

Anne shrugged. 'We have very little option, Jonny.' She used his childhood diminutive deliberately. 'I suggest you have more faith in your sister and keep your fingers crossed. Frankly, there's bugger all else we can do.'

Eleven

IN DRIBS AND drabs, as messages got through, Walsh's men assembled on the grass in front of the ice house to make their reports. The day was at its hottest and the company shed their jackets gratefully and sat or reclined on the ground like family men at the beach. McLoughlin, lying now on his stomach, frowned into the middle distance like an anxious father with far-off boisterous children. Sergeant Robinson, oblivious to anyone's needs but his own, guzzled happily on a packet of sandwiches and gave the whole the spurious air of an impromptu picnic.

In the background the brambles which had once flourished as a magnificent green curtain quietly leached their sap through shattered stems and turned brown in the sun.

Walsh drew out his handkerchief and wiped the sweat from his forehead. 'Let's hear what you've got then,' he snarled into the contented silence as if he had already made the suggestion once and been ignored. He was sitting with his legs stretched wide apart and a notebook on the ground between his knees. He turned to a blank page. 'Shoes,' he said, making a pencilled note then tapping the brown shoes in the bag beside him. 'Who went up to the house?'

'I did, sir,' said one of Jones's search party. 'Fred Phillips takes size ten and his feet are about as broad as they are long. He took off his boots to show me.' He chuckled at the memory. 'He's not just built like an elephant, he's got feet to match.' He caught Walsh's eye and peered hurriedly at the shoes in the bag. He shook his head. 'No chance. I doubt he'd even get those over his big toes. Jonathan Maybury takes size nine.' He looked up. 'Incidentally, he and Mrs Goode's daughter have arrived, sir. They're with their mothers now.'

Walsh murmured acknowledgement as he jotted down the sizes. 'OK, Robinson, what have you got?'

The DS crammed the last of his sandwich into his mouth and fished out his pad. 'Promotion,' he muttered under his breath to the man next to him.

'What was that?' demanded Walsh coldly.

'Sorry, sir, wind,' replied Robinson, thumbing through his pages. 'I hit upon a mine of information, sir. I'll put it all in my report, but the important bits are these: one, these woods are used regularly by local courting couples, have been for years apparently; two, David Maybury had a hundred copies of a booklet printed, showing a map of the grounds and giving a potted history of the place.' He glanced at Walsh. 'He wanted to attract tourists,' he explained, 'and gave the booklets away to anyone in the village who would pass them on.'

'Damn,' said the Chief Inspector with feeling. 'Have you got a copy?'

'Not yet. It was the landlord at the pub who told me about it and he's looking for his copies now. If he finds them, he'll give me a ring.'

'Anything else?'

'Do me a favour, sir, I've hardly started,' said Nick Robinson plaintively. 'I asked about strangers. Several people remembered seeing an old tramp hanging around the village about two, three months ago but I couldn't get a definite date on him. He had money because he bought a couple of drinks in the pub.'

'I've a date, sir,' Constable Williams interrupted eagerly. 'He knocked at two houses on the council estate asking for food and money. The first was an old lady called Mrs Hogarth who gave him a sandwich; the second was a Mrs Fowler who sent him off with a flea in his ear because he came in the middle of her son's birthday party. The twenty-seventh of May,' he finished triumphantly. 'I've got a good description, too. He shouldn't be too hard to find. Old brown trilby, green jacket and, this is the clincher, bright pink trousers.'

Walsh was doubtful. 'There's probably no connection. Tramps are two a penny round here in the summer. They follow the sun and the scenic routes just like the tourists. Any more?'

DS Robinson caught a sardonic gleam in McLoughlin's eye which told him what he'd already guessed, that the old man was in another of his moods. God rot his soul, he thought. It was like working with a yo-yo, up one minute, down the next. Any other time and all his efforts of the morning would have earned him a pat on the back. As things stood now, he'd be lucky if he got away with a kick in the pants.

He returned to his notebook. 'I followed a lead I was given and spoke to one of the condom users,' he went on. 'He comes up here with his girlfriend when it's warm enough, usually around eleven o'clock – '

'Name,' snapped Walsh.

'Sorry, sir. Promised I wouldn't reveal his name, not unless it became absolutely necessary for a prosecution and, even then, not without his permission.' In Sergeant Robinson's view, Paddy Clarke's threat to string him up by the balls had been no idle one. The big man had offered no reasons for his promiscuity but Robinson had guessed them when Mrs Clarke returned unexpectedly as he was leaving. She was big, meaty and domineering with a brittle smile and hard eyes. A Gorgon who wore the trousers. God knows, Robinson had thought, no one could blame Paddy for wanting something soft, sweet and compliant to cuddle from time to time.

'Go on,' said Walsh.

'I asked him if he'd seen anything unusual up here in the last six months. Seen, no, he said, but heard, yes. According to him it's normally pretty quiet, the odd owl or nightjar, dogs barking in the distance, that sort of thing.' He consulted his notebook. 'On two occasions in June, during the first two weeks, he reckons, he and his girlfriend were – and I'm quoting him, sir – "scared shitless by the most god-awful racket you've ever heard. Like souls crying out in hell." The first time it happened, his girlfriend was so frightened she took to her heels and ran. He followed pretty sharpish and when they reached the road, she told him she'd left her knickers behind.'

A muted snigger rippled round the seated men like a soft breeze through the grass. Even Walsh smiled. 'What was it, did they know?'

'They sussed it the second time. They came up a week later and it happened again but to a much lesser degree. This time, my man hung on to his girl and made her listen. It was cats yowling and spitting, either at each other or something else – he thought he could hear growling as well. He couldn't say where it was coming from, but it was fairly close.' He looked at Walsh. 'They've been up several times since but it's not happened again.'

McLoughlin stirred himself. 'The colony of feral cats at the farm,' he said, 'fighting over the body. If that's right and the date's accurate it gives us the beginnings of a timescale. Our victim was murdered during or before the first week in June.'

'How sure is your man of his dates?' Walsh asked Robinson.

'Pretty sure. He's going to check with the girlfriend but he remembers it being during that spell of very hot weather at the beginning of June, said the ground was dry as a bone both times so he didn't need to take anything for them to lie on.'

Walsh made some notes on his pad. 'Is that it?'

'I've had some conflicting reports about the three women up here. Almost everyone agrees they're lesbians and that they try to seduce the village girls into lesbian orgies. But two of them – in my view, sir, the two most sensible – said it was malicious rubbish. One's an old lady in her seventies or eighties who knows them pretty well, the other's my informant. He said that Anne Cattrell's had so many lovers she could give Fiona Richmond lessons on sex.' He took a cigarette out and lit it, glancing through the smoke at McLoughlin. 'If it's true, sir, it might give us another angle. *Crime passionnel*, or whatever the Frogs call it. It strikes me she's gone out of her way to make us think she's only interested in women. Why? Could be because she's done away with a jealous lover and doesn't want us to make the connection.'

'Your informant's talking crap,' McLoughlin said

bluntly. 'Everyone knows they're lesbians. Hell, I've heard more old jokes about that than I can remember.' Jack Booth had had a fund of them. 'It's hardly something new that Miss Cattrell's invented for our benefit. And if it's not true, why do they pretend it is? What on earth do they gain by it?'

Walsh was stuffing tobacco into his pipe. 'Your problem, Andy, is that you generalise too much,' he said acidly. 'The fact that everyone knows something doesn't make it true. Everyone knew my brother was a tight-fisted bastard until he died and we discovered he'd been paying out two hundred quid a year for fifteen years to educate some black kids in Africa.' He nodded approvingly at Robinson. 'You may have something, Nick. Personally, I couldn't give a monkey's what their sexual habits are and, from what I've seen of them, they couldn't give a monkey's what people say or think about them. Which is why' – he glared at McLoughlin – 'they wouldn't trouble to deny or confirm anything. But,' he continued thoughtfully, lighting his pipe, 'I *am* interested in the fact that Anne Cattrell's been shoving lesbianism down our throats since we got here. What's her motive?' He fell silent.

DS Robinson waited a moment. 'Let me have a go at her, sir. A new face, she might open up. No harm in trying.'

'I'll think about it. Has anyone else got anything?'

A constable raised a hand. 'Two people I spoke to reported hearing a woman sobbing one night, sir, but they couldn't remember how long ago.'

'Two people in the same house?'

'No, that's why I thought it worth mentioning. Different houses. There's a couple of farm cottages just off the East Deller road, belong to Grange Farm. Both sets of occupants remembered hearing the woman but said they didn't do anything about it because they thought it was a lovers' tiff. Neither cottage could remember exactly when it was.'

'Go and see them again,' said Walsh abruptly. 'You, too, Williams. Find out if they were watching telly when it happened, what programme was on, were they eating supper? Or if they were in bed, how late was it, were they awake because it was hot, because it was raining? Anything to give us an idea of time and date. If she wasn't sobbing because she'd just killed a man, she might have been sobbing because she'd just seen him killed.' He pushed himself awkwardly to his feet, gathering his notebook and jacket as he did so. 'McLoughlin, you come with me. We're going to have a chat with Mrs Thompson. Jones, you and your squad pack up here and get everything back to the Station. You can take an hour's break, then I want you all here for a search of the house. There'll be warrants on my desk,' he told Jones. 'Bring them with you.' He turned to Nick Robinson. 'OK, lad, you go and have a quiet little chat about sex with Ms Cattrell but don't go putting the wind up her. If she did chop our body up, I want to be able to prove it.'

'Leave it to me, sir,'

Walsh smiled his reptilian smile. 'Just remember one thing, Nick. In her time she's eaten Special Branch men for breakfast. You represent a small bag of peanuts.'

The door opened after some moments to reveal a drab little woman in a high-buttoned, long-sleeved black dress. She had sorrowful eyes and a pinched mouth. A gold cross on a long chain lay between her flat breasts and she needed only a coif and an open prayer book to complete the picture of devoted suffering.

Walsh proffered his identity card. 'Mrs Thompson?' he asked.

She nodded but didn't bother to look at the card.

'Chief Inspector Walsh and Sergeant McLoughlin. Could we come in? We'd like to ask you some questions about your husband's disappearance.'

She pinched her lips into an unattractive moue. 'But I've told the police all I know,' she whispered, the sorrowful eyes welling with tears. 'I don't want to think about it any more.'

Walsh groaned inwardly. His wife would be like this, he thought, if anything happened to him. Inadequate, tearful, irritating. He smiled kindly. 'We'll only keep you a minute,' he assured her.

Reluctantly, she pulled the door wide and gestured towards the living-room, though *living*-room, thought McLoughlin as he entered it, was a misnomer. It was clean to the point of obsession and bare of anything that might display character or individuality, no books, no ornaments, no pictures, not even a television. In his mind's eye, he compared it with the vivid and colourful room that Anne Cattrell lived in. If the two rooms were an outward expression of the inner person, he had no doubt who was the more interesting. Living with Mrs Thompson would be like living with an empty shell.

They sat on the sterile chairs. Mrs Thompson perched on the edge of the sofa, crumpling a lace handkerchief between her fingers, dabbing her eyes with it from time to time. Inspector Walsh took his pipe from his pocket, glanced around the room as if noticing it for the first time, then put the pipe away again.

'What size shoes does your husband take?' he asked the little woman.

Her eyes opened wide and she stared at him as if he'd made an improper suggestion. 'I don't understand,' she whispered.

Walsh felt his irritation mounting. If Thompson had done a runner, who could blame him? The woman was ridiculous. 'What size shoes does your husband take?' he asked again patiently.

'Does?' she repeated. 'Does? Have you found him

then? I've been so sure he was dead.' She became quite animated. 'He's lost his memory, hasn't he? It's the only explanation. He'd never leave me, you know.'

'No, we haven't found him, Mrs Thompson,' said the Inspector firmly, 'but you reported him missing and we are doing our best to trace him for you. It would help if we knew his shoe size. The missing person's report says size eight. Is that correct?'

'I don't know,' she said vacantly. 'He always bought his shoes himself.' She peeped at him from under her lashes and, rather shockingly, flashed him a coy smile.

McLoughlin leaned forward. 'Could you take me upstairs, Mrs Thompson, and we'll find out from the pairs he left behind?'

She shrank into the sofa. 'I couldn't possibly,' she said. 'I don't know you. It was a young policewoman who came before. Where is she? Why isn't she here?'

Inspector Walsh counted to ten and considered that Daniel Thompson must have been a saint. 'How long have you been married?' he asked curiously.

'Thirty-two years,' she whispered.

The man *was* a saint, he thought. 'Could you pop up and fetch a pair of his shoes?' he suggested. 'Sergeant McLoughlin and I will wait down here for you.'

She accepted this without demur and slipped out of the room, shutting the door behind her as if the door would somehow stop them were they really intent on raping her in her bedroom. Walsh raised his eyebrows to heaven. 'She needs her head examined.'

McLoughlin replied seriously, 'She's ill. Looks to me as if her husband's disappearance has sent her off the rails. Don't you think we ought to get her some help?'

Walsh pondered. 'There was a vicarage a few houses down, wasn't there? We'll stop off on our way back to the Grange.'

They looked up as the door opened again and Mrs Thompson reappeared with a pair of highly polished black leather shoes clasped against her chest. 'Size eight,' she said, 'and a narrow fitting. I never realised what dainty feet he had. He wasn't a short man, you know.'

Reluctantly, Walsh opened his briefcase and produced the clear plastic bag containing the brown shoes. He placed the shoes, in the bag, on the flat of one hand and held them out for the woman to examine. 'Are these your husband's shoes, Mrs Thompson? Do you remember him having a pair like this?'

There was no hesitation in her reply. 'Certainly not,' she said. 'My husband wouldn't dream of wearing co-respondent shoes.'

'The white patches are where the shoes have got damp, Mrs Thompson, not white leather. The shoes were uniformly brown once.'

'Oh.' She moved closer, then after a few moments, shook her head. 'No, I've never seen them before. They're certainly not Daniel's. He had only one pair of brown shoes and he was wearing them the day he' – she gave a little sob – 'the day he vanished.' She used the sodden scrap of lace to dab at her eyes again. 'They were very expensive Italian shoes with pointed toes. Nothing like those. He was very conscientious about his appearance,' she finished.

Walsh put the shoes back in his briefcase. 'When you reported your husband missing, Mrs Thompson, you said he'd had some business worries recently. What exactly did you mean?'

She shied away from him as if he'd tried to touch her. 'He wouldn't leave me,' she said again.

'Of course he wouldn't, Mrs Thompson, but pressure at work does make some men act irrationally. Perhaps he couldn't cope with his problems and needed time on his own to sort them out. Is that what you meant?'

Tears poured from the sorrowful eyes in a flood. She wore her despair like a tatty cardigan, something she had grown used to and was comfortable with in spite of its ugliness. She sank on to the sofa. 'His business is bankrupt,' she explained. 'He owes money all over the place. It's all being sorted out by his assistant but people – creditors – keep ringing me. There's nothing I can do. I've told them he's dead.'

'How do you know?' asked Walsh gently.

'He wouldn't leave me,' she said, 'not if he was alive.'

Walsh looked at McLoughlin and nodded towards the door. They stood up. 'Thank you for giving us your time, Mrs Thompson. There's just one thing. Has your husband ever been to Streech Grange or had dealings with the people living there?'

Her lips thinned to an angry slit. 'Is that where those awful women live?' she spat. Walsh nodded. 'Daniel would sooner walk into the lion's den' – she fingered her cross – 'than be contaminated by their sin.' She kissed the cross and started to undo the buttons of her dress.

'Fair enough,' said Walsh with some embarrassment. 'We'll let ourselves out.'

Andy McLoughlin paused in the living-room doorway and looked back at her. 'We're going to ask the Vicar to pop round and see you, Mrs Thompson. It might do you good to have a chat with him.'

The Vicar listened to the expressions of police concern with ill-disguised panic. 'Frankly, Inspector, there's nothing I can do. Believe me, our little community has bent over backwards to assist poor Mrs Thompson. We've enlisted the aid of her doctor and a social worker, but they're powerless to act unless she herself requests psychiatric help. She's not mad, you see, nor, in the accepted sense, even depressed. In fact, outwardly, she's coping magnificently.' He had a pronounced Adam's apple which bobbed up and down as he spoke. 'It's only when people visit her, particularly men, that she acts – er – strangely. The doctor's sure it's only a matter of time before she snaps out of it.' He wrung his hands. 'The truth is neither he nor I like to go there any more. She seems to have developed sex and religious mania. I'll send my wife, though to be honest her last encounter with Mrs Thompson was less than happy, some accusation about seeing me in church with only my socks and shoes on.' The Adam's apple crowded nervously towards his chin. 'Poor woman. Such a tragedy for her. Leave it with me, Inspector. I'm sure it's only a matter of time, of coming to terms with Daniel's disappearance. There must be a text to deal with it. Leave it with me.'

Detective Sergeant Robinson rang Anne's doorbell and waited. The door was slightly ajar and a voice called: 'Come in,' from a distance. He went down the corridor to the room at the end. Anne was sitting at her desk, a pencil tucked behind her ear, one booted foot propped on an open drawer and tapping in time to 'Jumping Jack Flash' playing quietly from her stereo. She looked up and waved him to an empty chair. 'I'm Anne Cattrell,' she said, taking the pencil from behind her ear and marking a correction on a page of typed paper. 'Vaginal Orgasm – Fact or Fiction' had struggled its way towards some sort of climax on five sheets of A4.

He sat down. 'Detective Sergeant Robinson,' he introduced himself.

She smiled. 'What can I do for you?'

Hell, he thought, she's OK – more than OK. With her cap of dark hair and wide-spaced eyes, she reminded him of Audrey Hepburn. From the way McLoughlin had talked the previous evening, he'd been expecting a real dog. 'It's not much,' he said, 'just something that doesn't square.'

'Fire away. Does the music worry you?'

'No. One of my favourites,' he said truthfully. 'It's like this, Miss Cattrell, both you and the majority of people in Streech village have made out that you and your friends are lesbians.' He paused.

'Go on.'

'Yet when I mentioned it to Mr Clarke at the pub this morning, he roared with laughter and said, though not in quite these words, that you were very definitely heterosexual.'

'What were his actual words?' she asked curiously.

He noticed the full ashtray on her desk. 'Do you mind if I smoke, Miss Cattrell?'

She offered him one of hers. 'Be my guest.' She watched him light the cigarette in silence.

'He said you've had more men than I've had hot dinners,' he said in a rush.

She chuckled. 'Yes, that well-worn cliché sounds like Paddy. So, you want to know if I'm a lesbian, and if I'm not why I've given the impression that I am.' He could almost hear her mind clicking. 'Why would a woman give people reason to despise her unless it's to put them off the track of something else?' She levelled her pencil at him. 'You think I've murdered one of my lovers and left him to rot in the ice house.' Her hands were as small and delicate as a child's.

'No,' he lied gamely. 'To be honest, it's not very important one way or the other, it's just something that's puzzled us. Also,' he went on, taking a shot in the dark, 'I took to Mr Clarke more than any of the others I spoke to, and I can't really believe he's the one who's wrong.'

'Clever of you,' said Anne appreciatively. 'In matters unconnected with sex, Paddy has more sense in his little finger than the whole of Streech put together.'

'Well?' he asked.

'Was his wife there when you spoke to him?'

He shook his head. 'We spoke entirely in confidence though what he said about you was intended to be passed on. He said he was fed up with the b– er – rubbish that was spoken about the three of you.'

'Bullshit?' she supplied helpfully.

'Yes.' He grinned boyishly. 'Actually, I met his wife as I was leaving. She scared the hell out of me.'

Anne lit a cigarette. 'She was a nun once and

incredibly pretty. She met Paddy in church and he swept her off her feet and persuaded her to break her vows. She's never forgiven him for it. As she gets older, her fall from grace assumes larger and larger proportions. She thinks it's God's punishment that she hasn't any children.' She was amused by his astonishment.

'You're having me on?' He couldn't believe Mrs Clarke had ever been pretty.

Her dark eyes sparkled. 'God's truth, m'lud.' She blew a smoke ring into the air. 'Fifteen years ago she set Paddy on fire. The spark's still there. It flashes out occasionally when she forgets herself, though Paddy can't see it. He's accepted the surface image and forgotten that nine-tenths of her lies hidden.'

'You could say that about anyone,' Robinson pointed out.

'You could indeed.'

'Jumping Jack Flash' had given way to 'Mother's Little Helper'. Her foot tapped out a new rhythm.

He waited for a moment but she didn't go on. 'Was Mr Clarke's information about you correct, Miss Cattrell?'

'Hopelessly wrong on numbers unless your mother's deprived you of hot dinners, but the general drift's accurate.'

'So why did you tell Sergeant McLoughlin you were a lesbian?'

She made another pencilled note on the page. 'I

didn't,' she said, without looking up. 'He heard what he wanted to hear.'

'He's not a bad sort,' he said lamely, wondering why he felt a need to defend McLoughlin. 'He's been going through a rough patch lately.'

She raised her eyes. 'Is he a friend of yours?'

Robinson shrugged. 'I suppose so. He's done me some favours, stood by me a couple of times. We have the odd drink together.'

Anne found his answer depressing. Who listened, she wondered, when a man needed to talk? Women had friends; men, it seemed, had drinking companions. 'Whatever I said wouldn't have made any difference,' she told the Sergeant. 'It doesn't matter twopence to this case whether we bonk women every night or men every night. Or if,' she waved her pencil at her bookcase, 'we go to bed for the simple pleasure of reading ourselves to sleep. When you've solved your murder, you'll see I'm right.' She bent to her corrections once more.

Twelve

CHIEF INSPECTOR WALSH gathered his men about him on the drive in front of the Grange and divided them into four groups. Three to search the properties inside, and a fourth to comb the outhouses behind the kitchen, the garage block, the greenhouses and the cellars. Robinson had come out of the house to join them.

'What are we looking for, sir?' asked one man.

Walsh handed some typed sheets round the group. 'Read these pointers, then use your common sense. If anyone here is connected with this murder, they are not going to make you a free gift of their involvement so keep your wits about you and your eyes open. The important facts to remember are these: one, our man died approximately ten weeks ago; two, he was stabbed; three, his clothes and dentures were removed; four, and most importantly, it would help if we knew who the hell he was. David Maybury and Daniel Thompson seem the most likely contenders and there's a brief description of both of them on those sheets.' He paused to let the men read the descriptions. 'You will notice that in terms of height, colouring and shoe size, the two are not dissimilar, but bear in mind, please, that Maybury will have aged ten years since his description was written. I shall head up the search in Mrs Maybury's house, McLoughlin will take Miss Cattrell, Jones, Mrs Goode and Robinson will mastermind the outhouses. If anyone finds anything, notify me immediately.'

With a sense of reluctance, McLoughlin presented himself and his two men outside Anne's door and rang her bell. Nick Robinson's crowing account of his chat with her had set a pile-driver beating in his head. 'Got your wires crossed there, old son,' Nick had said breathily into his ear. 'Given half a chance, I'd have a shot myself. They always say the bright ones are the least inhibited.'

McLoughlin, starved of alcohol, poked stiff fingers into the fat man's beer gut and listened to the satisfying ejection of air. 'You mean they stick a knife between your ribs when the performance is lousy,' he hissed into the other man's face.

Robinson notched up a direct hit and chuckled between deep breaths. 'I wouldn't know. I never have that problem.'

McLoughlin tried to remember a time when his head hadn't hurt, when shutters stayed open in his mind, and when he hadn't felt sick. His feelings seesawed violently between intense dislike of Anne coupled with certainty that she was responsible for the mangled body in the ice house, and a hot shame that set the sweat pouring under his arms whenever he thought of his behaviour of the morning. He bunched his fist till the knuckles gleamed white. 'So why did she say she was a dyke?'

With a wary eye on the fist, Nick Robinson took a pace or two backwards. 'Claims she didn't. Face it, Andy, she reckons you're a pompous ass so she took the piss.' And it'll do you good, he thought. He liked McLoughlin, he had no reason not to, but the man fancied himself a cut above the rest of them which was why his wife's desertion had come so hard. The joke was that the Station had known about it for days, ever since Jack Booth had spilled the beans to Bob Rogers, but they had waited tactfully for McLoughlin to tell them himself. He never had. For two weeks he had come in every morning with a ferocious hangover and rambling stories about what Kelly had said or done the night before. Only his pride was hurt, they all knew it, and that not for much longer the way the WPCs were queuing up to get between his sheets. The clever money was on WPC Brownlow. And for Nick, fat, prematurely bald and with a penchant for WPC Brownlow himself, Anne's indifference to McLoughlin had been a soothing balm.

*

Anne opened the door and gestured them inside. McLoughlin removed the search warrant from his briefcase and gave it to her. She read it through carefully before handing it back with a shrug. There was no change in her manner towards him, no indication to him or his colleagues that he had overstepped that invisible mark beyond which behaviour is censured.

'Go ahead,' she said, nodding towards the small staircase leading to her upper rooms. 'I'll be in my study if you want me.' She returned to her desk in the big sunlit room. 'I Can't Get No Satisfaction' throbbed in the amplifiers.

Her spare room revealed nothing. McLoughlin doubted if it had been used for months, even years. There was a depression in the counterpane of one of the twin beds which implied that Benson or Hedges had found a comfortable retreat there, but no indication of a human presence. They moved on to her bedroom.

'Not bad,' said one of the men approvingly. 'The wife's just paid a fortune for pink frills, white melamine and mirrors. Can't get into the bloody bedroom now. Bet we could have done something like this for half the price.' He ran his hand along the front of a low oak chest.

The room gave an impression of space because it contained so little: only the chest, a delicate wicker chair, and a low double bed with a pile of pillows and a bottle-green duvet. In a recess in one corner was a built-in wardrobe. A white carpet stretched to infinity with no line to show where carpet ended and white skirting boards began. Huge colour close-ups of glorious flowers against jet-black backgrounds marched in a brilliant band round white walls. The room both challenged the eye and relaxed it.

'You two go through the chest and wardrobe,' said McLoughlin. 'I'll have a look in the bathroom.' He retreated gratefully to the normality of a pale pink bathroom but found nothing exceptional, unless two tins of shaving foam, a large packet of disposable razors and three used toothbrushes could be considered unusual possessions for a spinster. As he turned to the door, the corner of his eye caught a movement behind him. He spun sharply, heart struggling like a live thing in his mouth, and hardly recognised himself in the drawn and angry man who stared out of the mirror. He flicked the tap and splashed water over his face, dabbing it dry with a towel which smelt of roses. His head ached unbearably. He was at war with himself and the effort of trying to hold the warring parts together was destroying him. It was nothing to do with Kelly. The thought, unprompted, surprised him. It was inside him and had been inside him for a long time, a simmering rage that he could neither direct nor control, but which Kelly's departure had fired.

He went into the bedroom.

'Here's something, Sarge,' said DC Friar. He was on the bed, reclining against the pillows in a posture absurdly reminiscent of Manet's 'Olympia'. He held a small leather-bound book in one hand and was chuckling over it. 'Jesus, it's obscene.'

'Off,' said McLoughlin with a jerk of his head. He watched the man slide his feet reluctantly to the floor. 'What is it?'

'Her diary. Listen to this. "I cannot look on a penis, post-ejaculation, in a condom without laughing. I am transported immediately to my childhood and the time when my father's finger turned septic. He constructed a finger-stall out of industrial polythene – 'to keep an eye on the bugger' – and summoned my mother and me to witness the exciting climax when the finger, after much squeezing, burst. It was a jolly occasion." Jesus, that's sick!' He twitched the book out of McLoughlin's reach. 'And this one, listen to this one – ' he flicked a page – "Phoebe and Diana sunbathed nude on the terrace today. I could have watched them for hours, they were so beautiful."' Friar grinned. 'She's a dirty little bugger, isn't she? I wonder if the other two know she's a peeper.' He looked up and was surprised by the expression of distaste on McLoughlin's face. He took it for prudery. 'I was reading the entries for end of May, beginning of June,' he said. 'Take a look at June second and third.'

McLoughlin turned the pages. Her handwriting

was black and strong and not always legible. He found Saturday, June 2nd. She had written: 'I have looked into the grave and eternity frightens me. I dreamed there was awareness after death. I hung alone in a great darkness, unable to speak or move, but knowing' (this word was underscored three times) 'that I had been abandoned to exist for ever without love and without hope. I could only yearn, and the pain of my yearning was terrible. I shall keep my light on tonight. Just at the moment, the darkness frightens me.' He read on. June 3rd: 'Poor Di. "Conscience does make cowards of us all." Should I have told her?' June 4th: 'P. is a mystery. He tells me he screws fifty women a year, and I believe him, yet he remains the most considerate of lovers. Why, when he can afford to take women for granted?'

McLoughin snapped the diary shut in his palm. 'Anything else? Anything on her clothes?' The two men shook their heads. 'We'll tackle the living-room.'

Anne looked up as they went in. She saw the diary in McLoughlin's hand and a faint colour washed her cheeks. Damn, she thought. Why, of all things, had she forgotten that? 'Is that necessary?' she asked him.

'I'm afraid so, Miss Cattrell.' The Stones struck a final chord which lingered as a vibration in the air before fading into silence.

'There's nothing in it,' she said. 'Nothing that will help you, at least.'

DC Friar muttered into his colleague's ear, loud enough for McLoughlin to hear. 'Like hell there isn't! It's packed with fucking information!'

He wasn't prepared for the sudden grip of McLoughlin's fingers on the underside of his upper arm. They bit into the tender flesh like iron marlin-spikes, gouging, probing, unrelenting in their vicious-ness. Quite unwittingly, he had reminded McLoughlin of Jack Booth.

A head taller than Friar, McLoughlin smiled gently down on him. His voice, curling lovingly round the Scots vernacular, murmured softly and sweetly: '"Ye ugly, creepin blastit wonner, Detested, shunn'd by saunt and sinner, How daur ye set a fit upon her, sae fine a Lady! Gae somewhere else and seek your dinner, on some poor body."' There was no emotion in his dark face but his knuckles whitened. 'Recognise that, Friar?'

The DC pulled himself free with an effort and rubbed his arm. He looked thoroughly startled. 'Give over, Sarge,' he muttered uncomfortably. 'I didn't understand a bloody word.' He looked to the other constable for support but Jansen was staring at his feet. He was new to Silverborne and Andy McLoughlin scared the shit out of him.

McLoughlin placed his briefcase on the corner of Anne's desk and opened it. 'It's from a poem by Robert Burns,' he told Friar affably. 'It's called "To A Louse". Now, Miss Cattrell,' he went on, turning his attention to her, 'this is a murder investigation. Your diary will help us establish your movements during the last few months.' He removed a pad of receipts and wrote on the top one. 'It will be returned as soon as we've finished with it.' He tore off the piece of paper and held it out to her and, for a brief moment, his eyes looked into hers and saw the laughter in them. A surge of warmth lapped around the frozen heart of his solitude. She bent her head to study the receipt and his gaze was attracted to the soft curls round the base of her neck, tiny inverted question marks which posed as many problems for him as she did herself. He wanted to touch them.

'I don't record my movements in that diary,' she told him after a moment, 'only my thoughts.' She looked up and her eyes laughed still. 'It's poor fare, Sergeant, just bees in my bonnet. I fear ye'll dine but sparely on sic a place.'

He smiled. Burns had written his poem after seeing a louse on a lady's bonnet in church. 'Ye've nae got the accent, Miss Cattrell. Ye grate ma lug wi' your crabbet sound.' She laughed out loud, and he hooked his foot round a chair and drew it forward to sit on. It was such a tiny face, he thought, and so expressive. Too expressive? Did sorrow come as easily as laughter? 'You recorded some interesting thoughts in your diary on June second. You wrote' – he pictured the written page in his mind – '"I have looked into the grave and eternity frightens me."' He examined her closely.

'Why did you write that, Miss Cattrell, and why did you write it then?'

'No reason. I often write about death.'

'Had you just seen inside a grave?'

'No.'

'Does death frighten you?'

'Not in the least. It annoys me.'

'In what way?'

Her eyes were amused. They would always betray her, he thought. 'Because I'll never know what happened next. I want to read the whole book, not just the first chapter. Don't you?'

Yes, he thought, I do. 'Yet you feared it at the beginning of June. Why?'

'I don't remember.'

'"I dreamed there was awareness after death,"' he prompted her. 'You went on to say that you would keep your light on that night because the darkness frightened you.'

She thought back. 'I had a dream and my dreams are very real. That one was particularly vivid. I woke early, when it was still dark, and I couldn't think where I was. I thought the dream was true.' She shrugged. 'That's what frightened me.'

'You told Mrs Goode something on June third which troubled her conscience. What was that?'

'Did I?' He opened the diary and read the extract to her. She shook her head. 'It was probably something trivial. Di has a sensitive conscience.'

'Perhaps,' he suggested, 'you'd decided to tell her about the corpse you'd found in the ice house?'

'No, it certainly wasn't that.' Her eyes danced wickedly. 'I'd remember that.'

He was silent for a moment. 'Tell me why you don't feel sorry for that wretched man out there, Miss Cattrell.'

She turned away to look for a cigarette. 'I do feel sorry for him.'

'Do you?' He picked up her lighter and flicked the flame for her. 'You've never said so. Neither has Mrs Maybury nor Mrs Goode. It's hardly normal. Most people would have expressed some sympathy, said "Poor man" as the minimum gesture of regret. The only emotion any of you has shown so far is irritation.'

It was true, she thought. How stupid they had been. 'We save our sympathies for ourselves,' she told him coolly. 'Compassion is a frail thing. It dies at the first touch of frost. You would have to live at Streech Grange to understand that.'

'You depress me. I assumed compassion was one of your muses.' He splayed his hands on the desk, then stood up. 'You would have felt sorry for a stranger, I think. But you knew him and you didn't like him, did you?' His chair scraped back. 'Right, Friar, Jansen, let's get on with it. We'll be as quick as we can, Miss Cattrell. At the end I will ask you to go upstairs with a WPC who will search you for anything you may have concealed in your clothing. You are welcome to stay while we work in here but, if you prefer to wait outside, one of the constables will wait with you.'

She puffed a smoke ring into the air and stabbed its centre with the end of her cigarette. 'Oh, I'll stay, Sergeant,' she told him. 'Police searches are meat and drink to me. It should run to a couple of thousand words on a woman's page somewhere. I rather fancy a headline like THE PRY TRADE or LICENCE TO SNOOP. What do you think?'

Sallow-faced bitch, he thought, as he watched the smoke drift from her mouth. The room stank of her cigarettes. 'Please yourself, Miss Cattrell.' He turned away. The blood swelled and throbbed and thickened in his head till he thought only a scream would relieve its pressure.

They went through everything with a fine-tooth comb and with infinite patience. Inside books, behind pictures, beneath chairs, through drawers; they ran long needles into the earth in the plant pots, felt for lumps under the fitted carpet, upended the sofa and poked deftly into its soft cushions; and when they had finished, the room looked exactly as it had done before they started. Anne, who had been moved courteously from her place behind her desk, was duly impressed.

'Very professional,' she told them. 'I congratulate you. Is that it?'

'Not quite,' said McLoughlin. 'Would you open the safe for me, please?'

She gave him a startled look. 'What on earth makes you think I've got a safe?'

He walked over to the oak-panelled mantelpiece which was an exact replica of the one in the library. He pressed on the edge of the middle panel and slid it back, revealing the dull green metal of a wall-safe with a chromium handle and lock. He glanced at Friar and Jansen. 'I found the one in the library this morning,' he said. 'Neat, isn't it?' He couldn't look at her. Her panic, brief though it had been, had shocked him.

She walked back to her desk, collecting her thoughts. She had always believed Phoebe the better judge of character, but it was Diana who was scared of McLoughlin.

'Would you open it, please?' he asked her again.

She took an unbroached packet of cigarettes from a carton of two hundred in her top drawer and tore the seal off it. He watched her patiently, saying nothing.

'Just who do you think you are?' snapped DC Friar angrily. 'You heard the Sergeant. Open the bloody safe.'

She ignored him, flipped the lid of the packet and turned the whole thing upside down, shaking a key into the palm of her hand. 'How are you on Spenser?' she asked McLoughlin with a quirky smile. '"A man by nothing is so well betrayed as by his manners." It might have been written for your friend here.'

She's stalling, he thought, she's afraid, and I hate

her. God, how I hate her. 'The safe, please, Miss Cattrell.'

She walked over with a tiny shrug, unlocked the door and pulled it open. The safe was empty except for a carving knife with a blood-stained rag wrapped around its handle. The blade was black and crusted. McLoughlin felt sick. For all his anger, he hadn't wanted this. With a detached part of his mind, he wondered if he was ill. His head was burning as if he had a fever. He leant his shoulder against the mantelpiece to steady himself. 'Can you explain this, please?' He heard his voice from a distance, harsh and unnatural.

'What's to explain?' she asked, taking out a cigarette and lighting it.

What indeed? The shutter clicked open and shut, open and shut, behind his eyes. He glanced at the cigarette packet on the desk. 'Let's start with why you went to so much trouble to hide the key?'

'Habit.'

'That's a lie, Miss Cattrell.'

Tension had tightened the skin around his nose and mouth, giving him a curiously flat look. She thought of the steel hawser she had once seen in Shanghai, winding on to a huge capstan and drawing a crippled tanker into the docks. As the slack was taken up, it had risen from the concrete, shaking itself free of dust as it thinned and tautened, and then had come a moment of pure horror when it snapped under the strain and whipped with frightening speed through the defenceless flesh of a man's neck. He had seen it coming, she remembered, had put up his hands to protect himself. She looked at McLoughlin and felt an urge to do the same. 'I want to phone my solicitor,' she said. 'I will not answer any more questions until he gets here.'

McLoughlin stirred. 'Friar, find Inspector Walsh for me and ask him to come to Miss Cattrell's wing, will you? Tell him it's urgent, tell him she wants to make a phone call. Jensen' – he flicked his head towards the French windows – 'rustle up a WPC for a strip search. You'll find Brownlow somewhere outside.' He waited till the two men had left then turned to the mantelpiece and stood staring at the open safe. After a moment he swung the door to and put his hands on the mantelpiece, lowering his head to look into the unlit fire. It was a gas replica of a real fire and the artificial coals were peppered with cigarette ash and dog-ends. 'You should put them in a bin,' he murmured. 'They'll leave marks when they burn.'

She craned her neck to see what he was looking at. 'Oh, those. I keep meaning to hoover them up.'

'I thought Mrs Phillips did the hoovering.'

'She does, but she discriminates against certain messes, or more accurately the makers of certain messes, and won't touch them with a barge pole.'

He turned to look at her, resting his elbow on the

mantelpiece. He was shaking like a man with ague. 'I see.' He didn't, of course. What sort of discrimination did Molly go in for? Racial? Religious? Class?

'She discriminates on moral grounds,' Anne told him. Had he spoken his thoughts aloud? He couldn't remember, his head ached so much. 'She's a good old-fashioned Puritan, only truly happy when she's miserable. She can't understand why the rest of us don't feel the same way.'

'Like my mother,' he said.

She gave her throaty chuckle. 'Probably. Mine doesn't bother, thank God. I couldn't do battle with two of them.'

'Does she live near here?'

Anne shook her head. 'The last I heard of her she was in Bangkok. She remarried after my father died and set off round the world with husband mark two. I've rather lost track of them, to be honest.'

That hurt, he thought. 'When did you last see her?'

She didn't answer immediately. 'A long time ago.' She drummed her fingers impatiently on her desk. 'Give me one good reason why I should wait for the Inspector's permission to make this telephone call.'

Her voice vibrated with irritation. It made him laugh. Laughter swept over him like a kind of madness, wild, uncontrollable, joyous. He put a hand to his streaming eyes. 'I'm sorry,' he said. 'I'm so sorry. There is no good reason. Please. Be my guest.' The words, appallingly slurred, seemed to echo in his head and, even to his own ears, he sounded drunk. He clung to the mantelpiece and felt the hearth lurch beneath his feet.

'I suppose it hasn't occurred to you,' observed Anne at his shoulder, as she shoved a chair behind his legs and folded him neatly on to it with the pressure of one small hand on the nape of his neck, 'that it might be worth eating from time to time.' She abandoned him to rummage through her bottom drawer. 'Here,' she said, a moment later, pressing an unwrapped Mars bar into his hand. 'I'll get you something to drink.' She took a bottle of mineral water from a small drinks cabinet, poured a tumblerful and carried it back to him.

His hand, clasping the Mars bar, hung loosely between his knees. He made no attempt to eat it. He couldn't have moved, even if he'd wanted to.

'Oh, shit!' she said crossly, putting the glass on a table and squatting on the floor in front of him. 'Look, McLoughlin, you're a pain in the bloody arse, you really are. If you're trying to drink yourself into early retirement, fine, that's your choice – God knows why you joined the police force in the first place. You should be writing a biography of Francis Bacon or Rabbie Burns or something equally sensible. But if you're not trying for the chop, then do yourself a favour. Any minute now, that little toe-rag you sent off in search of the Inspector is going to come back through my door, and he'll wet himself when he sees you like this. Take my word for it, I know the type. And if there's anything left of you when Walsh has finished, then your friend the constable is going to piss all over it. He'll do it again and again and again, and he'll have an orgasm every time he does it. I promise you, you won't enjoy the experience.'

In her own way she was beautiful. He could drown quite happily in those soft brown eyes. He took a bite out of the Mars bar and chewed on it thoughtfully. 'You're a bloody awful liar, Cattrell.' He moved his head gently from side to side. 'You told me compassion was a frail thing, but I think you've just broken my neck.'

Thirteen

THERE WAS AN atmosphere in the room. Walsh smelled it the minute he stepped inside. McLoughlin was by the window, hands resting on the sill, looking out over the terrace and the long sweep of lawn; Miss Cattrell sat at her desk, doodling, her boots propped on her open bottom drawer, her lower lip protruding aggressively. She looked up as he approached. 'Well, thank God for small mercies!' she snapped. 'I want to phone my solicitor, Inspector, I want to do it now, and I refuse to answer any more questions until he gets here.' She looked very cross.

Anger, thought Walsh with surprise. Somehow, it hadn't smelled like anger. 'I hear you,' he said equably, 'but why would you want to do that?'

McLoughlin opened the French windows to let in Jansen and WPC Brownlow. His legs, seeping sawdust, belonged to somebody else; his stomach, reawakened by the Mars bar, was clawing at itself in a search for further nourishment; his heart was gambolling about his wilting frame like a healthy spring lamb. He felt rather pleased with himself. 'Miss Cattrell,' he said, his voice quite steady, 'would you agree to WPC Brownlow searching you now, while I explain the position to Inspector Walsh?'

'No,' she snapped again, 'I would not. I refuse to co-operate any further until my solicitor gets here.' She tapped a pencil angrily on the desk-top. 'And I'm bloody well not going to say any more in front of you, either, or those creeps you brought with you.' She glared at Walsh. 'I object to this very strongly. It's bad enough having your personal things mauled over, but to have them mauled over by men is the pits. You must have some women on your force. I refuse to talk to anyone but women.'

Walsh hid his excitement well but McLoughlin, with his new clarity of vision, could see the Inspector's scrawny tail wagging. 'Are you making a formal complaint against Sergeant McLoughlin and his team?' Walsh asked.

She glanced at Friar. 'I don't know. I'll wait until my solicitor gets here.' She reached for her telephone and started dialling. 'But my objection stands, so, if you want my co-operation, I suggest you find me some women.'

The Chief Inspector jerked his head towards the door. 'Friar, Jansen, wait in the corridor. Sergeant McLoughlin, gather together what you've found and bring it outside. Brownlow, stay here.' He stood back, eyes narrowing, as he watched McLoughlin launch himself off the wall and plough firmly across the floor. There was something wrong, something he couldn't quite put his finger on. He darted sharp glances about the room.

Anne was murmuring into the telephone. 'Hold on a moment, Bill' – she cupped her hand over the receiver – 'I'd like to remind you, Sergeant,' she said icily, 'that you haven't given me a receipt for what's in my safe. The only receipt I have is the one for my diary.'

Jesus, woman, thought McLoughlin, give me a break. I'm not Charles Atlas, I'm the puny one who gets sand kicked in his face. He bowed ironically. 'I'll make one out now, Miss Cattrell.'

She ignored him and returned to her phone call, listening for a moment. 'Dammit, Bill,' she exploded angrily into the mouthpiece, 'considering how much you charge, you might make the effort to get here a bit sooner. Hell, I may not be one of your fancy London clients, but I always pay on the nail. For God's sake, you can make it in under two hours if you pull your finger out.'

Bill Stanley, long-time friend as well as solicitor, grinned at the other end of the line. He had just told her he'd drop everything to be with her in an hour. 'I could make it three hours,' he suggested.

'That's a bit more like it,' she growled. 'OK, I'll ask him.' She turned to the Inspector. 'Are you planning to take me down to the Police Station? My solicitor wants to know where to come.'

'That's entirely up to you, Miss Cattrell. Frankly, I'm a little puzzled at the moment as to why you want your solicitor present.' McLoughlin turned round with the carving-knife and rag neatly secured in a polythene bag. 'Ah!' said Walsh with ill-concealed glee. 'Well, that does rather suggest you can help us in our enquiries. As long as you understand there is no duress involved, I think it will be simpler for everyone if we pursue our questioning at the Station.'

'Silverborne Police Station,' she told her solicitor. 'No, don't worry, I won't say anything till you get there.' She hung up and snatched the second receipt from McLoughlin. 'And there'd better be nothing of mine hidden in that briefcase,' she said spitefully. 'I've yet to meet a policeman who didn't have sticky fingers.'

'That's enough, Miss Cattrell,' said Walsh sharply, wondering how McLoughlin had managed to keep his temper with her. But perhaps he hadn't and perhaps that explained the tension in the air. 'I draw the line at unwarranted abuse against my officers. Constable Brownlow will wait with you while I have a couple of words with Sergeant McLoughlin in the corridor.' He walked stiffly from the room. 'Right,' he said, when the door had closed behind them, 'let's see what you've got.' He held out his hand for the polythene bag.

'It's like I told you, sir,' said Friar eagerly. 'She was hiding it in her safe. And then there's the diary, with talk about death and graves and God knows what else.'

'Andy?'

He supported himself against the wall. 'I'm not sure.' He shrugged.

'Not sure about what?' demanded Walsh impatiently.

'I suspect we're being had, sir.'

'Why?'

'A feeling. She's not a fool and it was very easy.'

'Friar?'

'That's balls, sir. The diary was easy, I grant you that, but the knife was well hidden. Jansen went all along that wall and missed the safe completely.' He threw a look of grudging acknowledgement in McLoughlin's direction. 'It was the Sergeant spotted it.'

Walsh thought deeply for several moments. 'Well, either way we're committed now, so if we're being had, let's find out why. Jansen, you take this back to the Station and get it fingerprinted before I bring Miss Cattrell in. Friar, cut along and give them a hand outside. Andy, I suggest you take over from me in Mrs Maybury's wing.'

'With respect, sir,' McLoughlin murmured, 'wouldn't it be a better idea if I went through her diary? Friar's right, there are some strange references in there.'

Walsh looked at him closely for a moment, then nodded. 'Perhaps you're right. Pick out anything you think relevant and have it on my desk before I talk to her.' He went back into the room, closing the door behind him.

Friar dogged McLoughlin's heels down the corridor. 'You jammy bastard!'

McLoughlin grinned evilly. 'Privilege has its perks, Friar.'

'You reckon she's going to make a complaint?'

'I doubt it.'

'Yeah.' Friar paused to light a cigarette. 'Jansen and me are clear, whichever way you look at it.' He called after McLoughlin: 'But I'd sure as hell like to know where those marks on her neck came from.'

McLoughlin drove straight to a transport café on the outskirts of Silverborne and ate and ate till he could eat no more. He kept his mind deliberately on his food and, when an errant thought popped in, he chased it out again. He was at peace with himself for the first time in months. When he'd finished, he went back to his car, reclined the seat and went to sleep.

*

Jonathan was hanging round the front door when Anne was ushered out by Walsh and WPC Brownlow. He moved aggressively into their path and Walsh had no difficulty recognising in him the gangling boy who had protected his mother so fiercely all those years ago.

'What's going on?' he demanded.

Anne laid a hand on his arm. 'I'll be back in two or three hours at the most, Jon. There's nothing to worry about, I promise. Tell your Ma I've phoned Bill Stanley and he's coming straight down.' She paused for a moment. 'And make sure she takes the phone off the hook and gets Fred to lock the front gates. The story's bound to be out by now and there'll be pressmen all over the place.' She gave him a long, straight look. 'It's a safe bet she'll be worrying, Jon, so try and take her mind off it. Play her some records or something.' She spoke over her shoulder as Walsh led her towards a car. 'Pat Boone and "Love Letters in the Sand". That's always a safe bet when you want to take Phoebe's mind off something. You know how she adores Pat Boone. And don't hang about, will you?'

He nodded. 'OK. Take care, Anne.'

He waved disconsolately as she was driven away, then retreated thoughtfully through the front door. As far as he was aware, his mother had never listened to a

Pat Boone record in her life. '*Don't hang about, will you?*' He walked towards Anne's door, took a quick look about him, then turned the handle and trod softly down her corridor. He eased her living-room door open and peered around it. The room was empty. '*Safe bet*,' she had said that twice. '*Love Letters.*' It was the work of seconds to slip the hidden catches, take a firm grasp on the chromium handle and slide the whole safe out. It weighed virtually nothing, being made of aluminium. He rested it on one hip while he plunged his hand into the dark recess in the chimney breast and retrieved a large brown envelope. He flicked it on to the nearest easy chair, then carefully repositioned the safe and thrust it back into place. As he stuffed the envelope into the front of his jacket, it occurred to him that something or someone must have frightened Anne pretty badly to make that hiding place unsafe. And why on earth should she worry over some love letters? It was odd. As he left by the French windows, he heard the door into Anne's wing open and close and the sound of footsteps in the corridor. He tip-toed across the terrace and out of sight.

He found Phoebe and Diana in the main drawing-room. They were murmuring quietly on the sofa, heads together, gold hair and red hair interwoven like threads in a tapestry. He was suddenly jealous of their intimacy. Why did his mother confide in Diana before him? Didn't she trust him? He had shouldered the guilt for ten years. Wasn't that long enough for her?

Sometimes, he felt, it was only Anne who treated him like an adult.

'They've taken Anne,' he announced laconically.

They nodded, unsurprised. 'We were watching,' said Phoebe. She gave Jonathan a comforting smile. 'Don't worry, darling. I have more sympathy for the police than I do for her. They'll find that two hours in the ring with Mike Tyson would be preferable to half an hour in Anne's company when she's fighting her corner. She's phoned Bill, I hope.'

'Yes.' He went to the window and looked out on to the terrace. 'Where's Lizzie?' he asked them.

'She's gone with Molly,' said Diana. 'They're searching the Lodge now.'

'Is Fred there, too?'

'Fred's standing guard by the gates,' said Phoebe. 'It seems the press have arrived in force. He's keeping them at bay.'

'That reminds me. Anne said to take the phone off the hook.'

Diana stood up and walked over to the mantelpiece, retrieving a dog-end from behind a clock there. She struck a match and lit the crumpled tip. 'Already done.' She squinted at the pathetic half-inch of tube and puffed inexpertly.

Phoebe exchanged a glance with Jonathan and laughed. 'I'll go and get a decent one from Anne's room,' she said, pushing herself out of the sofa. 'She's bound to have some lying around and I do hate to see you suffer.' She left the room.

Diana dropped the dog-end into the fireplace. 'She's going to bring me one and I'm going to smoke it, and it'll be my second one today. Tomorrow it'll be three and so on till I'm hooked again. I must be mad. You're a doctor, Jon. Tell me not to.'

He walked over, mollified by her sudden need of him, and put an arm round her shoulders. 'Not a doctor yet and you wouldn't take any notice of me anyway. How does it go? "A prophet is not without honour, save in his own country and in his own house." Smoke, if it helps. I'd say stress is just as bad for you as nicotine.' It was like cuddling an older Elizabeth, he thought. They were so alike: in their looks, in their constant search for reassurance, in the ironic twist they gave to everything. It explained so well why they didn't get on.

He squeezed her arm and let her go, moving back to the window. 'Have all the police gone?'

'Except for the ones at the Lodge, I think. Poor Molly. It'll take her months to get over having her long johns inspected by the fuzz. She'll probably wash them all several times before she wears them again.'

'Lizzie will calm her ruffled feathers,' he said.

She gave his back a speculative glance. 'Do you see much of Elizabeth in London?' she asked him.

He didn't turn round. 'On and off. We have lunch

together sometimes. She works pretty anti-social hours, you know. She's in the casino till nearly dawn most nights.' It was tragic, he thought, how much there was about a daughter you could never tell her mother. You couldn't describe the exquisite pleasure of waking at four in the morning to find her warm naked body rhythmically arousing yours. You couldn't explain that just to think about her made you horny or that one of the reasons you loved her was because, whenever you slipped your hand between her thighs, she was wet with longing for you. Instead, you had to say you rarely saw her, pretend indifference, and the mother would never know of the fire her daughter could kindle. 'I should think I see more of her down here,' he said, turning round.

'She doesn't tell me anything about her life in London,' said Diana with regret. 'I assume she gets taken out but I don't know and I don't ask.'

'Is that because you don't want to know or you think she wouldn't tell you?'

'Oh, because she wouldn't tell me, of course,' she said. 'She knows I don't want her to repeat my mistake and marry too young. If she is serious about someone, I'll be the last to know, and by then it'll be too late for me to urge caution. My own fault entirely,' she said. 'I quite see that.'

Phoebe came back and tossed an opened packet of cigarettes at Diana. 'Would you believe they've left that child on guard in Anne's room? PC Williams, the one Molly's taken a shine to. He's had orders to stay there until further notice. Insisted on taking every one of these fags out to have a look at it.' She crossed to the telephone and replaced the receiver. 'I must have been out of my mind,' she went on. 'Jane's due in at Winchester some time this afternoon or evening. I told her to ring when she got there. We'll just have to put up with nuisance calls until we hear from her.'

With a grimace, Jonathan opened the French windows and stepped out on to the terrace. 'I'm going to take the dogs for a walk. I think I'll try and find Lizzie. See you later.' He put his fingers to his lips and gave a piercing whistle before setting off down the garden.

Just then the telephone rang. Phoebe picked it up and listened for a moment. 'No comment,' she said, replacing the receiver. A few seconds later it began to ring again.

Benson and Hedges cavorted around him, waggling their bottoms and barking, as if a walk was a rarity. He struck out towards the woodland between the Grange and Grange Farm, flinging a stick every now and then to please the scampering dogs. His direction took him past the ice house and he watched with distaste as they made a beeline for it, only to whine and scratch with frustration outside the sealed door. He went on, pausing regularly to turn and scan the way he had come, whistling to the dogs to keep up.

When he reached the two-hundred-year-old oak, standing majestically in its clearing in the middle of the wood, he took off his jacket and sat down, relaxing his back into a natural concave in the wrinkled bark. He remained there for half an hour, listening, watching, until he was satisfied that the only witnesses to what he was about to do were dogs and wild creatures.

He stood up, removed the envelope from inside his folded jacket and popped it through a narrow slit into a hollow in the oak's great trunk where a branch had died and been discarded in infancy. Only Jane, who had swarmed with him through the leafy panoply when they were children, knew the secrets of the hidey-hole.

He whistled up the straying dogs and went back to the house.

'Can I talk to you, darling?'

Elizabeth, halfway up the stairs to her bedroom, looked reluctantly at her mother. 'I suppose so.' She had just got back from the Lodge and was tired and irritable. Molly's unspoken distress over the police search had upset her.

'We'll leave it if it's not a good time.'

Elizabeth came slowly down the stairs. 'What's the matter?'

'Everything.' Diana gave a hollow laugh. 'What isn't the matter? I could answer that more easily.'

Elizabeth followed her into their sitting-room. It was a room like Anne's, but with a very different character, less startling, more conventional, with a gold carpet and classic floral prints in tones of russet and gold at the windows and on the chairs. A dwindling sun fingered the colours with a mellow glow.

'Tell me,' said Elizabeth as she watched Jonathan cross the terrace with Benson and Hedges and disappear through Phoebe's French windows.

Diana told her and, as the shadows lengthened, Elizabeth's distress grew.

Inspector Walsh glanced at his watch and, with an inward sigh, shouldered open the door of Interview Room Number Two. It was nine fifteen. He looked sourly from Anne to her solicitor.

Bill Stanley was a great bear of a man with ungroomed ginger hair sprouting everywhere, even on his knuckles, and an air of shabbiness. From his card he was with a top London firm, no doubt earning a packet, so the black pin-striped suit, crumpled and frayed at the cuffs, was presumably some sort of statement – equality with the huddled masses, perhaps

– although why he chose to wear it over a yellowed string vest, Walsh couldn't imagine. He made a mental note to check up on him. In thirty years of rubbing shoulders with the legal profession, he had never seen the like of B. R. Stanley, LLB. The card was probably a forgery.

'You can go home now, Miss Cattrell. There's a car waiting for you.'

She gathered her bits and pieces together and stuffed them carelessly into her handbag. 'And my other things?' she asked him.

'They will be returned to you tomorrow.'

Bill unfolded himself from his chair, stretched his huge hands to the ceiling and yawned. 'I can take you home, if you'd prefer it, Anne.'

'No, it's late. You get back to Polly and the children.'

He straightened his shoulders and the snap as the bones locked into place was loud in the small room. 'This is going to cost you an arm and a leg, my girl – it's goodbye to fifty quid every time I draw breath, remember – so what do you say? Shall we sue? I'm game.' He beamed. 'We're embarrassed for choice really. Harassment, abuse of police powers, damage to your professional reputation, loss of self-esteem, loss of earnings. I always enjoy litigation cases when I've had a chance to see both teams in action.'

Her eyes gleamed. 'Would I win?'

'Good lord, yes. I've hit the opposition for six off far stickier wickets.'

Walsh, who had found Bill's wisecracks increasingly irritating, spluttered angrily. 'The law is not a joke, Mr Stanley. I regret any inconvenience Miss Cattrell may have suffered, but in the circumstances I don't see that we could have acted any differently. It was her choice to have you present while she answered questions and, frankly, had it not taken you three hours to get here, this could all have been dealt with very much more quickly.'

'Couldn't make it any sooner, old man,' said Bill, poking a finger through his string vest and scratching his bear-hairy chest. 'My day for child-minding. Can't abandon the brood to their own devices. They'd slaughter each other the minute I was out of the house. Mind you, you might have a point. Don't relish accusations of sloppiness floating around in open court.' He gave Anne's shoulder a friendly squeeze with his great paw. 'I'll give you a discount. It's less fun but probably more sensible.'

Walsh gobbled furiously. 'I've a damn good mind to charge you both with wasting police time.'

Laughter shook the solicitor's huge frame as he opened the door for Anne and ushered her out. 'No, no, Inspector. I do the charging. Indecent, isn't it? I win whichever way you look at it.' He escorted her to the front door where a police car was waiting, took her face in his hands and bent to whisper in her ear. 'That little farce is going to cost you fifty smackers to one of the AIDS charities, plus an explanation.'

She patted his cheek. 'I needed someone to hold my hand,' she told him.

He grunted his amusement. 'Bollocks! I'd have been angry if I hadn't wanted to find out what the hell was going on and if I hadn't been waiting for a chance to meet that bastard Walsh.' The smile faded from his voice. 'Give me a ring tomorrow and I'll come down and talk to the three of you. Murder is a dangerous game, Anne, even for the spectators. It's too easy to get dragged in. Phoebe knows that better than anyone.' He put his hand on her bottom and propelled her towards the car. 'Give her my love, and Diana too.' He waved goodbye, then walked to his own car and set off back to London and his weekly night-shift in a shelter for the homeless.

Andy McLoughlin lingered in his car on the other side of the road. It was parked in the twilight zone between two pools of orange lamplight and he had seen without being seen. His hands shook on the steering wheel. God, he needed a drink. Had she kissed him? It was difficult to be sure. Did it matter anyway? It was their easy understanding, the way their bodies had leant against each other in uncomplicated friendship that had rocked him. He didn't want her love.

He eased himself out of the car and went inside in search of Walsh. 'How did it go?'

The Inspector was standing at his office window, glowering into the night. 'Did you see them? They've just gone.'

'No.'

'Damned solicitor took three hours to get here, arrived sporting a filthy string vest and looking like the hairy man of Borneo. Matter of fact, I'm highly doubtful about his credentials.' He took out his pipe. 'You were quite right, Andy. It was beef blood. We were being had. Why?'

McLoughlin lowered himself into a chair. 'A diversion. To draw you away from the rest of the house.'

Walsh walked back to his desk and sat down. 'Possibly. In that case it didn't work. There wasn't a stone left unturned by the time we'd finished.' There was a long silence before he tapped his pipe on a sheaf of letters in front of him. 'Jones found this little lot in Mrs Goode's studio.' He pushed the papers towards McLoughlin and waited while the Sergeant skimmed through them. 'Interesting, don't you think?'

'Did Jonesy question her about them?'

'Tried to. She said it was none of his business, that she'd got her fingers burnt and preferred to forget it, certainly had no intention of answering questions on the matter.' He fingered tobacco into the bowl of the pipe. 'When he told her he would have to take the letters, she lost her temper and tried to snatch them back.' There was a twinkle of amusement in his eye as he lit the tobacco and sucked in warm smoke. 'Two PCs had to restrain her while he removed them to his car.'

'And I thought she was the least volatile of the three. What about Mrs Maybury?'

'Good as gold. She took herself off to the greenhouse and spent most of the afternoon rooting Pelargonium cuttings while we turned her house inside out and found nothing.' Noises of succulent contentment puttered from his mouth. 'I've detailed a couple of lads to tout those shoes round the menders. It's a long shot but someone might remember re-heeling them. I don't care what Mrs Thompson says – let's face it, she's so damn cuckoo she wouldn't recognise her own reflection if it didn't have a halo round it – those shoes are the missing Daniel's. Size eight and brown. Too much of a coincidence.'

McLoughlin forced his pricking eyes to stay open as he re-read the top letter. It was undated and very brief. 'Monday. My dear Diana, Of course I regret what's happened, but my hands are tied. If it will help I can come out on Thursday to discuss the position with you. Yours ever, Daniel.' The address was Larkfield, East Deller, and scored across the page in angry writing was: 'Meeting confirmed.' The previous letter, a carbon copy of a demand from Diana for an up-to-date statement of Daniel Thompson's business, was dated Friday, 20th May.

'So when did he go missing?'

'Thursday, twenty-fifth of May,' said Walsh with satisfaction, 'the very day he had arranged an appointment with Mrs Goode.'

'So why didn't you bring her in with Miss Cattrell?'

'I can only cope with one at a time, lad. She'll keep another twelve hours. At the moment I'm rather more interested in why Miss Cattrell went to such extraordinary lengths to get herself brought in for questioning. Any ideas?'

McLoughlin looked at the floor and shook his head.

Fourteen

ANNE WAS DOG-TIRED. Her body had been pumping adrenaline for several hours, exciting her brain, racing her heart, keeping her at a peak of almost intolerable stimulation. Her reaction when she sank into the back of the warm police car was immediate and total. She fell asleep, upright at first but ending in a flat ungainly sprawl along the length of the seat when the driver took a bend too fast. Thus, the photographers outside the unlit gates of Streech Grange missed the picture they had been waiting for: Murder Enquiry – Journalist In Questioning Drama. They had seen too many police cars come and go to be interested in one without a passenger. Fred, sitting doggedly on an old deckchair at the padlocked gates, was not so easily fooled. He let the car in, satisfied himself with a momentary flash of his torch that it contained Anne, then with a sigh of relief resumed his seat. His clutch was safely in the nest. When the police car had gone he could retire to bed.

Barely awake, Anne let herself in through the front door and staggered sleepily across the carpet. Outside, with a new passenger in the shape of PC Williams, now relieved from guard duty, the police car grated away across the gravel. Anne leaned against the wall for a moment to collect her scattered wits. Behind Phoebe's door, she heard the warning bark of the dogs. The next moment, Jane Maybury precipitated herself into the hall and flung herself on her godmother. Together, they collapsed in a heap on the floor where Anne lay, eyes closed, and trembling.

'My God,' said Jane, turning to her mother who had appeared in the doorway behind her, 'there's something wrong with her. Jon!' she shrilled with alarm. 'Come quick. Anne's ill.'

'I'm not ill,' said the shaking body, opening its eyes. 'I'm laughing.' She sat up. 'God, I am *knackered.* Get off me, you great dollop,' she said, giving the girl a kiss, 'and get me a brandy. I'm suffering severe post-interrogation trauma.'

Phoebe hauled her to her feet and marched her into the drawing-room while Jane fetched a brandy. Anne folded happily on to the sofa and beamed about her. 'What's the matter? You all look as if you've been sucking lemons.'

Diana pulled a face. 'We've been worried sick, you idiot.'

'You should have more faith,' said Anne sternly, accepting the brandy from Jane. 'And how's my god-daughter?' She examined the girl circumspectly while she warmed her glass.

Jane smiled. 'I'm fine.' She was still too thin but Anne was pleased to see that her face had filled out and lost some of its tension.

'You look it,' she agreed.

Phoebe turned to Jonathan. 'Shall we have that celebration we promised ourselves?'

'Sure thing. I'll raid the cellar. What does anyone fancy? Château Lafite '78 or those last bottles of the '75 Champagne? Anne, you choose.'

'The Lafite. Champagne on top of brandy will make me puke.'

He looked questioningly at his mother. 'Shall I drive down and get Fred and Molly to join us? It hasn't been much fun for them either.'

Phoebe nodded. 'Good idea.' She held out a hand to Elizabeth who was sitting slightly apart on the tapestry stool. 'You go too, Lizzie darling. Molly can say no to all of us, and does regularly, but she won't refuse you.' She looked pointedly at Jonathan.

'Come on,' he said. 'You, too, Jane.' They went out.

Phoebe walked over to the mantelpiece. 'I wish David had never used the cellar for storing his wretched imports.'

Anne sniffed her brandy. 'Why? I bless his memory for it regularly.'

'Exactly,' agreed Phoebe dryly, 'so do I. It's very

upsetting.' She glanced at Diana. 'Lizzie's worried about something. Is it Molly and Fred?'

'No. I'm afraid it's me.'

'Why?'

Diana attempted a laugh which didn't work. 'Because I told her I'd be the next one in the police mincing machine.' She swung to face Anne. 'Why did they take you in?'

'They found the safe and it had some incriminating evidence in it.' Anne chuckled into her brandy. 'A bloody carving-knife, wrapped in a bloody rag.' She stirred her glass in her hands, warming it. 'It was straight out of Enid Blyton, but they all got very excited and I refused to answer any more questions till Bill arrived.'

'You're mad,' said Phoebe decidedly. 'What on earth were you up to?'

Mischief lit Anne's dark eyes. 'To tell you the truth, I didn't think they'd find the safe, and if it hadn't been for the Sergeant, they wouldn't have done.' She shrugged. 'Hell, you know me. I always put in an insurance policy, just in case.'

Diana groaned. 'You *are* mad. I do wish you'd take this whole thing a bit more seriously. God knows what they're thinking now. What was it you didn't want them to find?'

'Nothing too desperate,' said Anne easily. 'The odd document or two which probably oughtn't to be in my possession.'

'Well,' said Phoebe, 'I can't understand why you aren't still at the Police Station undergoing a grilling. That's more than Walsh ever had on me and he never let up for a minute.'

Anne sipped her brandy and looked from one to the other with laughter spilling out of her eyes. 'You didn't have my trump card. Bill did his stuff brilliantly. You should have seen him. Walsh damn nearly popped a blood vessel when he finally turned up. He was wearing his string vest.' She dabbed at her eyes and examined Diana's face through damp lashes. It was still very strained.

'It's a game with you, isn't it?' said Diana accusingly. 'I wouldn't mind so much, if I didn't think it was me they'll come down on. You are a fool, you know.'

Anne shook her head. 'What can they possibly have on you?'

Diana sighed. 'Nothing really, except that I've made a prize arsehole of myself.' She smiled unhappily at the two women. 'I hoped you'd never find out. It makes me look such an idiot.'

'It *must* be bad then,' said Anne lightly.

Phoebe squatted on her haunches with her back to the fireplace. 'It can't be worse than Anne's toy-boy, can it?' She looked at her friend and giggled. 'Do you remember him? He still had adolescent acne. You thought he was the bee's knees for about a week.'

Anne, whose earlier hysteria was still perilously close

to the surface, snorted stinging brandy through her nose. She gasped with pain and laughter. 'You mean Wayne Gibbons? A temporary aberration, I assure you. It was his whole-hearted commitment to the cause that attracted me.'

'Yes, but what cause? You looked worn out when he finally left.'

Anne mopped her running eyes. 'You know he's on a study course in Russia now? I had a letter from him not so long ago. It dwelt in extreme and tedious length on the subject of his constipation. I gather he hadn't had any green vegetables since Christmas.' She shuddered. 'God knows what it's done to his acne.' She turned to Diana with a grin. 'It can't be worse than Phoebe's wrestling match by the village pond with that ridiculous Dilys Barnes woman – the one whose daughter fornicates in our bushes. No question about that. Phoebe really looked a fool.'

In spite of herself, Diana laughed. 'Yes, that was funny.' She looked at Phoebe's smiling face. 'You should never have tackled her in a sarong.'

'How was I to know she was going to start a fight?' Phoebe protested. 'Also, it wasn't actually Mrs Barnes who pulled it off. It was Hedges. He got over-excited and did a runner with the damn thing between his teeth.'

Anne was shaking with tension-releasing laughter. 'It was the way you came stomping up the drive in your wellies, purple in the face, boobs bouncing all over the shop and with only a pair of knickers on. God, it was funny. I wish I'd seen the fight. And what were you doing wearing wellies with a sarong, anyway?'

Phoebe's eyes sparkled. 'It was hot, hence the sarong, and I wanted some pondweed from the village pond, hence the wellies. Absurd woman. She ran away screaming. I think she thought I'd taken the dress off myself in order to rape her.' She patted Diana's knee. 'If you've made a laughing-stock of yourself, it's hardly the end of the world.'

'Laughing-stock's right,' said Diana, 'Oh, hell! I'm never going to live it down. It's too bloody embarrassing. I wouldn't mind so much if I wasn't supposed to have good judgement in these things.'

Anne and Phoebe exchanged puzzled glances. 'Tell us,' prompted Phoebe.

Diana put her head between her hands. 'I was persuaded into parting with ten thousand quid,' she muttered. 'Half my savings straight down the drain, apart from anything else.'

Anne whistled sympathetically. 'That's rough. No chance of getting it back?'

'None. He's done a bunk.' She chewed her bottom lip. 'From the way they piled into my correspondence, I suspect the police think they've found him in our ice house.'

'Oh lord!' said Phoebe with feeling. 'No wonder Lizzie's worried. Who is this man?'

'Daniel Thompson. He got my name from that design consultant in Winchester, the one who helped me with the Council offices. He's an engineer, lives in East Deller. Have you come across him?'

Phoebe shook her head. 'You should have gone to the police yourself,' she said. 'It sounds to me as though you've been conned by this creep.'

'No,' said Diana tiredly, staring at her hands, 'it wasn't a con. I invested in a business he was running, all very legitimate and above board, but the bloody thing's gone bust and my money with it. Looking back, I must have been mad but it seemed like such a good idea at the time. It could have revolutionised interior design if it'd taken off.'

'Why on earth didn't you talk to us about it?'

'I would have done but it came up during that week in January when you were both away and I was holding the fort here. Another backer pulled out at the last minute and I had twenty-four hours to make up my mind. By the time you got back I'd rather forgotten about it, then things started to turn sour and I decided to keep mum. I wouldn't be telling you now if the police hadn't found out about it.'

'What business was it?'

Diana groaned. 'You'll laugh.'

'No, we won't.'

She gave them a ferocious glare. 'I'll throttle you if you do.'

'We won't.'

'See-through radiators,' she said.

The watcher in the garden was masturbating in an ecstasy of voyeuristic thrill. How many times had he spied on these cunts, preyed on them, seen them nude? Once he had creepy-crawled the house. His hand moved in mounting frenzy until, with convulsive shudders, he climaxed into his handkerchief. He held the sodden cloth to his face to muffle his giggles.

'I'm off to bed,' said Anne, putting her glass on a tray with the exaggerated care of the tipsy. 'Apart from anything else, I'm pissed. I happily volunteer to wash up in the morning, but tonight I'm off games. I'd break the lot,' she explained owlishly.

'Have you eaten anything this evening, Miss Cattrell?' scolded Molly.

'Not a thing.'

Molly muttered angrily. 'I'll have words with that Inspector in the morning. What a way to treat people.'

Anne paused on her way to the door. 'They brought me a corned beef sandwich,' she said, scrupulously fair. 'I didn't fancy it. There's something about corned beef.' She thought for a moment. 'It's the texture. Moist but crumbly. Reminds me of dog shit.' With a wave, she departed.

Diana, who was watching Molly's face, held her glass in front of her mouth to hide her smile. Even after eight years of Anne's careless bombardment, Molly's sensibilities were still so easily shocked.

Anne drank a pint of water in the kitchen, took a banana from the fruit bowl and wandered, eating it, through the hall and down the corridor. She switched on the lights in her sitting-room and collapsed gratefully into an armchair, tossing the banana skin into the waste-paper basket. She sat for some time, her weary brain in neutral, while the water slowly diluted the effects of the alcohol. After half an hour she began to feel better.

What a day! She had been shitting bricks at the Police Station, wondering if Jon had picked up her hint, and she thought now that she had probably panicked unnecessarily. Could McLoughlin be that sharp? Surely not. The room had been searched by experts – two, three years ago – when Special Branch suspected her of having a leaked MOD document in her possession. They had found the safe but not the secret cache behind it. She rubbed her eyes. Jon had whispered to her that he'd put the envelope somewhere outside where it would never be found. If that were true, she was tempted to let it stay there, wherever 'there' was. She hadn't asked for details. She ran hot and cold every time she thought of the contents of that envelope. God, she was a fool, but, at the time, a photographic record of that terrible brick tomb had made sense. She beat her fist against her head. Supposing Jon had opened it? But he hadn't, she told herself firmly. She could tell by the look in his eyes that he hadn't. But if he had? She thrust the thought away angrily.

McLoughlin held a fretful fascination for her. She kept going back to him, worrying at him, like a tongue against a loosening tooth. That business in front of the mantelpiece? Was it all a blind to cover his interest in the safe? She had looked into his face and seen only a deep, deep hurt, but an expression was only an expression, after all. She rubbed her eyes again. If only, she thought, if only, if only – There was a scream inside her, a scream that was as vast and as silent as the vast silence of space. Was her life always to be a series of *if onlys*?

There was a sharp tap on her French window.

She was so startled she flung her arm out and knocked her wrist on the occasional table beside her. She swung round, massaging the bruise, eyes straining into the night's blackness. A face was pressed against the window, eyes shielded from the bright glare of her lamps by a cupped hand. Fear flooded her mouth with sickly bile and the remembered stench of urine swamped her nostrils.

'Did I frighten you?' asked McLoughlin, easing open the unlocked window when she didn't get up.

'You gave me a shock.'

'I'm sorry.' Some shock he thought.

'Why didn't you come to the front door?' Even her lips were bloodless.

'I didn't want to disturb Mrs Maybury.' He closed the glass doors behind him. 'The light's on in her bedroom. She'd have to have come downstairs to let me in.'

'We've each got a front doorbell. If you press the one with my name on, I'm the only one who hears it.' But he knew that already, didn't he?

'Can I sit down?'

'No,' she said sharply. He shrugged and walked towards the fireplace. 'All right, yes, sit down. What are you doing here?'

He didn't sit down. 'I wanted to talk to you.'

'What about?'

'Anything. Eternity. Rabbie Burns. Safes.' He paused. 'Why are you so frightened of me?'

He wouldn't have believed she had any more blood to lose from her face. She didn't answer. He gestured towards the mantelpiece. 'May I?' He took her silence for permission and slid back the oak panelling. 'Someone's been here before me,' he said conversationally. 'You?' He looked at her. 'No, not you. Someone else.' He grasped the chrome handle and gave a strong pull. Too strong. Jonathan had forgotten to snap home the catches and the safe came out in a rush, sending McLoughlin staggering backwards. With a small laugh he lowered it to the floor and peered into the empty hole. 'Are you going to tell me what was in here?'

'No.'

'Or who removed whatever it was?'

'No.'

He ran his fingers down the side of the safe and located the spring catches. 'Very neat.' He swung it back into position and shoved it home. 'But you've been taking it in and out far more often than it was ever designed for. You're wearing away the ledge.' He pointed to the bottom of the door. 'It isn't parallel with the mantelpiece any more. It should be resting on a concrete lintel. Bricks are no good, they're too soft, too easily crumbled.' He slid the oak panelling into place and folded himself into the chair opposite her. 'One of Mrs Maybury's building efforts?' he suggested.

She ignored that. 'How did you know it wasn't the mantelpiece that was out of true?' Some of the colour had trickled back into her lips.

'I didn't, not until I opened the panel just now, but whoever's been at it in the meantime put it back even more carelessly than you did. Judging by the unsecured catches, they were presumably in a hurry. What was in there?'

'Nothing. You're imagining things.' They sat in silence looking at each other. 'Well?' demanded Anne finally.

'Well what?'

'What are you planning to do about it?'

'Oh, I don't know. Find out who cleaned it out, I suppose, and ask them a few questions. It shouldn't be too hard. The field isn't very wide, is it?'

'You'll end up with egg on your face,' she said tartly. 'The Inspector phoned through for a constable to be in here all the time I was away.' He liked her better when she fought back. 'So in that case, how could anyone have tampered with the safe? It must have dropped of its own accord.'

'That explains the hurry,' was all he said. He sank deeper into his chair and rested his chin on steepled fingers.

'I've nothing to tell you. You're wasting your time.'

He closed his eyes. 'Oh, you've got lots to tell me,' he murmured. 'Why you came to Streech. Why Mrs Phillips calls this house a fortress. Why you have nightmares about death.' He opened his eyes a fraction to look at her. 'Why you panic every time your safe is mentioned and why you like to divert interest away from it.'

'Did Fred let you in?'

'No, I climbed the wall at the bottom.'

Her eyes were deeply wary. 'Why would you do that?'

He shrugged. 'There's a barrage of photographers at your gate. I didn't particularly want to be seen coming in.'

'Did Walsh send you?'

She was as taut as piano wire. He reached out and took her hand, playing with her fingers briefly before letting them drop. 'I'm not your enemy, Cattrell.'

A smile flickered. 'I'll bet that's what Brutus said as he stuck the knife into Caesar. I'm not your enemy, Caesar, and, hell, old chap, it's nothing personal, I just happen to love Rome more.' She stood up and walked to the window. 'If you're not my enemy, McLoughlin, then drop me, drop all of us, from the enquiry and look for your murderer somewhere else.' The moon was pouring herself in a shimmering libation about the garden. Anne pressed her forehead against the cold glass and stared out at the awesome beauty of what lay beyond. Black roses with coronas of silver; the lawn glittering like an inland sea; a weeping willow, its leaves and branches wrought in sparkling tracery. 'But you can't do that, can you? You're a policeman and you love justice more.'

'How can I answer that?' he teased her. 'It's based on so many false premisses that it's entirely hypothetical. I sympathise with personal vengeance. I told you that this morning.'

She smiled cynically into the glass. 'Are you telling me you wouldn't have arrested Fred and Molly for murdering Donaghue?'

'No. I would have arrested them.'

She looked at him with surprise. 'That's a more honest answer than I expected.'

'I wouldn't have had any choice,' he said dispassionately. 'They wanted to be arrested. They sat there with the body, waiting for the police to come.'

'I see.' She smiled faintly. 'You make the arrest but you shed crocodile tears while you're doing it. That's a great way of salving your conscience, isn't it?'

He stood up and walked across to look down into her face. 'You helped me,' he said simply, putting his hands on her shoulders. 'I'd like to help you. But I can't if you won't trust me.'

He was so damn transparent, she thought, with his state-of-the-art cunning. She chuckled amiably. Two could play at this game. 'Trust *me*, McLoughlin. I don't need your help. I am as innocent of personal revenge and murder as a newborn baby.'

Abruptly, as if she were no more than a rag doll, he lifted her off her feet and twisted her towards the light, examining every inch of her face. As a face, it wasn't that special. She had laughter lines etched deeply round her eyes and mouth, frown lines on her forehead, but there was no menace lurking in her dark eyes, no shutters closed on nefandous secrets. Her skin gave off a faint scent of roses. He let go with one hand and ran the tips of his fingers along the curve of her jaw and down the soft line of her neck before, as abruptly, releasing her. 'Did you cut his balls off?'

She hadn't expected that. She straightened her sleeves. 'No.'

'You could be lying through your teeth,' he murmured, 'and I can't see it.'

'That's probably because I'm telling the truth. Why do you find that so hard to believe?'

'Because,' he growled angrily, 'my damn crotch is ruling my brain at the moment and lust is hardly an indicator of innocence.'

Anne glanced down and gave a gurgle of laughter. 'I see your problem. What do you plan to do about it?'

'You tell me. Cold showers?'

'God no. That would be Molly's choice. My advice is, when you've got an itch, scratch it.'

'I'd enjoy it a little more if you scratched it.'

Her black eyes danced. 'Did you have the sense to eat something?'

'Sausage and chips about five hours ago.'

'Well, I'm starving. I haven't eaten since lunchtime. There's an Indian take-away a couple of miles down the road. How do you fancy discussing your options over a Vindaloo?'

He lifted his hand to caress the curls round the base of her neck. The need to touch her was like an addiction. He was crazy, he didn't believe a damn word she said, but he couldn't help himself.

She saw the look in his eyes. 'I'm not your type, McLoughlin,' she warned. 'I am selfish, self-opinionated and entirely self-centred. I am independent, incapable of sustaining relationships and am often unfaithful. I dislike babies and housework and I can't cook. I am an intellectual snob with unconventional philosophies and left-wing politics. I don't conform, so I'm an embarrassment. I smoke like a chimney, am often rude, loathe getting tarted up and I fart very loudly in bed.'

He dropped his hand and grinned down at her. 'And on the plus side?'

'There isn't a plus side,' she said, suddenly serious, 'not for you. I'll get bored, I always do, and when something better comes along, as it surely will, I'll dump you just as I've dumped everyone else. We'll have a halfway decent bonk from time to time, but you'll pay heavily in emotion for what you can buy free of strings in Southampton. Is that what you want?'

He regarded her thoughtfully. 'Is this a regular turnoff, or am I privileged?'

She smiled. 'Regular. I like to be fair.'

'And what's the drop-out rate at this stage?'

'Low,' she said ruefully. 'A few sensible ones leg it. The rest plunge in thinking they're going to change me. They don't. You won't.' She watched his expression. 'Getting cold feet?'

'Well, I can't say I fancy it much,' he admitted. 'It sounds horribly like the relationship I had with my wife, dull, stifling and leading nowhere. I had no idea you were so narrow-minded. Put in "frightened to explore" after "selfish, self-opinionated and self-centred", and I guarantee the drop-out rate, pre-copulation, will astonish you.' He took her arm and steered her towards the window.

'Let's eat,' he said. 'My judgement's better on a full stomach. I'll decide then whether I want to sow my seed in sterile ground.'

She pulled away. 'Go fuck yourself, McLoughlin.'

'Getting cold feet, Cattrell?'

She laughed. 'I'll turn off the lights.' She slipped back to the door and plunged the room into darkness. He took out his torch and waited by the windows. As she approached, she neatly avoided a small table with a bronze statuette of a naked woman on it. 'Me,' she said. 'When I was a nubile seventeen-year-old. I had a bit of a thing going with the sculptor during one school holidays.'

He lit it with the torch and studied it with interest. 'Nice,' he said appreciatively.

She chuckled as she followed him out. 'The figure or the sculpture?'

'Both. Do you lock these doors?' he asked, sliding them to behind him.

'I can't, not from the outside. They'll be all right.'

He put a hand on the back of her neck and walked her across the terrace on to the lawn. An owl hooted in the distance. He looked back at the house to get his bearings and half-turned her to the left. 'This way,' he said, flashing the torch ahead of them. 'I parked the car in a lane that runs along the corner.' Beneath his fingers he could feel the tightness of her skin. They walked in silence until they entered the woodland bordering the lawn. Away to their left, something scuttered noisily through the undergrowth. Her skin leapt with fear, jolting him as violently as it jolted her. 'For God's sake, woman,' McLoughlin growled, swinging his torch beam among the trees. 'What's the matter with you?'

'Nothing.'

'Nothing?' He shone the torch into her eyes, suddenly angry. 'You've buried yourself alive, erected a mountain of barbed wire over the mound, and you call it nothing. She's not worth it. Can't you see that? What the hell can she ever have done for you that you have to sacrifice your whole life in exchange? For Christ's sake, do you enjoy dying by inches? What happened to the Anne Cattrell who seduced sculptors in her school holidays? Where's the thorn in the Establishment's flesh who stormed citadels single-handed?'

She pushed the torch away and her teeth gleamed momentarily as she smiled. 'It was fun while it lasted, McLoughlin, but I did tell you not to try and change me.'

She was gone so fast that even his torch beam couldn't follow her.

Fifteen

HE LET HER go and set off back to his car. He knew that if he went after her, her windows would be locked. He felt regret and relief in equal measure, like the suicide playing Russian roulette who hears the hammer click against an empty chamber. The Station was lousy with women wanting to console him. To hold a loaded gun to his temple by seeking his consolation with her was madness. He swiped in angry frustration at the branches of a tree and ripped the flesh on the side of his hand. He sucked the blood and swore profusely. He was in a mess, and he knew it. He needed a drink.

An owl screeched. Somewhere, far away, he thought he heard voices. He turned his head to listen but the silence only thickened about him. He shrugged and walked on, and it came again, a thread of sound, insubstantial – imagined? The skin on his scalp prickled uneasily. Damn the woman, he thought. If he went back, she would laugh at him.

He was cursing himself for a fool by the time he reached the terrace. He had seen no one, the house was in darkness and Anne was obviously already tucked up in bed. He flashed his torch across the flagstones and lit up her half-opened French window. With a frown, he walked over to it and shone his torch round the interior. He found her almost immediately. He thought she was asleep until he saw the blood glistening in her velvet cap of hair.

After the first paralysing moment of shock, he set to with such speed that time became elastic. In ten seconds he had worked up a sweat that would be rare after an hour's strenuous effort. His torch beam found a table lamp which he switched on as he sank to his knees beside the crumpled heap of clothes. He felt for a pulse in her neck, couldn't find one; laid his head on her chest, no heartbeat. With one fluid movement he rolled the tiny body over, shoved a hand under her neck, pinched her nostrils closed and began mouth-to-mouth respiration. He needed help. The part of his brain that wasn't directly concerned with the resuscitation directed him backwards, drawing the lifeless body with him, feeling with his feet for the table with the bronze statuette. He found it. While he continued the regular in-flows of air, he gave a vicious backward kick and sent the heavy bronze smashing through the plate-glass window. The glass exploded outwards on to the terrace, shattering the silence of the night and sending Benson and Hedges into a frenzy of alarm in another part of the house. He realised with a sense of desperation that he was getting no response. Her face was grey, her lips blue. He placed the heel of his right hand over her breast bone and with the heel of his left hand pressed down, rocking forward, arms straight. While his mouth was free, he shouted for help. After five compressions, he gave her another mouth-to-mouth respiration, before returning to the heart massage. As he rocked forward on the third compression, he saw Jonathan press his fingers against the colourless neck and feel for the pulse.

'Give her another breath,' said Jonathan. 'There's a very faint pulse. My bag, Mum. It's in the hall.'

McLoughlin breathed again into her lungs and, this time, when he turned his head to look at her chest it fluttered weakly. 'Keep going,' said Jonathan, 'one breath every five seconds until she's breathing normally. You're doing great.' He took his bag from a white-faced Phoebe. 'Get some blankets,' he told her. 'Hot-water bottles, anything to keep her warm. And get an ambulance.' He took out his stethoscope, pulled open Anne's shirt and listened for the heartbeat. 'Brilliant,' he said warmly. 'It's weak, but there.' He pinched her cheek and watched with relief as the sluggish blood tinged it faintly pink. Her breathing began to take on a regular rhythm. Gently, he pushed McLoughlin off. 'OK,' he said. 'I think she's under her own steam now. We'll put her in the recovery position.' With the Sergeant's help he pulled her arm across her midriff, then rolled her on to her front, turning her face gently to one side and bending her nearest arm and leg at the elbow and knee. Her breathing was slow but even. She muttered something into the carpet and opened her eyes.

'Hey, McLoughlin,' she said distinctly before giving a huge yawn and falling asleep.

McLoughlin's face was running with sweat. He sat back and wiped it with his shirt sleeve. 'Can't you give her something?'

'Nothing to give. I'm not qualified yet. Don't worry. She's doing all right.'

McLoughlin pointed to the bloody hair. 'She may have a fractured skull.'

Phoebe had come in quietly with a pile of blankets which she spread over the prone figure. She popped her own hot-water bottle at the feet. 'Diana's on the phone for an ambulance. Jane's run down to wake Fred and get the gates open.' She squatted by Anne's head. 'Is she going to be all right?'

'I don't – ' Jonathan began.

'Your daughter's outside?' McLoughlin interrupted, staggering to his feet.

Phoebe stared at him. 'She's gone to the Lodge. They're not on the phone.'

'Is anyone with her?'

Phoebe's face turned pale. 'No.'

'Jesus!' swore McLoughlin, thrusting past her. 'Ring the police for God's sake, get some cars up here.

I don't want to tackle a bloody maniac on my own.' He shouted back to them as he ran down Anne's corridor: 'Tell them someone's tried to murder your friend and may have a go at your daughter. Tell them to get a fucking move on.'

He ran past Diana and burst out of the front door, his sweat turning ice-cold in the night air. It was four hundred yards to the gates and he reckoned Jane was a couple of minutes ahead of him. He set off at a blistering pace. Two minutes was an eternity to kill a woman, he thought, when a second was all it needed to smash an unsuspecting skull. The drive was in pitch darkness with the overhanging trees and bushes blocking out even the weak light of a shrouded moon. He swore at himself for not bringing his torch as he blundered unseeingly into the stinging branches at the edge of the way. He set off again, this time using the crown of the road for his guide, eyes straining to adjust themselves to the night. It was several seconds before he realised that the bobbing yellow pin-point in the distance ahead of him was a torch beam. The drive had straightened out.

'Jane!' he yelled. 'Stop! Wait there.' He pounded on.

The torch swung round to point in his direction. The beam wobbled as if the hand that held it was unsteady.

'I'm a police officer,' he called, his lungs straining. 'Stay there.'

He slowed to a walk as he approached her, hands held placatingly in front of him, chest heaving. The torchlight, wavering frantically now, danced across his face and dazzled him. He fished for his warrant card in his trouser pocket, holding it in front of him like a talisman. With a groan he put his hands on his knees, bent forward and whooped for breath.

'What's the m-matter?' she stammered in a shrill, frightened voice.

'Nothing,' he said, straightening. 'I didn't think you should come alone, that's all. Could you shine the torch on the ground? You're blinding me.'

'Sorry,' She dropped her hand to her side and he saw she was wearing a dressing-gown and carpet slippers.

'Let's go,' he suggested. 'It can't be far now. Shall I take the torch?'

She passed it to him and he caught a brief glimpse of her in its gleam as he turned to light the way ahead. She was like a bloodless ghost, white-faced and insubstantial with a cloud of dark hair. She looked absolutely terrified.

'Please don't be frightened. Your mother knows me,' he said inadequately as they went on. 'She agreed I should come after you.' They could see the black mass of the Lodge in the distance.

She tried to speak but it was a second or two before the sound came. 'I could hear b-breathing,' she wobbled out.

'That was my lungs gasping,' he said, attempting a joke.

'No,' she whispered, 'it wasn't you.' Her step faltered and he swung the beam towards her. She plucked pathetically at her dressing-gown. 'I've got my nightie on.' Her lips were trembling uncontrollably. 'I thought it was my father.'

McLoughlin caught her as she slumped in a dead faint. In the distance, carried on the wind, came the faint sough of a siren.

'What did she mean, Mrs Maybury?' McLoughlin was leaning wearily against the Aga, watching Phoebe make tea.

Anne had been rushed to hospital with Jonathan and Diana in attendance. Jane was asleep in bed with Elizabeth watching over her. Police were swarming all over the garden in search of a suspect. Phoebe, under pressure from McLoughlin, was answering questions in the kitchen.

She had her back to him. 'She was frightened. I don't suppose she meant anything by it.'

'She wasn't frightened, Mrs Maybury, she was terrified, and not of me. She said: "I've got my nightie on. I thought it was my father."' He moved round so that he was facing her. 'Forgetting for the moment that she hasn't seen her father for ten years, why should she associate him with the fact that she was wearing a nightie? And why should it terrify her? She said she heard breathing.'

Phoebe refused to meet his eyes. 'She was upset,' she said.

'Are you going to make me ask Jane when she wakes up?' he demanded brutally.

She raised her lovely face. 'You'd do that, I suppose.' She made as if to push her spectacles up her nose, then realised she hadn't got them on and dropped her hand to the table.

'Yes,' he said firmly.

With a sigh, she poured two cups of tea. 'Sit down, Sergeant. You may not know it but you look dreadful. Your face is covered in scratches and your shirt's torn.'

'I couldn't see where I was going,' he explained, taking a chair and straddling it.

'I gathered that.' She was silent for a moment. 'I don't want you asking Jane questions,' she said quietly, taking the other chair, 'even less so after tonight. She couldn't cope. You'll understand that because I think you've guessed already what she meant by her remark.' She looked at him enquiringly.

'Your husband abused her sexually,' he said.

She nodded. 'I blame myself because I had no idea what he was doing. I found out one night when I came home early from work. I was the evening receptionist at the doctor's surgery,' she explained. 'We needed the money. David had sent Johnny to a boarding prep-school. That day I had flu and Dr

Penny sent me home and told me to go to bed. I walked in on my poor little Jane's rape.' Her face was quite impassive as if, long ago, she had realised the futility of nurtured anger. 'His violence had always been directed at me,' she went on, 'and in a way I asked for it. While he was beating me, I could be certain he wasn't touching the children. Or I thought I could.' She gave a mirthless laugh. 'He took full advantage of my naivety and Jane's terror of him. He had been raping her systematically since she was seven years old and he kept her quiet by telling her he would kill me if she ever said anything. She believed him.' She fell silent.

'Did you kill him?'

'No.' She raised her eyes to his. 'I could have done quite easily. I would have, if I'd had anything to kill him with. A child's bedroom doesn't lend itself to murder weapons.'

'What happened?'

'He ran away,' she said unemotionally. 'We never saw him again. I reported him missing three days later after several people had phoned to say he hadn't kept appointments. I thought it might look odd if I didn't.'

'Why didn't you tell the police the truth about him?'

'Would you, Sergeant, with a severely disturbed child your only witness? I wasn't going to let her be questioned, nor was I going to give the police a motive for a murder I didn't commit. She was under a psychiatrist for years because of what happened. When she became anorexic, we thought she was going to die. I'm only telling you now to protect her from further distress.'

'Have you any idea what happened to your husband?'

'None. I've always hoped he killed himself but, frankly, I doubt he had the guts. He loved inflicting pain on others but couldn't take it himself.'

'Why did he run away?'

She didn't answer immediately. 'I honestly don't know,' she said at last. 'I've thought about it often. I think, perhaps, for the first time in his life he was afraid.'

'Of what? The police? Prosecution?'

She smiled grimly, but didn't answer.

McLoughlin toyed with his teacup. 'Someone tried to murder Miss Cattrell,' he said. 'Your daughter thought she heard her father. Could he have come back?'

She shook her head. 'No, Sergeant, David would never come back.' She looked him straight in the eye as she brushed a strand of red hair from her forehead. 'He knows if he did, I'd kill him. I'm the one he's afraid of.'

A very irritable Walsh sat in Anne's armchair and watched a policeman photographing prints on the outside of what was left of the French windows. It was a job that couldn't be put off till the morning in case it rained. The broken slivers of glass on the flagstones had been covered with weighted-down polythene. 'There are going to be dozens of prints,' he muttered to McLoughlin. 'Apart from anything else, half the Hampshire police force have left their grubby paw marks round the shop.' McLoughlin was examining the carpet by the French windows, looking for blood spots. He moved across to the desk. 'Anything?' Walsh demanded.

'Nothing.' His eyes were red-rimmed with exhaustion.

'So what happened here, Andy?' Walsh cast a speculative eye over his Sergeant, before glancing at his watch. 'You say you found her at eleven forty or thereabouts. It is now one thirty and we have come up with some vague sounds in the distance and a woman with a fractured skull. What's your guess?'

McLoughlin shook his head. 'I haven't got one, sir. I wouldn't even know where to start. We'd better pray she comes round soon and can tell us something.'

Walsh levered himself out of the chair and shuffled over to the window. 'Haven't you finished yet?' he demanded of the man outside.

'Just about, sir.' He took a last photograph and lowered his camera.

'I'll leave someone here overnight and you can do the inside tomorrow.' Walsh watched while the man packed up his equipment and left, carefully skirting the broken glass, then he shuffled back to the chair, playing up his age. He took out his pipe and began the process of filling it, watching McLoughlin closely from beneath the angry jut of his brows. 'All right, Sergeant,' he snapped, 'now you can tell me just what the hell you've been up to. I don't like the smell of this one little bit. If I find you've been getting your priorities mixed, by God you'll be for the high jump.'

Exhaustion and jangling nerves combined in a prolonged yawn. 'I was trying to steal a bit of a march, sir. I thought there might be promotion in it.' Bold, bare-faced lies, he thought, nothing too concrete, not even a half-truth that Walsh could check up on. If Phoebe could get away with it, then so could he.

Walsh's frown deepened. 'Go on.'

'I came over the wall at the bottom to see what happened when she came back from the Station. I must have got here by about ten forty-five. The others had all gone to bed but Miss Cattrell was sitting in that chair you're sitting in. She finally switched off her downstairs light at about eleven fifteen. I hung around for another ten minutes then set off for the car. I hadn't gone far when I thought I heard voices, so I came back to investigate. Her window was slightly open. I shone my torch round inside and found her there.' He jerked his head towards the middle of the room.

Walsh champed thoughtfully on the stem of the

pipe. 'It was lucky you did. Mrs Maybury said you were giving her heart massage when she came in. You probably saved her life.' He lit the pipe and studied the Sergeant through the smoke. 'Is this the truth?'

McLoughlin gave another huge yawn. He couldn't control them. 'It's the truth, sir,' he said wearily. Why was he trying to protect himself? This morning he would have welcomed an excuse to go. Perhaps he just wanted to know the end of the story, or perhaps he wanted vengeance.

Walsh was deeply suspicious. 'If I find there's something been going on between the two of you, you'll be up on a discipline charge so damned fast you'll wonder what happened. She's a suspect in a murder enquiry.'

The dark face cracked into a grin. 'Do me a favour, sir, she's been treating me like Vlad the Impaler since I called her a dyke.' He yawned again. 'But I appreciate the compliment. In view of the bashing it's taken in the past couple of weeks, it does my ego good that you think I can pull a reluctant bird after twenty-four hours. Kelly wouldn't agree with you,' he finished bitterly.

Walsh grunted, 'Was it you who hit her?'

McLoughlin didn't have to feign surprise. 'Me? Why would *I* want to hit her?'

'To get even. You're in the mood for it.'

He stared at Walsh for a moment, then shook his head. 'That's not the way I'd choose,' he said. 'But if

Jack Booth ever turns up with a hole in his head, that might be down to me.'

The Inspector nodded. 'So what was Miss Cattrell doing for the half hour you watched her?'

'She sat in that armchair, sir.'

'And did what?'

'Nothing. I presume she was thinking.'

'You say the Maybury woman made no bones about wanting to kill her husband. Would she kill her friend too?'

'Possibly. If she was angry enough. But what was her motive?'

'Revenge? Perhaps she thought Miss Cattrell had talked to us.'

McLoughlin shook his head slowly. 'I imagine she knows Miss Cattrell better than that.'

'Mrs Goode? The Phillipses? The children?'

'Same question, sir. What was the motive?'

Walsh stood up. 'I suggest we start looking,' he said acidly, 'before we all end up on point-duty. A weapon would be helpful. I want this entire house turned upside down, Sergeant. You can lead the search till Nick Robinson gets here. He'll be my number two in this investigation.' He looked at his watch. 'You'll be concentrating on the Maybury file. Be in my office at ten tomorrow morning. There's a pattern to all of this and I want it found.'

'With respect, sir, I believe I can make a more valuable contribution here.'

'You'll do as you're told in future, Sergeant,' the older man snapped angrily. 'I'm not sure what your game is, but I don't like people who try to steal a march over me.'

McLoughlin shrugged. 'Then I urge you not to get too sold on a pattern, sir. Mrs Maybury has told you what she thinks happened and, as I pointed out this morning, Mrs Phillips describes this house as a fortress. Why?'

Walsh eyed him thoughtfully for a moment then walked to the door. 'You're being conned by some very professional liars, lad. If you don't sharpen up, you're going to look very foolish indeed.'

Sixteen

THERE WAS A new sense of urgency about police activities. They moved into top gear with alacrity, demonstrating all too clearly that there was another gear to move into. It was as if the attempted murder of a known woman was on a different scale from the murder of an anonymous male stiff in the garden. Anne would have found it disquieting, except that she was in a coma in Intensive Care and knew nothing about it. Walsh would have denied it vigorously, but his irascible temper flayed his men instead when, after a thorough search of the house and grounds, they failed to come up with anything.

In the press, Streech Grange was likened, quite inappropriately, to 10 Rillington Place, as a setting for mass murder and decomposing remains. To Anne's friends, the burden of their association with it was heavy. In retrospect, their previous interrogations had the relaxed air of a social gathering. After the assault on Anne, the gloves came off and they were grilled dry. Walsh was looking for a pattern. Logic told him there was one. The odds against three unconnected mysteries in one house were so incalculable as to be beyond consideration.

For the children, it was a new experience altogether. As yet none of them had been questioned and it came like a baptism of fire. Jonathan hated his sense of impotence, of being involved in something over which he had no control. He was surly and uncooperative and treated the police with a sort of weary disdain. Walsh wanted nothing so much as to kick him up the backside, but after two hours of questioning he was satisfied there was nothing more he could get out of him. Jonathan had vindicated the three youngsters of the assault on Anne. According to him, they had changed into their nightclothes after the impromptu Lafite party, wrapped themselves in duvets and curled up in Jane's room to watch the late film on her television. The shattering glass, followed by McLoughlin's shouts for help, had startled them. No, they had heard nothing before that, but then the television had been quite loud. Walsh questioned Elizabeth. She was nervous but helpful. When asked for her movements on the previous evening, her account tallied exactly with Jonathan's down to the most trivial detail. Jane, after a day's respite, gave a similar story. Unless they were in some fantastic and well-organised conspiracy, they had had nothing to do with the attempt on Anne's life.

For Phoebe it was a case of déjà vu. The only difference this time was that her interrogators now had information she had withheld from them ten years previously. She answered them with the same stolid patience she had shown before, annoyed them with her unshakeable composure and refused to be drawn when they needled her on the subject of her husband's perversions.

'You say you blame yourself for not knowing what he was doing to your daughter,' said Walsh on more than one occasion.

'Yes, I do,' she answered. 'If I had known earlier, perhaps I could have minimised the damage.'

He got into the habit of leaning forward for the next question, waiting for the tell-tale flicker of weakening resolve. 'Weren't you jealous, Mrs Maybury? Didn't it madden you that your husband preferred sex with your daughter? Didn't you feel degraded?'

She always paused before she answered, as if she were about to agree with him. 'No, Inspector,' she would say. 'I had no such feelings.'

'But you've said you could easily have murdered him.'

'Yes.'

'Why did you want to murder him?'

She smiled faintly at this. 'I should have thought it was obvious, Inspector. If I had to, I'd kill any animal I found savaging my children.'

'Yet you say you didn't kill your husband.'

'I didn't have to. He ran away.'

'Did he come back?'

She laughed. 'No, he didn't come back.'

'Did you kill him and leave him to rot in the ice house?'

'No.'

'It would have been a sort of justice, wouldn't it?'

'It certainly would.'

'The Phillipses, or should I say Jeffersons, believe in that kind of justice, don't they? Did they do it for you, Mrs Maybury? Are they your avenging arm?'

It was always at this point that Phoebe's anger threatened to spill over. The first time he put the question it had come like a blow to the solar plexus. Afterwards, she was better prepared, though it still required iron self-control to keep from tearing and gouging at his hated face. 'I suggest you ask Mr and Mrs Phillips that,' she always said. 'I wouldn't be so presumptuous as to answer anything on their behalf.'

'I'm asking you for an opinion, Mrs Maybury. Are they capable of exacting vengeance for you and your daughter?'

A pitying smile would curl her lips. 'No, Inspector.'

'Was it you who struck down Miss Cattrell? You say you were in bed, but we only have your word for it. Was she going to reveal something you didn't want revealed?'

'Who was she going to reveal it to? The police?'

'Perhaps.'

'You're such a fool, Inspector.' She smiled humourlessly. 'I've told you what I think happened to Anne.'

'Guesswork, Mrs Maybury.'

'Perhaps, but in view of what happened to me nine years ago, not unlikely.'

'You never reported it.'

'You wouldn't have believed me if I had. You'd have accused me of doing it to myself. In any case, nothing would have induced me to have you back in the house, not once I'd got rid of you. In some ways I was luckier than Anne. My scars were all internal.'

'It's too convenient. You must think me very gullible.'

'No,' she said honestly, 'narrow-minded and vindictive.'

'Because I don't share your taste for melodrama? Your daughter is very vague about what frightened her. Even Sergeant McLoughlin only *thinks* he heard someone. I'm a realist. I prefer to deal in fact, not female neurosis.'

She studied him with a new awareness. 'I never realised how much you dislike women. Or is it just me, Inspector? The idea that I might be getting my just deserts really appeals to you, doesn't it? Would I have saved myself all this misery if I'd said "yes" ten years ago?'

Invariably it was Walsh who became angry. Invariably, after a bout of questioning, Phoebe would get in her car and drive to the hospital to sit at Anne's bedside, massaging her hands and talking to her, willing her back to consciousness.

Diana's interrogations probed and prodded her connection with Daniel Thompson. She couldn't control her anger against Walsh in the way that Phoebe did and she frequently lost her temper. Even so, after two days, he could still detect no flaws in her story.

He tapped the pile of correspondence. 'It's perfectly clear from your letters that you were furious with him.'

'Of course I was furious,' she snapped. 'He had squandered ten thousand pounds of my money.'

'Squandered?' he repeated. 'But he was doing his best, wasn't he?'

'Not in my view.'

'Didn't you have the business checked before you agreed to invest in it?'

'We've already been through all this, for God's sake. Don't you listen to anything?'

'Answer the question, please, Mrs Goode.'

She sighed. 'I wasn't given much time. I spent a day going through the company books. They seemed in order, so I made over the cheque for ten thousand. Satisfied?'

'So why do you say he squandered your money?'

'Because as I got to know him, I realised he was supremely incompetent, may even have been an out-

and-out rogue. The figures I saw had been heavily massaged. For example, I now think he inflated the company's assets by overvaluing his stock and I have discovered he was also using his employees' National Insurance contributions to keep the business afloat. The order books I saw were full, yet after three months he had sold virtually nothing and the little stock he had at his factory apparently had nowhere to go. His PR was a joke. He kept saying that word-of-mouth would spread and the thing would take off.'

'And that made you angry?'

'God give me strength,' she said, raising her hands to heaven. 'Do you need it spelled out? It made me livid. I was conned.'

'Do you know anything about Mr Thompson's disappearance?'

'For the last time, no. N-O, no.'

'But you knew he'd disappeared before we told you.'

'Yes, Inspector, I knew. He was supposed to come here to explain what was going on.' She leaned forward and banged her fist on the letters. 'You've got the date and the time in front of you. He never turned up. I rang his office and was told he wasn't there. I rang his home and was given a flea in my ear by his wife. I rang his offices again a couple of days later and was told Mrs Thompson had reported him missing. I went to the office the next day to find some very angry employees who had not been paid for three weeks and had just discovered that their insurance contributions had not been paid for nearly a year. There has been no sign of Daniel Thompson since. The business is bankrupt and a lot of people, not just me, are owed a considerable amount of money.'

'Frankly, Mrs Goode, anyone who invests money in see-through radiators should expect to lose it.'

Ice-blue eyes, he thought, had a capacity for murderous dislike that the greens and browns lacked. The epithets she now applied to him were unprintable.

'It's your pride that's hurt, isn't it?' he said with interest. 'Your amour-propre. I can easily imagine you killing someone who made a fool of you.'

'Can you?' she snapped. 'Then you've an overactive imagination. No wonder the police have such a poor detection record.'

'I think Mr Thompson did come here, Mrs Goode, and I think you got as angry with him as you are with me, and you hit out at him.'

She laughed. 'Have you ever seen him? No? Well, take it from me, he's built like a tank. Ask his silly wife if you don't believe me. If I'd hit him, he'd have hit me back and I'd still be sporting the bruises.'

'Were you sleeping with him?'

'I'll make a confession,' she conceded. 'I found Daniel even less fanciable than I find you. He had wet lips, very like yours. I don't like wet lips. Does that answer your question?'

'His wife denied any connection between him and the Grange.'

'That doesn't surprise me. I've only met her once. She didn't approve of me.'

'Did Fred and Molly know about this investment of yours?'

'No one here knew.'

'Why not?'

'You know bloody well.'

'You didn't want to look a fool.'

She didn't bother to answer.

'Perhaps Fred and Molly did your dirty work for you, Mrs Goode?'

She massaged the beginnings of a headache. 'What a nasty manipulative man you are.'

'Did they, Mrs Goode?'

She studied him thoughtfully. 'No,' she said. 'And if you ever dare ask me that question again, I'll hit you.'

'And be arrested for assault?'

'It would be worth it,' she said.

'You're a very aggressive woman, aren't you? Did you take out your aggressions on Miss Cattrell?'

She punched him on the nose.

Jonathan tapped his mother on the shoulder, then bent forward and looked at Anne. 'How is she?' She was off the critical list and had been removed from

Intensive Care to a side room on a surgical ward. She was attached via a catheter and a plastic tube to an intravenous drip.

'I don't know. She's very restless. She's opened her eyes once or twice, but she's not seeing anything.'

He squatted on the floor beside her. 'You're going to have to leave her for a bit, I'm afraid. Diana needs you.'

'Surely not.' Phoebe frowned.

''Fraid so. She's been arrested.'

She was visibly surprised. 'Diana? Whatever for?'

'Assault on a police officer. She punched Inspector Walsh and gave him a nose bleed. She's been carted off to the nick.'

Phoebe's mouth dropped open. 'Oh, lord, how funny,' she said, beginning to laugh. 'Is he all right?'

'Bloody but unbowed.'

'I'll come. We'd better get hold of poor Bill again.' She looked down at Anne. 'Nothing I can do for you at the moment, old girl. Keep fighting. We're all rooting for you.'

'I'll bring Jane in later,' said Jonathan. 'She wants to come.'

They walked into the corridor. 'Is she up to it?'

'I'd say so. She's coped fantastically since it happened. We had a long chat this afternoon. She was more objective than I've ever known her. Ironically, the whole thing may have done her some good, silver linings and all that, made her realise she's tougher than she thought she was. She likes the Sergeant, by the way. If they want to question her again, we should press for him to do it.'

'Yes,' said Phoebe. 'Apart from anything else, he saved Anne's life. That would always commend him to Jane. She dotes on her godma.'

Jonathan linked his arm through his mother's. 'She dotes on you, too. We all do.'

Phoebe gave her rich laugh. 'Only because you haven't discovered my clay feet yet.'

'No,' he said seriously. 'It's because you've never pretended they were anything else.'

They walked on and disappeared round a bend in the corridor. Behind them, Andy McLoughlin inched with the embarrassment of the eavesdropper from where he had been hiding in a recessed doorway.

Damn Walsh and his bloody pattern, he thought. Logic was fallible. It had to be.

He showed his warrant card to the Sister. 'Miss Cattrell?' he asked. 'Any change?'

'Not really. She's getting restless and opening her eyes which is a good sign but, as I told the Inspector, you'll be wasting your time if you want to interview her. She could come out of it any moment or she could be like this for a day or two. We'll let you know as soon as she's up to talking.'

'I'll stay for a few minutes, if that's all right. You never know.'

'She's in side ward two. Chat to her,' the Sister

encouraged. 'Might as well make yourself useful while you're here.'

He hadn't seen her since she had been taken away in the ambulance and he was shocked. She was even smaller than he remembered, a tiny, shrunken thing with bandaged head and ugly, sallow skin. But, even unconscious, she seemed to be smiling at some private joke of her own. He felt no lust – how could he? – but his heart warmed with a sense of recognition as if he had known her a long time. He pulled the chair close to her pillows and started to speak. There was no hesitation for he knew, without thinking, just what would give her pleasure. After half an hour he ran dry and looked at his watch. She had moved once or twice, like a child in her sleep, but her eyes had stayed firmly closed. He pushed his chair back. 'That's it, Cattrell. Time's up, I'm afraid. I'll see if I can get you alone again tomorrow.' He touched her cheek with his fingertips.

'You're a mean sod,' she mumbled. 'Give me "Tam o' Shanter".' She opened one eye and glared at him. 'I'm dying.'

'You've been awake all the time,' he accused her.

She opened the other eye and there was a twinkle amidst the confusion. 'Was Phoebe here?'

He nodded.

'I remember Phoebe being here. Am I at home?'

'You're in hospital,' he told her.

'Oh, shit. I hate hospitals. What day is it?'

'Friday. You've had a two-day snooze.'

That worried her. 'What happened?'

'I'll find a nurse.' He started to get up.

'You bloody well won't,' she growled. 'I hate nurses too. What happened?'

'Someone hit you. Tell me what you remember.'

She knit her brows into a deep furrow. 'Curry,' she said experimentally.

He gripped her hand tightly. 'Can we forget the curry, Cattrell?' he asked her. 'It'll be easier all round if you never saw me that evening.'

She wrinkled her forehead. 'But what happened? Who found me?'

He rubbed her fingers. 'I found you, but I've had the devil's own job explaining to Walsh what I was doing there. I can hardly admit to carnal designs on a suspect.' He searched her face. 'Do you understand what I'm saying? I want to stay on the case, Anne. I want justice.'

'Of course I bloody understand.' Humour danced in the dark eyes and he wanted to hug her. 'I can chew gum and walk at the same time, you know.' She thought deeply. 'I remember now. You were telling me how to live my life.' She looked at him accusingly. 'You had no right, McLoughlin. As long as I can live with myself, that's all that matters.'

He raised her fingertips and brushed them softly across his lips. 'I'm learning. Give me time. Tell me what else you remember?'

'I ran all the way back,' she said with an effort of concentration. 'I opened the window, I remember that. And then' – she frowned – 'I heard something, I think.'

'Where?'

'I don't remember.' She looked worried. 'What happened then?'

'Someone hit you on the back of the head.'

She looked dazed. 'I don't remember.'

'I found you inside your room.'

A heavy hand descended on his shoulder and made him jump. 'You've no business to be asking her questions, Sergeant,' said the Sister angrily. 'Get me Dr Renfrew,' she called to a nurse in the corridor. 'Out,' she told McLoughlin.

Anne looked at her with unalloyed horror and clung to his hand. 'Don't you dare go,' she whispered. 'I've seen her picture on *World at War* and she wasn't fighting for the Allies.'

He turned and raised his hands in helpless resignation.

'Is there anything I should remember?' she asked him. 'I wouldn't want to confuse the Inspector.'

His eyes softened. 'No, Miss Cattrell. You just concentrate on getting better and leave the remembering to me.'

She winked sleepily. 'I'll do that.'

*

DS Robinson was after promotion. He had gone diligently door-to-door again, looking for leads to Anne's assailant, but he had come up against the proverbial brick wall. No one had seen or heard anything on that night, except the ambulance, and they'd all heard that. He had had another pint with Paddy Clarke, this time under the beady eye of Mrs Clarke. He had found her immensely intimidating, more so since Anne's revelation that she had once been a nun. Paddy assured him they had looked for the map of the grounds but hadn't found it and, with Mrs Clarke breathing over his shoulder, he expressed complete ignorance of Streech Grange and its inhabitants. In particular, he knew nothing at all about Anne Cattrell. Nick Robinson didn't press him. Frankly, he didn't rate his chances if he got caught up between Mr and Mrs Clarke and he was unashamedly attached to his balls.

There was nothing to stop him going home now. By rights, he was off-duty. Instead, he turned his car in the direction of Bywater Farm and one Eddie Staines. So far, Mrs Ledbetter's information had paid dividends. No harm in giving her another whirl.

The farmer pointed him to the cow-sheds where Eddie was cleaning up after the evening's milking. He found Eddie leaning on a rake and carelessly chatting up an apple-cheeked girl who giggled inanely at everything he said. They fell silent as Nick Robinson approached and looked at him curiously.

'Mr Staines?' he asked, producing his warrant card. 'Can I have a word?'

Eddie winked at the girl. 'Sure,' he said. 'Would bollocks do?'

The girl shrieked her mirth. 'Ooh, Eddie! You are funny!'

'Preferably in private,' continued Robinson, making a mental note of Eddie's riposte for his own future use.

'Buzz off, Suzie. I'll see you later in the pub.'

She went reluctantly, scuffing her boots through the muck in the yard, looking over her shoulder in the hopes of being invited back. For Eddie, it was clearly a case of out of sight out of mind. 'What do you want?' he asked, raking soiled straw into a heap while he spoke. He was wearing a sleeveless tee-shirt which gave full expression to the muscles of his shoulders.

'You've heard about the murder at the Grange?'

'Who hasn't?' said Staines, uninterestedly.

'I'd like to ask you a few questions about it.'

Staines leant on his rake and eyed the detective. 'Listen, mate, I've already told your lot all I know and that's nothing. I'm a farmhand, a salt-of-the-earth prole. The likes of me don't mix with the people at the Grange.'

'No one said you did.'

'Then what's the point of asking me questions?'

'We're interested in anyone who's been into the grounds in the last couple of months.'

Staines resumed his raking. 'Not guilty.'

'That's not what I've heard.'

The young man's eyes narrowed. 'Oh, yeah? Who's been blabbing?'

'It's common knowledge you take your girlfriends up there.'

'You trying to pin something on me?'

'No, but there's a chance you may have seen or heard something that could help us.' He offered the man a cigarette.

Eddie accepted a light. He appeared to be thinking deeply for several minutes. 'Happen I did then,' he said surprisingly.

'Go on.'

'Seems you've been asking my sister questions about a woman crying one night. Seems you've been back a couple of times.'

'The farm cottages on the East Deller road?'

'That's right. Maggie Trewin's my sister, lives in number two. Her man works up at Grange Farm. She tells me you want to know which night this – woman' – he put a derisory emphasis on the word – 'was crying.'

Robinson nodded.

'Well, now,' said Staines, blowing perfect smoke rings into the air above his head, 'I can probably tell you, but I'd want a guarantee my brother-in-law'll never know where you got it from. No court appearances, nothing like that. He'd skin me alive if he knew I'd been up there and he'd not give up till he found out who I was with.' He shook his head morosely. 'It's more'n my life's worth.' His brother-in-law's young sister was the apple of his eye.

'I can't guarantee no court appearances,' said Robinson. 'If the prosecution serves a writ on you, you'll have to attend. But it may never happen. The woman may have no bearing on the case.'

'You reckon?' Staines snorted. 'More'n I do.'

'I could take you in for questioning,' said Robinson mildly.

'Wouldn't get you nowhere. I won't say nothing till I'm certain Bob Trewin won't find out. He'd kill me, no mistake.' He flexed his muscles and returned to his raking.

Nick Robinson wrote his name and the address of the Police Station on a page of his notebook. He tore it out and handed it to Staines. 'Write down what happened and when, and send it to me unsigned,' he suggested. 'I'll treat it as an anonymous tip-off. That way no one will know where it came from.'

'You'll know.'

'If you don't,' Robinson warned, 'I'll come back and next time I'll bring the Inspector. He won't take no for an answer.'

'I'll think on it.'

'You do that.' He started to leave. 'I suppose you weren't up there three nights ago?'

Staines hefted a lump of dung to the top of his straw pile. 'You suppose right.'

'One of the women was attacked.'

'Oh, yeah?'

'You hadn't heard?'

Staines shrugged. 'Maybe.' He cast a sideways glance at the detective. 'One of her girlfriends did it, bound to be. Bitches fight like the devil when they're roused.'

'So you didn't hear or see anything that night?'

Eddie turned his back to attack the farthest corner of the shed. 'Like I just said, I wasn't there.'

Now, why don't I believe you, Robinson wondered, as he picked his way with distaste through the cow dung in the yard. The apple-cheeked girl giggled as he passed her by the gate then, like a moth to the flame, she dashed back to the cow-sheds and the arms of her philanderer.

Seventeen

WALSH WAS STILL nursing a bloody nose when McLoughlin got back to the Station. It had long since stopped bleeding but he persisted in holding his blood-stained handkerchief to it. McLoughlin, who hadn't overheard that part of Phoebe's and Jonathan's conversation, looked at him in surprise.

'What happened?' he asked.

'Mrs Goode hit me, so I arrested her for assault,' said Walsh maliciously. 'That soon wiped the smile off her face.'

McLoughlin sat down. 'Is she still here?'

'No, dammit. Mrs Maybury persuaded her to apologise and I let her go with a caution. Bloody women,' he said. He stuffed the handkerchief into his pocket. 'We've had a result on the shoes. Young Gavin Williams turned up an old cobbler in East Deller who does it for pin money.'

McLoughlin whistled. 'And?'

'Daniel Thompson's for sure. The old boy keeps

records, bless him. Writes a description of the shoes – in this case, made a special note of the different coloured laces – what needs to be done, name of owner and the dates they come in and go out. Thompson collected them a week before he went missing.' Walsh fingered his nose tenderly. 'The time-scale's perfect. It's not looking good for Mrs Goode.' He chuckled at his witticism. 'If we can find just one person who saw him going into the Grange – ' He let the thought hang in the air while he took out his pipe and started to clean it with cheerful industry. 'How do you fancy Miss Cattrell for that part? She went through the little pantomime with her solicitor to steer us away from her friend, then panicked her friend by letting on how much she knew.' He tapped the pipe against his head. 'Goodbye Miss Cattrell.'

'No chance,' said McLoughlin decidedly, watching the pipe-cleaner turn black with tar. 'I dropped into the hospital on my way here. She's come round. I've sent Brownlow down to sit with her.'

'Has she now? Did you speak to her?'

'Briefly, before I was booted out by the Sister. She needs a good sleep, apparently, before she can answer questions.'

'Well?' demanded Walsh sharply. 'What did she say?'

'Nothing much. The whole thing's a complete blank to her.' He examined his nails. 'She did say she thought she heard something outside.'

Walsh grunted suspiciously. 'Suits your case rather neatly, doesn't it?'

McLoughlin shrugged. 'You're barking up the wrong tree, sir, and if you hadn't tied my hands I'd have proved it by now.'

There was malice in the older man's voice. 'Jones has taken his team over the ground twice and they haven't found anything.'

'Then let me have a look. I'm wasting my time on the Maybury file. No one I've spoken to so far knew anything about his penchant for little girls. Jane appears to be the only one. It's a dead end, sir.'

Walsh dropped the fouled pipe-cleaner into his waste-paper basket and glared at his Sergeant with open dislike. McLoughlin's admission that he had been trying to steal a march rankled with him, all the more because his own grip on the case was so tenuous. He was deeply suspicious of the man in front of him. What did McLoughlin know that *he* didn't? Had he found the pattern? 'You'll stick with that file till you've talked to everyone who knew Maybury,' he said angrily. 'It's a whole new line of enquiry and I want it thoroughly explored.'

'Why?'

Walsh's brows snapped together. 'What do you mean, why?'

'Where will it lead us?'

'To Maybury's murderer.'

McLoughlin looked at him with amusement. 'She's

got the better of you, sir, and there's damned all you can do about it. Raking over dead ashes isn't going to produce a prosecution. He terrorised one child and that was his own daughter, and now he's dead. My guess is he's buried in that garden somewhere, possibly in one of the flowerbeds at the front. She does those herself. Fred is never allowed near them. I think you were right and she hid the body in the ice house till the coast was clear and I doubt very much if, after ten years, there's anything left for us to find. Those dogs of hers are rather partial to human remains.'

Walsh plucked at his lips. 'I'm keeping an open mind. Webster still hasn't proved to my satisfaction that it wasn't Maybury in the ice house.'

McLoughlin gave a derisive snort. 'A minute ago you were convinced it was Daniel Thompson. For God's sake, sir, face up to the fact that you've got a *closed* mind on this whole thing. Result, we're all working with one hand behind our backs.' He leaned forward. 'There is no pattern, or not the sort you're looking for. You're trying to force unrelated facts to fit and you're making a mess of it.'

A panic of indecision gripped Walsh's belly. It was true, he thought. There was too much pressure. Pressure from within him to close the Maybury case once and for all, pressure from the media for eye-catching headlines, pressure from above to find quick solutions. And, always, the unrelenting pressure from below as the new bloods challenged for his job. He eyed McLoughlin covertly as he fingered tobacco into his pipe bowl. He had liked and trusted this devil once, he reminded himself, when the devil was shackled to a tiresome wife and troubled by his inadequacies. 'What do you suggest?'

McLoughlin, who had been up for three nights in a row, rubbed his tired eyes vigorously. 'A constant watch on Streech Grange. I'd suggest a minimum of two in each shift. Another thorough search of the grounds, but concentrated up near the Lodge. And, finally, let's be done with Maybury and put our energies into pursuing the Thompson angle.'

'With Mrs Goode as chief suspect?'

McLoughlin pondered for a moment or two. 'We can't ignore her certainly, but it doesn't feel right.'

Walsh touched his sore nose tenderly. 'It feels very right to me, lad.'

Mrs Thompson greeted them with her look of long-suffering martyrdom and showed them into the pristine but characterless room. McLoughlin had a sense of going back in time, as if the intervening days hadn't happened and they were about to explore the same conversation in the same way and with the same results. Walsh produced the shoes, no longer in their polythene bag, but with the odd meagre dusting of powder where an attempt had been made to bring up fingerprints and had failed. He put them on a low coffee table for her to look at.

'You said these weren't your husband's shoes, Mrs Thompson,' he accused her mildly.

Her hands fluttered to the cross on her bosom. 'Did I? But of course they're Daniel's.'

Walsh sighed. 'Why did you tell us they weren't?'

The awful tears swam into her eyes and drizzled over her cheeks. 'The devil whispers in my ear.' Her fingers fumbled at her shirt buttons.

'Give me strength,' muttered Walsh.

McLoughlin stood up abruptly and walked to a telephone in one corner. 'Pull yourself together, Mrs Thompson,' he ordered sharply. 'If you don't, I shall call for an ambulance and have you taken into hospital.'

She shrank into her chair as if he had slapped her.

Walsh frowned angrily at his Sergeant. 'Are these the shoes Mr Thompson was wearing when he disappeared?' he asked the woman gently.

She examined them closely. 'No,' she said.

'Are you sure? You told us the other day he had only one pair of brown shoes and he was wearing them the day he went.'

Her eyelids fluttered uncontrollably. 'Did I?' she gasped. 'How very odd. I don't believe I was feeling quite well the last time you came. Daniel loved brown shoes. You can have a look in his cupboard if you like.

He had pairs and pairs.' She waved her hand at the table. 'No, these are the ones Daniel gave to the tramp.'

Walsh closed his eyes. His threadbare case against Diana was disintegrating. 'What tramp?' he demanded.

'We didn't ask his name,' she said. 'He came to the door, begging. The shoes were on the stairs to go up and Daniel said he could have them.'

'When was this?'

She produced the lace handkerchief and touched it to her eyes. 'The day before he left. I remember it very clearly. Daniel was a saint, you know. In spite of all his troubles he had time for a poor beggarman.'

Walsh took some papers from his briefcase and flicked through them. 'You reported your husband missing on the night of the twenty-fifth of May,' he said. 'So this tramp came on the twenty-fourth.'

'He must have done,' she said through her tears.

'What time was it?'

She looked helpless. 'Oh, I couldn't remember that. Some time during the day.'

'Why was your husband at home during the day, Mrs Thompson?' asked McLoughlin, looking at his diary. 'The twenty-fourth was a Wednesday. Shouldn't he have been at work?'

She pouted. 'His beastly business,' she said viciously. 'All his worries came from that. It wasn't his fault, you know. People expected too much of him. He stopped going in towards the end,' she admitted lamely.

'Can you give me a description of this tramp?' asked Walsh.

'Oh, yes,' she said. 'He'll be able to help you, I'm sure. He was wearing a pair of pink trousers and an old brown hat.' She thought back. 'He was about sixty, I suppose, not much hair and he smelled terribly. He was very drunk.' She paused, a thought suddenly occurring to her. 'But you must have found him already,' she said, 'or why would you have the shoes?'

Walsh picked them up and turned them over. 'You said your husband had no connection with the women at Streech Grange, yet one of them, Mrs Goode, invested money in his business.'

A shadow crossed her face. 'I didn't know.'

'Mrs Goode claims to have met you,' Walsh went on.

There was a long silence. 'Possibly, I do recall talking to someone of that name three or four months ago in the street. Daniel told me she was a client.' A glint sharpened in her eye. 'Brassy blonde woman, over-dressed, with a come-hither look.'

'Yes,' said Walsh who found the description inept but entertaining.

'She rang me,' said Mrs Thompson, pursing her lips in disapproval, 'wanting to know where Daniel was. I told her to mind her own business.' She pinioned the Inspector with a basilisk's glare. 'Did she have something to do with Daniel's disappearance?'

'We've been going through your husband's books,' said McLoughlin glibly from his corner. 'We noted the discrepancy. It puzzled us.'

'I didn't know she was one of them.' She held her handkerchief to dry eyes. 'Now you tell me she invested money in his company?' The floodgates opened and this time her tears were of real distress. 'How could he?' she sobbed. 'How could he? Such terrible women.'

Walsh looked at McLoughlin and stood up. 'We'll be off now, Mrs Thompson. Thank you for your help.'

She tried without success to stem the flood.

'Have you thought about going away at all?' the younger man asked.

She gave a long shuddering sigh. 'The Vicar's arranged a holiday,' she said. 'I'm going to a hotel by the seaside at the end of the week, just for a few days' rest. It won't do any good though, not without Daniel.'

McLoughlin looked very thoughtful as he closed the door behind him.

Chief Inspector Walsh ground his teeth with fury as he jerked the clutch on his brand new Rover and promptly stalled. 'What are you looking so damned cheerful about? We've just lost our only promising lead.'

McLoughlin waited until the car was moving. 'Who was in charge of the case at the beginning?'

'If you mean Thompson's disappearance, it was Staley.'

'Did he do a thorough job? Did he check Mrs Thompson?'

'Checked everything. I've been through the file.'

'Does he know about our body?'

'He does.'

'And it hasn't made him suspicious?'

'No. Her alibi's too good. She took Mr T. to Winchester station where he boarded a train to London. Various people remember seeing him during the journey and one remembers seeing him on the platform at Waterloo. After dropping him off, Mrs T. went straight to East Deller Church where she took part in a twenty-four-hour fast with other members of the congregation. The saintly Daniel was due to join her there at six o'clock on his return from London where, incidentally, he was supposed to be raising a loan to keep the business afloat. He never came back. At ten o'clock, the Vicar's wife took Mrs T. home to Larkfield and waited with her while she telephoned office, friends and acquaintances. At nearly midnight, Mrs Vicar rang the police and stayed with Mrs T., who was by then quite hysterical, through the night and most of the following day. Daniel has not been seen since he got off the train in London.'

'But her alibi's only good for the twenty-fifth and twenty-sixth. Supposing he came back later?'

Walsh manoeuvred his way into the traffic on a roundabout. 'Why would he, if he'd gone to the lengths of doing the bunk in the first place? Staley reckons he planned to kill two birds with one stone – get shot of the awful wife and duck out of the bankruptcy. He hopped into the bog at Waterloo, reversed his mac, stuck on a false moustache and went to ground with whatever he'd managed to stash away from the business. For what it's worth, Thompson's number two at the radiator firm said he wasn't in the least surprised Thompson legged it, he only wondered why it had taken him so long. According to him, Thompson had no balls and less bottle and from the moment things began to get dicey, he looked like running.'

McLoughlin picked at a fingernail. 'You must have thought he had a good reason for coming back, sir. Otherwise, how could Mrs Goode have killed him?'

'Yes, well, Mrs Goode's a damn sight more attractive than that silly bitch back there. I felt there was a good chance he staged his disappearance in order to throw in his lot with a blonde bombshell.'

'But when he turned up on her doorstep, Mrs Goode, who was down by ten thousand, found she didn't fancy him as much as she thought she did and stuck a knife into him?'

'Something like that.'

McLoughlin laughed out loud. 'Sorry, sir.' He thought for a moment. 'The Thompsons don't have any children, do they?'

'No.'

'OK, let's say you've been married to a man for thirty-odd years. He's been the be-all and end-all of your existence and he suddenly deserts you.' He paused for further thought.

'Go on.'

'I'll need to think it through properly but something along these lines. Daniel does a runner because the business has gone down the chute and he can't cope. He hangs around in London for a bit but finds that living off his wits there is worse than facing the music at home, so he comes back. Meanwhile, Mrs Thompson has discovered, because Mrs Goode telephones and tells her that Daniel was supposed to have gone to Streech Grange, that her husband has been seeing another woman, worse, a woman steeped in sin. She's very near the edge already and this sends her right over. Bear in mind she's a religious fanatic, her marriage has been a sham and she's had several days to sit and brood. What's she going to do when Daniel comes home unexpectedly?'

'Yes,' agreed Walsh thoughtfully. 'That works quite nicely. But how did she get the body to the ice house?'

'I don't know. Perhaps she persuaded him to go there when he was alive. But it's entirely logical for her to leave the body somewhere in Streech Grange, the site of Daniel's sin, and it's logical for her to have stripped him and chopped him about a bit so that we'd think it was David Maybury. She'd see that as retribution against the evil women – she probably thought they were all in it – who'd ruined her life. Do we have a follow-up on that report of someone crying near the Grange Farm cottages?'

'We do, but it's not very helpful. Both sets of occupants agreed it was after midnight because they were in bed, and they both agreed it was during the spell of hot weather that spanned the last week in May and the first two weeks in June. One lot said it was May, the other lot said it was the second week in June. Yer pays yer money and takes yer choice.'

'It's all too nebulous. We need a fix on some dates. Did Staley search the Thompsons' house?'

'Twice, once on the night of his disappearance and again about two weeks later.'

McLoughlin frowned. 'Why the second time?'

'Well, it's interesting that. He had an anonymous tip-off that Mrs T. had lost her marbles, butchered Daniel and hidden him under the floorboards. He turned up out of the blue one day, a couple of weeks into June, and went through the house with a magnifying glass. He found nothing except one sex-starved little woman who kept following him from room to room and making advances. He's convinced it was Mrs Thompson who made the tip-off.'

'Why?'

Walsh chuckled. 'He reckons she fancied him.'

'Perhaps her conscience was troubling her.'

Walsh pulled into the kerb outside the Police Station. 'It's all very well, Andy, but where do those blasted shoes fit in? If Daniel was wearing them, why did she leave them in the grounds? And if he wasn't, how did they get there?'

'Yes,' mused McLoughlin. 'I've been wondering about that. I can't help feeling she's telling the truth about the shoes. There must have been a tramp, you know. The description was too fluent and it matches the one Nick Robinson came up with. I remember the pink trousers.' He raised an enquiring eyebrow. 'I could try and trace him.'

'Waste of time,' muttered Walsh. 'Even if you found him, what could he tell you?'

'Whether or not Mrs Thompson's telling lies.'

'Hmm.' He hunched his shoulders over the steering wheel. 'I've had an awful thought.' He looked sick.

McLoughlin glanced at him.

'You don't suppose those damn women have been right all along, do you? You don't suppose this miserable tramp went into the ice house and had a heart attack?'

'What happened to his pink trousers?'

Walsh's face cleared. 'Yes, yes, of course. All right, then, see if you can find him.'

'I'll have to give up on the Maybury file.'

'Temporarily,' growled Walsh.

'And I want to take a team to search Streech grounds again.' He saw thunder clouds gathering across the Inspector's face. 'With a view to linking Mrs Thompson with the ice house,' he finished dispassionately.

Elizabeth stood in her favourite position, by the long window in her mother's room, watching the shadows lengthen on the terrace. She wondered how many times she had stood just so in just that place, watching. 'I shall have to go back,' she said at last. 'They won't keep the job open indefinitely.'

'You haven't any holiday owing?' asked Diana, glad that the silence was finally broken.

'Not spare. I'm going to the States for two weeks at the end of September. It leaves me with nothing to play with.' She turned round. 'I'm sorry, Mum.'

Diana shook her head. 'No need to be. Will you be staying with your father?'

Elizabeth nodded. 'It's three years since I've seen him,' she excused herself, 'and the flight's booked.'

What a gulf of misunderstanding lay between them,

Diana thought, and all because they found each other so hard to talk to. When she thought back over the years, she realised their conversations had been polite but safe, never touching on anything that might lead to embarrassment. In one way, Phoebe had been lucky. There had been no division of loyalties for her children, no lingering love for their father, no need for her to justify why he had deserted them.

'Would you like a drink?' She walked over to a mahogany cabinet.

'Are you having one?'

'Yes.'

'OK. I'll have a gin and tonic.'

Diana poured the drinks and took the glasses over to the window. 'Cheers.' She perched on the back of a chair and joined her daughter's contemplation of the terrace. It was easier, on the whole, not to look at her. 'For years I couldn't think about your father without getting angry. When his letters arrived for you and I saw his handwriting, I used to get so tensed up my jaw would ache for hours. I kept wondering what Miranda had that I hadn't.' She gave a short laugh. 'That's when I first understood what "grinding your teeth" meant.' She paused. 'It took me a while but I've got over it. Now I try to remember the good times. Is she nice? I never met her, you know.'

Elizabeth's attention was riveted on the antics of a sparrow on the flagstones outside, as if in its small person it was about to provide an answer to the mysteries of the universe. 'It wasn't all his fault,' she said defensively.

'No, it wasn't. Actually, in many ways it was more my fault. I took him for granted. I assumed he was the sort of man who could cope with a working wife, and he wasn't. He particularly disliked competing with me as a business partner. I don't blame him. He couldn't help that, any more than I could help wanting a career after you were born. The truth is, we should never have married. We were far too young and neither of us knew what we were doing. Phoebe feels the same. She married David because she was pregnant with Jonathan, and propriety amongst the middle classes twenty years ago dictated marriage. I married your father for virtually the same reasons. I wanted to go to the States with him and my parents wouldn't hear of my going as his mistress.' She sighed. 'God knows, Lizzie, we've all lived to regret it. We made a mess of each other's lives because we didn't have the courage to raise two fingers to convention.'

The girl stared at the sparrow. 'If you regret the marriage, do you also regret its consequence?'

'Do you mean, do I regret you?'

'Of course,' she snapped angrily. 'The two are rather closely linked, wouldn't you say?' The hurt ran deep.

Diana sought carefully for the right words. 'When you were born, I used to be driven mad by people asking: Who does she take after? Is she like you or Steven? My answer was always the same: Neither. I couldn't understand why they needed to tie you to one or other of us. To me, from the moment you drew breath, you were an individual with your own character, your own looks, your own way of doing things. I love you because you're my daughter and we've grown up together, but much more than that I actually like you. I like Elizabeth Goode.' She brushed a speck of dust from the girl's sleeve where it rested on the chair beside her. 'You exist in your own right. You're not a consequence of a marriage.'

'But I *am*,' the girl cried. 'Don't you see that? I am what you and Dad have made me.'

Diana looked at her. 'No, you were bolshy as a baby. I had to put you on solids when you were about eight weeks old because you wouldn't stop yelling for food. Steven always called you "The Despotic Diaper" because you had us both so well trained. Whatever makes you think now that you were born without personality and had to be fashioned by two untrained people? God knows, you've a horrible shock coming if you think babies don't have minds of their own.'

Elizabeth smiled. 'You know what I mean.'

'Yes,' her mother conceded, 'I know what you mean.' She was silent for a moment. 'The truth is, I should have thought this one out before. On the one hand, I've been patting myself on the back for having a strong-minded, independent daughter even if she is a bit wilful; on the other, I've been nagging at you not to make my mistakes.' She smiled ruefully. 'Sorry, darling. Hardly a consistent position.'

'Phoebe's just the same,' said Elizabeth. 'It must be a common maternal weakness.'

Diana laughed. 'What does Phoebe do?'

'Haven't you noticed? Whenever Jonathan takes a drink she quietly marks the level in the bottle with a felt-tip pen. She thinks he's never noticed.'

'Well, I haven't,' said Diana in some surprise. 'How extraordinary. Why does she do it?'

'Because his father drank too much. She's watching like a hawk to make sure Jonathan doesn't do the same.'

God, and I can't blame her, thought Diana, yet how foolish her actions seemed when looked at objectively. 'Does Jonathan understand?' she asked curiously.

'I think so.'

'Do you understand?'

'Yes, but that's not to say you or Phoebe are right. My own view is you're both getting your knickers in a twist over something that may never happen.'

'I'll drink to that,' said Diana, clinking her glass against her daughter's, but if she hoped this new fragile accord would lead to confidences, she was disappointed. Elizabeth had kept her own counsel too long to give it free expression on such tenuous beginnings.

'She *is* nice,' said Elizabeth unexpectedly. 'Very different from you. She's short and rather dumpy and she wears pinafore dresses all the time. She cooks very well. Dad's put on about two stone since he married her.' She smiled. 'None of his shirts do up any more, or they didn't three years ago.'

Good lord, thought Diana, so that's what he wanted. She thought of the slim young man she had married with the cadaverous good looks and the designer clothes, and she chuckled. 'Poor old Steven.'

'He's very happy,' her daughter protested, quick to see a criticism.

Diana held up her hands in mock surrender. 'I'm sure he is and I'm glad. Very glad,' she said, and she was.

'I suppose I'll have to ask the police if it's all right for me to go back to London,' Elizabeth hazarded after a moment.

'When do you want to go?'

'Straight after lunch tomorrow. Jon said he'd drive me to the station.'

'We'll ask Walsh in the morning,' said Diana. 'He's sure to be up here bright and early to rap me over the knuckles for this afternoon's little naughtiness.'

'Oh, Mum,' scolded Elizabeth as if she were speaking to a child, 'you will be careful, won't you? You've got such a temper when you're angry. Frankly, I think you're damn lucky to have got off as lightly as you did.'

'Yes,' agreed Diana meekly, marvelling at how rapidly roles reversed.

Elizabeth pursed her lips. 'Jon got into a fight today,' she announced surprisingly, 'but don't tell Phoebe. She'll have a fit.'

'Where?'

'Silverborne. Some yobbos recognised him from that photo in the local newspaper, the one taken outside the hospital the night Anne was attacked. They called him a lessies' pimp, so he bopped one of them in the eye and took to his heels.' She smiled. 'I was rather impressed when he told me. I didn't think he had it in him.'

Diana thought of David Maybury. Jonathan had it in him all right.

Eighteen

WITHIN TWENTY-FOUR hours Anne had made such a rapid recovery that she was suffering severe nicotine withdrawal symptoms and announced her intention of discharging herself. Jonathan told her not to be such a fool. 'You nearly died. If it hadn't been for the Sergeant, you probably would have done. Your body needs time to recover and get over the shock.'

'Damn,' she said roundly, 'and I can't remember a thing about it. No near-death experiences, no free-floating on the ceiling, no tunnels with shining lights at the end. What an absolute bugger. I could have written it all up. That's what comes of being an atheist.'

Jonathan, who for various reasons had come to view McLoughlin as a bit of a hero, certainly not all to do with coming to Anne's rescue, took her to task. 'Have you thanked him?'

She scowled from him to the WPC beside the bed. 'What for? He was only doing his job.'

'Saving your life.'

She glowered. 'Frankly, the way I feel at the moment, it wasn't worth saving. Life should be effortless, painless and fun. None of those apply here. It's a gulag, run by sadists.' She nodded in the direction of the ward. 'That Sister should be locked up. She laughs every time she sticks the needles into me and trills that she's doing it for my own good. God, I need a fag. Smuggle some in for me, Jonny. I'll puff away under the sheets. No one will know.'

He grinned. 'Until the bed goes up in flames.'

'There you are, you're laughing,' she accused. 'What's the matter with everyone? Why do you all find it so hilarious?'

WPC Brownlow, on duty on the other side of the bed, sniggered.

Anne cast a baleful eye upon her. 'I don't even know what you're doing here,' she snapped. 'I've told you all I can remember, which is absolutely zero.' She had been unable to talk freely to anyone, which was undoubtedly why the bloody woman had been stationed there, and it was driving her mad.

'Orders,' said the WPC calmly. 'The Inspector wants someone on hand when your memory comes back.'

Anne closed her eyes and thought of all the ways she could murder McLoughlin the minute she got her hands on him again.

He for his part had collated the information on the

tramp and relayed his description through the co
He rang a colleague in Southampton and asked h
for a favour, to check round the hostels there.

'What makes you think he came here?'

'Logic,' said McLoughlin. 'He was heading your way and your Council's more sympathetic to the homeless than most in this area.'

'But two months, Andy. He'll have been on his way weeks ago.'

'I know. It's a good description though. Someone might remember him. If we had a name, it'd make things easier. See what you can do.'

'I'm pretty busy at the moment.'

'Aren't we all. Cheers.' He put an end to the grumbles by the simple expedient of replacing the receiver, abandoned a cup of congealing plastic coffee and left in a hurry before his friend could ring back with a string of excuses. With a light conscience, he set off for the Grange and a chat with Jane Maybury who had announced herself ready to answer questions.

He asked her if she would prefer to have her mother present, but she shook her head and said no, it wasn't necessary. Phoebe, with a faintly troubled smile, showed them into her drawing-room and closed the door. They sat by the French windows. The girl was very pale, with a skin like creamy alabaster, but McLoughlin guessed this was her natural colouring. She was wearing a pair of faded jeans and a baggy tee-shirt with BRISTOL CITY emblazoned across the chest. He thought how incongruous it looked on the waif-like body.

She read his mind. 'It's the triumph of hope over experience,' she said. 'I go in for a lot of that.'

He smiled. 'I suppose everyone does, one way or another. If at first you don't succeed and all that.'

She settled herself a little nervously. 'What do you want to ask me?'

'Just a few things but, first, I want you to understand that I have no desire to distress you. If you find my questions upsetting, please say so and we'll stop. If at any point you decide you'd rather talk to a policewoman, again just tell me and I'll arrange it.'

She nodded. 'I understand.'

He took her back to the night of the assault and quickly ran through her account of watching television and hearing the sound of the breaking glass. 'Your brother was the first to go downstairs, I think you said.'

'Yes. He decided it was a burglar and told Lizzie and me to stay where we were until he called for us.'

'But did you stay?'

'No. Lizzie insisted on going downstairs after him to get through to Diana's wing. We didn't know at that stage which window had been broken. I said I'd check Mum's rooms and Jon ran through to where you were.'

'What happened then?'

'Mum and Diana arrived in the hall at the same

time as us. Mum followed Jonathan. I checked this room, Diana checked the library and Lizzie the kitchen. When I got back to the hall, Mum was running downstairs with some blankets and a hot-water bottle and yelling at Diana to call an ambulance. I said, someone ought to warn Fred to open the gate and Mum said, of course, she hadn't thought of that.' She spread her hands in her lap. 'So I took the torch from the hall table and left.'

'Why you? Why didn't Mrs Goode's daughter go?'

She shrugged. 'It was my idea. Anyway, Lizzie hadn't come back from the kitchen.'

'You weren't frightened? You didn't think of waiting for her to go with you?'

'No,' she said, 'it never occurred to me.' She was surprised now that it hadn't. She thought about it. 'To be honest, there was nothing to be frightened of. Mum just said Anne was ill. I suppose I thought she'd got an appendix or something. I just kept thinking what a nuisance it was that we had to keep the reporters at bay by locking the gates.' Her voice rose. 'And it's not as if I've never been up the drive before on my own. I've done it hundreds of times, and in the dark. I sometimes go and chat to Molly when Fred goes to the pub.'

'Fine,' he said unemotionally. 'That's all very logical.' He smiled encouragement. 'You're a fast runner. I had the devil's own job to catch you and I was going like a train.'

She unknit her fingers from the tangled bottom of her tee-shirt. 'I was worried about Anne,' she admitted. 'I keep telling her she's going to drop dead of cancer any minute. I had this ghastly thought that that was exactly what she'd done. So I put a spurt on.'

'You're fond of her, aren't you?'

'Anne's good news,' she said. 'Live and let live, that's her motto. She never interferes or criticises, but I suppose it's easier for her. She doesn't have children to worry about.'

'My mother's a worrier,' lied McLoughlin, thinking the only thing Mrs McLoughlin Snr ever worried about was whether she was going to be late for Bingo.

Jane put her chin in her hands. 'Mum's an absolute darling,' she confided naively, 'but she still thinks I need protection. Anne keeps telling her to let me fight my own battles.' She twisted a lock of the long dark hair round her finger.

He crossed his legs and pushed himself down into the chair, deliberately relaxed. 'Battles?' he teased gently. 'What battles do you have?'

'Silly things,' she assured him. 'Molehills to you, mountains to me. They'd make you laugh.'

'I shouldn't think so. You're just as likely to laugh at some of my battles.'

'Tell me,' she demanded.

'All right.' He looked at her smiling, trusting face and he thought, pray God there is nothing you can tell me or that smile will never come again. 'The worst battle I ever had was with my mother when I was about your age,' he told her. 'I'd sneaked my girlfriend into my bedroom for a night of passion. Ma walked in on us in the middle.'

'Golly,' she breathed. 'Why didn't you lock the door?'

'No key.'

'How embarrassing,' said Jane with feeling.

'Yes, it was,' he said reminiscently. 'My girlfriend hopped it and I had to do battle with the old dragon in the nuddy. She gave me two choices: if I swore on oath I'd never do it again, I'd be allowed to stay; if I refused to swear, then she'd boot me out just as I was.'

'What did you do?'

'Guess,' he invited.

'You left, starkers.'

He pointed his finger at her with thumb cocked. 'Got it in one.'

She was like a wide-eyed child. 'But where did you get clothes from? What did you do?'

He grinned. 'I hid in the bushes until all the lights went out, then I took a ladder from the shed and climbed up to my bedroom. The window was open. It was very easy. I crept back into bed, had a decent night's kip and scarpered with a suitcase before she got up in the morning.'

'Do you still see her?'

'Oh, yes,' he said, 'I do my duty Sunday lunches.

To tell you the truth, I think she regretted it afterwards. The house became very quiet when I left.' He was silent for a moment. 'Your turn now,' he said.

She giggled. 'That's not fair. Your battle was funny, mine are all pathetic. Things like: Will I or will I not eat my mashed potato? Am I working too hard? Shouldn't I go out and enjoy myself?'

'And do you?'

'Go out and enjoy myself?' He nodded. 'Not much.' Her lips twisted cynically and made her look older. 'Mum's idea of my enjoying myself is to go out with boys. I don't find that enjoyable.' Her eyes narrowed. 'I don't like men touching me. Mum hates that.'

'It's not surprising,' he said. 'She must feel it's her fault.'

'Well, it's not,' she said dismissively, 'and I wish she'd realise it. The hardest thing in the world is to cope with someone else's guilt.'

'What do you think happened to your father, Jane?'

The question hung in the air between them like a bad smell. She turned away and looked out of the window and he wondered if he had pushed too fast and lost her. He hoped not, as much for her own sake as for the sake of the enquiry.

'I'll tell you what happened the night he left,' she said at last, speaking to the window. 'I remember it very clearly but even my psychiatrist doesn't know all of it. There are bits I kept back, bits that at the time didn't fit the pattern and which I left out.' She paused for a moment. 'I hadn't thought about it for ages until the other night. Since then I've thought of nothing else, and I think now that what I left out may be important.'

She spoke slowly and clearly as though, having geared herself to tell the story, she saw no point in making it garbled. She told him how, after her mother had left for work, her father had run her bath. That was the signal, she said, that he intended to have sex with her. It was a routine he had established and which she had learned to accept. She described the entire process without a flicker of emotion and McLoughlin guessed she had rehearsed it many times on the psychiatrist's couch. She spoke of her father's approaches and her removal to her bedroom as if she were commentating on a chess game.

'But he did something different that night,' she said, turning her dark gaze on the Sergeant.

He found his voice. 'What was it?'

'He told me he loved me. He'd never done that before.'

McLoughlin was shocked. So much pain and without a word of love. Yet, after all, what good would kind words have done except make the man a hypocrite? 'Why do you think that's important?' he asked dispassionately.

'Let me finish the story,' she suggested, 'and perhaps it will strike you, too.' Before raping her this time, he had given her a present, carefully wrapped in tissue paper. 'He'd never done that before either.'

'What was it?'

'A little teddy-bear. I used to collect them. When he had finished,' she said, dismissing the entire incident in four words, 'he stroked my hair and said he was sorry. I asked him why because he'd never apologised before, but my mother came in and he never answered.' She fell silent and stared at her hands.

He waited but she didn't go on. 'What happened then?' he asked after several minutes.

She gave a mirthless laugh. 'Nothing really. They just looked at each other for what seemed like hours. In the end, he got off the bed and pulled up his trousers.' Her voice was brittle. 'It was like one of those awful Whitehall farces. I do remember my mother's face. It was frozen, like a statue's. She was very pale except for the bruise on her face where he hit her the day before. She only moved after he'd left the room, then she lay beside me on the bed and hugged me. We stayed like that all night and in the morning he'd gone.' She shrugged. 'We've never seen him again.'

'Did she say anything to him?' he asked.

'No. She didn't need to.'

'Why not?'

'You know that expression "if looks could kill".' He nodded. 'That was what was frozen on her face.' She bit her lip. 'What do you think?'

She caught him off guard. He so nearly said, I think your mother killed him. 'About what?' he asked her.

She showed her disappointment. 'It seems so obvious to me. I hoped it would strike you, too.' There was a hunger in the thin face, a yearning for something that he didn't understand.

'Hang on,' he said firmly. 'Give me a minute to think about it. You know the story backwards. This is the first time I've heard it, remember.' He looked at the notes he had been taking and cudgelled his brain to find what she wanted him to find. He had ringed the three things she said her father had never done before: love, present, apology. What was their significance? Why did she think he had done them? Why *had* he done them? Why would any father tell his daughter he loved her, give her a present and regret his unkindnesses? He looked up and laughed. It was stunningly obvious, after all. 'He was planning to leave anyway. He was saying goodbye. That's why he disappeared without trace. He'd arranged it all beforehand.'

She let out a long sigh. 'Yes, I think so.'

He leaned forward excitedly. 'But do you know why he would want to disappear?'

'No. I don't.' She sat up straight and pushed the hair back off her face. 'All I do know, Sergeant, is that it wasn't my fault.' A slow smile curved her lips. 'You can't imagine how good that makes me feel.'

'But surely no one's ever suggested it was?' The idea appalled him.

'When I was eight years old, my mother caught me in bed with my father. My father ran away because of it and my mother was labelled a murderess. At the age of ten, my brother's personality changed. He stopped being a child and took his father's place. He was sworn to secrecy about what had happened and has never mentioned his father again.' She played with her fingers. 'My mother's guilt has been an irrelevancy beside mine.' She raised her eyes. 'What happened the other night was a blessing in disguise. For years I've sat with a psychiatrist who has done his level best to intellectualise me out of my feelings of guilt. To a certain extent he succeeded and I pushed it all to the back of my mind. I was the victim, not the culprit. I was manipulated by someone I had been taught to respect. I played the role that was demanded of me because I was too young to understand I had a choice.' She paused briefly. 'But the other night, perhaps because I was so frightened, it all came back to me with amazing clarity. For the first time, I realised how the pattern had changed the night he left. For the first time, I didn't need to consciously justify my innocence, because I saw that the misery and uncertainty of the last ten years would have happened anyway, whether my mother had found us or not.'

'Have you told her all this?'

'Not yet. I will after you've gone. I wanted someone else to reach the same conclusion I had.'

'Tell me what happened when you were going to the Lodge,' he encouraged. 'You said you heard breathing.'

She compressed her lips in thought. 'It's a bit of a blur now,' she admitted. 'I was fine till I came to the beginning of the long straight bit leading to the gates. I slowed down as I came round the bend because I was getting a stitch and I heard what sounded like someone letting out a long breath, the sort of sound you make when you've been holding your breath for hiccups. It seemed to be very close. I was so frightened, I started to run again. Then I heard running footsteps and someone shouting.' She looked at him sheepishly. 'That was you. You scared me out of my wits. Now I'm not sure I heard breathing at all.'

'OK,' he said. 'It's not important. And when you said you thought it was your father, that was just because you were frightened? There wasn't anything about the breathing that reminded you of him?'

'No,' she said. 'I can't even remember what he looked like. It was so long ago and Mum's burnt all his photos. I couldn't possibly recognise his breathing.' She watched him gather his bits and pieces together. 'Have I been any good?'

'Good?' On impulse, he reached forward and gave her hands a quick impersonal squeeze. 'I'd say your godma's going to be pretty pleased with you, young lady. Forget about fighting battles, you've just scaled your own Mount Everest. And it's all downhill from now on.'

Phoebe was sitting on a garden seat beside the front door, chin in hands, staring unseeingly at the flower-beds which bordered the gravel drive. 'May I join you?' he asked her.

She nodded.

They sat in silence for some minutes. 'The dividing line between a fortress and a prison is a fine one,' he remarked softly. 'And ten years is a long time. Do you not think, Mrs Maybury, that you've served your sentence?'

She sat up straight and gestured bitterly in the direction of Streech Village and beyond. 'Ask them,' she said. 'It was they who put up the barbed wire.'

'Was it?'

Instinctively, defensively, she pressed her glasses up her nose. 'Of course. It was never my choice to live like this. But what do you do when people turn against you? Beg them to be kind?' She gave a harsh laugh. 'I wouldn't do it.'

He stared at his hands. 'It wasn't your fault,' he said quietly. 'Jane understands that. He was what he was. Nothing you did or didn't do would have made any difference.'

She withdrew into herself and let the silence lengthen. Above them swallows and house martins dipped and darted and a lark swelled its little throat and sang. At long last she took a handkerchief from her sleeve and held it to her eyes. 'I don't think I like you very much,' she said.

He looked at her. 'We all carry our burden of guilt – it's human nature. Listen to anyone newly bereaved or divorced and you'll hear the same story – if only I had done this . . . if only I hadn't done that . . . if only I had been kinder . . . if only I had realised. Our capacity for self-punishment is enormous. The trick is to know when to stop.' He rested a light hand on her shoulder. 'You've been punishing yourself for far too long. Can you not see that?'

She turned her face away from him. 'I should have known,' she said into her handkerchief. 'He was hurting her and I should have known.'

'How could you have known? You're no different from the rest of us,' he told her brutally. 'Jane loved you, she wanted to protect you. If you blame yourself, you take away everything she tried to do for you.'

There was another long silence while she fought to control her tears. 'I'm her mother. There was only me to save her, but when she needed me I never came. I can't bear to think about it.' A convulsive tremor rocked the shoulder beneath his hand.

He didn't stop to consider whether it was a good idea but reacted instinctively, drawing her into the fold of his arm and letting her weep. They were not the first tears she had shed, he guessed, but they were the first she had shed for her lost self, that self who had come into an enchanted world, wide-eyed and sure that she could do anything. The triumph of the human condition was to face one small defeat after another and to survive them relatively intact. The tragedy, as for Phoebe, was to face the worst defeat too soon and never to recover. His heart, still bruised and battered, ached for her.

He stopped his car on the bend before the straight stretch of drive and got out. Close, Jane had said, which meant in all probability crouched among the rhododendron bushes along the edge of the way. His searches so far had been disappointing. While he had set a team to scour the ice house for a link with Mrs Thompson, he himself had gone on hands and knees about the terrace for signs of Anne's attacker. If what he believed had happened, there would have been ample evidence of it. But Walsh was right. Bar some dislodged bricks and a cigarette end which was a brand that neither Fred nor Anne smoked, there was nothing. No weapon – he'd examined every brick and stone minutely for bloodstains; no footprints – the lawn was too hard from lack of rain and the flagstones too clean from Molly's regular sweepings; no blood, not even the tiniest speck, to prove that Anne had been hit outside and not inside. He had begun to wonder if he'd put too much faith in Phoebe's certainty – ten years was a long time and people changed – and she admitted herself it had only happened the once. But if she were wrong or if she were lying? He couldn't bring himself to explore either alternative. Not yet.

He sank to hands and knees again and began to inch along the drive. If there *was* anything, it wouldn't be easy to find. A team had been over here once without success but then he had told them to concentrate further down, near where he had caught her and where, for one brief moment, he had had the feeling that he and Jane were being watched. He crawled along the left-hand side, knees aching, eyes constantly alert, but after half an hour he had found nothing.

He sat back wearily on his heels and swore at the injustice of it. Just once, he thought, let me be lucky. Just once, let something come my way that I haven't had to work my bloody butt off for.

He moved to the right-hand side of the drive and inched back towards the bend. Predictably, he was almost at the car before he found it. He took a deep breath and thumped his fist on the tarmac, growling and shaking his head from side to side like a mad dog. Had he only started on the right-hand side, he would have found the damn thing over an hour ago and saved himself a lot of trouble.

'You all right, son?' asked a voice.

McLoughlin looked over his shoulder to find Fred staring at him. He grinned self-consciously and stood up. 'Fine,' he assured him. 'I've just found the bastard who did for Miss Cattrell.'

'I don't see him,' muttered Fred, eyeing McLoughlin doubtfully.

McLoughlin crouched down and parted the bushes, sweeping leaves away from something on the ground. 'Look at that. The forensic boys are going to have a field day.'

With much panting and heaving Fred squatted beside him. 'Well, I'll be blowed,' he said, 'it's a Paddy Clarke Special.'

Nestling in the débris under the rhododendron, beautifully camouflaged, was an old-fashioned stone beer bottle with a dark brown crust clinging to its bottom. McLoughlin, who had been thinking only in terms of some decent fingerprints and what looked like the imprint of a trainer in the soft damp earth beneath the dense bushes, flicked him a curious glance. 'What on earth is a Paddy Clarke Special?'

Fred lumbered unhappily to his feet. 'There's no harm in it, not really. It's more of a hobby than a business, though I don't s'pose the tax man would agree. He's got a room at the back of his garage where he makes it. Uses only traditional materials and leaves it to mature till it has the kick of a horse and tastes like nectar. There's not a beer to touch Paddy's Special.' He stared glumly at the rhododendron. 'You have to drink it on the premises. He sets great store by those bottles, says they breathe flavour in a way glass never does.' He looked immensely troubled. 'I've never known him let one out of the pub.'

'What's he like? The type to beat up women?'

The old man shuffled his feet. 'No, never that. He's a good sort. Mind you, the wife's got little time for him on account of he's married and not too particular about his vows, but – hit Miss Cattrell?' He shook his head. 'No, he'd not do that. He and she are' – he looked away – 'friends, as you might say.'

An entry in Anne's diary swam before his eyes. '*P. is a mystery. He tells me he screws fifty women a year, and I believe him, yet he remains the most considerate of lovers.*' 'Does he smoke?'

Fred, who had supplied Paddy with many a cigarette over the years, thought the question odd. 'Other people's,' he said warily. 'His wife's a bit of a tyrant, doesn't approve of smoking.'

McLoughlin pictured her fireplace awash with cigarette ends. 'Don't tell me,' he said gloomily, 'let me guess. He looks like Rudolph Valentino, Paul Newman and Laurence Olivier, all rolled into one.' He opened his car door and reached for his radio.

'Tut, tut, tut,' clicked Fred impatiently. 'He's a big man, dark, full of life, clever in his way. Always reminds me of the one who plays *Magnum*.'

Tom Selleck! I hate him, thought McLoughlin.

*

Sergeant Jones was leaving the Station as McLoughlin came in. 'You know that tramp you're after, Andy?'

'Mm.'

'Got a sighting from your friend the Vicar in East Deller. Wife claims she gave him a cup of tea.'

'Any idea of a date?'

'No, but the Vicar remembers he was writing a sermon at the time and was annoyed by the disturbance, found himself praying to the Good Lord for deliverance from tramps, then had to reprimand himself for his lack of charity.'

McLoughlin chuckled. 'That sounds like the Vicar all right.'

'Apparently he always writes his sermons on a Saturday while he's watching the sport on telly. Any good?'

'Could be, Nick, could be.'

Nineteen

THE PHONE RANG on McLoughlin's desk the following morning. 'You're a jammy bastard, Andy. I've got a lead on that tramp of yours,' said his mate in Southampton. 'One of the uniformed sergeants recognised the description. Seems he picked up the old boy about a week ago and took him to a new hostel out Shirley way. No guarantee he's still there but I'll give you the address. You can check it out for yourself. He's called Wally Ferris and he's a regular down here during the summer. Sergeant Jordan's known him for years.' McLoughlin wrote down the address, Heaven's Gate Hostel, and thanked him. 'You owe me one,' said the other cheerfully and hung up.

Heaven's Gate was a large detached Victorian house, probably much sought after in the days before motor cars, but its appeal was diminished now by the busy thoroughfare which mewled and milled about its front door.

Wally Ferris bore no resemblance to the description

McLoughlin had circulated, except in age and height. He was clean. Scrubbed rosy cheeks and gleaming pate with frill of washed hair dazzled above a white shirt, black slacks and highly polished shoes. He looked, for all the world, like an elderly schoolboy on his first day in class. They met in the sitting-room and Wally gestured to a chair.

'Take a pew,' he invited.

McLoughlin showed his disappointment. 'No point,' he said. 'To be honest, I don't think you're the person I'm looking for.'

Wally did a rapid about-turn and beetled for the door. 'Suits me, son. I'm not comfortable wiv bluebottles and that's a fact.'

'Hold on,' said McLoughlin. 'At least, let's establish it.'

Wally turned and glowered at him. 'Make yer bleeding mind up. I'm only 'ere because the lady of the 'ouse arst me. She's scratched my back, in a manner o' speaking, so I'm scratching 'ers. What you after?'

McLoughlin sat down. 'Take a pew,' he said, echoing Wally.

'Gawd, you're a shilly-shallyer and no mistake. Can't make yer mind up, can yer.' He perched on a distant chair.

'What were you wearing when you came here?' asked McLoughlin.

'None of your effing business.'

'I can ask the lady of the house,' said McLoughlin. 'What's it to you, anyway?'

'Just answer. The sooner you do, the sooner I'll leave you in peace.'

Wally sucked his teeth noisily. 'Green jacket, brown 'at, black shoes, blue jumper and pink trews,' he reeled off.

'Did you have them long?'

'Long enough.'

'How long?'

'All different. 'Ad the 'at and jacket near on five years, I'd say.'

'The trousers?'

'Twelve monfs or so. Bit on the bright side but a good fit. 'Ere, you're not finking I nicked 'em, are you? I was give 'em.' He looked thoroughly indignant.

'No, no,' said McLoughlin soothingly. 'Nothing like that. The truth is, Wally, we're trying to trace a man who's disappeared and we think you may be able to help us.'

Wally planted his feet firmly on the ground, one in front of the other beneath his chair, poised to take flight. 'I don't know nuffink about nuffink,' he said with absolute conviction.

McLoughlin raised his hands in a conciliatory gesture. 'Don't panic, Wally. As far as we know, there's no crime involved. The man's wife asked us to find him. She says you came to the house the day before he disappeared. All we're wondering is if you remember going there, and if you saw or heard anything that might help us find out why he went.'

Wally's rheumy eyes looked his suspicion. 'I go to a lot of 'ouses.'

'These two gave you a pair of brown shoes.'

Something like relief flickered across the wizened features. 'If the wife was there, why can't she tell you why 'er old man went?' he asked reasonably.

'She's become very ill since her husband went,' said McLoughlin, stretching the truth like a rubber band. 'She hasn't been able to tell us much at all.'

'What's this chap done?'

'Nothing, except lose all his money and run away.'

That struck a chord with Wally, 'Poor bastard. Does 'e want to be found?'

'I don't know. What do you think? His wife certainly wants him back.'

Wally considered for several minutes. 'No one bovvered to come looking for me,' he said in the end. 'Sometimes I wished they 'ad 'ave done. They was glad to see the back of me, and that's the trufe. Go on then. Arst yer questions.'

It took over an hour, but in the end McLoughlin had a clear picture of Wally's movements during the last week in May, or as clear as the old man could make it, bearing in mind he had been tight most of the time. 'I was give a fiver,' he explained. 'Some old geezer in the middle of Winchester popped it in me 'and. Put the lot on a gee-gee called Vagrant, didn't

I. Came up eleven to one. Ain't 'ad so much cash for years. Kept me plastered for free weeks 'fore it ran out.'

He had hung around Winchester for most of the three weeks, then, when he was down to his last few quid, he'd made his way along the back roads to Southampton in search of new pickings. 'I like the villages,' he said. 'Reminds me of cycling holidays in my youf.' He remembered stopping at the pub in Streech. 'It was pissing down,' he explained. 'Landlord was a decent sort, gave me no bovver.' Paddy's wife, by contrast, was a fat old cow whom, for unspecified reasons, Wally didn't take to, but he winked ferociously a couple of times as he mentioned her. At three o'clock, they turned him out into the rain. 'Ain't no fun when it's wet,' he said lugubriously, 'so I took meself off to a little shelter I know of and spent the afternoon and night there.'

'Where?' asked McLoughlin when the old man fell silent.

'Never did no 'arm,' said Wally defensively. 'No call for anyone to complain.'

'There haven't been any complaints,' said McLoughlin encouragingly. 'I won't rat on you, Wally. As far as I'm concerned, if you behave yourself, you can use it as often as you like.'

Wally pursed his lips into a pink rosette. 'There's a big 'ouse there. Easy as winking to pop over the wall. Been in the garden a few times, never seen no one.'

He gave McLoughlin a speculative look to see if he was interested. He was. 'There's a sort of man-made cave near the woods,' he went on. 'Can't fink what it's for but it's got some bricks stacked in it. The door's 'idden by a big bramble but it's a doddle to creep in be'ind it. I always take bracken in wiv me to give me a good kip. 'Ere, why you looking like that?'

McLoughlin shook his head. 'No reason. I'm just interested. Have you any idea what day this was, Wally?'

'Gawd knows, son.'

'And you didn't see anyone when you were in the garden?'

'Not a soul.'

'Was this cave in darkness?'

'Well, there ain't no electricity, if that's what you mean, but while it's light you can see. If the door's ajar, of course,' he added.

McLoughlin wondered how to put the next question. 'And the place was empty except for this stack of bricks you mentioned?'

'What you getting at?'

'Nothing. I'm just trying to get a clear picture.'

'Then yes. It was empty.'

'And what happened the next morning?'

'Hung around till lunchtime, didn't I?'

'In the cave?'

'No. In the woods. Nice and peaceful, it was. Then I got to feeling peckish, so I 'opped over the wall and looked about for somefing to eat.' He had knocked on several doors, without much success.

'Why didn't you buy something with your winnings?' asked McLoughlin, fascinated.

Wally was intensely scornful. 'Do me a favour,' he admonished. 'Why pay for somefink you can get free? It's booze they won't give away. Anyway, I 'adn't much winnings left and that's a fact.'

He had found a group of houses on the outskirts of Streech where 'an old bat' had given him a sandwich. The council houses, McLoughlin thought. 'Did you try anyone else?' he asked.

'Young lass told me to push off. Gawd knows, I sympathised wiv 'er. There was a dozen nippers yelling their 'eads off in 'er front room.' He abandoned Streech as a dead duck at that point and set off down the road. After about an hour, he came to another village. 'Don't recall the name, son, but there was a vicarage. Always good for a touch, they are.' He had roused the Vicar's wife and persuaded her out of a cup of tea and some cake. 'Nice little woman, but she came over sanctimonious. That's the trouble wiv vicarages. You can always get a bite but you has to take the lecture wiv it. I scarpered sharpish.' It had begun to rain again. 'Strange wevver, I can tell yer. 'Ot as blazes most of the time, but every now and then there was a funder storm. You know the sort. Fat rain, I calls it. Flashes of lightning and great claps of funder.' He had looked around for shelter. 'Not a blooming fing. Nice little boxes wiv neat garages. No help to me. Then I comes to this bigger house, set back a bit. I fought I'd explore the back, see if there was a shed. I sneaks down the side and lo and be'old there's just what I'm looking for, nice little shed wiv no one in sight. I opens the door and pops inside.' He stopped.

'And?' prompted McLoughlin.

A cunning gleam had appeared in the old man's eyes. 'Seems like I'm giving you a lot of information for nuffink, son. What's in it for me?'

'A fiver,' said McLoughlin, 'if what you tell me's worth it.'

'Ten,' said Wally. He glanced behind him at the closed door then leaned forward confidentially. 'To tell you the trufe, son, it's a bit claustrophobic this place. The lady of the 'ouse does 'er best but there's no fun. Know what I mean. A tenner'd give me a day out. I've been 'ere a week for Gawd's sake. I've 'ad more fun in prison.'

McLoughlin considered the morality of giving Wally the wherewithal to turn his back on Heaven's Gate and concluded that Wally was on the point of scarpering whatever happened. You can't teach an old dog new tricks. Ten pounds would give him a start at least. 'Done,' he said. 'What happened when you went into this shed?'

'Looked around for somefink to sit on, didn't I,

make meself comfortable while I was there. Found this feller 'iding at the back be'ind some boxes. When 'e realised I'd seen 'im, 'e came over all 'oity-toity and ordered me off 'is property. I arst, reasonable like, why I should imagine 'e was the owner when 'e was skulking in the shed same as me. 'E got properly riled and called me a few names. In the middle of it, this woman comes out of the kitchen door to see what the noise is. I explains the situation and she tells me the geezer's 'er 'usband and 'e's in the shed looking for a paintbrush.' Wally pulled a wry face. 'They must've fought I was born yesterday. The paintbrushes was all laid out neat and tidy on a workbench at the side. The geezer was 'iding, no mistake. Anyway, I sees my opportunity. They wants rid of me and they'd pay up to see me go. I got a bottle of whisky, a decent pair of shoes and twenty quid out of it. Tried for more but they turned nasty and I reckoned it was time to skedaddle. This the feller you're looking for?'

McLoughlin nodded. 'Sounds like it. Can you describe him?'

Wally's brow wrinkled. 'Five tennish, fat, grey 'air. 'E 'ad nancy feet for a man. The shoes they gave me didn't 'alf pinch.'

'What did the woman look like?'

'Mousey little fing, sorrowful eyes, but Gawd she 'ad a temper. Lammed into me and 'er old man somefink rotten for making a noise.' He looked suddenly thoughtful. 'Not that we was, mind you. Froughout the 'ole fing, we spoke in whispers.' He shook his head. 'Bats the pair of 'em.'

McLoughlin was jubilant. Got you, Mrs T., he thought. 'Where did you go then?'

A thoughtful expression crossed Wally's face. 'There's a saying, son. A bird in the 'and is worf two in the bush. It had stopped raining but I 'ad this feeling we was in for anover funder storm. I fought to meself I've a bottle o' whisky and nowhere cosy to drink it. If I push on, 'oo's to say if I'll find a dry place for the night. So I 'ightailed it back to the cave at the big 'ouse and passed a 'alfway decent night.' He considered McLoughlin out of the corner of his eyes. 'The next day, I finks to myself, I've a few quid in me pocket and I've 'ad nuffink decent to eat for days, so I 'eaded off towards Silverborne. There's a nice café on the road – '

'Did you leave anything behind?' McLoughlin cut in.

'Like what?' asked the old man sharply.

'Like the shoes?'

'Dumped 'em in the woods,' said Wally scornfully. 'Damn fings gave me corns a right drubbing. That's where experience comes in. A young bloke would've chucked the old pair out before 'e'd properly tried the new. Then 'e'd've been in agony till 'e found some more.'

McLoughlin tucked his notebook into his pocket. 'You've been a great help, Wally.'

'That it?'

McLoughlin nodded.

'Where's my tenner?'

McLoughlin took a ten-pound note out of his wallet and stretched it between his fingers. 'Listen to me, Wally. I'm going to give you ten pounds now as a token of good faith, but I want you to stay here another night because I may want to talk to you again. If you do, I'll come back tomorrow morning with another ten, making twenty in all.' He held out the tenner. 'Is it a deal?'

Wally got up and pounced on the note, secreting it in the depths of his shirt. 'Are you on the level, son?'

'I'll give you an IOU if you like.'

Wally made as if to spit on the carpet, then thought better of it. 'Be about as much use to me as a mug of water,' he said. 'OK, son, it's a deal. But if you don't come back first fing, I'm off.' His eyes narrowed. 'Don't you go telling the lady of the 'ouse, mind. I've 'ad my fill of good works this week. They don't know when to leave a bloke alone in this place.'

McLoughlin chuckled. 'Your secret's safe with me, Wally.'

'I spotted the *pattern*,' said McLoughlin to Walsh, with a tinge of irony which brought a glitter to the older man's eyes, 'when I marked the houses which reported seeing the tramp.' He pointed to small red crosses on the map in front of them. 'If you remember, Nick Robinson had two reports. One from a woman in Clementine Cottage who said the tramp passed her house and went into the pub, which meant he was coming from the direction of Winchester. The next from the landlord at the pub who said he stayed until closing time then ambled off in the lee of the wall round the Grange estate, in other words heading towards East Deller.' He traced his finger along the printed road. 'The next reports we had of him were PC Williams's. He said an elderly woman had given the tramp a sandwich and a young woman had turned him away because it was her son's birthday. They both live on the council estate which is to the west of Streech and on the East Deller road. The date the young woman gave was May twenty-seventh. But when we spoke to Mrs Thompson she told us he'd visited them in East Deller on the twenty-fourth. That would have meant he had doubled back on himself for some reason to come through Streech three days later from the direction of Winchester.'

Walsh gathered together the remnants of his authority and buttoned them about himself with as much dignity as he could muster. 'I went into all this myself,' he lied. 'The fact that we found the shoes at the Grange implies he did just that.'

'I agree, so we needed another sighting in East

Deller, with a date, if possible. Jonesy went out there to see what he could dig up. He had a chat with our friend the Vicar who told Jonesy he was writing a sermon when the tramp called at the vicarage. The Vicar couldn't give a date but he always writes his sermons on a Saturday. OK, now only two people have offered a definite date, May twenty-fourth, supplied by Mrs Thompson, a Wednesday, and May twenty-seventh, the day of the birthday party, a Saturday. Wally is adamant he went from the council estate in Streech to the vicarage and the Thompsons at East Deller which puts him there on Saturday, May twenty-seventh. So why did Mrs T. lie about the date?'

'Get on with it,' ordered Walsh impatiently.

'Because, in face of her blatant lie, we had proved the shoes were her husband's and she had to explain why they were no longer in her possession. She opted for the truth this time, or as near the truth as damn it, and invited us to corroborate the story by giving us a description of the tramp. Remember, we never told her where we found the shoes. For all she knew we got them from the tramp himself.' He collected his thoughts. 'Now she could be sure, if we had the tramp, that he would say he'd seen her husband. So to give us the actual day of his visit would be tantamount to telling us her husband was alive and well and living in East Deller after she'd reported him missing. Bang would go her alibi. So she advanced the tramp's visit by three days. It was a gamble but it damn nearly paid off. Wally hasn't a clue when he went through, and if it wasn't for the child's birthday, neither would we. No one else can remember the date.' He paused for a moment. 'It's going to come as a nasty shock when we tell her where Wally dumped the shoes. In her wildest nightmares she couldn't believe it would be at the scene of her proposed crime.'

Walsh stood up. 'Poetic justice, I say. But I'd like to know how she persuaded him to lie low and how she got him to the ice house.'

'Use your charm and she'll probably tell us,' said McLoughlin.

Twenty

MRS THOMPSON OPENED the door with a smile of welcome. She was dressed to go out in a neat blue suit and white gloves but there was a sad, rather dated air about her as if her fashion sense had expired with the '50s. Two suitcases stood behind her in the hall. Splashes of rouge on her cheeks and a touch of lipstick gave her face a bogus gaiety but when she saw the gathered policemen her mouth drooped tragically.

'O-oh.' She breathed her disappointment. 'I thought it was the Vicar.'

'May we come in?' asked Walsh. Her inadequacies repulsed as effectively as cheap perfume.

'So many of you,' she whispered. 'Has the devil sent you?'

Walsh took her arm and eased her backwards, allowing his men in behind. 'Shall we go into the sitting-room, Mrs Thompson? No point in standing around on the doorstep.'

She put up a feeble resistance. 'What is this?' she

beseeched, eyes welling, little heels digging into the hall carpet. 'Please don't touch me.'

McLoughlin slipped his hand under her other arm and, together, they whisked her through the sitting-room door and into a chair. While McLoughlin kept her seated with a firm hand on her shoulder, Walsh directed his men to a thorough search of the house and garden. He flashed the warrant under her eyes before tucking it back into his jacket pocket and sitting in the chair opposite her.

'Well, now, Mrs Thompson,' he said genially. 'Off for your little rest by the sea?'

She shook McLoughlin's hand from her shoulder but remained seated. 'I'm expecting the Vicar at any moment to take me to the station,' she announced with dignity. McLoughlin noticed a thinning patch in her hair. He found it oddly embarrassing as if she had taken off part of her clothing and revealed something best kept hidden.

'Then I suggest we don't beat around the bush,' announced Walsh. 'We wouldn't want to keep him waiting.'

'Why are you here? Why are your men searching my house?'

Walsh steepled his fingers in his lap. 'You remember that tramp you told us about, Mrs Thompson?' She gave a brief nod. 'We've found him.'

'Good. Then you'll know I was telling you the truth about dear Daniel's generosity.'

'Indeed, yes. He also happened to mentioned that Mr Thompson gave him a bottle of whisky and twenty pounds.'

The sad eyes lit with pleasure. 'I told you Daniel was a saint. He would have given the shirt off his back if the man had asked for it.'

McLoughlin took the chair next to Walsh and leaned forward aggressively. 'The tramp's name is Wally Ferris. I've had a long talk with him. He says you and Mr Thompson wanted rid of him, that's why you were so generous.'

'The ingratitude,' she gasped, her lips parting on a tremor. 'What did our Lord say? "Give to the poor and you shall have treasure in Heaven." My poor Daniel has earned his place there by his kindness. The same cannot be said of this tramp.'

'He also said,' continued McLoughlin doggedly, 'that he found your husband hiding in the shed outside.'

She tittered behind her hand like a teenager. 'Actually,' she said, looking directly at him, 'it was the other way round. Daniel found the tramp hiding in the shed. He went out to look for a paintbrush and tripped over a bundle of old clothes behind some boxes at the back. Imagine his surprise when the bundle spoke.'

Her words carried conviction and McLoughlin knew a sudden doubt. Had he relied too heavily on an old man who, by his own admission, lived in an alcoholic haze? 'Wally claims it was raining while he was in your shed. I've checked with the local meteorological office and they have no record of any rainfall on Wednesday, twenty-fourth May. The storms began two days later and lasted on and off for the next three days.'

'Poor man,' she murmured. 'I told Daniel at the time we should have tried to get him to a doctor. He was drunk and very confused. You know, he asked me if I was his sister. He thought I'd come looking for him at last.'

'But, Mrs Thompson,' said Walsh, allowing surprise into his voice, 'if he was as drunk as you say, why did you give him a bottle of whisky? Were you not compounding his already severe problems?'

She cast her eyes to the ceiling. 'He begged us in tears, Inspector. Who were we to refuse? Judge not and you shall not be judged. If the poor man chooses to kill himself with demon alcohol, I have no right to condemn him.'

'But you do have the right to speed up the process, I suppose,' said McLoughlin sarcastically.

'He's a sad little man whose only comfort lies in a whisky bottle,' she said quietly. 'It would have been cruel to deny him his comfort. We gave him money to spend on food, shoes for his feet and we urged him to seek help for his addiction. There was not much more we could do. My conscience is clear, Sergeant.'

'Wally claims he came here on Saturday, May twenty-seventh.' Walsh spoke casually.

She wrinkled her forehead and thought for a moment. 'But it can't have been,' she said with genuine puzzlement. 'Daniel was here. Didn't we decide it was the twenty-fourth?'

McLoughlin was fascinated by her performance. It occurred to him that she had expunged the memory of murder from her mind and had convinced herself that the story she told was the real one. If that was so, they were going to have the devil's own job bringing a prosecution. With only Wally's testimony, backed by the woman in the council house, they wouldn't stand a chance. They needed a confession.

'The date is corroborated by an independent witness,' he told her.

'Really?' she breathed. 'How extraordinary. I don't remember seeing anyone with him and we are so secluded here.' She fingered her cross and gazed at him with reproachful eyes. 'Who could it be, I wonder?'

Walsh cleared his throat noisily. 'Would it interest you to know where we found your husband's shoes, Mrs Thompson?'

'Not really,' she assured him. 'I assume from the things you've said that the tramp – Wally – discarded them as useless. I find that hurtful to my dear Daniel's memory.'

'You're very sure he's dead, aren't you?' said McLoughlin.

She produced her lace hankie like a magician and dabbed at the inevitable tears. 'He would never leave me,' came the refrain.

'We found the shoes in the woods at Streech Grange, not far from the ice house,' said Walsh, watching her closely.

'Did you?' she asked politely.

'Wally spent the night of the twenty-seventh of May in the ice house and abandoned the shoes in the woods the next morning as he left.'

She lowered the handkerchief and looked with curiosity from one to the other. 'Really,' she commented. Her expression was one of bafflement. 'Is that significant?'

'You do know we've found a corpse in Streech Grange ice house, don't you?' McLoughlin remarked brutally. 'It is male, aged between fifty and sixty, broad build, grey hair and five feet ten inches tall. He was murdered two months ago, around the time your husband went missing.'

Her amazement was utter. For several seconds a kaleidoscope of emotions transformed her face. The two men watched closely, but if guilt was there, it was impossible to isolate. To the forefront was surprise. 'I had no idea,' she said, 'no idea at all. No one's said anything to me. Whose corpse is it?'

McLoughlin turned to Walsh and raised a despairing eyebrow. 'It's been in all the newspapers, Mrs Thompson,' said the Inspector, 'and on the local television news. You could hardly have missed it. The body has decomposed to such an extent that we have not yet been able to identify it. We have our suspicions, however.' He studied her pointedly.

She was taking deep breaths as though breathing were difficult. The rouge stood out on her cheeks in bright spots. 'I don't have a television,' she told them. 'Daniel used to get a paper at work and tell me all the news when he came home.' She struggled for air. 'God,' she said surprisingly, holding a hand to her chest, 'they've all been keeping it from me, protecting me. I had no idea. No one's said a word.'

'No idea we'd found the body, or no idea there was a body to find?' asked McLoughlin.

She digested the implications of this for a moment. 'No idea there was one, of course,' she snapped, eyeing him with dislike. She calmed her breathing with a conscious effort and tightened her lips into their customary thin lines. She addressed herself to Walsh. 'I now understand your interest in Daniel's shoes,' she told him. A small tic had started above her lip. 'You are assuming they are connected in some way with this body you've found.'

'Perhaps,' he said guardedly.

A gleam of triumph showed in her eyes. 'Yet this

tramp you've found has proved they can't be. You say he spent the night of the twenty-seventh in the – what did you call it?'

'Ice house.'

'In the ice house. I assume he wouldn't have stayed if the dead body had been there, too, so he must have abandoned the shoes before the body ever got there.' She seemed to relax slightly. 'I cannot see a connection, merely a bizarre coincidence.'

'You're absolutely right,' agreed Walsh. 'In that sense, there is no connection.'

'Then why have you been asking me questions?'

'The bizarre coincidence led us to the tramp, Mrs Thompson, and to some interesting facts about you and your husband. We can prove he was alive in this house two days after you reported him missing and well outside the time for which you'd provided yourself with an alibi. Mr Thompson has not been seen since, and a week ago we were presented with an unidentifiable body, corresponding to his description and less than four miles away. Frankly, we can make out an excellent case against you for the murder of your husband on or after the twenty-eighth of May.'

The tic came faster. 'It can't be Daniel's body.'

'Why not?' demanded McLoughlin.

She was silent, gathering her thoughts.

'Why not?' he pressed.

'Because I had a letter from him about two weeks ago.' Her shoulders slumped and she started to weep again. 'It was a beastly letter, telling me how much he hated me and what a bad wife I'd – '

McLoughlin cut her short. 'Will you show us the letter, please?'

'I can't,' she sobbed. 'I burnt it. He'd written such vile things.'

There was a knock on the door and one of the uniformed policemen came in. 'We've been through the house and garden, sir.' He shook his head at Walsh's questioning look. 'Nothing yet. There's still this room to do and Mrs Thompson's cases. They're locked. We'll need the keys.'

The little woman grabbed her handbag and held it to her middle. 'I will not give you the keys. You will not search my cases. They contain my underwear.'

'Fetch me a WPC,' instructed the Inspector. He leaned towards Mrs Thompson. 'I'm sorry, but you've no choice in the matter. If you prefer it, I will ask the WPC to bring the cases in here and you may watch while she examines the contents.' He held out his hand. 'The keys, please.'

'Oh, very well,' she said crossly, delving into her handbag and producing two small keys tied together with a white ribbon. 'Personally, I think the whole thing's outrageous. I intend to make a strong complaint to the Chief Constable.'

Walsh wasn't surprised she objected to having her underwear scrutinised. Pieces of filmy black lacework, more at home in a brothel, he would have thought, than in the luggage of this drab, boring woman, were held up for inspection. But a truth he had discovered during his career was that some of the unlikeliest women possessed attractive lingerie. His own wife was a case in point. She had come to bed every night of their married lives in silks or soft satins, with only him to appreciate the effect. And for a long time he *had* appreciated it and done his best to show it, before years of indignant rejection had taught him that Mrs Walsh did not don her lingerie for his benefit but for some private delight of her own. And he had long since given up trying to discover what that was.

The WPC shook her head as she re-locked the cases. 'Nothing there, sir.'

'I did tell you,' said Mrs Thompson. 'Heaven knows what you think you're looking for.'

'Your handbag, please.'

She relinquished it with a moue of disgust. The constable emptied the contents carefully on to the coffee table, felt the soft leather bag for anything hidden in the lining, then sorted through the various objects. She glanced enquiringly at Walsh. 'Seems OK, sir.'

He gestured to her to return everything to the bag. 'Would you rather wait outside while we search this room?' he asked Mrs Thompson.

She settled herself deeply into her chair, gripping the cushion beneath her as if she expected to be wrestled from it. 'I would not, Inspector.'

As the search got under way, Walsh returned to the questioning. 'You say you've had a letter from your husband. Why haven't you mentioned this before?'

She cringed away from him, tucking herself sideways into a tight ball in the chair. 'Because I have only my pride left. I didn't want anyone to know how shamefully he's treated me.' She dabbed at her dry eyes.

'What was the postmark?' asked McLoughlin.

'London, I think.'

'Presumably the letter was handwritten,' he mused. 'He wouldn't have access to a typewriter.'

She nodded. 'It was.'

'What sort of envelope?'

She thought for a moment. 'White,' she told him.

McLoughlin laughed. 'It won't wash, you know. You can't just keep pulling lies out of the hat and expect us to applaud your ingenuity. We'll check with your postman. In a place like this you'll have had the same postman for years, it's probably the chap who runs the little shop-cum-post-office near the church. Your letters will have been a source of great interest to him in the last couple of months. He's probably scrutinised every one carefully in the hopes of being first with news of the errant Daniel. You won't persuade us your husband's still alive by dreaming up letters, Mrs Thompson.'

She glanced beyond him to where the woman constable was going through the sideboard. 'Ask the postman, Sergeant. You'll find I'm telling you the truth.' She spoke with sincerity, but the look in her eyes was as level and calculating as any he'd seen. 'If only I'd known what was in your mind, I'd have told you about the letter the first time you came.'

McLoughlin stood up and leaned over her, resting his hands on the arms of her chair. 'Why were you so shocked to hear about the body at the ice house? If you know your husband's alive, it couldn't mean anything to you.'

'This man's threatening me,' she snapped at Walsh. 'I don't like it.' She cringed deep into the chair.

'Back off, Andy.'

'With pleasure.' Without warning, he hooked his hand under her arm and stepped back sharply. She popped out of the chair like a champagne cork, then wriggled and spat with ferocity. He clung on to a flailing arm, dodged a swipe from the other and felt warm spittle smear his cheek. 'The chair, sir,' he called. 'She's hiding something.'

'Got it.'

McLoughlin took a grip on both her arms, arching his body away to avoid the kicking points of her shoes. 'Come on, you sods,' he shouted angrily at the two constables. 'She's pulverising me. Who's got the handcuffs, for God's sake?'

'Bastard!' she screamed. 'Bloody fucking bastard!' She rolled another ball of spittle into her mouth and launched it at him. To his immense disgust, it caught his lip and dribbled inside.

The constables, galvanised out of frozen inactivity, snapped on the handcuffs and pushed the woman on to the sofa. She looked at McLoughlin's vain attempts to get rid of the venom and laughed. 'Serves you bloody right. I hope you catch something.'

'Looks like I've caught you,' he said grimly. He turned to Walsh. 'What is it?'

Walsh handed him a thin envelope. 'She must have slipped it out of her bag when we were gawping at her blasted knickers.' He chuckled good-humouredly. 'Waste of time, dear lady. We'd have found it eventually.'

McLoughlin opened the envelope. Inside were two aeroplane tickets, made out to Mr and Mrs Thompson, for a flight to Marbella that evening. 'Where's he been hiding all this time?' he asked her.

'Go to hell!'

'Mrs Thompson! Mrs Thompson!' exclaimed a shocked voice from the doorway. 'Some control, I beg you.'

She laughed. 'Go and play with yourself, you silly little man.'

'Is she mad?' asked the horrified Vicar.

'In a manner of speaking,' said Inspector Walsh cheerfully.

Twenty-One

ANNE LAUGHED AS McLoughlin told the story. Colour had returned to her face and lively enjoyment sparkled in her eyes. The only visible reminder that she'd been attacked was the brilliant red and white spotted scarf that she had tied, bandit-style, over her bandage. Against medical advice, she had discharged herself the day before, maintaining that five days in hospital was the absolute maximum that a sentient drug addict could tolerate. Bowing to the inevitable, Phoebe had brought her home after extracting a promise that she would do precisely as she was told. Anne gave the promise readily. 'Just lead me to a cigarette,' she said, 'and I'll do anything you say.'

What she didn't know was that Phoebe had also assumed responsibility for her safety. 'If she leaves hospital, Mrs Maybury, we won't be able to protect her,' Walsh had pointed out, 'any more than we can protect you. We simply haven't enough men to patrol

Streech Grange. I shall be advising her to stay put in hospital, just as I've advised you to move out.'

'Don't waste your breath, Inspector,' Phoebe told him contemptuously. 'Streech is our home. If we had to rely on you to protect us it wouldn't be worth living in.'

Walsh shrugged. 'You're a very foolish woman, Mrs Maybury.'

Diana, who was in the room with them, was incensed. 'My God, you really are the pits,' she snapped. 'Two days ago you didn't believe a word Phoebe told you. Now, because Sergeant McLoughlin took the trouble to find some evidence, you tell her she's a fool for not running away on your bloody say-so. Well, let me tell you this, the only thing that's changed in the last two days is your mind.' She stamped her foot in exasperation. 'Why the hell should we run away today when we didn't run away yesterday or the day before that? The danger's the same for God's sake. And who do you imagine has been protecting us all this time?'

'Who, Mrs Goode?'

She turned her back on him.

'We've been protecting ourselves of course,' said Phoebe coolly, 'and we'll go on doing it. The dogs are the best safeguard we've got.'

Anne was propped on pillows in her favourite armchair, her feet resting on Phoebe's tapestry stool, an old donkey jacket which passed for a dressing-gown round her shoulders, a pencil stuck behind one ear. She was, McLoughlin thought, completely careless of other people's opinions. The message was simple: I am what you see; take it or leave it. He wondered if it came from supreme self-confidence or total indifference. Whatever it was, he wished he shared it. For his own part, he still felt the need of others' approval.

'So where was Mr Thompson hiding?' she asked him.

'She wouldn't tell us, but it wasn't very difficult to find him. He turned up like a lamb, for the seven-thirty flight to Marbella.'

'Skedaddling with the loot?'

McLoughlin nodded. Once caught and identified by Wally as the man in the shed, Daniel Thompson had offered to co-operate. The idea had come to them, he said, when they had found a book in the library describing the life of luxury enjoyed by British embezzlers on the Spanish riviera. Thompson's engineering business was on the decline and he had complained to his wife about the injustice of having to work his balls off to keep it alive when other men, faced with the same problem, simply absconded with the capital and lived it up in the sun. The answer was simple, announced Mrs T., they too would follow the sun. They had no dependants, she had never liked England, positively loathed East Deller where the community was worthy and stultifying, and she had no intention of spending the next ten years scrimping and saving to keep Daniel's business from going broke.

'The most extraordinary thing,' said Thompson reminiscently, 'was how easy it was to persuade people to invest in transparent radiators. It just proved to me how much money and how little sense there is floating around in the South.' He reminded McLoughlin of Arthur Daley.

'What do you make transparent radiators from?' he'd asked him curiously.

'Toughened, heatproof glass,' said Thompson, 'the same sort of stuff they use for those saucepans. The idea was to add dyes to the water in the expansion tank and watch them flow through the system.'

'Mrs Goode said it could have revolutionised interior design.'

The saintly Daniel sighed. 'That was the terrible irony of it all. I think she may have been right. I opted for the idea because while it was feasible to make the things, it was also absurd enough to make bankruptcy a likely possibility. Imagine my surprise when, without any publicity, it started to take off. By that time, of course, it was too late. To turn the business into a success then would have presented enormous difficulties. On top of which, Maisie – the wife' – he explained helpfully – 'had set her heart on the Costa del Sol. Sad, really,' he mused with a faraway look in his eyes. 'They might well have made my fortune and we could have retired to the sun anyway.'

'Why did you bother with the disappearing act? Why not simply pack up, both of you, and go?'

Mr Thompson beamed. 'Moonlight flits worry people,' he said, 'make them suspicious, and we didn't want the Spanish to take against us. They're not as easy-going as they used to be. While Maisie remained, everyone merely felt sorry for her for having married so weak and inept a man.'

'So where have you been for the last two months?'

'East Deller,' he said, as if surprised by the question, 'until two nights ago when I went to a B & B so Maisie could pack up. Your visits were becoming a little too frequent for comfort.'

'You were hiding in your own house?'

He nodded. 'It was quite safe. Maisie phoned me at my hotel in London after the police had searched the house and garden the first time. I came home during the night of the twenty-sixth and lay low in the attic. We reckoned that was safer than my being on the loose with my description floating about.'

'Wally saw you in the shed,' McLoughlin pointed out.

'That was a mistake,' he admitted. 'We thought the shed would be the best hiding place because it would be easier to escape from if the police turned up unexpectedly. Of course it was also the easiest place for someone to walk into. Not that any normal person walking in would have mattered,' he said without rancour. 'Maisie had hidden me behind a stack of old boxes, no way I'd have been seen by a casual visitor.' He tapped two pudgy forefingers together. 'But the silly old fool was looking for a place to hide himself. I don't know who got the worse shock when he pulled the boxes aside, him or me.'

'The police made two searches,' McLoughlin said. 'How did they miss you the second time?'

'Because we were expecting it. We worked out if the police made a surprise search and found nothing, they'd conclude I really had run away because of my business problems and abandoned Maisie to fend for herself. So Maisie made an anonymous phone call to stimulate another search. It was a nerve-racking two days waiting for it, but we were ready when it came. I simply hopped over the fence at the bottom of the garden and crouched in a bush in our neighbours' orchard until Maisie gave me the all-clear.' He smiled amiably. He was, as Diana had described him, built like a tank. The smile split his chubby face into two half moons, the lower half pendulous with double chins. 'After that we had no more trouble till you turned up with those shoes. Until then my disappearance had been a nine-day wonder.'

McLoughlin acknowledged he was right. 'You were taking a gamble, though. Neighbours must have been popping in all the time.'

'Not after Maisie developed her wonderfully outrageous sex mania,' said Thompson. 'The women kept coming for a few days out of kindness, but it's amazing how rapidly embarrassment alienates people. Maisie should have gone on the stage, I've always said it. We got the idea of the attic from Anne Frank's diary,' he volunteered.

'And she really didn't know about the body in the ice house? I find that extraordinary.'

'It was a damn nuisance,' said Thompson, showing annoyance for the first time. 'She couldn't be seen to change her habits. If she had rented a telly or started buying papers, people might have thought she was taking an interest again. Wrong image, do you see?'

McLoughlin nodded. 'And no one told her because they were afraid the body was yours.'

Daniel sighed. 'Hoist with our own petard.'

'Why did you leave it so long to fly out? You could have gone weeks ago.'

'We were greedy,' confessed Thompson. 'We wanted the money from selling the house. You're talking over a quarter of a million pounds for a property like that. It was the icing on the gingerbread. The plan was for Maisie to become more and more depressed until the obvious solution was to sell the house and move somewhere smaller which had no memories for her. No one would have questioned it. If the truth be told, they'd have been relieved to see the back of her. Then, with the money safely under our belts, we were off on a ferry to France and from there to sunny Spain.'

'And you were intending to use your own passports?'

The other man nodded.

'You'd been reported missing, Mr Thompson. You'd have been stopped.'

'Oh, I don't think so, Sergeant,' he said comfortably. 'Six months on, brouhaha died down, hundreds of people on day trips, a middle-aged couple with a common name. What would they have against me anyway? My wife could testify I was no longer missing. And it's not as though there's a warrant out for my arrest, is there?' He cocked his head on one side and considered the Sergeant with amusement.

'No,' McLoughlin admitted.

'I was incompetent,' said Thompson. 'I admit it freely. But no one person lost very much money through my failure.' He folded his hands across his plump stomach. 'My employees have all found other jobs and the Inland Revenue has agreed to honour their National Insurance contributions which I so rashly – how shall I put it? – "borrowed" to keep the business afloat.' He winked outrageously. 'I give credit to my number two for that. He's done all the negotiations on their behalf, or so Maisie tells me. Splendid chap, great organisational flair, full of integrity. He's sorted out the mess I made and wound up the business. Mind you, he's said some harsh words to Maisie on the phone, called me an amateurish bungler, but I don't hold it against him.' He flicked a speck of dust from his jumper. 'My investors took a gamble on me which was sadly misplaced, but they have cheerfully cut their losses and moved on to more lucrative ventures. I'm delighted. It saddened me to have failed them.'

'Hang on,' said McLoughlin sharply. 'You didn't fail them, Mr Thompson. You embezzled their money.'

'Who says so?'

'You admitted it yourself.'

'When?'

McLoughlin turned to WPC Brownlow who had been taking shorthand notes. 'Find that bit where he said he got the idea from British embezzlers living in Spain.'

She flicked back through her notebook. 'He didn't actually say *he* was an embezzler,' she admitted after a couple of minutes, 'only that his business was in decline.'

'Skip on a few pages,' said McLoughlin. 'He said it was ridiculously easy to get people to invest in the radiator idea.'

'It was,' said Thompson. 'It was a good idea.'

'Dammit all,' exploded McLoughlin. 'You said it was absurd enough to make bankruptcy likely.'

'And I was proved right. That's just what happened.'

'You didn't go bankrupt because it wouldn't work. You salted the money away. You said yourself it could have been a great success.'

Thompson sighed. 'I'm sure it would have been, too, if I'd had more business sense. My problem, as I've tried to explain to you, is incompetence. Are you going to arrest us, Sergeant?'

'Yes, Mr Thompson, I bloody well am.'

'On what charge?'

'Wasting police time, for a kick-off, while I find someone who's willing to press a more serious charge.'

'Who?'

'One of your creditors, Mrs Goode.'

'I'll get my solicitor to discuss an out-of-court settlement with her,' he said comfortably. 'Much more satisfactory than pursuing me through the courts.'

'I'll get your wife on an assault charge.'

'Poor Maisie. She's demented, you know.' He winked with enormous enjoyment. 'Doesn't know what she's doing half the time. A short spell of treatment with a sympathetic doctor will do her far more good than a police prosecution. The Vicar will agree with me on that.'

'You're a pair of rogues.'

'Harsh words, Sergeant. The truth is I'm a coward who couldn't face the disappointment of those who'd put their trust in me. I ran away and hid. Contemptible, I agree, but hardly criminal.' His gaze was level and sincere, but his double chins wobbled. Whether from mirth or contrition, McLoughlin couldn't say.

By the end of his account, Anne was laughing so much it hurt. 'Did you let them go?'

He grinned sheepishly. 'It was like trying to hold on to a couple of eels. Every time you thought you'd got a grip, they wriggled out of it. They're back home now, but due to answer a charge of obstruction in a couple of weeks' time. Meanwhile, I've got on to his number two, who's hopping mad at being taken for a ride, and told him to go through the books with an accountant and look for straightforward embezzlement.'

'He won't find it,' said Anne, mopping her eyes. 'Mr Thompson sounds like a real pro. It'll all be neatly tied up in a villa in Spain by now.'

'Perhaps.' McLoughlin stretched his arms above his head, then subsided comfortably into his chair. He had been up all night again and he was tired.

Jane had told Anne that McLoughlin was in the wrong job. Why? Anne had asked. Because he was over-sensitive to other people's problems. Anne watched him through the smoke from her cigarette. She had none of her god-daughter's naivety so her appraisal was untinged by sentiment. Lust after him she might, but it in no way affected her objectivity. He was not troubled by over-sensitivity towards others, she concluded, but by over-sensitivity towards himself, a trap, in Anne's view, that far too many men fell into. To burden oneself with a socially acceptable image was to put oneself in a strait-jacket. She wondered when McLoughlin had last had a good laugh at himself – if ever. Life for him, she thought, was a series of hurdles which had to be taken cleanly. To touch one would represent failure.

'What are you thinking?' he asked.

'I was wondering why men take themselves so seriously.'

'I didn't know they did.'

'I'm trying to think if I've ever met one who doesn't. Your Mr Thompson sounds a likely candidate.' She waggled her toes on the tapestry stool. 'A woman's problems centre round her biological programming. Without her willingness to reproduce and nurture a new generation, the species would die out. Her frustrations come from the species' unwillingness to recognise the sacrifices she makes for the general good. You don't get paid by a grateful government for being on duty twenty-four hours a day to raise a family; you don't get an MBE for training your children to be good citizens; nine times out of ten even your children don't thank you for your efforts, but chuck in your face that they didn't ask to be born anyway.' She tapped the end of her cigarette against the ashtray and chuckled. 'It's a dog's life being a mother. There's no management structure to speak of, no independent arbitrator, no dismissal procedure for repeated offences and no promotion prospects. Emotional blackmail and sexual harassment are rampant and backhanders commonplace.' Her eyes gleamed as she leant forward. 'No man would tolerate it. His self-esteem would suffer.'

McLoughlin cursed himself silently for being a fool. He should have trusted his first impressions and steered clear. She would have to be very special in bed to make it worth his while to sit through feminist claptrap to get her there. After all, he thought, was there really so much difference between her and his absent wife? The complaints were the same, merely more fluent and better articulated from Anne. He vowed to become celibate. He had neither the inclination nor the energy to wage war every time he felt randy. If the price of pleasure was capitulation, he could do without it. He'd had to grovel past his wife's headaches and stay awake through low-budget late films for Saturday night sex. He was damned if he'd do it for a woman he wasn't tied to.

He stood up abruptly and unleashed his pent-up rage and disappointment. 'Let me tell you something, *Ms* Cattrell. I'm sick to death of hearing women complain about their lot. You're all so bloody strident about what a grand time men have and how badly we treat you.' He walked to the fireplace and leaned both hands on the mantelpiece, staring into the unlit fire. 'Do you think yours is the only sex to suffer from biological programming? The burden on men to perform is infinitely greater. If we weren't programmed to sow our seed, female disinclination would have wiped out the human race centuries ago. You try persuading a woman to have sex. It costs money, effort, emotional commitment and the trauma of regular rejection. If a man wants to do his bit by society, he has to spend a lifetime in chains flogging his guts out to keep his woman content and well fed so that she first agrees to have his offspring and then looks after them properly when she's got them.' He turned to look at her. 'It's humiliating and degrading,' he said with bitterness. 'My procreative chemistry is no different from a dog's. Nature compels us both to eject sperm into a fertile female, the difference is that he doesn't have to justify why he wants to do it whereas I do. Think about that next time you feel like sneering at male self-esteem. It's fragile in the extreme. You're damn right I take myself seriously. I bloody well have to. I've only my office left where rules of behaviour still apply and where I don't have to tie myself in knots to achieve the goals set for me.'

She took an apple from the bowl beside her and tossed it to him. 'You're doing great, McLoughlin. In a minute you'll be telling me you'd rather be a woman.'

He looked at her, saw the amused lift of her lips and laughed. 'I damn nearly did. You're winding me up.'

'No,' she said with a smile, 'I'm winding you down. Life is pure farce from beginning to end, with a little black comedy thrown in for shade. If it was anything else, mankind would have stuck his collective head in the gas oven years ago. No one could tolerate seventy years of tragedy. When I die – probably of cancer – Jane has promised to put on my tombstone: "Here lies Anne Cattrell who laughed her way through it. The joke was on her but at least she knew it."' She tossed another apple into the air and caught it. 'In a couple of weeks, if you last the pace, you could be as cynical as I am, McLoughlin. You'll be a happy man, my son.'

He sat down with the apple clenched between his teeth and drew his briefcase towards him. 'You're not all cynic,' he said, speaking round the apple.

She smiled. 'What makes you say that?'

'I've read your diary.' He snapped the locks on the briefcase, half-opened it and withdrew the slim volume.

She watched him curiously. 'Did you enjoy it?'

'Was I supposed to?'

'No,' she said tartly. 'I didn't write it for publication.'

'Good thing too,' he said frankly. 'It needs editing to make it readable.'

She glared at him. 'You would know, I suppose?' She was incredibly hurt. Her writing, even the writing she did for herself, mattered to her.

'I can read.'

'I can hold a paintbrush. That doesn't make me an expert on art.' She looked pointedly at her watch. 'Shouldn't you be trying to solve a murder? As far as I can see you're still no nearer finding out who the body belongs to or, for that matter, who hit me on the head.' She couldn't give a damn what he thought, he was only a policeman, so why did her stomach feel as if it had just bounced off the floor?

He munched on his apple. 'P. needs editing out,' he told her. 'P. ruins it.' He flicked the diary into her lap. 'The carving-knife is still at the Station, awaiting your signature. I rescued this early on to prevent Friar sneaking it out to photocopy the rude bits.' He was sitting with his back to the windows and his eyes, shadowed, gave nothing away. She couldn't tell if he was joking.

'Pity. Friar might have appreciated it.'

'Tell me about P., Anne.'

She eyed him cautiously. 'What do you want to know?'

'Would he have attacked you?'

'No.'

'Sure? Perhaps he's the jealous type. It was one of his Special Brew bottles that was used to hit you, and I'm told he never lets them out of the pub.'

She could deny that P. and Paddy were one – the prospect of McLoughlin meeting the P. he had read about rather appalled her – but that would be coy, and Anne was never coy. 'I'm positive,' she said. 'Have you spoken to him?'

'Not yet. We only got confirmation of the forensic results this morning.' The match on Anne's blood and hair proved the bottle was the weapon, but the other results were disappointing. A smudged set of fingerprints round the neck and an incomplete footprint built up from barely seen depressions in the ground. It wasn't enough to take them any further.

Anne wished she knew what he was thinking. Was he a harsh judge? Would he ever understand how Paddy, just because he always came back, however irregularly, made Streech bearable? Somehow she doubted it, for, in spite of his strange attraction to her, McLoughlin was a conventional man. The attraction wouldn't last, she knew that. Sooner or later he would snap back into character and then she would be remembered only as a brief madness. And for Anne, there would be just Paddy, once again, to remind her that the walls of Streech Grange were not totally impenetrable. Tired tears pricked at the back of her eyes. 'He's a kind man,' she said, 'and he understands everything.'

If McLoughlin understood, he didn't show it. He left without saying goodbye.

Paddy was hefting empty beer barrels at the rear of the pub. He eyed McLoughlin thoughtfully as he swung another barrel effortlessly atop the pile. 'Can I help you?'

'Detective Sergeant McLoughlin, Silverborne Police.' Imagination had created in McLoughlin's mind a huge, muscular Adonis with the magnetic attraction of the North Pole and the brain of Einstein. The reality was a big, rather overweight, hairy man in a tatty jumper and seated trousers. The jealous fire dimmed perceptibly in McLoughlin's belly. He showed Paddy a photograph of the stone beer bottle, taken after its removal from the undergrowth. 'Do you recognise it?'

Paddy squinted briefly at the picture. 'Maybe.'

'I'm told you bottle your Special in it.'

For a moment they scented the air suspiciously like two powerful mongrels poised to defend their territory. Then Paddy chose to back off. He shrugged good-humouredly. 'OK, yes, it looks like one of mine,' he said, 'but it's a hobby. I'm writing a book on traditional beer-making methods to make damn sure the old ways aren't forgotten.' His gaze was level and without guile. 'I host the odd tasting session where I give it away to the locals to get their opinions.' He studied the other's dark face, looking for a reaction. 'All right, so I may have asked for a donation from time to time towards my costs. That's not unreasonable, it's an expensive hobby.' He found the other's silence irritating. 'Dammit, man, haven't your lot got more important things to exercise your minds at the moment? Who gave it to you anyway? I'll skin the bastard.'

'Is it true you never let these bottles out of the pub, Mr Clarke?' McLoughlin asked coldly.

'Yes, it's true, and I'd bloody well like to get my hands on the bugger who took it. Who was it?'

McLoughlin tapped the black stain round the bottom of the monochrome bottle. 'That's blood, Mr Clarke, Miss Cattrell's blood.'

The big man became very still. 'What the hell is this?'

'It's the weapon that was used to beat a woman's skull in. I thought you might know how it found its way into her garden.'

Paddy opened his mouth to say something, then sank abruptly on to the nearest barrel. 'Jesus Christ! Those bottles weigh a ton. I heard she was all right, but Jesus!'

'How did the bottle get into her garden, Mr Clarke?'

Paddy took no notice. 'Robinson said she'd had a knock on the head. I thought it was concussion. Those bloody wankers keep calling it concussion.'

'What wankers?'

'Journalists.'

'Someone fractured her skull.'

Paddy stared at the ground. 'Is she all right?'

'They used one of your bottles to do it.'

'Goddammit, man, I asked you a question.' He

surged to his feet and stared angrily into McLoughlin's face. 'Is she all right?'

'Yes. But why are you so interested? Did you hit her harder than you meant to?'

Anger flared briefly in Paddy's face. He glanced towards the kitchen door to make sure it was closed. He lowered his voice. 'You're on the wrong track. Anne's a friend of mine. We go back a long way. She'll tell you I wouldn't hurt her.'

'It was dark. Perhaps you thought it was Mrs Goode or Mrs Maybury.'

'Don't be a fool, man. I go back a long way with them, too. Hell, they're all friends of mine.'

McLoughlin's mouth dropped open. 'All three of them?'

'Yes.'

'You're telling me you sleep with all three of them?'

Paddy made damping gestures with his hands. 'Keep your voice down for God's sake. Who said anything about sleeping with anybody? It's damn lonely up there. I keep each one company from time to time, that's all.'

McLoughlin shook with laughter as the jealous flame spluttered and died. 'Do they know?'

Paddy sensed the lack of hostility and grinned. 'I don't know. It's not the sort of thing you ask, is it?' He made a snap judgement. 'Will your conscience allow you a bottle of Special? We might as well drink it before Customs and Excise get their miserable paws on it. And while we're enjoying it, I'll give you a list of all my Special customers. I never let strangers near it, so I know each customer personally. The bastard you're looking for has to be one of them, and I rather think I know who it is. There's only one person in this village who's stupid enough and vindictive enough.' He led McLoughlin across the yard and into the room behind the garage where the rich smell of fermenting malt tingled in the nose. 'To tell you the truth, I've often toyed with the idea of doing the thing properly and going into full legal production. Maybe this is the push I needed. The wife can take over the pub licence, she's a far better landlord than I am.' He took two unopened bottles, removed the clamped rubber stoppers and with immense care poured a deep amber liquid with a foaming white head into two straight-sided glasses. He handed one to McLoughlin. 'Be advised by me, Sergeant.' There was a twinkle in his eye. 'You have all the time in the world, so approach it the way you approach your women. Slowly, lovingly, patiently, and with infinite respect. Because if you don't, you'll be flat on the floor within three mouthfuls, wondering what hit you.'

'Is that your secret?'

'It is.'

McLoughlin raised his glass. 'Cheers.'

*

The letter was waiting on Detective Sergeant Robinson's desk when he arrived that morning. The handwriting on the envelope was childish and unformed, the postmark local. He ripped it open eagerly and spread the lined paper flat on the desk in front of him. The lines were covered in the same unformed script, a rambling, hard-to-read account of a bizarre happening one night in the middle of May. Eddie Staines, anonymously, had come up trumps.

> You been asking about a woman when and so forth. It were a Sunday. Know that becos my girls relijus and took some purswading becos she'd been to comunion. Must of been May 14 as May 12 is my birthday and it was by way of a late pressent. We did it in Grange woods as per normal. We left after 12 and wolked along the wall by the farm. We heard this waleing and weeping on the other side. My girl wanted to beet it but I hopped up for a look. Well you got it rong see. It was a man not a woman and he was rocking about and banging his head. Mad as a hatter if you ask me. I shone the torch on him and said was he all write. He said fuck off so I did. I seen the descripshun of the dead bloke. Sounds write to me. He had long grey hair anyways. Forgot about it till reesently. Thing is I knew him. Couldn't put a name to him mind just knew his face from sumwere. But it weren't no one

reglar if you follow. Reckon now it was Mayberry. Thats all.

With promotion signs flickering in his eyes, Sergeant Robinson rang through to Walsh. He had a momentary qualm about his promise of anonymity – there was no way he could keep Eddie's identity secret now – but it was only momentary. When all was said and done, Eddie had not threatened to string him up by his balls.

Twenty-Two

MCLOUGHLIN THREW OPEN the glass doors of the Police Station and let the heat from outside billow in behind him like a swelling spinnaker. Paddy's Special, taken slowly, lovingly and with immense respect, was swirling nicely in his brain. '"Now's the day and now's the hour,"' he roared. '"See the front of battle lour." Where's Monty? I need troops.'

The Desk Sergeant gave a grunt of amusement. There *was* a certain skinny similarity between Walsh and Montgomery. 'On manoeuvres.'

'Hell!'

'Someone's identified the body.'

'And?'

'David Maybury. The Inspector's wetting himself.'

Shock waves drove the alcohol from McLoughlin's brain. Goddammit, he thought, it couldn't be. He'd come to love those women. The pain of loving them gnawed at his insides like a half-starved rat. 'Where's he gone?'

The other shook his head. 'No idea. Presumably questioning the witness. He and Nick took off like scalded cats about two hours ago.'

'Well, he's wrong.' His voice was harsh. 'It's not Maybury. Tell him that if he gets back before I do, will you?'

Not bloody likely, thought the Desk Sergeant, watching the angry young man shoulder open the doors and surge out on to the pavement. If McLoughlin was intent on self-destruction, he had no plans to go with him. He glanced at his watch and saw with relief that his shift was nearly over.

McLoughlin pulled Anne bodily out of her chair and shook her till her teeth rattled. 'Was it David Maybury?' he shouted at her. 'Was it?' he spat.

She didn't say anything and, with a groan, he pushed her from him. The donkey jacket slipped from her shoulders, leaving her clad only in a pair of men's pyjamas that were far too big for her. She looked oddly pathetic, like a child playing at being an adult. 'I don't know,' she said with dignity. 'The body was unrecognisable, but I shouldn't think it was David. He's not likely to have come back here after ten years, assuming he was still alive.'

'Don't play games, Anne,' he said angrily. 'You saw the body before it rotted. Who was it?'

She shook her head.

'Someone's ID'd it. They say it's David Maybury.'

She licked her lips but didn't answer.

'Help me.'

'I can't.'

'Can't or won't?'

'Does it matter?'

'Yes,' he said bitterly, 'it matters to me. I believed in you. I believed in all of you.'

Her face twisted. 'I'm sorry.'

He gave a savage laugh. 'You're sorry? Jesus Christ!' He gripped her arms again, his long fingers curling into the flesh. 'Don't you understand, you little bitch? I trusted you. I've put my head on the line for you. Dammit, you owe me.'

There was a long silence. When she spoke, her voice was brittle. 'Well, hey, McLoughlin, never let it be said that Cattrell doesn't pay her debts.' She pulled the cord on her pyjama trousers and let them slither to the floor. 'Go ahead. Screw me. That's all you were ever interested in, wasn't it? A good fuck. Just like your precious boss ten years ago.'

The sands shifted under his feet. He raised his hands to her throat and stroked the soft white flesh of her neck.

'You didn't know?' Her eyes glittered as she put her hands between his wrists and thrust them apart to break his grip. 'The horny little bastard made Phoebe a proposition – a nice clean line drawn under the investigation in return for a weekly screw. Oh, he wasn't quite so vulgar. He dressed it up a bit.' She mimicked Walsh's voice. 'She was alone and vulnerable. He wanted to protect her. Her beauty had touched him. She deserved something better after her husband's brutal treatment.' Her lip curled in derision. 'She turned him down and told him where to stick his protection.' A strident note made her voice unattractive. 'My God, but she was naive. She never considered for one moment that the man held her future in his hands.'

'I don't believe this.'

She walked across to her armchair and took a cigarette from the packet on the arm. 'Why not?' she asked coolly, flicking her lighter. 'What makes you think you have a monopoly on wanting to ball murder suspects?' Her eyes mocked him. 'God knows what it is, but there's something very attractive about us. Perhaps it's the uncertainty.'

He shook his head. 'What did you mean when you said he held her future in his hands? You said she was naive.'

'Oh, for pity's sake,' she countered scornfully. 'Who told the world and his wife that Phoebe killed her husband? Who briefed the press, McLoughlin?'

He looked very thoughtful. 'She could have sued.'

'Who?'

'The newspapers.'

'She was never libelled. They weren't so crude as to call her a murderess. They referred to her as "an avid gardener" in one sentence, then in the next revealed that the police were digging up the flowerbeds. And all neatly sign-posted for them by your boss.'

'Why didn't she put in a complaint?' He saw the expression on her face and held up his hands. 'Don't say it. Her word against his and he was a Detective Inspector.' He lapsed into silence. 'So what happened?'

She drew on her cigarette and raked him with angry eyes. 'Walsh couldn't produce the goods because of course David had never been murdered, so the investigation was eventually stopped. It was then the fun started. She found herself on the wrong end of a malicious smear campaign and there wasn't a soul in this bloody place who would give her the time of day. She was on the verge of a nervous breakdown by the time I moved in. Jonny, at the age of eleven, had started to wet his bed and Jane – ' She searched his face. 'It's going to happen again. That bastard is going to throw Phoebe to the wolves a second time.' She looked pale beneath the scarlet bandanna.

'Why didn't you tell me all this at the beginning?'

'Would you have believed me?'

'No.'

'And now?'

'Maybe.' He eyed her for a long time, rubbing his jaw in thoughtful silence. 'You're a good journalist, Anne. Couldn't you have written Phoebe's side of it and got her off the hook?'

'You tell me how I can do that without giving Jane as her alibi and I'll write it. Phoebe would burn at the stake before she let her daughter become a sideshow for ghouls. Me, too, if it comes to that.' She inhaled deeply. 'It's not an alibi anyway. Jane might have fallen asleep.'

He nodded. 'In that case, why are you so sure he left this house alive?'

She turned away to stub out her cigarette. 'Why are *you* so sure?' She looked back at him. 'You are, aren't you?'

'Yes.'

'Because someone claims now it was David in the ice house?'

'No.'

'Why then?'

He looked at her for a long moment. 'Because you chose to bury yourself in Streech Grange. That's how I know he walked out of here alive.'

'I don't know what you're talking about.'

'You're a bloody awful liar, Cattrell.'

'I wish you wouldn't keep saying that,' she said crossly, stamping her foot, 'and I'm freezing.'

'So, stop waggling your fanny at me and put some clothes on,' he said reasonably, reaching down for her pyjama trousers and tossing them across to her. He watched while she put them on. 'It's a nice fanny, Cattrell,' he murmured, 'but I only came for the truth. I got rather more than I bargained for.'

*

He drove to the forensic laboratories and searched out Dr Webster in his office. 'I was passing,' he said. 'I wondered if you'd had any new ideas on that corpse of ours.'

If Dr Webster found this approach a little unorthodox, he didn't remark on it. 'I've the full report here,' he said, tapping a folder on the desk beside him. 'The typist finished this morning. You can take a copy back with you if you like.' He chuckled. 'Mind you, I don't think it's going to please George much, but there we are, he will push for instant opinions and they're not always accurate. Made any progress?'

McLoughlin made a see-saw motion with his hand. 'Not much. Our most promising lead turned up alive. Now we're in the dark again.'

'In that case I doubt that anything I've managed to piece together is going to help you much. Give me a description, better still a photograph, and I'll say yea or nay to whether he's on my slab. But I can't tell you who he is. George is on the phone every day, yelling for results, but miracles take time. Fresh bodies are one thing, bits of old shoe leather need patience to sort out.'

'What about Maybury?'

The pathologist grunted impatiently. 'You're all obsessed with that wretched man. Of course it's not Maybury. And you can tell George I've taken a second opinion and it agrees with mine. Facts are facts,' he grumbled, 'and in this case they are not open to interpretation.'

McLoughlin breathed deeply through his nose. 'How do you know?'

'Too old. I've done a lot of work on the X-rays and the fusion's more advanced than I thought. I'm sure now we're looking at a sixty-five to seventy-year-old. The bottom line's sixty. Maybury would be what? Fifty-four, fifty-five?'

'Fifty-four.'

Webster reached for the folder and removed some photographs. 'In the report, I've come down against mutilation but it's only an opinion and I'm prepared to be proved wrong. There *are* some scratches on the bone that might have been made with a sharp knife, but my own view is it wasn't.' He pointed to one of the photographs. 'Clearly rat droppings.'

McLoughlin nodded. 'Anything else?'

'I'm in two minds about how he died. It really depends on whether he was wearing any clothes at the time of his death. Have you sorted that one out yet?'

'No.'

'I scraped up a lot of earth from the floor round the body. We've analysed it but, frankly, there's a negligible amount of blood in it.'

McLoughlin frowned. 'Go on.'

'Well, that makes it very difficult for me to say with any certainty how he died. If he was nude and he was stabbed, the ground would have been saturated with blood. If he was fully clothed and stabbed, then the clothes would have soaked up most of the blood. You'll have to find his clothes.'

'Hang on a minute, Doctor. You're saying that if he was nude he couldn't have been stabbed, but if he was clothed he might have been?'

'In essence, that's right. There's an outside chance animals might have licked the floor but you'll never get a prosecution on that.'

'Does Chief Inspector Walsh know this?'

Webster peered at him over his glasses. 'Why do you ask that?'

McLoughlin rumpled his hair. 'He hasn't mentioned it.' Or had he? McLoughlin could remember very little of what Walsh had said that first night. 'OK. Supposing he was nude. How did he die?'

Webster pursed his lips. 'Old age. Cold. From the little that's left, it's impossible to say. I couldn't find any traces of barbiturates or asphyxia, but – ' He shrugged, and tapped the photographs. 'Shoe leather. Find the clothes. They'll tell you more than I can.'

McLoughlin put his hands on the desk and hunched his shoulders. 'We've been conducting a murder enquiry on the basis that he was stabbed in the belly. Now you're telling me he could have died of natural causes. Have you any idea how many hours I've worked in the last week?'

The pathologist chuckled. 'About half as many as

I have, at a rough guess. I've pulled out the stops on this one. Good grief, man, we don't get cases like this every day. Most bodies have at least ninety per cent of their constituent parts. In any case, until you produce some intact and unstained clothes to prove me wrong, stabbing still looks the most likely. Old men, wandering around nude in search of an ice house to freeze to death in, are quite outside my experience.'

McLoughlin straightened. 'Touché. Any more surprises?'

'Just a little bit of fun which I've tacked on to the end of the report, so I don't want you coming back and accusing me of putting ideas into your head.' He chuckled. 'I had another look in the ice house yesterday. It's been sealed for over a week now and the temperature's dropped considerably. The door's as old as the hills but it still fits perfectly. I was impressed. Obviously an extraordinarily efficient method of storing ice. Very cold and very sterile. Must have kept for months.'

'And?'

The doctor turned his attention to some letters in front of him. 'I've speculated on what sort of condition he would have been in if the door had remained closed until the gardener found him.' He scratched his name in spidery writing on the top letter. 'Surprisingly good, I think. I'd like to have seen it. Purely out of scientific interest, of course.'

He raised his head. McLoughlin and the report had gone.

Sergeant Bob Rogers, who had switched to the afternoon shift after a two-day break and was now on duty at the desk, looked up as McLoughlin came in through the front doors. 'Ah, Andy. The very man.' He held up the description of Wally Ferris that had circulated round the county. 'This tramp you're looking for.'

'Found him. Matter of fact, as soon as I've seen the Inspector, I'm off after him again.'

'Good, then you can bring him in. He's on our missing persons' list.'

McLoughlin walked slowly across the floor. 'You've got Wally Ferris down as a missing person? But he's been on the road for years.'

Rogers frowned and turned the list for McLoughlin to look at. 'See for yourself. The description here fits the one you put out to a T.'

McLoughlin looked at what was written. 'Did Walsh see this?'

'Left it with him the first night.'

McLoughlin reached for the telephone. 'Do me a favour, Bob. The next time you see me too hung over to double-check what that bastard does' – he pointed to his chin – 'hit me here.'

*

He slouched in a chair in the Chief Inspector's office and watched the thin, bloodless lips dribble smoke. Imperceptibly, the face had changed. Where respect had once fleshed it with a genial wisdom, contempt had uncovered its malice. Phrases registered here and there – 'definitely Maybury' . . . 'young man recognised him' . . . 'in the ice house two weeks' . . . 'tramp must have seen him there' . . . 'you missed it completely' . . . 'writing a report' . . . 'domestic problems can't excuse your negligence' – but the bulk of what was said passed over McLoughlin's head. He stared unblinkingly at Walsh's face and thought about the teeth behind the smile.

Walsh jabbed his pipe stem angrily at his Sergeant. 'DS Robinson is out rounding up Wally Ferris now and by God, there are going to be no mistakes this time.'

The younger man stirred. 'What will you do? Show him a photograph of Maybury and suggest he was the dead man? Wally will agree with you just to get out of here.'

'Staines has already made the identification. If Wally confirms it, we're on safe ground.'

'How old is Staines?'

'Twenty-fiveish.'

'So he was fifteen when he last saw Maybury? And he claims to have recognised him in the dark? You'll never get a prosecution on that.'

'It's a good case,' said Walsh calmly. 'We've motive, means and opportunity, plus a wealth of circumstantial evidence. Mutilation to obscure identity, lamb bones to tempt scavengers to the ice house, the removal of the clothes to hinder investigation, Fred's obliteration of tracks and evidence. With all that and the positive IDs, she'll confess this time, I think.'

McLoughlin rubbed his unshaven jaw and yawned. 'You're forgetting the forensic evidence. That's not so easy to fabricate. Webster won't lie for you.'

Walsh's ferocious brows snapped together. 'What's that supposed to mean?'

'You know damn well – *sir*. The dead man was too old to be Maybury. And what happened to all the blood?'

Walsh eyed him with intense dislike. 'Get out of here!' he growled.

There was humour in the dark face. 'Are you going to tell her defence barrister to bugger off every time he asks a reasonable question?'

'The blood was on the clothes, presumably destroyed with them,' said Walsh tightly. 'As to Webster's interpretation of his skull X-rays, it is just that, an interpretation. The discrepancy between his position and mine is six years. I say fifty-four. He says sixty. He's wrong. Now get out.'

McLoughlin shrugged and stood up, reaching into his pocket and removing a piece of folded paper. 'The missing persons' list,' he said, dropping it on to the desk. 'I took a photocopy. It's yours. Keep it as a memento.'

'I've seen it.'

McLoughlin studied the pink scalp through the thinning hair. He remembered liking this man once. But that was before Anne's revelations. 'So I gather. Bob Rogers showed it to you the night the body was discovered. The case, for all it ever was a case, should have been over by the morning.'

Walsh stared at him for a moment, then took the paper and unfolded it. There were the same five names and descriptions, but with 'Since Traced' scrawled across Daniel Thompson's box. The two young women were of no consequence because of their sex, which left the Asian lad, Mohammed Mirahmadi, who was too young, and the semi-senile Keith Chapel, sixty-eight, who had walked out of his warden-run hostel five months before, wearing a green jacket, blue jumper and bright pink slacks. A tight, cold fist gripped at Walsh's insides. He laid the paper on the desk. 'The tramp didn't come into it until the next day,' he muttered. 'And how could this old man know about Streech Grange or the ice house?'

McLoughlin stabbed at the box with his finger. 'Look at his initials,' he said. 'Keith Chapel. K.C. I rang the warden of his hostel. The old boy used to ramble on endlessly about a garage he'd owned and what a success it was until a woman spread lies about him and he was forced to sell up. You knew all about it. Dammit, it was you who prompted Mrs Goode to tell the story.'

'Only by hearsay,' Walsh muttered. 'I never met the man. He was gone by the time Maybury disappeared. I thought Casey was a name. Everyone called him Casey. It's in the file as Casey.'

'You're damn right it's in the file. For a bit of hearsay, you gave it a hell of an airing. Great story, shame about the facts. Was that about the size of it?'

'It's not my fault if people thought she killed her parents. We just recorded what they told us.'

'Like hell you did! You fed it to them first. Jesus, you even hoicked it out for my benefit the other evening. And I believed it.' He shook his head. 'What did she do, for pity's sake? Laugh? Call you a dirty old man? Threaten to tell your wife?' He waited for a moment. 'Or couldn't she hide her revulsion?'

'You're suspended,' Walsh whispered. His hands quivered with a life of their own.

'What for? Uncovering the truth?' He slammed his palm on to the missing persons' list. 'You bastard! You had the bloody nerve to accuse me of negligence. Those trousers should have registered with you. You heard them described twice in twelve hours. How many men wear pink slacks, for Christ's sake? You knew a man had been reported missing wearing pink trousers. And it wasn't difficult to find Wally. If I'd had that information when I spoke to him – ' He shook his head angrily and reached for his briefcase. 'There's Dr Webster's final report.' He flung it on to the desk. 'Judging by the fact that Wally felt K.C.'s clothes were fit to wear, I think we can safely assume they were neither ripped with a knife nor blood-soaked. The poor old chap probably died of cold.'

'He went missing five months ago,' muttered the Inspector. 'Where was he for the first two months?'

'In a cardboard box in a subway, I should think, just like all the other poor sods this bloody awful society rejects.'

Walsh moved restlessly. 'And Maybury? You know all the answers. So where's Maybury?'

'I don't know. Living it up in France, I expect. He seems to have had enough contacts out there through his wine business.'

'She killed him.'

McLoughlin's eyes narrowed. 'The bastard ran away when the money dried up and left her and his two small children to carry the can. It was planned, for God's sake.' He was silent for a moment. 'I can't think of one good reason why he would have wanted to punish them but, if he did, he must have been praying for a shit like you to turn up.' He walked to the door.

'What are you going to do?' The words were barely above a whisper.

McLoughlin didn't answer.

*

On his way down the corridor, he bumped into Nick Robinson and Wally Ferris. He gave the old man a friendly punch on the shoulder. 'You might have left him his underpants, you old rogue.'

Wally shuffled his feet and cast sideways glances at both policemen. 'You lot gonna charge me then?'

'What with?'

'Didn't do no 'arm, not really. Wet frough I was wiv all that flamin' rain and 'im sittin' there quiet as a mouse. To tell you the trufe I didn't click to 'im bein' dead, not for a while. Put 'im down as one of my sort, but wiv a screw loose. There's a lot like that who've 'ad too much mefs and too little whisky. 'Ad quite a chat wiv 'im one way and anuvver.' He pulled a lugubrious face. ''E didn't 'ave no underpants, son, didn't 'ave nuffink 'cept the 'fings 'e'd folded up and put on the floor beside 'im.' He gave McLoughlin a sly peep. 'Didn't see no 'arm in taking 'em, not when 'e didn't need 'em and I did. Bloody parky, it was. I put 'em on over me own cloves.'

Nick Robinson, who had had no success in getting Wally to talk, snorted. 'You're saying he was sitting there stark naked, dead as a dodo, and you had a chat with him?'

'It was company,' muttered Wally defensively, 'an' it was a while before I got used to the gloom in the cave. You see some funny fings in my line of business.'

'Pink elephants mostly, I should think.' Robinson

looked enquiringly at McLoughlin. 'What's all this about the clothes?'

'You'll find out. What do you reckon he died of, Wally?'

'Gawd knows. Cold, I should fink. That place is freezin' wiv ve door closed, an' 'e'd wedged a brick against it. I 'ad to push pretty 'ard to get it open. It weren't nuffink nasty. 'E 'ad a smile on 'is face.'

There was a sharp indrawn breath from Robinson. 'But there was blood, wasn't there?'

Wally's old eyes looked shocked. 'Course there weren't no blood. I wouldn't 'ave stayed if there was blood. 'E was in lovely shape. On the white side per'aps but that was natural. It was dark wiv all the rain outside.' He wrinkled his nose. 'Whiffed a bit, but I didn't 'old it against 'im. Dare say I didn't smell too good meself.'

It was like something out of a Samuel Beckett play, thought McLoughlin. Two old men sitting in semi-darkness, chatting – one nude and dead, the other sodden, and in more ways than one. He didn't doubt for a minute that Wally had spent the night with K.C., rambling happily about this and that. Wally loved to talk. Was it a horrible shock, he wondered, to find in the sober morning light that he'd been chatting with a corpse? Probably not. Wally, he was sure, had seen many worse things. 'So did you shut the door again when you left?'

The old man pulled thoughtfully at his lower lip.

'Sort of.' He seemed to be weighing the problem in his mind. 'That's to say, I did the first time. The first time I shut it. Seemed to me 'e wanted to be left in peace or 'e wouldn't 'ave wedged a brick against it. Then that geezer in the shed gave me the whisky, an' I 'ad a few mouffuls, an' I got to finking about proper burials an' such. Seemed wrong some'ow to leave 'im wivout a chance of a few good words bein' said for 'im, wouldn't want it personally, so I nips back and opens the door. Reckoned 'e'd 'ave more chance of bein' found wiv ve door open.'

It would be cruel, McLoughlin thought, to tell him that by opening the door he had let in the heat, the dogs, the rats and putrefaction. He hoped Walsh wouldn't do it.

'And that,' Wally finished firmly, 'is all I knows. Can I go now?'

'Not likely,' said Nick Robinson, 'the Inspector wants a word with you.' He took a firm grip on Wally's arm and looked enquiringly at McLoughlin. 'How about filling me in?'

McLoughlin grinned evilly. 'Let's just say, you got your wires crossed, old son.'

Twenty-Three

HE FOLDED HIMSELF wearily into his car and sat for some time staring blankly through the windscreen. Some words of Francis Bacon kept repeating themselves in his mind like a memory-jerk mnemonic. 'Revenge is a kind of wild justice. The more man's nature runs to it, the more ought law to weed it out.' He rubbed his gaunt face. He had told Anne he sympathised with personal vengeance but he knew now that wasn't true. The end result of an 'eye for an eye' was a world gone blind. With a sigh, he fired the motor and drew out into the traffic.

He lived in a modern box on a large estate to the north-west of Silverborne where every house was depressingly similar and where individuality expressed itself only in what colour you chose to paint your front door. It had satisfied him once. Before he had seen Streech Grange.

'Hello, Andy,' said Kelly. She was standing irresolutely by the kitchen sink, mop in hand, washing the dirty dishes he had left untouched for ten days. He had forgotten how stunning she was and how easily that fabulous body had once been able to turn him on.

'Hello.'

'Pleased to see me?'

He shrugged. 'Sure. Look, you don't need to do those. I was planning to tackle them over the weekend. I haven't been around much this week.'

'I know. I've been trying to phone you.'

He went to the fridge and took out a piece of cheese from among the opened tins of furred tomatoes and sliced cling peaches. He held it out to her. 'Want some?' She shook her head, so he ate the whole lump before looking at his watch. 'I've a phone call to make, then I'll grab a quick shower before I go out.' He waved his arm to encompass the whole house. 'Take your time and take what you like.' He smiled without hostility. 'Except my books and my two boat paintings. You won't quibble over those, will you? You always said they were only good for gathering dust.' So much so that they had been relegated, along with him, to the spare room.

He was on his way to the stairs when his conscience smote and he turned round. 'Look, really, don't do the washing-up. It's not necessary. I'd have done it myself if I'd had the time.' He smiled again. 'You'll ruin your nail varnish.'

Her mouth trembled. 'Jack and me, it didn't work.'

She flung herself after him and burrowed her sweet-smelling head into his chest. 'Oh, Andy, I've missed you. I want to come home. I want to come home so much.'

An awful lethargy stole over him then, like the lethargy a drowning man must feel in the moment before he gives up. His eyes looked into the middle distance above her head, seeking straws. There were none. He held her for a second or two, then gently disentangled himself. 'Come home,' he said. 'It's yours as much as mine.'

'You're not angry?'

'Not at all. I'm glad.'

Her wonderful eyes shone like stars. 'Your mother said you would be.'

Straws, he thought, were useless to drowning men. It was the unquenchable longing for life that kept heads above water. 'I'll have that shower, then I'll be off,' he said. 'I'll fetch the books and the paintings tomorrow, and maybe the records I bought before we were married.' He glanced through the sitting-room door at the chromium coffee table, the oatmeal carpet, the net curtains, the white formica wall units and the dainty pastel three-piece suite, and he thought, no one has ever lived here. He shook his head. 'There's nothing else I want.'

She caught him by the arm. 'You *are* angry.'

His dark face cracked into a grin. 'No. I'm glad. I needed a push. I hate this place. I always have done.

It's so' – he sought for a word – 'sterile.' He looked at her with compassion. 'Like our marriage.'

She dug her fingers into his arm. 'I knew you'd bring that up, you bastard. But it's not my fault. You never wanted kids any more than I did.'

He removed her hands. 'That wasn't quite the sterility I was referring to.'

She was bitter. 'You've found someone else.'

He moved to the telephone, took a piece of paper from his pocket and dialled the number written on it. 'McLoughlin,' he said into the mouthpiece. 'We've identified the body. That's it, all over the newspapers tomorrow, so if he's any sense he'll lie low. Yes, it'll have to be tonight. Damn right, I want him. Let's just say I take what he did personally. So can you swing it?' He listened for a moment. 'Just make the point that they've got away with murder again. I'll be with you by ten.' He looked up and caught Kelly's eye.

Water had gathered in great droplets round the mascaraed lashes. 'Where will you go?'

'I don't know yet. Maybe Glasgow.'

Tears turned to anger, and her anger lashed out at him as it always had done. 'You've left that bloody job, haven't you? After all the begging I did for you to leave, you've left it because someone else asked you.'

'No one's asked me, Kelly, and I haven't left it, not yet.'

'But you will.'

'Maybe.'

'Who is she?'

He found he wanted to hurt her, so there must be some feeling left. Perhaps there always would be. Seven years, however sterile, had left their mark. 'She's my rose,' he said, 'my red, red rose.' And Kelly, who had heard enough of hated Rabbie Burns to last a lifetime, felt a knot of panic tighten round her heart.

Phoebe rocked Diana's shoulder and prodded her into wakefulness. 'We've got visitors,' she whispered. 'I need help.' Somewhere in the darkness behind her came the low growls of the dogs.

Diana squinted at her out of one eye. 'Turn the light on,' she said sleepily.

'No, I don't want them to know we're awake.' She bundled Diana's dressing-gown on to her chest. 'Come on, old girl, get a move on.'

'Have you called the police?' Diana sat up and shrugged her arms into the dressing-gown.

'No point. It'll be over one way or another long before the police get here.' Phoebe switched on a small torch and pointed it at the floor. 'Come on,' she urged, 'we haven't much time.'

Diana pulled on her slippers and padded after her. 'Why are the dogs here? Why aren't they outside? And where's McLoughlin?'

'He didn't come tonight.' She sighed. 'The one night we needed him, he didn't turn up.'

'So what are you planning to do?'

Phoebe lifted her shotgun from where she had propped it outside Diana's bedroom door. 'I'm going to use this,' she said, leading the way downstairs, 'and I don't want to shoot the dogs by mistake. It'll be their turn to have a go if the bastards manage to break in.'

'Lord, woman,' muttered Diana, 'you're not intending to kill anyone, are you?'

'Don't be a fool.' She crept across the hall and into her drawing-room. 'I'm going to scare the shit out of the creeps. They didn't get rid of me last time. They won't get rid of me now.' She gestured Diana to one side of the curtains and, switching off the torch, took up a position on the other side. 'Keep your eyes peeled. If you see anyone on the far side of the terrace, let me know.'

'I'm going to regret this,' Diana groaned, twitching the curtain aside and peering into the darkness. 'I can't see a bloody thing. How do you know they're out there?'

'Benson came in through the cellar window and woke me. I trained him to do it after the first time these yobs had a go at me.' She patted the old dog's head. 'You're such a good boy, aren't you. It's years since I've had you patrolling the grounds and you haven't forgotten.' The sound of the dog's tail swishing backwards and forwards across the carpet was loud in the quiet room. Hedges, unborn at the time of David Maybury's disappearance, crouched by his mistress's feet, muscles tensed for when his turn came. Phoebe scanned the wide terrace for signs of movement. 'Your eyes will soon adjust.'

'There *is* someone,' said Diana suddenly. 'By the right-hand wall. Do you see him?'

'Yes. There's another coming round Anne's wing.' She gripped her shotgun firmly. 'Can you unlock the windows without making a noise?'

For a brief moment Diana hesitated, then she shrugged and applied herself carefully to the key. Phoebe, she argued, knew all there was to know about hell. She had been there. She wouldn't willingly go back a second time. In any case, the adrenaline was racing in her as strongly as it was racing in Phoebe. It was backs-against-the-wall time, she thought, when everyone, even rabbits, showed their teeth. 'OK,' she whispered, as the lock clicked quietly open. She peeped past the edge of the curtain again. 'Oh, lord,' she breathed, 'there are dozens of them.'

Black figures crouched along the edge of the terrace like a troop of apes, but to think of them as such was to demean the animals. It is only man, with his single evolutionary advancement of reason, who takes pleasure in other people's pain. Diana's mouth went dry. There was something unbelievably chilling in mob hysteria where individual accountability was subordinate to the group.

'Hardly dozens; five, six at the most. When I say, "Now," open the door wide.' Phoebe gave a wild laugh. 'We'll put the old adage to the test and wait till we see the whites of their eyes. I've always wanted to try it.'

There was confusion in the huddled mass as they seemed to crowd together about the terrace wall, then separate again. 'What are they doing?' asked Diana.

'Pulling bricks off the top by the look of it. Keep your head down if they start throwing them.'

One of the crouching group seemed to be the leader. He used his arms to direct his troop, half to go down one side of the terrace, half to take the other side. 'Now,' muttered Phoebe urgently. 'I don't want them splitting up.'

Diana twisted the handle and thrust the door open. Phoebe was through it in a second, her tall figure melting into the shadows. She had raised the heavy stock to her shoulder and was about to sight down the barrel when one large hand clamped itself over her mouth and another plucked the gun from her grasp.

'I wouldn't if I were you, madam,' whispered Fred's soft voice in her ear. He kept his hand firmly over her mouth and used his forearm on her shoulder to force her to her knees. Bent double, he laid the shotgun noiselessly on the flagstones then, urging her upright again, he caught her round the waist as if she were no more than a piece of thistledown, and lifted her through the drawing-room windows. He felt Diana's presence, rather than saw it. 'Not a sound,' he cautioned her in a tight whisper, 'and close the window, if you please.'

'But, Fred – ' she began.

'Do as I say, Mrs Goode. Do you want madam hurt?'

Thoroughly shaken, Diana did as he said.

Ignoring Phoebe's biting teeth, Fred hauled her unceremoniously across the room and bundled her into the hall. Diana pursued him. 'What are you doing?' she demanded fiercely, buffeting him around his shoulders with bunched fists. 'Put Phoebe down this minute.' Benson and Hedges, alarmed by Diana's tone, threw themselves against Fred's legs.

'This door, too, Mrs Goode, if you please.'

She caught a handful of his sparse hair and tugged hard. 'Let her go,' she grunted.

With a sigh of pain, he swung round, carrying both women with him, and kicked the door to with his foot. Seconds later the French windows shattered inwards into a thousand pieces. 'There,' he said amiably, setting Phoebe carefully on the floor and removing his hand from her mouth. 'We're all right now, I think. If you wouldn't mind, Mrs Goode, that *is* a little painful. Thank you.' He fished a handkerchief from his pocket and wrapped it round his bleeding fingers. 'Good boys,' he murmured, fondling the dogs' muzzles, 'that's the ticket. I don't say I'm not annoyed about another window needing new glass, but this time we'll make sure it's paid for.' He opened the door. 'Would you excuse me, madam? I'd hate to miss the fun.'

Speechlessly, the two women watched his great bulk pad lightly across the broken glass and step out on to the terrace. Beyond, lit by brilliant moonlight, was a scene from Hieronymus Bosch. A grotesque tangle of misshapen figures writhed in hideous and noisy confusion upon the lawn. As Fred, with a blood-curdling roar, charged across the terrace and launched himself atop the mêlée, Phoebe took in the situation at a glance, whistled up Hedges and pointed to one flying fugitive who had managed to pull himself free. 'Off you go, boy.' Hedges, barking his excitement, bounded across the grass, bowled his man over and pranced about him, howling his achievement to the moon. Benson, not to be outdone, waddled on to the terrace, sat comfortably on his haunches and raised his old muzzle in joyous unison.

The row from dogs and flailing bodies was deafening.

'Men!' exclaimed Diana in Phoebe's ear and Phoebe, with adrenaline still running rampant in her bloodstream, burst into tears of laughter.

Twenty-Four

THE CONFUSION WAS short-lived. By the time Diana thought of switching on the drawing-room lights, the half dozen vandals had thrown in the towel and were being herded across the terrace by a panting semi-circle of McLoughlin, young PC Gavin Williams, out of uniform, Jonathan, Fred and Paddy Clarke.

'Inside,' ordered McLoughlin curtly. 'You're all nicked.'

Stripped of their menace by the glare of the overhead lamps, they were an unprepossessing bunch of shuffling, sweaty youths with surly faces and evasive eyes. Diana knew them all by sight as lads from the village, but she could put a name to only two of them, Eddie Staines and nineteen-year-old Peter Barnes, son of Dilys and brother to Emma. She looked them over in amazement. 'What have we ever done to you? I don't even know who most of you are.'

Barnes was a good-looking young man, tall, athletic, an ex-public school boy, now working in his father's print business in Silverborne. He sneered at her but didn't answer. Eddie Staines and the remaining four stared fixedly at the floor.

'It's a reasonable enough question,' said McLoughlin evenly. 'What have these ladies ever done to you?'

Barnes shifted his gaze. 'Which ladies?' he asked insolently. 'Do you mean the dykes?'

Barnes's voice, unaccented, interested McLoughlin. The shouts on the lawn had all carried the strangled vowels of the working class. A slight shake of his head kept Diana quiet. 'I was referring to Mrs Maybury and her friends,' he said in the same even tone. 'What have they ever done to you?' He searched the line of unresponsive faces. 'All right, for the moment you will be charged with aggravated assault on the owner of Streech Grange.'

'We never touched her,' complained Eddie Staines.

'Shut up,' said Barnes.

'Never touched who?'

'Her. Mrs Maybury.'

'I didn't say you did.'

'What was all that aggravated assault crap?'

'She's not the owner of Streech Grange,' McLoughlin pointed out. 'Mr Jonathan Maybury and his sister own this property.'

'Oh.' Eddie frowned. 'We thought it was the dyke's.'

McLoughlin arched an eyebrow. 'Do you mean Mrs Maybury?'

'You soft in the head, or what?'

'That,' murmured McLoughlin mildly, 'would appear to be your privilege. Eddie Staines, is it?'

'Yeah.'

'Keep your big mouth shut, you ignorant turd,' Barnes grated through clenched teeth.

A cold gleam lit McLoughlin's eyes. 'Well, well, Paddy, you were right. It's the jumped-up little oik who calls the shots. So what's his problem?'

'His mother,' was Paddy's laconic reply.

The boy threw him a murderous glance.

Paddy gave an indifferent shrug. 'I'm sorry for you, lad. If you'd had half your sister's sense, you'd have got by. You'd have raised two fingers to that stupid bitch with her twisted ambitions, and you'd have kept your sanity. Try asking yourself who Emma's really screwing when she comes up here and spreads her legs.' He glanced at McLoughlin. 'Ever heard the expression, a beggar on horseback? A beggar comes into a bit of money, buys a horse to raise himself up, only to find he can't ride the damn thing. That's Dilys Barnes. She came a cropper when she set her sights too high and moved the family into Streech. No harm in that, of course. It's a free country. But you don't, if you've any sense, treat one end of the village like muck because you think they're beneath you, while you lick the backsides of the other end and brandish your painfully transparent family tree under their noses. That way, you alienate everybody.'

Peter's face worked unpleasantly. 'Bastard!' he hissed.

Paddy let it pass. 'People laughed at her, of course. They would. Social climbing's a spectator sport in a place like this, and Dilys was never any good at it.' He stroked his chin. 'She's a very unintelligent woman. She couldn't grasp the first rule, that class is in inverse proportion to its relevance.' His eyes flickered over Peter. 'You'll need a translation, lad. The classier you are the less you have to talk about it.'

Barnes bunched his fists. 'Fuck you, Paddy. Cheap Irish trash, that's all you are.' Fleetingly, McLoughlin had the odd impression that the boy was enjoying himself.

A deep laugh rumbled in Paddy's throat. 'I'll take it as a compliment, lad. It's a long time since anyone's recognised the Irish in me.' He dodged a flying fist. 'Jesus Christ!' he said crossly. 'You're even more stupid than your mother, despite your fancy education and the puffed-up ideas she's given you.' He wagged a finger at Phoebe. 'It's your fault, woman. You made a laughing-stock of her and, believe me, you don't do that to the Dilys Barneses of this world. She has a poisoned callus on her soul for every slight, true or imagined, that she's suffered, and the biggest and the most venomous is the one you gave her. She's fed her venom to this little creep by the bucket-load.'

Phoebe looked at him in astonishment. 'I hardly

know her. She made a scene by the village pond once but I was far too angry to laugh.'

'Before David went missing,' he prompted. 'He did the real damage. He repeated the story in the pub and it was all round the village before you could say Jack Robinson.'

Phoebe stared at him blankly and shook her head.

He reached down to scratch the ears of the old Labrador lying at his feet. 'When Benson was little more than a puppy, Dilys caught him humping her Pekinese.' His eyes twinkled encouragingly. 'Harangued you over the telephone for not keeping him under better control.'

'Oh, good God!' Phoebe clapped her hands to her face. 'Not my Barnes pun. But it was a joke,' she protested. 'You're not going to tell me she took it personally. I was referring to her Peke. The damn thing was on heat and she let it out, reeking of pheromones.'

Paddy's great chuckle boomed about the room, stirring the heightened adrenalin into a responsive froth.

Phoebe's voice shook. 'It was all her fault anyway. She would keep calling Benson a dirty dog.' Quite unconsciously, she took on the refined tones of Dilys Barnes. '"Your dirty dog should be ashamed of himself, Mrs Maybury." God, it was funny. She couldn't bring herself to say that Benson had rogered her ghastly bitch.' She wiped her eyes on her sleeve. 'So I said, I was very sorry but, as she knew better than I, you couldn't stop dirty dogs poking into smelly barns.' She looked up, caught Diana's eye and laughed out loud. The room quivered.

Eddie Staines, not too bright but with a well-developed sense of humour, grinned broadly. 'That's good. Never heard it before. That why they call old man Barnes "the dirty dog" then? God, struth!' He doubled up as Peter Barnes, without any warning, swung a booted foot and kicked him in the groin. 'Ah, Jesus!' He backed away, clutching his balls.

McLoughlin watched this little sally with amused detachment. 'And presumably Dilys got lumbered with Smelly?' he said to Paddy.

The big man grinned. 'For a month or two, maybe. Far as I recall, Dirty Dog stuck to Tony longer than Smelly Barnes stuck to Dilys, but the damage was done. Takes herself too seriously, you see. When you're eaten up with frustrated ambition, there's no room for humour.' His eyes rested on the bitter young face of the boy. 'Respectability,' he said with heavy irony, 'it's a sickness with her. With this one, too. They won't be laughed at.'

And that, McLoughlin knew, was as far as Paddy could take him. He had been suspicious enough of Peter Barnes to set him up, but he had no proof that the lad had struck Anne any more than he had proof that Dilys initiated all the slander against Phoebe. 'She's far too cunning,' he had said that morning.

'She's a type. Pathologically jealous. You come across them now and then. They're usually women, invariably inadequate and their spite is always directed against their own sex because that's the sex they're jealous of. They are completely vicious. As often as not, the target is their own daughter.'

'So why single out Mrs Maybury?' McLoughlin had asked.

'Because she was the first lady of Streech and you buggers dropped her in the shit. For ten years, Dilys has been wetting herself because she can look down on Mrs Maybury of Streech Grange. God knows, she was never going to do it any other way.'

'What did she do?'

'Piled shit on shit, of course. People were ready to believe anything after you lot left, and murder was the least of the garbage Dilys fed them.'

'What a sewer you live in, Paddy.' McLoughlin spoke quietly, his voice level.

The big man surprised him. 'If it is, it's Phoebe's fault,' he had observed. 'She's the focus for it all. Whatever the rights and wrongs, any normal woman would have sold up and moved on. The Grange isn't worth the price she's had to pay for it.'

No, McLoughlin thought, Paddy was wrong about that. The Grange was worth whatever Phoebe had to pay, and she would go on paying because it was cheap at the price. The real cost was being borne by the people who loved her. He glanced across at her with a sudden irritation. God damn the woman! People loved her or hated her. The one thing no one seemed to feel was indifference.

'OK,' he said abruptly into the silence, 'you' – he jerked a finger at Eddie Staines – 'are going to listen to a few home truths. You're not the brightest thing on two legs but you have to be brighter than this dickhead here.' He scowled at Barnes, then held up a finger. 'Number one, Eddie. Mrs Maybury did not murder her parents. Colonel and Mrs Gallagher died because their brakes didn't work, and their brakes didn't work because K.C. hadn't serviced the car properly. Had he done so, he would have found the corroded brake hose. Got that?'

'Yeah, but who corroded it?' asked Eddie triumphantly. 'That's the question.'

'Read the coroner's report,' said McLoughlin wearily. 'Colonel Gallagher took the car to K.C. *because* the brakes felt soft. He wrote a note to that effect and the note, in his handwriting, is in the file. K.C. ignored it.' He held up a second finger. 'Number two. Mr David Maybury walked out of this house alive ten years ago. No one murdered him. He legged it because he had finally run through all of Mrs Maybury's money and he didn't fancy working for his living.'

'So who's arguing? Saw the bugger myself three months ago. Mind you, he's dead now.' Eddie glared at Phoebe. 'Hell of a way to get your own back, lady.'

McLoughlin held up a third finger. 'Number three, Eddie. That man wasn't David Maybury.'

He looked sceptical. 'Oh, yeah?'

'Oh, yeah. It was K.C. And it's not a matter for debate. It is a matter of proven fact.'

There was a long silence. Very slowly, recognition dawned. 'Hell, happen it was, too. Knew I knew him. But that Inspector of yours was damn sure it was Maybury.'

Paddy snorted. 'The only people who are ever damn sure of anything are idiots and politicians. Same difference, some would say.'

They could almost follow Eddie's thought processes in the contortions of his face. 'Still, I don't see it makes much difference. We're back to square one. If it was K.C. she did in this time, then stands to reason she did her old man in ten years ago. The only proof you thought she didn't was that I thought the old guy was him. You follow me?'

'I follow you,' McLoughlin told him. 'But the whole thing stinks. Didn't it occur to you that if it was Maybury this time, then you've been beating up on an innocent woman for ten years?'

'There was her parents – ' He broke off as his brain caught up with his mouth. 'Yeah, well, as I say, we're back to square one now.'

'Anything but. Mrs Maybury didn't kill K.C., Eddie. You did.'

'Cobblers!'

'He wasn't murdered. He died of cold, starvation and self-neglect. You were the last person to see him alive. If you'd offered him a hand he wouldn't be dead now. He needed help, and you didn't give it to him.'

'Now listen here, mister. You trying to set me up or something? The Inspector said he was stabbed in the gut.'

Between the Scylla of Barnes and the Charybdis of Walsh, was it any wonder, thought McLoughlin, that Phoebe had retreated into her fortress? Without a twinge of regret, he rode rough-shod over Walsh's thirty years on the Force. 'The Inspector greased a few palms and was over-promoted,' he said bluntly. 'It happens in the police just as it happens everywhere else. They'll give him early retirement as a result of this cock-up and get shot of him.'

'Jesus!' said Eddie, impressed by so much honesty from a policeman.

'You cretin,' muttered Peter Barnes. 'He's running bloody rings round you.'

McLoughlin ignored him. 'Number four, Eddie,' he went on. 'When you and the scum you associate with come up here for a spot of queer-bashing, you miss the mark. There are no queers living in Streech Grange. Who told you there were?'

'It's common knowledge.' Eddie looked uncomfortable. 'The three dykes. The three witches.

They're always called one or the other.' He darted a quick glance at Peter Barnes. 'Me, I'm not into queer-bashing.'

'I see.' McLoughlin transferred his attention to Barnes. 'So it's you who's not keen on queers.' He yawned suddenly and rubbed his eyes. 'What happened? Someone try it on at that school you went to?' He saw the sudden pinching round the boy's nostrils and his brooding face cracked into a grin. 'Don't tell me you enjoyed it, and now you're busting a gut to prove you didn't.'

'Fucking perverts,' the boy blurted out. 'They make me sick.' He spat at Phoebe. 'Fucking perverts. They should be locked up.' A well of loathing seemed to overflow. 'I hate them.'

Something malignant stirred in the depths of McLoughlin's dark eyes. He took a lightning step forward and clamped his hand across Barnes's mouth, digging his fingers and thumb into the soft flesh of the cheeks and forcing the boy up on to the balls of his feet. 'I find you extremely offensive,' he said softly. 'You're a moronic little psychopath and in my book it's the likes of you who should be locked up, not the likes of Oscar Wilde. The only contribution you will ever make to society will be a negative one when you pass your prejudices and your miserably inadequate IQ to a succeeding generation.' He levered Barnes up another inch. 'In addition it makes me very angry to hear these women referred to as perverts. Do you understand me?'

Barnes tried to speak but the words stuck in his throat. McLoughlin dug his fingers deeper and Barnes nodded vigorously.

'Good.' McLoughlin unlocked his fingers and pushed him away with the heel of his hand. He favoured Staines with a friendly smile. 'I hope you can see where all this is leading, Eddie. You do realise I am giving you the benefit of the doubt. I am assuming you genuinely believed these people were guilty of something.'

Eddie's good-humoured face puckered in worried concentration. 'Listen, mister, I just came along to see justice done. I swear to God that's all I came for.' He waved a hand at the other youths. 'That's all any of us came for. We got the call you were letting her off again. This queer-bashing stuff, that's Peter's kick.' He flicked a shy look at Phoebe and Diana. 'Jesus, it doesn't make sense anyway. If you're not queer, why do you go along with it?'

Diana rolled her eyes to Heaven. 'Do you know, I've often wondered that myself.' She turned to Phoebe. 'I've forgotten, old thing, why do we go along with it?'

Phoebe's rich laugh tumbled from her mouth. 'Don't be such a fool.' She looked at Eddie and raised her hands helplessly. 'We've never had a choice.

Hardly anyone ever speaks to us. Those who do, know all about us. Those who don't, assume whatever they want to assume. You have assumed we're gay.' Her eyes laughed softly. 'Bar copulating naked by the village pond with a series of men, I don't see how we could ever prove we weren't. In any case, would you have thought any better of us if you'd known we preferred men?'

'Yeah,' said Eddie with an appreciative wink. 'I bloody well would. Mind you,' he continued thoughtfully, 'none of this explains what happened to your old man. If the only reason he legged it was because the money'd dried up why didn't he get you off the hook when he read what was happening to you? It only needed a phone call to the police.'

There was an awkward silence.

'You talk as if the man had a clear conscience,' said McLoughlin at last. Out of the corner of his eye he saw the colour drain from Jonathan's set face. Dammit, he thought. Whichever way you turned, you were always caught between the rock and the hard place. 'It's sub judice, Eddie, which is why we've never released details. But I can tell you this, the minute the man re-surfaces he will be prosecuted.' He shrugged. 'For the moment you'll just have to take my word that it suits his book if everyone thinks he's dead. He was a villain. We'll find him one day.'

Even Paddy looked impressed.

'Jesus!' said Eddie again. 'Je – sus!' He scrunched

his foot on some broken glass. 'Listen, lady,' he offered, 'about these windows.' He gestured to the youths behind him. 'We'll clear up and put some new ones in. It's only fair.'

'You can do better than that, Eddie,' said McLoughlin pleasantly. 'It's names we want. Let's start with who attacked Miss Cattrell?'

Eddie shook his head with genuine regret. 'I can guess, same as you can, but if it's proof you need, then I can't help you. Like I said, queer-bashing doesn't turn me on.' He indicated one of his mates. 'Me and Bob took a couple of birds to the flicks that night. I don't know about the rest of them.'

A chorus of denials greeted this statement.

'Not me. I was watching telly with my folks.'

'Jesus, Eddie, I was round your sister's place. You bloody know that.'

'Fuck that. I only heard about it the next morning, same as you.'

Above their heads, McLoughlin caught Paddy's eye and saw his own disappointment mirrored there. The truth had an unmistakable ring about it. 'And what about you?' he asked Peter Barnes, knowing the little bastard would get away with it. 'Where were you?'

Barnes grinned. 'I was with my mother all evening until half-past midnight. Then I went to bed. She'll sign a statement if you ask her nicely.' He raised his middle finger and jabbed it in the air at Paddy. 'That's to you and your beggar crap, shithead.' He giggled and crooked his arm over his other fist, thrusting the finger skyward. 'And that's to your pathetic little set-up. What a joke. It was so fucking transparent, a blind man could have seen through it. You think I haven't creepy-crawled this place, seen the tame fuzz they've got watching over them?' He giggled again.

Alarm bells rang in McLoughlin's head. What the hell sort of psychopath was this boy? A Charles Manson freak? Je – sus! 'Creepy-crawled', he knew, was an expression the Charles Manson Family had used to describe the way they had entered Sharon Tate's house before they murdered her. 'So what brought you up here?' he asked, loosing some handcuffs from his jacket pocket. 'Gives you a buzz, does it, being arrested?'

'It sure as hell gives me a buzz to see you cretins screw up. That's got to be worth a slapped wrist and a fine any day. Hell, it was a bit of high spirits. Dad'll ante-up for the damage.'

There was a moment of silence before Jonathan's cool voice spoke from the shattered window. 'That seems reasonable,' he said. 'In return, I'll ante-up for the damage I'm going to do to you.'

It was the element of surprise that held everyone frozen. Like a slow motion sequence they watched him cross the room, release the safety catch on his mother's shotgun, shove the barrel between Barnes's legs and pull the trigger. The explosion left them deaf. Through a dense cloud of dust they saw, rather than heard, the screams that issued from the boy's writhing mouth. They watched the pool of liquid collect on the floor at his feet.

McLoughlin, stunned, tried to intervene, only to find a pair of thick arms clamped around his chest, holding him back. 'Jon!' he yelled, his voice muffled by the ringing echoes in his ears. 'For God's sake! He's not worth it!'

'Leave him be, sir.' It was Fred's voice. 'He's waited a long time for this.'

Shocked beyond belief, McLoughlin watched Jonathan Maybury drive Peter Barnes against the wall and ram the shotgun into the boy's screaming mouth.

Twenty-Five

GAP-TOOTHED WHERE the windows yawned, its finery ruffled by birdshot, the old house slumbered on, a silent witness to many worse things in its four-hundred-year history. Within half an hour, three patrol cars had arrived to ferry the culprits to the Station with PC Gavin Williams in firm but reluctant charge. 'It's down to you, Sarge,' he protested. 'You should be taking them in.'

'*Nn-nn.* They're all yours. I've some unfinished business here.'

'What do I do about Maybury, Sarge?'

McLoughlin folded his arms and didn't say anything.

'Barnes is bound to mention it.'

'Let him.'

'Shouldn't we charge Maybury?'

'What with? Accidental discharge of a licensed firearm?'

'You'll never get away with that. Eddie, for one, knows it wasn't an accident.'

McLoughlin was amused. 'I think you'll find Eddie's somewhat disenchanted with Peter Barnes. Apart from anything else, he doesn't take kindly to being set up as a fall-guy for Barnes's warped sense of humour. He tells me he and his mates were looking the other way when the accident happened.'

Williams looked worried. 'What do I say?'

'That's up to you, Gavin. I can't help you I'm afraid. When the gun went off, I had my back turned, taking down the names and addresses of the intruders. After that I couldn't see anything for dust.'

'Hell, Sarge!'

'I thought you were taking down the names and addresses of all the witnesses to the vandalism. It's standard police procedure in incidents of this sort.'

The constable pulled a wry face. 'And how do you explain Barnes's confession? I mean if it was just an accident why would he want to stitch himself up? Jesus, Sarge, he was so bloody terrified, he was pissing all over the floor.'

McLoughlin clapped him amiably on the shoulder. 'Is that right, Gavin? I couldn't see a damn thing because of the dust in my eyes. So don't ask me what loosened his tongue, because I couldn't tell you, unless it was the shock of the gun going off. Explosions react on people in different ways. Left me temporarily blinded but with my ears working overtime. Some sort of compensation effect, I imagine.

Couldn't see worth a damn, but I heard every word the little weasel said.'

Williams shook his head. 'I was in a blue funk. I thought the doctor shot his balls off.'

So did I, thought McLoughlin. So did I. And so it seemed had Peter Barnes. Swept back by the violence of Jonathan's assault and numbed by the blast of the shotgun between his legs which had discharged itself harmlessly into Phoebe's drawing-room wall, he had burst into tears of self-pity as Jonathan rammed the barrel against his teeth and threatened to pull the second trigger. 'I didn't mean to do it,' he babbled. 'I was creepy-crawling the house. I didn't mean to do it. I didn't mean to do it,' he screamed. 'She came back. The silly bitch came back. I had to hit her.'

Jonathan's finger whitened on the trigger. 'Now tell me about nine years ago.'

'Oh, God, help me! Somebody help me!' The front of his trousers was saturated with urine.

'TELL ME!' roared Jonathan, his face white and drawn with rage. 'Someone ransacked this house. WHO WAS IT?'

'It was my dad,' the boy screamed, sobbing convulsively. 'He got drunk with some friends.' His eyes widened alarmingly as Jonathan started to squeeze the trigger. 'It's not my fault. Mum's always giggling about it. It's not my fault. It was my dad.' His eyes rolled into the back of his head and he collapsed on the floor.

Jonathan lowered the gun and looked across at McLoughlin. 'We never knew who it was. Mum, Jane and I locked ourselves in the cellar and waited till they'd gone. I have never been so frightened in my life. We could hear them shouting and breaking all the furniture. I thought they were going to kill us.' He shook his head and looked down at the twitching boy. 'I swore I'd make them pay if I ever found out who they were. They used the house as a toilet and wrote "Murdering Bitch" all over the walls in tomato ketchup. I was only eleven. I thought it was blood.' His jaw tightened.

McLoughlin shook off Fred's bear hug and started to slap the dust out of his clothes. 'That was a hell of a close shave, Jon. What happened, for God's sake? Did you trip on some broken glass or something?'

'That's it, Sergeant,' said Fred impassively. 'I was watching. Could have been quite nasty if young Jon hadn't kept his wits about him.'

'Yes, well, do something with the flaming thing before it goes off again.' He watched Fred take the gun, break it open and remove the second cartridge. 'Oh, for Christ's sake, Barnes, get up and stop belly-aching. You're damn lucky Dr Maybury had the good sense to keep the barrel down.' He hauled him to his feet and snapped on the handcuffs. 'You're under arrest. Constable Williams will read you your rights.'

The boy was still sobbing. 'He tried to kill me.'

'There's gratitude for you,' said Paddy, shaking

plaster from his hair. 'Jon nearly blows his own foot off to protect the little scum and all he can do is accuse him.' He looked at Jonathan's stricken face, saw the obvious danger signals, and glanced across at Fred with a Gary Lineker finger to eye gesture.

Calmly Fred took the boy's arm and steered him towards the door into the hall. 'I suggest we check on the rest of the house, sir. I don't like the idea of Miss Cattrell alone upstairs.' He closed the door firmly behind them.

Half an hour, thought McLoughlin, and it seemed more like a year. He smoothed the stubble on his jaw and stared thoughtfully at the young constable. 'I can't help you, Gavin. You're a good copper and it's not my place to tell you what to do. You must make your own decision.'

The young man glanced through the drawing-room door where Fred was helping Phoebe restore order. 'I agreed to do the patrols with you because of him and the old lady really. They're decent folks. Seemed wrong to abandon them to yobbos.'

'I agree,' said McLoughlin dryly.

He frowned. 'If you want my opinion, the Chief Inspector's got some explaining to do on this one. You should hear what Molly has to say about when she and Fred first came here. The house had been totally vandalised. Mrs Maybury and the two kids were living in one bedroom which Miss Cattrell and the lad, Jonathan, had managed to clean up. According to Molly, Mrs Maybury and Jane were so shell-shocked by the whole thing they didn't know if they were coming or going. Molly says you could still smell the piss even after three months, and the mould on the tomato ketchup had started to grow inwards, into the walls. It took them weeks to scrub the place clean. What's the Chief got against them, Sarge? Why wouldn't he believe them?'

Because, thought McLoughlin, he couldn't afford to. It was Walsh himself who, all those years ago, had created the climate of hate in which this woman and her two young children could be terrorised. For him, and for whatever reason, Phoebe had always been guilty, and his prolonged and hostile hounding of her had led inevitably to others meting out justice when he failed to prove it himself. 'He's a small man, Gavin,' was all he said.

'Well, I don't like it and I'm going to say something. It's not what I joined the Force for. I asked Molly why they didn't call the police in when it happened, and do you know what she said? "Because madam knew better than to ask help from the enemy."' He scuffed his foot shyly against the floor. 'I'm planning to take Molly and Fred around and about a bit, no fuss, nothing like that, but I'd like them to know we're not all enemies.'

McLoughlin smiled down on the bent head. If

Williams wanted to wrap up his affection in the guise of community policing, that was fine with him. 'I'm told she makes a damn good lardy cake.'

'Bloody brilliant!' The young eyes sparkled. 'You should try some.'

'I will.' He pushed the lad towards the front door and the waiting cars. 'It won't do Eddie and his mates any harm to spend the night in a police cell, so book 'em and lock 'em up. If Mrs Maybury wants to press charges in the morning, then we'll fill out all the sheets then. But I don't think she will. She laid the first stone of a bridge this evening.'

'And Barnes?'

'Keep him on ice for me. I'll be in first thing tomorrow morning. I'll take his statement myself. And Gavin?'

'Yes?'

'He would have talked anyway. He couldn't have resisted it. He's too arrogant to keep quiet for long. You'll see. Tomorrow, without any pressure from me, he'll give us the whole works.'

A weight seemed to drop from the lad's shoulders. 'Yeah. Anything else I should do?'

'Bell his parents in a couple of hours, three o'clock, say, tell them we're holding their son, and get them down to the Station. But, whatever you do, don't let them talk to him. Keep them waiting through the dark hours till I get there. Just tell them he's confessed to ten years of persecution. I want them softened up.'

Williams looked doubtful. 'You'll never get a prosecution after ten years, will you?'

'No.' McLoughlin grinned. 'But for a few hours, I can sure as hell make them think I will.'

Paddy was another who took his leave reluctantly. 'You'll have to come out of retreat now,' he told Phoebe and Diana. 'One way and another the door's been forced. It's a damn good thing too. It's time you made a bit of an effort. Come down to the pub tomorrow. It's as good a place as any to start.' He shook hands with McLoughlin. 'Jack in the job, Andy, and join me in starting a brewery. It'll need a strong hand at the helm.'

'I don't know the first thing about brewing.'

'I wouldn't want you for your brewing skills. That's my province. Organise the business, find me customers, get the whole thing rolling. You'd be good at that. I need someone I can trust.'

McLoughlin grinned. 'You mean someone Customs and Excise trusts? You're too anarchic for me, Paddy. I'd be a nervous wreck in three months, trying to remember what I was supposed to be hiding.'

Paddy gave a roar of laughter and punched him on the shoulder. 'Think about it, old son. I enjoy your company.' He left.

Jonathan had retreated to an armchair where he sat in embarrassed silence, studiously avoiding everyone's gaze. His anger had long since abated and he was desperately trying to come to terms with what he had done to Peter Barnes. He could find no excuses for his violence. Fred coughed politely. 'If there's nothing more I can do, madam,' he said to Phoebe, 'I'll be heading back to the Lodge. The wife and young Jane will be wondering how we got on.' Jane had been sleeping at the Lodge with Molly for the past few nights while Fred patrolled the grounds with McLoughlin and PC Williams.

'Oh, Fred,' said Phoebe with genuine contrition, 'I'm so sorry. I am so sorry. I never really thought you were one of them. It was the shock. You do believe that, don't you? I'll take you down for your tetanus tomorrow.'

Fred looked at his bandaged hand, washed, disinfected, cried over and dressed by Phoebe and Diana amidst a welter of apology. 'I think, madam,' he said severely, 'that if one more word is said on this matter I shall be forced to give in my notice. I can stand a lot of things, but I can't stand fuss. Is that understood? Good. Now, if you will excuse me?'

'I'll drive you,' said Phoebe immediately.

'I'd rather the young doctor drove me, if that's all right. There's something I'd like his opinion on.'

The door closed behind them.

Phoebe turned away to hide the dampness in her eyes. 'God broke the mould after He made Fred and Molly,' she said gruffly. 'They never deserved any of this and yet they've stuck with us through thick and thin. I've made up my mind, Di,' she went on fiercely,

'I will brave that wretched pub tomorrow. Someone's got to make the first move and it might as well be me. Fred's been going there for years and no one, apart from Paddy, ever talks to him. I'm damn well going to do something about it.'

Diana looked at her friend's furious face. 'What, for instance? Hold your shotgun on them till they agree to talk?'

Phoebe laughed. 'No. I am going to let bygones be bygones.'

'Well, in that case, I'll come with you.' She looked at McLoughlin. 'Can we do that? It's all over now, isn't it? The Inspector was very curt over the phone but he seems to have absolved us.'

He nodded. 'Yes, you're absolved.'

'Was it suicide?' asked Phoebe.

'I doubt it. He was a confused old man whose memories of Streech survived all his other memories. I think he made his way back here, looking for somewhere to die.'

'But how could he possibly have known where the ice house was?'

'From the pamphlets your husband had printed. If you're touting for tourists, a garage is the obvious place to leave them. On paper, K.C. probably knew this garden better than you did.'

'Still. To remember it after all this time.'

'But the memory is like that,' said Diana. 'Old people remember every detail of their childhood but can't remember what they had for breakfast.' She shook her head. 'I never knew the man but I've always felt very bitter about what happened to Phoebe's parents and the lies he told afterwards. Still' – she shrugged – 'to die like that, alone and with nothing. It's very sad. It may sound silly, but I wish he hadn't taken his clothes off. It makes it worse, somehow, as if he were pointing out the futility of living. Naked we're born and naked we die. I have this awful feeling that, for him, everything that happened in between was worthless.'

McLoughlin stretched. 'I wouldn't get too sentimental about that, if I were you, Mrs Goode. We've only Wally's word for it that the corpse was nude. I think he's probably a little ashamed of himself. There's a world of difference between taking some unwanted, folded clothes and undressing a corpse to rob it.' He looked at his watch. 'Anything else?'

'We'd like to thank you,' said Phoebe.

'What for?'

'Everything. Jane. Jonathan. Anne. Us.'

He nodded and made for the door into the hall. The two women looked at each other.

'You will be coming back, won't you?' said Diana in a rush.

He laughed quietly. 'If I have to, I will.'

'What's that supposed to mean?'

Phoebe chuckled. 'I think it means that he wasn't

planning on leaving. He can't come back if he's never gone, can he?'

The gun-shot and shouting had dragged Anne from a deep barbiturate-induced sleep to a lighter sleep where dreams enacted themselves in glorious Technicolor. There were no nightmares, just an endless parade of places and faces, some only half-remembered, which fluttered across the screen of her sleeping mind in surrealistic juxtaposition. And, somewhere, irritatingly, McLoughlin was tapping the double-glazing in the windows of a huge citadel and telling her it needed two people to lift it if they weren't to be buried alive.

She sat up with a start and looked at him. Her bedside light was on. 'I dreamt that Jon and Lizzie were getting married,' she said, isolating the one memory from the cloud of others which vanished for ever.

He pulled up the wicker chair and sat on it. 'Given time and room to breathe, perhaps they will.'

She thought about that. 'You don't miss much, do you?'

'That depends. We've caught your assailant.' He stretched out his long legs and gave her all the details. 'Paddy wants me to join him in starting a brewery.'

She smiled. 'Do you like him?'

'He's a bastard.'

'But do you like him?'

He nodded. 'He's his own man. I like him very much.'

'Will you join him?'

'I shouldn't think so. It would be too easy to get addicted to that Special of his.' He looked at her through half-closed lids. 'Jon's going back to London tomorrow. He asked me to find out if you wanted your love letters returned. He says he can try and fish them out before he goes.'

She looked at her hands. 'Do you know where he's put them?'

'I gather they're in a fissure in the old oak tree behind the ice house. He's a little worried about whether or not he can retrieve them. He asked me to give him a hand.' He studied her face. 'Should I, Cattrell?'

'No. Let them stay there.' She raised her head to look at him. 'When I'm firing on all cylinders again I'll take some cement and stick it into every crack in the oak tree so the damn things never see the light of day again. I had to ask Jon to hide them – he was the only one there when Walsh took me away – but he's the last person in the world I want looking at them. Oh God, I wish they *were* love letters.' She fell silent.

'What are they?'

'Photographs.'

'Of David Maybury?' She nodded. 'After Phoebe

had killed him?' She nodded again. 'One of your famous insurance policies, I suppose.'

She sighed. 'I never thought we'd get away with it. I kept a record in case the body was found and Phoebe needed a defence.' Her face clouded. 'I developed them myself. Awful, awful pictures, showing David two weeks after Phoebe killed him, showing Phoebe herself, looking so damn mad you wouldn't believe it was the same woman, showing what the vandals did to the house, showing the tomb I built in the cellar. I never want to see them again.'

'Tell me, Anne.'

She took a deep breath. 'David came back the night after the house had been ransacked. It was inevitable he would turn up some time, but to choose that night – ' She shook her head. 'Not that he knew, of course. He wouldn't have come back if he'd known. The doors were barred with stacked-up furniture, so he came in through the cellar window. Phoebe was in the kitchen and she heard him stumbling around in the dark downstairs.' Her eyes searched his. 'You must understand how frightened she was. She thought the drunks had come back to kill her and the children.'

'I do understand.'

'She picked up the heaviest thing she could find, the wood-chopping axe by the Aga, and when he came through the cellar door she split his head in two.'

'Did she recognise him?'

'You mean, did she know it was David when she killed him? I shouldn't think so. It all happened too fast. She certainly recognised him afterwards.'

There was a long silence. 'You could have brought the police in then,' he said at last. 'With the evidence of what had happened the night before, she could have pleaded self-defence. She would have got off with no trouble at all.'

She stared at her hands. 'I would have done if I'd known about it. But Jon didn't phone me for a fortnight.' She raised her hands to her eyes to block out the nightmare pictures. 'Phoebe has absolutely no recollection of that two-week period. The only thing she had the sense to do before she went into shock was to shove David's body back down the cellar steps and bolt the door. The children have never known about it. Jon only phoned me because for two weeks she had kept them all locked in her bedroom, living on a diet of tinned food that she'd rescued from the larder. He took the key while she was asleep, let himself out of the bedroom and kept ringing my number till I answered.' Tears welled in her eyes, spilling over her tired lids, as she remembered. 'He was only eleven, hardly more than a baby really, and he said he was doing his best but he thought Jane and Mummy needed a proper person to look after them.' She dashed the tears from her eyes. 'Oh God, I'm sorry. It just makes me cry every time I think of it. He must have been so frightened. I came straight down.'

She looked suddenly very tired. 'I couldn't possibly go to the police, McLoughlin. She was completely off her head and Jon and Jane would hardly speak. I thought Phoebe had vandalised the house herself *after* killing David. There was no way of proving which came first. And if I thought that, what the hell conclusion would Walsh have come to? It was a nightmare. All I could think of doing was to put the children before everything else, because that is what Phoebe's father had asked me to do when he set up the trust. And putting them first, I decided, meant keeping their mother out of a prison hospital.' She sighed. 'So, over a period of days, I bought small quantities of grey stone from DIY shops all over South Hampshire. I had to be able to fit it in Phoebe's car. I didn't dare get anyone to deliver. Then I locked myself in the cellar and bricked that revolting, stinking mess that had once been David behind a fake wall.' She gagged on bile. 'He's still there. The wall has never been disturbed. Diana went down and checked after Fred found that thing in the ice house. We were so afraid he had somehow got out.'

'Does Fred know?'

'No. Only Diana, Phoebe and I.'

'And Phoebe knows what she did?'

'Oh, yes. It took a while, but she remembered it all

in the end. She wanted to confess about four years ago, but we persuaded her out of it. Jane at fourteen was down to four and a half stone. Diana and I said her peace of mind was more important than Phoebe's.' She took another deep breath. 'It meant we've never been able to sell the Grange, of course. Sod's Law predicts that whoever buys it will want to rip the guts out of the cellar to put in a jacuzzi.' She smiled faintly. 'At times it has been quite unbearable. But when I look at the three of them now, I know it was all worth it.' Her damp eyes pleaded for a reassurance she would never put into words.

He took one of her hands. 'What can I say, woman? Except that next time I tell you how to run your life, remind me that you know best.' He played with her fingers, pulling at them. 'I could use your photographs of the house to smash Walsh and Barnes for what they've done to Phoebe.'

'No,' she said immediately. 'No one knows they exist, except you and me. Phoebe and Diana don't know. Let's leave them where they are. I see death too often in my nightmares as it is. Phoebe wouldn't want it, anyway. Walsh was right. She did kill David.'

He nodded and looked away. It was a while before he spoke. 'My wife came back to me tonight.'

She forced herself to smile. 'Are you glad?'

'As a matter of fact I am.' She tried to extract her hand tactfully from his, but he wouldn't let her.

'Then I'm pleased for you. Will it work this time, do you think?'

'Oh, yes. I'm toying with the idea of leaving the police force. What do you think?'

'It'll make things easier at home. The divorce rate amongst policemen is phenomenal.'

'Forget the practicalities. Advise me, for myself.'

'I can't,' she said. 'It's something you will have to decide for yourself. All I can say is that, whatever decision you come to, make sure it's one you can live with.' She looked at him shyly. 'I was mistaken before, you know. I think you were probably right to go into the police, and I think the police would be the poorer without you.'

He nodded. 'And you? What will you do now?'

She smiled brightly. 'Oh, the usual. Storm a few citadels, seduce a sculptor or two.'

He grinned. 'Well, before you do that, will you give me a hand in the cellar one night? I think it's time that wall came down, and David Maybury left this house for good. Don't worry. It won't be unpleasant. After nine years there will be very little left and this time we'll get rid of him properly.'

'Wouldn't it be better to leave well alone?'

'No.'

'Why not?'

'Because, Cattrell, if Phoebe isn't freed of him, you and Diana will be tied to this house for ever.'

She looked into a private darkness beyond him. How little he understood. They would always be tied now. It had been too long. They had lost the confidence to start again.

He gave her fingers a last squeeze and stood up. 'I'd better make tracks for bed then.'

She nodded, her eyes over-bright. 'Goodbye, McLoughlin. I wish you luck, I really do.'

He scratched the side of his face. 'I suppose you couldn't lend me a pillow? And maybe a toothbrush from the bathroom?'

'What for?'

'I've got nowhere to sleep, woman. I told you, my wife came back. I'm damned if I'm spending another seven years with someone whose favourite colour is beige. I walked out.' He watched her smile. 'I thought I'd shack up with a friend this time.'

'What sort of friend?'

'Oh, I don't know. How about a cynical, selfish intellectual snob, who can't sustain relationships, doesn't conform and embarrasses people?'

She laughed quietly. 'It's all true.'

'Of course it is. We've a lot in common. It's not a bad description of me either.'

'You'd hate living here.'

'About as much as you do, probably. How does Glasgow sound?'

'What would we do there?'

'Explore, Cattrell, explore.'

Her eyes danced. 'Are you going to take no for an answer, McLoughlin?'

'No.'

'Well what the hell are you waiting for then?'

THE
Sculptress

For Roland and Philip

Prologue

Southern Evening Herald, January, 1988

Twenty-Five Years for Brutal Murders

At Winchester Crown Court yesterday, Olive Martin, 23, of 22 Leven Road, Dawlington, was sentenced to life imprisonment for the brutal murders of her mother and sister, with a recommendation that she serve twenty-five years. The judge, who referred to Martin as 'a monster without a grain of humanity', said that nothing could excuse the savagery she had shown to two defenceless women. The murder of a mother by her daughter was the most unnatural of crimes and demanded the strongest penalty that the law could impose. The murder of a sister by a sister was no less heinous. 'Martin's butchery of the bodies,' he went on, 'was an unforgivable and barbarous desecration that will rank in the annals of crime as an act of supreme evil.' Martin showed no emotion as sentence was passed. . .

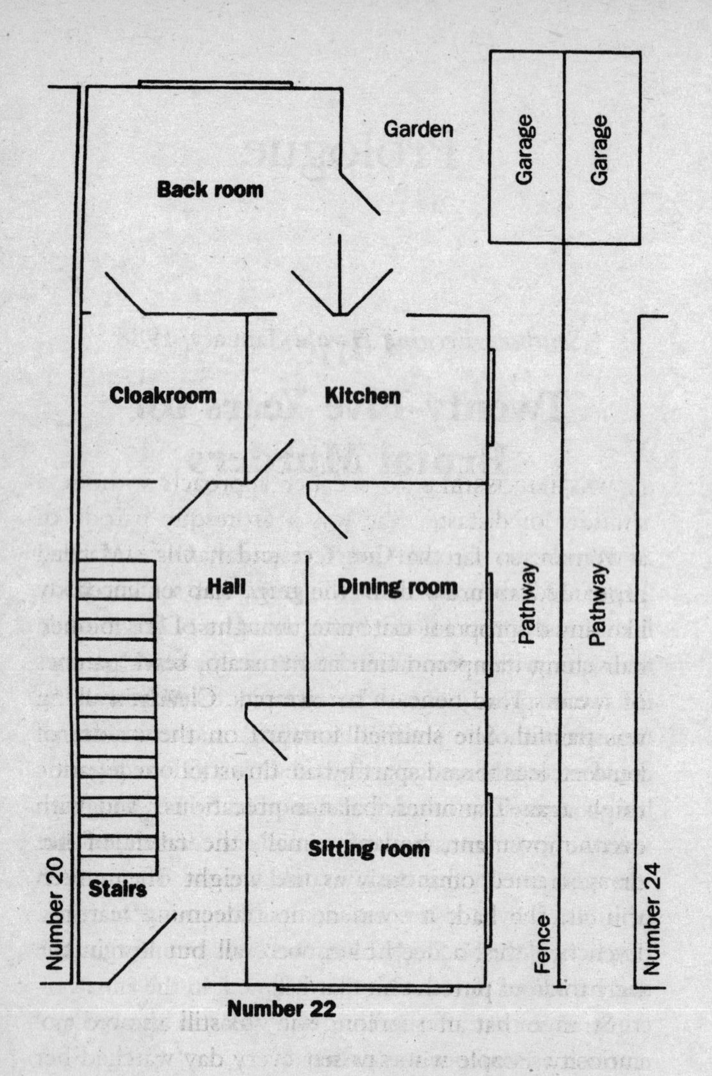

Ground-floor plan of Number 22 Leven Road, Dawlington, Southampton, as it was at the time of the murders. Drawn by the present owner for Miss Rosalind Leigh.

One

IT WAS IMPOSSIBLE to see her approach without a shudder of distaste. She was a grotesque parody of a woman, so fat that her feet and hands and head protruded absurdly from the huge slab of her body like tiny disproportionate afterthoughts. Dirty blonde hair clung damp and thin to her scalp, black patches of sweat spread beneath her armpits. Clearly, walking was painful. She shuffled forward on the insides of her feet, legs forced apart by the thrust of one gigantic thigh against another, balance precarious. And with every movement, however small, the fabric of her dress strained ominously as the weight of her flesh shifted. She had, it seemed, no redeeming features. Even her eyes, a deep blue, were all but lost in the ugly folds of pitted white lard.

Strange that after so long she was still an object of curiosity. People who saw her every day watched her progress down that corridor as if for the first time. What was it that fascinated them? The sheer size of a woman who stood five feet eleven and weighed over twenty-six stones? Her reputation? Disgust? There were no smiles. Most watched impassively as she passed, fearful perhaps of attracting her attention. She had carved her mother and sister into little pieces and rearranged the bits in bloody abstract on her kitchen floor. Few who saw her could forget it. In view of the horrific nature of the crime and the fear that her huge brooding figure had instilled in everyone who had sat in the courtroom she had been sentenced to life with a recommendation that she serve a minimum of twenty-five years. What made her unusual, apart from the crime itself, was that she had pleaded guilty and refused to offer a defence.

She was known inside the prison walls as the Sculptress. Her real name was Olive Martin.

Rosalind Leigh, waiting by the door of the interview room, ran her tongue around the inside of her mouth. Her revulsion was immediate as if Olive's evil had reached out and touched her. *My God*, she was thinking, and the thought alarmed her, *I can't go through with this.* But she had, of course, no choice. The gates of the prison were locked on her, as a visitor, just as securely as they were locked on the inmates. She pressed a shaking hand to her thigh where the muscles were jumping uncontrollably. Behind her, her all but empty briefcase, a testament to her lack of preparation for this meeting, screamed derision at her ill-considered assumption that conversation with Olive could develop like any other. It had never occurred to her, not for one moment, that fear might stifle her inventiveness.

Lizzie Borden took an axe and gave her mother forty whacks. When she saw what she had done, she gave her father forty-one. The rhyme churned in her brain, over and over, numbingly repetitive. *Olive Martin took an axe and gave her mother forty whacks. When she saw what she had done she gave her sister forty-one . . .*

Roz stepped away from the door and forced herself to smile. 'Hello, Olive. I'm Rosalind Leigh. Nice to meet you at last.' She held out her hand and shook the other's warmly, in the hope, perhaps, that by demonstrating an unprejudiced friendliness she could quell her dislike. Olive's touch was token only, a brief brush of unresponsive fingers. 'Thank you.' Roz spoke to the hovering prison officer briskly. 'I'll take it from here. We have the Governor's permission to talk for an hour.' *Lizzie Borden took an axe . . .* Tell her you've changed your mind. *Olive Martin took an axe and gave her mother forty whacks . . .* I can't go through with this!

The uniformed woman shrugged. 'OK.' She dropped the welded metal chair she was carrying carelessly on to the floor and steadied it against her knee. 'You'll need this. Anything else in there will collapse the minute she sits on it.' She laughed amiably. An attractive woman. 'She got wedged in the flaming toilet last year and it took four men to pull her out again. You'd never get her up on your own.'

Roz manoeuvred the chair awkwardly through the doorway. She felt at a disadvantage, like the friend of warring partners being pressured into taking sides. *But Olive intimidated her in a way the prison officer never could.* 'You will see me using a tape-recorder during this interview,' she snapped, nervousness clipping the words brusquely. 'The Governor has agreed to it. I trust that's in order.'

There was a short silence. The prison officer raised an eyebrow. 'If you say so. Presumably someone's taken the trouble to get the Sculptress's agreement. Any problems, like, for example, she objects violently' – she drew a finger across her throat before tapping the pane of glass beside the door which allowed the officers a clear view of the room – 'then bang on the window. Assuming she lets you, of course.' She smiled coolly. 'You've read the rules, I hope. You bring nothing in for her, you take nothing out. She can smoke your cigarettes in the interview room but she can't take any away with her. You do not pass messages for her, in or out, without the Governor's permission. If in doubt about anything, you refer it to one of the officers. Clear?'

Bitch, thought Roz angrily. 'Yes, thank you.' But it wasn't anger she felt, of course, it was fear. Fear of being shut up in a confined space with this monstrous creature who stank of fat woman's sweat and showed no emotion in her grotesquely bloated face.

'Good.' The officer walked away with a broad wink at a colleague.

Roz stared after her. 'Come in, Olive.' She chose the chair furthest from the door deliberately. It was a statement of confidence. She was so damn nervous she needed a wee.

The idea for the book had been delivered as an ultimatum by her agent. 'Your publisher is about to wash his hands of you, Roz. His precise words were, "She has a week to commit herself to something that will sell or I shall remove her from our lists." And, though I hate to rub your nose in it, I am within a whisker of doing the same thing.' Iris's face softened a little. Berating Roz, she felt, was like beating your head against a brick wall, painful and completely ineffective. She was, she knew, the woman's best friend – her *only* friend, she thought sometimes. The barrier of barbed wire that Roz had erected around herself had deterred all but the most determined. People rarely even asked after her these days. With an inward sigh, Iris threw caution to the winds. 'Look, sweetheart, you really can't go on like this. It's unhealthy to shut yourself away and brood. Did you think about what I suggested last time?'

Roz wasn't listening. 'I'm sorry,' she murmured,

her eyes maddeningly vacant. She saw the irritation on Iris's face and forced herself to concentrate. Iris, she thought, had been lecturing again. But really, Roz wondered, why did she bother? Other people's concern was so exhausting, for her and for them.

'Did you ring that psychiatrist I recommended?' Iris demanded bluntly.

'No, there's no need. I'm fine.' She studied the immaculately made-up face, which had changed very little in fifteen years. Someone had once told Iris Fielding that she looked like Elizabeth Taylor in *Cleopatra*. 'A week's too short,' Roz said, referring to her publisher. 'Tell him a month.'

Iris flicked a piece of paper across her desk. 'You've run out of room to manoeuvre, I'm afraid. He's not even prepared to give you a choice of subject. He wants Olive Martin. Here's the name and address of her solicitor. Find out why she wasn't sent to Broadmoor or Rampton. Find out why she refused to offer a defence. And find out what made her commit the murders in the first place. There's a story there somewhere.' She watched the frown on Roz's face deepen and shrugged. 'I know. It's not your sort of thing, but you've brought this on yourself. I've been pressing you for months to produce an outline. Now it's this or nothing. To tell you the truth, I think he's done it on purpose. If you write it, it will sell, if you refuse to write it because it's pure sensationalism, then he's found a good excuse to drop you.'

Roz's reaction surprised her. 'OK,' she said mildly, taking the piece of paper and tucking it into her handbag.

'I thought you'd refuse.'

'Why?'

'Because of the way the tabloids sensationalized what happened to *you*.'

Roz shrugged. 'Maybe it's time someone showed them how to handle human tragedy with dignity.' She wouldn't write it, of course – she had no intention of writing anything any more – but she gave Iris an encouraging smile. 'I've never met a murderess before.'

Roz's application to visit Olive Martin for the purposes of research was passed on by the Prison Governor to the Home Office. It was several weeks before permission was given in a grudging processed letter from a civil servant. While Martin had consented to the visits, she reserved the right at any time to withdraw consent, without reason and without prejudice. It was emphasized that the visits had been authorized only on the understanding that there would be no breaches of the prison regulations, that the Governor's word would be final in all circumstances, and that Ms Leigh would be held liable should she contribute in any way to an undermining of prison discipline.

Roz found it hard to look at Olive. Good manners and the woman's ugliness precluded staring and the monstrous face was so flat, so unresponsive, that her eyes kept sliding off it like butter off a baked potato. Olive, for her part, watched Roz greedily. Attractive looks put no such limitations on staring – quite the reverse, they invite it – and Roz was, in any case, a novelty. Visitors were rare in Olive's life, particularly ones who came without the reforming baggage of missionary zeal.

After the cumbersome business of getting her seated, Roz gestured towards the tape-recorder. 'If you remember, I mentioned in my second letter that I'd like to record our chats. I presumed when the Governor gave permission for it that you'd agreed.' Her voice was pitched too high.

Olive shrugged a kind of acquiescence.

'You've no objections, then?'

A shake of the head.

'Fine. I'm switching on now. Date, Monday, April twelve. Conversation with Olive Martin.' She consulted her all too sketchy list of questions. 'Let's start with some factual details. When were you born?'

No answer.

Roz looked up with an encouraging smile, only to be confronted by the woman's unblinking scrutiny. 'Well,' she said, 'I think I have that detail already. Let's see. Eighth of September, nineteen sixty-four, which makes you twenty-eight. Am I right?' No response. 'And you were born in Southampton General, the first of Gwen and Robert Martin's two daughters. Your sister, Amber, came along two years later on the fifteenth of July, nineteen sixty-six. Were you pleased about that? Or would you rather have had a brother?' Nothing.

Roz did not look up this time. She could feel the weight of the woman's eyes upon her. 'Your parents liked colours, obviously. I wonder what they would have called Amber if she'd been a boy?' She gave a nervous giggle. 'Red? Ginger? Perhaps it was a good thing the baby was another girl.' She listened to herself in disgust. *Goddamnit, why the hell did I agree to this!* Her bladder was hurting.

A fat finger reached out and switched off the tape-recorder. Roz watched it with a horrible fascination. 'There's no need to be so frightened,' said a deep, surprisingly cultured voice. 'Miss Henderson was teasing you. They all know I'm completely harmless. If I wasn't, I'd be in Broadmoor.' A strange rumbling noise vibrated the air. A laugh? Roz wondered. 'Stands to reason, really.' The finger hovered over the switches. 'You see, I do what normal people do when I have objections to something. I express them.' The finger moved to *Record* and gently pushed the button. 'Had Amber been a boy they would have called him Jeremy after my mother's father. Colour didn't come into it. In actual fact, Amber was christened Alison. I called her Amber because, at the age of two, I couldn't get my tongue round the "*l*" or the "*s*". It suited her. She had lovely honey-blonde hair, and as she grew up she always answered to Amber and never to Alison. She was very pretty.'

Roz waited a moment until she was sure she had her voice under control. 'Sorry.'

'That's all right. I'm used to it. Everyone is afraid at first.'

'Does that upset you?'

A flicker of amusement twitched the fatness round her eyes. 'Would it upset you?'

'Yes.'

'Well, then. Have you got a cigarette?'

'Sure.' Roz took an unopened pack from her brief-case and pushed it across the table with a box of matches. 'Help yourself. I don't smoke.'

'You would if you were in here. Everyone smokes in here.' She fumbled her way into the cigarette packet and lit up with a sigh of contentment. 'How old are you?'

'Thirty-six.'

'Married?'

'Divorced.'

'Children?'

Roz shook her head. 'I'm not the maternal type.'

'Is that why you got divorced?'

'Probably. I was more interested in my career. We went our separate ways very amicably.' Absurd, she thought, to bother with pain management in front of

Olive but the trouble was that if you told a lie often enough it became a truth, and the hurt only returned occasionally, in those strange, disorientating moments of wakening when she thought she was still at home with a warm body wrapped in her arms, hugging, loving, laughing.

Olive blew a smoke ring into the air. 'I'd have liked children. I got pregnant once but my mother persuaded me to get rid of it. I wish I hadn't now. I keep wondering what sex it was. I dream about my baby sometimes.' She gazed at the ceiling for a moment, following the wisp of smoke. 'Poor little thing. I was told by a woman in here that they wash them down the sink – you know, when they've vacuumed them out of you.'

Roz watched the big lips suck wetly on the tiny cigarette and thought of foetuses being vacuumed out of wombs. 'I didn't know that.'

'About the sink?'

'No. That you'd had an abortion.'

Olive's face was impassive. 'Do you know anything about me?'

'Not much.'

'Who've you asked?'

'Your solicitor.'

Another wheeze rumbled up through the caverns of her chest. 'I didn't know I had one.'

'Peter Crew,' said Roz with a frown, pulling a letter from her briefcase.

'Oh, him.' Olive's tone was contemptuous. 'He's a creep.' She spoke with undisguised venom.

'He says here he's your solicitor.'

'So? Governments say they care. I haven't heard a word from him in four years. I told him to get stuffed when he came up with his wonderful idea to get me an indefinite stay at Broadmoor. Slimy little sod. He didn't like me. He'd have wet himself with excitement if he could have got me certified.'

'He says' – Roz skimmed through the letter without thinking – 'ah, yes, here it is. "Unfortunately Olive failed to grasp that a plea of diminished responsibility would have ensured her receiving the sort of help in a secure psychiatric unit that would, in all probability, have meant her release into society within, at the most, fifteen years. It has always been obvious to me—" ' She came to an abrupt stop as sweat broke out across her back. *Any problems like, for example, she objects violently* . . . Was she completely out of her mind? She smiled weakly. 'Frankly, the rest is irrelevant.'

' "It has always been obvious to me that Olive is psychologically disturbed, possibly to the point of paranoid schizophrenia or psychopathy." Is that what it says?' Olive stood the glowing butt of her cigarette on the table and took another from the packet. 'I don't say I wasn't tempted. Assuming I could have got the court to accept that I was temporarily insane when I did it, I would almost certainly be a free woman by now. Have you seen my psychological reports?' Roz shook her head. 'Apart from an unremitting compulsion to eat, which is generally considered abnormal – one psychiatrist dubbed it a tendency to severe self-abuse – I am classified "normal".' She blew out the match with a gust of amusement. 'Whatever normal means. You've probably got more hang-ups than I have but I assume you fall into a "normal" psychological profile.'

'I wouldn't know,' said Roz, fascinated. 'I've never been analysed.' *I'm too frightened of what they might find.*

'You get used to it in a place like this. I reckon they do it to keep their hand in and it's probably more fun talking to a mother-hacker than a boring old depressive. I've had five different psychiatrists put me through the hoops. They love labels. It makes the filing system easier when they're trying to sort out what to do with us. I create problems for them. I'm sane but dangerous, so where the hell do they put me? An open prison's out of the question in case I get out and do it again. The public wouldn't like that.'

Roz held up the letter. 'You say you were tempted. Why didn't you go along with it if you thought there was a chance of getting out earlier?'

Olive didn't answer immediately but smoothed the shapeless dress across her thighs. 'We make choices. They're not always right but, once made, we have to live with them. I was very ignorant before I came here. Now I'm streetwise.' She inhaled a lungful of smoke. 'Psychologists, policemen, prison officers, judges, they were all out of the same mould. Men in authority with complete control of my life. Supposing I'd pleaded diminished responsibility and they'd said this girl can never get better. Lock the door and throw away the key. Twenty-five years amongst sane people was so much more attractive to me than a whole life with mad ones.'

'And what do you think now?'

'You learn, don't you? We get some real nut cases in here before they're transferred on. They're not so bad. Most of them can see the funny side.' She balanced a second dog-end next to her first. 'And I'll tell you something else, they're a damn sight less critical than the sane ones. When you look like me, you appreciate that.' She scrutinized Roz from between sparse blonde eyelashes. 'That's not to say I'd have pleaded differently had I been more *au fait* with the system. I still think it would have been immoral to claim I didn't know what I was doing when I knew perfectly well.'

Roz made no comment. What can you say to a woman who dismembers her mother and sister and then calmly splits hairs over the morality of special pleading?

Olive guessed what she was thinking and gave her wheezy laugh. 'It makes sense to me. By my own standards, I've done nothing wrong. It's only the law, those standards set by society, that I've transgressed.'

There was a certain biblical flourish about that last phrase, and Roz remembered that today was Easter Monday. 'Do you believe in God?'

'No. I'm a pagan. I believe in natural forces. Worshipping the sun makes sense. Worshipping an invisible entity doesn't.'

'What about Jesus Christ? He wasn't invisible.'

'But he wasn't God either.' Olive shrugged. 'He was a prophet, like Billy Graham. Can you swallow the garbage of the Trinity? I mean, either there's one God or there's a mountainful of them. It just depends on how imaginative you feel. I, for one, have no cause to celebrate that Christ is Risen.'

Roz, whose faith was dead, could sympathize with Olive's cynicism. 'So, if I understand you correctly, you're saying there is no absolute right or wrong, only individual conscience and the law.' Olive nodded. 'And your conscience isn't troubling you because you don't think you've done anything wrong.'

Olive looked at her with approval. 'That's it.'

Roz chewed her bottom lip in thought. 'Which means you believe your mother and sister deserved to die.' She frowned. 'Well, I don't understand, then. Why didn't you put up a defence at your trial?'

'I had no defence.'

'Provocation. Mental cruelty. Neglect. They must

have done *something* if you felt you were justified in killing them.'

Olive took another cigarette from the pack but didn't answer.

'Well?'

The intense scrutiny again. This time Roz held her gaze.

'Well?' she persisted.

Abruptly, Olive rapped the window pane with the back of her hand. 'I'm ready now, Miss Henderson,' she called out.

Roz looked at her in surprise. 'We've forty minutes yet.'

'I've talked enough.'

'I'm sorry. I've obviously upset you.' She waited. 'It was unintentional.'

Olive still didn't answer but sat impassively until the Officer came in. Then she grasped the edge of the table and, with a shove from behind, heaved herself to her feet. The cigarette, unlit, clung to her lower lip like a string of cotton wool. 'I'll see you next week,' she said, easing crabwise through the door and shambling off down the corridor with Miss Henderson and the metal chair in tow.

Roz sat on for several minutes, watching them through the window. Why had Olive balked at the mention of justification? Roz felt unreasonably cheated – it was one of the few questions she had wanted an answer to – and yet . . . Like the first stirrings of long dormant sap, her curiosity began to reawaken. God knows, there was no sense to it – she and Olive were as different as two women could be – but she had to admit an odd liking for the woman.

She snapped her briefcase closed and never noticed that her pencil was missing.

Iris had left a breathy message on the answerphone. 'Ring me with all the dirt . . . Is she perfectly ghastly? If she's as mad and as fat as her solicitor said, she must be terrifying. I'm agog to hear the gory details. If you don't phone, I shall come round to the flat and make a nuisance of myself . . .'

Roz poured herself a gin and tonic and wondered if Iris's insensitivity was inherited or acquired. She dialled her number. 'I'm phoning because it's the lesser of two evils. If I had to watch you drooling your disgusting prurience all over my carpet, I should be sick.' Mrs Antrobus, her bossy white cat, slithered round her legs, stiff tailed and purring. Roz winked down at her. She and Mrs Antrobus had a relationship of long standing, in which Mrs Antrobus wore the trousers and Roz knew her place. There was no persuading Mrs A. to do anything she didn't want.

'Oh, goody. You liked her, then?'

'What a revolting woman you are.' She took a sip

from her glass. 'I'm not sure that *like* is quite the word I would use.'

'How fat is she?'

'Grotesque. And it's sad, not funny.'

'Did she talk?'

'Yes. She has a very pukka accent and she's a bit of an intellectual. Not at all what I expected. Very sane, by the way.'

'I thought the solicitor said she was a psychopath.'

'He did. I'm going to see him tomorrow. I want to know who gave him that idea. According to Olive, five psychiatrists have diagnosed her normal.'

'She might be lying.'

'She's not. I checked with the Governor afterwards.' Roz reached down to scoop Mrs Antrobus against her chest. The cat, purring noisily, licked her nose. It was only cupboard love. She was hungry. 'Still, I wouldn't get too excited about this, if I were you. Olive may refuse to see me again.'

'Why, and what's that awful row?' demanded Iris.

'Mrs Antrobus.'

'Oh God! The mangy cat.' Iris was diverted. 'It sounds as if you've got the builders in. What on earth are you doing to it?'

'Loving it. She's the only thing that makes this hideous flat worth coming back to.'

'You're mad,' said Iris, whose contempt for cats was matched only by her contempt for authors. 'I can't think why you wanted to rent it in the first place. Use the money from the divorce and get something decent. Why might Olive refuse to see you?'

'She's unpredictable. Got very angry with me suddenly and called a halt to the interview.'

She heard Iris's indrawn gasp. 'Roz, you wretch! You haven't blown it, I hope.'

Roz grinned into the receiver. 'I'm not sure. We'll just have to wait and see. Got to go now. Bye-ee.' She hung up smartly on Iris's angry squeaking and went into the kitchen to feed Mrs Antrobus. When the phone rang again, she picked up her gin, moved into her bedroom, and started typing.

Olive took the pencil she had stolen from Roz and stood it carefully alongside the small clay figure of a woman that was propped up at the back of her chest of drawers. Her moist lips worked involuntarily, chewing, sucking, as she studied the figure critically. It was crudely executed, a lump of dried grey clay, unfired and unglazed but, like a fertility symbol from a less sophisticated age, its femininity was powerful. She selected a red marker from a jar and carefully coloured in the slab of hair about the face, then, changing to a green marker, filled in on the torso a rough representation of the silk shirtwaisted dress that Roz had been wearing.

To an observer her actions would have appeared

childish. She cradled the figure in her hands like a tiny doll, crooning over it, before replacing it beside the pencil which, too faintly for the human nose, still carried the scent of Rosalind Leigh.

Two

PETER CREW'S OFFICE was in the centre of Southampton, in a street where estate agents predominated. It was a sign of the times, thought Roz, as she walked past them, that they were largely empty. Depression had settled on them, as on everything else, like a dark immovable cloud.

Peter Crew was a gangling man of indeterminate age, with faded eyes and a blond toupee parted at the side. His own hair, a yellowish white, hung beneath it like a dirty net curtain. Every so often, he lifted the edge of the hair-piece and poked a finger underneath to scratch his scalp. The inevitable result of so much ill-considered stretching was that the toupee gaped perpetually in a small peak above his nose. It looked, Roz thought, like a large chicken perched on top of his head. She rather sympathized with Olive's contempt for him.

He smiled at her request to tape their conversation, a studied lift of the lips which lacked sincerity. 'As you please.' He folded his hands on his desk. 'So, Miss Leigh, you've already seen my client. How was she?'

'She was surprised to hear she still had a solicitor.'

'I don't follow,'

'According to Olive, she hasn't heard from you in four years. Are you still representing her?'

His face assumed a look of comical dismay but, like his smile, it lacked conviction. 'Good Heavens. Is it as long as that? Surely not. Didn't I write to her last year?'

'You tell me, Mr Crew.'

He fussed to a cabinet in the corner and flicked through the files. 'Here we are. Olive Martin. Dear me, you're right. Four years. Mind you,' he said sharply, 'there's been no communication from her either.' He pulled out the file and brought it across to his desk. 'The law is a costly business, Miss Leigh. We don't send letters for fun, you know.'

Roz lifted an eyebrow. 'Who's paying, then? I assumed she was on Legal Aid.'

He adjusted his yellow hat. 'Her father paid, though, frankly, I'm not sure what the position would be now. He's dead, you know.'

'I didn't know.'

'Heart attack a year ago. It was three days before anyone found him. Messy business. We're still trying to sort out the estate.' He lit a cigarette and then abandoned it on the edge of an overflowing ashtray.

Roz pencilled a doodle on her notepad. 'Does Olive know her father's dead?'

He was surprised. 'Of course she does.'

'Who told her? Obviously, your firm didn't write.'

He eyed her with the sudden suspicion of an unwary rambler coming upon a snake in the grass. 'I telephoned the prison and spoke to the Governor. I thought it would be less upsetting for Olive if the news was given personally.' He became alarmed. 'Are you saying she's never been told?'

'No. I just wondered why, if her father had money to leave, there's been no correspondence with Olive. Who's the beneficiary?'

Mr Crew shook his head. 'I can't reveal that. It's not Olive, naturally.'

'Why naturally?'

He tut-tutted crossly. 'Why do you think, young woman? She murdered his wife and younger daughter and condemned the poor man to live out his last years in the house where it happened. It was completely unsaleable. Have you any idea how tragic his life became? He was a recluse, never went out, never received visitors. It was only because there were milk bottles on the doorstep that anyone realized there was something wrong. As I say, he'd been dead for three days. Of course he wasn't going to leave money to Olive.'

Roz shrugged. 'Then why did he pay her legal bills? That's hardly consistent, is it?'

He ignored the question. 'There would have been difficulties, in any case. Olive would not have been allowed to benefit financially from the murder of her mother and her sister.'

Roz conceded the point. 'Did he leave much?'

'Surprisingly, yes. He made a tidy sum on the stock market.' His eyes held a wistful regret as he scratched vigorously under his toupee. 'Whether through luck or good judgement he sold everything just before Black Monday. The estate is now valued at half a million pounds.'

'My God!' She was silent for a moment. 'Does Olive know?'

'Certainly, if she reads the newspapers. The amount has been published and, because of the murders, it found its way into the tabloids.'

'Has it gone to the beneficiary yet?'

He frowned heavily, his brows jutting. 'I'm afraid I'm not at liberty to discuss that. The terms of the will preclude it.'

Roz shrugged and tapped her teeth with her pencil. 'Black Monday was October eighty-seven. The murders happened on September ninth, eighty-seven. That's odd, don't you think?'

'In what way?'

'I'd expect him to be so shell-shocked that stocks and shares would be the last thing he'd worry about.'

'Conversely,' said Mr Crew reasonably, 'that very fact would demand that he find something to occupy his mind. He was semi-retired after the murders. Perhaps the financial pages were his only remaining interest.' He looked at his watch. 'Time presses. Was there anything else?'

It was on the tip of Roz's tongue to ask why, if Robert Martin had made a killing on the stock exchange, he had chosen to live out his days in an unsaleable house. Surely a man worth half a million could have afforded to move, irrespective of what his property was worth? What, she wondered, was in that house to make Martin sacrifice himself to it? But she sensed Crew's hostility to her and decided that discretion was the better part of valour. This man was one of the few sources of corroborative information open to her and she would need him again, even though his sympathies clearly lay more with the father than the daughter. 'Just one or two more questions this morning.' She smiled pleasantly, a studied use of charm as insincere as his. 'I'm still feeling my way on this, Mr Crew. To tell you the truth, I'm not yet convinced there's a book in it.' And what an understatement that was. She wasn't intending to write anything. Or was she?

He steepled his fingers and tapped them together impatiently. 'If you remember, Miss Leigh, I made that very point in my letter to you.'

She nodded gravely, pandering to his ego. 'And as I told you, I don't want to write Olive's story simply to cover the pages with lurid details of what she did.

But one part of your letter implied an angle that might be worth pursuing. You advised her to plead not guilty to murder on the grounds of diminished responsibility. Had that succeeded, you suggested, she would have been found guilty of manslaughter and would, in all probability, have been sentenced to indefinite detention. I think you went on to estimate ten to fifteen years in a secure unit if she had been given psychiatric treatment and had responded favourably to it.'

'That is correct,' he agreed. 'And I think it was a reasonable estimate. Certainly she would have served nothing like the twenty-five year sentence the judge recommended she serve.'

'But she rejected your advice. Do you know why?'

'Yes. She had a morbid fear of being locked up with mad people and she misunderstood the nature of indefinite detention. She was convinced that it meant endless, and, try as we might, we could not persuade her otherwise.'

'In that case, why didn't you lodge a not guilty plea on her behalf? The very fact that she couldn't grasp what you were telling her implies that she wasn't capable of pleading for herself. You must have thought she had a defence or you wouldn't have suggested it.'

He smiled grimly. 'I don't quite understand why, Miss Leigh, but you seem to have decided that we failed Olive in some way.' He scribbled a name and address on a piece of paper. 'I suggest you talk to this man before you come to any more erroneous conclusions.' He flicked the paper in her direction. 'He's the barrister we briefed for her defence. Graham Deedes. In the event, she outmanoeuvred us and he was never called to defend her.'

'But why? How could she outmanoeuvre you?' She frowned. 'I'm sorry if I sound critical, Mr Crew, and please believe me, you are wrong in assuming I have reached any unfavourable conclusions.' But was that really true? she wondered. 'I am simply a perplexed onlooker asking questions. If this Deedes was in a position to raise serious doubts over her quote *sanity* unquote, then surely he should have insisted that the court hear her defence whether she wanted it or not. Not to put too fine a point on it, if she was bonkers then the system had a duty to recognize the fact, even if she herself thought she was sane.'

He relented a little. 'You're using very emotive language, Miss Leigh – there was never a question of pleading insanity, only diminished responsibility – but I do take your point. I used the word outmanoeuvred advisedly. The simple truth is that a few weeks before the scheduled date of her trial, Olive wrote to the Home Secretary demanding to know whether she had the right to plead guilty or whether, under British law, this right was denied her. She claimed that undue pressure was being brought to bear to force a lengthy trial that would do nothing to help her but only prolong the agony for her father. The trial date was postponed while tests were carried out to discover if she was fit to plead. She was ruled eminently fit and was allowed to plead guilty.'

'Good Lord!' Roz chewed her lower lip. 'Good Lord!' she said again. 'Were they right?'

'Of course.' He noticed the forgotten cigarette with a curl of ash dripping from its end and, with a gesture of annoyance, stubbed it out. 'She knew exactly what the consequences would be. They even told her what sort of sentence to expect. Nor would prison have come as any surprise to her. She spent four months on remand before the trial. Frankly, even had she agreed to defend herself the result would still have been the same. The evidence for a plea of diminished responsibility was very flimsy. I doubt we could have swung a jury.'

'And yet in your letter you said that, in spite of everything, you are still convinced she's a psychopath. Why?'

He fingered the file on his desk. 'I saw the photographs of Gwen and Amber's bodies, taken before their removal from the kitchen. It was a slaughterhouse running with blood, the most horrifying scene I have ever witnessed. Nothing will ever convince me that a psychologically stable personality could wreak such atrocity on anyone, let alone on a mother and sister.' He rubbed his eyes. 'No, despite what the psychiatrists say – and you must remember, Miss Leigh, that whether or not psychopathy is a diagnosable disease is under constant debate – Olive Martin is a dangerous woman. I advise you to be extremely wary in your dealings with her.'

Roz switched off her tape-recorder and reached for her briefcase. 'I suppose there's no doubt that she did it.'

He stared at her as if she had said something dirty. 'None at all,' he snapped. 'What are you implying?'

'It just occurs to me that a simple explanation for the discrepancy between the psychiatric evidence of Olive's normality and the quite *ab*normal nature of the crime is that she didn't do it but is covering for whoever did.' She stood up and gave a small shrug in face of his tight-lipped expression. 'It was just a thought. I agree it makes little sense, but nothing about this case makes much sense. I mean, if she really *is* a psychopathic murderess she wouldn't have cared tuppence about putting her father through the mill of a trial. Thank you for your time, Mr Crew. I can see myself out.'

He held up a hand to hold her back. 'Have you read her statement, Miss Leigh?'

'Not yet. Your office promised to send it to me.'

He sorted through the file and took out some stapled sheets of paper. 'This is a copy you may keep,' he told her, passing the pages across the desk. 'I urge you to read it before you go any further. It will persuade you, I think, as it persuaded me, of Olive's guilt.'

Roz picked up the papers. 'You really don't like her, do you?'

His eyes hardened. 'I have no feelings for her, one way or the other. I merely question society's rationale in keeping her alive. She kills people. Don't forget that, Miss Leigh. Good day to you.'

It took Roz an hour and a half to drive back to her flat in London and for most of that time Crew's words – *She kills people* – obscured all other thoughts. She took them out of context and wrote them large across the screen of her mind, dwelling on them with a kind of grim satisfaction.

It was later, curled up in an armchair, that she realized the journey home was a complete blank. She had no recollection, even, of leaving Southampton, a city she wasn't familiar with. *She* could have killed someone, crushing them under the wheels of her car, and she wouldn't have been able to remember when or how it happened. She stared out of her sitting-room window at the dismal grey façades opposite, and she wondered quite seriously about the nature of diminished responsibility.

Statement made by Olive Martin
9.9.87 – 9.30 p.m.
Present: DS Hawksley, DS Wyatt,
E.P. Crew (Solicitor)

My name is Olive Martin. I was born on 8th September, 1964. I live at 22 Leven Road, Dawlington, Southampton. I am employed as a clerk in the Department of Health and Social Security in Dawlington High Street. Yesterday was my birthday. I am twenty-three years old. I have always lived at home. My relationship with my mother and sister has never been close. I get on well with my father. I weigh eighteen and a half stone and my mother and sister have always teased me about it. Their nickname for me was Fattie-Hattie, after Hattie Jacques, the actress. I am sensitive to being laughed at for my size.

Nothing was planned for my birthday and that upset me. My mother said I wasn't a child any more and that I must organize my own treats. I decided to show her I was capable of doing something on my own. I arranged to have today off work with the idea of taking the train to London and spending the day sight-seeing. I did not organize the treat for yesterday, my birthday, in case she had planned a surprise for the evening which is what she did for my sister's twenty-first birthday in July. She did not. We all spent the evening quietly watching television. I went to bed feeling very upset. My parents gave me a pale pink jumper for my birthday present. It was very unflattering and I didn't like it. My sister gave me some new slippers which I did like.

I woke up feeling nervous about going to London on my own. I asked Amber, my sister, to phone in sick and come with me. She has been working in *Glitzy*, a fashion boutique in Dawlington, for about a month. My mother got very angry about this and stopped her. We had an argument over breakfast and my father left for work in the middle of it. He is fifty-five and works three days a week, as a book-keeper for a private haulage company. For many years he owned his own garage. He sold it in 1985 because he had no son to take it over.

The argument became very heated after he left, with my mother blaming me for leading Amber astray. She kept calling me Fattie and laughing at me for being too wet to go to London alone. She said I had been a disappointment to her from the day I was born. Her shouting gave me a headache. I was still very upset that she had done nothing for my birthday and I was jealous because she had given Amber a birthday party.

I went to the drawer and took out the rolling pin. I hit her with it to make her be quiet, then I hit her again when she started screaming. I might have stopped then but Amber started screaming because of what I had done. I had to hit her too. I have never liked noise.

I made myself a cup of tea and waited. I thought I had knocked them out. They were both lying on the floor. After an hour I wondered if they were dead. They were very pale and hadn't moved. I know that if you hold a mirror to someone's mouth and there is no mist on it afterwards it means they are dead. I used the mirror from my handbag. I held it to their mouths for a long time but there was no mist. Nothing.

I became frightened and wondered how to hide the bodies. At first, I thought of putting them in the attic, but they were too heavy to carry upstairs. Then I decided the sea would be the best place as it's only two miles from our house, but I can't drive and, anyway, my father had taken the car. It seemed to me that if I could make them smaller I could fit them into suitcases and carry them that way. I have cut chickens into portions many times. I thought it would be easy to do the same thing with Amber and my mother. I used an axe that we kept in the garage and a carving knife from the kitchen drawer.

It wasn't at all like cutting up chickens. I was tired by two o'clock and I had only managed to take off the heads and the legs and three of the arms. There was a lot of blood and my hands kept slipping. I knew my father would be home soon and that I could never finish by then as I still had to carry the pieces to the sea. I realized it would be better to ring the police and admit what I had done. I felt much happier once I had made this decision.

It never occurred to me to leave the house and pretend that someone else had done it. I don't know why except that my mind was set on hiding the bodies. That's all I thought about. I did not enjoy cutting them up. I had to undress them so I could see where the joints were. I did not know I'd mixed the pieces up. I rearranged them out of decency, but there was so much blood that I couldn't tell which body was which. I must have put my mother's head on Amber's body by mistake. I acted alone.

I am sorry for what I have done. I lost my temper and behaved stupidly. I confirm that everything written here is true.

Signed – OLIVE MARTIN

The statement was a photocopy, covering three typed sheets of A4. On the reverse of the last sheet was a photocopied extract from what was presumably the pathologist's report. It was brief, just a concluding paragraph, and there was no indication to show who had written it.

The injuries to the heads are entirely consistent with a blow or blows from a heavy solid object. These were inflicted before death and were not fatal. While there is no forensic evidence to suggest

> that the rolling pin was the weapon used, there is none to prove it wasn't. Death in both cases was caused by severance of the carotid artery during the decapitation process. Examination of the axe revealed considerable rusting beneath the blood stains. It is highly probable that it was blunt before it was used to dismember the bodies. The extensive bruising around the cuts on Amber Martin's neck and trunk indicate three or four strikes with an axe before the carving knife was used to cut the throat. It is unlikely that she ever regained consciousness. In Mrs Gwen Martin's case, however, the lacerations to her hands and forearms, inflicted before death, are consistent with her regaining consciousness and trying to defend herself. Two stabbing incisions below the jawline imply two failed attempts before her throat was successfully cut with the knife. These attacks were carried out with savage ferocity.

Roz read the pages through then put them on the table beside her and stared into the middle distance. She felt very cold. *Olive Martin took an axe* . . . Oh, God! No wonder Mr Crew called her a psychopath. Three or four strikes with a blunted axe and Amber was still alive! Bile rose in her throat, nauseous, bitter, gagging. *She must stop thinking about it.* But she couldn't, of course. The muffled thuds of metal bouncing off soft flesh boomed loudly in her brain.

How dark and shadowy the flat was. She reached out abruptly and snapped on a table lamp but the light did nothing to dispel the vivid pictures that crowded her imagination, nightmare visions of a madwoman, frenzied by blood-lust. And the bodies . . .

How far had she committed herself to writing this book? Had she signed anything? Had she received an advance. She couldn't remember and a cold fist of panic squeezed her insides. She was living in a twilight world where so little mattered that day followed day with nothing to distinguish their passing. She thrust herself out of her chair and paced about the floor, cursing Iris for bouncing her, cursing herself for her own insanity, and cursing Mr Crew for not sending her the statement when she'd first written to him.

She seized the telephone and dialled Iris's number. 'Have I signed anything on the Olive Martin book? Why? Because I damn well can't write it, that's why. The woman scares the bloody shit out of me and I am not visiting her again.'

'I thought you liked her.' Iris spoke calmly through a mouthful of supper.

Roz ignored this comment. 'I've got her statement here and the pathologist's report, or his conclusions at least. I should have read them first. I'm not doing it. I will not glorify what she did by writing a book about it. My God, Iris, they were alive when she cut their heads off. Her poor wretched mother tried to ward off the axe. It's making me sick just thinking about it.'

'OK.'

'OK what?'

'Don't write it.'

Roz's eyes narrowed suspiciously. 'I thought you'd argue at least.'

'Why? One thing I've learnt in this business is that you can't force people to write. Correction. You can if you're persistent and manipulative enough, but the result is always below par.' Roz heard her take a drink. 'In any case, Jenny Atherton sent me the first ten chapters of her new book this morning. It's all good stuff on the inherent dangers of a poor self-image, with obesity as number one confidence crippler. She's unearthed a positive goldmine of film and television personalities who've all sunk to untold depths since gaining weight and being forced off camera. It's disgustingly tasteless, of course, like all Jenny's books, but it'll sell. I think you should send all your gen – sorry about the pun – to her. Olive would make rather a dramatic conclusion, don't you think, particularly if we can get a photograph of her in her cell.'

'No chance.'

'No chance of getting a photograph? Shame.'

'No chance of my sending anything to Jenny Atherton. Honestly, Iris,' she stormed, losing her temper, 'you really are beneath contempt. You should be working for the gutter press. You believe in exploiting anyone just as long as they bring in the cash. Jenny Atherton is the last person I'd allow near Olive.'

'Can't see why,' said Iris, now chewing heartily on something. 'I mean if you don't want to write about her and you're refusing ever to visit her again because she makes you sick, why cavil at somebody else having a bash?'

'It's the principle.'

'Can't see it, old thing. Sounds more like dog in the manger to me. Listen, I can't dally. We've got people in. At least let me tell Jenny that Olive's up for grabs. She can start from scratch. It's not as though you've got very far, is it?'

'I've changed my mind,' Roz snapped. 'I will do it. Goodbye.' She slammed the receiver down.

At the other end of the line, Iris winked at her husband. 'And you accuse me of not caring,' she murmured. 'Now, what could have been more caring than that?'

'Hobnailed boots,' Gerry Fielding suggested acidly.

Roz read Olive's statement again. 'My relationship with my mother and sister was never close.' She reached for her tape-recorder and rewound the tape, flicking to and fro till she found the piece she wanted. 'I called her Amber because, at the age of two, I couldn't get my tongue round the "*l*" or the "*s*". It suited her. She had lovely honey-blonde hair, and as she grew up she always answered to Amber and never to Alison. She was very pretty . . .'

It meant nothing of course, in itself. There was no unwritten law that said psychopaths were incapable of pretending. Rather the reverse, in fact. But there was a definite softening of the voice when she spoke about her sister, a tenderness which from anyone else Roz would have interpreted as love. And why hadn't she mentioned the fight with her mother? Really, that was very odd. It could well have been her justification for what she did that day.

The chaplain, quite unaware that Olive was behind him, started violently as a large hand fell on his shoulder. It wasn't the first time she had crept up on him and he wondered again, as he had wondered before, how she managed to do it. Her normal gait was a painful shuffle which set his teeth on edge every time he heard its approach. He steeled himself and turned with a friendly smile. 'Why, Olive, how nice to see you. What brings you to the chapel?'

The bald eyes were amused. 'Did I frighten you?'

'You startled me. I didn't hear you coming.'

'Probably because you weren't listening. You must listen first if you want to hear, Chaplain. Surely they taught you that much at theological college. God talks in a whisper at the best of times.'

It would be easier, he thought sometimes, if he

could despise Olive. But he had never been able to. He feared and disliked her but he did not despise her. 'What can I do for you?'

'You had some new diaries delivered this morning. I'd like one.'

'Are you sure, Olive? These are no different from the others. They still have a religious text for every day of the year and last time I gave you one you tore it up.'

She shrugged. 'But I need a diary so I'm prepared to tolerate the little homilies.'

'They're in the vestry.'

'I know.'

She had not come for a diary. That much he could guess. But what did she plan to steal from the chapel while his back was turned? What *was* there to steal except Bibles and prayer books?

A candle, he told the Governor afterwards. Olive Martin took a six-inch candle from the altar. But she, of course, denied it, and though her cell was searched from top to bottom, the candle was never found.

Three

GRAHAM DEEDES WAS young, harassed, and black. He saw Roz's surprise as she came into his room, and he frowned his irritation. 'I had no idea black barristers were such a rarity, Miss Leigh.'

'Why do you say that?' she asked curiously, sitting down in the chair he indicated.

'You looked surprised.'

'I am, but not by your colour. You're much younger than I expected.'

'Thirty-three,' he said. 'Not so young.'

'No, but when you were briefed to appear for Olive Martin you can only have been twenty-six or twenty-seven. That *is* young for a murder trial.'

'True,' he agreed, 'but I was only the junior. The QC was considerably older.'

'But you did most of the preparation?'

He nodded. 'Such as there was. It was a very unusual case.'

She took her tape-recorder from her bag. 'Have you any objections to being recorded?'

'Not if you intend to talk about Olive Martin.'

'I do.'

He chuckled. 'Then I've no objections, for the simple reason that I can tell you virtually nothing about her. I saw the woman once, on the day she was sentenced, and I never even spoke to her.'

'But I understood you were preparing a diminished responsibility defence. Didn't you meet her in the course of doing that?'

'No, she refused to see me. I did all my work from material her solicitor sent me.' He smiled ruefully. 'Which wasn't much, I have to say. We would, quite literally, have been laughed out of court if we'd had to proceed, so I was quite relieved when the judge ruled her guilty plea admissible.'

'What arguments would you have used if you had been called?'

'We planned two different approaches.' Deedes considered for a moment. 'One, that the balance of her mind was temporarily disturbed – as far as I recall it was the day after her birthday and she was deeply upset because instead of paying her attention the family teased her about being fat.' He raised his eyebrows in query and Roz nodded. 'In addition, I believe, she made a reference in her statement to not liking noise. We did manage to find a doctor who was prepared to give evidence that noise can cause such violent distress in some people that they may act out of character in trying to stop it. There was no psychiatric or medical evidence, however, to prove that Olive was of this type.' He tapped his forefingers together. 'Two, we were going to work backwards from the appalling savagery of the crime and invite the court to draw what we hoped to persuade them was an inescapable inference – that Olive was a psychopath. We hadn't a cat's chance on the balance of her mind argument, but the psychopathy' – he made a see-saw motion with one hand – 'maybe. We found a professor of psychology who was prepared to stick his neck out after seeing the photographs of the bodies.'

'But did he ever *talk* to her?'

He shook his head. 'There wasn't time and she wouldn't have seen him anyway. She was quite determined to plead guilty. I assume Mr Crew told you that she wrote to the Home Office demanding an independent psychiatric report to prove that she was competent to plead?' Roz nodded. 'After that there was really nothing we could do. It was an extraordinary business,' he mused. 'Most defendants fall over themselves to come up with excuses.'

'Mr Crew seems convinced she's a psychopath.'

'I think I'd agree with him.'

'Because of what she did to Amber and her mother? You don't have any other evidence?'

'No. Isn't that enough?'

'Then how do you explain that five psychiatrists

have all diagnosed her normal?' Roz looked up. 'She's had several sessions, as far as I can gather, in the prison.'

'Who told you this? Olive?' He looked sceptical.

'Yes, but I spoke to the Governor afterwards and she verified it.'

He shrugged. 'I wouldn't place too much reliance on it. You'd have to see the reports. It depends who wrote them and why they were testing her.'

'Still, it's odd, don't you think?'

'In what way?'

'You'd expect some measurable level of sociopathic behaviour over a period of time if she was a psychopath.'

'Not necessarily. Prison may be the sort of controlled environment that suits her. Or perhaps her particular psychopathy was directed against her family. Something brought it on that day and once rid of them, she settled down.' He shrugged again. 'Who knows? Psychiatry is hardly an exact science.' He was silent for a moment. 'In my experience, well-adjusted people don't hack their mothers and their sisters to death. You do know they were still alive when she set to with the axe?' He smiled grimly. 'She knew it, too. Don't imagine she didn't.'

Roz frowned. 'There is another explanation,' she said slowly, 'but the trouble is, while it fits the facts, it's too absurd to be credible.'

He waited. 'Well?' he asked at last.

'Olive didn't do it.' She saw his amused disbelief and hurried on. 'I'm not saying I go along with it, I'm just saying that it fits the facts.'

'*Your* facts,' he pointed out gently. 'It seems to me you're being a little selective in what you choose to believe.'

'Maybe.' Roz remembered her extremes of mood of the previous evening.

He watched her for a moment. 'She knew a great deal about the murders for someone who wasn't responsible for them.'

'Do you think so?'

'Of course. Don't you?'

'She doesn't say anything about her mother trying to ward off the axe and the carving knife. But that must have been the most frightening part. Why didn't she mention it?'

'Shame. Embarrassment. Traumatic amnesia. You'd be surprised how many murderers blot what they've done from their memories. Sometimes it's years before they come to terms with their guilt. In any case, I doubt the struggle with her mother was as frightening for Olive as you suggest. Gwen Martin was a tiny woman, five feet at the most, I would think. Physically, Olive took after her father, so containing her mother would have been easy for her.' He saw the hesitation in Roz's eyes. 'Let me put a question to *you*. Why would Olive confess to two murders she didn't commit?'

'Because people do.'

'Not when they have their lawyers present, Miss Leigh. I accept that it happened, which is why new rules were introduced governing the taking of evidence, but Olive did not fall into the category of either forced confession or having her confession subsequently tampered with. She had legal representation throughout. So I repeat, why would she confess to something she didn't do?'

'To protect someone else?' She was relieved they weren't in court. He was a bruising cross-examiner.

'Who?'

She shook her head. 'I don't know.'

'There was no one else except her father, and he was at work. The police had him thoroughly checked and his alibi was unbreakable.'

'There was Olive's lover.'

He stared at her.

'She told me she'd had an abortion. Presumably, then, she must have had a lover.'

He found that very entertaining. 'Poor Olive.' He laughed. 'Well, I guess an abortion is as good a way as any of keeping her end up. Especially' – he laughed again – 'if everyone believes her. I shouldn't be too gullible, if I were you.'

She smiled coldly. 'Perhaps it's you who is being gullible by subscribing to the cheap male view that a woman like Olive could not attract a lover.'

Deedes studied her set face and wondered what

was driving her. 'You're right, Miss Leigh, it was cheap, and I apologise.' He raised his hands briefly, then dropped them again. 'But this is the first I have heard about an abortion. Let's just say it strikes me as a little unlikely. And somewhat convenient, perhaps? It's not something you can ever really check, is it, not without Olive's permission. If laymen were allowed to browse through other people's medical records some very delicate secrets might be exposed.'

Roz regretted her waspish remark. Deedes was a nicer man than Crew and hadn't deserved it. 'Olive mentioned an abortion. *I* assumed the lover. But perhaps she was raped. Babies can be conceived as easily in hate as in love.'

He shrugged. 'Beware of being used, Miss Leigh. Olive Martin dominated the court the day she appeared in it. I had the impression then, and still have it, that it was *we* who were dancing to *her* tune not she to ours.'

Dawlington was a small eastern suburb of Southampton, once an isolated village, now swallowed up in the great urban expansion of the twentieth century. It maintained an identity of a sort by the busy trunk-roads that gave it tarmac boundaries but, even so, the place was easy to miss. Only a tired peeling shop sign, advertising *Dawlington Newsagents*, alerted Roz to the fact that she had left one suburb and entered another. She drew into the kerb before a left-hand turning and consulted her map. She was, presumably, in the High Street and the road to the left – she squinted at the sign – was Ainsley Street. She ran her finger across the grid. 'Ainsley Street,' she muttered. 'Come on, you bugger, where are you? OK. Leven Road. First right, second left.' With a glance in her driving mirror, she pulled out into the traffic and turned right.

Olive's story, she thought, grew odder by the minute, as she studied number twenty-two, Leven Road, from her parked car. Mr Crew had said the house was unsaleable. She had imagined something out of a Gothic novel, twelve months of dereliction and decay since the death of Robert Martin, a house condemned by the haunting horror in its kitchen. Instead, the reality was a cheerful little semi, freshly painted, with pink, white, and red geraniums nodding in boxes beneath its windows. Who, she wondered, had bought it? Who was brave enough (or ghoulish enough?) to live with the ghosts of that tragic family? She double-checked the address from press cuttings she had put together that morning in the archives basement of the local newspaper. There was no mistake. A black and white photograph of 'The House of Horror' showed this same neat semi, but without its window-boxes.

She climbed out of the car and crossed the road. The house remained stubbornly silent to her ring on the doorbell, so she went next door and tried there. A young woman answered with a sleepy toddler clinging round her neck. 'Yes?'

'Hello,' said Roz, 'I'm sorry to bother you.' She indicated towards her right. 'It's your neighbours I really want to talk to but there's no one in. Have you any idea when they might be back?'

The young woman thrust out a hip to support the child more easily and subjected Roz to a penetrating glare. 'There's nothing to see, you know. You're wasting your time.'

'I'm sorry?'

'They pulled the innards out of the house and revamped the whole of the inside. They've done it up nice. There's nothing to see, no blood stains, no spirits roaming about, nothing.' She pressed the child's head against her shoulder, a casual, proprietary gesture, a statement of tender motherhood at odds with the hostility in her voice. 'You want to know what I think? You should see a psychiatrist. It's the likes of you who're the real sick people of society.' She prepared to close the door.

Roz raised her palms in a gesture of surrender. She smiled sheepishly. 'I haven't come to gawp,' she said. 'My name is Rosalind Leigh and I'm working in co-operation with the late Mr Martin's solicitor.'

The woman eyed her suspiciously. 'Oh, yeah? What's his name?'

'Peter Crew.'

'You could of got it from the paper.'

'I have a letter from him. May I show it to you? It will prove I am who I say I am.'

'Go on then.'

'It's in the car. I'll fetch it.' She retrieved her brief-case hurriedly from the boot, but when she got back, the door was closed. She rang several times and waited for ten minutes on the doorstep, but it was obvious the young woman had no intention of answering. From a room above came the wail of a baby. Roz listened to the mother's soothing tones as she climbed the stairs, then, thoroughly annoyed with herself, she retreated to the car and pondered her next step.

The press cuttings were disappointing. It was names she wanted, names of friends or neighbours, even old school teachers, who could give her back-ground detail. But the local newspaper had, like the nationals, sensationalized the crime's horror without uncovering any details about Olive's life or why she might have done it. There were the usual quotes from 'neighbours' – all anonymous and all wise after the event – but they were so uniformly unenlightening that Roz suspected imaginative journalism at work.

> 'No, I'm not surprised,' said a neighbour, 'shocked and appalled, yes, but not surprised. She was a strange girl, unfriendly, kept herself to herself. Not like the sister. She was the attractive, outgoing one. We all liked Amber.' 'The parents found her very

difficult. She wouldn't mix or make friends. She was shy, I suppose, because of her size but she had a way of looking at you that wasn't normal.'

Beyond the sensationalism, there had been nothing to write about. There was no police investigation to report – Olive had phoned them herself, had confessed to the crime in the presence of her solicitor, and had been charged with murder. Because she had pleaded guilty there had been no salacious details from a lengthy trial, no names of friends or associates to draw on, and her sentencing had rated a single paragraph under the headline: twenty-five years for brutal murders. A conspiracy of journalistic apathy seemed to surround the whole event. Of the five cardinal Ws of the journalist's creed – Where?, When?, What?, Who?, and Why? – the first four had been amply covered. Everyone knew what had happened, who had done it, where, and when. But no one, it seemed, knew why. Nor, and this was the real puzzle, had anyone actually asked. Could teasing alone really drive a young woman to such a pitch of anger that she would hack her family to pieces?

With a sigh, Roz switched on the radio and fed Pavarotti into the tape-deck. Bad choice, she thought, as 'Nessun Dorma' flooded the car and brought back bitter memories of a summer she would rather forget. Strange how a piece of music could be so evocative, but then the path to separation had been choreographed around the television screen with 'Nessun Dorma' triggering the stops and starts of their rows. She could remember every detail of every World Cup football match. They were the only peaceful periods in a summer of war. How much better, she thought wearily, if she had called a halt then instead of dragging the misery out to its far more terrible conclusion.

A net curtain, in the semi to the right, number 24, twitched behind a Neighbourhood Watch sticker which proclaimed itself loudly against the glass. A case, Roz wondered, of locking the stable door after the horse had bolted? Or was that same net curtain twitching the day Olive wielded her chopper? Two garages filled the gap between the houses, but it was possible the occupants had heard something. '*Olive Martin took an axe and gave her mother forty whacks . . .*' The words circled in her brain as they had done, on and off, for days.

She resumed her contemplation of number 22, but watched the net curtain out of the corner of her eye. It moved again, plucked by prying fingers, and she felt unreasonably irritated by the busybody spying on her. It was an empty, wasted life that had time to stand and stare. What sort of interfering old bitch inhabited there, she wondered? The frustrated spinster who got off on voyeurism? Or the bored and boring wife with nothing better to do than find fault? Then something clicked inside her head, a realignment of thought like the points on a railway line. Just the sort of busybody she wanted, of course, but why had that not occurred to her immediately? Really, she worried about herself. She spent so much time in neutral now, just listening to the footfalls, leading nowhere, that echoed in her memory.

A frail old man opened the door, a small, shrunken person with transparent skin and bowed shoulders. 'Come in, come in,' he said, standing back and ushering her into his corridor. 'I heard what you said to Mrs Blair. She won't talk to you, and I'll tell you something else, it wouldn't help you if she did. They only came four years ago when the first youngster was on the way. Didn't know the family at all and, as far as I know, never spoke to poor old Bob. What shall I say? She's got a nerve. Typical of today's youngsters. Always wanting something for nothing.' He muttered on, leading the way into his living room. 'Resents living in a goldfish bowl but forgets that they got the house for a pittance just because it *was* a goldfish bowl. Ted and Dorothy Clarke virtually gave the place away because they couldn't stand it any longer. What shall I say? Ungrateful girl. Imagine what it's like for those of us who've always lived here. No bargains for us. We have to put up with it, don't we? Sit down. Sit down.'

'Thank you.'

'You're from Mr Crew, you say. They found the child yet?' He stared into her face with disconcertingly bright blue eyes.

Roz stared back, her mind racing. 'That's not my province,' she said carefully, 'so I'm not sure where they are on that one. I'm conducting a follow-up of Olive's case. You did know that Mr Crew is still representing her?'

'What's to represent?' he asked. His eyes strayed in disappointment. 'Poor little Amber. They should never have made her give it up. I said it would cause trouble.'

Roz sat very still and stared at the worn carpet.

'People don't listen, of course,' he said crossly. 'You give them well-meant advice and they tell you you're interfering. What shall I say? I could see where it would lead.' He fell into a resentful silence.

'You're talking about the child,' said Roz at last.

He looked at her curiously. 'If they'd found him, you'd know.'

It was a boy, then. 'Oh, yes.'

'Bob did his best but there's rules about these things. They'd signed him away, given up their stake, so to speak. You'd think it was different where money's concerned, but there's no contest for the likes of us against the government. What shall I say? They're all thieves.'

Roz made what she could of this speech. Was he talking about Mr Martin's will? Was this child

(Amber's child?) the beneficiary? On the pretext of looking for a handkerchief, she opened her bag and surreptitiously switched on her tape-recorder. This conversation, she felt, was going to be tortuous. 'You mean,' she tried tentatively, 'that the government will get the money?'

'Course.'

She nodded wisely. 'Things aren't exactly stacked in our favour.'

'Never are. Damn thieves. Take every last penny off you. And what for? To make sure the skivers go on breeding like rabbits at the expense of the rest of us. Makes you sick. There's a woman in the council houses has five children, and all by different fathers. What shall I say? They're all worthless. Is that the sort of breeding stock we want in this country? Good-for-nothings, with not a brain between them. Where's the sense in encouraging a woman like that? Should have sterilized her and put a stop to it.'

Roz was noncommittal, unwilling to be drawn down a cul-de-sac, even more unwilling to antagonize him. 'I'm sure you're right.'

'Course I'm right, and it'll be the death of the species. Before the dole, she'd have starved to death and her brood with her, and quite right too. What shall I say? It's the survival of the fittest in this world. There's no other species mollycoddles its rotten apples the way we do, and certainly none that pays its rotten apples to produce more rotten apples. Makes you sick. How many children have you got?'

Roz smiled faintly. 'None, I'm afraid. I'm not married.'

'See what I mean?' He cleared his throat noisily. 'Makes you sick. What shall I say? It's your sort, decent sort, should have the children.'

'How many do you have, Mr – er—?' She made a play of consulting her diary, as if looking for his name.

'Hayes. Mr Hayes. Two lads. Fine boys. Grown up now, of course. Only the one granddaughter,' he added morosely. 'It's not right. I keep telling them they've a duty to their class but I could be pissing in the wind – excuse my French – for all the good it does.' His face set into familiar lines of irritation. His obsession was clearly a deep-seated one.

Roz knew she had to take the plunge or one hobby horse would follow another as inexorably as night follows day. 'You're a very perceptive man, Mr Hayes. Why were you so sure that making Amber give up her son would cause trouble?'

'Stands to reason there'd come a time when he was wanted again. It's sod's law, isn't it? The minute you throw something out, that's the minute you find you needed it after all. But it's too late by then. It's gone. My wife was one, forever throwing things away, pots of paint, carpet, and two years later you needed to patch. Me, I hoard. What shall I say? I value everything.'

'So, are you saying Mr Martin wasn't bothered about his grandson before the murders?'

He touched the end of his nose with thumb and forefinger. 'Who's to say? He kept his own counsel, did Bob. It was Gwen who insisted on signing the kid away. Wouldn't have it in the house. Understandable, I suppose, in view of Amber's age.'

'How old was she?'

He frowned. 'I thought Mr Crew knew all this.'

She smiled. 'He does but, as I told you, it's not my province. I'm just interested, that's all. It seems so tragic.'

'It is that. Thirteen,' he said wistfully. 'She was thirteen. Poor little kid. Didn't know anything about anything. Some lout at the school was responsible.' He jerked his head towards the back of his house. 'Parkway Comprehensive.'

'Is that the school Amber and Olive went to?'

'Hah!' His old eyes were amused. 'Gwen wouldn't have stood for that. She sent them to the posh Convent where they learnt their times tables and didn't learn the facts of life.'

'Why didn't Amber have an abortion? Were they Catholics?' She thought again about Olive and foetuses being washed down the sink.

'They didn't know she was pregnant, did they? Thought it was puppy fat.' He cackled suddenly. 'Rushed her off to hospital with suspected appendicitis and out pops a bouncing baby boy. They got away with it, too. Best kept secret I've ever come across. Even the nuns didn't know.'

'But you knew,' she prompted.

'The wife guessed,' he said owlishly. 'It was obvious something untoward had happened, and not appendicitis neither. Gwen was well-nigh hysterical the night it happened and my Jeannie put two and two together. Still, we know how to keep our mouths shut. No reason to make life harder for the kid. It wasn't her fault.'

Roz did some rapid mental arithmetic. Amber was two years younger than Olive which would have made her twenty-six if she were still alive. 'Her son's thirteen,' she said, 'and due to inherit half a million pounds. I wonder why Mr Crew can't find him. There must be records of the adoption.'

'I heard they'd found traces.' The old man clicked his false teeth with disappointment. 'But, there, it was probably just rumour, Brown Australia,' he muttered with disgust, as if that explained everything. 'I ask you.'

Roz allowed this cryptic remark to pass unchallenged. Time enough to puzzle over it later without claiming ignorance yet again. 'Tell me about Olive,' she invited. 'Were you surprised that she did what she did?'

'I hardly knew the girl.' He sucked his teeth. 'And you don't feel surprised when people you know get hacked to death, young lady, you feel bloody sick. It did for my Jeannie. She was never the same afterwards, died a couple of years later.'

'I'm sorry.'

He nodded, but it was clearly an old wound that had healed. 'Used to see the child come and go but she wasn't a great talker. Shy, I suppose.'

'Because she was fat?'

He pursed his lips thoughtfully. 'Maybe. Jeannie said she was teased a lot, but I've known fat girls who've been the life and soul of the party. It was her nature, I think, to look on the black side. Never laughed much. No sense of humour. That sort doesn't make friends easily.'

'And Amber did?'

'Oh, yes. She was very popular.' He glanced back down the passages of time. 'She was a pretty girl.'

'Was Olive jealous of her?'

'Jealous?' Mr Hayes looked surprised. 'I've never thought about it. What shall I say? They always seemed very fond of each other.'

Roz shrugged her bewilderment. 'Then why did Olive kill her? And why mutilate the bodies? It's very odd.'

He scowled suspiciously. 'I thought you were representing her. You should know if anyone does.'

'She won't say.'

He stared out of the window. 'Well, then.'

Well then what? 'Do you know why?'

'Jeannie reckoned it was hormones.'

'Hormones?' Roz echoed blankly. 'What sort of hormones?'

'You know.' He looked embarrassed. 'Monthly ones.'

'Ah.' PMT? she wondered. But it was hardly a subject she could pursue with him. He was of a generation where menstruation was never mentioned. 'Did Mr Martin ever say why he thought she did it?'

He shook his head. 'The subject didn't arise. What shall I say? We saw very little of him afterwards. He talked about his will once or twice, and the child – it was all he thought about.' He cleared his throat again. 'He became a recluse, you know. Wouldn't have anyone in the house, not even the Clarkes, and there was a time when Ted and he were close as brothers.' His mouth turned down at the corners. 'It was Ted started it, mind. Took against Bob for some reason and wouldn't go in. And others followed suit, of course, the way they do. Reckon I was his only friend at the end. It was me as realized something was wrong, seeing the milk bottles outside.'

'But why did he stay? He was rich enough to let number twenty-two go for peanuts. You'd have thought he'd go anywhere rather than stay with the ghosts of his family.'

Mr Hayes muttered to himself. 'Never understood it myself. Perhaps he wanted his friends about him.'

'You said the Clarkes moved. Where did they go?'

He shook his head. 'No idea. They upped and went

one morning without a word to anyone. A removal van took out their furniture three days later and the house stood empty for a year till the Blairs bought it. Never heard a word from them since. No forwarding address. Nothing. What shall I say? We were good friends, the six of us, and I'm the only one left now. Strange business.'

Very strange, thought Roz. 'Can you remember which estate agent sold the house?'

'Peterson's, but you won't learn anything from them. Little Hitlers,' he said, 'all bursting with self-importance. Told me to mind my own business when I went in and asked what was what. It's a free world, I pointed out, no reason why a man shouldn't ask after his friends, but oh, no, they had instructions of confidentiality or some such rubbish. What shall I say? Made out it was me the Clarkes were cutting their ties with. Hah! More likely Bob, I told them, or ghosts. And they said if I spread those sort of rumours, they'd take action. You know who I blame. The estate agents' federation, if there is one, which I doubt . . .' He rambled on, venting his spleen out of loneliness and frustration.

Roz felt sorry for him. 'Do you see much of your sons?' she asked when he drew to a halt.

'Now and then.'

'How old are they?'

'Forties,' he said after a moment's thought.

'What did they think of Olive and Amber?'

He pinched his nose again and waggled it from side to side. 'Never knew them. Left home long before either of the girls reached their teens.'

'They didn't baby-sit or anything like that?'

'My lads? You wouldn't catch them baby-sitting.' His old eyes moistened, and he nodded towards the sideboard where photographs of two young men in uniform crowded the surface. 'Fine boys. Soldiers.' He thrust out his chest. 'Took my advice and joined up. Mind, they're out of jobs now, what with the bloomin' regiment being cut from under them. It makes you sick when you think them and me's served Queen and country for nigh on fifty years between us. Did I tell you I was in the desert during the war?' He looked vacantly about the room. 'There's a photograph somewhere of Churchill and Monty in a jeep. We all got one, us boys who were out there. Worth a bob or two, I should think. Now where is it?' He became agitated.

Roz picked up her briefcase. 'Don't worry about it now, Mr Hayes. Perhaps I could see it next time I come.'

'You coming back?'

'I'd like to, if it's no trouble.' She took a card from her handbag, flicking the switch on the recorder at the same time. 'That's my name and telephone number. Rosalind Leigh. It's a London number but I'll be down here regularly over the next few weeks, so if you feel like a chat' – she smiled encouragingly and stood up – 'give me a ring.'

He regarded her with astonishment. 'A chat. Goodness me. A youngster like you has better things to do with her time.'

Too right, she thought, but I do need information. Her smile, like Mr Crew's, was false. 'I'll be seeing you then, Mr Hayes.'

He pushed himself awkwardly out of his chair and held out a marbled hand. 'It's been a pleasure meeting you, Miss Leigh. What shall I say? It's not often an old man sees charming young ladies out of the blue.'

He spoke with such sincerity that she felt chastened by her own lack of it. Why, oh why, she wondered, was the human condition so damn bloody?

Four

ROZ FOUND THE local convent with the help of a policeman. 'That'll be St Angela's,' he told her. 'Left at the traffic lights and left again. Large red-brick building set back from the road. You can't miss it. It's the only decent piece of architecture still standing round there.'

It reared in solid Victorian magnificence above its surrounding clutter of cheap concrete obsolescence, a monument to education in a way that none of the modern prefabricated schools could ever be. Roz entered the front door with a sense of familiarity, for this was a schooling she recognized. Glimpses through classroom doors of desks, blackboards, shelves of books, attentive girls in neat uniforms. A place of quiet learning, where parents could dictate the sort of education their daughters received simply by threatening to remove the pupils and withhold the fees. And whenever parents had that power the requirements were always the same: discipline, structure, results.

She peeped through a window into what was obviously the library. Well, well, no wonder Gwen had insisted on sending the girls here. Roz would put money on Parkway Comprehensive being an unruly bedlam where English, History, Religion and Geography were all taught as the single subject of General Studies, spelling was an anachronism, French an extra-curricular activity, Latin unheard of, and Science a series of chats about the greenhouse effect. . .

'Can I help you?'

She turned with a smile. 'I hope so.'

A smart woman in her late fifties had paused in front of a door marked Secretary. 'Are you a prospective parent?'

'I wish I were. It's a lovely school. No children,' she explained at the woman's look of puzzled enquiry.

'I see. So how can I help you?'

Roz took out one of her cards. 'Rosalind Leigh,' she introduced herself. 'Would it be possible for me to talk to the headmistress?'

'Now?' said the woman in surprise.

'Yes, if she's free. If not, I can make an appointment and come back later.'

The woman took the card and read it closely. 'May I ask what you want to talk about?'

Roz shrugged. 'Just some general information about the school and the sort of girls who come here.'

'Would you be the Rosalind Leigh who wrote *Through the Looking Glass* by any chance?'

Roz nodded. *Through the Looking Glass*, her last book and her best, had sold well and won some excellent reviews. A study of the changing perceptions of female beauty down the ages, she wondered now how she had ever managed to summon the energy to write it. A labour of love, she thought, because the subject had fascinated her.

'I've read it.' The other smiled. 'I agreed with very few of your conclusions but it was extremely thought-provoking none the less. You write lovely prose, but I'm sure you know that.'

Roz laughed. She felt an immediate liking for the woman. 'At least you're honest.'

The other looked at her watch. 'Come into my office. I have some parents to see in half an hour, but I'm happy to give you general information until then. This way.' She opened the secretary's door and ushered Roz through to an adjoining office. 'Sit down, do. Coffee?'

'Please.' Roz took the chair indicated and watched her busy herself with a kettle and some cups. 'Are you the headmistress?'

'I am.'

'They were always nuns in my day.'

'So you're a convent girl. I thought you might be. Milk?'

'Black and no sugar, please.'

She placed a steaming cup on the desk in front of Roz and sat down opposite her. 'In fact I am a nun.

Sister Bridget. My order gave up wearing the habit quite some time ago. We found it tended to create an artificial barrier between us and the rest of society.' She chuckled. 'I don't know what it is about religious uniforms, but people try to avoid you if they can. I suppose they feel they have to be on their best behaviour. It's very frustrating. The conversation is often so stilted.'

Roz crossed her legs and relaxed into the chair. She was unaware of it but her eyes betrayed her. They brimmed with all the warmth and humour that, a year ago, had been the outward expression of her personality. Bitterness, it seemed, could only corrode so far. 'It's probably guilt,' she said. 'We have to guard our tongues in case we provoke the sermon we know we deserve.' She sipped the coffee. 'What made you think I was a convent girl?'

'Your book. You get very hot under the collar about established religions. I guessed you were either a lapsed Jew or a lapsed Catholic. The Protestant yoke is easier to discard, being far less oppressive in the first place.'

'In fact I wasn't a lapsed anything when I wrote *Through the Looking Glass*,' said Roz mildly. 'I was a good Catholic still.'

Sister Bridget interpreted the cynicism in her voice. 'But not now.'

'No. God died on me.' She smiled slightly at the look of understanding on the other woman's face.

'You read about it, I suppose. I can't applaud your taste in newspapers.'

'I'm an educator, my dear. We take the tabloids here as well as the broadsheets.' She didn't drop her gaze or show embarrassment, for which Roz was grateful. 'Yes, I read about it and I would have punished God, too. It was very cruel of Him.'

Roz nodded. 'If I remember right,' she said, reverting to her book, 'religion is confined to only one chapter of my book. Why did you find my conclusions so hard to agree with?'

'Because they are all drawn from a single premiss. As I can't accept the premiss, then I can't agree with the conclusions.'

Roz wrinkled her brow. 'Which premiss?'

'That beauty is only skin deep.'

Roz was surprised. 'And you don't think that's true?'

'No, not as a general rule.'

'I'm speechless. And you a nun!'

'Being a nun has nothing to do with it. I'm streetwise.'

It was an unconscious echo of Olive. 'You really believe that beautiful people are beautiful all the way through? I can't accept that. By the same token ugly people are ugly all the way through.'

'You're putting words into my mouth, my dear.' Sister Bridget was amused. 'I am simply questioning the idea that beauty is a surface quality.' She cradled her coffee cup in her hands. 'It's a comfortable thought, of course – it means we can all feel good about ourselves – but beauty, like wealth, is a moral asset. The wealthy can afford to be law abiding, generous and kind. The very poor cannot. Even kindness is a struggle when you don't know where your next penny is coming from.' She gave a quirky smile. 'Poverty is only uplifting when you can choose it.'

'I wouldn't disagree with that, but I don't see the connection between beauty and wealth.'

'Beauty cushions you against the negative emotions that loneliness and rejection inspire. Beautiful people are prized – they always have been, you made that point yourself – so they have less reason to be spiteful, less reason to be jealous, less reason to covet what they can't have. They tend to be the focus of all those emotions, rarely the instigators of them.' She shrugged. 'You will always have exceptions – most of them you uncovered in your book – but, in my experience, if a person is attractive then that attractiveness runs deep. You can argue which comes first, the inner beauty or the outer, but they do tend to walk together.'

'So if you're rich and beautiful the pearly gates will swing open for you?' She smiled cynically. 'That's a somewhat radical philosophy for a Christian, isn't it? I thought Jesus preached the exact opposite. Something like it's easier for a camel to pass through the eye of a needle than for a rich man to enter the kingdom of heaven.'

Sister Bridget laughed good-humouredly. 'Yours was obviously an excellent convent.' She stirred her coffee absent-mindedly with a biro. 'Yes, He did say that but, if you put it in context, it supports my view, I think, rather than detracts from it. If you remember, a wealthy young man asked Him how he could have eternal life. Jesus said: keep the commandments. The youth answered: I have kept them, since childhood, but what more can I do. If you want to be perfect, said Jesus – and I emphasize the *perfect* – sell all you have and give it to the poor, *then* follow me. The young man went away sorrowing because he had many possessions and could not bring himself to sell them. It was then Jesus made the reference to the camel and the eye of the needle. He was, you see, talking about perfection, not goodness.' She sucked the end of her biro. 'In fairness to the young man, I have always assumed that to sell his possessions would have meant selling houses and businesses with tenants and employees in them, so the moral dilemma would have been a difficult one. But what I think Jesus was saying was this: so far you have been a good man, but to test how good you really are, reduce yourself to abject poverty. Perfection is to follow me and keep the commandments when you are so poor that stealing and lying are a way of life if you want to be sure of waking up the next morning. An impossible goal.' She sipped her coffee. 'I could be wrong, of course.' There was a twinkle in her eye.

'Well, I'm not going to argue the toss with you on that,' said Roz bluntly. 'I suspect I'd be on a hiding to nothing. But I reckon you're on very bumpy ground with your beauty is a moral asset argument. What about the pitfalls of vanity and arrogance? And how do you explain that some of the nicest people I know are, by no stretch of the imagination, beautiful?'

Sister Bridget laughed again, a happy sound. 'You keep twisting my words. I have never said that to be nice you have to be beautiful. I merely dispute your assertion that beautiful people are *not* nice. My observation is that very often they are. At the risk of labouring the point, they can afford to be.'

'Then we're back to my previous question. Does that mean ugly people are very often not nice?'

'It doesn't follow, you know, any more than saying poor people are invariably wicked. It just means the tests are harder.' She cocked her head on one side. 'Take Olive and Amber as a case in point. After all, that's why you've really come to see me. Amber led a charmed life. She was quite the loveliest child I've ever seen and with a nature to match. Everyone adored her. Olive, on the other hand, was universally unpopular. She had few redeeming features. She was greedy, deceitful, and often cruel. I found her very hard to like.'

Roz made no attempt to deny her interest. The

conversation had, in any case, been about them from the beginning. 'Then you were being tested as much as she was. Did you fail? Was it impossible to like her?'

'It was very difficult until Amber joined the school. Olive's best quality was that she loved her sister, without reserve and quite unselfishly. It was really rather touching. She fussed over Amber like a mother hen, often ignoring her own interests to promote Amber's. I've never seen such affection between sisters.'

'So why did she kill her?'

'Why indeed? It's time that question was asked.' The older woman drummed her fingers impatiently on the desk. 'I visit her when I can. She won't tell me, and the only explanation I can offer is that her love, which was obsessional, turned to a hate that was equally obsessional. Have you met Olive?'

Roz nodded.

'What did you make of her?'

'She's bright.'

'Yes, she is. She could have gone to university if only the then headmistress had managed to persuade her mother of the advantages. I was a lowly teacher in those days.' She sighed. 'But Mrs Martin was a decided woman, and Olive very much under her thumb. There was nothing we, as a school, could do to make her change her mind. The two girls left together, Olive with three good A-levels and Amber with four rather indifferent O-levels.' She sighed again. 'Poor Olive. She went to work as a cashier in a supermarket while Amber, I believe, tried her hand at hairdressing.'

'Which supermarket was it?'

'Pettit's in the High Street. But the place went out of business years ago. It's an off-licence now.'

'She was working at the local DHSS, wasn't she, at the time of the murders?'

'Yes and doing very well, I believe. Her mother pushed her into it, of course.' Sister Bridget reflected for a moment. 'Funnily enough, I bumped into Olive quite by chance just a week or so before the murders. I was pleased to see her. She looked' – she paused – 'happy. Yes, I think happy is exactly the word for it.'

Roz let the silence drift while she busied herself with her own thoughts. There was so much about this story that didn't make sense. 'Did she get on with her mother?' she asked at last.

'I don't know. I always had the impression she preferred her father. It was Mrs Martin who wore the trousers, of course. If there were choices to be made, it was invariably she who made them. She was very domineering, but I don't recall Olive voicing any antagonism towards her. She was a difficult woman to talk to. Very correct, always. She appeared to watch every word she said in case she gave herself away.' She shook her head. 'But I never did find out what it was that needed hiding.'

There was a knock on the connecting door and a

woman popped her head inside. 'Mr and Mrs Barker are waiting, Sister. Are you ready for them?'

'Two minutes, Betty.' She smiled at Roz. 'I'm sorry. I'm not sure I've been very helpful. Olive had one friend while she was here, not a friend as you or I would know it, but a girl with whom she talked rather more than she did with any of the others. Her married name is Wright – Geraldine Wright – and she lives in a village called Wooling about ten miles north of here. If she's willing to talk to you then I'm sure she can tell you more than I have. The name of her house is Oaktrees.'

Roz jotted down the details in her diary. 'Why do I have the feeling you were expecting me?'

'Olive showed me your letter the last time I saw her.'

Roz stood up, gathering her briefcase and handbag together. She regarded the other woman thoughtfully. 'It may be that the only book I can write is a cruel one.'

'I don't think so.'

'No, I don't think so either.' She paused by the door. 'I've enjoyed meeting you.'

'Come and see me again,' said Sister Bridget. 'I'd like to know how you get on.'

Roz nodded. 'I suppose there's no doubt that she did it?'

'I really don't know,' said the other woman slowly. 'I've wondered, of course. The whole thing is so shocking that it *is* hard to accept.' She seemed to come to a conclusion. 'Be very careful, my dear. The only certainty about Olive is that she lies about almost everything.'

Roz jotted down the name of the arresting officer from the press clippings and called in at the police station on her way back to London. 'I'm looking for a DS Hawksley,' she told the young constable behind the front desk. 'He was with this division in nineteen eighty-seven. Is he still here?'

He shook his head. 'Jacked it in, twelve – eighteen months ago.' He leaned his elbows on the counter and eyed her over with an approving glance. 'Will I do instead?'

Her lips curved involuntarily. 'Perhaps you can tell me where he went?'

'Sure. He opened a restaurant in Wenceslas Street. Lives in the flat above it.'

'And how do I find Wenceslas Street?'

'Well, now' – he rubbed his jaw thoughtfully – 'by far the easiest way is to hang around for half an hour till the end of my shift. I'll take you.'

She laughed. 'And what would your girlfriend say to that?'

'A ruddy mouthful. She's got a tongue like a chain-saw.' He winked. 'I won't tell her if you won't.'

'Sorry, sunshine. I'm shackled to a husband who

hates policemen only marginally less than he hates toy-boys.' Lies were always easier.

He grinned. 'Turn left out of the station and Wenceslas Street is about a mile down on the left. There's an empty shop on the corner. The Sergeant's restaurant is bang next door to it. It's called the Poacher.' He tapped his pencil on the desk. 'Are you planning to eat there?'

'No,' she said, 'it's purely business. I don't intend to hang around.'

He nodded approval. 'Wise woman. The Sergeant's not much of a cook. He'd have done better to stick with policing.'

She had to pass the restaurant to reach the London road. Rather reluctantly she pulled into its abandoned car park and climbed out of the car. She was tired, she hadn't planned on talking to Hawksley that day, and the young constable's light-hearted flirtation depressed her because it had left her cold.

The Poacher was an attractive red-brick building, set back from the road with the car park in front. Leaded bay windows curved out on either side of a solid oak door and wistaria, heavy with buds, grew in profusion across the whole façade. Like St Angela's Convent it was at odds with its surroundings. The shops on either side, both apparently empty, their windows a repository for advertising stickers, complemented each other in cheap post-war pragmatism but did nothing for the old faded beauty in their midst. Worse, a thoughtless council had allowed a previous owner to erect a two-storey extension behind the red-brick frontage, and it gloomed above the restaurant's tiled roof in dirty pebble-dashed concrete. An attempt had been made to divert the wistaria across the roof but, starved of sunlight by the jutting property to the right, the probing tendrils showed little enthusiasm for reaching up to veil the dreary elevation.

Roz pushed open the door and went inside. The place was dark and deserted. Empty tables in an empty room, she thought despondently. Like her. Like her life. She was on the point of calling out, but thought better of it. It was all so peaceful and she was in no hurry. She tiptoed across the floor and took a stool at a bar in the corner. A smell of cooking lingered on the air, garlicky, tempting, reminding her that she hadn't eaten all day. She waited a long time, unseen and unheard, a trespasser upon another's silence. She thought about leaving, unobtrusively, as she had come, but it was strangely restful and her head drooped against her hand. Depression, an all too constant companion, folded its arms around her again, and turned her mind, as it often did, to death. She would do it one day. Sleeping pills or the car. The car, always the car. Alone, at night, in the rain. So easy just to turn the wheel and find a peaceful oblivion. It would be justice of a sort. Her head hurt where the hate swelled and throbbed inside it. God, what a mess she had become. If only someone could lance her destructive anger and let the poison go. Was Iris right? Should she see a psychiatrist? Without warning, the terrible unhappiness burst like a flood inside her, threatening to spill out in tears.

'Oh, shit!' she muttered furiously, dashing at her eyes with the palms of her hands. She scrabbled in her bag for her car keys. 'Shit! Shit! And more bloody shit! Where the hell are you?'

A slight movement caught her attention and she lifted her head abruptly. A shadowy stranger leant against the back counter, quietly polishing a glass and watching her.

She blushed furiously and looked away. 'How long have you been there?' she demanded angrily.

'Long enough.'

She retrieved her keys from the inside of her diary and glared at him briefly. 'What's that supposed to mean?'

He shrugged. 'Long enough.'

'Yes, well, you're obviously not open yet, so I'll be on my way.' She pushed herself off the stool.

'Suit yourself,' he said with supreme indifference. 'I was just about to have a glass of wine. You can go or you can join me. I'm easy either way.' He turned his back on her and uncorked a bottle. The colour receded from her cheeks.

'Are you Sergeant Hawksley?'

He lifted the cork to his nose and sniffed it appreciatively. 'I was, once. Now I'm just plain Hal.' He turned round and poured the wine into two glasses. 'Who's asking?'

She opened her bag again. 'I've got a card somewhere.'

'A voice would do just as well.' He pushed one of the glasses towards her.

'Rosalind Leigh,' she said shortly, propping the card against the telephone on the bar.

She stared at him in the semi-darkness, her embarrassment temporarily forgotten. He was hardly a run of the mill restaurateur. If she had any sense, she thought, she would take to her heels now. He hadn't shaved and his dark suit hung in rumpled folds as if he'd slept in it. He had no tie and half the buttons on his shirt were missing, revealing a mass of tight black curls on his chest. A swelling contusion on his upper left cheek was rapidly closing the eye above it, and thick dried blood encrusted both nostrils. He raised his glass with an ironic smile. 'To your good health, Rosalind. Welcome to the Poacher.' There was a lilt to his voice, a touch of Geordie, tempered by long association with the South.

'It might be more sensible to drink to your good

health,' she said bluntly. 'You look as though you need it.'

'To us then. May we both get the better of whatever ails us.'

'Which, in your case, would appear to be a steamroller.'

He fingered the spreading bruise. 'Not far off,' he agreed. 'And you? What ails you?'

'Nothing,' she said lightly. 'I'm fine.'

'Sure you are.' His dark eyes rested kindly on her for a moment. 'You're half alive and I'm half dead.' He drained his glass and filled it again. 'What did you want with Sergeant Hawksley?'

She glanced about the room. 'Shouldn't you be opening up?'

'What for?'

She shrugged. 'Customers.'

'Customers,' he echoed thoughtfully. 'Now there's a beautiful word.' He gave a ghost of a chuckle. 'They're an endangered species, or haven't you heard? The last time I saw a customer was three days ago, a skinny little runt with a rucksack on his back who was scratching about in search of a vegetarian omelette and decaffeinated coffee.' He fell silent.

'Depressing.'

'Yes.'

She eased herself on to the stool again. 'It's not your fault,' she said sympathetically. 'It's the recession. Everyone's going under. Your neighbours already have, by the look of it.' She gestured towards the door.

He reached up and flicked a switch at the side of the bar. Muted lamplight glowed around the walls, bringing a sparkle to the glasses on the tables. She looked at him with alarm. The contusion on his cheek was the least of his problems. Bright red blood was seeping from a scab above his ear and running down his neck. He seemed unaware of it. 'Who did you say you were?' His dark eyes searched hers for a moment then moved past her to search the room.

'Rosalind Leigh. I think I should call an ambulance,' she said helplessly. 'You're bleeding.'

She had a strange feeling of being outside herself, quite remote from this extraordinary situation. Who was this man? Not her responsibility, certainly. She was a simple bystander who had stumbled upon him by accident. 'I'll call your wife,' she said.

He gave a lop-sided grin. 'Why not? She always enjoyed a good laugh. Presumably she still does.' He reached for a tea-towel and held it to his head. 'Don't worry, I'm not going to die on you. Head wounds always look worse than they are. You're very beautiful. "From the east to western Ind, No jewel is like Rosalind." '

'It's Roz and I'd rather you didn't quote that,' she said sharply. 'It annoys me.'

He shrugged. '*As You Like It.*'

She sucked in an angry breath. 'I suppose you think that's original.'

'A tender nerve, I see. Who are we talking about?' He looked at her ring finger. 'Husband? Ex-husband? Boyfriend?'

She ignored him. 'Is there anyone else here? Someone in the kitchen? You should have that cut cleaned.' She wrinkled her nose. 'In fact you should have this *place* cleaned. It stinks of fish.' The smell, once noticed, was appalling.

'Are you always this rude?' he asked curiously. He rinsed the tea-towel under a tap and watched the blood run out of it. 'It's me,' he said matter of factly. 'I went for a ride on a ton of mackerel. Not a pleasant experience.' He gripped the edge of the small sink and stood staring into it, head lowered in exhaustion, like a bull before the *coup de grâce* of the matador.

'Are you all right?' Roz watched him with a perplexed frown creasing her forehead. She didn't know what to do. It wasn't her problem, she kept telling herself, but she couldn't just walk away from it. Supposing he passed out? 'Surely there's someone I can call,' she insisted. 'A friend. A neighbour. Where do you live?' But she knew that. In the flat above, the young policeman had said.

'Jesus, woman,' he growled, 'give it a rest, for Christ's sake.'

'I'm only trying to help.'

'Is that what you call it? It sounded more like

nagging to me.' He was alert suddenly, listening to something she couldn't hear.

'What's the matter?' she asked, alarmed by his expression.

'Did you lock the door after you?'

She stared at him. 'No. Of course I didn't.'

He dowsed the lights and padded across to the entrance door, almost invisible in the sudden darkness. She heard the sound of bolts being thrust home.

'Look—' she began, getting off her stool.

He loomed up beside her and put an arm around her shoulder and a finger to her lips. 'Quiet, woman.' He held her motionless.

'But—'

'Quiet!'

A car's headlamps swept across the windows, slicing the darkness with white light. The engine throbbed in neutral for a moment or two, then the gears engaged and the vehicle drove away. Roz tried to draw away but Hawksley's arm only gripped her more firmly. 'Not yet,' he whispered.

They stood in silent immobility among the tables, statues at a spectral feast. Roz shook herself free angrily. 'This is absolutely absurd,' she hissed. 'I don't know what on earth is going on but I'm not staying like this for the rest of the night. Who was in that car?'

'Customers,' he said regretfully.

'You're mad.'

He took her hand. 'Come on,' he whispered, 'we'll go upstairs.'

'We will not,' she said, snatching her hand away. 'My God, doesn't anyone think about anything except screwing these days.'

Amused laughter fanned her face. 'Who said anything about screwing?'

'I'm going.'

'I'll see you out.'

She took a deep breath. 'Why do you want to go upstairs?'

'My flat's up there and I need a bath.'

'So what do you want me for?'

He sighed. 'If you remember, Rosalind, it was you who came in here asking for me. I've never met a woman who was so damn prickly.'

'Prickly!' she stuttered. 'My God, that's rich. You stink to high heaven, you've obviously been in a fight, you plunge us into total darkness, moan about not having any customers and then turn them away when they do come, make me sit for five minutes without moving, try to manhandle me upstairs . . .' She paused for breath. 'I think I'm going to be sick,' she blurted out.

'Oh, great! That's all I need.' He took her hand again. 'Come on. I'm not going to rape you. To tell you the truth I haven't the strength at the moment. What's wrong?'

She stumbled after him. 'I haven't eaten all day.'

'Join the club.' He led her through the darkened kitchen and unlocked a side door, reaching past her to switch on some lights. 'Up the stairs,' he told her, 'and the bathroom's on the right.'

She could hear him double-locking the door behind her as she collapsed on the lavatory seat and pressed her head between her knees, waiting for the waves of nausea to pass.

The light came on. 'Here. Drink this. It's water.' Hawksley squatted on the floor in front of her and looked into her white face. She had skin like creamy alabaster and eyes as dark as sloes. A very cold beauty, he thought. 'Do you want to talk about it?'

'What?'

'Whatever's making you so unhappy.'

She sipped the water. 'I'm not unhappy. I'm hungry.'

He put his hands on his knees and pushed himself upright. 'OK. Let's eat. How does sirloin steak sound?'

She smiled weakly. 'Wonderful.'

'Thank God for that! I've got a freezer full of the flaming stuff. How do you like it?'

'Rare but—'

'But what?'

She pulled a face. 'I think it's the smell that's making me sick.' She put her hands to her mouth. 'I'm sorry but I really think it would be better if you got cleaned up first. Mackerel-flavoured sirloin doesn't appeal over much.'

He sniffed at his sleeve. 'You don't notice it after a while.' He turned the taps on full and emptied bath foam into the running water. 'There's only the one loo, I'm afraid, so if you're going to puke you'd better stay there.' He started to undress.

She stood up hurriedly. 'I'll wait outside.'

He dropped his jacket on to the floor and unbuttoned his shirt. 'Just don't be sick all over my carpets,' he called after her. 'There's a sink in the kitchen. Use that.' He was easing the shirt carefully off his shoulders, unaware that she was still behind him, and she stared in horror at the blackened scabs all over his back.

'What happened to you?'

He pulled the shirt back on. 'Nothing. Scoot. Make yourself a sandwich. There's bread on the side and cheese in the fridge.' He saw her expression. 'It looks worse than it is,' he said prosaically. 'Bruising always does.'

'What happened?'

He held her gaze. 'Let's just say I fell off my bike.'

With a contemptuous smile, Olive extracted the candle from its hiding place. They had given up body searches after a woman haemorrhaged in front of one of the Board of Visitors following a particularly aggressive probing of her vagina for illicit drugs. The Visitor had been a MAN. (Olive always thought of men in capital letters.) No woman would have fallen for it. But MEN, of course, were different. Menstruation disturbed them, particularly if the blood flowed freely enough to stain the woman's clothes.

The candle was soft from the warmth of her body and she pulled off the end and began to mould it. Her memory was good. She had no doubt of her ability to imbue the tiny figure with a distinct individuality. This one would be a MAN.

Roz, preparing sandwiches in the kitchen, looked towards the bathroom door. The prospect of questioning Hawksley about the Olive Martin case unnerved her suddenly. Crew had become very annoyed when she questioned *him*; and Crew was a civilized man – in so far as he did not look as if he'd spent half an hour in a dark alley having the shit beaten out of him by Arnold Schwarzenegger. She wondered about Hawksley. Would he be annoyed when he learnt that she was delving into a case he had been involved with? The idea was an uncomfortable one.

There was a bottle of champagne in the fridge. On the rather naïve assumption that another injection of alcohol might make Hawksley more amenable, Roz put it on a tray with the sandwiches and a couple of glasses.

'Were you saving the champagne?' she asked brightly – *too brightly?* – placing the tray on the lavatory seat lid and turning round.

He was lying in a welter of foam, black hair slicked back, face cleaned and relaxed, eyes closed. ''Fraid so,' he said.

'Oh.' She was apologetic. 'I'll put it back then.'

He opened one eye. 'I was saving it for my birthday.'

'And when's that?'

'Tonight.'

She gave an involuntary laugh. 'I don't believe you. What's the date?'

'The sixteenth.'

Her eyes danced wickedly. 'I still don't believe you. How old are you?' She was unprepared for his look of amused recognition and couldn't stop the adolescent flush that tinged her pale cheeks. He thought she was flirting with him. *Well – dammit! – maybe she was.* She had grown weary of suffocating under the weight of her own misery.

'Forty. The big four-o.' He pushed himself into a sitting position and beckoned for the bottle. 'Well, well, this is jolly.' His lips twitched humorously. 'I wasn't expecting company or I'd have dressed for the occasion.' He unbound the wire and eased out the cork, losing only a dribble of bubbly into the foam before filling the glasses that she held out to him. He lowered the bottle to the floor and took a glass. 'To life,' he said, clinking hers.

'To life. Happy birthday.'

His eyes watched her briefly, before closing again as he leant his head against the back of the bath. 'Eat a sandwich,' he murmured. 'There's nothing worse than champagne on an empty stomach.'

'I've had three already. Sorry I couldn't wait for the sirloin. You have one.' She put the tray beside the bottle and left him to help himself. 'Do you have a laundry basket or something?' she asked, stirring the heap of stinking clothes with her toe.

'They're not worth saving. I'll chuck 'em out.'

'I can do that.'

He yawned. 'Bin bags. Second cupboard on the left in the kitchen.'

She carried the bundle at arm's length and sealed the lot into three layers of clean white plastic. It took only a few minutes but when she went back he was asleep, his glass clasped in loose fingers against his chest.

She removed it carefully and put it on the floor. What now? she wondered. She might have been his sister, so unaroused was he by her presence. Go or stay? She had an absurd longing to sit quietly and watch him sleep but she was nervous of waking him.

He would never understand her need to be at peace, just briefly, with a man.

Her eyes softened. It was a nice face. No amount of battering and bruising could hide the laughter lines, and she knew that if she let it it would grow on her and make her pleased to see it. She turned away abruptly. She had been nurturing her bitterness too long to give it up as easily as this. God had not been punished enough.

She retrieved her handbag from where she'd dropped it beside the lavatory and tiptoed down the stairs. But the door was locked and the key was missing. She felt more foolish than concerned, like the embarrassed eavesdropper trapped inside a room whose only object is to escape without being noticed. He must have put the wretched thing in his pocket. She crept back up to the kitchen to scrabble through the dirty clothes bundle but the pockets were all empty. Perplexed, she stared about the work surfaces, searched the tables in the sitting-room and bedroom. If keys existed, they were well hidden. With a sigh of frustration, she pulled back a curtain to see if there was another way out, a fire escape or a balcony, and found herself gazing on a window full of bars. She tried another window and another. All were barred.

Predictably, anger took over.

Without pausing to consider the wisdom of what she was doing, she stormed into the bathroom and shook him violently. 'You bastard!' she snapped. 'What the hell do you think you're playing at! What are you? Some kind of Bluebeard. I want to get out of here. Now!'

He was hardly awake before he'd smashed the champagne bottle against the tiled wall, caught her by the hair, and thrust the jagged glass against her neck. His bloodshot eyes blazed into hers before a sort of recognition dawned and he let her go, pushing her away from him. 'You stupid bitch,' he snarled. 'Don't you ever do that again.' He rubbed his face vigorously to clear it of sleep.

She was very shaken. 'I want to go.'

'So what's stopping you?'

'You've hidden the key.'

He looked at her for a moment, then started to soap himself. 'It's on the architrave above the door. Turn it twice. It's a double lock.'

'Your windows are all barred.'

'They are indeed.' He splashed water on his face. 'Goodbye, Ms Leigh.'

'Goodbye.' She made a weak gesture of apology. 'I'm sorry. I thought I was a prisoner.'

He pulled out the plug and tugged a towel off the rail. 'You are.'

'But – you said the key—'

'Goodbye, Ms Leigh.' He splayed his hand against the door and pushed it to, forcing her out.

*

She should not be driving. The thought hammered in her head like a migraine, a despairing reminder that self-preservation was the first of all the human instincts. But he was right. She *was* a prisoner and the yearning to escape was too strong. So easy, she thought, so very, very easy. Successive headlamps grew from tiny distant pinpoints to huge white suns, sweeping through her windscreen with a beautiful and blinding iridescence, drawing her eyes into the heart of their brilliance. The urge to turn the wheel towards the lights was insistent. How painless the transition would be at the moment of blindness and how bright eternity. *So easy . . . so easy . . . so easy . . .*

Five

OLIVE TOOK A cigarette and lit it greedily. 'You're late. I was afraid you wouldn't come.' She sucked down the smoke. 'I've been dying for a bloody fag.' Her hands and shift were filthy with what looked like dried clay.

'Aren't you allowed cigarettes?'

'Only what you can buy with your earnings. I always run out before the end of the week.' She rubbed the backs of her hands vigorously and showered the table with small grey flakes.

'What is that?' Roz asked.

'Clay.' Olive left the cigarette in her mouth and set to work, plucking the smears from her bosom. 'Why do you think they call me the Sculptress?'

Roz was about to say something tactless, but thought better of it. 'What do you make?'

'People.'

'What sort of people? Imaginary people or people you know?'

There was a brief hesitation. 'Both.' She held Roz's gaze. 'I made one of you.'

Roz watched her for a moment. 'Well, I just hope you don't decide to stick pins into it,' she said with a faint smile. 'Judging by the way I feel today, somebody else is at that already.'

A flicker of amusement crossed Olive's face. She abandoned the smears and fixed Roz with her penetrating stare. 'So what's wrong with you.'

Roz had spent a weekend in limbo, analysing and re-analysing until her brain was on fire. 'Nothing. Just a headache, that's all.' And that was true as far as it went. Her situation hadn't altered. She was still a prisoner.

Olive screwed her eyes against the smoke. 'Changed your mind about the book?'

'No.'

'OK. Fire away.'

Roz switched on the tape-recorder. 'Second conversation with Olive Martin. Date: Monday, April nineteen. Tell me about Sergeant Hawksley, Olive, the policeman who arrested you. Did you get to know him well? How did he treat you?'

If the big woman was surprised by the question, she didn't show it, but then she didn't show anything very much. She thought for some moments. 'Was he the dark-haired one? Hal, I think they called him.'

Roz nodded.

'He was all right.'

'Did he bully you?'

'He was all right.' She drew on her cigarette and stared stolidly across the table. 'Have you spoken to him?'

'Yes.'

'Did he tell you he threw up when he saw the bodies?' There was an edge to her voice. Of amusement? Roz wondered. Somehow, amusement didn't quite square.

'No,' she said. 'He didn't mention that.'

'He wasn't the only one.' A short silence. 'I offered to make them a pot of tea but the kettle was in the kitchen.' She transferred her gaze to the ceiling, aware, perhaps, of having said something tasteless. 'Matter of fact, I liked him. He was the only one who talked to me. I might have been deaf and dumb for all the interest the others showed. He gave me a sandwich at the police station. He was all right.'

Roz nodded. 'Tell me what happened.'

Olive took another cigarette and lit it from the old one. 'They arrested me.'

'No. I mean before that.'

'I called the police station, gave my address, and said the bodies were in the kitchen.'

'And before that?'

Olive didn't answer.

Roz tried a different tack. 'The ninth of September, eighty-seven, was a Wednesday. According to your statement you killed and dismembered Amber and your mother in the morning and early afternoon.' She watched the woman closely. 'Did none of the neighbours hear anything, come and investigate?'

There was a tiny movement at the corner of one eye, a tic, hardly noticeable amidst the fat. 'It's a man, isn't it?' said Olive gently.

Roz was puzzled. 'What's a man?'

Sympathy peeped out from between the puffy, bald lids. 'It's one of the few advantages of being in a place like this. No men to make your life a misery. You get the odd bit of bother, of course, husbands and boyfriends playing up on the outside, but you don't get the anguish of a daily relationship.' She pursed her lips in recollection. 'I always envied the nuns, you know. It's so much easier when you don't have to compete.'

Roz played with her pencil. Olive was too canny to discuss a man in her own life, she thought, assuming there had ever been one. *Had she told the truth about her abortion?* 'But less rewarding,' she said.

A rumble issued from the other side of the table. 'Some reward you're getting. You know what my father's favourite expression was? The game is not worth the candle. He used to drive my mother mad with it. But it's true in your case. Whoever it is you're after, he's not doing you any good.'

Roz drew a doodle on her pad, a fat cherub inside a balloon. Was the abortion a fantasy, a perverted link in Olive's mind with Amber's unwanted son? There was a long silence. She pencilled in the cherub's smile and spoke without thinking. 'Not whoever,' she said, 'whatever. It's what I want, not who I want.' She regretted it as soon as she'd said it. 'It's not important.'

Again there was no response and she began to find Olive's silences oppressive. It was a waiting game, a trap to make her speak. And then what? The toe-curling embarrassment of stammered apologies.

She bent her head. 'Let's go back to the day of the murders,' she suggested.

A meaty hand suddenly covered hers and stroked the fingers affectionately. 'I know about despair. I've felt it often. If you keep it bottled up, it feeds on itself like a cancer.'

There was no insistence in Olive's touch. It was a display of friendship, supportive, undemanding. Roz squeezed the fat, warm fingers in acknowledgement then withdrew her hand. *It's not despair*, she was going to say, *just overwork and tiredness.* 'I'd like to do what you did,' she said in a monotone, 'and kill someone.' There was a long silence. Her own statement had shocked her. 'I shouldn't have said that.'

'Why not? It's the truth.'

'I doubt it. I haven't the guts to kill anyone.'

Olive stared at her. 'That doesn't stop you wanting to,' she said reasonably.

'No. But if you can't summon the guts then I don't think the will is really there.' She smiled distantly. 'I can't even find the guts to kill myself and sometimes I see that as the only sensible option.'

'Why?'

Roz's eyes were over bright. 'I hurt,' she said simply. 'I've been hurting for months.' *But why was she telling Olive all this instead of the nice safe psychiatrist Iris had recommended?* Because Olive would understand.

'Who do you want dead?' The question vibrated in the air between them like a tolled bell.

Roz thought about the wisdom of answering. 'My ex-husband,' she said.

'Because he left you?'

'No.'

'What did he do?'

But Roz shook her head. 'If I tell you, you'll try to persuade me I'm wrong to hate him.' She gave a strange laugh. 'And I need to hate him. Sometimes I think it's the only thing that's keeping me alive.'

'Yes,' said Olive evenly. 'I can understand that.' She breathed on the window and drew a gallows in the mist with her finger. 'You loved him once.' It was a statement, expecting no reply, but Roz felt compelled to answer.

'I can't remember now.'

'You must have done.' The fat woman's voice became a croon. 'You can't hate what you never loved, you can only dislike it and avoid it. Real hate, like real love, consumes you.' With a sweep of her large palm she wiped the gallows from the window. 'I suppose,' she went on, matter of factly, 'you came to see me to find out whether murder is worth it.'

'I don't know,' Roz said honestly. 'Half the time I'm in limbo, the other half I'm obsessed by anger. The only thing I'm sure of is that I'm slowly falling apart.'

Olive shrugged. 'Because it's inside your head. Like I said, it's bad to keep things bottled up. It's a pity you're not a Catholic. You could go to confession and feel better immediately.'

Such a simple solution had never occurred to Roz. 'I was a Catholic, once. I suppose I still am.'

Olive took another cigarette and placed it reverently between her lips like a consecrated wafer. 'Obsessions,' she murmured, reaching for a match, 'are invariably destructive. That, at least, I have learnt.' She spoke sympathetically. 'You need more time before you can talk about it. I understand. You think I'll pick at the scab and make you bleed again.'

Roz nodded.

'You don't trust people. You're right. Trust has a way of rebounding. I know about these things.'

Roz watched her light the cigarette. 'What was your obsession?'

She flicked Roz a strangely intimate look but didn't answer.

'I needn't write this book, you know, not if you don't want me to.'

Olive smoothed her thin blonde hair with the back of her thumb. 'It'll upset Sister Bridget if we give up now. I know you've seen her.'

'Does that matter?'

Olive shrugged. 'It might upset *you* if we give up now. Does *that* matter?'

She smiled suddenly and her whole face brightened. How very *nice* she looked, thought Roz. 'Maybe, maybe not,' she said. 'I'm not convinced myself that I want to write it.'

'Why not?'

Roz pulled a face. 'I should hate to turn you into a freak side-show.'

'Aren't I that already?'

'In here perhaps. Not outside. They've forgotten all about you outside. It may be better to leave it that way.'

'What would persuade you to write it?'

'If you tell me why.'

The silence grew between them. Ominous. 'Have they found my nephew?' Olive asked at last.

'I don't think so.' Roz frowned. 'How did you know they were looking for him?'

Olive gave a hearty chuckle. 'Cell telegraph. Everyone knows everything in here. There's bugger-all else to do except mind other people's business, and we all have solicitors and we all read the newspapers and everyone talks. I could have guessed anyway. My father left a lot of money. He would always leave it to family if he could.'

'I spoke to one of your neighbours, a Mr Hayes. Do you remember him?' Olive nodded. 'If I understood him right, Amber's child was adopted by some people called Brown who've since emigrated to Australia. I assume that's why Mr Crew's firm is having so much difficulty in tracing him. Big place, common name.' She waited for a moment but Olive didn't say anything. 'Why do you want to know? Does it make a difference to you whether he's found or not?'

'Maybe,' she said heavily.

'Why?'

Olive shook her head.

'Do you want him found?'

The door crashed open, startling them both. 'Time's up, Sculptress. Come on, let's be having you.' The officer's voice boomed about the peaceful room, tearing the fabric of their precarious intimacy. Roz saw her own irritation reflected in Olive's eyes. But the moment was lost.

She gave an involuntary wink. 'It's true what they say, you know. Time does fly when you're enjoying yourself. I'll see you next week.' The huge woman lumbered awkwardly to her feet.

'My father was a very lazy man, which is why he let my mother rule the roost.' She rested a hand against the door jamb to balance herself. 'His other favourite saying, because it annoyed her so much, was:

never do today what can always be done tomorrow.' She smiled faintly. 'As a result, of course, he was completely contemptible. The only allegiance he recognized was his allegiance to himself, but it was allegiance without responsibility. He should have studied existentialism.' Her tongue lingered on the word. 'He would have learnt something about man's imperative to choose and act wisely. We are all masters of our fate, Roz, including you.' She nodded briefly then turned away, drawing the prison officer and the metal chair into her laborious, shuffling wake.

Now what, Roz wondered, watching them, was that supposed to mean?

'Mrs Wright?'

'Yes?' The young woman held the front door half open, a restraining hand hooked into her growling dog's collar. She was pretty in a colourless sort of way, pale and fine drawn with large grey eyes and a swinging bob of straw-gold hair.

Roz offered her card. 'I'm writing a book about Olive Martin. Sister Bridget at your old convent school suggested you might be prepared to talk to me. She said you were the closest friend Olive had there.'

Geraldine Wright made a pretence of reading the card then offered it back again. 'I don't think so, thank you.' She said it in the sort of tone she might have used to a Jehovah's Witness. She prepared to close the door.

Roz held it open with her hand. 'May I ask why not?'

'I'd rather not be involved.'

'I don't need to mention you by name.' She smiled encouragingly. 'Please, Mrs Wright. I won't embarrass you. That's not the way I work. It's information I'm after, not exposure. No one will ever know you were connected with her, not through me or my book at least.' She saw a slight hesitancy in the other woman's eyes. 'Ring Sister Bridget,' she urged. 'I know she'll vouch for me.'

'Oh, I suppose it's all right. But only for half an hour. I have to collect the children at three thirty.' She opened the door wide and pulled the dog away from it. 'Come in. The sitting room's on the left. I'll have to shut Boomer in the kitchen or he won't leave us alone.'

Roz walked through into the sitting room, a pleasant, sunny space with wide patio doors opening out on to a small terrace. Beyond, a neat garden, carefully tended, merged effortlessly into a green field with distant cows. 'It's a lovely view,' she said as Mrs Wright joined her.

'We were lucky to get it,' said the other woman with some pride. 'The house was rather out of our price range, but the previous owner took a bridging loan on another property just before the interest rates went through the roof. He was so keen to be shot of this one we got it for twenty-five thousand less than he was asking. We're very happy here.'

'I'm not surprised,' said Roz warmly. 'It's a beautiful part of the world.'

'Let's sit down.' She lowered herself gracefully into an armchair. 'I'm not ashamed of my friendship with Olive,' she excused herself. 'I just don't like talking about it. People are so persistent. They simply won't accept that I knew nothing about the murders.' She examined her painted fingernails. 'I hadn't seen her, you know, for at least three years before it happened and I certainly haven't seen her since. I really can't think what I can tell you that will be of any use.'

Roz made no attempt to record the conversation. She was afraid of scaring the woman. 'Tell me what she was like at school,' she said, taking out a pencil and notepad. 'Were you in the same form?'

'Yes, we both stayed on to do A-levels.'

'Did you like her?'

'Not much.' Geraldine sighed. 'That does sound unkind, doesn't it? Look, you really won't use my name, will you? I mean, if there's a chance you will, I just won't say any more. I should hate Olive to know how I really felt about her. It would be so hurtful.'

Of course it would, thought Roz, but why would you care? She took some headed notepaper from her briefcase, wrote two sentences on it and signed it.

' "I, Rosalind Leigh, of the above address, agree to treat all information given to me by Mrs Geraldine Wright of Oaktrees, Wooling, Hants, as confidential. I shall not reveal her as the source of any information, either verbally or in writing, now or at any time in the future." There. Will that do?' She forced a smile. 'You can sue me for a fortune if I break my word.'

'Oh dear, she'll guess it's me. I'm the only one she talked to. At school, anyway.' She took the piece of paper. 'I don't know.'

God, what a ditherer! It occurred to Roz then that Olive may well have found the friendship as unrewarding as Geraldine appeared to have done. 'Let me give you an idea of how I'll use what you tell me, then you'll see there's nothing to worry about. You've just said you didn't like her much. That will end up in the book as something like: "Olive was never popular at school." Can you go along with that?'

The woman brightened. 'Oh, yes. That's absolutely true anyway.'

'OK. Why wasn't she popular?'

'She never really fitted in, I suppose.'

'Why not?'

'Oh dear.' Geraldine shrugged irritatingly. 'Because she was fat, perhaps.'

This was going to be like drawing teeth, slow and extremely painful. 'Did she try to make friends or didn't she bother?'

'She didn't really bother. She hardly ever said

anything, you know, just used to sit and stare at everyone else while they talked. People didn't like that very much. To tell you the truth, I think we were all rather frightened of her. She was very much taller than the rest of us.'

'Was that the only reason she scared you? Her size?'

Geraldine thought back. 'It was a sort of over-all thing. I don't know how to describe it. She was very quiet. You could be talking to someone and you'd turn round to find her standing right behind you, staring at you.'

'Did she bully people?'

'Only if they were nasty to Amber.'

'And did that happen often?'

'No. Everyone liked Amber.'

'OK.' Roz tapped her pencil against her teeth. 'You say you were the only one Olive spoke to. What sort of things did you talk about?'

Geraldine plucked at her skirt. 'Just things,' she said unhelpfully. 'I can't remember now.'

'The sort of things all girls talk about at school.'

'Well, yes, I suppose so.'

Roz gritted her teeth. 'So you discussed sex, and boys, and clothes, and make-up?'

'Well, yes,' she said again.

'I find that hard to believe, Mrs Wright. Not unless she's changed a great deal in ten years. I've met her, you know. She's not remotely interested in trivia and she doesn't like talking about herself. She wants to know about me and what I do.'

'That's probably because she's in prison and you're her only visitor.'

'I'm not, in actual fact. Also, I am told that most prisoners do the exact opposite when someone visits them. They talk about themselves nineteen to the dozen because it's the only time they get a sympathetic hearing.' She raised a speculative eyebrow. 'I think it's Olive's nature to quiz the person she's talking to. I suspect she's always done it, and that's why none of you liked her very much. You probably thought she was nosy.' Pray God, I'm right, she thought, because this one, who's about as manipulable as putty, will say I am regardless.

'How funny,' said Geraldine. 'Now you mention it, she did ask a lot of questions. She was always wanting to know about my parents, whether they held hands and kissed, and whether I'd ever heard them making love.' She turned her mouth down. 'Yes, I remember now, that's why I didn't like her. She was forever trying to find out how often my parents had sex, and she used to push her face up close when she asked, and stare.' She gave a small shudder. 'I used to hate that. She had such greedy eyes.'

'Did you tell her?'

'About my parents?' Geraldine sniggered. 'Not the truth, certainly. I didn't know myself. Whenever she asked, I always said, yes, they'd had sex the night before, just to get away from her. Everyone did. It became a silly sort of game in the end.'

'Why did she want to know?'

The woman shrugged. 'I always thought it was because she had a dirty mind. There's a woman in the village who's just the same. The first thing she says to anyone is, "Tell me all the gossip," and her eyes light up. I hate that sort of thing. She's the last person to hear what's going on, of course. She puts people's backs up.'

Roz thought for a moment. 'Did Olive's parents kiss and cuddle?'

'Lord, no!'

'You're very certain.'

'Well, of course. They loathed each other. My mother said they only stayed together because he was too lazy to move out and she was too mercenary to let him.'

'So Olive was looking for reassurance?'

'I'm sorry?'

'When she asked you about your parents,' said Roz coolly, 'she was looking for reassurance. The poor kid was trying to find out if hers were the only ones who didn't get on.'

'Oh,' said Geraldine in surprise. 'Do you think so?' She made a pretty little moue with her lips. 'No,' she said, 'I'm sure you're wrong. It was the sex bits she wanted to know about. I told you, her eyes had a greedy look.'

Roz let this pass. 'Did she tell lies?'

'Yes, that was another thing.' Memories chased themselves across her face. 'She was always lying. How odd, I'd forgotten that. In the end, you know, nobody ever believed anything she said.'

'What did she lie about?'

'Everything.'

'What in particular? Herself? Other people? Her parents?'

'Everything.' She saw the impatience in Roz's face. 'Oh dear, it's so hard to explain. She told stories. I mean, she couldn't open her mouth without telling stories. Oh dear, let me see now. All right, she used to talk about boyfriends that didn't exist, and she said the family had been on holiday to France one summer but it turned out they'd stayed at home, and she kept talking about her dog, but everyone knew she didn't have a dog.' She pulled a face. 'And she used to cheat, of course, all the time. It was really annoying that. She'd steal your homework out of your satchel when you weren't looking and crib your ideas.'

'She was bright, though, wasn't she? She got three A-levels.'

'She passed them all but I don't think her grades were anything to shout home about.' It was said with a touch of malice. 'Anyway, if she was so bright, why couldn't she get herself a decent job? My mother said it was embarrassing going to Pettit's and being served by Olive.'

Roz looked away from the colourless face to gaze out over the view from the window. She let some moments pass while common sense battled with the angry reproaches that were clamouring inside her head. After all, she thought, she could be wrong. And yet . . . And yet it seemed so clear to her that Olive must have been a deeply unhappy child. She forced herself to smile. 'Olive was obviously closer to you than anyone else, except, perhaps, her sister. Why do you think that was?'

'Oh, goodness, I haven't a clue. My mother says it's because I reminded her of Amber. I couldn't see it myself, but it's true that people who saw the three of us together always assumed Amber was my sister and not Olive's.' She thought back. 'Mother's probably right. Olive stopped following me around quite so much when Amber joined the school.'

'That must have been a relief.' There was a certain acidity in her tone, mercifully lost on Geraldine.

'I suppose so. Except' – she added this as a wistful afterthought – 'nobody dared tease when Olive was with me.'

Roz watched her for a moment. 'Sister Bridget said Olive was devoted to Amber.'

'She was. But then everyone liked Amber.'

'Why?'

Geraldine shrugged. 'She was nice.'

Roz laughed suddenly. 'To be frank, Amber's

beginning to get up my nose. She sounds too damn good to be true. What was so special about her?'

'Oh dear.' She frowned in recollection. 'Mother said it was because she was willing. People put on her, but she never seemed to mind. She smiled a lot, of course.'

Roz drew her cherub doodle on the notepad and thought about the unwanted pregnancy. 'How was she put upon?'

'I suppose she just wanted to please. It was only little things, like lending out her pencils and running errands for the nuns. I needed a clean sports shirt once for a netball match, so I borrowed Amber's. That sort of thing.'

'Without asking?'

Surprisingly, Geraldine blushed. 'You didn't need to, not with Amber. She never minded. It was only Olive who got angry. She was perfectly beastly about that sports shirt.' She looked at the clock. 'I shall have to go. It's getting late.' She stood up. 'I haven't been very helpful, I'm afraid.'

'On the contrary,' said Roz, pushing herself out of her chair, 'you've been extremely helpful. Thank you very much.'

They walked into the hall together.

'Did it never seem odd to you,' Roz asked as Geraldine opened the front door, 'that Olive should kill her sister?'

'Well, yes, of course it did. I was terribly shocked.'

'Shocked enough to wonder if she actually did it? In view of all you've said about their relationship it seems a very unlikely thing for her to do.'

The wide grey eyes clouded with uncertainty. 'How strange. That's just what my mother always said. But if she didn't do it, then why did she say she did?'

'I don't know. Perhaps because she makes a habit of protecting people.' She smiled in a friendly way. 'Would your mother be prepared to talk to me, do you think?'

'Oh Lord, I shouldn't think so. She hates anyone even knowing I was at school with Olive.'

'Will you ask her anyway? And if she agrees, phone me at that number on the card.'

Geraldine shook her head. 'It would be a waste of time. She won't agree.'

'Fair enough.' Roz stepped through the door and on to the gravel. 'What a lovely house this is,' she said with enthusiasm, looking up at the clematis over the porch. 'Where were you living before?'

The other woman grimaced theatrically. 'A nasty modern box on the outskirts of Dawlington.'

Roz laughed. 'So coming here was by way of a culture shock.' She opened the car door. 'Do you ever go back to Dawlington?'

'Oh, yes,' said the other. 'My parents still live there. I see them once a week.'

Roz tossed her bag and briefcase on to the back

seat. 'They must be very proud of you.' She held out a hand. 'Thank you for your time, Mrs Wright, and please don't worry, I shall be very careful how I use the information you've given me.' She lowered herself on to the driver's seat and pulled the door to. 'There's just one last thing,' she said through the open window, her dark eyes guileless. 'Can I have your maiden name so I can cross you off the school list Sister Bridget gave me? I don't want to go troubling you again by mistake.'

'Hopwood,' said Geraldine helpfully.

It wasn't difficult to locate Mrs Hopwood. Roz drove to the library in Dawlington and consulted the local telephone directory. There were three Hopwoods with Dawlington addresses. She made a note of these with their numbers, found a telephone box and rang each in turn, claiming to be an old friend of Geraldine's and asking to speak to her. The first two denied any knowledge of such a person, the last, a man's voice, told her that Geraldine had married and was now living in Wooling. He gave her Geraldine's telephone number and told her, rather sweetly, how nice it had been to talk to her again. Roz smiled as she put down the receiver. Geraldine, she thought, took after her father.

*

This impression was forcibly confirmed when Mrs Hopwood rattled her safety chain into place and opened the front door. She eyed Roz with deep suspicion. 'Yes?' she demanded.

'Mrs Hopwood?'

'Yes.'

Roz had planned a simple cover story but, seeing the hard glint in the woman's eyes, decided to abandon it. Mrs Hopwood was not the type to take kindly to flannel. 'I'm afraid I bamboozled your daughter and your husband into giving away this address,' she said with a slight smile. 'My name's—'

'Rosalind Leigh and you're writing a book about Olive. I know. I've just had Geraldine on the phone. It didn't take her long to put two and two together. I'm sorry but I can't help you. I hardly knew the girl.' But she didn't close the door. Something – curiosity? – kept her there.

'You know her better than I do, Mrs Hopwood.'

'But I haven't chosen to write a book about her, young woman. Nor would I.'

'Not even if you thought she was innocent?'

Mrs Hopwood didn't answer.

'Supposing she didn't do it? You've considered that, haven't you?'

'It's not my affair.' She started to close the door.

'Then whose affair is it, for God's sake?' demanded Roz, suddenly angry. 'Your daughter paints a picture of two sisters, both of whom were so insecure that one told lies and cheated to give herself some status and the other was afraid to say no in case people didn't like her. What the hell was happening to them at home to make them like that? And where were you then? Where was anybody? The only real friend either of them had was the other.' She saw the thin compression of the woman's lips through the gap in the door and she shook her head contemptuously. 'Your daughter misled me, I'm afraid. From something she said I thought you might be a Samaritan.' She smiled coldly. 'I see you're a Pharisee, after all. Goodbye, Mrs Hopwood.'

The other clicked her tongue impatiently. 'You'd better come in, but I'm warning you, I shall insist on a transcript of this interview. I will not have words put into my mouth afterwards simply to fit some sentimental view you have of Olive.'

Roz produced her tape-recorder. 'I'll tape the whole thing. If you have a recorder you can tape it at the same time, or I can send you a copy of mine.'

Mrs Hopwood nodded approval as she unhooked the chain and opened the door. 'We have our own. My husband can set it up while I make a cup of tea. Come in, and wipe your feet, please.'

Ten minutes later they were ready. Mrs Hopwood took natural control. 'The easiest way is for me to tell you everything I remember. When I've finished you can ask me questions. Agreed?'

'Agreed.'

'I said I hardly knew Olive. That's true. She came here perhaps five or six times in all, twice to Geraldine's birthday parties, and on three or four occasions to tea. I didn't take to her. She was a clumsy girl, slow, impossible to talk to, lacking in humour, and, frankly, extremely unattractive. This may sound harsh and unkind but there you are – you can't pretend feelings that you don't have. I wasn't sorry when her friendship with Geraldine died a natural death.' She paused to collect her thoughts.

'After that, I really had very little to do with her. She never came to this house again. I heard stories, of course, from Geraldine and Geraldine's friends. The impression I formed was very much along the lines you set out earlier – a sad, unloved, and unlovely child, who had resorted to boasting about holidays she hadn't taken and boyfriends she didn't have to make up for unhappiness at home. The cheating, I think, was the result of her mother's constant pressure to do well, as indeed was the compulsive eating. She was always plump but during her adolescence her eating habits became pathological. According to Geraldine, she used to steal food from the school kitchen and cram it, in its entirety, into her mouth, as if she were afraid someone would take it away from her before she had finished.

'Now, you would interpret this behaviour, I imagine, as a symptom of a troubled home background.' She looked enquiringly at Roz, who nodded.

'Yes, well, I think I'd agree with you. It wasn't natural, and nor was Amber's submissiveness, although I must stress I never witnessed either girl in action, so to speak. I am relating only what I was told by Geraldine and her friends. In any event, it did trouble me, mostly because I had met Gwen and Robert Martin when I went to collect Geraldine on the few occasions she was invited to their house. They were a very strange couple. They hardly spoke. He lived in a downstairs room at the back of the house and she and the two girls lived at the front. As far as I could make out, virtually all contact between them was conducted through Olive and Amber.' Seeing Roz's expression, she stopped. 'No one's told you this yet?'

Roz shook her head.

'I never did know how many people were aware of it. She kept up appearances, of course, and, frankly, had Geraldine not told me she had seen a bed in Mr Martin's study, I wouldn't have guessed what was going on.' She wrinkled her brow. 'But it's always the way, isn't it? Once you begin to suspect something, then everything you see confirms that suspicion. They were never together, except at the odd parents' evening, and then there would always be a third party with them, usually one of the teachers.' She smiled self-consciously. 'I used to watch them, you know, not out of malice – my husband will confirm that – but just to prove myself wrong.' She shook her head. 'I came to the conclusion that they simply loathed each other. And it wasn't just that they never spoke, they couldn't bring themselves to exchange *anything* – touches, glances – anything. Does that make sense to you?'

'Oh, yes,' said Roz with feeling. 'Hatred has as strong a body language as love.'

'It was she, I think, who was the instigator of it all. I've always assumed he must have had an affair which she found out about, though I must stress I don't know that. He was a nice looking man, very easy to talk to, and, of course, he got out and about with his job. Whereas she, as far as I could see, had no friends at all, a few acquaintances perhaps, but one never came across her socially. She was a very controlled woman, cold and unemotional. Really rather unpleasant. Certainly not the type one could ever grow fond of.' She was silent for a moment. 'Olive was very much her daughter, of course, both in looks and personality, and Amber his. Poor Olive,' she said with genuine compassion. 'She did have very little going for her.'

Mrs Hopwood looked at Roz and sighed heavily. 'You asked me earlier where I was while all this was going on. I was bringing up my own children, my dear, and if you have any yourself you will know it's hard enough to cope with them, let alone interfere with someone else's. I do regret now that I didn't say anything at the time, but, really, what could I have done? In any case, I felt it was the school's responsibility.' She spread her hands. 'But there you are, it's so easy with hindsight, and who could possibly have guessed that Olive would do what she did? I don't suppose anyone realized just how disturbed she was.' She dropped her hands to her lap and looked helplessly at her husband.

Mr Hopwood pondered for a moment. 'Still,' he said slowly, 'there's no point pretending we've ever believed she killed Amber. I went to the police about that, you know, told them I thought it was very unlikely. They said my disquiet was based on out-of-date information.' He sucked his teeth. 'Which of course was true. It was five years or so since we'd had any dealings with the family, and in five years the sisters could well have learned to dislike each other.' He fell silent.

'But if Olive didn't kill Amber,' Roz prompted, 'then who did?'

'Gwen,' he said with surprise, as if it went without saying. He smoothed his white hair. 'We think Olive walked in on her mother battering Amber. That would have been quite enough to send her berserk, assuming she had retained her fondness for the girl.'

'Was Gwen capable of doing such a thing?'

They looked at each other. 'We've always thought so,' said Mr Hopwood. 'She was very hostile towards Amber, probably because Amber was so like her father.'

'What did the police say?' asked Roz.

'I gather Robert Martin had already suggested the same thing. They put it to Olive and she denied it.'

Roz stared at him. 'You're saying Olive's father told the police that he thought his wife had battered his younger daughter to death and that Olive then killed her mother?'

He nodded.

'God!' she breathed. 'His solicitor never said a word about that.' She thought for a moment. 'It implies, you know, that Gwen had battered the child before. No man would make an accusation like that unless he had grounds for it, would he?'

'Perhaps he just shared our disbelief that Olive could kill her sister.'

Roz chewed her thumbnail and stared at the carpet. 'She claimed in her statement that her relationship with her sister had never been close. Now, I might go along with that if I accept that in the years after school they drifted apart, but I can't go along with it if her own father thought they were still so close that Olive would kill to revenge her.' She shook her head. 'I'm damn sure Olive's barrister never got to hear about this. The poor man was trying to conjure a defence out of thin air.' She looked up. 'Why did Robert Martin give up on it? Why did he let her plead guilty? According to her she did it to spare him the anguish of a trial.'

Mr Hopwood shook his head. 'I really couldn't say. We never saw him again. Presumably, he somehow became convinced of her guilt.' He massaged arthritic fingers. 'The problem for all of us is trying to accept that a person we know is capable of doing something so horrible, perhaps because it shows up the fallibility of our judgement. We knew her before it happened. You, I imagine, have met her since. In both cases, we have failed to see the flaw in her character that led her to murder her mother and sister, and we look for excuses. In the end, though, I don't think there are any. It's not as if the police had to beat her confession out of her. As far as I understand it, it was they who insisted she wait till her solicitor was present.'

Roz frowned. 'And yet you're still troubled by it.'

He smiled slightly. 'Only when someone pops up to stir the dregs again. By and large we rarely think about it. There's no getting away from the fact that she signed a confession saying she did it.'

'People are always confessing to crimes they didn't commit,' countered Roz bluntly. 'Timothy Evans was hanged for his confession, while downstairs Christie went on burying his victims under the floorboards. Sister Bridget said Olive lied about everything, you and your daughter have both cited lies she told. What makes you think she was telling the truth in this one instance?'

They didn't say anything.

'I'm so sorry,' said Roz with an apologetic smile. 'I don't mean to harangue you. I just wish I understood what it was all about. There are so many inconsistencies. I mean why, for example, did Robert Martin stay in the house after the deaths? You'd expect him to move heaven and earth to get out of it.'

'You must talk to the police,' said Mr Hopwood. 'They know more about it than anyone.'

'Yes,' Roz said quietly, 'I must.' She picked up her cup and saucer from the floor and put them on the table. 'Can I ask you three more things? Then I'll leave you in peace. First, is there anyone else you can think of who might be able to help me?'

Mrs Hopwood shook her head. 'I really know very little about her after she left school. You'll have to trace the people she worked with.'

'Fair enough. Second, did you know that Amber had a baby when she was thirteen years old?' She read the astonishment in their faces.

'Good Heavens!' said Mrs Hopwood.

'Quite. Third . . .' She paused for a moment, remembering Graham Deedes' amused reaction. Was it fair to make Olive a figure of fun? 'Third,' she repeated firmly, 'Gwen persuaded Olive to have an abortion. Do you know anything about that?'

Mrs Hopwood looked thoughtful. 'Would that have been at the beginning of eighty-seven?'

Roz, unsure how to answer, nodded.

'I was having problems of my own with a prolonged menopause,' said Mrs Hopwood, matter of factly. 'I bumped into her and Gwen quite by chance at the hospital. It was the last time I saw them. Gwen was very jumpy. She tried to pretend they were there for a gynaecological reason of her own but I couldn't help noticing that it was clearly Olive who had the problem. The poor girl was in tears.' She tut-tutted crossly. 'What a mistake not to let her have it. It explains the murders, of course. They must have happened around the time the baby would have been due. No wonder she was disturbed.'

Roz drove back to Leven Road. This time the door to number 22 stood ajar and a young woman was clipping the low hedge that bordered the front garden. Roz drew her car into the kerb and stepped out. 'Hi,' she said, holding out her hand and shaking the other's firmly. Immediate, friendly contact, she hoped, would stop this woman barring the door to her as her neighbour had done. 'I'm Rosalind Leigh. I came the other day but you were out. I can see your time's precious so I won't stop you working, but can we talk while you're doing it?'

The young woman shrugged as she resumed her clipping. 'If you're selling anything, and that includes religion, then you're wasting your time.'

'I want to talk about your house.'

'Oh, Christ!' said the other in disgust. 'Sometimes I wish we'd never bought the flaming thing. What are you? Psychical bloody research? They're all nutters.

They seem to think the kitchen is oozing with ecto-plasm or something equally disgusting.'

'No. Far more earthbound. I'm writing a follow-up report on the Olive Martin case.'

'Why?'

'There are some unanswered questions. Like, for example, why did Robert Martin remain here after the murders?'

'And you're expecting me to answer that?' She snorted. 'I never even met him. He was long dead before we moved in. You should talk to old Hayes' – she jerked her head towards the adjoining garages – 'he's the only one who knew the family.'

'I have talked to him. He doesn't know either.' She glanced towards the open front door but all she could see was an expanse of peach wall and a triangle of russet carpet. 'I gather the house has been gutted and redecorated. Did you do that yourselves or did you buy it after it was done?'

'We did it ourselves. My old man's in the building trade. Or was,' she corrected herself. 'He was made redundant ten, twelve months ago. We were lucky, managed to sell our other house without losing too much, and bought this for a song. Did it without a mortgage, too, so we're not struggling the way some other poor sods are.'

'Has he found another job?' Roz asked sympathetically.

The young woman shook her head. 'Hardly. Building's all he knows and there's precious little of that at the moment. Still, he's trying his best. Can't do more than that, can he?' She lowered the shears. 'I suppose you're wondering if we found anything when we gutted the house.'

Roz nodded. 'Something like that.'

'If we had, we'd have told someone.'

'Of course, but I wouldn't have expected you to find anything incriminating. I was thinking more in terms of impressions. Did the place look loved, for example? Is that why he stayed? Because he loved it?'

The woman shook her head. 'I reckon it was more of a prison. I can't swear to it because I don't know for sure, but my guess is he only used one room and that was the room downstairs at the back, the one that was attached to the kitchen and the cloakroom with its own door into the garden. Maybe he went through to the kitchen to cook, but I doubt it. The connecting door was locked and we never found the key. Plus, there was an ancient Baby Belling still plugged into one of the sockets in that room, which the house clearers couldn't be bothered to take, and my bet is he did all his cooking on that. The garden was nice. I think he lived in the one room and the garden, and never went into the rest of the house at all.'

'Because the door was locked?'

'No, because of the nicotine. The windows were so thick with it that the glass looked yellow. And the ceiling' – she pulled a face – 'was dark brown. The smell of old tobacco was overpowering. He must have smoked non-stop in there. It was disgusting. But there were no nicotine stains anywhere else in the house. If he ever went beyond the connecting door, then it can't have been for very long.'

Roz nodded. 'He died of a heart attack.'

'I'm not surprised.'

'Would you object to my taking a look inside?'

'There's no point. It's completely different. We knocked out any walls that weren't structural and changed the whole layout downstairs. If you want to know what it looked like when he was here, then I'll draw you a plan. But you don't come in. If I say yes to you, then there's no end to it, is there? Any Tom, Dick, or Harry can demand to put his foot through our door.'

'Point taken. A plan would be more helpful, anyway.' She reached into the car for a notepad and pencil and passed it across.

'It's much nicer now,' said the self-possessed young woman, drawing with swift strokes. 'We've opened up the rooms and put some colour into them. Poor Mrs Martin had no idea at all. I think, you know, she was probably rather boring. There.' She passed the notepad back. 'That's the best I can do.'

'Thank you,' said Roz studying the plan. 'Why do you think Mrs Martin was boring?'

'Because everything – walls, doors, ceilings, *everything* – was painted white. It was like an operating theatre, cold and antiseptic, without a spot of colour. And she didn't have pictures either, because there were no marks on the walls.' She shuddered. 'I don't like houses like that. They never look lived in.'

Roz smiled as she glanced up at the red-brick façade. 'I'm glad it's you who bought it. I should think it feels lived in now. I don't believe in ghosts myself.'

'Put it this way, if you want to see ghosts, you'll see them. If you don't, you won't.' She tapped the side of her head. 'It's all in the mind. My old dad used to see pink elephants but no one ever thought *his* house was haunted.'

Roz was laughing as she drove away.

Six

THE CAR PARK of the Poacher was as deserted as before but this time it was three o'clock in the afternoon, lunchtime was over, and the door was bolted. Roz tapped on the window pane but, getting no response, made her way round to the alley at the back where the kitchen door must be. It stood ajar and from inside came the sound of singing.

'Hello,' she called. 'Sergeant Hawksley?' She put her hand on the door to push it wider and almost lost her balance when it was whipped away from her. 'You did that on purpose!' she snapped. 'I could have broken my arm.'

'Good God, woman,' he said in mock disgust. 'Can't you open your mouth without nagging? I'm beginning to think I did my ex-wife an injustice.' He crossed his arms, a fish slice dangling from one hand. 'What do you want this time?'

He had a peculiar talent for putting her at a disadvantage. She bit back an angry retort. 'I'm sorry,' she said instead. 'It's just that I nearly fell over. Look, are you busy at the moment or can I come in and talk to you?' She examined his face warily for signs of further damage but there were none that hadn't been there before.

'I'm busy.'

'What if I came back in an hour? Could you talk then?'

'Maybe.'

She gave a rueful smile. 'I'll try again at four.'

He watched her walk up the alleyway. 'What are you going to do for an hour?' he called after her.

She turned round. 'I expect I'll sit in the car. I've some notes to work on.'

He swung the fish slice. 'I'm cooking *steak au poivre* with some lightly steamed vegetables and potatoes fried in butter.'

'Bully for you,' she said.

'There's enough for two.'

She smiled. 'Is that an invitation or a refined form of torture?'

'It's an invitation.'

She came back slowly. 'Actually, I'm starving.'

A slight smile warmed his face. 'So what's new?' He took her into the kitchen and pulled out a chair at the table. He eyed her critically as he turned the gas up under some simmering pans. 'You look as if you haven't had a square meal in days.'

'I haven't.' She recalled what the young policeman had said. 'Are you a good cook?'

He turned his back on her without answering, and she regretted the question. Talking to Hawksley was almost as intimidating as talking to Olive. She couldn't speak, it seemed, without treading on a nerve. Except for a muted thank you when he poured her a glass of wine she sat in uncomfortable silence for five minutes, wondering how to open the conversation. She was highly doubtful that he would greet her proposed book on Olive with any enthusiasm.

He placed the steaks on warmed plates, surrounded them with fried whole potatoes, steamed mangetout, and baby carrots, and garnished them with the juices from the pan. 'There,' he said, whisking a plate in front of Roz, apparently unaware of her discomfort, 'that'll put some colour in your cheeks.' He sat down and attacked his own plate. 'Well, come on, woman. What are you waiting for?'

'A knife and fork.'

'Ah!' He pulled open a drawer in the table and slid some cutlery across. 'Now, get stuck in and don't yatter while you're eating. Food should be enjoyed for its own sake.'

She needed no further bidding but set to with a will. 'Fabulous,' she said at last, pushing her empty plate to one side with a sigh of contentment. 'Absolutely fabulous.'

He arched a sardonic eyebrow. 'So what's the verdict? Can I cook or can I cook?'

She laughed. 'You can cook. May I ask you something?'

He filled her empty glass. 'If you must.'

'If I hadn't turned up would you have eaten all that yourself?'

'I might have drawn the line at one steak.' He paused. 'Then again I might not. I've no bookings for tonight and they don't keep. I'd probably have eaten them both.'

She heard the trace of bitterness in his voice. 'How much longer can you stay open without customers?' she asked incautiously.

He ignored the question. 'You said you wanted to talk to me,' he reminded her. 'What about?'

She nodded. Apparently, he had no more desire than she to lick wounds in public. 'Olive Martin,' she told him. 'I'm writing a book about her. I believe you were one of the arresting officers.'

He didn't answer immediately but sat looking at her over the rim of his wine glass. 'Why Olive Martin?'

'She interests me.' It was impossible to gauge his reaction.

'Of course.' He shrugged. 'She did something completely horrific. You'd be very unnatural if you didn't find her interesting. Have you met her?'

She nodded.

'And?'

'I like her.'

'Only because you're naïve.' He stretched his long arms towards the ceiling, cracking the joints in his shoulders. 'You steeled yourself to delve in the sewer, expecting to pull out a monster, and you've landed yourself something comparatively pleasant instead. Olive's not unusual in that. Most criminals are pleasant most of the time. Ask any prison officer. They know better than anyone that the penal system relies almost entirely on the goodwill of the prisoners.' His eyes narrowed. 'But Olive hacked two completely innocent women to death. The fact that she presents a human face to you now doesn't make what she did any less horrific.'

'Have I said it does?'

'You're writing a book about her. Even if you castigate her, she will still be something of a celebrity.' He leaned forward, his tone unfriendly. 'But what about her mother and sister? Where is the justice for them in giving their murderer the thrill and the kudos of being written about?'

Roz dropped her eyes. 'It does worry me,' she admitted. 'No, that's wrong.' She looked up. 'It *did* worry me. I'm a little more sure now of where I'm heading. But I take your point about her victims. It's all too easy to focus on Olive. She's alive and they're dead, and the dead are difficult to recreate. You have to rely on what other people tell you, and just as their perceptions at the time were not always accurate, neither are their memories now.' She sighed. 'I still have reservations – there's no point in pretending I don't – but I need to understand what happened that day before I can make up my mind.' She fingered the stem of her wine glass. 'I think I may very well be naïve but I'd need convincing that that is a bad thing. I could argue, with considerable justification, that anyone delving regularly in sewers must come up jaundiced.'

'What's that supposed to mean?' He was amused.

She looked at him again. 'That what Olive did shocks you but doesn't surprise you. You've known, or known of, other people who've done similar things before.'

'So?'

'So you never established *why* she did it. Whereas I, being naïve' – she held his gaze – 'am surprised as well as shocked and I want to know why.'

He frowned. 'It's all in her statement. I can't remember the exact details now, but she resented not being given a birthday party, I think, and then blew a fuse when her mother got angry with her for persuading the sister to ring in sick the next day. Domestic violence erupts over the most trivial things. Olive's motives were rather more substantial than some I've known.'

Roz bent down to open her briefcase. 'I've a copy of her statement here.' She handed it across and waited while he read it through.

'I can't see your problem,' he said at last. 'She makes it clear as crystal why she did it. She got angry, hit them, and then didn't know how to dispose of the bodies.'

'That's what she says, I agree, but it doesn't mean it's *true*. There's at least one blatant lie in that statement and possibly two.' She tapped her pencil on the table. 'In the first paragraph she says that her relationship with her mother and sister had never been close but that's been flatly contradicted by everyone I've spoken to. They all say she was devoted to Amber.'

He frowned again. 'What's the other lie?'

She leaned over with her pencil and put a line by one of the middle paragraphs. 'She says she held a mirror to their lips to see if there was any mist. According to her, there wasn't, so she proceeded to dismember the bodies.' She turned the pages over. 'But here, according to the pathologist, Mrs Martin put up a struggle to defend herself before her throat was cut. Olive makes no mention of that in her statement.'

He shook his head. 'That doesn't mean a damn thing. Either she decided to put a gloss on the whole affair out of belated shame, or shock simply blotted the less acceptable bits out of her memory.'

'And the lie about not getting on with Amber? How do you explain that away?'

'Do I need to? The confession was completely voluntary. We even made her wait until her solicitor arrived to avoid any hint of police pressure.' He drained his glass. 'And you're not going to try and argue that an innocent woman would confess to a crime like this?'

'It's happened before.'

'Only after days of police interrogation and then, when it comes to the trial, they plead not guilty and deny their statement. Olive did neither.' He looked amused. 'Take it from me, she was so damned relieved to get it all off her chest she couldn't confess fast enough.'

'How? Did she deliver a monologue or did you have to ask questions?'

He clasped his hands behind his neck. 'Unless she's changed a great deal I should imagine you've already discovered that Olive doesn't volunteer information easily.' He cocked his head enquiringly. 'We had to ask questions but she answered them readily enough.' He looked thoughtful. 'For most of the time she sat and stared at us as if she were trying to engrave our faces on her memory. To be honest, I live in terror of her getting out and doing to me what she did to her family.'

'Five minutes ago you described her as comparatively pleasant.'

He rubbed his jaw. 'Comparatively pleasant as far as *you* were concerned,' he corrected her. 'But you were expecting something inhuman, which is why you find it difficult to be objective.'

Roz refused to be drawn again down this blind alley. Instead she took her recorder from her briefcase and put it on the table. 'Can I tape this conversation?'

'I haven't agreed to talk to you yet.' He stood up abruptly and filled a kettle with water. 'You'd do better,' he said after a moment, 'to ring Detective Sergeant Wyatt. He was there when she gave her statement, and he's still on the Force. Coffee?'

'Please.' She watched him select a dark Arabica and spoon the grounds into a cafetière. 'I really would rather talk to you,' she said evenly. 'Policemen are notoriously difficult to pin down. It could take me weeks to get an interview with him. I won't quote you, I won't even name you, if you'd rather I didn't, and you can read the final draft before it goes to print.' She gave a hollow laugh. 'Assuming it ever gets that far. What you say may persuade me not to write it.'

He looked at her, absent-mindedly scratching his chest through his shirt, then made up his mind. 'All right. I'll tell you as much as I can remember but you'll have to double-check everything. It's a long time ago and I can't vouch for my memory. Where do I start?'

'With her telephone call to the police.'

He waited for the kettle to boil, then filled the cafetière and placed it on the table. 'It wasn't a 999 call. She looked up the number in the book and dialled the desk.' He shook his head, remembering. 'It started out as a farce because the sergeant on duty couldn't make head or tail of what she was saying.'

He was shrugging into his jacket at the end of his shift when the desk sergeant came in and handed him a piece of paper with an address on it. 'Do me a favour, Hal, and check this out on your way home. It's Leven Road. You virtually pass it. Some madwoman's been bawling down the phone about chicken legs on her kitchen floor.' He pulled a face. 'Wants a policeman to take them away.' He grinned. 'Presumably she's a vegetarian. You're the cookery expert. Sort it out, there's a good chap.'

Hawksley eyed him suspiciously. 'Is this a wind-up?'

'No. Scout's honour.' He chuckled. 'Look, she's obviously a mental case. They're all over the place, poor sods, since the Government chucked 'em on to the streets. Just do as she asks or we'll have her phoning all night. It'll take you five minutes out of your way.'

Olive Martin, red eyed from weeping, opened the door to him. She smelt strongly of B.O. and her bulky shoulders were hunched in unattractive despair. So much blood was smeared over her baggy T-shirt and trousers that it took on the property of an abstract pattern and his eyes hardly registered it. And why should they? He had no premonition of the horror in store. 'D.S. Hawksley,' he said with an encouraging smile, showing her his card. 'You rang the police station.'

She stepped back, holding the door open. 'They're in the kitchen.' She pointed down the corridor. 'On the floor.'

'OK. We'll go down and have a look. What's your name, love?'

'Olive.'

'Right, Olive, you lead the way. Let's see what's upset you.'

Would it have been better to know what was in there? Probably not. He often thought afterwards that he could never have entered the room at all if he'd been told in advance that he was about to step into a human abattoir. He stared in horror at the butchered bodies, the axe, the blood that ran in rivers across the floor, and his shock was so great that he could hardly breathe for the iron fist that thrust against his diaphragm and squeezed the breath from his lungs. The room reeked of blood. He leant against the door jamb and sucked desperately at the sickly, cloying air, before bolting down the corridor and retching over and over again into the tiny patch of front garden.

Olive sat on the stairs and watched him, her fat moon face as white and pasty as his. 'You should have brought a friend,' she told him miserably. 'It wouldn't have been so bad if there'd been two of you.'

He held a handkerchief to his lips as he used his radio to summon assistance. While he spoke he eyed her warily, registering the blood all over her clothes. Nausea choked him. Je-*sus*! JESUS! How mad was she? *Mad enough to take the axe to him?* 'For God's sake, make it quick,' he shouted into the mouthpiece. 'This is an emergency.' He stayed outside, too frightened to go back in.

She looked at him stolidly. 'I won't hurt you. There's nothing to be afraid of.'

He mopped at his forehead. 'Who are they, Olive?'

'My mother and sister.' Her eyes slid to her hands. 'We had a row.'

His mouth was dry with shock and fear. 'Best not talk about it,' he said.

Tears rolled down her fat cheeks. 'I didn't mean it to happen. We had a row. My mother got so angry with me. Should I give my statement now?'

He shook his head. 'There's no hurry.'

She stared at him without blinking, her tears drying in dirty streaks down her face. 'Will you be able to take them away before my father comes home?' she asked him after a minute or two. 'I think it would be better.'

Bile rose in his throat. 'When do you expect him back?'

'He leaves work at three o'clock. He's part-time.'

Hal glanced at his watch, an automatic gesture. His mind was numb. 'It's twenty to now.'

She was very composed. 'Then perhaps a policeman could go there and explain what's happened. It would be better,' she said again. They heard the wail of approaching sirens. 'Please,' she said urgently.

He nodded. 'I'll arrange it. Where does he work?'

'Carters Haulage. It's in the Docks.'

He was passing the message on as two cars, sirens shrieking, swept round the corner and bore down on number 22. Doors flew open all along the road and curious faces peered out. Hal switched off the radio and looked at her. 'All done,' he said. 'You can stop worrying about your father.'

A large tear slipped down her blotchy face. 'Should I make a pot of tea?'

Hal thought of the kitchen. 'Better not.'

The sirens stilled as policemen erupted from the cars. 'I'm sorry to cause so much bother,' she said into the silence.

She spoke very little after that, but only, thought Hal on reflection, because nobody spoke to her. She was packed into the living room, under the eye of a shocked W.P.C., and sat in bovine immobility watching the comings and goings through the open door. If she was aware of the mounting horror that was gathering about her, she didn't show it. Nor, as time passed and the signs of emotion faded from her face, did she display any further grief or remorse for what she had done. Faced with such complete indifference, the consensus view was that she was mad.

'But she wept in front of you,' interrupted Roz. 'Did *you* think she was mad?'

'I spent two hours in that kitchen with the pathologist, trying to work out the order of events from the blood splashes over the floor, the table, the kitchen units. And then, after the photographs had been taken, we embarked on the grisly jigsaw of deciding which bit belonged to which woman. Of course I thought she was mad. No normal person could have done it.'

Roz chewed her pencil. 'That's begging the question, you know. All you're really saying is that the act itself was one of madness. I asked you if, from your experience of her, you thought Olive was mad.'

'And you're splitting hairs. As far as I could see, the two were inextricably linked. Yes, I thought Olive was mad. That's why we were so careful to make sure her solicitor was there when she made her statement. The idea of her getting off on a technicality and spending twelve months in hospital before some idiot psychiatrist decided she was responding well enough to treatment to be allowed out scared us rigid.'

'So did it surprise you when she was judged fit to plead guilty?'

'Yes,' he admitted, 'it did.'

*

At around six o'clock attention switched to Olive. Areas of dried blood were lifted carefully from her arms and each fingernail was minutely scraped before she was taken upstairs to bathe herself and change into clean clothes. Everything she had been wearing was packed into individual polythene bags and loaded into a police van. An inspector drew Hal to one side.

'I gather she's already admitted she did it.'

Hal nodded. 'More or less.'

Roz interrupted again. 'Less is right. If what you said earlier is correct, she did not admit anything. She said they'd had a row, that her mother got angry, and she didn't mean it to happen. She didn't say she had killed them.'

Hal agreed. 'I accept that. But the implication was there which is why I told her not to talk about it. I didn't want her claiming afterwards that she hadn't been properly cautioned.' He sipped his coffee. 'By the same token, she didn't deny killing them, which is the first thing an innocent person would have done, especially as she had their blood all over her.'

'But the point is, you assumed her guilt before you knew it for a fact.'

'She was certainly our prime suspect,' he said drily.

*

The inspector ordered Hal to take Olive down to the station. 'But don't let her say anything until we can get hold of a solicitor. We'll do it by the book. OK?'

Hal nodded again. 'There's a father. He'll be at the nick by now. I sent a car to pick him up from work but I don't know what he's been told.'

'You'd better find out then, and, for Christ's sake, Sergeant, if he doesn't know, then break it to him gently or you'll give the poor sod a heart attack. Find out if he's got a solicitor and if he's willing to have him or her represent his daughter.'

They put a blanket over Olive's head when they took her out to the car. A crowd had gathered, lured by rumours of a hideous crime, and cameramen jostled for a photograph. Boos greeted her appearance and a woman laughed. 'What good's a blanket, boys? You'd need a bloody marquee to cover that fat cow. I'd recognize her legs anywhere. What you done, Olive?'

Roz interrupted again when he jumped the story on to his meeting with Robert Martin at the police station.

'Hang on. Did she say anything in the car?'

He thought for a moment. 'She asked me if I liked her dress. I said I did.'

'Were you being polite?'

'No. It was a vast improvement on the T-shirt and trousers.'

'Because they had blood on them?'

'Probably. No,' he contradicted himself, ruffling his hair, 'because the dress gave her a bit of shape, I suppose, made her look more feminine. Does it matter?'

Roz ignored this. 'Did she say anything else?'

'I think she said something like: "That's good. It's my favourite." '

'But in her statement, she said she was going to London. Why wasn't she wearing the dress when she committed the murders?'

He looked puzzled. 'Because she was going to London in trousers, presumably.'

'No,' said Roz stubbornly. 'If the dress was her favourite, then that's what she would have worn for her trip to town. London was her birthday treat to herself. She probably had dreams of bumping into Mr Right on Waterloo station. It simply wouldn't occur to her to wear anything but her best. You need to be a woman to understand that.'

He was amused. 'But I see hundreds of girls walking around in shapeless trousers and baggy T-shirts, particularly the fat ones. I think they look grotesque but they seem to like it. Presumably they're making a statement about their refusal to pander to conventional standards of beauty. Why should Olive have been any different?'

'Because she wasn't the rebellious type. She lived at home under her mother's thumb, took the job her mother wanted her to take, and was apparently so unused to going out alone for the day that she had to beg her sister to go with her.' She drummed her fingers impatiently on the table. 'I'm right. I know I am. If she wasn't lying about the trip to London then she should have been wearing her dress.'

He was not impressed. 'She was rebellious enough to kill her mother and sister,' he remarked. 'If she could do that, she could certainly go to London in trousers. You're splitting hairs again. Anyway, she might have changed to keep the dress clean.'

'But she definitely intended to go to London? Did you check that?'

'She certainly booked the day off work. We accepted that London was where she was going because, as far as we could establish, she hadn't mentioned her plans to anyone else.'

'Not even to her father?'

'If she did, he didn't remember it.'

Olive waited in an interview room while Hal spoke to her father. It was a difficult conversation. Whether he had schooled himself to it, or whether it was a natural trick of behaviour, Robert Martin reacted little to anything that was said to him. He was a handsome man but, in the way that a Greek sculpture is handsome, he invited admiration but lacked warmth or attraction. His curiously impassive face had an unlined and ageless quality, and only his hands, knotted with arthritis, gave any indication that he had passed his middle years. Once or twice he smoothed his blond hair with the flat of his hand or touched his fingers to his tie, but for all the expression on his plastic features Hal might have been passing the time of day. It was impossible to gauge from his expression how deeply he was shocked or whether, indeed, he was shocked at all.

'Did you like him?' asked Roz.

'Not much. He reminded me of Olive. I don't know where I am with people who hide their feelings. It makes me uncomfortable.'

Roz could identify with that.

Hal kept detail to a minimum, informing him only that the bodies of his wife and one of his daughters had been discovered that afternoon in the kitchen of his house, and that his other daughter, Olive, had given the police reason to believe she had killed them.

Robert Martin crossed his legs and folded his hands calmly in his lap. 'Have you charged her with anything?'

'No. We haven't questioned her either.' He watched the other man closely. 'Frankly, sir, in view of the serious nature of the possible charges we think she should have a solicitor with her.'

'Of course. I'm sure my man, Peter Crew, will come.' Mild enquiry twitched his brows. 'What's the procedure? Should I telephone him?'

Hal was puzzled by the man's composure. He wiped a hand across his face. 'Are you sure you understand what's happened, sir?'

'I believe so. Gwen and Amber are dead and you think Olive murdered them.'

'That's not quite accurate. Olive has implied that she was responsible for their deaths but, until we take a statement from her, I can't say what the charges will be.' He paused for a moment. 'I want you to be quite clear on this, Mr Martin. The Home Office pathologist who examined the scene had no doubts that considerable ferocity was used both before and after death. In due course, I'm afraid to say, we will have to ask you to identify the bodies and you may, when you see them, feel less charitably inclined towards any possible suspect. On that basis, do you have any reservations about your solicitor representing Olive?'

Martin shook his head. 'I would be happier dealing with someone I know.'

'There may be a conflict of interests. Have you considered that?'

'In what way?'

'At the risk of labouring the point, sir,' said Hal

coldly, 'your wife and daughter have been brutally murdered. I imagine you will want the perpetrator prosecuted?' He lifted an eyebrow in enquiry and Martin nodded. 'Then you may well want a solicitor yourself to ensure that the prosecution proceeds to your satisfaction, but if your own solicitor is already representing your daughter, he will be unable to assist you because your interests will conflict with your daughter's.'

'Not if she's innocent.' Martin pinched the crease in his trousers, aligning it with the centre of his knee. 'I am really not concerned with what Olive may have implied, Sergeant Hawksley. There is no conflict of interest in my mind. Establishing her innocence and representing me in pressing for a prosecution can be done by the same solicitor. Now, if you could lend me the use of a telephone, I will ring Peter Crew, and afterwards, perhaps you will allow me to talk to my daughter.'

Hal shook his head. 'I'm sorry, sir, but that won't be possible, not until we've taken a statement from her. You will also be required to make a statement. You may be allowed to speak to her afterwards, but at the moment I can't guarantee it.'

'And that,' he said, recalling the incident, 'was the one and only time he showed any emotion. He looked quite upset, but whether because I'd denied him access to Olive or because I'd told him he'd have to make a statement, I don't know.' He considered for a moment. 'It must have been the denial of access. We went through every minute of that man's day and he came out whiter than white. He worked in an open-plan office with five other people and, apart from the odd trip to the lavatory, he was under someone's eye the whole day. There just wasn't time for him to go home.'

'But you did suspect him?'

'Yes.'

Roz looked interested. 'In spite of Olive's confession?'

He nodded. 'He was so damn cold blooded about it all. Even identifying the bodies didn't faze him.'

Roz thought for a moment. 'There was another conflict of interest which you don't seem to have considered.' She chewed her pencil. 'If Robert Martin was the murderer, he could have used his solicitor to manipulate Olive into confessing. Peter Crew makes no secret of his dislike of her, you know. I think he regrets the abolition of capital punishment.'

Hal folded his arms, then smiled in amusement. 'You'll have to be very careful if you intend to make statements like that in your book, Miss Leigh. Solicitors are not required to like their clients, they merely have to represent them. In any case, Robert Martin dropped out of the frame very rapidly. We toyed with the idea that he killed Gwen and Amber before he went to work and Olive then set about disposing the bodies to protect him, but the numbers didn't add up. He had an alibi even for that. There was a neighbour who saw her husband off to work a few minutes before Martin himself left. Amber and Gwen were alive then because she spoke to them on their doorstep. She remembered asking Amber how she was getting on at Glitzy. They waved as Martin drove away.'

'He could have gone round the corner and come back again.'

'He left home at eight-thirty and arrived at work at nine. We tested the drive and it took half an hour.' He shrugged. 'As I said, he was whiter than white.'

'What about lunch? Could he have gone back then?'

'He had a pint and a sandwich in the local pub with two men from the office.'

'OK. Go on.'

There was little more to tell. In spite of Crew's advice to remain silent, Olive agreed to answer police questions, and at nine-thirty, expressing relief to have got the whole thing off her chest, she signed her statement and was formally charged with the murder of her mother and sister.

Following her remand into custody on the morning of the next day, Hal and Geoff Wyatt were given the task of detailing the police case against her. It was a straightforward collating of pathological, forensic, and police evidence, all of which, upon examination, supported the facts given in Olive's statement. Namely that, acting alone, she had, on the morning of the ninth of September, 1987, murdered her mother and sister by cutting their throats with a carving knife.

Seven

THERE WAS A lengthy silence. Hal splayed his hands on the scrubbed deal table and pushed himself to his feet. 'How about some more coffee?' He watched her industrious pen scribbling across a page of her notebook. 'More coffee?' he repeated.

'Mm. Black, no sugar.' She didn't look up but went on writing.

'Sure, baas. Don't mind me, baas. I'se just de paid help, baas.'

Roz laughed. 'Sorry. Yes, thank you, I'd love some more coffee. Look, if you can just bear with me for a moment, I've a few questions to ask and I'm trying to jot them down while the thing's still fresh.'

He watched her while she wrote. Botticelli's *Venus*, he had thought the first time he saw her, but she was too thin for his liking, hardly more than seven stone and a good five feet six. She made a fabulous clothes'-horse, of course, but there was no softness to hug, no comfort in the tautly strung body. He wondered if her slenderness was a deliberate thing or if she lived on her nerves. The latter, he thought. She was clearly a woman of obsessions if her crusade for Olive was anything to go by. He put a fresh cup of coffee in front of her but stayed standing, cradling his own coffee cup between his hands.

'OK,' she said, sorting out the pages, 'let's start with the kitchen. You say the forensic evidence supported Olive's statement that she acted alone. How?'

He thought back. 'You have to picture that place. It was a slaughter house, and every time she moved she left footprints in the congealing blood. We photographed each one separately and they were all hers, including the bloody prints that her shoes left on the carpet in the hall.' He shrugged. 'There were also bloody palm-prints and fingerprints over most of the surfaces where she had rested her hands. Again all hers. We did raise other fingerprints, admittedly, including about three, I think, which we were never able to match with any of the Martins or their neighbours, but you'd expect that in a kitchen. The gas man, the electricity man, a plumber maybe. There was no blood on them so we inclined to the view that they had been left in the days prior to the murder.'

Roz chewed her pencil. 'And the axe and the knife? I suppose they had only her fingerprints.'

'Actually no. The cutting weapons were so smeared that we couldn't get anything off them at all.' He chuckled at her immediate interest. 'You're chasing red herrings. Wet blood is slippery stuff. It would have been very surprising if we *had* found some perfect prints. The rolling pin had three damn good ones, all hers.'

She made a note. 'I didn't know you could take them off unpolished wood.'

'It was solid glass, two feet long, a massive thing. I suppose if we were surprised by anything it was that the blows she struck with it hadn't killed Gwen and Amber. They were both tiny women. By rights she should have smashed their skulls with it.' He sipped his coffee. 'It leant some credence to her story, in fact, that she only tapped them lightly in the first instance to make them shut up. We were afraid she might use that in her defence to get the charge reduced to manslaughter, the argument being that she slit their throats *only* because she believed they were already dead and she was trying to dismember them in panic. If she could then go on to show that the initial blows with the rolling pin were struck with very little force – well, she might almost have persuaded a jury that the whole thing was a macabre accident. Which is one good reason, by the way, why she never mentioned the fight with her mother. We did push her on that, but she kept insisting that no mist on the mirror meant they were dead.' He pulled a face. 'So I spent a very unpleasant two days working with the pathologist and the bodies, going step by step through what actually happened. We ended up with enough evidence of the fight Gwen put up to save her life to press a murder charge. Poor woman. Her hands and arms were literally cut to ribbons where she had tried to ward off the blows.'

Roz stared into her coffee for some minutes. 'Olive was very kind to me the other day. I can't imagine her doing something like that.'

'You've never seen her in a rage. You might think differently if you had.'

'Have you seen her in a rage?'

'No,' he admitted.

'Well, I find it difficult even to imagine that. I accept she's put on a lot of weight in the last six years but she's a heavy, stolid type. It's highly strung, impatient people who lose their tempers.' She saw his scepticism and laughed. 'I know, I know, amateur psychology of the worst kind. Just two more questions then I'll leave you in peace. What happened to Gwen and Amber's clothes?'

'She burnt them in one of those square wire incinerators in the garden. We retrieved some scraps from the ashes which matched the descriptions that Martin gave of the clothes the two women had been wearing that morning.'

'Why did she do that?'

'To get rid of them, presumably.'

'You didn't ask her?'

He frowned. 'I'm sure we must have done. I can't remember now.'

'There's nothing in her statement about burning clothes.'

He lowered his head in reflection and pressed a thumb and forefinger to his eyelids. 'We asked her why she took their clothes off,' he murmured, 'and she said they had to be naked or she couldn't see where to make the cuts through the joints. I think Geoff then asked her what she had done with the clothes.' He fell silent.

'And?'

He looked up and rubbed his jaw pensively. 'I don't think she gave an answer. If she did, I can't remember it. I have a feeling the information about the scraps in the incinerator came in the next morning when we made a thorough search of the garden.'

'So you asked her then?'

He shook his head. 'I didn't, though I suppose Geoff may have done. Gwen had a floral nylon overall that had melted over a lump of wool and cotton. We had to peel it apart into its constituent elements but there was enough there that was recognizable. Martin ID'd the bits and so did the neighbour.' He stabbed a finger in the air. 'There were some buttons, too. Martin recognized those straightaway as being from the dress his wife had been wearing.'

'But didn't you wonder why Olive took time out to burn the clothes? She could have put them in the suitcases with the bodies and dumped the whole lot in the sea.'

'The incinerator certainly wasn't burning at five o'clock that night or we'd have noticed it; therefore disposing of the clothes must have been one of the first things she did. She wouldn't have seen it as taking time out because at that stage she probably still thought dismembering two bodies would be comparatively easy. Look, she was trying to get rid of evidence. The only reason she panicked and called us in was because her father was coming home. If it had been just the three women living in that house she could have gone through with her plan, and we'd have had the job of trying to identify some bits and pieces of mutilated flesh found floating in the sea off Southampton. She might even have got away with it.'

'I doubt it. The neighbours weren't stupid. They'd have wondered why Gwen and Amber were missing.'

'True,' he conceded. 'What was the other question?'

'Did Olive's hands and arms have a lot of scratches on them from her fight with Gwen?'

He shook his head. 'None. She had some bruising but no scratches.'

Roz stared at him. 'Didn't that strike you as odd? You said Gwen was fighting for her life.'

'She had nothing to scratch with,' he said almost apologetically. 'Her fingernails were bitten to the quick. It was rather pathetic in a woman of her age. All she could do was grip Olive's wrists to try and keep the knife away. That's what the bruises were. Deep finger-marks. We took photographs of them.'

With an abrupt movement Roz squared her papers and dropped them into her briefcase. 'Not much room for doubt then, is there?' she said, picking up her coffee cup.

'None at all. And it wouldn't have made any difference, you know, if she'd kept her mouth shut or pleaded not guilty. She would still have been convicted. The evidence against her was overwhelming. In the end, even her father had to accept that. I felt quite sorry for him then. He became an old man overnight.'

Roz glanced at the tape, which was still running. 'Was he very fond of her?'

'I don't know. He was the most undemonstrative person I've ever met. I got the impression he wasn't fond of any of them but' – he shrugged – 'he certainly took Olive's guilt very badly.'

She drank her coffee. 'Presumably the post-mortem revealed that Amber had had a baby when she was thirteen?'

He nodded.

'Did you pursue that at all? Try and trace the child?'

'We didn't see the need. It had happened eight years before. It was hardly likely to have any bearing on the case.' He waited, but she didn't say anything. 'So? Will you go on with the book?'

'Oh, yes,' she said.

He looked surprised. 'Why?'

'Because there are more inconsistencies now than there were before.' She held up her fingers and ticked them off point by point. 'Why was she crying so much when she telephoned the police station that the desk sergeant couldn't understand what she was saying? Why wasn't she wearing her best dress for London? Why did she burn the clothes? Why did her father think she was innocent? Why wasn't he shocked by Gwen and Amber's deaths? Why did she say she didn't like Amber? Why didn't she mention the fight with her mother if she intended to plead guilty? Why were the blows from the rolling pin so comparatively light? Why? Why? Why?' She dropped her hands to the table with a wry smile. 'They may very well be red herrings but I can't get rid of a gut feeling that there's something wrong. Ultimately, perhaps, I cannot square your and her solicitor's conviction that Olive was mad with the assessments of five psychiatrists who all say she's normal.'

He studied her for some minutes in silence. 'You accused me of assuming her guilt before I knew it for a fact, but you're doing something rather worse. You're assuming her innocence *in spite of* the facts. Supposing you manage to whip up support for her through this book of yours – and in view of the way the judicial system is reeling at the moment, that's not as unlikely as it should be – have you no qualms about releasing someone like her back into society?'

'None at all, if she's innocent.'

'And if she isn't, but you get her out anyway?'

'Then the law is an ass.'

'All right, if she didn't do it, who did?'

'Someone she cared about.' She finished her coffee and switched off the tape. 'Anything else just doesn't make sense.' She shut the recorder into her briefcase and stood up. 'You've been very kind to give up so much of your time. Thank you, and thank you for the lunch.' She held out a hand.

He took it gravely. 'My pleasure, Miss Leigh.' Her fingers, soft and warm in his, moved nervously when he held them too long, and he thought she seemed suddenly rather afraid of him. It was probably for the best. One way and another, she spelt trouble.

She walked to the door. 'Goodbye, Sergeant Hawksley. I hope the business picks up for you.'

He gave a savage smile. 'It will. This is what's known as a temporary blip, I assure you.'

'Good.' She paused. 'There's just one last thing. I understand Robert Martin told you he thought the more likely scenario was that Gwen battered Amber, and Olive then killed Gwen trying to defend her sister. Why did you dismiss that possibility?'

'It didn't hold water. The pathologist established that both throats were cut with the same hand. The size, depth, and angle of the wounds were consistent with one attacker. Gwen wasn't just fighting for herself, you know, she was fighting for Amber, too. Olive is completely ruthless. You would be very foolish to forget that.' He smiled again but the smile didn't reach his eyes. 'If you'll take my advice you'll abandon the whole thing.'

Roz shrugged. 'I tell you what, Sergeant' – she gestured towards the restaurant – 'you mind your business, and I'll mind mine.'

He listened to her heels tapping away down the alley, then reached for the telephone and dialled. 'Geoff,' he snapped into the mouthpiece, 'get down here, will you? We need to talk.' His eyes hardened as he listened to the voice at the other end. 'Like hell it's not your problem. I'm damned if I'll be the fall guy for this one.'

Roz glanced at her watch as she drove away. It was four thirty. If she pushed it she might catch Peter Crew before he went home for the day. She found a parking space in the centre of Southampton and arrived at his office just as he was leaving.

'Mr Crew!' she called, running after him.

He turned with his unconvincing smile, only to frown when he saw who it was. 'I've no time to talk to you now, Miss Leigh. I have an engagement.'

'Let me walk with you,' she urged. 'I won't delay you, I promise.'

He gave a nod of acquiescence and set off again,

the hair of his toupee bobbing in time to his steps. 'My car isn't far.'

Roz did not waste time on pleasantries. 'I gather Mr Martin left his money to Amber's illegitimate son. I have been told' – she stretched the truth like a piece of elastic – 'that he was adopted by some people called Brown who have since emigrated to Australia. Can you tell me if you've made any progress in finding him?'

Mr Crew shot her an annoyed glance. 'Now where did you find that out, I wonder?' His voice clipped the words angrily. 'Has someone in my practice been talking?'

'No,' she assured him. 'I had it from an independent source.'

His eyes narrowed. 'I find that hard to believe. May I ask who it was?'

Roz smiled easily. 'Someone who knew Amber at the time the baby was born.'

'How did they know the name?'

'I've no idea.'

'Robert certainly wouldn't have talked,' he muttered. 'There are rules governing the tracing of adopted children, which he was well aware of, but even allowing for that he was passionate on the subject of secrecy. If the child were to be found he didn't want any publicity surrounding the inheritance. The stigma of the murders could follow the boy all his life.' He shook his head crossly. 'I must insist, Miss

Leigh, that you keep this information to yourself. It would be gross irresponsibility to publish it. It could jeopardize the lad's future.'

'You really do have quite the wrong impression of me,' said Roz pleasantly. 'I approach my work with immense care, and I do not set out to expose people for the sake of it.'

He turned a corner. 'Well, be warned, young lady. I shan't hesitate to take out an injunction against your book if I think it justified.' A gust of wind lifted the toupee's peak and he pressed it firmly to his head like a hat.

Roz, a step or two behind him, scurried alongside. 'Fair enough,' she said, biting back her laughter. 'So, on that basis, could you answer my question? Have you found him yet? Are you anywhere near finding him?'

He padded on doggedly. 'Without wishing to be offensive, Miss Leigh, I don't see how that information can help you. We have just agreed you won't be publishing it.'

She decided to be straight with him. 'Olive knows all about him, knows her father left him his money, knows you're looking for him.' She lifted her hands at his expression of irritation. 'Not, in the first instance, from me, Mr Crew. She's very astute and what she hadn't guessed for herself she picked up on the prison grapevine. She said her father would always leave money to family if he could so it hardly required much imagination to guess that he would try and trace Amber's child. Anyway, whether or not you've had any success seems to matter to her. I hoped you could tell me something that would set her mind at rest.'

He stopped abruptly. 'Does she want him found?'

'I don't know.'

'Hm. Perhaps she thinks the money will come to her in the absence of the named beneficiary?'

Roz showed her surprise. 'I don't think that's ever occurred to her. It couldn't, anyway, could it? You made that point before.'

Mr Crew set off again. 'Robert did not insist that Olive should be kept in the dark. His only instruction was that we should avoid distressing her unnecessarily. Wrongly, perhaps, I assumed that knowledge of the terms of the will *would* distress her. However, if she is already acquainted with them – well, well, you can leave that with me, Miss Leigh. Was there anything else?'

'Yes. Did Robert Martin ever visit her in prison?'

'No. I'm sorry to say he never spoke to her again after she was charged with the murders.'

Roz caught his arm. 'But he thought she was innocent,' she protested with some indignation, 'and he paid her legal bills. Why wouldn't he see her? That was very cruel, wasn't it?'

There was a sharp gleam in the man's eyes. 'Very cruel,' he agreed, 'but not on Robert's part. It was

Olive who refused to see him. It drove him to his death, which, I think, was her intention all along.'

Roz frowned unhappily. 'You and I have very different views of her, Mr Crew. I've only experienced her kindness.' The frown deepened. 'She did know he wanted to see her, I suppose.'

'Of course. As a prosecution witness he had to apply to the Home Office for special permission to visit her, even though she was his daughter. If you contact them they'll verify it for you.' He moved on again and Roz had to run to keep up with him.

'What about the inconsistencies in her statement, Mr Crew? Did you ask her about them?'

'What inconsistencies?'

'Well, for example, the fact that she doesn't mention the fight with her mother but claims Gwen and Amber were dead before she started to dismember them.'

He cast an impatient glance at his watch. 'She was lying.'

Roz caught at his arm again and forced him to stop. 'You were her solicitor,' she said angrily. 'You had a duty to believe her.'

'Don't be naïve, Miss Leigh. I had a duty to *represent* her.' He shook himself free. 'If solicitors were required to believe everything their clients told them there would be little or no legal representation left.' His lips thinned in distaste. 'In any case I did believe her. She said she killed them and I accepted it. I had to. In spite of every attempt I made to suggest she said nothing, she insisted on making her confession.' His eyes bored into hers. 'Are you telling me now that she denies the murders?'

'No,' Roz admitted, 'but I don't think the version she gave the police is the correct one.'

He studied her for a moment. 'Did you talk to Graham Deedes?' She nodded. 'And?'

'He agrees with you.'

'The police?'

She nodded again. 'One of them. He also agrees with you.'

'And doesn't that tell you anything?'

'Not really. Deedes was briefed by you and never even spoke to her and the police have been wrong before.' She brushed a curl of red hair from her face. 'Unfortunately, I don't have your faith in British justice.'

'Obviously not.' Crew smiled coolly. 'But your scepticism is misplaced this time. Good day to you, Miss Leigh.' He loped away up the wind-swept street, the absurd toupee held in place under his hand, his coat-tails whipping about his long legs. He was a comical figure, but Roz did not feel like laughing. For all his idiotic mannerisms he had a certain dignity.

She telephoned St Angela's Convent from a payphone but it was after five o'clock and whoever answered said Sister Bridget had gone home for the evening. She called Directory Enquiries for the DSS number in Dawlington, but, when she tried it, the office had closed for the night and there was no answer. Back in her car she pencilled in a rough timetable for the following morning, then sat for some time with her notebook propped against the steering-wheel, running over in her mind what Crew had told her. But she couldn't concentrate. Her attention kept wandering to the more attractive lure of Hal Hawksley in the Poacher's kitchen.

He had an unnerving trick of catching her eye when she wasn't expecting it, and the shock to her system every time was cataclysmic. She thought 'going weak at the knees' was something invented by romantic authoresses. But the way things were, if she went back to the Poacher, she'd need a Zimmer frame just to make it through the door! *Was she mad?* The man was some sort of gangster. Whoever heard of a restaurant without customers? People had to eat, even in recessions. With a rueful shake of her head, she fired the engine and set off back to London. *What the hell, anyway!* Sod's law predicated that because thoughts of him filled her mind with erotic fantasies his thoughts of her (if he thought about her at all) would be anything but libidinous.

London, when she reached it, was fittingly clogged

and oppressive with Thursday night rush-hour traffic.

An older motherly inmate, elected by the others, paused nervously by the open door. The Sculptress terrified her but, as the girls kept saying, she was the only one Olive would talk to. You remind her of her mother, they all said. The idea alarmed her, but she *was* curious. She watched the huge brooding figure, clumsily rolling a cigarette paper around a meagre sprinkling of tobacco, for several moments before she spoke. 'Hey, Sculptress! Who's the redhead you're seeing?'

Except for a brief flick of her eyes, Olive ignored her.

'Here, have one of mine.' She fished a pack of Silk Cut from her pocket and proffered it. The response was immediate. Like a dog responding to the ringing tap of its dinner plate, Olive shuffled across the floor and took one, secreting it in the folds of her dress somewhere. 'So who's the redhead?' persisted the other.

'An author. She's writing a book about me.'

'Christ!' said the older woman in disgust. 'What she want to write about you for? I'm the one got bloody stitched up.'

Olive stared at her. 'Maybe I did, too.'

'Oh, sure,' the other sniggered, tapping her thigh. 'Now pull the other one. It's got frigging bells on.'

A wheeze of amusement gusted from Olive's lips. 'Well, you know what they say: you can fool some of the people all of the time and all of the people some of the time . . .' She paused invitingly.

'But not all of the people all of the time,' the woman finished obligingly. She wagged her finger. 'You haven't got a prayer.'

Olive's unblinking eyes held hers. 'So who needs prayers?' She tapped the side of her head. 'Find yourself a gullible journalist, then use a bit more of this. Even *you* might get somewhere. She's an opinion-former. You fool her and she fools everyone else.'

'That stinks!' declared the woman incautiously. 'It's only the bloody psychos they're ever interested in. The rest of us poor sods can go hang ourselves for all they care.'

Something rather unpleasant shifted at the back of Olive's tiny eyes. 'Are you calling me a psycho?'

The woman smiled weakly and retreated a step. 'Hey, Sculptress, it was a slip of the tongue.' She held up her hands. 'OK? No harm done.' She was sweating as she walked away.

Behind her, using her bulk to obscure what she was doing from prying eyes, Olive took the clay figure she was working on from her bottom drawer and set her ponderous fingers to moulding the child on its mother's lap. Whether it was intentional or whether she hadn't the skill to do it differently, the mother's crude hands, barely disinterred from the clay, seemed to be smothering the life from the baby's plump, round body.

Olive crooned quietly to herself as she worked. Behind the mother and child, a series of figures, like grey gingerbread men, lined the back of the table. Two or three had lost their heads.

He sat slumped on the steps outside the front door of her block of flats, smelling of beer, his head buried in his hands. Roz stared at him for several seconds, her face blank of expression. 'What are you doing here?'

He had been crying, she saw. 'We need to talk,' he said. 'You never talk to me.'

She didn't bother to answer. Her ex-husband was very drunk. There was nothing they could say that hadn't been said a hundred times before. She was so tired of his messages on her answerphone, tired of the letters, tired of the hatred that knotted inside her when she heard his voice or saw his handwriting.

He plucked at her skirt as she tried to pass, clinging to it like a child. 'Please, Roz. I'm too pissed to go home.'

She took him upstairs out of an absurd sense of past duty. 'But you can't stay,' she told him, pushing him on to the sofa. 'I'll ring Jessica and get her to come and collect you.'

'Sam's sick,' he muttered. 'She won't leave him.'

Roz shrugged unsympathetically. 'Then I'll call a cab.'

'No.' He reached down and jerked the jackplug from its socket. 'I'm staying.

There was a raw edge to his voice which was a warning, if she had chosen to heed it, that he was in no mood to be trifled with. But they had been married too long and had had too many bruising rows for her to allow him to dictate terms. She had only contempt for him now. 'Please yourself,' she said. 'I'll go to a hotel.'

He stumbled to the door and stood with his back to it. 'It wasn't my fault, Roz. It was an accident. For God's sake, will you stop punishing me?'

Eight

ROZ CLOSED HER eyes and saw again the tattered, pale face of her five-year-old daughter, as ugly in death as she had been beautiful in life, her skin ripped and torn by the exploding glass of the windscreen. Could she have accepted it more easily, she wondered as she had wondered so many times before, if Rupert had died too? Could she have forgiven him, dead, as she could not forgive him, alive? 'I never see you,' she said with a tight smile, 'so how can I be punishing you? You're drunk and you're being ridiculous. Neither of which conditions is any way out of the ordinary.' He had an unhealthy and uncared-for look which fuelled her scorn and made her impatient. 'Oh, for God's sake,' she snapped, 'just get out, will you? I don't feel anything for you any more and, to be honest, I don't think I ever did.' But that wasn't true, not really. 'You can't hate what you never loved,' Olive had said.

Tears slithered down his drink-sodden face. 'I weep for her every day, you know.'

'Do you, Rupert? I don't. I haven't the energy.'

'Then you didn't love her as much as I loved her,' he sobbed, his body heaving to control itself.

Roz's lips curled contemptuously. 'Really? Then why your indecent haste to provide her replacement? I worked it out, you know. You must have impregnated your precious Jessica within a week of walking away unscathed from the – *accident.*' She larded the word with sarcasm. 'Is Sam a good replacement, Rupert? Does he wind your hair round his finger the way Alice used to do? Does he laugh like her? Does he wait by the door for you and hug your knees and say: "Mummy, Mummy, Daddy's home"?' Her anger made her voice brittle. 'Does he, Rupert? Is he everything Alice was and more? Or is he nothing like her and that's why you have to weep for her every day?'

'He's a baby, for Christ's sake.' He clenched his fists, her hatred mirrored in his eyes. 'God, you're a fucking bitch, Roz. I never set out to replace her. How could I? Alice was Alice. I couldn't bring her back.'

She turned away to look out of the window. 'No.'

'Then why do you blame Sam? It wasn't his fault either. He doesn't even know he had a half-sister.'

'I don't blame Sam.' She stared at a couple, lit by orange light, on the other side of the road. They held each other tenderly, stroking hair, stroking arms, kissing. How naïve they were. They thought love was kind. 'I resent him.'

She heard him blunder against her coffee table. 'That's just bloody spite,' he slurred.

'Yes,' she said quietly, more to herself than to him, her breath misting the glass, 'but I don't see why you should be happy when I am not? You killed my daughter but you got away with it because the law said you'd suffered enough. I've suffered far more and my only crime was to let my adulterous husband have access to his daughter because I knew she loved him and I didn't want to see her unhappy.'

'If you'd only been more understanding,' he wept, 'it would never have happened. It was your fault, Roz. You're the one who really killed her.' She didn't hear his approach. She was turning back into the room when his fist smashed against her face.

It was a shabby, sordid fight. Where words had failed them – the very predictability of their conversations meant they were always forearmed – they hit and scratched instead in a brutish desire to hurt. It was a curiously passionless exercise, motivated more by feelings of guilt than by hate or revenge, for at the back of both their minds was the knowledge that it was the failure of their marriage, the war they had conducted between themselves, that had led Rupert to accelerate away in frustrated anger with their daughter, unstrapped, upon the back seat. And who could have foreseen the car that would hurtle out of control across a central reservation and, under the force of its impact, toss a helpless five-year-old through shards of broken glass, smashing her fragile skull as she went? An act of God, according to the insurance company. But for Roz, at least, it had been God's final act. He and Alice had perished together.

Rupert was the first to stay his hand, aware, perhaps, that the fight was an unequal one or because, quite simply, he had sobered up. He crawled away to sit huddled in a corner. Roz fingered the tenderness round her mouth and licked blood from her lips, then closed her eyes and sat for several minutes in restful silence, her murderous anger assuaged. They should have done this a long time ago. She felt at peace for the first time in months, as if she had exorcised her own guilt in some way. She should, she knew, have gone out to the car that day and strapped Alice into the seat herself, but instead she had slammed the front door on them both and retreated to the kitchen to nurse her hurt pride with a bottle of gin and an orgy of tearing up photographs. Perhaps, after all, she had needed to be punished too. Her guilt had never been expiated. Her own atonement, a private rending of herself, had brought about her disintegration and not her redemption.

Enough, she saw now, was enough. *'We are all masters of our fate, Roz, including you.'*

She pushed herself gingerly to her feet, located the jackplug and inserted it back into its socket. She glanced at Rupert for a moment, then dialled Jessica. 'It's Roz,' she said. 'Rupert's here and he needs collecting, I'm afraid.' She heard the sigh at the other end of the line. 'It's the last time, Jessica, I promise.' She gave a hint of a laugh. 'We've declared a truce. No more recriminations. OK, half an hour. He'll be waiting for you downstairs.' She replaced the receiver. 'I mean it, Rupert. It's over. It was an accident. Let's stop blaming each other and find some peace at last.'

Iris Fielding's insensitivity was legendary but even she was shocked by the sight of Roz's battered face the next day. 'God, you look awful!' she said bluntly, making straight for the drinks cabinet and pouring herself a brandy. As an afterthought she poured one for Roz. 'Who did it?'

Roz closed the door and limped back to the sofa.

Iris drained her glass. 'Was it Rupert?' She proffered the second glass to Roz who shook her head to the brandy and the question.

'Of course it wasn't Rupert.' She lowered herself carefully on to the sofa, half lying, half sitting, while Mrs Antrobus stalked across the soft fluff of her dressing-gowned chest to butt her chin with an affectionate head. 'Could you feed Mrs A. for me? There's an opened tin in the fridge.'

Iris glowered at Mrs Antrobus. 'Horrible flea-bitten creature. Where were you when your mistress needed you?' But she disappeared into the kitchen and rattled a saucer anyway. 'Are you sure it wasn't Rupert?' she asked again when she re-emerged.

'No. Not his style at all. The fights we have are entirely verbal and infinitely more bruising.'

Iris looked thoughtful. 'You've always told me how supportive he's been.'

'I lied.'

Iris looked even more thoughtful. 'So who was it?'

'Some creep I picked up at a wine bar. He was more fanciable with his clothes on than off, so I told him to get stuffed and he took exception.' She saw a question in Iris's eyes and smiled cynically through her split lip. 'No, he didn't rape me. My virtue is intact. I defended it with my face.'

'Hm. Well, far be it from me to criticize, my love, but wouldn't it have been more sensible to defend your face with your virtue? I'm not a great believer in fighting over lost causes.' She drank Roz's brandy. 'Did you call the police?'

'No.'

'A doctor?'

'No.' She put a hand on the telephone. 'And you're not calling them either.'

Iris shrugged. 'So what have you been doing all morning?'

'Trying to work out how I could get by without calling anyone. At midday, I realized I couldn't. I've used all my aspirin, I've no food in the house, and

I'm not going out looking like this.' She raised bruised and suspiciously bright eyes. 'So I thought of the least shockable and the most egocentric person I know and I telephoned her. You'll have to go out shopping for me, Iris. I need enough to last me a week.'

Iris was amused. 'I would never deny that I'm egocentric but why is that important?'

Roz bared her teeth. 'Because you're so wrapped up in yourself you'll have forgotten all about this by the time you get home. Plus, you're not going to pressure me into doing the right thing and nailing the little bastard. It wouldn't reflect well on your agency if one of your authors was in the habit of bringing home pick-ups from wine bars.' She clenched both hands over the telephone and Iris watched her knuckles whiten under the strain.

'True,' she agreed calmly.

Roz relaxed a little. 'I really couldn't bear it, you know, if this got out, and it will if doctors or the police are involved. You know the bloody press as well as I do. Any excuse, and they'll plaster their front pages all over again with pictures of Alice in the wreckage.' Poor little Alice. Malign providence had put a freelance photographer beside the dual carriageway when she was tossed like a rag doll from Rupert's car. His dramatic shots – published, according to the tabloid editors, as a tragic reminder to other families of the importance of wearing seat belts – had been

Alice's most lasting memorial. 'You can imagine the sordid parallels they'll draw. MOTHER DISFIGURED LIKE DAUGHTER. I couldn't survive it a second time.' She fished in her pocket and produced a shopping list. 'I'll write you a cheque when you come back. And whatever you do, don't forget the aspirin. I'm in agony.'

Iris tucked the shopping list into her bag. 'Keys,' she said, holding out her hand. 'You can go to bed while I'm out. I'll let myself back in.'

Roz pointed to her keys on a shelf by the door. 'Thank you,' she said, 'and, Iris—' She didn't finish.

'And, Iris, what?'

She made an attempt at a wry grimace but abandoned it because it was too painful. 'And, Iris, I'm sorry.'

'So am I, old thing.' She gave an airy wave and let herself out of the flat.

For reasons best known to herself, Iris returned a couple of hours later with the shopping and a suitcase. 'Don't look at me like that,' she said severely, administering aspirin in a glass of water. 'I intend to keep an eye on you for a day or two. For entirely mercenary purposes, of course. I like to guard my investments closely. And anyway,' she scratched under Mrs Antrobus's chin, 'someone's got to feed this revolting moggy for you. You'll only start howling if it dies of starvation.'

Roz, depressed and very lonely, was touched.

Detective Sergeant Geoff Wyatt toyed unhappily with his wine glass. His stomach was playing up, he was very tired, it was Saturday, he would rather have been at a Saints' football match, and the sight of Hal tucking into a plateful of rare steak needled him. 'Look,' he said, trying to keep the irritation out of his voice, 'I hear what you're saying but evidence is evidence. What are you expecting me to do? Tamper with it?'

'It's hardly evidence if it was tampered with at the outset,' Hal snapped. 'It was a frame, for Christ's sake.' He pushed his plate away. 'You should have had some,' he said acidly. 'It might have improved your temper.'

Wyatt looked away. 'There's nothing wrong with my temper and I ate before I got here.' He lit a cigarette and glanced towards the door into the restaurant. 'I've never felt comfortable in kitchens, not since seeing those women on Olive's floor. Too many murder weapons and too much bloody meat about the place. Couldn't we go next door?'

'Don't be a fool,' said Hal curtly. 'Damn it, Geoff, you owe me a few one way and another.'

Wyatt sighed. 'How's it going to help you if I get suspended for doing dodgy favours for an ex-copper?'

'I'm not asking for dodgy favours. Just get the pressure taken off. Give me a breathing space.'

'How?'

'You could start by persuading the Inspector to back off.'

'And that's not dodgy?' His mouth turned down. 'Anyway, I've tried. He's not playing. He's new, he's honest, and he doesn't like anyone who bends the rules, particularly policemen.' He tapped ash on the floor. 'You should never have left the Force, Hal. I did warn you. It's very lonely outside.'

Hal rubbed his unshaven face. 'It wouldn't be so bad if my erstwhile colleagues didn't keep treating me like a criminal.'

Wyatt stared at the remains of the steak on Hal's plate. He felt very queasy. 'Well, if it comes to that, you shouldn't have been so damn careless, then they wouldn't have to.'

Hal's eyes narrowed unpleasantly. 'One of these days you're going to wish you hadn't said that.'

With a shrug, Wyatt ground his cigarette against his shoe and tossed the butt into the sink. 'Can't see it, old son. I've been shitting my backside off ever since the Inspector rumbled you. It's made me ill, it really has.' He pushed back his chair and stood up. 'Why the hell did you have to cut corners instead of doing it by the book the way you were supposed to?'

Hal nodded towards the door. 'Out,' he said, 'before I rip your two-faced head off.'

'What about that check you wanted me to run?'

Hal fished in his pocket and removed a piece of paper. 'That's her name and address. See if there's anything on her.'

'Like what?'

Hal shrugged. 'Anything that will give me a lever. This book she's writing is too well timed.' He frowned. 'And I don't believe in coincidence.'

One of the few advantages of being fat was that it was easier to hide things. Another bulge here or there passed unnoticed and the soft cavity between Olive's breasts could accommodate itself to almost anything. In any case, she had noticed very early on that the officers preferred not to search her too diligently on the rare occasions when they thought it necessary. She had assumed at first that they were frightened of her, but she soon came to recognize that it was her fatness that inhibited them. Politically correct thinking within the prison service meant that while they were free to say what they liked about her behind her back they had to guard their tongues in her presence and treat her with a modicum of respect. Thus the helpful legacy of her anguished tears during strip-searches at the beginning, when her huge, repulsive body shook with distress, was a reluctance on the part of the screws now to do anything more than a perfunctory running of their hands down the sides of her shift.

But she had problems. Her small family of wax figures, absurdly cheerful in their painted cottonwool wigs and strips of dark material which she had wound around them like miniature suits, kept softening against the warmth of her skin and losing their shape. With infinite patience, she set her awkward fingers to remoulding them, first removing the pins which skewered the wigs to each of the heads. She wondered idly if the one of Roz's husband looked anything like him.

'What a ghastly place this is,' said Iris, gazing critically about the bleak grey walls of Roz's flat from her place on the vinyl sofa. 'Haven't you ever felt the urge to liven it up a bit?'

'No. I'm just passing through. It's a waiting room.'

'You've been here twelve months. I can't think why you don't use the money from the divorce and buy yourself a house.'

Roz rested her head against the back of her chair. 'I like waiting rooms. You can be idle in them without feeling guilty. There's nothing to do except wait.'

Thoughtfully, Iris put a cigarette between her brilliant red lips. 'What are you waiting for?'

'I don't know.'

She flicked a lighter to the tip of her cigarette while her penetrating eye-lined gaze fixed uncomfortably on Roz. 'One thing does puzzle me,' she said. 'If it wasn't Rupert, then why did he leave another tearful message on my answerphone, telling me he had behaved badly?'

'Another?' Roz stared at her hands. 'Does that mean he's done it before?'

'With tedious regularity.'

'You've never mentioned it.'

'You've never asked me.'

Roz digested this for some moments in silence, then let out a long sigh. 'I've been realizing recently how dependent I've become on him.' She touched her sore lip. 'His dependence hasn't changed, of course. It's the same as it always was, a constant demand for reassurance. Don't worry, Rupert. It's not your fault, Rupert. Everything will be all right, Rupert.' She spoke the words without emphasis. 'It's why he prefers women. Women are more sympathetic.' She fell silent.

'How does that make you dependent on him?'

Roz gave a slight smile. 'He's never left me alone long enough to let me think straight. I've been angry for months.' She shrugged. 'It's very destructive. You can't concentrate on anything because the anger won't go away. I tear his letters up without reading them, because I know what they'll say, but his handwriting sets my teeth on edge. If I see him or hear him, I start shaking.' She gave a hollow laugh. 'You can become obsessed by hatred, I think. I could have moved a long time ago but, instead, I stay here waiting for Rupert to make me angry. That's how I'm dependent on him. It's a prison of sorts.'

Iris wiped her cigarette end round the rim of an ashtray. Roz was telling her nothing she hadn't worked out for herself a long time ago, but she had never been able to put it into words for the simple reason that Roz had never let her. She wondered what had happened to bring the barbed wire down. Clearly, it was nothing to do with Rupert, however much Roz might like to think it was. 'So how are you going to break out of this prison? Have you decided?'

'Not yet.'

'Perhaps you should do what Olive has done,' said Iris mildly.

'And what's that?'

'Let someone else in.'

Olive waited by her cell door for two hours. One of the officers, wondering why, paused to talk to her. 'Everything all right, Sculptress?'

The fat woman's eyes fixed on her. 'What day is it?' she demanded.

'Monday.'

'That's what I thought.' She sounded angry.

The officer frowned. 'Are you sure there's nothing wrong?'

'There's nothing.'

'Were you expecting a visitor?'

'No. I'm hungry. What's for tea?'

'Pizza.' Reassured, the officer moved on. It made sense. There were few hours in the day when Olive *wasn't* hungry, and the threat of withholding her meals was often the only way to control her. A medical officer had tried to persuade her once of the benefits of dieting. He had come away very shaken and never tried again. Olive craved food in the way others craved heroin.

In the end Iris stayed for a week and filled the sterile waiting room of Roz's life with the raucous baggage of hers. She ran up a colossal telephone bill phoning her clients and customers at home and abroad, piled the tables with magazines, dropped ash all over the floor, imported armfuls of flowers which she abandoned in the sink when she couldn't find a vase, left the washing-up in tottering stacks on the kitchen work-tops, and regaled Roz, when she wasn't doing something else, with her seemingly inexhaustible flow of anecdotes.

Roz said her farewells on the following Thursday afternoon with some relief and rather more regret. If nothing else, Iris had shown her that a solitary life was emotionally, mentally, and spiritually deadening. There was, after all, only so much that one mind could encompass, and obsessions grew when ideas went unchallenged.

Olive's destruction of her cell that night took the prison by surprise. It was ten minutes before the duty governor was alerted and another ten before a response was possible. It required eight officers to restrain her. They forced her to the ground and brought their combined weight to bear on her, but as one remarked later: 'It was like trying to contain a bull elephant.'

She had wreaked complete havoc on everything. Even the lavatory bowl had shattered under a mighty blow from her welded metal chair which, bent and buckled, had been discarded amongst the shards of porcelain. The few possessions which had adorned her chest of drawers lay broken across the floor and anything that could be lifted had been hurled in fury against the walls. A poster of Madonna, ripped limb from limb, lay butchered on the floor.

Her rage, even under sedation, continued long into the night from the confines of an unfurnished cell, designed to cool the tempers of ungovernable inmates.

'What the hell's got into her?' demanded the duty governor.

'God knows,' said a shaken officer. 'I've always said she should be in Broadmoor. I don't care what the psychiatrists say, she's completely mad. They've no business to leave her here and expect us to look after her.'

They listened to the muffled bellowings from

behind the locked door. 'BI-ITCH! BI-ITCH! BI-ITCH!'

The duty governor frowned. 'Who's she talking about?'

The officer winced. 'One of us, I should think. I wish we could get her transferred. She puts the wind up me, she really does.'

'She'll be fine again tomorrow.'

'Which is why she puts the wind up me. You never know where you are with her.' She tucked her hair back into place. 'You noticed none of her clay figures were touched except the ones she's already mutilated?' She smiled cynically. 'And have you seen that mother and child she's working on? The mother's only smothering her baby, for God's sake. It's obscene. Presumably it's supposed to be Mary and Jesus.' She sighed. 'What do I tell her? No breakfast if she doesn't calm down?'

'It's always worked in the past. Let's hope nothing's changed.'

Nine

THE FOLLOWING MORNING, a week later than planned, Roz was shown through to a clerical supervisor at the Social Security office in Dawlington. He regarded her scabby lip and dark glasses with only mild curiosity and she realized that for him her appearance was nothing unusual. She introduced herself and sat down. 'I telephoned yesterday,' she reminded him.

He nodded. 'Some problem that goes back over six years, you said.' He tapped his forefingers on the desk. 'I should stress we're unlikely to be able to help. We've enough trouble chasing current cases, let alone delving into old records.'

'But you were here six years ago?'

'Seven years in June,' he said without enthusiasm. 'It won't help, I'm afraid. I don't remember you or your circumstances.'

'You wouldn't.' She smiled apologetically. 'I was a little economical with the truth on the telephone. I'm not a consumer. I'm an author. I'm writing a book about Olive Martin. I need to talk to someone who knew her when she worked here and I didn't want a straight refusal down the phone.'

He looked amused, glad perhaps that he was spared an impossible search for lost benefits. 'She was the fat girl down the corridor. I didn't even know what her name was until it appeared in the paper. As far as I remember, I never exchanged more than a dozen words with her. You probably know more about her than I do.' He crossed his arms. 'You should have said what you wanted. You could have saved yourself a drive.'

Roz took out her notebook. 'That doesn't matter. It's names I need. People who did speak to her. Is there anyone else who's been here as long as you?'

'A few, but no one who was friendly with Olive. A couple of reporters came round at the time of the murders and there wasn't a soul who admitted to passing anything more than the time of day with her.'

Roz felt his distrust. 'And who can blame them?' she said cheerfully. 'Presumably it was the gutter press looking for a juicy headline. I HELD THE HAND OF A MONSTER or something equally tasteless. Only publicity seekers or idiots allow themselves to be used by Wapping to boost their grubby profits.'

'And your book won't make a profit?' There was a dry inflection in his voice.

She smiled. 'A very modest one by newspaper standards.' She pushed her dark glasses to the top of her head, revealing her eyes and the yellow rings around them. 'I'll be honest with you. I was dragooned into this research by an irritable agent demanding copy. I found the subject distasteful and was prepared to abandon it after a token meeting with Olive.' She looked at him, turning her pencil between her fingers. 'Then I discovered that Olive was human and very likeable, so I kept going. And almost everyone I've spoken to has given a similar answer to you. They hardly knew her, they never talked to her, she was just the fat girl down the corridor. Now, I could write my book on that theme alone, how social ostracism led a lonely, unloved girl to turn in a fit of frenzied anger on her teasing family. But I'm not going to because I don't think it's true. I believe there's been a miscarriage of justice. I believe Olive is innocent.'

Surprised, he reassessed her. 'It shocked us rigid when we heard what she'd done,' he admitted.

'Because you thought it out of character?'

'Totally out of character.' He thought back. 'She was a good worker, brighter than most, and she didn't clock-watch like some of them. OK, she was never going to set the world alight, but she was reliable and willing and she didn't make waves or get involved in office politics. She was here about eighteen months and while no one would have claimed her as a bosom friend she made no enemies either. She was one of those people you only think about when you want something done and then you remember them with relief because you know they'll do it. You know the type?'

She nodded. 'Boring but dependable.'

'In a nutshell, yes.'

'Did she tell you anything about her private life?'

He shook his head again. 'It was true what I said at the beginning. Our paths rarely crossed. Any contact we had was work related and even that was minimal. Most of what I've just told you was synthesized from the amazed reactions of the few who did know her.'

'Can you give me their names?'

'I'm not sure I can remember.' He looked doubtful. 'Olive would know them better than I do. Why don't you ask her?'

Because she won't tell me. She won't tell me anything. 'Because,' she said instead, 'I don't want to hurt her.' She saw his look of puzzlement and sighed. 'Supposing doors get slammed in my face and I'm given the cold shoulder by Olive's so-called friends. She's bound to ask me how I got on, and how would I answer her? Sorry, Olive, as far as they're concerned you're dead and buried. I couldn't do that.'

He accepted this. 'All right, there is someone who might be willing to help you but I'm not prepared to give you her name without her permission. She's elderly, retired now, and she may not want to be involved. If you give me five minutes, I'll telephone and see how she feels about talking to you.'

'Was she fond of Olive?'

'As much as anyone was.'

'Then will you tell her that I don't believe Olive murdered her mother and sister and that's why I'm writing the book.' She stood up. 'And please impress on her that it's desperately important I talk to someone who knew her at the time. So far I've only managed to trace one old school friend and a teacher.' She walked to the door. 'I'll wait outside.'

True to his word, he was five minutes. He joined her in the corridor and gave her a piece of paper with a name and address on it. 'Her name's Lily Gainsborough. She was the cleaner-cum-tea-lady in the good old days before privatized cleaning and automatic coffee machines. She retired three years ago at the age of seventy, lives in sheltered accommodation in Pryde Street.' He gave her directions. 'She's expecting you.' Roz thanked him. 'Give my regards to Olive when you see her,' he said, shaking her hand. 'I had more hair and less flab six years ago, so a description won't be much use, but she might remember my name. Most people do.'

Roz chuckled. His name was Michael Jackson.

'Of course I remember Olive. Called her "Dumpling", didn't I, and she called me "Flower". Get it, dear? Because of my name, Lily. There wasn't an ounce of harm in her. I never believed what they said she done and I wrote and told her so when I heard where they'd sent her. She wrote me back and said I was wrong, it was all her fault and she had to pay the penalty.' Old wise eyes peered short-sightedly at Roz. 'I understood what she meant, even if no one else did. She never did it but it wouldn't have happened if she'd not done what she shouldn't have. More tea, dear?'

'Thank you.' Roz held out her cup and waited while the frail old lady hefted a large stainless steel teapot. A relic from her job on the tea trolley? The tea was thick and charged with tannin, and Roz could hardly bring herself to drink it. She accepted another indigestible scone. 'What did she do that she shouldn't have?'

'Upset her mum, that's what. Took up with one of the O'Brien boys, didn't she?'

'Which one?'

'Ah, well, that I'm not too sure about. I've always thought it was the baby, young Gary – mind, I only saw them together once and those boys are very alike. Could have been any of them.'

'How many are there?'

'Now you're asking.' Lily pursed her mouth into a wrinkled rosebud. 'It's a big family. Can't keep track of them. Their mum must be a grandmother twenty times over and I doubt she's reached sixty yet.

Gyppos, dear. Bad apples the lot of them. In and out of prison that regular you'd think they owned the place. The mum included. Taught them to steal soon as they could walk. The kids kept being taken off her, of course, but never for very long. Always found their way home. Young Gary was sent to a boarding school – approved schools, they was called in my day – did quite well by all accounts.' She crumbled a scone on her plate. 'Till he went home, that is. She had him back on the thieving quicker than you can say knife.'

Roz thought for a moment. 'Did Olive tell you she was going out with one of them?'

'Not in so many words.' She tapped her forehead. 'Put two and two together, didn't I? She was that pleased with herself, lost some weight, bought some pretty dresses from that boutique her sister went to work in, dabbed some colour on her face. Made herself look quite bonny, didn't she? Stood to reason there was a man behind it somewhere. Asked her once who it was and she just smiled and said, "No names no pack drill, Flower, because Mummy would have a fit if she ever found out." And then, two or three days later, I came across her with one of the O'Brien boys. Her face gave her away, as sunny as the day is long it was. That was him all right – the one she was soppy over – but he turned away as I passed, and I never did know exactly which O'Brien he was.'

'But what made you think it was an O'Brien anyway?'

'The uniform,' said Lily. 'They all wore the same uniform.'

'They were in the Army?' asked Roz in surprise.

'Leathers, they call them.'

'Oh, I see. You mean they're bikers, they ride motorbikes.'

'That's it. Hell's Angels.'

Roz drew her brows together in a perplexed frown. She had told Hal with absolute conviction that Olive was not the rebellious type. But Hell's Angels, for God's sake! Could a convent girl get more rebellious than that? 'Are you sure about this, Lily?'

'Well, as to being sure, I don't know as I'm sure about anything any more. There was a time when I was sure that governments knew better how to run things than I did. Can't say as I do these days. There was a time when I was sure that if God was in his heaven all would be right with the world. Can't say as I think that now. If God's there, dear, He's blind, deaf, and dumb, far as I'm concerned. But, yes, I am sure my poor Dumpling had fallen for one of the O'Briens. You'd only to look at her to see she was head over heels in love with the lad.' She compressed her lips. 'Bad business. Bad business.'

Roz sipped the bitter tea. 'And you think it was the O'Brien lad who murdered Olive's mother and sister?'

'Must have been, mustn't it? As I said, dear, bad apples.'

'Did you tell the police any of this?' asked Roz curiously.

'I might have done if they'd asked, but I didn't see no point in volunteering the information. If Dumpling wanted them kept out, then that was her affair. And, to tell you the truth, I wasn't that keen to run up against them. Stick together, they do, and my Frank had passed on not many months before. Wouldn't have stood a chance if they'd come looking, would I?'

'Where do they live?'

'The Barrow Estate, back of the High Street. Council likes to keep 'em together, under their eye so to speak. It's a shocking place. Not an honest family there, and they're not all O'Briens neither. Den of thieves, that's what it is.'

Roz took another thoughtful sip from her cup. 'Are you prepared to let me use this information, Lily? You do realize that if there's anything in it it could help Olive.'

'Course I do, dear. Why would I tell you otherwise?'

'The police would become involved. They'd want to talk to you.'

'I know that.'

'In which case your name would be out, and the O'Briens could still come looking for you.'

The old eyes appraised her shrewdly. 'You're only a slip of a thing, dear, but you've survived a beating by the look of it. Reckon I can too. In any case,' she went on stoutly, 'I've spent six years feeling bad about not speaking up, and I was that glad when young Mick phoned and said you was coming, you wouldn't believe. You go ahead, dear, and don't mind about me. It's safer here, anyway, than my old place. They could have set the whole thing alight and I'd have been dead long before anyone'd have thought of phoning for help.'

If Roz had expected to see a chapter of Hell's Angels rampaging about the Barrow Estate she was disappointed. At lunchtime on a Friday it was an unexceptional place, where only the odd dog barked and young women, in ones and twos, pushed babies in prams piled high with shopping for the weekend. Like too many council estates there was a naked and uncared for look about it, a recognition that what it offered was not what its tenants wanted. If individuality was present in these dull uniform walls then it was inside, away from view. But Roz doubted its existence. She had a sense of empty spaces marking time where people waited for somebody else to offer them something better. Like her, she thought. Like her flat.

As she drove away she passed a large school, advertising itself with a tired sign beside the gate. Parkway Comprehensive. Children milled about the tarmac, the sound of their voices loud in the warm air. Roz slowed the car to watch them for a moment. Groups of children played the same games whichever school they went to, but she could see why Gwen had turned her nose up at Parkway and had sent her girls to the convent. Its close proximity to the Barrow Estate would worry even the most liberal of parents, and Gwen certainly wasn't that. But it was ironic, if what Lily and Mr Hayes had said was true, that both Gwen's daughters had succumbed to the attractions of this other world. Was that in spite of or because of their mother? she wondered.

She told herself she needed a tame policeman to give her the low-down on the O'Briens, and her road led inevitably to the Poacher. Being lunchtime the door to the restaurant was unlocked, but the tables were as empty as ever. She selected one well away from the window and sat down, her dark glasses firmly in place.

'You won't need those,' said Hawksley's amused voice from the kitchen doorway. 'I don't intend to put the lights on.'

She smiled, but did not remove the glasses. 'I'd like to order some lunch.'

'OK.' He held the door wide. 'Come into the kitchen. It's more comfortable in there.'

'No, I'll have it in here.' She stood up. 'At the table in the window. I'd like the door open and' – she looked for amplifiers and found them – 'some loud music, preferably jazz. Let's liven the place up a bit. Nobody wants to eat in a morgue, for God's sake.' She seated herself in the window.

'No,' he said, an odd inflection in his voice. 'If you want lunch, you eat it in here with me. Otherwise, you go somewhere else.'

She studied him thoughtfully. 'This has nothing to do with the recession, has it?'

'What hasn't?'

'Your non-existent customers.'

He gestured towards the kitchen. 'Are you going or staying?'

'Staying,' she said, standing up. What was this all about? she wondered.

'It's really none of your concern, Miss Leigh,' he murmured, reading her mind. 'I suggest you stick to what you know and leave me to deal with my affairs in my own way.' Geoff had phoned through the results of his check the previous Monday. 'She's kosher,' he had said. 'A London-based author. Divorced. Had a daughter who died in a car accident. No previous connections with anyone in the area. Sorry, Hal.'

'OK,' Roz said mildly, 'but you must admit it's very intriguing. I was effectively warned off eating here by a policeman when I went to the station to find out where you were. I've been wondering why ever since. With friends like that you don't really need enemies, do you?'

His smile didn't reach his eyes. 'Then you're very

brave to accept my hospitality a second time.' He held the door wide.

She walked past him into the kitchen. 'Just greedy,' she said. 'You're a better cook than I am. In any case, I intend to pay for what I eat unless, of course' – her smile didn't reach her eyes either – 'this isn't a restaurant at all, but a front for something else.'

That amused him. 'You've an overactive imagination.' He pulled out a chair for her.

'Maybe,' she said, sitting down. 'But I've never met a restaurateur before who barricades himself behind bars, presides over empty tables, has no staff, and looms up in the dark looking like something that's been fed through a mincing machine.' She arched her eyebrows. 'If you didn't cook so well, I'd be even more inclined to think this wasn't a restaurant.'

He leaned forward abruptly and removed her dark glasses, folding them and laying them on the table. 'And what should I deduce from this?' he said, unexpectedly moved by the damage done to her beautiful eyes. 'That you're not a writer because someone's left his handprints all over your face?' He frowned suddenly. 'It wasn't Olive, was it?'

She looked surprised. 'Of course not.'

'Who was it, then?'

She dropped her gaze. 'No one. It's not important.'

He waited for a moment. 'Is it someone you care about?'

'No.' She clasped her hands loosely on the table top. 'Rather the reverse. It's someone I don't care about.' She looked up with a half smile. 'Who beat you up, Sergeant? Someone *you* care about?'

He pulled open a fridge door and examined its contents. 'One of these days your passion for poking your nose into other people's business is going to get you into trouble. What do you fancy? Lamb?'

'I really came to see you for some more information,' she told him over coffee.

Humour creased his eyes. He really was extraordinarily attractive, she thought, wistfully aware that the attraction was all one way. Lunch had been a friendly but distant meal, with a large sign between them saying: so far and no further. 'Go on, then.'

'Do you know the O'Brien family? They live on the Barrow Estate.'

'Everyone knows the O'Briens.' He frowned at her. 'But if there's a connection between them and Olive I'll eat my hat.'

'You're going to have galloping indigestion then,' she said acidly. 'I've been told she was going out with one of the sons at the time of the murders. Probably Gary, the youngest. What's he like? Have you met him?'

He linked his hands behind his head. 'Someone's winding you up,' he murmured. 'Gary is marginally brighter than the rest of them, but I'd guess his educational level is still about fourteen years old. They are the most useless, inadequate bunch I've ever come across. The only thing they know how to do is petty thieving and they don't even do that very well. There's Ma O'Brien and about nine children, mostly boys, all grown up now, and, when they're not in prison, they play box and cox in a three-bedroomed house on the estate.'

'Aren't any of them married?'

'Not for long. Divorce is more prevalent in that family than marriage. The wives usually make other arrangements while their men are inside.' He flexed his laced fingers. 'They produce a lot of babies, though, if the fact that a third generation of O'Briens has started appearing regularly in the juvenile courts is anything to go by.' He shook his head. 'Someone's winding you up,' he said again. 'For all her sins Olive wasn't stupid and she'd have to have been brain-dead to fall for a jerk like Gary O'Brien.'

'Are they really as bad as that?' she asked him curiously. 'Or is this police animosity?'

He smiled. 'I'm not police, remember? But they're that bad,' he assured her. 'Every patch has families like the O'Briens. Sometimes, if you're really unlucky, you get an estateful of them, like the Barrow Estate, when the council decides to lump all its bad apples into one basket and then expects the wretched police to throw a cordon round it.' He gave a humourless laugh. 'It's one of the reasons I left the Force. I got sick to death of being sent out to sweep up society's messes. It's not the police who create these ghettos, it's the councils and the governments, and ultimately society itself.'

'Sounds reasonable to me,' she said. 'In that case why do you despise the O'Briens so much? They sound as if they need help and support rather than condemnation.'

He shrugged. 'I suppose it's because they've already had more help and support than you or I will ever be offered. They take everything society gives them and then demand more. There's no quid pro quo with people like that. They put nothing in to compensate for what they've had out. Society owes them a living and, by God, they make sure society pays, usually in the shape of some poor old woman who has all her savings stolen.' His lips thinned. 'If you'd arrested those worthless shits as often as I have, you'd despise them, too. I don't deny they represent an underclass of society's making, but I resent their unwillingness to try and rise above it.' He saw her frown. 'You look very disapproving. Have I offended your liberal sensibilities?'

'No,' she said with a twinkle in her eye. 'I was just thinking how like Mr Hayes you sound. Remember him? "What shall I say?" ' – she mimicked the old man's soft burr – ' "They should all be strung up from the nearest lamppost and shot." ' She smiled when he laughed.

'My sympathies with the criminal classes are a trifle frayed at the moment,' he said after a moment. 'More accurately, my sympathies in general are frayed.'

'Classic symptoms of stress,' she said lightly, watching him. 'Under pressure we always reserve our compassion for ourselves.'

He didn't answer.

'You said the O'Briens are inadequate,' Roz prompted. 'Perhaps they can't rise above their situation.'

'I believed that once,' he admitted, toying with his empty wine glass, 'when I first joined the police force, but you have to be very naïve to go on believing it. They're professional thieves who simply don't subscribe to the same values as the rest of us hold. It's not a case of *can't*, but more a case of *won't*. Different ball game entirely.' He smiled at her. 'And if you're a policeman who wants to hold on to the few drops of human kindness that remain to you, you get out quick the minute you realize that. Otherwise you end up as unprincipled as the people you're arresting.'

Curiouser and curiouser, thought Roz. So he had little sympathy left for the police either. He gave the impression of a man under siege, isolated and angry within the walls of his castle. But why should his friends in the police have abandoned him? Presumably he had had some. 'Have any of the O'Briens been charged with murder or GBH?'

'No. As I said, they're thieves. Shoplifting, pick-pocketing, house burglaries, cars, that sort of thing. Old Ma acts as a fence whenever she can get her hands on stolen property but they're not violent.'

'I was told they're all Hell's Angels.'

He gave her an amused look. 'You've been given some very duff information. Are you toying with the idea, perhaps, that Gary did the murders and Olive was so besotted with him that she took the rap on his behalf?'

'It doesn't sound very plausible, does it?'

'About as plausible as little green men on Mars. Apart from anything else, Gary is scared of his own shadow. He was challenged once during a burglary – he didn't think anyone was in the house – and he burst into tears. He could no more have cut Gwen's throat while she was struggling with him than you or I could. Or for that matter, than his brothers could. They're skinny little foxes, not ravening wolves. Who on earth have you been talking to? Someone with a sense of humour, obviously.'

She shrugged, suddenly out of patience with him. 'It's not important. Offhand, do you know the O'Briens' address? It would save me having to look it up.'

He grinned. 'You're not planning on going there?'

'Of course I am,' she said, annoyed by his amusement. 'It's the most promising lead I've had. And now that I know they're not axe-wielding Hell's Angels, I'm not so worried about it. So what's their address?'

'I'll come with you.'

'Think again, sunshine,' she said roundly. 'I don't want you queering my pitch. Are you going to give me the address or must I look it up?'

'Number seven, Baytree Avenue. You can't miss it. It's the only house in that road with a satellite dish. Nicked for sure.'

'Thank you.' She reached for her handbag. 'Now, if we can just settle my bill, I'll leave you in peace.'

He unfolded himself from his chair and walked round to draw hers back. 'On the house,' he said.

She stood up and regarded him gravely. 'But I'd like to pay. I didn't come here at lunchtime just to scrounge off you and, anyway' – she smiled – 'how else can I show my appreciation of your cooking? Money always speaks louder than words. I can say it was fabulous, like the last time, but I might just be being polite.'

He raised a hand as if he was going to touch her, then dropped it abruptly. 'I'll see you out,' was all he said.

Ten

ROZ DROVE PAST the house three times before she could pluck up enough courage to get out and try the door. In the end it was pride that led her up the path. Hal's amusement had goaded her. A tarpaulined motorbike was parked neatly on a patch of grass beside the fence.

The door was opened by a bony little woman with a sharp, scowling face, her thin lips drawn down in a permanently dissatisfied bow. 'Yes?' she snapped.

'Mrs O'Brien?'

''Oo's asking?'

Roz produced a card. 'My name's Rosalind Leigh.' The sound of a television blared out from an inner room.

The woman glanced at the card but didn't take it. 'Well, what do you want? If it's the rent, I put it in the post yesterday.' She folded her arms across her thin chest and dared Roz to dispute this piece of information.

'I'm not from the council, Mrs O'Brien.' It occurred to her that the woman couldn't read. Apart from her telephone number and address, Roz's card had only her name and her profession on it. Author, it stated clearly. She took a flyer. 'I work for a small independent television company,' she said brightly, her mind searching rapidly for some plausible but tempting bait. 'I'm researching the difficulties faced by single parents with large families. We are particularly interested in talking to a mother who has problems keeping her sons out of trouble. Society is very quick to point the finger in these situations and we feel it's time to redress the balance.' She saw the lack of comprehension on the woman's face. 'We'd like to give the mother a chance to give her side of the story,' she explained. 'There seems to be a common pattern of continual harassment and interference from people in authority – social services, the council, the police. Most mothers we've spoken to feel that if they'd been left alone they wouldn't have had the problems.'

A gleam of interest lit the other's eyes. 'That's true enough.'

'Are you willing to take part?'

'Maybe. 'Oo sent you?'

'We've been conducting some research in the local courts,' she said glibly. 'The name O'Brien popped up quite frequently.'

'Not surprised. Will I get paid?'

'Certainly. I'd need to talk to you for about an

hour now to get a rough idea of your views. For that you will receive an immediate cash payment of fifty pounds.' Ma would turn her nose up at anything less, she thought. 'Then, if we think your contribution is valuable and if you agree to be filmed, we will pay you at the same hourly rate while the cameras are here.'

Ma O'Brien pursed her meagre lips and proceeded to splatter aitches about the place. 'Han hundred,' she said, 'hand h'I'll do it.'

Roz shook her head. Fifty pounds would clean her out anyway. 'Sorry. It's a standard fee. I'm not authorized to pay any more.' She shrugged. 'Never mind. Thank you for your time, Mrs O'Brien. I've three other families on my list. I'm sure one of them will jump at the chance to get their own back at authority and earn some money while they're doing it.' She turned away. 'Look out for the programme,' she called over her shoulder. 'You'll probably see some of your neighbours on it.'

'Not so 'asty, Mrs. Did I say no? Course I didn't. But I'd be a mug not to try for more hif there was more to be 'ad. Come in. Come in. What d'you say your name was?'

'Rosalind Leigh.' She followed Ma into a sitting room and took a chair while the little woman turned off the television and flicked aimlessly at some non-existent dust on the set. 'This is a nice room,' said Roz, careful to keep the surprise from her voice. A three-piece suite of good quality burgundy leather ringed a pale Chinese rug in pinks and greys.

'All bought and paid for,' snapped Ma.

Roz didn't doubt her for a moment. If the police spent as much time in her house as Hal had implied, then she was hardly likely to furnish it with hot goods. She took out her tape-recorder. 'How do you feel about my recording this conversation? It'll be a useful gauge for the sound man when he comes to set levels for filming, but if the microphone puts you off then I'm quite happy to make notes instead.'

'Get on with you,' she said, perching on the sofa. 'I'm not afraid of microphones. We've got a karaoke next door. You gonna ask questions or what?'

'That's probably easiest, isn't it? Let's start with when you first came to this house.'

'Ah, well, now, they was built twenty year ago, near enough, and we was the first family hin. There was six of us, including my old man, but 'e got nicked shortly after and we never seen 'im again. The old bastard buggered hoff when they let 'im out.'

'So you had four children?'

'Four in the 'ouse, five in care. Bloody hinterference, like you said. Kept taking the poor little nippers hoff me, they did. Makes you sick, it really does. They wanted their ma, not some do-good foster mother who was only in it for the money.' She hugged herself. 'I always got them back, mind. They'd turn up on my doorstep, regular as clockwork, no matter 'ow many times they was taken away. The council's tried everything to break us up, threatened me with a one-roomed flat even.' She sniffed. ''Arassment, like you said. I remember one time . . .'

She required little prompting to tell her story but rambled on with remarkable fluency for nearly three-quarters of an hour. Roz was fascinated. Privately she dismissed at least fifty per cent of what she was hearing, principally because Ma blithely maintained that her boys were and always had been innocent victims of police frames. Even the most gullible of listeners would have found that difficult to swallow. Nevertheless, there was a dogged affection in her voice whenever she referred to her family and Roz wondered if she was really as callous as Lily had painted her. She certainly portrayed herself as a hapless victim of circumstances beyond her control, though whether this was something she genuinely believed or whether she was saying what she thought Roz wanted to hear, Roz couldn't tell. Ma, she decided, was a great deal smarter than she let on.

'Right, Mrs O'Brien, let me see if I've got it right,' she said at last, interrupting the flow. 'You've got two daughters, both of whom are single parents like you, and both of whom have been housed by the council. You have seven sons. Three are currently in prison, one is living with his girlfriend, and the remaining three live here. Your oldest child is Peter, who's thirty-six, and your youngest is Gary, who's twenty-five.'

She whistled. 'That was some going. Nine babies in eleven years.'

'Two sets of twins in the middle. Boy and a girl each time. Mind, it was 'ard work.'

Unmitigated drudgery, thought Roz. 'Did you want them?' she asked curiously. 'I can't think of anything worse than having nine children.'

'Never 'ad much say in it, dear. There weren't no abortion in my day.'

'Didn't you use contraceptives?'

To her surprise, the old woman blushed. 'Couldn't get the 'ang of them,' she snapped. 'The old man tried a rubber once but didn't like it and wouldn't do it again. Old bugger. No skin off 'is nose if I kept falling.'

It was on the tip of Roz's tongue to ask why Ma couldn't get the hang of contraceptives when the penny dropped. If she couldn't read and she was too embarrassed to ask how to use them, they'd have been useless to her. Good God, she thought, a little education would have saved the country a fortune where this family was concerned. 'That's men for you,' she said lightly. 'I noticed a motorbike outside. Does that belong to one of the boys?'

'Bought and paid for,' came the belligerent refrain. 'It's Gary's. Motorbike mad, 'e is. There was a time when three of the boys 'ad bikes, now it's just Gary. They was all working for one of them messenger companies till the bloody coppers went round and got them sacked. Victimization, pure and simple. 'Ow's a man to work hif the police keep waving 'is record under the boss's noses. Course, they lost the bikes. They was buying them on the never-never and they couldn't keep up the payments.'

Roz made sympathetic noises. 'When was that? Recently?'

'Year of the gales. I remember the electricity was off when the boys came 'ome to say they'd been given the push. We'd got one blooming candle.' She firmed her lips. 'Bloody awful night, that was. Depressing.'

Roz kept her expression as neutral as she could. Was Lily right, after all, and Hal wrong? 'The nineteen eight-seven gales,' she said. 'The first ones.'

'That's it. Mind, it 'appened again two years later. No electricity for a week the second time, hand you get no compensation for the 'ardship neither. I tried and the buggers told me hif I didn't pay what I owed they'd cut me hoff for good and all.'

'Did the police give a reason for getting your boys the sack?' asked Roz.

'Hah!' Ma sniffed. 'They never give reasons for nothing. It was victimization, like I said.'

'Did they work for the messenger company long?'

Old eyes regarded her suspiciously. 'You're mighty interested all of a sudden.'

Roz smiled ingenuously. 'Only because this was an occasion when three of your family were trying to go straight and build careers for themselves. It would make good television if we could show that they were denied that opportunity because of police harassment. Presumably it was a local firm they were working for?'

'Southampton.' Ma's mouth became an inverted horseshoe. 'Bloody silly name it 'ad too. Called theirselves Wells-Fargo. Still, the boss was a ruddy cowboy so maybe it wasn't so silly after all.'

Roz suppressed a smile. 'Is it still in business?'

'Last I 'eard, it was. That's it. You've 'ad your 'our.'

'Thank you, Mrs O'Brien.' She patted the tape-recorder. 'If the producers like what they hear I might need to come back and talk to your sons. Would that be acceptable, do you think?'

'Don't see why not. Can't see them sneezing at fifty quid apiece.' Ma held out her hand.

Dutifully, Roz took two twenty-pound notes and a ten from her wallet and laid them on the wrinkled palm. Then she started to gather her things together. 'I hear Dawlington's quite famous,' she remarked chattily.

'Oh yeah?'

'I was told Olive Martin murdered her mother and sister about half a mile down the road.'

'Oh, 'er,' said Ma dismissively, standing up. 'Strange girl. Knew 'er quite well at one time. Used to clean for the mother when she and 'er sister were nippers. She took a real fancy to Gary. Used to pretend 'e was 'er doll whenever I took 'im halong with me. There was only three years between them but she was nearly twice as big as my skinny little runt. Strange girl.'

Roz busied herself with sorting out her briefcase. 'It must have been a shock hearing about the murders then. If you knew the family, that is.'

'Can't say I gave it much thought. I was only there six month. Never liked *'er.* She only took me on for a bit of snobbery, then got rid of me the minute she found hout my old man was in the nick.'

'What was Olive like as a child. Was she violent to your Gary?'

Ma cackled. 'Used to dress 'im up in 'er sister's frocks. God, 'e looked a sight. Like I said, she treated 'im like a doll.'

Roz snapped the locks on her briefcase and stood up. 'Were you surprised she became a murderess?'

'No more surprised by that than by anything else. There's nowt so queer as folk.' She escorted Roz to the front door and stood, arms akimbo, waiting for her to leave.

'It might make an interesting introduction to the programme,' Roz mused, 'the fact that Gary was a doll-substitute for a notorious murderess. Does he remember her?'

Ma cackled again. 'Course 'e remembers 'er. Carried messages between 'er and 'er fancy man, didn't 'e, when she was workin' for the Social.'

*

Roz made a beeline for the nearest telephone. Ma O'Brien either wouldn't or couldn't elaborate on her tantalizing statement and had closed the door abruptly when pressed for information on Gary's whereabouts. Roz dialled Directory Enquiries and asked for Wells-Fargo in Southampton, then used her last fifty pence to call the number she was given. A bored female voice on the other end gave her the company's address and some directions on how to find it. 'We close in forty minutes,' was the woman's parting shot.

By dint of parking on a double yellow line and shrugging off the prospect of a parking ticket Roz made it to the Wells-Fargo office with ten minutes to spare. It was a dingy place, approached through a doorway between two shops and up a flight of uncarpeted stairs. Two anaemic Busy Lizzies and an ancient Pirelli calendar were the only spots of colour against the yellowed walls. The bored female voice resolved itself into a bored-looking middle-aged woman who was counting the seconds to the start of her weekend.

'We don't often see customers,' she remarked, filing her nails. 'I mean if they can bring their package here they might just as well deliver it themselves.' It was an accusation, as if she felt Roz were wasting company time. She abandoned her nails and held out a hand. 'What is it and where's it for?'

'I'm not a customer,' said Roz. 'I'm an author and I'm hoping you can give me some information for a book I'm writing.' Stirrings of interest animated the other's face so Roz pulled forward a chair and sat down. 'How long have you been working here?'

'Too long. What sort of book?'

Roz watched her closely. 'Do you remember Olive Martin? She murdered her mother and sister in Dawlington six years ago.' She saw immediate recognition in the woman's eyes. 'I'm writing a book about her.'

The woman returned to her nails but didn't say anything.

'Did you know her?'

'God, no.'

'Did you know *of* her? Before the murders, that is. I've been told one of your messengers delivered letters to her.' It was true enough. The only trouble was that she didn't know if Gary was working for Wells-Fargo when he did it.

A door to an inner office opened and a man fussed out. He looked at Roz. 'Did this lady want to see me, Marnie?' His fingers ran involuntarily up and down his tie, playing it like a clarinet.

The nail file vanished from sight. 'No, Mr Wheelan. She's an old friend of mine. Popped in to see if I've time for a drink before I go home.' She stared hard at Roz, her eyes demanding support. There was a curious intimacy in her expression as if she and Roz already shared a secret.

Roz smiled amiably and glanced at her watch. 'It's

nearly six now,' she said. 'Half an hour won't delay you too much, will it?'

The man made shooing motions with his hands. 'You two get on then. I'll lock up tonight.' He paused in the doorway, his forehead wrinkling anxiously. 'You didn't forget to send someone to Hasler's, did you?'

'No, Mr Wheelan. Eddy went two hours ago.'

'Good, good. Have a nice weekend. What about Prestwick's?'

'All done, Mr Wheelan. There's nothing outstanding.' Marnie raised her eyes to heaven as he closed the door behind him. 'He drives me mad,' she muttered. 'Fuss, fuss, fuss, all the time. Come on, quick, before he changes his mind. Friday evenings are always the worst.' She scurried across to the door and started down the stairs. 'He hates weekends, that's his trouble, thinks the business is going to fold because we have two consecutive days without orders. He's paranoid. Had me working Saturday mornings last year till he realized we were simply sitting around twiddling our thumbs because none of the offices we deal with open on a Saturday.' She pushed through the bottom door and stepped out on to the pavement. 'Look, we can forget about that drink. I'd like to get home in reasonable time for once.' She looked at Roz, measuring the other's reaction.

Roz shrugged. 'Fine. I'll go and talk to Mr Wheelan about Olive Martin. He doesn't seem to be in any hurry.'

Marnie tapped her foot impatiently. 'You'll get me sacked.'

'*You* talk to me then.'

There was a long pause while the other woman considered her options. 'I'll tell you what I know, as long as you keep it to yourself,' she said at last. 'Is that a deal? It's not going to help you one little bit, so you won't need to use it.'

'Suits me,' said Roz.

'We'll talk as we walk. The station's this way. If we hurry I might be able to catch the six thirty.'

Roz caught her arm to hold her back. 'My car's over there,' she said. 'I'll drive you instead.' She took Marnie across the road and unlocked the passenger door. 'OK,' she said, getting in the other side and starting the engine. 'Fire away.'

'I did know of her, or at least I knew of *an* Olive Martin. I can't swear it's the same one because I never saw her, but the description sounded right when I read about her in the newspaper. I've always assumed it was the same person.'

'Who gave you her description?' asked Roz, turning into the main road.

'There's no point asking questions,' snapped Marnie. 'It'll just take longer. Let me tell the story my way.' She collected her thoughts. 'I said back there that we hardly ever see customers. Sometimes office managers come in to suss out what sort of operation we run, but normally it's all done by telephone. Somebody wants something delivered, they phone us and we dispatch a rider, simple as that. Well, one lunchtime, when Wheelan was out getting his sandwiches, this man came into the office. He had a letter that he wanted delivered that afternoon to a Miss Olive Martin. He was prepared to pay over the odds if the dispatch rider would hang around outside where she worked and give it to her quietly as she was leaving. He was absolutely adamant that it wasn't to be taken inside and said he was sure I understood why.'

Roz forgot herself. 'And did you?'

'I assumed they were having an affair and that neither of them wanted people asking questions. Anyway, he gave me a twenty-quid note for the one letter, and we're talking six years ago, remember, plus a very good description of Olive Martin, right down to the clothes she was wearing that day. Well, I thought it was a one-off and as that old bastard Wheelan pays peanuts at the best of times, I pocketed the cash and didn't bother to record the transaction. Instead, I got one of our riders who lived in Dawlington to do it freelance, as it were, on his way home. He got ten for doing virtually nothing and I kept the other ten.' She motioned with her hand. 'You take the next right at the traffic lights and then right at the roundabout.'

Roz put on her indicator. 'Was that Gary O'Brien?'

Marnie nodded. 'I suppose the little sod's been talking.'

'Something like that,' said Roz, avoiding a direct answer. 'Did Gary ever meet this man?'

'No, only Olive. It turned out he'd known her before – she used to look after him when he was a child or something – so he had no trouble recognizing her and didn't bungle the job by trying to give the letter to the wrong woman. Which, considering what an oaf he was, I thought he might do. Pull in here.' She glanced at her watch as Roz drew to a halt. 'That's grand. OK, well, the upshot of the whole thing going so smoothly was that Olive's bloke started to use us quite regularly. All in all we must have delivered about ten letters in the six months before the murders. I think he realized we were doing it on the side because he always came in at lunchtime after Wheelan had gone out. I reckon he used to wait until he saw the old fool leave.' She shrugged. 'It stopped with the murders and I've never seen him since. And that's all I can tell you except that Gary got really nervous after Olive was arrested and said we should keep our mouths shut about what we knew or the police would be down on us like a ton of bricks. Well, I wasn't keen to say anything anyway, not because of the police but because of Wheelan. He'd have burst a blood vessel if he'd found out we'd been running a bit of private enterprise behind his back.'

'But didn't the police turn up anyway about a month later to warn Wheelan against the O'Brien brothers?'

Marnie looked surprised. 'Who told you that?'

'Gary's mother.'

'First I've heard of it. As far as I know they just got bored. Gary wasn't so bad because he loved his motorbike but the other two were the most work-shy creeps I've ever come across. In the end they were skiving off so often that Wheelan sacked the lot. It's about the only decision he's ever made that I agreed with. God, they were unreliable.' She checked her watch again. 'To tell you the truth it amazed me that Gary delivered Olive's letters so conscientiously. I did wonder if he had a bit of a yen for her himself.' She opened the car door. 'I'll have to go.'

'Hang on,' said Roz sharply. 'Who was this man?'

'No idea. We dealt in cash and he never gave his name.'

'What did he look like?'

'I'll miss my train.'

Roz leant across and pulled the door to. 'You've got ten minutes and if you don't give me a decent description I'll go straight back to your office and spill the beans to Wheelan.'

Marnie shrugged petulantly. 'He was fifty-odd, old enough to be her father if the age they gave for her in the paper was right. Quite good-looking in a smarmy sort of way, very clean cut and conservative. He had a posh accent. He smoked. He always wore a suit and tie. He was about six foot and he had blond hair. He never said very much, just sort of waited for me to speak, never smiled, never got excited. I remember his eyes because they didn't go with his hair. They were very dark brown. And that's it,' she said firmly. 'I don't know any more about him and I don't know anything at all about her.'

'Would you recognize him from a photograph?'

'Probably. Do you know him then?'

Roz drummed her fingers on the steering-wheel. 'It doesn't make any sense but it sounds exactly like her father.'

Eleven

THE OFFICER ON the gate checked Roz's name against his list the following Monday, then picked up the telephone. 'The Governor wants to see you,' he said, dialling a number.

'What for?'

'I wouldn't know, miss.' He spoke into the telephone. 'Miss Leigh's here for Martin. There's a note that she's to see the Governor first. Yes. Will do.' He pointed with his pencil. 'Straight through the first set of gates and you'll be met the other side.'

It was horribly reminiscent of being hauled before the headmistress at school, thought Roz, waiting nervously in the secretary's office. She was trying to remember if she'd broken any rule. *Bring nothing in and take nothing out. Don't pass messages.* But she had done that, of course, when she spoke to Crew about the will. The slimy little toad must have ratted on her!

'You can go in now,' the secretary told her.

The Governor gestured towards a chair. 'Sit down, Miss Leigh.'

Roz lowered herself into the easy chair, hoping she looked less guilty than she felt. 'I wasn't expecting to see you.'

'No.' She studied Roz for a moment or two, then seemed to reach a decision. 'There's no point beating about the bush. Olive has had her privileges suspended and we think you may be the indirect cause of the suspension. According to the log-book you didn't come in last week, and I'm told Olive was very upset about it. Three days later she destroyed her cell and had to be sedated.' She saw Roz's surprise. 'She's been very volatile ever since and, under the circumstances, I am not happy about letting you back in. I think it's something I need to discuss with the Home Office.'

God! Poor old Olive! Why on earth didn't I have the sense to phone? Roz folded her hands in her lap and collected her thoughts rapidly. 'If it was three days before she did anything, what makes you think it was because of my not turning up? Did she say it was?'

'No, but we're stumped for any other explanation and I'm not prepared to risk your safety.'

Roz mulled this over for a moment or two. 'Let's assume for a moment you're right – though I should emphasize that I don't think you are – then if I don't show up again won't that distress her even more?' She leaned forward. 'Either way it would be more sensible to let me talk to her. If it *was* to do with my non-appearance then I can reassure her and calm her down; if it *wasn't*, then I see no reason why I should be punished with Home Office delays and wasted journeys when I haven't contributed to Olive's disturbance.'

The Governor gave a slight smile. 'You're very confident.'

'I've no reason not to be.'

It was the Governor's turn to reflect. She studied Roz in silence for some time. 'Let's be clear,' she said finally, 'about what sort of woman Olive really is.' She tapped her pencil on the desk. 'I told you when you first came here that there was no psychiatric evidence of psychopathy. That was true. It means that when Olive butchered her mother and sister she was completely sane. She knew exactly what she was doing, she understood the consequences of her act, and she was prepared to go ahead with it, despite those consequences. It also means – and this is peculiarly relevant to you – that she cannot be cured because there is nothing to cure. Under similar circumstances – unhappiness, low self-image, betrayal, in other words whatever triggers her anger – she would do the same thing again with the same disregard for the consequences because, in simple terms, having weighed them up, she would consider the consequences worth the action. I would add, and again this is peculiarly relevant to you, that the consequences are far less daunting to her now than they would have been six years ago. On the whole Olive enjoys being in prison. She has security, she has respect, and she has people to talk to. Outside, she would have none of them. And she knows it.'

It *was* like being up before her old headmistress. The confident voice of authority. 'So what you're saying is that she would have no qualms about taking a swipe at me because an additional sentence would only mean a longer stay here? And she would welcome that?'

'In effect, yes.'

'You're wrong,' said Roz bluntly. 'Not about her sanity. I agree with you, she's as sane as you or I. But you're wrong about her being a danger to me. I'm writing a book about her and she wants that book written. If it *is* me she's angry with, and I stress again that I don't think it is, then her interpretation of my non-appearance last week may be that I've lost interest, and it would be very poor psychology to let her go on thinking it.' She composed her arguments. 'You have a notice at the gate, presumably all prisons do. It's a declaration of policy. If I remember right, it includes something about helping prison inmates to lead law-abiding lives both inside prison and outside. If that has any meaning at all, and isn't simply a piece of decorative wallpaper to appease the reformers, then how can you justify provoking further punishable outbursts from Olive by denying her visits which the

Home Office has already approved?' She fell silent, worried about saying too much. However reasonable the woman might be, she could not afford to have her authority challenged. Few people could.

'Why does Olive want this book written?' asked the Governor mildly. 'She hasn't sought public notoriety before and you're not the first author to show an interest in her. We had several applications in the early days. She refused them all.'

'I don't know,' said Roz honestly. 'Perhaps it has something to do with her father's death. She claimed that one of her reasons for pleading guilty was to avoid putting him through the mill of a trial.' She shrugged. 'Presumably she felt a book would have been just as devastating to him, so waited till he died.'

The Governor was more cynical. 'Alternatively, while he was alive, her father was in a position to contest what she said; dead, he cannot. However, that is no concern of mine. My concern is with the ordered running of my prison.' She tapped her fingers impatiently on her desk. She had no desire at all to be drawn into a three-cornered dispute between herself, the Home Office, and Roz, but time-consuming correspondence with civil servants would pale into insignificance beside the murder of a civilian inside her prison. She had hoped to persuade Roz to abort the visit herself. She was surprised and, if the truth be told, rather intrigued by her own failure. *What was*

Rosalind Leigh getting right in her relationship with Olive that the rest of them were getting wrong? 'You may talk to her for half an hour,' she said abruptly, 'in the Legal Visits room, which is larger than the one you are used to. There will be two male officers present throughout the interview. Should either you or Olive breach any regulation of this prison, your visits will cease immediately and I will personally ensure that they will never resume. Is that understood, Miss Leigh?'

'Yes.'

The other nodded. 'I'm curious, you know. Are you raising her expectations by telling her your book will get her released?'

'No. Apart from anything else, she won't talk to me about the murders.' Roz reached for her briefcase.

'Then why are you so confident you're safe with her?'

'Because as far as I can make out I'm the only outsider she's met who's not frightened of her.'

Privately, she retracted that statement as Olive was ushered into the Legal Visits room by two large male officers who then retreated to the door behind Olive's back and stationed themselves on either side of it. The woman's look of dislike was chilling, and Roz recalled Hal saying to her that she might think differently about Olive if she ever saw her in a rage.

'Hi.' She held Olive's gaze. 'The Governor has allowed me to see you, but we're on trial, both of us. If we misbehave today my visits will be stopped. Do you understand?'

BITCH, Olive mouthed, unseen by the officers. FUCKING BITCH. But was she referring to Roz or the Governor? Roz couldn't tell.

'I'm sorry I didn't make it last Monday.' She touched her lip where the ugly scab still showed. 'I got thrashed by my miserable husband.' She forced a smile. 'I couldn't go out for a week, Olive, not even for you. I do have some pride, you know.'

Olive examined her stolidly for a second or two then dropped her eyes to the cigarette packet on the table. She plucked greedily at a cigarette and popped it between her fat lips. 'I've been on the block,' she said, flaring a match to the tip. 'The bastards wouldn't let me smoke. And they've been starving me.' She threw a baleful glance behind her. 'Bastards! Did you kill him?'

Roz followed her gaze. Every word she and Olive said would be reported back. 'Of course not.'

Olive smoothed the limp, greasy hair from her forehead with the hand that held the cigarette. A streak of nicotine staining along her parting showed she had done it many times before. 'I didn't think you would,' she said contemptuously. 'It's not as easy as it looks on the telly. You've heard what I did?'

'Yes.'

'So why have they let you see me?'

'Because I told the Governor that whatever you had done was nothing to do with me. Which it wasn't, was it?' She pressed one of Olive's feet with hers under the table. 'Presumably somebody else upset you?'

'Bloody Chaplain,' said Olive morosely. A bald eyelid drooped in a wink. 'Told me that God would do the rock'n'roll in heaven if I got down on my knees and said: "Alleluiah, I repent." Stupid sod. He's always trying to make religion relevant to modern criminals with low IQs. We can't cope with "There will be much rejoicing in heaven over one sinner that repenteth", so we get God will do the fucking rock'n'roll instead.' She listened with some satisfaction to the snorts of amusement behind her, then her eyes narrowed. I TRUSTED YOU, she mouthed at Roz.

Roz nodded. 'I assumed it was something like that.' She watched Olive's meaty fingers play with the tiny cigarette. 'But it was rude of me not to phone the prison and ask them to pass on a message. I had the mother and father of all headaches most of last week. You'll have to put it down to that.'

'I know you did.'

Roz frowned. 'How?'

With a flick of her fingers Olive squeezed the glowing head from the cigarette and dropped it into an ashtray on the table. 'Elementary, my dear Watson. Your ex gave you two black eyes if all that yellow round them isn't some weird sort of make-up. And headaches usually accompany black eyes.' But she was bored with the subject and fished an envelope abruptly from her pocket. She held it above her head. 'Mr Allenby, sir. Are you going to let me show this to the lady?'

'What is it?' asked one of the men, stepping forward.

'Letter from my solicitor.'

He took it from her raised hand, ignoring the two-fingered salute she gave him, and skimmed through it. 'I've no objections,' he said, placing it on the table and returning to his place by the door.

Olive prodded it towards Roz. 'Read it. He says the chances of tracing my nephew are virtually nil.' She reached for another cigarette, her eyes watching Roz closely. There was a strange awareness in them as if she knew something that Roz didn't, and Roz found it disturbing. Olive, it seemed, now held the initiative in this unnatural glasshouse relationship of theirs but why and when she had taken it, Roz couldn't begin to fathom. It was she, wasn't it, who had engineered this meeting against the odds?

Surprisingly, Crew had handwritten his letter in a neat, sloping script, and Roz could only assume he had composed it out of office hours and decided not to waste company time and money by having it typed. She found that oddly offensive.

Dear Olive,

I understand from Miss Rosalind Leigh that you are acquainted with some of the terms of your late father's will, principally those concerning Amber's illegitimate son. The bulk of the estate has been left in trust to the child although other provisions have been made in the event of failure on our part to trace him. Thus far, my people have met with little success and it is fair to say that we are increasingly pessimistic about our chances. We have established that your nephew emigrated to Australia with his family some twelve years ago when he was little more than a baby but, following their move from a rented flat in Sydney where they remained for the first six months, the trail goes cold. Unfortunately the child's adopted surname is a common one and we have no guarantee that he and his family remained in Australia. Nor can we rule out the possibility that the family decided to add to their name or change it entirely. Carefully worded advertisements in several Australian newspapers have produced no response.

Your father was most insistent that we should be circumspect in how we traced the child. His view, which I endorsed wholeheartedly, was that great damage could be done if there was any publicity associated with the bequest. He was very conscious of the shock his grandson might suffer if he learnt through an incontinent media campaign of his tragic association with the Martin family. For this reason, we have kept and will continue to keep your nephew's name a closely guarded secret. We are pressing on with our enquiries but, as your father stipulated a limited period for searches, the likelihood is that I, as executor, will be obliged to adopt the alternative provisions specified. These are a range of donations to hospitals and charities which care entirely for the needs and welfare of children.

Although your father never instructed me to keep the terms of his will from you, he was very concerned that you should not be distressed by them. It was for this reason that I thought it wiser to keep you in ignorance of his intentions. Had I known that you were already in possession of some of the facts, I should have corresponded sooner.

Trusting you are in good health,
Yours sincerely,
Peter Crew

Roz refolded the letter and pushed it back to Olive. 'You said last time that it mattered to you if your nephew was found, but you didn't enlarge on it.' She glanced towards the two officers, but they were showing little interest in anything except the floor.

She leaned forward and lowered her voice. 'Are you going to talk to me about it now?'

Olive jammed her cigarette angrily into the ashtray. She made no attempt to keep her voice down. 'My father was a terrible MAN.' Even in speech the word carried capital letters. 'I couldn't see it at the time but I've had years to think about it and I can see it now.' She nodded towards the letter. 'His conscience was troubling him. That's why he wrote that will. It was his way of feeling good about himself after the appalling damage he'd done. Why else would he leave his money to Amber's baby when he never cared shit for Amber herself?'

Roz looked at her curiously. 'Are you saying your father did the murders?' she murmured.

Olive snorted. 'I'm saying, why use Amber's baby to whitewash himself?'

'What had he done that needed whitewashing?'

But Olive didn't answer.

Roz waited a moment, then tried a different tack. 'You said your father would always leave money to family if he could. Does that mean there's other family he could have left it to? Or did you hope he'd leave it to you?'

Olive shook her head. 'There's no one. Both my parents were only children. And he couldn't leave it to me, could me?' She slammed her fist on the table, her voice rising furiously. 'Otherwise everyone would kill their fucking families!' The great ugly face leered at Roz. YOU WANTED TO, mouthed the sausage lips.

'Keep the volume down, Sculptress,' said Mr Allenby mildly, 'or the visit finishes now.'

Roz pressed a finger and thumb to her eyelids where she could feel her headache coming back. *Olive Martin took an axe* – she tried to thrust the thought away, but it wouldn't go – *and gave her mother forty whacks.* 'I don't understand why the will makes you so angry,' she said, forcing her voice to sound steady. 'If family was important to him who else is there except his grandson?'

Olive stared at the table, her jaw jutting aggressively. 'It's the principle,' she muttered. 'Dad's dead. What does it matter now what people think?'

Roz recalled something Mrs Hopwood had said. *'I've always assumed he must have had an affair . . .'* She took a shot in the dark. 'Do you have a half-brother or sister somewhere? Is that what you're trying to tell me?'

Olive found this amusing. 'Hardly. He'd have to have had a mistress for that and he didn't like women.' She gave a sardonic laugh. 'He did like MEN though.' Again the strange emphasis on the word.

Roz was very taken aback. 'Are you saying he was a homosexual?'

'I'm saying,' said Olive with exaggerated patience, 'that the only person I ever saw make Dad's face light up was our next-door neighbour, Mr Clarke. Dad used to get quite skittish whenever he was around.' She lit another cigarette. 'I thought it was rather sweet at the time, but only because I was too bloody thick to recognize a couple of queens when I saw them. Now I just think it was sick. It's no wonder my mother hated the Clarkes.'

'They moved after the murders,' said Roz thoughtfully. 'Vanished one morning without leaving a forwarding address. No one knows what happened to them or where they went.'

'Doesn't surprise me. I expect *she* was behind it.'

'Mrs Clarke?'

'She never liked him coming round to our house. He used to hop across the fence at the back and he and Dad would shut themselves in Dad's room and not come out for hours. I should think it must have worried her sick after the murders when Dad was all alone in the house.'

Images, gleaned from things people had said, chased themselves across Roz's mind. Robert Martin's vanity and his Peter Pan looks; he and Ted Clarke being as close as brothers; the room at the back with the bed in it; Gwen's keeping up appearances; her frigid flinching from her husband; the secret that needed hiding. It all made sense, she thought, but did it affect anything if Olive hadn't known it at the time?

'Was Mr Clarke his only lover, do you think?'

'How would I know? Probably not,' she went on,

contradicting herself immediately. 'He had his own back door in that room he used. He could have been out after rent-boys every night for all any of us would have known about it. I hate him.' She looked as if she were about to erupt again but Roz's look of alarm gave her pause. 'I hated him,' she repeated, before lapsing into silence.

'Because he killed Gwen and Amber?' asked Roz for the second time.

But Olive was dismissive: 'He was at work all day. Everyone knows that.'

Olive Martin took an axe . . . Are you raising her expectations by telling her your book will get her out? 'Did your lover kill them?' She felt she was being clumsy, asking the wrong questions, in the wrong way, at the wrong time.

Olive sniggered. 'What makes you think I had a lover?'

'Someone made you pregnant.'

'Oh, that.' She was scornful. 'I lied about the abortion. I wanted the girls here to think I was attractive once.' She spoke loudly as if intent on the officers hearing everything.

A cold fist of certainty squeezed at Roz's heart. Deedes had warned her of this four weeks ago. 'Then who was the man who sent you letters via Gary O'Brien?' she asked. 'Wasn't he your lover?'

Olive's eyes glittered like snakes' eyes. 'He was Amber's lover.'

Roz stared at her. 'But why would he send letters to you?'

'Because Amber was too frightened to receive them herself. She was a coward.' There was a brief pause. 'Like my father.'

'What was she frightened of?'

'My mother.'

'What was your father frightened of?'

'My mother.'

'And were you frightened of your mother?'

'No.'

'Who was Amber's lover?'

'I don't know. She never told me.'

'What was in his letters?'

'Love, I expect. Everyone loved Amber.'

'Including you?'

'Oh, yes.'

'And your mother. Did she love Amber?'

'Of course.'

'That's not what Mrs Hopwood says.'

Olive shrugged. 'What would she know about it? She hardly knew us. She was always fussing over her precious Geraldine.' A sly smile crept about her mouth, making her ugly. 'What does anybody know about it now except me?'

Roz could feel the scales peeling from her eyes in slow and terrible disillusionment. 'Is that why you waited till your father died before you would talk to anyone? So that there'd be no one left to contradict you?'

Olive stared at her with undisguised dislike then, with a careless gesture – hidden from the officers' eyes but all too visible to Roz – she removed a tiny clay doll from her pocket and turned the long pin that was piercing the doll's head. Red hair. Green dress. It required little imagination on Roz's part to endow the clay with a personality. She gave a hollow laugh. 'I'm a sceptic, Olive. It's like religion. It only works if you believe in it.'

'I believe in it.'

'Then more fool you.' She stood up abruptly and walked to the door, nodding to Mr Allenby to let her out. What had induced her to believe the woman innocent in the first place? And why, for Christ's sake, had she picked on a bloody murderess to fill the void that Alice had left in her heart?

She stopped at a payphone and dialled St Angela's Convent. It was Sister Bridget herself who answered. 'How may I help?' asked her comfortable lilting voice.

Roz smiled weakly into the receiver. 'You could say: "Come on down, Roz, I'll give you an hour to listen to your woes." '

Sister Bridget's light chuckle lost none of its warmth by transmission down the wire. 'Come on down, dear. I've a whole evening free and I like nothing better than listening. Are the woes so bad?'

'Yes. I think Olive did it.'

'Not so bad. You're no worse off than when you started. I live in the house next to the school. It's called Donegal. Totally inappropriate, of course, but rather charming. Join me as soon as you can. We'll have supper together.'

There was a strained note in Roz's voice. 'Do you believe in black magic, Sister?'

'Should I?'

'Olive is sticking pins into a clay image of me.'

'Good Lord!'

'And I've got a headache.'

'I'm not surprised. If I had just had my faith in someone shattered, I would have a headache, too. What an absurd creature she is! Presumably it's her way of trying to regain some semblance of control. Prison is soul destroying in that respect.' She tut-tutted in annoyance. 'Really quite absurd, and I've always had such a high esteem for Olive's intellect. I'll expect you when I see you, my dear.'

Roz listened to the click at the other end, then cradled the receiver against her chest. *Thank God for Sister Bridget* . . . She put the receiver back with two hands that trembled. *Oh, Jesus, Jesus, Jesus! THANK GOD FOR SISTER BRIDGET* . . .

*

Supper was a simple affair of soup, scrambled eggs on toast, fresh fruit and cheese, with Roz's contribution of a light sparkling wine. They ate in the dining room, looking out over the tiny walled garden where climbing plants tumbled their vigorous new growth in glossy green cascades. It took Roz two hours to run through all her notes and give Sister Bridget a complete account of everything she had discovered.

Sister Bridget, rather more rosy-cheeked than usual, sat in contemplative silence for a long time after Roz had finished. If she noticed the bruises on the other woman's face, she did not remark on them. 'You know, my dear,' she said at last, 'if I'm surprised by anything it is your sudden certainty that Olive is guilty. I can see nothing in what she said to make you overturn your previous conviction that she was innocent.' She raised mildly enquiring eyebrows.

'It was the sly way she smiled when she talked about being the only one who knew anything,' said Roz tiredly. 'There was something so unpleasantly knowing about it. Does that make sense?'

'Not really. The Olive I see has a permanently sly look. I wish she could be as open with me as she seems to have been with you, but I'm afraid she will always regard me as the guardian of her morals. It makes it harder for her to be honest.' She paused for a moment. 'Are you sure you're not simply reacting to her hostility towards you? It's so much easier to believe well of people who like us, and Olive made no secret of her liking for you on the two previous occasions you went to see her.'

'Probably.' Roz sighed. 'But that just means I'm as naïve as everyone keeps accusing me of being.' *Most criminals are pleasant most of the time*, Hal had said.

'I think you probably are naïve,' agreed Sister Bridget, 'which is why you've ferreted out information that none of the cynical professionals thought worth bothering with. Naïvety has its uses, just like everything else.'

'Not when it encourages you to believe lies, it doesn't,' said Roz with feeling. 'I was so sure she had told me the truth about the abortion, and if anything set me questioning her guilt it was that. A secret lover floating around, a rapist even' – she shrugged – 'either would have made a hell of a difference to her case. If he didn't do the murders himself, he might well have provoked them in some way. She cut that ground from under me when she told me the abortion was a lie.'

Sister Bridget looked at her closely for a moment. 'But when did she lie? When she told you about the abortion or, today, when she denied it?'

'Not today,' said Roz decisively. 'Her denial had a ring of truth which her admission never had.'

'I wonder. Don't forget, you were inclined to believe her the first time. Since when, everyone, except Geraldine's mother, has poured cold water on the idea. Subconsciously, you've been slowly conditioned to reject the idea that Olive could have had a sexual relationship with a man. That's made you very quick to accept that what she told you today was the truth.'

'Only because it makes more sense.'

Sister Bridget chuckled. 'It makes more sense to believe that Olive's confession was true but you've highlighted too many inconsistencies to take it at face value. She tells lies, you know that. The trick is to sort out fact from fiction.'

'But why does she lie?' asked Roz in sudden exasperation. 'What good does it do her?'

'If we knew that, we'd have the answer to everything. She lied as a child to shore up the image she wanted to project and to shield herself and Amber from her mother's angry disappointment. She was afraid of rejection. It's why most of us lie, after all. Perhaps she keeps on with it for the same reasons.'

'But her mother and Amber are dead,' Roz pointed out, 'and isn't her image diminished by denying she had a lover?'

Sister Bridget sipped her wine. She didn't respond directly. 'She may, of course, have done it to get her own back. I suppose you've considered that. I can't help feeling she's adopted you as a surrogate Amber or a surrogate Gwen.'

'And look what happened to them.' Roz winced. 'Getting her own back for what, anyway?'

'For missing a visit. You said that upset her.'

'I had good reason.'

'I'm sure you did.' The kind eyes rested on the bruises. 'That's not to say Olive believed you or, if she did, that a week of resentment could be cast off so easily. She may, quite simply, have wanted to spite you in the only way she could, by hurting you. And she's succeeded. You *are* hurt.'

'Yes,' Roz admitted, 'I am. I believed in her. But I'm the one who's feeling rejected, not Olive.'

'Of course. Which is exactly what she wanted to achieve.'

'Even if it means I walk away and abandon her for good?'

'Spite is rarely sensible, Roz.' She shook her head. 'Poor Olive. She must be quite desperate at the moment if she's resorting to clay dolls and outbursts of anger. I wonder what's brought it on. She's been very tetchy with me, too, these last few months.'

'Her father's death,' said Roz. 'There's nothing else.'

Sister Bridget sighed. 'What a tragic life his was. One does wonder what he did to deserve it.' She fell silent. 'I am disinclined to believe,' she went on after a moment, 'that this man who sent the letters was Amber's lover. I think I told you that I bumped into Olive shortly before the murders. I was surprised to see how nice she looked. She was still very big, of course, but she had taken such trouble with her appearance that she looked quite pretty. A different girl entirely from the one who'd been at St Angela's. Such transformations never come about in a vacuum. There's always a reason for them and, in my experience, the reason is usually a man. Then, you know, there is Amber's character to consider. She was never as bright as her sister and she lacked Olive's independence and maturity. I would be very surprised if, at the age of twenty-one, she had been able to sustain an affair with anybody for as long as six months.'

'But you said yourself, men can bring about amazing transformations. Perhaps she changed under his influence.'

'I can't deny that, but if he was Amber's lover, then I can point to a very definite lie that Olive has told you. She would know exactly what was in the letters, either because Amber would have told her or because she would have found a way to open them. She always pried into things that weren't her concern. It sounds so churlish to say it now, but we all had to be very careful of our personal possessions while Olive was at St Angela's. Address books and diaries, in particular, drew her like magnets.'

'Marnie at Wells-Fargo thought Gary O'Brien had a yen for Olive. Perhaps *he* was the man she was dressing up for.'

'Perhaps.'

They sat in silence for some time watching twilight fall. Sister Bridget's cat, a threadbare tabby of advanced years, had curled in a ball on Roz's lap, and she stroked it mechanically in time to its purrs with the same careless affection that she bestowed on Mrs Antrobus. 'I wish,' she murmured, 'there was some independent way of finding out whether or not she had the abortion, but I'd never be allowed within spitting distance of her medical records. Not without her permission, and probably not even then.'

'And supposing it turns out that she didn't have an abortion? Would that tell you anything? It doesn't mean she didn't have a man in her life.'

'No,' agreed Roz, 'but by the same token if she *did* have an abortion then there can be no doubt there *was* a man. I'd be so much more confident about pressing ahead if I knew a lover existed.'

Sister Bridget's perceptive eyes remained on her too long for comfort. 'And so much more confident about dropping the whole thing if you can be convinced he didn't. I think, my dear, you should have more faith in your ability to judge people. Instinct is as good a guide as written evidence.'

'But my instinct at the moment tells me she's guilty as hell.'

'Oh, I don't think so.' Her companion's light laughter rang about the room. 'If it did you wouldn't have driven all these miles to talk to me. You could have sought out your friendly policeman. He would have approved your change of heart.' Her eyes danced. 'I, on the other hand, am the one person you know who could be relied on to fight Olive's corner.'

Roz smiled. 'Does that mean you now think she didn't do it?'

Sister Bridget stared out of the window. 'No,' she said frankly. 'I'm still in two minds.'

'Thanks,' said Roz with heavy irony, 'and you expect me to have faith. That's a bit two-faced, isn't it?'

'Very. But you were chosen, Roz, and I wasn't.'

Roz arrived back at her flat around midnight. The telephone was ringing as she let herself in but after three or four bells the answerphone took over. Iris, she thought. No one else would call at such an unearthly hour, not even Rupert. She had no intention of speaking to her but, out of curiosity, she flicked the switch on the machine to hear Iris leave her message.

'I wonder where you are,' slurred Hal's voice, slack with drink and tiredness. 'I've been calling for hours. I'm drunk as a skunk, woman, and it's your fault. You're too bloody thin, but what the hell!' He gave a baritone chuckle. 'I'm drowning in shit here, Roz. Me and Olive both. Mad, bad and dangerous to know.' He sighed. '*From East to western Ind, no jewel is like Rosalind.* Who are you, anyway? Nemesis? You lied, you know. You said you'd leave me in peace.' There was the sound of a crash. 'Je-*sus*!' he roared into the telephone. 'I've dropped the bloody bottle.' The line was cut abruptly.

Roz wondered if her grin looked as idiotic as it felt. She switched the answerphone back to automatic and went to bed. She fell asleep almost immediately.

The phone rang again at nine o'clock the next morning. 'Roz?' asked his sober, guarded voice.

'Speaking.'

'It's Hal Hawksley.'

'Hi,' she said cheerfully. 'I didn't know you knew my number.'

'You gave me your card, remember.'

'Oh, yes. What can I do for you?'

'I tried you yesterday, left a message on your answerphone.'

She smiled into the receiver. 'Sorry,' she told him, 'the tape's on the blink. All I got was my ear-drums pierced by high-pitched crackling. Has something happened?'

His relief was audible. 'No.' There was a brief pause. 'I just wondered how you got on with the O'Briens.'

'I saw Ma. It cost me fifty quid but it was worth it. Are you busy today or can I come and chew your ear off again? I need a couple of favours: a photograph of Olive's father and access to her medical records.'

He was happy talking details. 'No chance on the

latter,' he told her. 'Olive can demand to see them but you'd have more chance breaking into Parkhurst than breaking into NHS files. I might be able to get hold of a photograph of him, though, if I can persuade Geoff Wyatt to take a photocopy of the one on file.'

'What about pictures of Gwen and Amber? Could he get photocopies of them too?'

'Depends how strong your stomach is. The only ones I remember are the post-mortem shots. You'll have to get on to Martin's executors if you want pictures of them alive.'

'OK, but I'd still like to see the post-mortem ones if that's possible. I won't try to publish them without the proper authority,' she promised.

'You'd have a job. Police photocopies are usually the worst you'll ever see. If your publisher can make a decent negative out of them, he probably deserves a medal. I'll see what I can do. What time will you get here?'

'Early afternoon? There's someone I need to see first. Could you get me a copy of Olive as well?'

'Probably.' He was silent for a moment. 'High-pitched crackling. Are you sure that's all you heard?'

Twelve

PETERSON'S ESTATE AGENCY in Dawlington High Street maintained a brave front, with glossy photographs turning enticingly in the window and bright lights inviting the punters in. But, like the estate agents in Southampton centre, the recession had taken its toll here, too, and one neat young man presided over four desks in the despondent knowledge that another day would pass without a single house sale. He jerked to his feet with robotic cheerfulness as the door opened, his teeth glittering in a salesman's smile.

Roz shook her head to avoid raising false hopes. 'I'm sorry,' she said apologetically. 'I haven't come to buy anything.'

He gave an easy laugh. 'Ah, well. Selling perhaps?'

'Not that either.'

'Very wise.' He pulled out a chair for her. 'It's still a buyer's market. You only sell at the moment if you're desperate to move.' He resumed his chair on the other side of the desk. 'How can I help?'

Roz gave him a card. 'I'm trying to trace some people called Clarke who sold their house through this agency three or four years ago and moved out of the area. None of their neighbours knows where they went. I was hoping you might be able to tell me.'

He pulled a face. 'Before my time, I'm afraid. What was the address of the house?'

'Number twenty, Leven Road.'

'I could look it up, I suppose. The file will be out the back if it hasn't been binned.' He looked at the empty desks. 'Unfortunately there's no one to cover for me at the moment so I won't be able to do it until this evening. Unless—' He glanced at Roz's card again. 'I see you live in London. Have you ever thought about buying a second property on the south coast, Mrs Leigh? We have a lot of authors down here. They like to escape to the peace and quiet of the country.'

Her mouth twitched. 'Miss Leigh. And I don't even own a first property. I live in rented accommodation.'

He spun his chair and pulled out a drawer in the filing cabinet behind him. 'Then let me suggest a mutually beneficial arrangement.' His fingers ran nimbly through the files, selecting a succession of printed pages. 'You read these while I search out that information for you. If a customer comes into the shop, offer them a seat and call for me. Ditto, if the phone rings.' He nodded to a back door. 'I'll leave that open. Just call "Matt" and I'll hear you. Fair?'

'I'm happy if you are,' she said, 'but I'm not planning on buying anything.'

'That's fine.' He walked across to the door. 'Mind you, there's one property there that would fit you like a glove. It's called Bayview, but don't be put off by the name. I shan't be long.'

Roz fingered through the pages reluctantly as if just touching them might induce her to part with her money. He had the soft insidiousness of an insurance salesman. Anyway, she told herself with some amusement, she couldn't possibly live in a house called Bayview. It conjured up too many images of net-curtained guest-houses with beak-nosed landladies in nylon overalls and lacklustre signs saying vacancies propped against the downstairs windows.

She came to it finally at the bottom of the pile and the reality, of course, was very different. A small whitewashed coastguard's cottage, the last of a group of four, perched on a cliff near Swanage on the Isle of Purbeck. Two up, two down. Unpretentious. Charming. Beside the sea. She looked at the price.

'Well?' asked Matt, returning a few minutes later with a folder under one arm. 'What do you think?'

'Assuming I could afford it, which I can't, I think I'd freeze to death in the winter from winds lashing in off the sea and be driven mad in the summer by streams of tourists wandering along the coastal path. According to your blurb it passes only a matter of yards from the fence. And that's ignoring the fact that I'd be rubbing shoulders with the inhabitants of the other three cottages, day in, day out, plus the frightening prospect of knowing that sooner or later the cliff will slip and take my very expensive cottage with it.'

He chuckled good-humouredly. 'I knew you'd like it. I'd have bought it myself if it wasn't too far to travel each day. The cottage at the other end has a retired couple in it in their seventies and the two in the middle are weekend cottages. They are situated in the middle of a small headland, well away from the cliff edges, and, frankly, the bricks will crumble long before the foundations do. As for the wind and the tourists, well, it's to the east of Swanage so it's sheltered from the prevailing winds, and the sort of tourists who walk that coastal path are not the sort to disturb your peace, simply because there is no public access beside these cottages. The nearest one is four miles away and you don't get noisy children or drunken lager louts tackling that sort of hike for the fun of it. Which leaves' – his boyish face split into a carefree smile – 'the problem of cost.'

Roz giggled. 'Don't tell me. The owners are so desperate to get rid of it they're prepared to give it away.'

'As a matter of fact, yes. Liquidity problems with

their business and this is only a weekend retreat. They'll take a twenty-thousand reduction if someone can come up with cash. Can you?'

Roz closed her eyes and thought of her fifty per cent share of the proceeds of divorce, sitting on deposit. Yes, she thought, I can. 'This is absurd,' she said impatiently. 'I didn't come in to buy anything. I'll hate it. It'll be far too small. And why on earth have you got it on your books? It's miles away.'

'We have a reciprocal arrangement with our other branches.' He had hooked his fish. Now he let her swim a little. 'Let's see what this file can tell us.' He drew it forward and opened it. 'Twenty, Leven Road. Owners: Mr and Mrs Clarke. Instructions: quick sale wanted; carpets and curtains included in asking price. Bought by Mr and Mrs Blair. Completion date: twenty-fifth Feb., eighty-nine.' He looked surprised 'They didn't pay very much for it.'

'It was vacant for a year,' said Roz, 'which would probably explain the low price. Does it give a forwarding address for the Clarkes?'

He read on: 'It says here: "Vendors have asked Peterson's not to divulge any information about their new whereabouts." I wonder why.'

'They fell out with their neighbours,' said Roz, economical as ever with the truth. 'But they must have given a forwarding address,' she remarked reasonably, 'or they wouldn't have asked for it to be withheld.'

He turned over several pages then carefully closed the file, leaving his finger to mark a place. 'We're talking professional ethics here, Miss Leigh. I am employed by Peterson's, and Peterson's were asked to respect the Clarkes' confidence. It would be very wrong to abuse a client's trust.'

Roz thought for a moment. 'Is there anything from Peterson's in writing saying they agreed to honour the Clarkes' request?'

'No.'

'Then I don't see that you're bound by anything. Confidences cannot be inherited. If they could, they would no longer be confidences.'

He smiled. 'That's a very fine distinction.'

'Yes.' She picked up the details of Bayview. 'Supposing I said I wanted to view this cottage at three o'clock this afternoon? Could you arrange it for me, using that telephone over there' – she nodded to the furthest desk – 'while I stay here looking through these other house details?'

'I could, but I'd take it very badly if you failed to keep the appointment.'

'My word's my bond,' she assured him. 'If I say I'm going to do something I always do it.'

He stood up, letting the file fall open on the desk. 'Then I'll phone our Swanage branch,' he told her. 'You will have to collect the key from them.'

'Thank you.' She waited until his back was turned,

then swung the file round and jotted down the Clarkes' address on her pad. Salisbury, she noted.

A few minutes later Matt resumed his seat and gave her a map of Swanage with Peterson's estate agency marked with a cross. 'Mr Richards is expecting you at three o'clock.' With a lazy flick of his hand he closed the Clarkes' file. 'I trust you will find your dealings with him as mutually satisfactory as you have found your dealings with me.'

Roz laughed. 'And I hope I don't, or I shall be considerably poorer by this evening.'

Roz approached the Poacher by the alleyway at the back and knocked on the kitchen door. 'You're early,' said Hal, opening it.

'I know, but I have to be in Swanage by three and if I don't leave fairly soon I won't make it. Have you any customers?'

He gave her a withering smile. 'I haven't even bothered to open up.'

She chose to ignore the sarcasm. 'Then come with me,' she said. 'Forget this place for a few hours.'

He didn't exactly jump at the invitation. 'What's in Swanage?'

She handed him the details of Bayview. 'A "des. res." overlooking the sea. I've committed myself to looking at it and I could do with some moral support or I might end up buying the wretched thing.'

'Then don't go.'

'I have to. It's by way of a quid pro quo,' she said obliquely. 'Come with me,' she urged, 'and say no whenever I look like saying yes. I'm a sucker for a soft sell and I've always wanted to live on a cliff by the sea and own a dog and go beachcombing.'

He looked at the price. 'Can you afford it?' he asked curiously.

'Just about.'

'Rich lady,' he said. 'Writing is obviously very profitable.'

'Hardly. That was by way of a pay-off.'

'Pay-off for what?' he asked, his eyes veiled.

'It's not important.'

'Nothing ever is in your life.'

She shrugged. 'So you don't want to come? Ah, well, it was only a thought. I'll go on my own.' She looked lonely suddenly.

He glanced behind him towards the restaurant, then abruptly reached his jacket off the back of the door. 'I'll come,' he told her, 'but I'm damned if I'll say no. It sounds like paradise, and the second best piece of advice my mother ever gave me was never get between a woman and what she wants.' He pulled the door to and locked it.

'And what was the best piece of advice?'

He dropped a casual arm across her shoulders – *could she really be as lonely as she looked? The thought saddened him* – and walked her up the alleyway. 'That happiness is no laughing matter.'

She gave a throaty chuckle. 'What's that supposed to mean?'

'It means, woman, that the pursuit of happiness deserves weighty consideration. It's the be-all and end-all of existence. Where is the sense in living if you're not enjoying it?'

'Earning Brownie points for the great hereafter, suffering being good for the soul and all that.'

'If you say so,' he said cheerfully. 'Shall we go in my car? It'll give you a chance to test out your theory.' He led her to an ancient Ford Cortina estate and unlocked the passenger door, pulling it half-open on screaming hinges.

'What theory?' she asked, squeezing inelegantly through the gap.

He shut the door. 'You'll soon find out,' he murmured.

They arrived with half an hour to spare. Hal drew into a parking space on the sea front and rubbed his hands. 'Let's have some fish and chips. We passed a kiosk about a hundred yards back and I'm ravenous. It's the fresh air that does it.'

Roz's head, tortoise-like, emerged from the collar of her jacket, slowly easing its frozen jaw and skewering him with gimlet eyes. 'Has this heap of junk got an MOT?' she grated.

'Of course it's got an MOT.' He slapped the steering-wheel. 'She's sound as a bell, just lacks a window or two. You get used to it after a while.'

'A window or two!' she spluttered. 'As far as I can see it hasn't got any windows at all except for the front one. I think I've caught pneumonia.'

'There's no pleasing some women. You wouldn't be whingeing like this if I'd whisked you down to the seaside on a beautiful sunny day in an open-topped cabriolet. You're being snotty-nosed just because it's a Cortina.' He gave an evil chuckle. 'And what about suffering being good for the soul? It's done bugger all for yours, my girl.'

She thrust the screeching door open as far as it would go and crawled out. 'For your information, Hawksley, it is *not* a beautiful sunny day' – she giggled – 'in fact it will probably turn out to be the coldest May day this century. And *had* this been a convertible, we could have stopped to put the top up. In any case, why aren't there any windows?'

He tucked her into the crook of his arm and set off towards the fish and chip kiosk. 'Someone smashed them,' he said matter of factly. 'I haven't bothered to replace them because there's a good chance it will happen again.'

She rubbed the end of her nose to restore the circulation. 'I suppose you're in hock to loan sharks.'

'And if I am?'

She thought of her money on deposit, untouched, going nowhere. 'I might be able to broker you out of your difficulties,' she suggested tentatively.

He frowned. 'Is this charity, Roz, or an offer to negotiate?'

'It's not charity,' she assured him. 'My accountant would have a fit if I offered charity.'

He dropped his arm abruptly. 'Why would you want to negotiate on my behalf? You don't know a damn thing about me.' He sounded angry.

She shrugged. 'I know you're in deep shit, Hawksley. I'm offering to help you out of it. Is that so terrible?' She walked on.

Hal, a step or two behind, cursed himself roundly. What sort of fool lowered his defences just because a woman looked lonely? But loneliness, of course, was the one thing guaranteed to strike a chord. There must have been times when he hadn't been lonely but he was damned, at the moment, if he could remember them.

Roz's delight in the cottage, masked by an unconvincing smile of bored indifference, announced itself loudly as she stared wide-eyed at the views from the windows, noted the double-glazing, admitted grudgingly that, yes, she had always liked open fireplaces, and, yes, she was quite surprised by the size of the rooms. She *had* expected them to be smaller. She poked for several minutes round the patioed garden, said it was a pity there wasn't a greenhouse, then, rather belatedly, obscured her enthusiasm behind a pair of dark glasses to examine a small rose-covered outhouse which was used by the present owners as a third bedroom, but which might, she supposed, at a pinch, serve as a sort of study–library.

Hal and Mr Richards sat on cast-iron chairs in front of the french windows, talking idly about very little and watching her. Mr Richards, thoroughly intimidated by Hal's brusque one-word answers, scented a sale but contained his excitement rather better than Roz.

He stood up when Roz had finished her inspection and, with a disarming smile, offered her his chair. 'I should perhaps have mentioned, Miss Leigh, that the present owners will consider selling the furniture with the house assuming, of course, a satisfactory price can be arranged. I understand none of it is more than four years old and the wear and tear has been minimal with weekend occupation only.' He glanced at his watch. 'Why don't I give you fifteen minutes to talk it over? I'll go for a stroll along the cliff path.' He vanished tactfully through the french windows and a moment later they heard the front door close.

Roz took off her glasses and looked at Hal. Her eyes were childlike in their enthusiasm. 'What do you think? Furniture, too. Isn't it fabulous?'

His lips twitched involuntarily. *Could this be acting?* It was damn good if it was. 'It depends what you want it for.'

'To live in,' she said. 'It would be so easy to work here.' She looked towards the sea. 'I've always loved the sound of waves.' She turned to him. 'What do you think? Should I buy it?'

He was curious. 'Will my opinion make a difference?'

'Probably.'

'Why?'

'Because common sense tells me it would be a mad thing to do. It's miles from everyone I know, and it's expensive for what it is, a pokey little two up, two down. There must be better ways of investing my money.' She studied his set face and wondered why her earlier offer to help had made him so hostile. He was a strange man, she thought. So very approachable as long as she steered clear of talking about the Poacher.

He looked past her towards the cliff-top where Mr Richards was just visible, sitting on a rock and having a quiet smoke. 'Buy it,' he said. 'You can afford it.' His dark face broke into a smile. 'Live dangerously. Do what you've always wanted to do. How did John Masefield put it? "I must down to the seas again, for the call of the running tide/Is a wild call and a clear call that may not be denied." So, live on your cliff by the sea and go beachcombing with your dog. As I said, it sounds like paradise.'

She smiled back, her dark eyes full of humour. 'But the trouble with paradise was that it was boring, which is why, when the one-eyed trouser-snake appeared, Eve was so damn keen to bite into the apple of knowledge.' He was a different man when he laughed. She caught a glimpse of the Hal Hawksley, hail-fellow-well-met, boon companion, who could, were his tables ever full, preside with confident conviviality among them. She threw caution to the winds. 'I wish you'd let me help you. I'd be lonely here. And where's the sense in paying a fortune to be lonely on a cliff?'

His eyes veiled abruptly. 'You really are free with your money, aren't you? Exactly what are you suggesting? A buy-out? A partnership? What?'

God, he was prickly! And he had accused her of it once. 'Does it matter? I'm offering to bail you out of whatever mess you're in.'

His eyes narrowed. 'The only certain thing you know about me, Roz, is that my restaurant is failing. Why would an intelligent woman want to throw good money after bad?'

Why indeed? She would never be able to explain it to her accountant whose idea of sensible living was minimum risk-taking, clean balance sheets, and tax advantageous pension plans. How would she even begin? 'There's this man, Charles, who reduces me to jelly every time I see him. But he's a damn good cook and he loves his restaurant and there's no logical reason why it should be going down the pan. I keep trying to lend him money but he throws it back in my face every time.' Charles would have her certified. She swung her bag on to her shoulder. 'Forget I mentioned it,' she said. 'It's obviously a sore nerve, though I can't imagine why.'

She started to get up but he caught her wrist in a grip of iron and held her in her seat. 'Is this another set-up, Roz?'

She stared at him. 'You're hurting me.' He released her abruptly. 'What are you talking about?' she asked, massaging her wrist.

'You came back.' He rubbed his face vigorously with both hands as if he were in pain. 'Why the hell do you keep coming back?'

She was incensed. 'Because you phoned,' she said. 'I wouldn't have come if you hadn't phoned. God, you're arrogant. They come two a penny like you in London, you know.'

His eyes narrowed dangerously. 'Then offer your money to them,' he said, 'and stop patronizing me.'

Tight-lipped, they took their leave of Mr Richards with false promises of phoning the next day, and drove off up the narrow coast road towards Wareham. Hal, all too conscious of the darkening clouds and the reduction in speed that wet tarmac would enforce on him, concentrated on his driving. Roz, crushed by his hostility which, like a tropical storm, had blown out of nowhere, withdrew into hurt silence. Hal had been gratuitously cruel, and knew it, but he was gripped by his own certainty that this trip had been engineered to get him out of the Poacher. And *God* was Roz good. She had every damn thing: looks, humour, intellect, and just enough vulnerability to appeal to his stupid chivalry. But *he* had phoned *her. Fool, Hawksley!* She would have come back, anyway. Someone had to offer him the stinking money. *Sh-i-it!* He slammed his fist against the steering-wheel. 'Why did you want me to come with you?' he demanded into the silence.

'You're a free agent,' she pointed out caustically. 'You didn't have to come.'

It started to rain as they reached Wareham, slanting stair-rods that drove in through the open windows.

'Oh, great!' announced Roz, clutching her jacket about her throat. 'The perfect end to a perfect day. I'll be soaked. I should have come on my own in my own car. I could hardly have had less fun, could I?'

'Why didn't you then? Why drag me out on a wild-goose chase?'

'Believe it or not,' she said icily, 'I was trying to do you a favour. I thought it would be good for you to escape for a couple of hours. I was wrong. You're even more touchy away from the place than you are in it.' He took a corner too fast and threw her against the door, grazing her leather jacket against the buckled chromium window strip. 'For God's sake,' she snapped crossly. 'This jacket cost me a fortune.'

He pulled into the kerb with a screech of rubber. 'OK,' he snarled, 'let's see what we can do to protect it.' He reached across her to take a book of road maps out of the dashboard pocket.

'What good will that do?'

'It will tell me where the nearest station is.' He thumbed through the pages. 'There's one in Wareham and the line goes to Southampton. You can take a taxi back to your car at the other end.' He fished out his wallet. 'That should be enough to pay your way.' He dropped a twenty-pound note into her lap then swung the car on to the road again. 'It's off to the right at the next roundabout.'

'You're a real sweetheart, Hawksley. Didn't your mother teach you any manners along with her little aphorisms about women and life?'

'Don't push your luck,' he growled. 'I'm on a very short fuse at the moment and it doesn't take much to rile me. I spent five years of marriage being criticized for every damn thing I did. I'm not about to repeat the experience.' He drew up in front of the station. 'Go home,' he told her, wiping a weary hand across his damp face. 'I'm doing you a favour.'

She put the twenty-pound note on the dashboard and reached for her handbag. 'Yes,' she agreed mildly, 'I think you probably are. If your wife stuck it out for five years, she must have been a saint.' She pushed the door open on its screaming hinges and eased round it, then bent down to look through the window, thrusting her middle finger into the air. 'Go screw yourself, Sergeant. Presumably it's the only thing that gives you any pleasure. Let's face it, no one else could ever be good enough.'

'Got it in one, Miss Leigh.' He nodded a curt farewell, then spun the wheel in a U-turn. As he drove away the twenty-pound note whipped like a bitter recrimination from the window and fell with the rain into the gutter.

Hal was cold and wet by the time he reached Dawlington, and his already evil temper was not improved to find her car still parked at the end of the alleyway where she had left it. He glanced past it, between the buildings, and saw that the back door of the Poacher stood ajar, the wood in splinters where a crowbar had been used to wrench it free of its frame. OH, *Jesus*! She *had* set him up. He knew a moment of total desolation – he was not as immune as he thought himself – before the need to act took over.

He was too angry for common sense, too angry to take even elementary precautions. He ran on light feet, thrust the door wide and weighed in with flailing fists, punching, kicking, gouging, oblivious to the blows that landed on his arms and shoulders, intent only on causing maximum damage to the bastards who were destroying him.

Roz, arriving thirty minutes later with Hal's sodden twenty-pound note clutched in one hand and a blistering letter of denunciation in the other, stared in disbelief at what she saw. The kitchen looked like a scene from Beirut in the aftermath of war. Deserted and destroyed. The table, up-ended, leant drunkenly against the oven, two of its legs wrenched free. Chairs, in pieces, lay amongst shards of broken crockery and jagged glass. And the fridge, tilted forward and balanced precariously on its open door, had poured its contents across the quarry tiling in streams of milk and congealed stock. She held a trembling hand to her lips. Here and there, splashes of bright red blood had tinged the spreading milk pink.

She looked wildly up the alleyway, but there was no one in sight. *What to do?* 'Hal!' she called, but her voice was little more than a whisper. 'Hal!' This time it rose out of control and, in the silence that followed, she thought she heard a sound from the other side of the swing doors into the restaurant. She stuffed the letter and the money into her pockets and reached inside the door for one of the table legs. 'I've called the police,' she shouted, croaky with fear. 'They're on their way.'

The door swung open and Hal emerged with a

bottle of wine. He nodded at the table leg. 'What are you planning to do with that?'

She let her arm fall. 'Have you gone mad? Did you do all this?'

'Am I likely to have done it?'

'Olive did.' She stared about her. 'This is just what Olive did. Lost her temper and destroyed her room. She had all her privileges taken away.'

'You're babbling.' He found a couple of glasses in an intact wall cupboard and filled them from the bottle. 'Here.' His dark eyes watched her closely. '*Have* you called the police?'

'No.' Her teeth chattered against the wine glass. 'I thought if you were a burglar you'd run away. Your hand's bleeding.'

'I know.' He took the table leg away from her and put it on top of the oven, then pulled forward the only intact chair from behind the back door and pressed her into it. 'What were you going to do if the burglar ran out this way?'

'Hit him, I suppose.' Her fear was beginning to subside. 'Is this what you thought I'd set you up for?'

'Yes.'

'God!' She didn't know what else to say. She watched while he found a broom and started to sweep the mess towards one corner. 'Shouldn't you leave that?'

'What for?'

'The police.'

He eyed her curiously. 'You said you hadn't called them.'

She digested this in silence for several seconds, then put her glass on the floor beside her. 'This is all a bit heavy for me.' She took the twenty-pound note from her pocket, but left the letter where it was. 'I only came back to give you this.' She held it out as she stood up. 'I'm sorry,' she said with an apologetic smile.

'What for?'

'Making you angry. I seem to have a knack for making people angry at the moment.' He moved towards her to take the money, but stopped abruptly at her look of alarm.

'Goddamnit, woman, do you think *I* did this?'

But he was speaking to thin air. Roz had taken to her heels down the alleyway and the twenty-pound note, once again, fluttered to the ground.

Thirteen

ROZ'S SLEEP THAT night was intermittent, fitful dozing between turbulent dreams. Olive with an axe, hacking kitchen tables to pieces. *I didn't think you would . . . it's not as easy as it looks on the telly . . .* Hal's fingers on her wrist, but his face the gleeful face of her brother as he gave her Chinese burns as a child. *Goddamnit, woman, do you think I did this . . .* Olive hanging from the gallows, her face the slimy grey of wet clay. *Have you no qualms about releasing someone like her back into society . . .* A priest with the eyes of Sister Bridget. *It's a pity you're not a Catholic . . . You could go to confession and feel better immediately . . . You keep offering me money . . . The law is an ass . . . Have you called the police . . .*

She woke in the morning to the sound of the phone ringing in her sitting room. Her head was splitting. She snatched up the receiver to shut off the noise. 'Who is it?'

'Well, that's a nice welcome, I must say,' remarked Iris. 'What's eating you?'

'Nothing. What do you want?'

'Shall I phone off,' said Iris sweetly, 'and call you back again in half an hour when you've remembered that I'm your friend and not some piece of dog's dirt that you've just scraped off your shoe?'

'Sorry. You woke me. I didn't sleep very well.'

'M'm, well, I've just had your editor on the phone pressing me for a date – and I don't mean an invitation to dinner. He wants a rough idea of when the book will be ready.'

Roz made a face into the receiver. 'I haven't started writing it yet.'

'Then you'd better get a move on, my darling, because I've told him it will be finished by Christmas.'

'Oh, Iris, for Heaven's sake. That's only six months away and I'm no further forward than the last time I spoke to you. Olive clams up every time we get to the murders. In fact I—'

'Seven months,' Iris cut in. 'Go and grill that dodgy policeman again. He sounds absolutely frightful and I'll bet you anything you like he framed her. They all do it. It boosts their quotas. The buzz word is productivity, darling, something that is temporarily absent from your vocabulary.'

*

Mrs Clarke listened to Roz's introductory speech about her book on Olive with an expression of complete horror. 'How did you find us?' she asked in a quavering voice. For no particular reason, Roz had pictured her in her fifties or early sixties. She was unprepared for this old woman, closer in age to Mr Hayes than to the age Robert and Gwen Martin would have been if they were still alive.

'It wasn't difficult,' she hedged.

'I've been so afraid.'

It was an odd reaction but Roz let it pass. 'Can I come in? I won't take up much of your time, I promise.'

'I couldn't possibly speak to you. I'm alone. Edward is shopping.'

'Please, Mrs Clarke,' she begged, her voice catching under the strain of her tiredness. It had taken two and a half hours to drive to Salisbury and locate their house. 'I've come such a long way to see you.'

The woman smiled suddenly and held the door wide. 'Come in. Come in. Edward made some cakes specially. He'll be so thrilled you found us.'

With a puzzled frown, Roz stepped inside. 'Thank you.'

'You remember Pussy, of course' – she waved at an ancient cat curled beneath a radiator – 'or was she after your time? I forget things, you know. We'll sit in the lounge. Edward,' she called, 'Mary's here.'

There was no response. 'Edward's gone shopping,' said Roz.

'Oh, yes.' She looked at Roz in confusion. 'Do I know you?'

'I'm a friend of Olive's.'

'I'm a friend of Olive's,' mimicked the old lady. 'I'm a friend of Olive's.' She lowered herself on to the sofa. 'Sit down. Edward's made some cakes specially. I remember Olive. We were at school together. She had long pigtails which the boys used to pull. Such wicked boys. I wonder what happened to them.' She looked at Roz again. 'Do I know you?'

Roz sat awkwardly in an armchair, weighing the ethics of questioning a vulnerable old woman with senile dementia. 'I'm a friend of Olive Martin,' she prompted. 'Gwen and Robert's daughter.' She studied the vacant blue eyes but there was no reaction. She was relieved. Ethics became irrelevant when asking questions was a nonsense. She smiled encouragingly. 'Tell me about Salisbury. Do you like living here?'

Their conversation was an exhausting one, filled with silences, chanting repetition, and strange inconsequential references that left Roz struggling to follow the thread. Twice, she had to divert Mrs Clarke from a sudden realization that she was a stranger, fearing that if she left she would find it impossible to get back in to talk to Edward. With part of her mind she wondered how he coped. Could you go on loving an empty shell when your love was neither reciprocated nor appreciated? Could there ever be enough flashes of lucidity to make the loneliness of caring worthwhile?

Her eye was drawn again and again to the wedding photograph above the mantelpiece. They had married comparatively late, she thought, judging by their ages. He looked to be in his forties, with most of his hair already missing. She looked a little older. But they stood shoulder to shoulder, laughing together out of the frame, two happy, healthy people, with not a care in the world, unaware – and how could they be? – that she carried the seeds of dementia. It was cruel to make a comparison but Roz couldn't help herself. Beside the celluloid woman, so alive, so vivid, so substantial, the real Mrs Clarke was a colourless, trembling shadow. Was this, Roz wondered, why Edward and Robert Martin had become lovers? She found the whole experience immensely depressing and when, at last, the sound of a key grated in the lock, it came like the welcome patter of rain on drought-hardened earth.

'Mary's come to see us,' said Mrs Clarke brightly as her husband entered the room. 'We've been waiting for cakes.'

Roz stood up and handed Mr Clarke one of her cards. 'I did tell her who I was,' she said quietly, 'but it seemed kinder to be Mary.'

He was old, like his wife, and entirely bald, but he still carried himself erect with shoulders squared. He towered above the woman on the sofa who shrank away from him in sudden fear, muttering to herself. Roz wondered if he ever lost his temper with her.

'I really don't leave her alone very often,' he answered defensively, as if she had accused him of it, 'but the shopping has to be done. Everyone's so busy and it's not fair to keep asking the neighbours.' He ran a hand across his bald head and read the card. 'I thought you were Social Services,' he said, this time accusing *her*. 'Author? We don't want an author. What good would an author be to us?'

'I was hoping you could help me.'

'I don't know the first thing about writing. Who gave you my name?'

'Olive did,' said Mrs Clarke. 'She's a friend of Olive's.'

He was shocked. 'Oh, no!' he said. 'No, no, no! You'll have to leave. I'm not having that dragged up again. It's an outrage. How did you get hold of this address?'

'No, no, no!' chanted his wife. 'It's an outrage. No, no, no!'

Roz held her breath and counted to ten, not sure if her sanity or her control would slip first. 'How on earth do you cope?' The words tumbled out as involuntarily as Mrs Clarke's did. 'I'm sorry.' She saw the strain in his face. 'That was unforgivably rude.'

'It's not so bad when we're alone. I just switch

off.' He sighed. 'Why have you come? I thought we'd put all that behind us. There's nothing I can do for Olive. Robert tried to help her at the time but it was all thrown back in his face. Why has she sent you here?'

'It's an outrage,' muttered the old woman.

'She hasn't. I'm here off my own bat. Look,' she said, glancing at Mrs Clarke, 'is there somewhere we can talk privately?'

'There's nothing to talk about.'

'But there is,' she said. 'You were a friend of Robert's. You must have known the family better than anyone. I'm writing a book' – she remembered belatedly that her explanations had been given to Mrs Clarke – 'and I can't do it if no one will tell me about Gwen and Robert.'

She had shocked him again. 'Gutter journalism,' he spat. 'I won't have anything to do with it. Leave now, or I shall call the police.'

Mrs Clarke gave a whimper of fear. 'Not the police. No, no, no. I'm afraid of the police.' She peered at the stranger. 'I'm afraid of the police.'

With reason, thought Roz, wondering if the shock of the murders had brought on the dementia. Was that why they had moved away? She picked up her briefcase and handbag. 'I'm no gutter journalist, Mr Clarke. I'm trying to help Olive.'

'She's beyond help. We all are.' He glanced at his wife. 'Olive destroyed everything.'

'I disagree.'

'Please go.'

The thin reedy voice of the old woman broke in on them. 'I never saw Gwen and Amber that day,' she cried plaintively. 'I lied. I lied, Edward.'

He closed his eyes. 'Oh, God,' he murmured, 'what did I ever do to deserve this?' His voice vibrated with repressed dislike.

'Which day?' Roz pressed.

But the moment of lucidity, if that is what it was, had passed. 'We've been waiting for cakes.'

Irritation and something else – relief? – passed across his face. 'She's senile,' he told Roz. 'Her mind's gone. You can't rely on anything she says. I'll show you out.'

Roz didn't move. 'Which day, Mrs Clarke?' she asked gently.

'The day the police came. I said I saw them but I didn't.' She furrowed her brow in perplexity. 'Do I know you?'

Mr Clarke seized Roz roughly by the arm and manhandled her towards the front door. 'Get out of my house!' he stormed. 'Haven't we suffered enough at the hands of that family?' He thrust her into the street and slammed the door.

Roz rubbed her arm reflectively. Edward Clarke, in spite of his age, was a good deal stronger than he looked.

*

She turned the problem in her mind throughout the long drive home. She was caught in the same dilemma that Olive kept posing her, the dilemma of belief. Was Mrs Clarke telling the truth? Had she lied to the police that day or was her senile recollection faulty? And if she had lied, did it make a difference?

Roz pictured herself in the Poacher's kitchen, listening to Hal talking about Robert Martin's alibi. 'We did wonder if he might have killed Gwen and Amber before he went to work and Olive then attempted to dispose of the bodies to protect him, but the numbers didn't add up. He had an alibi even for that. There was a neighbour who saw her husband off to work a few minutes before Martin himself left. Amber and Gwen were alive then because she spoke to them on their doorstep. She remembered asking Amber how she was getting on at Glitzy. They waved as Martin drove away.'

Mrs Clarke, thought Roz, it had to be. But how remiss of her not to question that statement before? Was it likely that Gwen and Amber would wave goodbye to Robert when so little love was lost between husband and wife? A sentence from Olive's statement pierced her thoughts like a sharp knife. *'We had an argument over breakfast and my father left for work in the middle of it.'*

So Mrs Clarke had been telling lies. But why? Why give Robert an alibi when, according to Olive, she saw him as a threat?

'There was a neighbour who saw her husband off to work a few minutes before Martin himself left . . .'

God, but she'd been blind. The alibi was Edward's.

She phoned Iris in a fever of excitement from a pay phone. 'I've cracked it, old thing. I know who did it and it wasn't Olive.'

'There you are, you see. Always trust your agent's instincts. I've had a fiver on you with Gerry. He'll be sick as a parrot about losing. So who did do it?'

'The neighbour, Edward Clarke. He was Robert Martin's lover. I think he killed Gwen and Amber out of jealousy.' Breathlessly, she rattled off her story. 'Mind you, I've still got to find a way of proving it.'

There was a lengthy silence at the other end.

'Are you still there?'

'Yes, I was just mourning my five pounds. I know you're excited, darling, but you'll have to sober up and give it a little more thought. If this Edward chopped up Gwen and Amber before Robert went to work, wouldn't Robert have stumbled across the bits in the kitchen?'

'Perhaps they did it together?'

'Then why didn't they kill Olive as well? Not to mention the small matter of why on earth Olive would want to shield her father's homosexual lover. It would make much more sense if Mrs Clarke lied to give Robert an alibi.'

'Why?'

'They were having a raging affair,' declared Iris. 'Mrs C. guessed Robert had done his wife in to give himself a free hand with her and lied through her teeth to protect him. You don't know for sure he was a homosexual. The schoolfriend's mother didn't think he was. Is Mrs C. attractive?'

'Not now. She was once.'

'There you are, then.'

'Why did Robert kill Amber?'

'Because she was there,' said Iris simply. 'I expect she woke up when she heard the fight and came downstairs. Robert would have had no option but to kill her as well. Then he skedaddled and left poor old Olive, who slept through it all, to face the music.'

Somewhat reluctantly, Roz went to see Olive.

'I wasn't expecting you, not after—' Olive left the rest of the sentence unsaid. 'Well, you know.' She smiled shyly.

They were back in their old room, unsupervised. The Governor's qualms, it seemed, had been laid to rest along with Olive's hostility. Really, thought Roz, the prison system never ceased to surprise her. She had foreseen enormous problems, particularly as it was a Wednesday and not her normal day, but there had been none. Access to Olive was once more unrestricted. She pushed forward the cigarette packet. 'You seem to be *persona grata* again,' she said.

Olive accepted a cigarette. 'With you, too?'

Roz arched an eyebrow. 'I felt better after my headache had gone.' She saw distress on the fat face. 'I'm teasing,' she said gently. 'And it was my fault anyway. I should have phoned. Have you had all your privileges restored?'

'Yes. They're pretty decent really, once you calm down.'

'Good.' Roz switched on her tape-recorder. 'I've been to see your next-door neighbours, the Clarkes.'

Olive studied her through the flame of the match, then tipped it thoughtfully towards her cigarette. 'And?'

'Mrs Clarke lied about seeing your mother and sister on the morning of the murders.'

'How do you know?'

'She told me.'

Olive wedged the cigarette firmly between her lips and drew in a lungful of smoke. 'Mrs Clarke's been senile for years,' she said bluntly. 'She had a thing about germs, used to rush about every morning scrubbing the furniture with Domestos and hoovering like mad. People who didn't know them thought she was the char. She always called me Mary which was her mother's name. I should imagine she's completely loopy by now.'

Roz shook her head in frustration. 'She is, but I'll swear she was lucid when she admitted lying. She's frightened of her husband, though.'

Olive looked surprised. 'She was never frightened of him before. If anything, he was more frightened of her. What did he say when she told you she'd lied?'

'He was furious. Ordered me out of the house.' She made a wry face. 'We got off to a bad start. He thought I was from the Social Services, spying on him.'

A wheeze of amusement eddied up through Olive's throat. 'Poor Mr Clarke.'

'You said your father liked him. Did *you*?'

She shrugged indifference. 'I didn't know him well enough to like him or dislike him. I suppose I felt sorry for him because of his wife. He had to retire early to look after her.'

Roz mulled this over. 'But he was still working at the time of the murders?'

'He carried on a small accountancy business from home. Other people's tax returns mostly.' She tapped ash on to the floor. 'Mrs Clarke set fire to their living room once. He was afraid to leave her alone after that. She was very demanding but my mother said most of it was an act to keep him tied to her apron strings.'

'Was that true, do you think?'

'I expect so.' She stood the cigarette on its end, as

was her habit, and took another. 'My mother was usually right.'

'Did they have children?'

Olive shook her head. 'I don't think so. I never saw any.' She pursed her lips. '*He* was the child. It was quite funny sometimes watching him scurrying about, doing what he was told, saying sorry when he got it wrong. Amber called him Puddleglum because he was wet and miserable.' She chuckled. 'I'd forgotten that until this minute. It suited him at the time. Does it still?'

Roz thought of his grip on her arms. 'He didn't strike me as being particularly wet,' she said. 'Miserable, yes.'

Olive studied her with her curiously penetrating gaze. 'Why have you come back?' she asked gently. 'You didn't intend to on Monday.'

'What makes you say that?'

'I saw it in your face. You thought I was guilty.'

'Yes.'

Olive nodded. 'It upset me. I hadn't realized what a difference it made to have someone believe I didn't do it. Politicians call it the feel-good factor.' Roz saw dampness on the pale lashes. 'You get used to being viewed as a monster. Sometimes I believe it myself.' She placed one of her disproportionate hands between her huge breasts. 'I thought my heart would burst when you left. Silly, isn't it?' Tears welled in her eyes.

'I can't remember being so upset about anything before.'

Roz waited a moment but Olive didn't go on. 'Sister Bridget knocked some sense into me,' she said.

A glow, like a rising candle flame, lit the fat woman's face. 'Sister Bridget?' she echoed in amazement. 'Does she think I didn't do it? I never guessed. I thought she came out of Christian duty.'

Oh hell, thought Roz, what does a lie matter? 'Of course she thinks you didn't do it. Why else would she keep pushing me so hard?' She watched the tremulous pleasure bring a sort of beauty to the awful ugliness that was Olive, and she thought, I've burnt my boats. I can never again ask her if she's guilty or if she's telling me the truth because, if I do, her poor heart *will* burst.

'I didn't do it,' said Olive, reading her expression.

Roz leaned forward. 'Then who did?'

'I don't know now. I thought I did at the time.' She stood her second cigarette beside the first and watched it die. 'At the time it all made sense,' she murmured, her mind groping into the past.

'Who did you think it was?' asked Roz after a while. 'Someone you loved?'

But Olive shook her head. 'I couldn't bear to be laughed at. In so many ways it's easier to be feared. At least it means people respect you.' She looked at Roz. 'I'm really quite happy here. Can you understand that?'

'Yes,' said Roz slowly, remembering what the Governor had said. 'Oddly enough, I can.'

'If you hadn't sought me out, I could have survived. I'm institutionalized. Existence without effort. I really don't know that I could cope on the outside.' She smoothed her hands down her massive thighs. 'People will laugh, Roz.'

It was a question more than a statement and Roz didn't have an answer, or not the reassuring answer that Olive wanted. People *would* laugh, she thought. There was an intrinsic absurdity about this grotesque woman loving so deeply that she would brand herself a murderess to protect her lover.

'I'm not giving up now,' she said firmly. 'A battery hen is born to exist. You were born to live.' She levelled her pen at Olive. 'And if you don't know the difference between existence and living then read the Declaration of Independence. Living means Liberty and the Pursuit of Happiness. You deny yourself both by staying here.'

'Where would I go? What would I do?' She wrung her hands. 'In all my life I've never lived on my own. I couldn't bear it, not now, not with everyone knowing.'

'Knowing what?'

Olive shook her head.

'Why can't you tell me?'

'Because,' said Olive heavily, 'you wouldn't believe me. No one ever does when I tell the truth.' She rapped on the glass to attract a prison officer's attention. 'You must find out for yourself. It's the only way you'll ever really know.'

'And if I can't?'

'I'm no worse off than I was before. I can live with myself, and that's all that really matters.'

Yes, thought Roz, at the end of the day it probably was. 'Just tell me one thing, Olive. Have you lied to me?'

'Yes.'

'Why?'

The door opened and Olive heaved herself upright with the customary shove from behind. 'Sometimes, it's safer.'

The telephone was ringing as she opened the door to the flat. 'Hi,' she said, thrusting it under her chin and taking off her jacket. 'Rosalind Leigh.' *Pray God it wasn't Rupert.*

'It's Hal. I've been ringing all day. Where the hell have you been?' He sounded worried.

'Chasing clues.' She leant her back against the wall for support. 'What's it to you, anyway?'

'I'm not psychotic, Roz.'

'You damn well behaved like it yesterday.'

'Just because I didn't call the police?'

'Among other things. It's what normal people do

when their property's been smashed up. Unless they've done it themselves, of course.'

'What other things?'

'You were bloody rude. I was only trying to help.'

He laughed softly. 'I keep seeing you standing by my door with that table leg. You're a hell of a gutsy lady. Shit scared, but gutsy. I've got those photographs for you. Do you still want them?'

'Yes.'

'Are you brave enough to collect them or do you want me to post them?'

'It's not bravery that's required, Hawksley, it's thick bloody skin. I'm tired of being needled.' She smiled to herself at the pun. 'Which reminds me, was it Mrs Clarke who said Gwen and Amber were alive after Robert went to work?'

There was a slight pause while he tried to see a connection. He couldn't. 'Yes, if she was the one in the attached semi.'

'She was lying. She says now that she didn't see them, which means Robert Martin's alibi is worthless. He could have done it before he went to work.'

'Why would she give Robert Martin an alibi?'

'I don't know. I'm trying to work it out. I thought at first she was alibiing her own husband, but that doesn't hold water. Apart from anything else, Olive tells me he was already retired so he wouldn't have gone to work anyway. Can you remember checking Mrs Clarke's statement?'

'Was Clarke the accountant? Yes?' He thought for a moment. 'OK, he ran most of his business from home but he also looked after the books of several small firms in the area. That week he was doing the accounts of a central heating contractor in Portswood. He was there all day. We checked. He didn't get home until after we had the place barricaded. I remember the fuss he made about having to park his car at the other end of the road. Elderly man, bald, with glasses. That the one?'

'Yes,' she said, 'but what he and Robert did during the day is irrelevant if Gwen and Amber were dead before either of the men left for work.'

'How reliable is Mrs Clarke?'

'Not very,' she admitted. 'What was the earliest estimate of death according to your pathologist?'

He was unusually evasive. 'I can't remember now.'

'Try,' she pressed him. 'You suspected Robert enough to check his alibi so he can't have been ruled out immediately on the forensic evidence.'

'I can't remember,' he said again. 'But if Robert did it, then why didn't he kill Olive as well? And why didn't she try and stop him? There must have been a hell of a row going on. She couldn't possibly have avoided hearing something. It's not that big a house.'

'Perhaps she wasn't there.'

*

The Chaplain made his weekly visit to Olive's room. 'That's good,' he said, watching her bring curl to the mother's hair with the point of a matchstick. 'Is it Mary and Jesus?'

She looked at him with amusement. 'The mother is suffocating her baby,' she said baldly. 'Is it likely to be Mary and Jesus?'

He shrugged. 'I've seen many stranger things that pass for religious art. Who is it?'

'It's Woman,' said Olive. 'Eve with all her faces.'

He was interested. 'But you haven't given her a face.'

Olive twisted the sculpture on its base and he saw that what he had taken to be curls at the side of the mother's hair was in fact a crude delineation of eyes, nose and mouth. She twisted it the other way and the same rough representation stared out from that side as well. 'Two-faced,' said Olive, 'and quite unable to look you in the eye.' She picked up a pencil and shoved it between the mother's thighs. 'But it doesn't matter. Not to MAN.' She leered unpleasantly. 'MAN doesn't look at the mantelpiece when he's poking the fire.'

Hal had mended the back door and the kitchen table, which stood in its customary place once more in the middle of the room. The floor was scrubbed clean, wall units repaired, fridge upright, even some chairs had been imported from the restaurant and placed neatly about the table. Hal himself looked completely exhausted.

'Have you had any sleep at all?' she asked him.

'Not much. I've been working round the clock.'

'Well, you've performed miracles.' She gazed about her. 'So who's coming to dinner? The Queen? She could eat it off the floor.'

To her surprise he caught her hand and lifted it to his lips, turning it to kiss the palm. It was an unexpectedly delicate gesture from such a hard man. 'Thank you.'

She was at a loss. 'What for?' she asked helplessly.

He released her hand with a smile. 'Saying the right things.' For a moment she thought he was going to elaborate, but all he said was: 'The photographs are on the table.'

Olive's was a mug-shot, stark and brutally unflattering. Gwen and Amber's shocked her as he had said they would. They were the stuff of nightmares and she understood for the first time why everyone had said Olive was a psychopath. She turned them over and concentrated on the head and shoulders' shot of Robert Martin. Olive was there in the eyes and mouth, and she had a fleeting impression of what might lie beneath the layers of lard if Olive could ever summon the will-power to shed it. Her father was a very handsome man.

'What are you going to do with them?'

She told him about the man who sent letters to

Olive. 'The description fits her father,' she said. 'The woman at Wells-Fargo said she'd recognize him from a photograph.'

'Why on earth should her father have sent her secret letters?'

'To set her up as a scapegoat for the murders.'

He was sceptical. 'You're plucking at straws. What about the ones of Gwen and Amber?'

'I don't know yet. I'm tempted to show them to Olive to shock her out of her apathy.'

He raised an eyebrow. 'I'd think twice about that if I were you. She's an unknown quantity, and you may not know her as well as you think you do. She could very easily turn nasty if you present her with her own handiwork.'

She smiled briefly. 'I know her better than I know you.' She tucked the photographs into her handbag and stepped out into the alleyway. 'The odd thing is you're very alike, you and Olive. You demand trust but you don't give it.'

He wiped a weary hand around his two-day growth of stubble. 'Trust is a two-edged sword, Roz. It can make you extremely vulnerable. I wish you'd remember that from time to time.'

Fourteen

MARNIE STUDIED THE photograph of Robert Martin for several seconds then shook her head. 'No,' she said, 'that wasn't him. He wasn't so good looking and he had different hair, thicker, not swept back, more to the side. Anyway, I told you, he had dark brown eyes, almost black. These eyes are light. Is this her father?'

Roz nodded.

Marnie handed the photograph back. 'My mother always said, never trust a man whose earlobes are lower than his mouth. It's the sign of a criminal. Look at his.'

Roz looked. She hadn't noticed it before because of the way his hair swept over them, but Martin's ears were almost unnaturally out of symmetry with the rest of his face. 'Did your mother know any criminals?'

Marnie snorted. 'Of course she didn't. It's just an old wives' tale.' She cocked her head to look at the picture again. 'Anyway, if there was something in it he'd be a Category A by now.'

'He's dead.'

'Perhaps he passed the gene on to his daughter. She's Category A all right.' She got busy with her nail file. 'Where did you get it, as a matter of interest?'

'The photograph? Why do you ask?'

Marnie tapped the top right-hand corner with her file. 'I know where it was taken.'

Roz looked where she was pointing. In the background beyond Martin's head was part of a lampshade with a pattern of inverted *y*s round its base. 'In his house, presumably.'

'Doubt it. Look at the sign round the shade. There's only one place anywhere near here has shades like that.'

The *y*s were lambdas, Roz realized, the international symbol of homosexuality. 'Where?'

'It's a pub near the waterfront. Goes in for drag acts.' Marnie giggled. 'It's a gay knocking-shop.'

'What's it called?'

Marnie giggled again. 'The White Cock.'

The landlord recognized the photograph immediately. 'Mark Agnew,' he told her. 'Used to come here a lot. But I haven't seen him in the last twelve months. What happened to him?'

'He died.'

The landlord pulled a long face. 'I shall have to go straight,' he said with weary gallows humour. 'What with AIDS and the recession I've hardly any customers left.'

Roz smiled sympathetically. 'If it's any consolation I don't think he died of AIDS.'

'Well, it is some consolation, lovey. He put himself about a bit, did Mark.'

Mrs O'Brien regarded her with deep displeasure. Time and her naturally suspicious nature had persuaded her that Roz was nothing to do with television but had come to worm information out of her about her sons. 'You've got a flaming cheek, I must say.'

'Oh,' said Roz with obvious disappointment, 'have you changed your mind about the programme?' Lies, she thought, worked if you kept repeating them.

'Programme, my arse. You're a bloody snooper. What you after? That's what I want to know.'

Roz took Mr Crew's letter out of her briefcase and handed it to the woman. 'I explained it as well as I could last time, but these are the terms of my contract with the television company. If you read it, you'll see that it sets out quite clearly the aims and objectives of the programme they want to make.' She pointed to Crew's signature. 'That's the director. He listened to the tape we made and liked what he heard. He'll be disappointed if you back out now.'

Ma O'Brien, presented with written evidence, was impressed. She frowned intelligently at the unintelligible words. 'Well,' she said, 'a contract makes a difference. You should of shown me this last time.' She folded it, preparatory to putting it in her pocket.

Roz smiled. 'Unfortunately,' she said, whisking it from Ma's fingers, 'this is the only copy I have and I need it for tax and legal purposes. If it's lost, none of us will get paid. May I come in?'

Ma compressed her lips. 'No reason not to, I suppose.' But suspicion died hard. 'I'm not hanswering hanything fishy, mind.'

'Of course not.' She walked into the sitting room. 'Is any of your family at home? I'd like to include them if possible. The more rounded the picture the better.'

Ma gave it some thought. '*Mike!*' she yelled suddenly. 'Get yourself down. There's a lady wants to talk to you. *Nipper!* In 'ere.'

Roz, who was only interested in talking to Gary, saw fifty-pound notes flying out the window by the bucket-load. She smiled with resignation as two skinny young men joined their mother on the sofa. 'Hi,' she said brightly, 'my name's Rosalind Leigh and I represent a television company which is putting together a programme on social deprivation . . .'

'I told them,' said Ma, cutting her short. 'No need for the sales pitch. Fifty quid per 'ead. That's right, isn't it?'

'As long as I get my money's worth. I'll need another good hour of chat and I'm only really prepared to pay fifty apiece if I can talk to your eldest son, Peter, and your youngest son, Gary. That way I get the broadest viewpoint possible. I want to know what difference it made to your older children being fostered out.'

'Well, you've got Gary,' said Ma, prodding the unprepossessing figure on her left, 'young Nipper 'ere. Pete's in the nick so you'll 'ave to make do with Mike. 'E's number three and spent as much time being fostered as Pete did.'

'Right, let's get on then.' She unfolded her list of carefully prepared questions and switched on her tape-recorder. The two 'boys', she noticed, had perfectly proportioned ears.

She spent the first half-hour talking to Mike, encouraging him to reminisce about his childhood in foster homes, his education (or, more accurately, lack of it through persistent truanting) and his early troubles with the police. He was a taciturn man, lacking even elementary social skills, who found it hard to articulate his thoughts. He made a poor impression and Roz, containing her impatience behind a forced smile, wondered if he could possibly have turned out any worse if Social Services had left him in the care of his mother. Somehow she doubted it. Ma, for all her sins and his, loved him, and to be loved was the corner-stone of confidence.

She turned with some relief to Gary, who had been listening to the conversation with a lively interest. 'I gather you didn't leave home till you were twelve,' she said, consulting her notes, 'when you were sent to a boarding school. Why was that?'

He grinned. 'Truanting, nicking, same as my brothers, only Parkway said I was worse and got me sent off to Chapman 'Ouse. It was OK. I learnt a bit. Got two CSEs before I jacked it in.'

She thought the truth was probably the exact opposite, and that Parkway had said he was a cut above his brothers and worth putting some extra effort into. 'That's good. Did the CSEs make it easier to find a job?'

She might have been talking about a trip to the moon for all the relevance a job seemed to have in his life. 'I never tried. We were doing all right.'

She remembered something Hal had said. 'They simply don't subscribe to the same values that the rest of us hold.' 'You didn't want a job?' she asked curiously.

He shook his head. 'Did *you*, when you left school?'

'Yes,' she said, surprised by the question. 'I couldn't wait to leave home.'

He shrugged, as perplexed by her ambition as she was perplexed by his lack of it. 'We've always stuck together,' he said. 'The dole goes a lot further if it's pooled. You didn't get on with your parents then?'

'Not enough to want to live with them.'

'Ah, well,' he said sympathetically, 'that would explain it then.'

Absurdly, Roz found herself envying him. 'Your mother told me you worked as a motorbike courier at one point. Did you enjoy that?'

'So-so. It was all right at the beginning but there's no fun driving a bike in town and it was all town work. It wouldn't 'ave been so bad if the bastard who ran it 'ad paid us enough to cover the cost of the bikes.' He shook his head. ''E was a mean sod. We 'ad 'em took off us after six months and that was it. No bikes, no work.'

Roz had now heard three different versions of how the O'Brien boys had lost their jobs at Wells-Fargo. Were any of them true, she wondered, or was it that they were all true, but seen from different perspectives? Truth, she thought, was not the absolute she had once believed it to be. 'Your mother told me,' she said with a look of innocent amusement, 'that you had a brush with a murderess while you were doing that job.'

'You mean Olive Martin?' Whatever qualms he had had on the matter at the time of the murders had obviously disappeared. 'Funny business, that. I used to deliver letters to her on a Friday evening from some bloke she was keen on, then – wham! – she did her folks in. Bloody shocked me to tell you the truth. 'Ad no idea she was a nutter.'

'But she must have been to hack her mother and sister to pieces.'

'Yeah.' He looked thoughtful. 'Never did understand it. She was all right. I knew 'er as a kid. She was all right then, as well. It was the bloody mother who was the cow and the stuck-up sister. Christ, she was a 'orrible little swine.'

Roz hid her surprise. *Everyone loved Amber.* How often had she heard that said? 'Maybe Olive had had enough and just snapped one day. It happens.'

'Oh,' he said with a dismissive shrug, 'that's not the bit I don't understand. It's why she didn't just go off with 'er fancy man instead. I mean, even if 'e was married, 'e could've set her up in a flat somewhere. 'E wasn't short of a bob or two judging by what 'e paid to have the letters delivered. Twenty quid a throw. 'E must have been bloody rolling in it.'

She chewed her pencil. 'Maybe she didn't do it,' she mused. 'Maybe the police got the wrong person. Let's face it, it wouldn't be the first time.'

Ma compressed her lips. 'They're all corrupt,' she said. 'Nick anyone for anythink these days. You don't want to be Irish in this country. You've no 'ope if you're Irish.'

'Still,' said Roz, looking at Gary, 'if Olive didn't do it, who did?'

'I'm not saying it wasn't 'er,' he said sharply. 'She

went guilty so she must of done it. All I'm saying is she didn't *need* to do it.'

Roz gave a careless shrug. 'Just lost her temper and didn't think. You'll probably find the sister provoked her. You said she was horrible.'

Surprisingly, it was Mike who spoke. 'Street angel, 'ouse devil,' he said. 'Like our Tracey.'

Roz smiled at him. 'What does that mean?'

Ma elucidated. 'A bitch to your family, a perfect darling to everybody else. But our Tracey's nothing like Amber Martin. I always said that child would come a cropper and I was right. You can't face two ways all your life and expect to get away with it.'

Roz showed her curiosity. 'You really did know the family quite well then. I thought you only worked there a short while.'

'So I did, but Amber took a fancy to one of the boys later' – she paused – 'though I'm blowed if I can remember at the moment which one. Was it you, Nipper?'

He shook his head.

'Chris,' said Mike.

'That's right,' agreed Ma, 'took a real shine to 'im and 'im to 'er. She'd sit in this room, pleased as punch with herself, making sheep's eyes at 'im and she can't 'ave been more than twelve or thirteen. 'E was – what? – fifteen, sixteen but, of course, any attention at that age is flattering and she was a pretty girl, I'll say that for 'er, *and* looked older than she was. Anyway, we saw the real Amber then. She treated Chris like a king and the rest of us like something the cat'd brought in. She had a tongue on 'er like I've never heard. Bitch, bitch, bitch, all the time.' She looked thoroughly indignant. 'Can't think 'ow I kept my 'ands off 'er but I did, for Chris's sake. Besotted, 'e was, poor lad. 'Er mother didn't know, of course. Put a stop to it straight away the minute she found out.'

Roz hoped her expression was less revealing than it felt. Did that make Chris O'Brien the father of Amber's illegitimate child? It made sense. Mr Hayes had referred to a lad from Parkway Comprehensive being responsible, and if Gwen had put a stop to the relationship then she would have known who to blame when a baby appeared. It would also explain the secrecy surrounding Robert Martin's efforts to trace his grandchild. Presumably the O'Briens had no idea that Chris had fathered a son nor that the son, if he could be found, was worth half a million pounds.

'It's fascinating,' she murmured, searching desperately for something to say. 'I've never met anyone so closely associated with a murder. Was Chris upset when Amber was killed?'

'No,' said Ma with an unfeeling chuckle. ''E 'adn't seen 'er in years. Gary was more upset for Olive, weren't you, love?'

He was watching Roz closely. 'Not really,' he said bluntly. 'I was jumpy about being roped in on it. I mean, I'd seen quite a bit of 'er one way and another.

Reckoned the cops'd be rounding up everyone she knew and grilling them.' He shook his head. ''Er bloke got off lightly. 'E'd've been 'auled in and no mistake if she'd named a few names to try and get off.'

'Did you ever meet him?'

'No.' His face became suddenly sly and he stared at Roz with an expression that said he saw right through her. 'I know where he took her for sex, though.' He gave a conspiratorial smile. 'What's it worth to you?'

She stared back. 'How do you know?'

'The silly sod used self-sticking envelopes. They're a doddle to open. I read one of the letters.'

'Did he sign it? Do you know his name?'

Gary shook his head. 'Something beginning with P. "All my love, P", was how it finished.'

Roz didn't bother with further pretence. 'Another fifty pounds,' she said, 'on top of the hundred and fifty I've already agreed to. But that's it. I'll be cleaned out.'

'OK.' He held out his hand in unconscious mimicry of his mother. 'Money up front.'

She took out her wallet and emptied it. 'Two hundred pounds.' She counted it on to his palm.

'I knew you wasn't from the television,' said Ma in disgust. 'I bloody knew it.'

'Well?' Roz demanded of Gary.

'It was on for Sunday at the Belvedere Hotel in

Farraday Street. "All my love, P." That's the Farraday Street in Southampton, in case you didn't know.'

The route to Southampton took Roz along Dawlington High Street. She had passed Glitzy boutique before the name registered, and nearly caused a pile-up by standing on her brakes in the middle of the road. With a cheerful wave to the furious man behind her, who was mouthing imprecations against women drivers, she drew into a side street and found a parking space.

Glitzy was something of a misnomer, she thought, as she pushed open the door. She had expected designer wear or, at the very least, clothes from the more expensive end of the market. But then, she was used to London boutiques. Glitzy catered very definitely for the cheaper end of the market, wisely recognizing that their customers would be predominantly teenage girls without the wherewithal or the transport to go shopping in the more stylish parts of Southampton.

Roz sought out the manager, a woman in her thirties with a splendid hairdo backcombed into a blonde beehive on top of her head. Roz handed her one of her cards and ran through her spiel about her book on Olive Martin. 'I'm trying to find someone who knew the sister, Amber,' she said, 'and I'm told she worked here during the month before she was murdered. Were you here then? Or do you know anyone who was?'

'No, love, sorry. Staff turns over very quickly in a place like this, young girls normally, doing a short stint till something better comes up. I don't even know who was manager then. You'll have to get on to the owners. I can give you their address,' she finished helpfully.

'Thank you. It's worth a shot, I suppose.'

The woman took her over to the cash desk and sorted through a card index. 'Funny, I remember those murders, but I never put two and two together. You know, that the sister had worked here.'

'She wasn't here very long and I'm not sure it was even reported. The press was more interested in Olive than in Amber.'

'Yeah.' She took out a card. 'Amber. It's not that common a name, is it?'

'I suppose not. It was a nickname, anyway. Her real name was Alison.'

The woman nodded. 'I've been here three years and for three years I've been pressing to have the staff toilet redecorated. The recession's their excuse for not doing it, same as it's their excuse for any wretched thing, from cuts in wages to cheap imported stock that's not even stitched properly. Anyway, the toilet's tiled and that's an expensive job, apparently, chipping off the old ones to put up new.' Roz smiled politely. 'Don't worry, love, it's to the point and I'm getting there. The reason I want new tiles is that someone took a chisel or something similar to the old ones. They scratched graffiti into the surface and then filled in the scratches with some sort of indelible ink. I've tried everything to get it out, bleach, oven cleaner, paint remover, you name it, love, I've tried it.' She shook her head. 'It can't be shifted. And why? Because whoever did it gouged so deep they cut right through the ceramic, and the china clay underneath just goes on absorbing dirt and stains. Every time I look at it, it gives me the shivers. Pure hate, that's what it was done with.'

'What does the graffiti say?'

'I'll show you. It's at the back.' She negotiated a couple of doors, then pushed open another and stood aside to let Roz pass. 'There. It sucks, doesn't it? And, you know, I've always wondered who Amber was. But it must be the sister, mustn't it? Like I say, Amber's not that common a name.'

It was the same two words, repeated ten or eleven times across the tiles, a violent inversion of the hearts and arrows that more usually adorned lavatory walls. **HATES AMBER . . . HATES AMBER . . . HATES AMBER.**

'I wonder who did it?' murmured Roz.

'Someone very sick, I should think. They certainly didn't want her to know, seeing how they've left their name off the front.'

'It depends how you read it,' said Roz thoughtfully.

'If it were set out neatly for you in a circle it would say Amber hates Amber hates Amber ad infinitum.'

The Belvedere was a typical back-street hotel, two substantial semis knocked together and entered via a flight of steps and a pillared front door. The place had an air of neglect as if its customers – sales reps for the main part – had deserted it. Roz rang the bell at the reception desk and waited.

A woman in her fifties emerged from a room at the back, all smiles. 'Good afternoon, madam. Welcome to the Belvedere.' She pulled the registration book towards her. 'Is it a room you're after?'

What terrible things recessions were, thought Roz. How long could people maintain this sad veneer of confident optimism when the reality was empty order books? 'I'm sorry,' she said. 'I'm afraid it isn't.' She handed over one of her cards. 'I'm a freelance journalist and I think someone I'm writing about may have stayed here. I was hoping you could identify her photograph for me.'

The woman tapped a finger on the book then pushed it away. 'Will what you write be published?'

Roz nodded.

'And will the Belvedere be mentioned if whoever it is did stay here?'

'Not if you'd rather it wasn't.'

'My dear, how little you know about the hotel

trade. Any publicity would be welcome at the moment.'

Roz laughed as she placed the photograph of Olive on the desk. 'If she came it would have been during the summer of eighty-seven. Were you here then?'

'We were.' The woman spoke with regret. 'We bought in eighty-six when the economy was booming.' She took a pair of glasses from her pocket and popped them on her nose, leaning forward to examine the photograph. 'Oh, yes, I remember her very well. Big girl. She and her husband came most Sundays during that summer. Used to book the room for the day and go home in the evening.' She sighed. 'It was a wonderful arrangement. We were always able to let the room again for the Sunday night. Double pay for one twenty-four-hour period.' She heaved another sigh. 'Chance'd be a fine thing now. I wish we could sell, I really do, but what with so many of the small hotels going bankrupt we wouldn't even get what we paid for it. Soldier on, that's all we can do.'

Roz brought her back to Olive by tapping the photograph. 'What did she and her husband call themselves?'

The woman was amused. 'The usual, I should think. Smith or Brown.'

'Did they sign in?'

'Oh, yes. We're very particular about our register.'

'Could I take a look?'

'Don't see why not.' She opened a cupboard under

the desk and sorted out the register for 1987. 'Now, let me see. Ah, here we are. Mr and Mrs Lewis. Well, well, they were more imaginative than most.' She twisted the book so that Roz could look at it.

She gazed at the neat script and thought: Got you, you bastard. 'This is the man's handwriting.' She knew already.

'Oh, yes,' said the woman. 'He always signed. She was a lot younger than he was and very shy, particularly at the beginning. She gained in confidence as time passed, they always do, but she never put herself forward. Who is she?'

Roz wondered if the woman would be so keen to help once she knew, but there was no point in keeping it from her. She would learn all the details the minute the book appeared. 'Her name's Olive Martin.'

'Never heard of her.'

'She's serving a life sentence for murdering her mother and sister.'

'Good lord! Is she the one who—' She made chopping motions with her hands. Roz nodded. 'Good Lord!'

'Do you still want the Belvedere mentioned?'

'Do I heck!' She beamed broadly. 'Of course I do! A murderess in our hotel. Fancy! We'll have a plaque put up in the bedroom. What are you writing exactly? A book? A magazine article? We'll provide photographs of the hotel and the room she stayed in. Well, well, I must say. How exciting! If only I'd known.'

Roz laughed. It was a cold-bloodedly ghoulish display of pleasure at another's misfortune but she couldn't find it in her heart to criticize. Only a fool would look a gift horse in the mouth. 'Before you get too excited,' she warned, 'the book probably won't be published for another year and it will be an exoneration of Olive, not a further condemnation. You see, I believe she's innocent.'

'Better and better. We'll have the book on sale in the foyer. I knew our luck had to turn eventually.' She beamed at Roz. 'Tell Olive she can stay here free of charge for as long as she likes the minute she gets out of prison. We always look after our regulars. Now, my dear, anything else I can help you with?'

'Do you have a photocopying machine?'

'We do. Every mod. con. here, you know.'

'Then may I have a copy of this entry in the register? And perhaps you could also give me a description of Mr Lewis.'

She pursed her lips. 'He wasn't very memorable. Early fifties. Blond, always wore a dark suit, a smoker. Any good?'

'Maybe. Did his hair look natural? Can you remember?'

The woman chuckled. 'There now, I'd forgotten. It never occurred to me till I took them in some tea one day and surprised him adjusting his wig in the mirror. I laughed afterwards, I can tell you. But it was a good one. I wouldn't have guessed just by looking at him. You know him then?'

Roz nodded. 'Would you recognize him from a photograph?'

'I'll try. I can usually remember a face when I see it.'

'Visitor for you, Sculptress.' The officer was in the room before Olive had time to hide what she was doing. 'Come on. Get a move on.'

Olive swept her wax figures into one hand and crushed them together in her palm. 'Who is it?'

'The nun.' She looked at Olive's closed fist. 'What have you got there?'

'Just plasticine.' She uncurled her fingers. The wax figurcs, carefully painted and clothed in coloured scraps, had merged into a multi-coloured mash, unidentifiable now as the altar candle they had sprung from.

'Well, leave it there. The nun's come to talk to you, not watch you play with plasticine.'

Hal was asleep at the kitchen table, body rigidly upright, arms resting on the table, head nodding towards his chest. Roz watched him for a moment through the window, then tapped lightly on the glass. His eyes, red-rimmed with exhaustion, snapped open to look at her and she was shocked by the extent of his relief when he saw who it was.

He let her in. 'I hoped you wouldn't come back,' he said, his face drawn with fatigue.

'What are you so frightened of?' she asked.

He looked at her with something like despair. 'Go home,' he said, 'this is none of your business.' He went to the sink and ran the cold-water tap, dowsing his head and gasping as the icy stream hit the back of his neck.

From the floor above came a sudden violent hammering.

Roz leapt a foot in the air. '*Oh, my God!* What was that?'

He reached out and gripped her arm, pushing her towards the door. 'Go home,' he ordered. 'Now! I don't want to have to force you, Roz.'

But she stood her ground. 'What's going on? What was that noise?'

'So help me,' he said grimly, 'I will do you some damage if you don't leave now.' But in outright contradiction to the words, he suddenly put his hands on either side of her face and kissed her. 'Oh, God!' he groaned, smoothing the tumbled hair from her eyes. 'I do not want you involved, Roz. *I do not want you involved.*'

She was about to say something when over his shoulder she saw the door into the restaurant swing open. 'Too late,' she said, turning him round. 'We've got company.'

Hal, horribly unprepared, showed his teeth in a wolfish grin. 'I've been expecting you,' he drawled. With a proprietary arm he eased Roz behind him and prepared to defend what was his.

There were four of them, large anonymous men in ski-masks. They said nothing, just weighed in indiscriminately with baseball bats, using Hal as a human target. It happened so fast that Roz was a spectator to their grisly sport almost before she realized it. She, it seemed, was too insignificant to concern them.

Her first angry impulse was to catch out at a flailing arm but the battering she had had at the hands of Rupert two weeks before persuaded her to use her brain instead. With trembling fingers she opened her handbag and removed the three-inch hatpin she had taken to carrying with her, thrusting it upwards into the buttock of the man nearest her. It drove in up to its ornate jade head and a soft groan issued from his mouth as he stood, completely paralysed with shock, the baseball bat slipping to the floor from his slackening fingers. No one noticed, except her.

With an exclamation of triumph she dived on it and brought it up in a swinging arc to smash against the man's balls. He sat on the floor and started to scream.

'I've got one, Hal,' she panted. 'I've got a bat.'

'Then use it, for Christ's sake,' he bellowed, going down under a rain of blows.

'Oh God!' Legs, she thought. She knelt on one knee, swiped at the nearest pair of trousers and crowed with triumph when she made contact. She took another swipe only to have her head jerked up as a hand seized her by the hair and started to pull it out by the roots. Shock and pain flooded her eyes with stinging tears.

Hal, on his hands and knees on the floor, his head protected by his shoulders, was only vaguely aware that the rapidity of the blows beating against his back had lessened. His brain was concentrated on the high-pitched screaming which he thought was coming from Roz. His anger was colossal, triggering such a surge of adrenalin that he exploded to his feet in an all-consuming fury and threw himself at the first man he saw, bearing him back against the gleaming ovens where a saucepan of fish stock bubbled gently. Oblivious to the blow which crashed with the force of a bus between his shoulder blades he bent his victim in an arc over the rings, grabbed the saucepan and upended the boiling liquid over the masked head.

He swung round to face the fourth man and fended off another blow with his forearm before smashing the cast-iron base of the saucepan into the side of an unprotected jaw. The eyes behind the mask registered the briefest glimmer of surprise before rolling helplessly into their sockets. The man was unconscious before he hit the floor.

Exhausted, Hal looked about for Roz. It was a moment or two before he found her, so disorientated was he by the noise of screaming which seemed to be filling the kitchen from every side. He shook his head to clear the fog and looked towards the door. He saw her almost immediately, her neck trapped in the hooked arm of the only man left with any fight in him. Her eyes were closed and her head lolled alarmingly to one side. 'If you make a move,' the man told Hal between jerky breaths, 'I'll break her neck.'

A hatred, so primeval that he couldn't control it, erupted like hot lava in Hal's brain. His actions were instinctive. He lowered his head and charged.

Fifteen

ROZ SWAM UP to a strange twilight world between oblivion and consciousness. She knew she was there in the room but she felt apart from it as if she were watching what was going on from behind thickened glass. Sound was muted. She had a vague memory of fingers clamping round her throat. And afterwards? She wasn't sure. It had, she thought, been very peaceful.

Hal's face loomed over her. 'Are you all right?' he asked from a great distance.

'Fine,' she murmured happily.

He smacked her on the cheek with the flat of his hand. 'That's my girl,' he told her, his voice muffled by cotton wool. 'Come on, now. Snap out of it. I need some help.'

She glared at him. 'I'll be up in a minute,' she said with dignity.

He hauled her to her feet. 'Now,' he said firmly, 'or we'll be back where we started.' He thrust a baseball bat into her hand. 'I am going to tie them up but you've got to protect my back while I'm doing it. I don't want one of these bastards surprising me.' He looked into her dazed eyes. 'Come on, Roz,' he said savagely, shaking her. 'Pull yourself together and show a bit of character.'

She took a deep breath. 'Has anyone ever told you what a complete and utter turd you are? I nearly died.'

'You fainted,' he said unemotionally, but his eyes were twinkling. 'Hit anything that moves,' he instructed her, 'except the one with his head under the tap. He's in enough agony already.'

Reality came rushing in on wings of sound. Moans and groans and running water. There *was* a man with his head under the tap. She caught a movement out of the corner of her eye and swung the baseball bat in terrified reaction, ramming home the hatpin that its unfortunate recipient was gingerly plucking from his bottom. His screams of reawakened agony were pitiful.

'Oh God!' she cried. 'I've done something awful.' Tears sprang into her eyes.

Hal finished trussing her putative killer, who had been knocked cold by his frenzied charge, and moved on to the other unconscious figure, winding twine expertly about the wrists and ankles. 'What's he yelling for anyway?' he demanded, tethering his victim to the table for good measure.

'He's got a pin in his bottom,' said Roz, her teeth chattering uncontrollably.

Hal approached the man warily. 'What sort of pin?'

'My mother's hatpin.' She gagged. 'I think I'm going to be sick.'

He saw the green ornamental head protruding from the man's Levis and felt a tiny twinge of sympathy. It didn't last. He left it there while he bound the man's wrists and ankles and tethered him, like his friend, to the table. It was almost as an afterthought that he gripped the jade and yanked the hatpin, grinning, from the quivering buttock. 'You arsehole,' he murmured cheerfully, tucking the pin into the front of his jumper.

'I feel ill,' said Roz.

'Sit down, then.' He took a chair and pressed her into it before moving to the back door and flinging it open. 'Out,' he ordered the man at the sink. 'Get yourself to hospital as fast as you can. If your friends have an ounce of decency they'll keep your name to themselves. If they haven't' – he shrugged – 'you've got about half an hour to get yourself admitted before the police come looking for you.'

The man needed no persuading. He launched himself into the fresh air of the alleyway and took to his heels.

With a groan of exhaustion, Hal shut the door and slithered to the floor. 'I need a rest. Do me a favour, sweetheart, and take off their masks. Let's see what we've got.'

Roz's head was aching intolerably where the roots of her hair had been loosened. She looked at him with burning eyes in a pasty white face. 'For your information, Hawksley,' she said icily, 'I'm just about out on my feet. It may have escaped your notice, but if it hadn't been for me you wouldn't have *got* anything.'

He gave a mighty yawn and winced as pain seared around his chest and back. Fractured ribs, he thought tiredly. 'I'll tell you this for free, Roz. As far as I'm concerned you are the most wonderful woman God ever made and I'll marry you if you'll have me.' He smiled sweetly. 'But at the moment I'm bushed. Be kind. Get off your high horse and take their ski-masks off.'

' "Words, words, mere words",' she murmured, but she did as he asked. The side of his face was already thickening where a baseball bat had split the skin. What the hell sort of state must his back be in? Covered in weals, probably, like the last time. 'Do you know any of them?' She studied the slack features of the unconscious man by the door. She had a fleeting impression she knew him, but his head moved and the impression vanished.

'No.' He'd seen her frown of brief recognition. 'Do you?'

'I thought I did,' she said slowly. 'Just for a

moment.' She shook her head. 'No. He probably reminded me of someone on the telly.'

Hal pushed himself to his feet and padded over to the sink, his stiffening body protesting at every step. He filled a bowl with water and sloshed it into the gaping mouth, watching the eyes flicker open. They were instantly alert, wary, guarded, all of which told Hal he wasn't likely to get anywhere by asking questions.

With a shrug of resignation, he looked at Roz. 'I need a favour.'

She nodded.

'There's a phonebox about two hundred yards down the main road. Take your car to it, dial 999, tell them the Poacher's been broken into, and then go home. Don't give your name. I'll call you the minute I can.'

'I'd rather stay.'

'I know.' His face softened. She was wearing her lonely look again. He reached out and ran the back of a finger down the line of her cheek. 'Trust me. I *will* call.'

She took a deep breath. 'How long do you want?'

He'd make it up to her one day, he thought. 'Fifteen minutes before you phone.'

She retrieved her handbag from the floor, cramming the contents inside and zippering it closed. 'Fifteen minutes,' she echoed, pulling the door open and stepping outside. She stared at him for a long moment then shut the door and walked away.

Hal waited until her footsteps faded. 'This,' he said gently, reaching for the hatpin, 'is going to be extremely painful.' He grasped the man's hair and forced him down until his face was flat against the floor. 'And I haven't got time for games.' He placed the weight of one knee across the man's shoulders then prised a finger straight in one of the bound fists and pushed the point of the hatpin between the flesh and the nail. He felt the finger flinch. 'You've got five seconds to tell me what the hell is going on before I push it home. One. Two. Three. Four. Five.' He breathed deeply through his nose, closed his eyes and shoved.

The man screamed.

Hal caught 'Foreclosures. You're costing money on the foreclosures' before a ton weight descended on the back of his head.

Sister Bridget, as imperturbable as ever, ushered Roz into her sitting room and sat her in a chair with a glass of brandy. Clearly Roz had been in another fight. Her clothes were filthy and dishevelled, her hair was a mess, and splotchy red marks on her neck and face looked very like the imprint of fingers. Someone, it seemed, was using her as a target for his spleen, though why she chose to put up with it Sister Bridget couldn't begin to imagine. Roz was as far removed from Dickens' Nancy as anyone could be, and had quite enough independence of spirit to reject the degrading life that a Bill Sykes offered.

She waited placidly while wave after wave of giggles spluttered from Roz's mouth.

'Do you want to tell me about it?' she asked at last, when Roz had composed herself enough to dab at her eyes.

Roz blew her nose. 'I don't think I can,' she said. 'It wasn't at all funny.' Laughter welled in her eyes again and she held the handkerchief to her mouth. 'I'm sorry to be a nuisance but I was afraid I'd have an accident if I tried to drive home. I think it's what's known as an adrenalin high.'

Privately, Sister Bridget decided it was a product of delayed shock, the natural healing process of mind over traumatized body. 'I'm pleased to have you here. Tell me how you're progressing on the Olive front. I saw her today but she wasn't very communicative.'

Grateful for something to take her mind off the Poacher, Roz told her. 'She did have a lover. I've found the hotel they used.' She peered at the brandy glass. 'It was the Belvedere in Farraday Street. They went there on Sundays during the summer of eighty-seven.' She took a sip from the glass then placed it hurriedly on the table beside her and slumped back into the chair, pressing shaking fingers to her temples.

'I'm terribly sorry,' she said, 'but I don't feel at all well. I've got the mother and father of all headaches.'

'I should imagine you have,' said Sister Bridget, rather more tartly than she had intended.

Roz massaged her aching temples. 'This ape tried to pull my hair out,' she murmured. 'I think that's what's done it.' She pressed an experimental hand to the back of her head and winced. 'There's some codeine in my handbag. You couldn't find them for me, could you? I think my head is about to explode.' She giggled hysterically. 'Olive must be sticking pins into me again.'

Tut-tutting with motherly concern, Sister Bridget administered three with a glass of water. 'I'm sorry, my dear,' she said severely, 'but I'm really very shocked. I can't forgive any man who treats a woman like a chattel and, harsh though it may sound, I find it almost as difficult to forgive the woman. Better to live without a man at all than to live with one who is only interested in the degradation of the spirit.'

Roz squinted through one half-closed eyelid, unable to take the glare of light from the window. How indignant the other woman looked, puffing her chest like a pouter pigeon. Hysteria nudged about her diaphragm again. 'You're very harsh all of a sudden. I doubt Olive saw it as degradation. Rather the reverse, I should think.'

'I'm not talking about Olive, my dear, I'm talking

about you. This ape you referred to. He isn't worth it. Surely you can see that?'

Roz shook with helpless laughter. 'I'm so sorry,' she said at last. 'You must think me incredibly rude. The trouble is I've been on an emotional rollercoaster for months.' She dabbed at her eyes and blew her nose. 'You must blame Olive for this. She's been a godsend. She's made me feel useful again.'

She saw the polite bewilderment on the other's face and sighed inwardly. Really, she thought, it was so much easier to tell lies. They were one dimensional and uncomplicated. '*I'm fine . . . Everything's fine . . . I like waiting rooms . . . Rupert's been very supportive over Alice . . . We went our separate ways amicably . . .*' It was the tangled web of truth, woven deep into the fragile stuff of character, that made life difficult. She wasn't even sure now what was true and what wasn't. Had she really hated Rupert that much? She couldn't imagine where she had found the energy. All she could really remember was how stifling the last twelve months had been.

'I'm completely infatuated,' she went on wildly as if that explained anything, 'but I've no idea if what I feel is genuine or just pie in the sky hoping.' She shook her head. 'I suppose one never really knows.'

'Oh, my dear,' said Sister Bridget, 'do be careful. Infatuation is a very poor substitute for love. It withers as easily as it flourishes. Love – *real* love – takes time to grow, and how can it do that in an atmosphere of brutality?'

'That's hardly his fault. I could have run away, I suppose, but I'm glad I didn't. I'm sure they'd have killed him if he'd been alone.'

Sister Bridget sighed. 'We seem to be talking at cross purposes. Do I gather the ape is not the man you're infatuated with?'

With streaming eyes, Roz wondered if there was any truth in the phrase *to die laughing.*

'You're very brave,' said Sister Bridget. 'I'd have assumed he was up to no good and run a mile.'

'Perhaps he is. I'm a very poor judge of character, you know.'

Sister Bridget laughed to herself. 'Well, it all sounds very exciting,' she said with a twinge of envy, taking Roz's dress from the tumble-drier and laying it on the ironing board. 'The only man who ever showed any interest in me was a bank clerk who lived three doors away from my parents. He was skin and bone, poor chap, with an enormous Adam's apple that crawled about his throat like a large pink beetle. I simply couldn't bear him. The Church was far more attractive.' She wet her finger and tapped it against the iron.

Roz, wrapped in an old flannelette nightie, smiled. 'And is it still?'

'Not always. But I wouldn't be human if I didn't have regrets.'

'Have you ever been in love?'

'Good Heavens, yes. More often than you have, I expect. Purely platonically, of course. I meet some very attractive fathers in my job.'

Roz chuckled. 'What sort of fathers? The cassocked variety or the ones in trousers?'

Sister Bridget's eyes danced wickedly. 'All I will say, as long as you promise not to quote me, is that I've always found cassocks a little off-putting and, with all the divorces there are these days, I spend more time talking to single men than, frankly, is good for a nun.'

'If things ever work out,' said Roz wistfully, 'and I have another daughter, I'll put her in your school so fast you won't know what hit you.'

'I shall look forward to it.'

'No. I don't believe in miracles. I did once.'

'I'll pray for you,' said Sister Bridget. 'It's time I had something to get my teeth into. I prayed for Olive and look what God sent me.'

'Now you're going to make me cry.'

She woke in the morning with brilliant sunlight bathing her face through a gap in Sister Bridget's spare-room curtains. It was too bright to look at so she cuddled down into the warmth of the duvet and listened instead. Ripples of birdsong swelled in glorious chorus from tiny feathered throats in the garden, and somewhere a radio murmured the news, but too low for her to make out the words. The smell of grilled bacon drifted tantalizingly from the kitchen downstairs, urging her to get up. She tingled with half-remembered vitality and wondered why she had allowed herself to stumble for so long through the blind fog of her depression. Life, she thought, was fabulous and the desire to live it too insistent to be ignored.

She waved goodbye to Sister Bridget, pointed the car towards the Poacher and switched on her stereo, feeding in Pavarotti. It was a very deliberate laying of a ghost. The rich voice surged in the speakers and she listened to it without regret.

The restaurant was deserted, no answer front or back to her knocking. She drove to the payphone she had used the night before and dialled the number, letting it ring for a long time in case Hal was asleep. When he didn't reply, she replaced the receiver and returned to her car. She wasn't concerned – frankly, Hal could look after himself rather better than any other man she had known – and she had more urgent fish to fry. From the dashboard pocket she took an expensive automatic camera with a powerful zoom lens – a legacy of the divorce – and checked it for film. Then, switching on the ignition, she drew out into the traffic.

She had to wait two hours, crouched uncomfortably on the back seat of her car, but she was well rewarded for her patience. When Olive's Svengali finally emerged from his front door he paused for a second or two and presented her with a perfect shot of his face. Magnified by the zoom lens, the dark eyes bored straight through her as she took the picture before they turned away to glance down between the avenue of trees to check for oncoming traffic. She felt the hairs pricking on the back of her neck. He couldn't possibly have seen her – the car was facing away from him with the camera lens propped on her handbag in the back window – but she shivered none the less. The photographs of Gwen and Amber's mutilated bodies, lying on the seat beside her, were a terrible reminder that she was stalking a psychopath.

She arrived back at her flat, hot and tired from the sweltering heat of unheralded summer. The wintry feel of three days before had melted into brilliant blue skies with a promise of more heat to come. She opened the windows of the flat and let in the roar of London traffic. More noticeable than usual, it made her think with a brief wistfulness of the peace and beauty of Bayview.

She checked her answerphone for messages while she poured a glass of water, only to find the tape as she had left it, blank. She dialled the Poacher and listened, this time with mounting anxiety, to the vain ringing at the other end. Where on earth was he? She chewed the knuckle of her thumb in frustration then phoned Iris.

'How would Gerry react if you asked him nicely to put on his solicitor's hat' – Gerald Fielding was a partner in a top London legal practice – 'ring Dawlington police station and make some discreet enquiries before everything winds down for the weekend?'

Iris was never one to beat about the bush. 'Why?' she demanded. 'And what's in it for me?'

'My peace of mind. I'm too twitched at the moment to write anything.'

'Hmm. Why?'

'I'm worried about my shady policeman.'

'*Your* shady policeman?' asked Iris suspiciously.

'That's right.'

Iris heard the amusement in her friend's voice. 'Oh, my God,' she said crossly, 'you haven't gone and fallen for him? He's supposed to be a source.'

'He is – of endless erotic fantasy.'

Iris groaned. 'How can you write objectively about

corrupt policemen if you've got the hots for one of them?'

'Who says he's corrupt?'

'He must be, if Olive's innocent. I thought you said he took her confession.'

'*It's a pity you're not a Catholic. You could go to confession and feel better immediately . . .*'

'Are you still there?' demanded Iris.

'Yes. Will Gerry do it?'

'Why can't you make the call yourself?'

'Because I'm involved and they might recognize my voice. I made them a 999 call.'

Iris groaned again. 'What on earth have you been up to?'

'Nothing criminal, at least I don't think so.' She heard the grunt of horror at the other end. 'Look, all Gerry has to do is ask a few innocent questions.'

'Will he have to lie?'

'A white lie or two.'

'He'll have a fit. You know Gerry. Breaks out in a muck sweat at the mere mention of falsehoods.' She sighed loudly. 'What a pest you are. You realize I shall have to bribe him with promises of good behaviour. My life won't be worth living.'

'You're an angel. Now, these are the only details Gerry needs to know. He's trying to contact his client, Hal Hawksley of the Poacher, Wenceslas Street, Dawlington. He has reason to believe the Poacher has been broken into and wonders if the police know where Hal can be contacted. OK?'

'No, it's not OK, but I'll see what I can do. Will you be in this evening?'

'Yes, twiddling my thumbs.'

'Well, try twiddling them round your keyboard,' said Iris acidly. 'I'm fed up with being the only one who does any meaningful work in this lopsided relationship of ours.'

She had had the film developed at a one-hour booth in her local High Street while she did some shopping. Now she spread the prints over her coffee table and studied them. She put the ones of Svengali, the two close-ups of his face and some full-length shots of his back as he walked away, to one side and smiled at the rest. She had forgotten taking them. Deliberately, she thought. They were of Rupert and Alice playing in the garden on Alice's birthday, a week before the accident. They had declared a truce that day, she remembered, for Alice's sake. And they had kept it, up to a point, although as usual the responsibility for refusing to be drawn had been Roz's. As long as she could keep her cool and smile while Rupert let slip his poisoned darts about Jessica, Jessica's flat, and Jessica's job, everything was hunky-dory. Alice's joy in having her parents back together again shone from the photographs.

Roz pushed them tenderly to one side and rummaged through her carrier bag of shopping, removing some cellophane, a paintbrush, and three tubes of acrylic paint. Then, munching into a pork pie, she set to work.

Every now and then she paused to smile at her daughter. She should have had the film developed before, she told Mrs Antrobus, who had curled contentedly into her lap. The rag doll of the newspapers had never been Alice. *This* was Alice.

'He's legged it,' said Iris baldly down the wire two hours later, 'and Gerry has been threatened with all sorts of nasties if he doesn't reveal his client's whereabouts the minute he knows them. There's a warrant out for the wretched man's arrest. Where on earth do you find these ghastly creatures? You should take up with a nice one, like Gerry,' she said severely, 'who wouldn't dream of beating up women or involving them in criminal activities.'

'I know,' agreed Roz mildly, 'but the nice ones are already taken. Did they mention what the charge is against Hal?'

'*Charges*, more like. Arson, resisting arrest, GBH, absconding from the scene of a crime. You name it, he's done it. If he gets in touch with you, don't bother to let me know. Gerry's already behaving like the man who knew the identity of Jack the Ripper but kept it quiet. He'll have a heart attack if he thinks I know where he is.'

'Mum's the word,' Roz promised.

There was a moment's silence. 'You might do better to hang up if he calls. There's a man in hospital with appalling facial burns, apparently, a policeman with a dislocated jaw, and when they arrived to arrest him he was trying to set fire to his restaurant. He sounds horribly dangerous to me.'

'I think you're probably right,' said Roz slowly, wondering what on earth had happened after she left. 'He's got a lovely arse, too. *Aren't* I the lucky one?'

'Cow!'

Roz laughed. 'Thank Gerry for me. I appreciate his niceness even if you don't.'

She went to sleep on the sofa in case she missed the phone when it rang. It occurred to her that he might not want to trust himself to an answer machine.

But the telephone remained stubbornly silent all weekend.

Sixteen

ON MONDAY MORNING, with the black dog of depression on her shoulder again, Roz went to the Belvedere Hotel and placed the photograph on the desk. 'Is this Mr Lewis?' she asked the proprietress.

The amiable woman popped on her glasses and took a good look. She shook her head apologetically. 'No, dear, I'm sorry. He doesn't ring a bell at all.'

'Try now.' She smoothed the cellophane across the photograph.

'Good heavens. How extraordinary. Yes, that's Mr Lewis all right.'

Marnie agreed. 'That's him. Dirty bugger.' She screwed up her eyes. 'It doesn't flatter him, does it? What would a young girl see in that?'

'I don't know. Uncritical affection perhaps.'

'Who is he?'

'A psychopath,' said Roz.

The other whistled. 'You want to be careful then.'

'Yes.'

Marnie tapped her carmined nails on the desk. 'Sure you don't want to tell me who he is in case you end up in bits on your kitchen floor?' She flicked Roz a speculative glance. There might, she thought, be some money in this somewhere.

Roz caught the glint in the other's eye. 'No thanks,' she said shortly. 'This is one piece of information I intend to keep to myself. I don't fancy my chances if he learns I'm close.'

'I won't blab,' said Marnie with a pout of injured innocence.

'You can't if I don't put temptation your way.' Roz tucked the photograph into her handbag. 'It would be irresponsible, anyway. You're a prime witness. He could just as easily come after *you* and chop *you* into little pieces.' She smiled coldly. 'I should hate to have that on my conscience.'

Roz returned to her car and sat for some minutes staring out of the window. If ever she had needed a tame ex-policeman to guide her through the maze of legal procedure, she thought, it was now. She was an amateur who could all too easily make mistakes and muck up the chances of a future prosecution. And where would that leave Olive? Languishing in prison, presumably. The verdict against her could only be overturned rapidly if someone else was convicted. On its own the seed of reasonable doubt would take years of germination before the Home Office would feel pressured enough to take notice. How long had the Birmingham Six had to wait for justice? The responsibility to get it right was frightening.

But, loath though she was to admit it, what weighed rather more heavily with her was the knowledge that she hadn't the courage to write the book while Olive's psychopathic lover remained at liberty. Try as she might, she could not get the pictures of Gwen and Amber out of her mind.

She slammed her fists against the steering-wheel. Where are you, Hawksley? *You bastard!* I was always there for you.

Graham Deedes, Olive's one-time barrister, walked into his chambers after a long day in court and frowned in irritation to find Roz parked on a seat outside his door. He looked pointedly at his watch. 'I'm in a hurry, Miss Leigh.'

She sighed, unfolding herself from the hard chair. 'Five minutes,' she begged. 'I've been waiting two hours.'

'No, I'm sorry. We have people coming to dinner and I promised my wife I wouldn't be late.' He opened his door and went inside. 'Ring and make an appointment. I'm in court for the next three days but

I may be able to fit you in towards the end of the week.' He prepared to shut her out.

She stood up and leaned her shoulder on the door jamb, holding the door open with one hand. 'Olive did have a lover,' she told him. 'I know who he is and I've had his photograph identified by two witnesses, one of whom is the owner of the hotel that he and Olive used throughout the summer before the murders. I have a witness who bears out Olive's claim to have had an abortion. The date she gave me implies that Olive's baby, had it lived, would have been born around the time of the murders. I have learned that two people, Robert Martin and the father of a friend of Olive's, quite independently of each other, told the police that Olive was incapable of murdering her sister. The scenario they both offered was that Gwen killed Amber – she didn't like Amber, apparently – and Olive killed Gwen. I admit the forensic evidence doesn't support that case but it proves that serious doubts existed even at the time which I don't think were brought to your attention.' She saw the impatience in his face and hurried on. 'For all sorts of reasons, principally because it was her birthday, I do not believe that Olive was in the house on the night before the murders and I *do* believe that Gwen and Amber were killed much earlier than the time Olive claims to have done it. I think Olive returned home some time during the morning or afternoon of the ninth, found the carnage in the kitchen, knew her lover was responsible, and was so overcome with shock and remorse that she confessed to the crime herself. I think she was very unsure of herself, very distressed, and didn't know how to cope when the main prop in her life, her mother, was so suddenly taken from her.'

He took some papers out of his desk and tucked them into his briefcase. He heard so many imaginative defences that he was more polite than interested. 'I assume you're suggesting that Olive and her lover spent her birthday night together in a hotel somewhere.' Roz nodded. 'Have you any proof of that?'

'No. They weren't registered at the hotel they usually used but that's not surprising. It was a special occasion. They may even have come up to London.'

'In that case why should she assume her lover was responsible? They would have gone back together. Even if he'd dropped her at a distance from her house he wouldn't have had time to do what was done.'

'He would if he'd walked out,' said Roz, 'and left her alone in the hotel.'

'Why would he do that?'

'Because she told him that but for her sister's earlier illegitimate baby and her mother's horror of it happening again he would by now be a proud father.'

Deedes looked at his watch. 'What illegitimate baby?'

'The one Amber had when she was thirteen. There's no dispute about that. The child is mentioned in Robert Martin's will. Gwen managed to hush it up but, as she couldn't hope to do the same thing with Olive, she persuaded her to abort.'

He clicked his tongue impatiently. 'This is all highly fanciful, Miss Leigh. As far as I can see, you've absolutely nothing to support these allegations and you can't go into print accusing somebody else of the murders without either some very strong evidence or enough capital behind you to pay a fortune in libel damages.' He looked at his watch again, torn between going and staying. 'Let's suppose for a moment your hypothesis is right. So, where was Olive's father while Gwen and Amber were being butchered in his kitchen? If I remember correctly he was in the house that night and left for work as usual the following morning. Are you suggesting he didn't know what had happened?'

'Yes, that's exactly what I'm suggesting.'

Deedes's pleasant face scowled in perplexity. 'That's absurd.'

'Not if he was never there. The only people who said he *was* were Olive, Robert himself, and the next-door neighbour, and she only mentioned him in the context of claiming that Gwen and Amber were still alive at eight thirty.'

He shook his head in complete bewilderment. 'So everybody's lying? That's too ridiculous. Why should the neighbour lie?'

Roz sighed. 'I know it's hard to swallow. I've had

a lot of time to think about it, so it's easier for me. Robert Martin was a closet homosexual. I've found the gay pub that he used for his pick-ups. He was well known there as Mark Agnew. The landlord recognized his picture immediately. If he was with a lover the night of the murders and went straight to work from there, he wouldn't have known anything about what had happened in the kitchen until he was told by the police.' She raised a cynical eyebrow. 'And he never had to reveal where he really was because Olive, who assumed he must have been in the house, claimed in her statement that she didn't attack her mother until after her father had left.'

'Hang on, hang on,' barked Deedes, as if he were haranguing a difficult witness, 'you can't have it both ways. A minute ago you were suggesting that Olive's lover dashed off in the middle of the night to have it out with Gwen.' He ran a smooth hand over his hair, collecting his thoughts. 'But, as Robert's body wasn't lying in the kitchen when Olive got back, she must have known he hadn't been there. Why claim in her statement he was?'

'Because he should have been. Look, it really doesn't matter what time her lover left her – the middle of the night, early morning – it's irrelevant as far as she was concerned. She didn't have a car, she was probably quite upset about being abandoned, plus she'd taken the day off work, presumably to spend it with her man, so the chances were she didn't get home till after lunch. She must have assumed her lover waited until Robert left for work before going in to tackle Gwen and Amber, so it was quite natural for her to include her father in her statement. He lived and slept downstairs in a back room but it doesn't appear to have occurred to any of them, except possibly Gwen, that he was slipping out at night for casual gay sex.'

He glanced at his watch for a third time. 'It's no good. I shall have to go.' He reached for his coat and folded it over his arm. 'You haven't explained why the neighbour lied.' He ushered her through the door and closed it behind them.

She spoke over her shoulder as she started down the stairs. 'Because I suspect that when the police told her Gwen and Amber had been murdered she jumped to the immediate conclusion that Robert had done it after a row over her husband.' She shrugged at his snort of disbelief. 'She knew all about the strained relationships in that house, knew that her husband spent hours shut up with Robert in the back room, knew jolly well, I should think, that Robert was a homosexual and by inference that her husband was one as well. She must have been beside herself until she heard that Olive had confessed to the murders. The scandal, if Robert had done it for love of Edward, would have been devastating, so, in a rather pathetic attempt to keep him out of it, she said that Gwen and Amber were alive after Edward left for work.' She led him across the hallway. 'Luckily for her the statement was never questioned because it tied in very neatly with what Olive said.'

They pushed through the main doors and walked down the front steps to the pavement. 'Too neatly?' he murmured. 'Olive's version is so simple. Yours is so complicated.'

'The truth always is,' she said with feeling. 'But in actual fact, all three of them only described what was, in effect, a normal Wednesday morning. Not so much neatness, then, as inevitability.'

'I go this way,' he said, pointing up towards Holborn Tube station.

'That's all right. I'll come with you.' She had to walk briskly to keep up with him.

'I don't understand why you're telling me all this, Miss Leigh. The person you should have gone to is Olive's solicitor, Mr Crew.'

She avoided a direct answer. 'You think I've got a case, then?'

He smiled good-humouredly, his teeth very white in his dark face. 'No, you're a long way off that. You may have the *beginnings* of a case. Take it to Mr Crew.'

'You're the barrister,' she persisted doggedly. 'If you were fighting Olive's corner, what would you need to convince a court she's innocent?'

'Proof that she could not have been in the house during the period of time that the murders happened.'

'Or the real murderer?'

'Or the real murderer,' he agreed, 'but I can't see you producing him very easily.'

'Why not?'

'Because there's no evidence against him. Your argument, presumably, is that Olive obscured all the evidence in order to take the blame on herself. She did it very successfully. Everything confirmed her as the guilty party.' He slowed down as they approached the Underground. 'So, unless your hypothetical murderer confesses voluntarily and persuades the police that he knew things that only the murderer could know, there's no way you can overturn Olive's conviction.' He smiled apologetically. 'And I can't see him doing that now, for the simple reason that he didn't do it at the time.'

She telephoned the prison from Holborn Tube station and asked them to tell Olive she wouldn't be in that evening. She had a feeling that things were about to blow up in her face, and the feeling centred on Olive.

It was late by the time she let herself in through the main door of her block. Unusually, the hall was in total darkness. She pressed the time switch to light the stairs and first-floor landing, and sighed when nothing happened. Another power cut, she thought.

She could have predicted it. Black was in tune with her mood. She sorted out the key to her flat, by touch, and groped her way up the stairs, trying to remember if she had any candles left over from the last time. With luck there was one in her kitchen drawer, otherwise this was going to be a long and tedious night.

She was fumbling blindly across her door with both hands, searching for the lock, when something rose up from the floor at her feet and brushed against her.

'*Aa-agh!*' she screamed, beating at it furiously.

Next second she was lifted bodily off the floor while a great palm clamped itself across her mouth. 'Ssh,' hissed Hal in her ear, shaking with laughter. 'It's me.' He kissed her on the nose. '*Ow!*' he roared, letting her go and bending over to clutch himself.

'Serves you right,' she said, scrabbling on the floor for her keys. 'You're lucky I didn't have my hatpin. Ah, got them.' She renewed her search for the lock and found it. 'There.' She tried the lights inside the door but the blackness remained impenetrable. 'Come on,' she said, catching his jacket and pulling him inside. 'I think there's a candle in the kitchen.'

'Everything all right?' called a quavering female voice from the floor upstairs.

'Yes, thank you,' Roz called back. 'I trod on something. How long has the power been off?'

'Half an hour. I've telephoned. There's a fuse gone in a box somewhere. Three hours they said. I told them I wouldn't pay my bill if it was any longer. We should take a stand. Don't you agree?'

'Absolutely,' said Roz, wondering who she was talking to. Mrs Barrett, perhaps. She knew their names from their mail but she rarely saw anyone. ''Bye now.' She closed her door. 'I'll try and find the candle,' she whispered.

'Why are we whispering?' Hal whispered back.

She giggled. 'Because one always does in the dark.'

He stumbled into something. 'This is ridiculous. The street lights aren't out, are they? Your curtains must be closed.'

'Probably.' She pulled open the kitchen drawer. 'I left early this morning.' She felt around the clutter of cotton reels and screwdrivers. 'I think I've found it. Have you any matches?'

'No,' he said patiently, 'otherwise I'd have lit one by now. Do you keep snakes by any chance?'

'Don't be silly. I have a cat.' *But where was Mrs Antrobus*? Her cries should have risen in joyful greeting when the key scraped in the lock. Roz made her way back to the door and groped for her briefcase where she kept the matches that she took in to the prison. She snapped the locks and poked amongst her papers. 'If you can find the sofa,' she told him, 'the curtains are behind it. There's a cord on the left-hand side.'

'I've found something,' he said, 'but it certainly isn't a sofa.'

'What is it?'

'I don't know,' he said cautiously, 'but whatever it is it's rather unpleasant. It's wet and slimy and it's wound itself round my neck. Are you sure you don't keep snakes?'

She gave a nervous laugh. 'Don't be an idiot.' Her fingers knocked against the matchbox and she snatched at it with relief. She struck a match and held it up. Hal was standing in the middle of the room, his head and shoulders swathed in the damp shirt she had washed that morning and hung on a coathanger from the lampshade. She shook with laughter. 'You knew it wasn't a snake,' she said, holding the candle to the spluttering match flame.

He found the cord and swished the curtains back to let in the orange glow from the street lamps outside. With that and the candlelight, the room sprang alive out of the pitch darkness. He gazed about him. Towels, clothes, carrier bags, and photographs lay in clutters on chairs and tables, a duvet sprawled half on and half off the sofa, dirty cups, and empty bags of crisps jostled happily about the floor. 'Well, this is nice,' he said, lifting his foot and prising off the remains of a half-eaten pork pie. 'I can't remember when I felt so much at home.'

'I wasn't expecting you,' she said, taking the pork pie with dignity and dropping it into a waste-paper basket. 'Or at least I thought you'd have the decency to warn me of your arrival with a phone-call first.'

He reached down to stroke the soft ball of white fur that was stretching luxuriously in its warm nest on the duvet. Mrs Antrobus licked his hand in approval before embarking on a comprehensive grooming. 'Do you always sleep on the sofa?' he asked Roz.

'There's no telephone in the bedroom.'

He nodded gravely but didn't say anything.

She moved over to him, the candle tilted to stop the hot wax burning her fingers. 'Oh, God, I'm so pleased to see you. You wouldn't believe. Where did you go? I've been worried sick.'

He lowered his weary forehead and pressed it against her sweet-smelling hair. 'Round and about,' he said, resting his wrists on her shoulders and running the softest of fingers down the lines of her neck.

'There's a warrant out for your arrest,' she said weakly.

'I know.' His lips brushed against her cheek, but so gently that their touch was almost unbearable.

'I'm going to set fire to something,' she groaned.

He reached down to pinch out the candle. 'You already have.' He cupped his strong hands about her bottom and drew her against his erection. 'The question is,' he murmured into the arch of her neck, 'should I have a cold shower before it spreads out of control?'

'Is that a serious question?' *Could* he stop now? *She* couldn't.

'No, a polite one.'

'I'm in agony.'

'You're supposed to be,' he said, his eyes glinting in the orange light. 'Damn it, woman, I've been in agony for weeks.'

Mrs Antrobus, ejected from the duvet, stalked indignantly into the kitchen.

Later, the lights came on, drowning the tiny flame of the candle which, rekindled, had started to splutter in its saucer on the table.

He stroked the hair from Roz's face. 'You are quite the most beautiful woman I've ever seen,' he said.

She smiled wickedly. 'And I thought I was too thin?'

His dark eyes softened 'I knew you were lying about that blasted answerphone.' He ran his hands over her silky arms, gripping them suddenly with urgent fingers. She was completely addictive. He plucked her up and sat her astride his lap. 'I've been dreaming about this.'

'Were they nice dreams?'

'Not a patch on the real thing.'

'Enough,' she said even later, sliding away from him and pulling on her clothes. 'What are you planning to do about this arrest warrant?'

He ignored the question and stirred the photographs on her coffee table. 'Is this your husband?'

'Ex-husband.' She threw him his trousers.

He pulled them on with a sigh, then isolated a close-up of Alice. 'And this must be your daughter,' he said evenly. 'She looks just like you.'

'Looked,' Roz corrected him. 'She's dead.'

She waited for the apology and the change of subject, but Hal smiled and touched a finger to the laughing face. 'She's beautiful.'

'Yes.'

'What was her name?'

'Alice.'

He examined the picture closely. 'I remember falling in love with a little girl just like her when I was six. I was very insecure and I used to ask her every day how much she loved me. She always answered in the same way. She would hold her hands out, like this' – he spread his palms apart, like a fisherman demonstrating the length of a fish – 'and say: this much.'

'Yes,' said Roz, remembering, 'Alice always measured love with her hands. I'd forgotten.'

She tried to take the photograph away, but he moved it out of her reach and tilted it to the light. 'There's a very determined glint in her eyes.'

'She liked her own way.'

'Sensible woman. Did she always get it?'

'Most times. She had very decided views. I remember once . . .' But she fell silent and didn't go on.

Hal shrugged into his shirt and started to button it. 'Like mother, like daughter. I bet she had you wound round her little finger before she could walk. I'd have enjoyed seeing someone get the better of you.'

Roz held a handkerchief to her streaming eyes. 'I'm sorry.'

'What for?'

'Being embarrassing.'

He pulled her against his shoulder and rested his cheek against her hair. What a terrible indictment of Western society it was, that a mother should be afraid to shed tears for her dead daughter in case she embarrassed someone.

'Thank you.' She saw the question in his eyes. 'For listening,' she explained.

'It was no hardship, Roz.' He could sense how insecure she was. 'Are you going to agonize over this all night and wake up tomorrow morning wishing you hadn't told me about Alice?'

He was far too perceptive. She looked away. 'I hate feeling vulnerable.'

'Yes.' He understood that. 'Come here.' He patted

his lap. 'Let me tell you about my vulnerabilities. You've been trying to prise them out of me for weeks. Now it's your turn to have a good laugh at my expense.'

'I won't laugh.'

'Ah!' he murmured. 'So that's what this is all about. You're a cut above me. I'll laugh at yours, but you won't laugh at mine.'

She put her arms about him. 'You're so like Olive.'

'I wish you'd stop comparing me with the mad-woman of Dawlington.'

'It's a compliment. She's a very nice person. Like you.'

'I'm not nice, Roz.' He held her face between his hands. 'I'm being prosecuted under the Health and Hygiene regulations. The Environmental Health Inspector's report describes my kitchen as the worst he's ever seen. Ninety-five per cent of the raw meat in the fridge was so rotten it was crawling with maggots. The dry foods should have been in sealed containers, but weren't, and rat droppings were found in all of them. There were open bags of rubbish in the larder. The vegetables had deteriorated so far they had to be discarded, and a live rat was discovered under the cooker.' He arched a weary eyebrow. 'I've lost all my customers because of it, my case comes up in six weeks, and I haven't a leg to stand on.'

Seventeen

ROZ DIDN'T SPEAK for some moments. She had invented a number of scenarios to account for what was happening at the Poacher, but never this. It would certainly explain his lack of customers. Who, in their right mind, would eat in a restaurant where the meat had been found crawling with maggots? She had. Twice. But she hadn't known about the maggots. It would have been more honest of Hal to tell her at the outset, she thought, her stomach protesting mildly over what might have gone into it. She felt his gaze upon her and quelled the treacherous stirrings firmly.

'I don't understand,' she said carefully. 'Is this a genuine prosecution? I mean, you appear to have been tried and judged already. How did your customers know what the Inspector found if the case hasn't been to court? And who are the men in ski-masks?' She gave a puzzled frown. 'I can't believe you'd be such a bloody fool, anyway, as to flout the hygiene regulations. Not to the extent of having an entire fridgeful of rotten meat and live rats running around the floor.' She laughed suddenly with relief and smacked a slender palm against his chest. 'You creep, Hawksley! It's a load of old flannel. You're trying to wind me up.'

He shook his head. 'I wish I were.'

She studied him thoughtfully for a moment then pushed herself off his lap and walked through to the kitchen. He heard the sound of a cork being drawn from a bottle and the clink of glasses. She took longer than she should have, and he recalled how his wife had always done the same thing – disappeared into the kitchen whenever she was hurt or disappointed. He had thought Roz different.

She reappeared finally with a tray. 'OK,' she said firmly, 'I've had a think.'

He didn't say anything.

'I do not believe you'd keep a dirty kitchen,' she told him. 'You're too much of an enthusiast. The Poacher is the fulfilment of a dream, not a financial investment to be milked for all its worth.' She poured him a glass of wine. 'And you accused me a week ago of setting you up again, which would imply you'd been set up before.' She filled the second glass for herself. 'Ergo, the rat and the rotten meat were planted. Am I right?'

'Right.' He sniffed the wine. 'But I would say that, wouldn't I?'

A very sore nerve, she thought. No wonder he didn't trust anyone. She perched on the edge of the sofa. 'Plus,' she went on, ignoring the comment, 'you've been beaten up twice to my knowledge, had your car windows smashed and the Poacher broken into.' She sipped her wine. 'So what do they want from you?'

He eased the still-bruised muscles in his back. 'Presumably they want me out, and fast. But I haven't a clue why or who's behind it. Six weeks ago I was a contented chef, presiding over a healthy little business without a care in the world. Then I came home from the markets at ten o'clock one morning to find my assistant being berated by the Environmental Health Inspector, my kitchen stinking to high heaven of corruption, and me on the wrong end of a prosecution.' He ruffled his hair. 'The restaurant was closed for three days while I cleaned it. My staff never came back after the closure. My customers, predominantly policemen and their families – which, incidentally, is how the news of the Inspector's visit got out – deserted in droves because they reckoned I'd been cutting corners to line my pockets, and the local restaurateurs are accusing me of giving the whole trade a bad name through my lack of professionalism. I've been effectively isolated.'

Roz shook her head. 'Why on earth didn't you report that break-in last Tuesday?'

He sighed. 'What good would it have done me? I couldn't tie it in to the Health Inspector's visit. I decided to work with some live bait instead.' He saw her bewilderment. 'I caught two of them at it, wrecking the place. I think it was a chance thing. They discovered the restaurant was empty and took their opportunity.' He laughed suddenly. 'I was so angry with you that I had them both upstairs, gagged and handcuffed to my window bars, before they even knew what had hit them. But they were a tough pair,' he said with genuine admiration. 'They weren't going to talk.' He shrugged. 'So I sat it out and waited for someone to come looking for them.'

No wonder he had been frightened. 'Why did you decide it was chance that brought them and not me?' she asked curiously. 'I'd have thought it was me every time.'

The laughter lines rayed out around his eyes. 'You didn't see yourself with that table leg. You were so terrified when the kitchen door opened, so relieved when you saw it was me, and so twitched when I told you I hadn't called the police. No one, but no one, is that good.' He took a mouthful of wine and savoured it for a moment. 'I'm in a catch twenty-two. The police don't believe me. They think I'm guilty, but trying to use clout or cunning to wriggle out of the prosecution. Even Geoff Wyatt, who was my partner and who knows me better than anyone, claims to have had the runs since he saw the Inspector's photographs. They all ate there regularly, partly because I gave them discounts and partly out of a genuine desire to see an ex-copper succeed.' He wiped a weary hand across his mouth. 'Now, I'm *persona non grata* and I can't really blame them. They feel they've been conned.'

'Why would you need to con them?'

'The recession.' He sighed. 'Businesses are going down like ninepins. There's no reason mine should have been immune. What's the first thing a restaurateur's likely to do when he's running out of money? Hang on to dodgy food and serve it up in a curry.'

There was a twisted logic to it. 'Won't your staff speak up for you?'

He smiled grimly. 'The two waitresses have agreed to, but the only one whose word might carry weight is my assistant chef, and he was last heard of heading for France.' He stretched his arms towards the ceiling, and winced as pain seared round his ribs. 'It wouldn't do me any good anyway. He must have been bought. Someone had to let whoever framed me into the kitchen and he had the only other key.' His eyes hardened. 'I should have throttled him when I had the chance but I was so damn shell-shocked I didn't put two and two together fast enough. By the time I had, he'd gone.'

Roz chewed her thumb in thought. 'Didn't that man tell you anything after I left? I assumed you were going to use my hatpin on him.'

Her candour brought a smile to his bleak face. 'I did, but he didn't make much sense. "You're costing money on the foreclosures." That's all he said.' He arched an eyebrow. 'Can you make anything of it?'

'Not unless the bank's about to pull the rug from underneath your feet.'

He shook his head. 'I borrowed the absolute minimum. There's no immediate pressure.' He drummed his fingers on the floor. 'Logically, he should have been referring to the businesses on either side of me. They've both gone bankrupt and in each case the lenders have foreclosed.'

'Well, that's it then,' said Roz excitedly. 'Someone wants all three properties. Didn't you ask him who it was and why?'

He rubbed the back of his head in tender recollection. 'I was clobbered before I had the chance. There was obviously a fifth man who went upstairs during the brawl to release Tweedledum and Tweedledee from the window bars. For all I know, it was that hammering we heard. Anyway, by the time I came to, a chip pan was in flames on the stove, the police had arrived in force, and my next-door neighbour was rabbiting on about how he'd had to call an ambulance because I'd tried to boil a customer in fish stock.' He grinned sheepishly. 'It was a blasted nightmare. So I hit the nearest copper and legged it through the restaurant. It was the only thing I could think of.' He looked at her. 'In any case the idea that someone was trying to get hold of the Poacher was the first thing I thought of. I checked out both the adjoining properties five weeks ago and there's no common factor between them. One was bought privately by a small retail chain and the other was sold at auction to an investment company.'

'They could be fronts. Did you go to Companies' House?'

'What do you think I've been doing for the last three days?' He gritted his teeth angrily. 'I've checked every damn register I can think of and I've got sweet FA to show for it. I don't know what the hell's going on except that the court case will be the last nail in the Poacher's coffin and presumably, at that point, someone will make me an offer to buy the place. Rather like you kept doing the other day.'

She let his anger slide past her. She understood it now. 'By which time it will be too late.'

'Precisely.'

They sat in silence for several minutes.

'Why were you beaten up the first time I saw you?' Roz asked at last. 'That must have followed on the Inspector's visit.'

He nodded. 'It was three or four days after I re-opened. They grabbed me off the doorstep when I unlocked the door. Same MO as you witnessed – men in ski-masks with baseball bats – but that time they shoved me in the back of a fish lorry, drove me ten miles into the New Forest, slapped me about a bit, then dumped me by the side of the road with no money and no cards. It took me all afternoon to walk home, because nobody fancied giving me a lift, and at the end of it' – he flicked her a sideways glance – 'I found Botticelli's *Venus* loitering palely among my tables. I really thought my luck had changed until Venus opened her mouth and turned into a Fury.' He ducked to avoid her hand. 'God, woman' – he grinned – 'I was out on my feet and you tore more strips off me than the bastards in the fish lorry. Rape, for Christ's sake! I could hardly put one foot in front of the other.'

'It's your own fault for having bars on your windows. Why do you, as a matter of interest?'

'They were there when I bought it. The chap before me had a wife who sleepwalked. I've been glad of them these last few weeks.'

She reverted to her former question. 'But it doesn't explain why, you know. I mean if the idea of the Inspector's visit was to get you to jack it in quickly, then they should have clobbered you the day you reopened, not four days later. And if they were happy to wait until the court case, then why clobber you at all?'

'I know,' he admitted. 'It made me very suspicious of you. I kept thinking you must be connected with it somehow but I had you checked and you seemed genuine enough.'

'Thanks,' she said drily.

'You'd have done the same.' A frown carved a deep furrow between his brows. 'You must admit it's damned odd the way everything blew up around the time you appeared.'

In all fairness, Roz could see it was. 'But you got stitched up,' she pointed out, 'before you or I had ever heard of each other. It must be coincidence.' She topped up his glass. 'And, anyway, the only common factor between you and me five weeks ago was Olive and you're not suggesting she's behind it. She's hardly confident enough to run a bath on her own, let alone mastermind a conspiracy to defraud you of the Poacher.'

He shrugged impatiently. 'I know. I've been over it a thousand times. None of it makes sense. The only thing I'm sure of is that it's about the neatest operation I've ever come across. I've had the ground cut from under me. I'm the fall guy and I can't even begin to get a fix on who's done it.' He scratched his stubble with weary resignation. 'So, Miss Leigh, how do you feel now about a failed restaurateur with convictions for health violation, GBH, arson, and resisting arrest? Because, barring miracles, that's what I'll be in three weeks.'

Her eyes gleamed above her wine glass. 'Horny.'

He gave an involuntary chuckle. It was the same gleam in the pictured eyes of Alice. 'You look just like your daughter.' He stirred the photographs again. 'You should have them all around the room to remind yourself of how beautiful she was. I would if she'd been mine.' He heard Roz's indrawn breath and glanced at her. 'Sorry. That was insensitive.'

'Don't be an oaf,' she said. 'I've just remembered where I've seen that man before. I knew I knew him. It's one of Mr Hayes's sons. You know, the old man who lived next door to the Martins. He had photographs of the family on his sideboard.' She clapped her hands. 'Is that a miracle, Hawksley, or is it a miracle? Sister Bridget's prayers must be working.'

She sat at her kitchen table and watched Hal work his magic on the meagre contents of her fridge. He had sloughed off his frustration like a used-up skin and was humming contentedly to himself as he interleaved bacon between thin slices of chicken breast and sprinkled them with parsley. 'You're not planning to stick my hatpin into Mr Hayes, are you?' she asked him. 'I'm sure he hasn't a clue what his beastly son's been up to. He's a dear old thing.'

Hal was amused. 'I shouldn't think so.' He covered the dish with silver foil and put it in the oven. 'But I'm damned if I can see at the moment how the jigsaw fits together. Why did Hayes Junior suddenly up the pressure on me if all he had to do was sit tight and wait for my prosecution?'

'Have him arrested and find out,' said Roz reasonably. 'If it was me, I'd have driven straight down, demanded an address off his father, and sent in the fuzz.'

'And you'd have got precisely nowhere.' He thought for a moment. 'You said you made a tape of your conversation with the old man. I'd like to listen to it. I can't believe it's coincidence. There has to be a stronger link. Why did they all get so twitched suddenly and start wielding baseball bats? It doesn't make sense.'

'You can listen to it now.' She brought her briefcase in from the hallway, located the tape, and set the recorder running on the table. 'We were talking about Amber's illegitimate son,' she explained as the old man's voice quavered out. 'He knew all about him, even down to the child's adopted name and what country he's in. Robert Martin's entire estate is his if they can find him.'

Hal listened with rapt attention. 'Brown?' he queried at the end. 'And living in Australia? How do you know he's right?'

'Because Olive's shitty solicitor threatened me with injunctions when I let on I knew.' She frowned. 'Mind you, I've no idea how Mr Hayes found out. Crew won't even give Olive the child's name. He's paranoid about keeping it secret.'

Hal removed a saucepan of rice from the cooker and drained it. 'How much did Robert Martin leave?'

'Half a million.'

'Christ!' He gave a low whistle. 'Christ!' he said

again. 'And it's all on deposit waiting for the child's appearance?'

'Presumably.'

'Who's the executor?'

'The solicitor, Peter Crew.'

Hal spooned the rice into a bowl. 'So what did he say when you tackled him about it? Did he admit they were on the child's track?'

'No. He just kept threatening me with injunctions.' She shrugged. 'But he wrote to Olive and told her the chances were minimal. There's a time limit, apparently, and if the child doesn't turn up the money goes to charity.' She frowned. 'He wrote that letter himself in long hand. I thought he was saving money but, you know, it's far more likely that he didn't want his secretary reading it. She would know if he was telling lies.'

'And meanwhile,' Hal said slowly, 'he is administering the estate and has access to the sort of capital that would be needed to buy up bankrupt businesses.' He stared past her head, his eyes narrowed. 'Plus, he's a solicitor, so probably has inside information on development plans and proposals.' He looked at Roz. 'It would amount to indefinite free credit, as long as no one turned up to claim Robert's money. When did you first go and see Crew?'

She was ahead of him. 'The day before you were beaten up.' Her eyes gleamed excitedly. 'And he was very suspicious of me, kept accusing me of jumping to unfavourable conclusions about his handling of Olive's case. I've got it all on tape.' She scrabbled through her cassettes. 'He said Olive couldn't inherit because she would not be allowed to benefit from Gwen and Amber's death. But, you know, if Olive were innocent' – she pounced triumphantly on the tape – 'it would be a whole new ball game. She could get leave to appeal against the will. And I remember saying to him at the end of the interview that one explanation for the discrepancies between the abnormality of the crime and the normality of Olive's psychiatric tests was that she didn't do it. God, it fits, doesn't it? First he learns that Amber's son is likely to surface and then I turn up, aggressively taking Olive's side. The Poacher must be awfully important to him.'

Hal took the chicken from the oven and put it on the table with the rice. 'You do realize your dear old man must be in it up to his neck? Crew would never have given him chapter and verse on Amber's child unless Hayes has some kind of hold on him.'

She stared at him for a long moment, then removed the Svengali photographs from her briefcase. 'Perhaps he knows Crew is using Robert's money. Or perhaps,' she said slowly, 'he knows who really murdered Gwen and Amber. Either or both could ruin Crew.' She fanned the pictures across the table. 'He was Olive's lover,' she said simply, 'and if I could find out so easily then so could anyone else. Including the police. You let her down, Hal, all of you. It's a betrayal of justice to assume someone's guilt before it's proved.'

Watery blue eyes regarded Roz with undisguised pleasure. 'Well, well. You came back. Come in. Come in.' He peered past her, frowning at Hal in half-recognition. 'Surely we've met before. What shall I say? I never forget a face. Now when could that have been?'

Hal shook the old man's hand. 'Six years ago,' he said pleasantly. 'I was on the Olive Martin case. Sergeant Hawksley.' The hand fluttered weakly in his, like a tiny bird, but only from old age and decrepitude, Hal thought.

Mr Hayes nodded vigorously. 'I remember now. Unhappy circumstances.' He fussed ahead of them into the sitting room. 'Sit down. Sit down. Any news?' He took a firm chair and sat bolt upright his head cocked enquiringly to one side. On the sideboard behind him his violent son smiled disarmingly into the camera.

Roz took her notebook from her handbag and switched on her recorder again. They had reached a mutual decision that Roz should ask the questions. For, as Hal had pointed out: 'If he knows anything, he's more likely to let it slip while talking to a – what shall I say? – charming young lady about Olive.'

'In fact,' she said in a gossipy voice which grated

on Hal but clearly appealed to Mr Hayes, 'there's quite a bit of news one way and another. Where would you like me to begin? With Olive? Or with Amber's baby?' She gave him an approving look. 'You were quite right about them finding traces, you know, in spite of there being thousands of Browns in Australia.'

'Ah,' he said, rubbing his hands, 'I knew they were close. That mean the lad will get the money? What shall I say? It's what Bob wanted. Fair upset him, it did, to think the government would get it all.'

'He made alternative provisions, you know, in case the boy wasn't found. It'll go to various children's charities.'

The old man's mouth compressed into a split of disgust. 'And we all know what sort of children they'll be. The worthless sort. The sort as are never going to make anything of theirselves but live off the rest of us till they drop. And you know who I blame. The social workers. They're namby-pamby when it comes to telling a woman she's had more children than's good for her.'

'Quite,' Roz interrupted hurriedly, reining in the inevitable hobby horse. She tapped her pencil on her notepad. 'Do you remember telling me that your wife thought Olive committed the murders because of hormones?'

He pursed his lips at the abrupt change of subject. 'Maybe.'

'Did your wife say that because she knew Olive had had an abortion the previous Christmas?'

'Maybe.'

'Do you know who the father was, Mr Hayes?'

He shook his head. 'Someone she met through work, we were told. Silly girl. Only did it to cock a snook at Amber.' He fingered his ancient mouth. 'Or that's what I reckoned anyway. Amber had a lot of boyfriends.'

So much for Mr Hayes and Crew in a conspiracy of silence, thought Roz. 'When did you find out about it?'

'Gwen told my Jeannie. She was that upset. Thought Olive was going to up and get married and abandon them all. It would have done for Gwen, that would. She couldn't have coped on her own.'

'Coped with what?'

'Everything,' he said vaguely.

'Housework, you mean?'

'Housework, cooking, bills, shopping. Everything. Olive did everything.'

'What did Gwen do?'

He didn't answer immediately, but seemed to be weighing something in his mind. He glanced across at Hal. 'You lot never did ask many questions. I might have said something if you had.'

Hal eased himself in his chair. 'At the time it was clear cut,' he said carefully. 'But Miss Leigh has unearthed a number of discrepancies which do tend to throw a different light on the affair. What would you have told us, had you been asked?'

Mr Hayes sucked at his false teeth. 'Well, for one thing, Gwen Martin drank too much. She had troubles, I can't deny that, kept up a good front, I can't deny that either, but she was a bad mother. She married beneath herself and it made her bitter. Felt life had dealt her a bad hand and she took it out on Bob and the girls. My Jeannie always said if it hadn't been for Olive the family would have fallen apart years before. It made us sick, of course, what she did, but everyone turns eventually and she was badly put upon one way and another. She shouldn't have killed them, though. Can't forgive that.'

'No,' said Roz thoughtfully. 'So what did Gwen do all day while the other three were out at work?'

The marbled hands fluttered a contradiction. 'Amber was at home more often than not. Work-shy, that one. Never stayed anywhere very long. Used to drive her mother mad listening to pop records at full blast and inviting boys up to her bedroom. She was a pretty girl but my Jeannie said she was difficult. Couldn't see it myself.' He smiled reminiscently. 'She was always charming to me. I had a soft spot for little Amber. But she got on with men, I think, better than she got on with women.' He peered at Roz. 'You asked me about Gwen. What shall I say, Miss Leigh? She kept up appearances. If you knocked on the door she was always smartly dressed, always held herself well, always spoke with icy correctness, but as often as not she was drunk as a lord. Strange woman. Never did know why she took to the bottle, unless it was the business of Amber's baby. She was a lot worse afterwards.'

Roz drew her cherub doodle. 'Robert Martin was an active homosexual but didn't want anyone to know,' she said bluntly. 'Perhaps that's what she found difficult to cope with.'

Mr Hayes sniffed. 'She drove him to it,' he said. 'There was nothing wrong with Bob that a loving wife wouldn't have put right. The two girls were his all right, so there was nothing untoward in the locker at the beginning, if you get my meaning. It was her turned him off women. She was frigid.'

Roz let that pass. Mr Hayes was too set in his views to see that what he said was nonsense and, in any case, there was probably some truth in the idea that Gwen was frigid. Roz found it difficult to believe that Robert Martin could ever have got as far as the altar with a woman who had a normal sexual drive. Her very normality would have been a threat to him. 'But if she was mourning Amber's baby,' she said in feigned puzzlement, 'I don't understand why she didn't try and get him back or at least establish contact with him? Presumably she knew who had adopted him or she wouldn't have been able to tell your Jeannie his name.'

He tut-tutted impatiently. 'It wasn't Jeannie told

me the name, it was my son, Stewart, six, seven weeks back. Knew I'd be interested, seeing as how me and Bob were pals.' He wagged a finger at her. 'You don't know much about adoption, that's for sure. Once you sign 'em away, that's it. You're not given a dossier. Gwen never knew who'd got him.'

Roz smiled easily. 'Does your son work for Mr Crew, then? I've not come across him. I thought he took after you and became a soldier.'

'Blooming Army didn't want him any more, did they?' he muttered crossly. 'Cutbacks there, like everywhere else. What shall I say? So much for loyalty to Queen and country. Course he doesn't work for Mr Crew. He's running a small security firm with his brother, but there's precious little work.' He flexed his arthritic fingers in annoyance. 'Trained soldiers and the best they can get is nightwatchmen jobs. Their wives aren't happy, not by a long chalk.'

Roz gritted her teeth behind another ingenuous smile. 'So how did he know the child's name?'

Archly, Mr Hayes tapped the side of his nose. 'No names no pack drill, young lady. Always best.'

Hal leaned forward aggressively and held up a hand. 'One moment, please, Miss Leigh.' He drew his brows together in a ferocious scowl. 'You do realize, Mr Hayes, that if your son doesn't work for Mr Crew then, strictly speaking, he's committed an offence by being in receipt of confidential information. The legal profession is bound by the same codes as the medical profession and if someone in Mr Crew's practice is talking to outsiders, then both he and the police would want to know about it.'

'Bah!' the old man snorted contemptuously. 'You never change, you lot. What shall I say? Quick as lightning to bang up the innocent while the bloody thieves wander around, free as birds, nicking anything they feel like nicking. You should do what you're being paid for, Sergeant, and not go round threatening old men. It was Mr Crew himself gave out that information. He told my lad and my lad told me. How's he supposed to know it's confidential if the blooming solicitor's telling everyone? Stands to reason he'd pass it on, seeing as how I was the only friend Bob had at the end.' He glared suspiciously from Hal to Roz. 'What you bring a policeman for, anyway?'

'Because there's some doubt of Olive's guilt,' said Roz glibly, wondering if being economical with the truth constituted deliberate impersonation of a police officer. 'This gentleman is holding a watching brief while I talk to people.'

'I see,' said Mr Hayes. But it was obvious he didn't.

'I'm nearly finished.' She smiled brightly. 'I found the Clarkes, by the way. Had a chat with them a week or so ago. Poor Mrs Clarke is completely senile now.'

The watery eyes looked amused. 'That doesn't surprise me. She was pretty far gone when I knew her. I sometimes thought my Jeannie was the only sensible woman in the road.'

'I gather Mr Clarke had to stay at home to look after her?' She raised her eyebrows in enquiry. 'But he spent more time with Robert than he spent with her. How friendly were they, Mr Hayes? Do you know?'

It was obvious he understood the point of her question. He chose – out of delicacy? – not to answer it. 'Good friends,' he muttered, 'and who can blame them? Bob's wife was a dipso and Ted's was the silliest creature I've ever met. Cleaned the house from top to bottom every day.' He gave a grunt of contempt. 'Hygiene mad, she was. Used to walk around in nothing but an overall, no undies in case she spread germs, swabbing everything with disinfectant.' He chuckled suddenly. 'Remember once she scrubbed the dining table with neat Domestos to sterilize it. Hah! Ted was hopping mad. He'd just paid for the thing to be french polished after Dorothy's last effort with boiling water. And now she's completely senile, you say. Not surprised. Not surprised at all.'

Roz sat with her pencil poised above her notepad. 'And can you say,' she asked after a moment, 'if Ted and Bob were lovers?'

'No. It weren't none of my business.'

'OK.' She gathered her things together. 'Thank you, Mr Hayes. I don't know if there's anything Mr Hawksley wants to ask you.' She looked at Hal.

He stood up. 'Only the name of your son's security firm, Mr Hayes.'

The old man eyed him suspiciously. 'What you want that for?'

'Just so I can put a quiet word in the right ear about the leak of privileged information.' He smiled coldly. 'Otherwise I shall have to report it and then there'll be an official complaint.' He shrugged. 'Don't worry. You have my word I won't make an issue out of it, not unless I have to.'

'The word of a policeman, eh? That's not something I'd want to rely on. Certainly not.'

Hal buttoned his jacket. 'It'll have to go through official channels then, and it'll be an inspector coming to see you next time.'

'What shall I say? Blooming blackmail, that's all this is. STC Security, Bell Street, Southampton. There now. Let's see if your word's worth something.'

Hal looked past him towards the photograph of his son. 'Thank you, Mr Hayes,' he said pleasantly. 'You've been very helpful.'

Eighteen

ROZ WALKED BACK to the car deep in thought. 'What's up?' Hal asked her.

'Just something he said.' She put her bag on the roof and stared into the middle distance, trying to pick up an elusive thread. 'It's no good. I'll have to go back through my notes.' She unlocked the door. 'So what do we do now? Go to the police?' She released Hal's door and he climbed in beside her.

'No. We'd be there all day answering questions and there's no guarantee they'd act at the end of it.' He thought for a moment. 'And it's no good tackling Crew either. If we're going to nail him we'll have to do it through Stewart Hayes and his security firm.'

Roz winced. 'We? Listen, Hawksley, I've already had my hair pulled out once by that gorilla. I'm not sure I fancy it a second time.' She meant it, too.

Hal put his hand on her shoulder and gave it a reassuring squeeze. 'If it's any consolation, I don't think I fancy it much either.' He could smell the scent of soap on her face and with a sigh he moved away. 'But we've got to get it settled one way or another,' he said coolly. 'I can't stand much more of this.'

Her insecurities resurfaced. 'Much more of what?'

'Sitting around in confined spaces with you,' he growled. 'It requires too much blasted self-control. Come on. Let's grasp the nettle. I'll phone Geoff Wyatt and see if I can persuade him to hold my hand while I offer the Poacher for sale.'

'Wouldn't it be easier just to have Hayes arrested?'

'What for?'

'Breaking and entering.'

'On what evidence?'

'Me,' she said. 'I can identify him.'

'He'll have an alibi by now.' He flicked a strand of hair from her cheek with a gesture of casual affection. 'We need to tempt Crew into the open.'

It was Roz's turn to sigh. In the cold light of morning, she was having doubts. 'It's all guesswork, Hal. Crew could be squeaky clean as far as the Poacher's concerned. Mr Hayes likes to give the impression he knows more than he does. It makes him feel important.'

'But it's the only scenario that makes sense.' He stroked his jaw and smiled at her with a confidence he didn't really feel. 'My nose is twitching. It's always a good sign.'

'Of what?'

'That I'm on the right track.'

'You'll lose the Poacher if you're wrong.'

'I'll lose it anyway.' He drummed his fingers on the dashboard. 'Come on,' he said abruptly. 'Let's go. Head for the city centre. Bell Street runs parallel with the main shopping area. We'll stop at the first telephone we see. And keep your eyes peeled for an electrical goods shop.'

She fired the engine and pulled out into the road. 'Why?'

'You'll find out.'

He dialled Dawlington police station and asked to be put through to Geoff Wyatt. 'It's Hal.' He let the angry recriminations run for a moment, then broke in. 'Save your breath. I'm trying to sort it now, but I need your help. What do you have on STC Security in Bell Street? No, I'll wait.' He propped the receiver under his chin and took out a notepad. 'OK. Hayes. Ex-Army. Clean as a whistle. You're sure? Right. Can you meet me there in half an hour?' More squeaks. 'For old time's sake, that's why. No, you bastard, I don't give a monkey's toss if you still feel sick. At the very least, you owe me for Sally. Half an hour.' He hung up.

Roz examined her fingernails with studied uninterest. 'Who's Sally?' she asked.

'My ex.'

'Why does he owe you for her?'

'He married her.'

'God!' She hadn't expected that.

He smiled at her startled expression. 'He did me a favour but doesn't know it. He thinks it's why I left the Force. His guilt is huge and extremely useful at times like this.'

'That's cruel.'

He lifted an eyebrow. 'It hurt at the time.'

'Sorry,' she said regretfully. 'I keep forgetting we both have pasts.'

He pulled her against him. 'The marriage was long dead, and Geoff didn't set out to poach Sally. He's a decent sort. He held her hand out of friendship, and ended up with more than he bargained for. And that's genuine gratitude talking, Roz, not bitterness.' He kissed her nose. 'Poor bastard. He had no idea what he was signing on for.'

'Olive's revenge,' she said slowly.

He frowned as he dialled Directory Enquiries. 'I don't follow.'

Roz gave a hollow laugh. 'She makes clay figures in her room and then sticks pins into them. She did one of me when she was angry with me. I had a migraine for a week.'

'When was that? Yes,' he said into the phone, 'STC Security, Southampton, please.'

'A couple of weeks ago.'

'Someone beat you up a couple of weeks ago,' he

pointed out. 'That's why you had a migraine.' He wrote a number on his pad and hung up.

'My ex-husband,' she agreed. 'I told Olive I wanted to kill him and he turned up out of the blue. I could have killed him, too, if I'd had a knife, or been better prepared. I was angry enough.' She shrugged. 'And then there's you and Crew and the Poacher, and Wyatt taking your wife, and her father dying. All people she blames for what's happened to her.'

He looked surprised. 'You don't really believe that, do you?'

She laughed. 'No, of course I don't.' But she did. Only she knew how much her head had hurt when Olive turned the pin.

'STC Security,' said a woman's bright voice at the other end of the wire.

Hal looked at Roz as he spoke. 'Good morning. I'd like to discuss security arrangements for my restaurant with Mr Stewart Hayes.'

'I'm not sure he's available to talk at the moment, sir.'

'He will be for me. Try his number and tell him that Hal Hawksley of the Poacher is on the line.'

'One moment, please.'

Several moments passed before she came back to him. 'Mr Hayes will talk to you now, Mr Hawksley.'

A bluff, friendly voice swelled down the wire. 'Good morning, Mr Hawksley. How may I help you?'

'You can't, Mr Hayes, but I can help you. You have a window of opportunity which will stay open for the length of time it takes me to reach your office. Roughly half an hour.'

'I don't understand.'

'I'm prepared to sell the Poacher, but at my price, and today. That's the only offer you'll ever get.'

There was a short silence. 'I'm not in the market for buying restaurants, Mr Hawksley.'

'But Mr Crew is, so I suggest you consult with him before you allow the window to close.'

There was another silence. 'I don't know any Mr Crew.'

Hal ignored this. 'Tell him the Olive Martin case is about to blow wide open.' He gave Roz a broad wink. 'She is already taking legal advice from another solicitor and is expected to lodge an appeal against the terms of her father's will within seven days on the grounds that she is innocent. Crew buys the Poacher today, at my price, or he doesn't buy it at all. You have half an hour, Mr Hayes.' He hung up.

Geoff was waiting on the pavement when they arrived. 'You didn't mention you were bringing company,' he said suspiciously, bending down to look through the open passenger window.

Hal introduced them. 'Sergeant Wyatt, Miss Rosalind Leigh.'

'Jesus, Hal,' he said in disgust. 'What on earth do you want to bring her for?'

'I fancy her.'

Geoff shook his head in exasperation. 'You're mad.'

Hal opened the door and got out. 'I trust you're referring to my motives in bringing her here. If I thought you were impugning my choice, I'd bop you on the nose.' He looked across the roof at Roz who had got out on the other side and was locking her door. 'I think you should stay in the car.'

'Why?'

'You might get your hair pulled.'

'So might you.'

'It's my battle.'

'And mine, if I'm really thinking of making this relationship permanent. Anyway, you need me. I'm the one with the Tampax.'

'They won't work.'

Roz chuckled at the expression on Geoff's face. 'They will. Trust me.'

Hal tipped a finger at Wyatt. 'Now you know why I brought her.'

'You're both bloody mad.' Geoff dropped his cigarette butt on to the pavement and ground it out beneath his heel. 'So what do you want me for? By rights I should be arresting you.' He eyed Roz curiously. 'I suppose he's told you everything.'

'I shouldn't think so,' she said cheerfully, walking round the back of the car. 'I only learnt half an hour ago that his ex-wife's name was Sally and you married her. So, on that basis, there must be an awful lot more still to come.'

'I was referring,' he said sourly, 'to the numerous prosecutions he's about to face when this little farce is over and I take him down the nick.'

'Oh, them.' She gave a dismissive wave. 'Bits of paper, that's all they are.'

Geoff, not altogether happy with his new marital arrangements, watched her amused exchange of glances with Hal and wondered why other people, infinitely less deserving than he, had all the luck. He listened to Hal's instructions for him with a hand pressed to his queasy stomach.

Roz had expected something seedy and run-down like the Wells-Fargo office: instead they walked into a clean, brightly painted reception with an efficient-looking receptionist behind an efficient-looking desk. Someone, she thought, had spent a great deal of money on STC Security. But who? And where had it come from?

Hal favoured the receptionist with his most charming smile. 'Hal Hawksley. Mr Hayes is expecting me.'

'Oh, yes.' She smiled in return. 'He said to show you straight in.' She leaned forward and pointed down the corridor. 'Third door on the left. Perhaps your friends would like to take a seat out here?' She indicated some chairs in the corner.

'Thank you, miss,' said Geoff. 'Don't mind if I do.' He hefted one as he passed and took it with him down the corridor.

'No,' she called, 'I didn't mean take one away.'

He beamed back at her as Hal and Roz disappeared through the third door without knocking and he stationed himself on the chair in the middle of the closed doorway. 'Very comfortable, I must say.' He lit a cigarette and watched, with some amusement, as she picked up the phone and put through a flustered call.

On the other side of the door, Stewart Hayes replaced the receiver. 'I gather from Lisa that you have a minder, Mr Hawksley. Would he be a policeman by any chance?'

'He would.'

'Ah.' He clasped his hands on his desk, apparently unconcerned. 'Sit down, please.' He smiled at Roz and gestured towards a chair.

Fascinated by him, she took it. This was not the man who had tried to strangle her. He was younger, better looking, bluff and friendly like his voice. The brother, she thought, recalling the photographs on the sideboard. He had his father's smile, with all its sincerity, his father's old-world charm, and under different circumstances she would have found him easy to like. Only his eyes, pale and carefully guarded, implied he had something to hide. Hal remained standing.

The smile embraced them both. 'OK, now perhaps you'd like to explain what you said over the telephone. I'll be honest with you' – his tone suggested he was about to be the exact opposite – 'I don't understand why I've been given half an hour to buy a restaurant *from* someone I've never met *for* someone I've never heard of, and all because a self-confessed murderess wants to contest her father's will.'

Hal glanced about the well-appointed office. 'Expensive,' he said. 'You and your brother are doing well.' He fastened speculative eyes on Hayes. 'Your father thinks you're on the breadline.'

Hayes gave a slight frown but didn't say anything.

'So how much does Crew pay for the baseball-bat treatment? It's risky so it won't come cheap.'

The pale eyes showed faint amusement. 'You've lost me, I'm afraid.'

'Your brother was very easy to identify, Hayes. Photographs of him litter your father's sideboard. But then Crew obviously never warned you about the loose cannon on board. Or perhaps you should have warned him. Does he know your father lived next door to Olive Martin?' He saw the other's incomprehension and nodded to Roz. 'This lady is writing a book about her. Crew was Olive's solicitor, I was her arresting officer, and your father was her neighbour.

Miss Leigh has visited us all and she recognized your brother from his snapshot. It is a much smaller world than you ever imagined.'

There was a tiny shift in the pale eyes, a flicker of annoyance. 'Mistaken identity. You'll never prove anything. It's your word against his and he was in Sheffield all last week.'

Hal shrugged well-feigned indifference. 'The window is closing. I came with a genuine offer.' He placed his hands on the desk and leaned forward aggressively. 'I think it runs something like this. Crew has been using Robert Martin's money to buy up bankrupt businesses cheap while he waits for the market to recover, but time's running out on him. Amber's child is not as dead and buried as he thought, and Olive is about to become a *cause célèbre* when Miss Leigh proves her innocent. Either she or her nephew, whoever gets in first, will demand a reckoning of Robert Martin's executor, namely Crew. But the recession has dragged on rather longer than he thought it would and he's in danger of being caught with his hands in the till. He needs to shift some property to make up the shortfall in his books.' He raised an eyebrow. 'What plans are there for the corner of Wenceslas Street, I wonder? A supermarket? Flats? Offices? He needs the Poacher to clinch the deal. I'm offering it to him. Today.'

Hayes wasn't so easily intimidated. 'The way I hear it, Hawksley, your restaurant is about to close anyway.

When it does, it will become a liability to you. At which point it will not be you who dictates terms, but whoever is willing to take it off your hands.'

Hal grinned and backed off. 'I'd say that rather depends on who goes down the chute first. Crew faces total extinction if his misappropriation of the Martin money comes to light before my bank decides to foreclose on the Poacher. Crew's taking a hell of a risk if he's backing me to lose.' He nodded to the telephone. 'He can save himself by clinching a deal on the Poacher today. Talk to him.'

Hayes pondered for a moment, then transferred his gaze to Roz. 'I presume you have a tape-recorder in your handbag, Miss Leigh. Would you oblige me by letting me have a look?'

Roz glanced up at Hal, and he nodded. She placed the bag with a bad grace on the desk in front of her.

'Thank you,' said Hayes politely. He opened it and removed the tape-recorder, making a cursory examination of the remaining contents of the handbag before snapping the recorder open and removing the cassette. He pulled the tape from between the rollers and cut it into pieces with a pair of scissors, then he stood up. 'You first, Hawksley. Let's just make sure there are no other little surprises.' He ran expert hands over Hal, then did the same with Roz. 'Good.' He gestured towards the door. 'Tell your minder to move his chair back to Reception and wait there.'

He resumed his seat and waited while Hal relayed

the message. After three minutes he used the telephone to establish that Wyatt was out of earshot.

'Now,' he said thoughtfully, 'there seem to be various courses open to me. One is to take you up on your offer.' He picked up a ruler and flexed it between his hands. 'I'm not inclined to do that. You could have put the Poacher on the market at any time in the last six weeks but you didn't, and this sudden urge of yours to sell makes me nervous.' He paused for a moment. 'Two, I can leave things to follow their natural course. The law is a joke and a slow joke at that, and there's only a fifty-fifty chance that Peter Crew's manipulations of Robert Martin's estate will surface before you sink.' He bent the ruler as far as it would go without breaking, then released it abruptly. 'I'm not inclined to do that either. Fifty-fifty is too close to call.' The pale eyes hardened. 'Three, and in many ways this is the most attractive, I can wish an unfortunate accident on the pair of you, thereby killing two birds with one stone.' He flicked a glance at Roz. 'Your death, Miss Leigh, would put Olive and this book you're writing, temporarily at least, on a back burner, and yours, Hawksley, would ensure the Poacher coming on the market. A neat solution, don't you think?'

'Very neat,' agreed Hal. 'But you're not going to do that either. There's still the child in Australia, after all.'

Hayes gave a faint laugh. An echo of his father.

'So what are you going to do?'

'Give you what you came for.'

Hal frowned. 'Which is?'

'Proof that you were framed.' He pulled open a drawer in his desk and removed a transparent polythene folder. Holding it by its top corners he shook the contents – a page of headed notepaper, showing creases where it had once been crumpled – on to his desk. The printed address was a house in one of the more expensive parts of Southampton and written across the page in Crew's handwriting were a series of short notes:

Re: Poacher	Cost £s
Pre-culture bad meat, rat excrement etc	1,000
Key b/door + guaranteed exit/France	1,000
Advance for set-up	5,000
If E H prosecution successful	5,000
Poacher foreclosure	80,000?
SUB-TOTAL	92,000
Site offer	750,000
Less Poacher	92,000
Less 1 Wenceslas St	60,000
Less Newby's	73,000
TOTAL	525,000

'It's genuine,' said Hayes, seeing Hal's scepticism. 'Crew's home address, Crew's handwriting' – he tapped the side of the note with his ruler – 'and his fingerprints. It's enough to get you off the hook but whether it's enough to convict Crew I don't know. That's your problem, not mine.'

'Where did you get it?'

But Hayes merely smiled and shook his head. 'I'm an ex-soldier. I like fall-back positions. Let's just say it came into my possession and, realizing its importance, I passed it on to you.'

Hal wondered if Crew knew the sort of man he had hired. Had this been intended for later blackmail? 'I don't get it,' he said frankly. 'Crew is bound to implicate you. So will I. So will Miss Leigh. One way or another you and your brother will get done. Why make it easy for us?'

Hayes didn't answer directly. 'I'm cutting my losses, Hawksley, and giving you your restaurant back. Be grateful.'

'Like hell, I'll be grateful,' said Hal angrily. His eyes narrowed suspiciously. 'Who's behind this foreclosure racket? You or Crew?'

'There's no racket. Foreclosures are a fact of life at the moment,' said the other. 'Anyone with a little capital can acquire property cheaply. Mr Crew was part of a small perfectly legal syndicate. Unfortunately, he used money that didn't belong to him.'

'So you run the syndicate?'

Hayes didn't answer.

'No racket, my arse,' said Hal explosively. 'The Poacher was never going to come on the market yet you still bought up the properties on either side.'

Hayes flexed the ruler again. 'You'd have sold eventually. Restaurants are appallingly vulnerable.' He gave a slight smile. 'Consider what would have happened if Crew had kept his nerve and sat it out till after your prosecution.' His eyes hardened. 'Consider what would have happened if my brother had told me about the approach Crew made to him. You and I would never have had this conversation for the simple reason that you would not have known who to have it with.'

The flesh crept on Hal's neck. 'The hygiene scam was going to happen anyway?'

The ruler, bent beyond endurance, snapped abruptly. Hayes smiled. 'Restaurants are appallingly vulnerable,' he said again. 'I repeat. Be grateful. If you are, the Poacher will flourish.'

'Which is another way of saying we must keep our mouths shut about your involvement.'

'Of course.' He looked almost surprised, as if the question went without asking. 'Because next time, the fire won't be confined to a chip pan, and you' – his pale eyes rested on Roz – 'and your lady friend won't be so lucky. My brother's pride was hurt. He's itching to have another go at the pair of you.' He pointed to the piece of notepaper. 'You can do what you like with Crew. I don't admire men without principle. He's a lawyer. He had a duty to a dead man's estate and he abused it.'

Hal, rather shaken, picked up the page by its corner and tucked it into Roz's handbag. 'You're no better, Hayes. You abused Crew's confidence when you told your father about Amber's child. But for that we'd never have put Crew in the frame.' He waited while Roz stood up and walked to the door. 'And I'll make damn sure he knows that when the police arrest him.'

Hayes was amused. 'Crew won't talk.'

'What's to stop him?'

He drew the broken ruler across his throat. 'The same thing that will stop you, Hawksley. Fear.' The pale eyes raked Roz from head to toe. 'But in Crew's case, it's his grandchildren he loves.'

Geoff followed them out on to the pavement. 'OK,' he ordered, 'give. What the hell's going on here?'

Hal looked at Roz's pale face. 'We need a drink.'

'Oh, no, you don't,' said Geoff aggressively. 'I've paid my dues, Hal, now you pay yours.'

Hal gripped him fiercely above the elbow, digging his fingers into the soft flesh. 'Keep your voice down, you cretin,' he muttered. 'There's a man in there who would take out your liver, eat it in front of you, and then start on your kidneys. And he'd smile while he was doing it. Where's the nearest pub?'

Not until they were settled in a tight corner of the

saloon, with empty tables all around them, was Hal prepared to speak. He delivered the story in clipped, staccato sentences, emphasizing Crew's role but referring to the intruders at the Poacher only as hired thugs. He finished by removing the note from Roz's handbag and laying it carefully on the table between them. 'I want this bastard screwed, Geoff. Don't even think about letting him worm his way out of it.'

Wyatt was sceptical. 'It's not much, is it?'

'It'll do.'

Wyatt slipped the page into his notebook and tucked it into his jacket pocket. 'So where does STC Security fit in?'

'It doesn't. Hayes got hold of that note for me. That's the extent of his firm's involvement.'

'Ten minutes ago he was going to eat my liver.'

'I was thirsty.'

Wyatt shrugged. 'You're giving me precious little to work with. I can't even guarantee you'll win the Environmental Health prosecution. Crew's bound to deny having anything to do with it.'

There was a silence.

'He's right,' said Roz abruptly, removing a packet of Tampax from her bag.

Hal grasped the hand holding the box and pressed it firmly to the table. 'No, Roz,' he said softly. 'Believe it or not, I care more about you than I do about the Poacher or about abstract justice.'

She nodded. 'I know, Hawksley,' Her eyes smiled

into his. 'The trouble is, I care about *you*, too. Which means we're in a bit of a fix. You want to save me and I want to save the Poacher, and the two would seem to be mutually exclusive.' She started to ease her hands from under his. 'So one of us must win this argument, and it's going to be me because this has nothing to do with abstract justice and everything to do with my peace of mind. I shall feel much happier with Stewart Hayes behind bars.' She shook her head as his hands moved to smother hers again. 'I won't be responsible for you losing your restaurant, Hal. You've gone through hell for it, and you can't give it up now.'

But Hal was no Rupert to be browbeaten or cajoled into doing what Roz wanted. 'No,' he said again. 'We're not playing intellectual games here. What Hayes said was *real.* And he's not threatening to kill you, Roz. He's threatening to maim you.' He lifted one hand to her face. 'Men like him don't kill because they don't need to. They cripple or they disfigure, because a live, broken victim is a more potent encouragement to others than a dead one.'

'But if he's convicted—' she began.

'You're being naïve again,' he cut in gently, smoothing the hair from her face. 'Even if he is convicted, which I doubt – ex-Army, first offence, hearsay evidence, Crew denying everything – he won't go to jail for any length of time. The worst that will happen will be twelve months for conspiracy to defraud, of which he'll serve six. More likely he will be given a suspended sentence. It wasn't Stewart who broke into the Poacher with a baseball bat, remember, it was his brother, and you will have to stand up in court and say that.' His eyes were insistent. 'I'm a realist, Roz. We'll go for Crew and raise enough doubts to get the Health charges lifted. After that' – he shrugged – 'I'll gamble that Hayes can be trusted to leave the Poacher alone.'

She was silent for a moment or two. 'Would you act differently if you'd never met me and I wasn't involved? And don't lie to me, Hal, please.'

He nodded. 'Yes,' he admitted. 'I would act differently. But you *are* involved, so the question doesn't arise.'

'OK.' She relaxed her hands under his and smiled. 'Thank you. I feel much happier now.'

'You agree.' Relieved, he lessened his pressure slightly and she seized the opportunity to snatch the Tampax box out of his grasp.

'No,' she said,'I don't.' She opened the box, removed some truncated cardboard tubes and upended it to disgorge a miniature voice-activated dictaphone. 'With luck' – she turned to Geoff Wyatt – 'this will have enough on it to convict Hayes. It was at full volume, sitting on his desk, so it should have caught him.'

She rewound the tape for a second or two and then pressed 'play'. Hal's voice was muffled by distance: '. . . *another way of saying we must keep our mouths shut about your involvement with the Poacher?*'

Hayes's, clear as a bell. '*Of course. Because next time, the fire won't be confined to the chip pan, and you and your lady friend won't be so lucky. My brother's pride was hurt. He's itching to have another go at the pair of you.*'

Roz switched it off and pushed it across the table towards Wyatt. 'Will it do any good?'

'If there's more like that, it will certainly help with Hal's prosecution, as long as you're prepared to give evidence to support it.'

'I am.'

He cast a glance at his friend, saw the tension on the other's face and turned back to Roz. 'But Hal's right in everything he's said, assuming I've understood the gist correctly. We *are* talking abstract justice here.' He picked up the dictaphone. 'At the end of the day – whatever sentence this man gets – if he still wants to revenge himself on you, he will. And there's nothing the police will be able to do to protect you. So? Are you sure you want me to take this?'

'I'm sure.'

Wyatt looked at Hal again and gave a helpless shrug. 'Sorry, old man. I did my best, but it looks like you've caught a tigress this time.'

Hal gave his baritone chuckle. 'Don't say it, Geoff, because I already know.'

But Wyatt said it anyway. 'You lucky, bloody sod.'

*

Olive sat hunched over her table, working on a new sculpture. Eve and her faces and her baby had collapsed under the weight of a fist, leaving the pencil pointing heavenward like an accusing finger. The Chaplain regarded the new piece thoughtfully. A bulky shape, roughly human and lying on its back, seemed to be struggling from its clay base. Strange, he thought, how Olive, with so little skill, made these figures work. 'What are you sculpting now?'

'MAN.'

He could, he thought, have predicted that. He watched the fingers roll a thick sausage of clay and plant it upright on the base at the figure's head. 'Adam?' he suggested. He had the feeling she was playing a game with him. There had been a surge of sudden activity when he entered her room, as if she had been waiting for him to break hours of stillness.

'Cain.' She selected another pencil and laid it across the top of the clay sausage, parallel with the recumbent man, pressing it down till it was held firmly. 'Faustus. Don Giovanni. Does it matter?'

'Yes, it does,' he said sharply. 'Not all men sell their souls to the devil, any more than all women are two-faced.'

Olive smiled to herself and cut a piece of string from a ball on the table. She made a loop in one end and fastened the other round the tip of the pencil so that the string hung down over the figure's head.

With infinite care, she tightened the loop about a matchstick. 'Well?' she demanded.

The Chaplain frowned. 'I don't know. The gallows?'

She set the matchstick swinging. 'Or the sword of Damocles. It amounts to the same thing when Lucifer owns your soul.'

He perched on the edge of the table and offered her a cigarette. 'It's not Man in general, is it?' he said, flicking his lighter. 'It's someone specific. Am I right?'

'Maybe.'

'Who?'

She fished a letter from her pocket and handed it to him. He spread the single page on the table and read it. It was a standard letter, personalized on a word processor, and very brief.

> Dear Miss Martin,
>
> Please be advised that unforeseen circumstances have obliged Mr Peter Crew to take extended leave from this practice. During his absence his clients' affairs will be covered by his partners. Please be assured of our continued assistance.
>
> Yours etc.

The Chaplain looked up. 'I don't understand.'

Olive inhaled deeply then blew a stream of smoke towards the matchstick. It spiralled wildly before slipping from the noose and striking the clay forehead. 'My solicitor's been arrested.'

Startled, he looked at the clay figure. He didn't bother to ask if she was sure. He knew the efficiency of the cell telegraph as well as she did. 'What for?'

'Wickedness.' She stubbed her cigarette into the clay. 'MAN was born to it. Even you, Chaplain.' She peeped at him to watch his reaction.

He chuckled. 'You're probably right. But I do my best to fight it, you know.'

She took another of his cigarettes. 'I shall miss you,' she said unexpectedly.

'When?'

'When they let me out.'

He looked at her with a puzzled smile. 'That's a long way off. We've years yet.'

But she shook her head and mashed the clay into a ball with the dog end in the middle. 'You never asked me who Eve was.'

The game again, he thought. 'I didn't need to, Olive. I knew.'

She smiled scornfully to herself. 'Yes, you would.' She examined him out of the corner of her eye. 'Did you work it out for yourself?' she asked. 'Or did God tell you? Look, my son, Olive strikes her reflection in the clay. Now help her to come to terms with her own duplicity. Well, don't worry, either way I shall remember what you did for me when I get out.'

What did she want from him? Encouragement that

she *would* get out, or rescuing from her lies? He sighed inwardly. Really, it would all be so much easier if he liked her, but he didn't. And *that* was his wickedness.

Nineteen

OLIVE REGARDED ROZ with deep suspicion. Contentment had brought a glow to the other woman's usually pale cheeks. 'You look different,' she said in an accusing tone as if what she saw displeased her.

Roz shook her head. 'No. Everything's the same.' Lies *were* safer sometimes. She was afraid Olive would regard her moving in with the police officer who arrested her as a betrayal. 'Did you get my message last Monday night?'

Olive was at her most unattractive, unwashed hair hanging limply about her colourless face, a smear of tomato ketchup ground into the front of her shift, the smell of her sweat almost unbearable in the small room. She vibrated with irritation, her forehead set in a permanent scowl, ready, it seemed to Roz, to reject anything that was said to her. She didn't answer.

'Is something wrong?' Roz asked evenly.

'I don't want to see you any more.'

Roz turned her pencil in her fingers. 'Why not?'

'I don't have to give a reason.'

'It would be polite,' said Roz in the same even tone. 'I've invested a great deal of time, energy, and affection in you. I thought we were friends.'

Olive's lip curled. 'Friends,' she hissed scathingly. 'We're not friends. You're Miss Wonderful making money out of doing her Lady Muck bit and I'm the poor sap who's being exploited.' She splayed her hands across the table top and tried to get up. 'I don't want you to write your book.'

'Because you'd rather be treated with awe in here than laughed at outside.' Roz shook her head. 'You're a fool, Olive. And a coward as well. I thought you had more guts.'

Olive pursed her fat lips as she struggled to rise. 'I'm not listening,' she said childishly. 'You're trying to make me change my mind.'

'Of course I am.' She rested her cheek against one raised hand. 'I shall write the book whether you want me to or not. I'm not afraid of you, you see. You can instruct a solicitor to take out an injunction to stop me, but he won't succeed because I shall argue that you're innocent, and a court will uphold my right to publish in the interests of natural justice.'

Olive slumped back on to her chair. 'I'll write to a Civil Liberties group. They'll support me.'

'Not when they find out I'm trying to get you released, they won't. They'll support *me*.'

'The Court of Human Rights, then. I'll say what you're doing is an invasion of my privacy.'

'Go ahead. You'll make me a fortune. Everyone will buy the book to find out what the fuss is all about. And if it's argued in a court, whichever one it is, I shall make damn sure this time that the evidence is heard.'

'What evidence?'

'The evidence that proves you didn't do it.'

Olive slammed a meaty fist on to the table. 'I did do it.'

'No, you didn't.'

'I *did*!' roared the fat woman.

'You did not,' said Roz, her eyes flashing with anger. 'When will you face up to the fact that your mother is dead, you silly woman.' She banged the table in her turn. 'She's not there for you any more, Olive, and she never will be, however long you hide in here.'

Two fat tears rolled down Olive's cheeks. 'I don't like you.'

Roz continued brutally. 'You came home, saw what your precious lover had done, and went into shock. And God knows, I don't blame you.' She took the mortuary photographs of Gwen and Amber from her bag and slapped them on the table in front of Olive. 'You adored your mother, didn't you? You always adore the people who need you.'

Olive's anger was enormous. 'That's *crap*, bloody fucking *crap*!'

Roz shook her head. 'I needed you. That's how I know.'

Olive's lip trembled. 'You wanted to know how it felt to kill someone, that's all you needed me for.'

'No.' Roz reached across and took a large, soft hand in hers. 'I needed someone to love. You're very easy to love, Olive.'

The woman tore the hand away and clamped it across her face. 'No one loves me,' she whispered. 'No one's ever loved me.'

'You're wrong,' said Roz firmly. 'I love you. Sister Bridget loves you. And we are not going to abandon you the minute you get out. You must trust us.' She closed her mind on the insidious voice that murmured warnings against a long-term commitment she could never keep and against well-meant lies that could so easily rebound on her. 'Tell me about Amber,' she went on gently. 'Tell me why your mother needed you.'

A sigh of surrender shuddered through the huge frame. 'She wanted her own way all the time, and if she didn't get it she made life hell for everyone. She told lies about things people did to her, spread awful stories, even hurt people sometimes. She poured boiling water down my mother's arm once to punish her, so we used to give in just to make life easy. She was as nice as pie as long as everyone did what she wanted.' She licked the tears from her lips. 'She never took responsibility, you see, but it got worse after the baby was born. Mum said she stopped maturing.'

'To compensate herself?'

'No, to excuse herself.' She twined her fingers in the front of her dress. 'Children get away with behaving badly so Amber went on behaving like a child. She was never told off for getting pregnant. We were too afraid of how she would react.' She wiped her nose with the back of her hand. 'Mum had made up her mind to take her to a psychiatrist. She thought Amber had schizophrenia.' She sighed heavily. 'Then they were killed and it didn't matter any more.'

Roz passed her a Kleenex and waited while she blew her nose. 'Why did she never behave badly at school?'

'She did,' said Olive flatly, 'if people teased her or took her things without asking. I used to have to get quite angry to stop them doing it, but most of the time I made sure no one got on her bad side. She was a lovely person as long as she wasn't crossed. Really,' she insisted, 'a lovely person.'

'The two faces of Eve.'

'Mum certainly thought so.' She took the cigarette packet out of Roz's open briefcase and stripped away the cellophane. 'I used to keep her with me when she wasn't in class. She didn't mind that. The older girls treated her like a pet and that made her feel special.

She had no friends of her own age.' She pulled some cigarettes on to the table and selected one.

'How did she hold down a job? You weren't there to protect her then.'

'She didn't. She never lasted anywhere longer than a month. Most of the time she stayed at home with Mum. She made Mum's life a misery.'

'What about Glitzy?'

Olive struck a match and lit the cigarette. 'The same. She'd only done three weeks and she was already talking about leaving. There was some trouble with the other girls. Amber got one of them sacked or something. I can't remember now. Anyway, that's when Mum said enough was enough, and she'd have to see a psychiatrist.'

Roz sat in thoughtful silence for some moments. 'I know who your lover was,' she said abruptly. 'I know that you spent Sundays at the Belvedere in Farraday Street and that you signed in as Mr and Mrs Lewis. I've had his photograph identified by the owner of the Belvedere and by the receptionist at Wells-Fargo. I think he abandoned you in a hotel the night of your birthday when you told him you had aborted his baby, and that he went straight to Leven Road to have it out with Amber and your mother whom he regarded as jointly responsible for the murder of the son or daughter he had always wanted. I think your father was out of the house that night and that the whole thing got out of hand. I think you came home a long time afterwards, discovered the bodies, and went to pieces because you thought it was all your fault.' She took one of Olive's hands in hers again and squeezed it tightly.

Olive closed her eyes and wept quietly, her soft skin caressing Roz's fingers. 'No,' she said at last, releasing the hand. 'It didn't happen like that. I wish it had. At least I'd know then why I did what I did.' Her eyes were curiously unfocused as if they were turned inwards upon herself. 'We didn't plan anything for my birthday,' she said. 'We couldn't. It wasn't a Sunday and Sundays were the only days we could ever be together. That was when his sister-in-law came over to give him some time away from his wife. They both thought he spent the day at the British Legion.' She smiled but there was no humour in it. 'Poor Edward. He was so afraid they'd find out and turn him off without a penny. It was her house and her money and it made him miserable. Puddleglum was such a good name for him, especially when he wore his silly wig. He looked just like a marshwiggle out of Narnia, tall and skinny and hairy.' She sighed. 'It was supposed to be a disguise, you know, in case anyone saw him. To me, it just looked funny. I liked him much better bald.' She sighed again. '*The Silver Chair* was Amber's and my favourite book when we were children.'

Roz had guessed. 'And you signed in as Mr and Mrs Lewis because it was C. S. Lewis who wrote it.

Were you afraid of Mrs Clarke finding out, or your parents?'

'We were afraid of everyone but mostly of Amber. Jealousy was a disease with her.'

'Did she know about your abortion?'

Olive shook her head. 'Only my mother knew. I never told Edward and I certainly didn't tell Amber. *She* was the only one who was allowed to have sex in our house. She did, too. All the time. Mum had to force her to take the pill every night so she didn't get pregnant again.' She pulled a long face. 'Mum was furious when I fell. We both knew Amber would go mad.'

'Is that why you had the abortion?'

'Probably. It seemed the only sensible solution at the time. I regret it now.'

'You'll have other chances.'

'I doubt it.'

'So what did happen that night?' asked Roz after a moment or two.

Olive stared at her unblinkingly through the smoke from her cigarette. 'Amber found the birthday present Edward had given me. It was well hidden but she used to pry into everything.' Her mouth twisted. 'I was always having to put things back that she'd taken. People thought I was the snooper.' She encircled her wrist with finger and thumb. 'It was an identity bracelet with a tiny silver-chair charm on it. He'd had the tag inscribed: u.r.n.a.r.n.i.a. Do you get it? You are

Narnia, Narnia being heaven.' She smiled self-consciously. 'I thought it was wonderful.'

'He was very fond of you.' It was a statement, not a question.

'I made him feel young again.' Tears squeezed from between the bald lids. 'We really didn't harm anyone, just conducted a quiet little affair now and then on Sundays which gave us both something to look forward to.' The tears flowed down her cheeks. 'I wish I hadn't done it now but it was nice to feel special. I never had before and I was so jealous of Amber. She had a lot of boyfriends. She used to take them upstairs. Mum was too frightened of her to say anything.' She sobbed loudly. 'They always laughed at me. I hate being laughed at.'

What a dreadful household it must have been, thought Roz, with each one desperately seeking love but never finding it. Would they have recognized it, anyway, if they had? She waited until Olive had composed herself a little. 'Did your mother know it was Edward?'

'No. I told her it was someone at work. We were very careful. Edward was my father's best friend. It would have devastated everyone if they'd known what we were doing.' She fell silent. 'Well, of course, it did devastate them in the end.'

'They found out.'

The sad head nodded. 'Amber guessed the minute she found the bracelet. I should have known she would. Silver chair, Narnia. The bracelet had to be from Puddleglum.' She sucked in a lungful of smoke.

Roz watched her for a moment. 'What did she do?' she asked when Olive didn't go on.

'What she always did when she was angry. Started a fight. She kept pulling my hair, I remember that. And screaming. Mum and Dad had to tear us apart. I ended up in a tug of war with my father gripping my wrists and tugging one way while Amber tugged my hair the other. All hell broke loose then. She kept yelling that I was having an affair with Mr Clarke.' She stared wretchedly at the table. 'My mother looked as if she was going to be sick – nobody likes the idea of old men getting excited about young girls – I used to see it in the eyes of the woman at the Belvedere.' She turned the cigarette in her fingers. 'But now, you know, I think it was because Mum knew that Edward and my father were doing it as well. That's what really made her sick. Makes *me* sick now.'

'Why didn't you deny it?'

Olive puffed unhappily on her cigarette. 'There was no point. She knew Amber was telling the truth. I suppose it's a kind of instinctive thing. You learn a fact and lots of other little bits and pieces, which didn't make sense at the time, suddenly slot into place. Anyway, all three of them started screeching at me then, my mother in shock, my father in fury.' She shrugged. 'I'd never seen Dad so angry. Mum let out about the abortion and he kept slapping my face and calling me a slut. And Amber kept screaming that he was jealous because he loved Edward, too, and it was so awful' – her eyes welled – 'that I left.' There was a rather comical expression on her face. 'And when I came back the next day there was blood everywhere and Mum and Amber were dead.'

'You stayed out all night?'

Olive nodded. 'And most of the morning.'

'But that's good,' said Roz leaning forward. 'We can prove that. Where did you go?'

'I walked to the beach.' She stared at her hands. 'I was going to kill myself. I wish I had now. I just sat there all night and thought about it instead.'

'Did anyone see you?'

'No. I didn't want to be seen. When it got light I hid behind a dinghy every time I heard someone coming.'

'What time did you get back?'

'About noon. I hadn't had anything to eat and I was hungry.'

'Did you speak to anyone?'

Olive sighed wearily. 'Nobody saw me. If they had I wouldn't be here.'

'How did you get into the house? Did you have a key?'

'Yes.'

'Why?' demanded Roz sharply. 'You said you left. I assumed you just walked out as you were.'

Olive's eyes widened. 'I knew you wouldn't believe

me,' she howled. 'No one believes me when I tell the truth.' She started to cry again.

'I do believe you,' said Roz firmly. 'I just want to get it straight.'

'I went to my room first and got my things. I only went out because they were all making so much noise.' She screwed her face in distress. 'My father was weeping. It was horrible.'

'OK. Go on. You're back at the house.'

'I let myself in and went down to the kitchen to get some food. I stepped in all the blood before I even knew it was there.' She looked at the photograph of her mother and the ready tears sprang into her eyes afresh. 'I really don't like to think about it too much. It makes me sick when I think about it.' Her lower lip wobbled violently.

'OK,' said Roz easily, 'let's concentrate on something else. What made you stay? Why didn't you run out into the road and call for help?'

Olive mopped at her eyes. 'I couldn't move,' she said simply. 'I wanted to, but I couldn't. I just stood there thinking how ashamed my mother would be when people saw her without her clothes on.' Her lip kept wobbling like some grotesque toddler's. 'I felt so ill. I wanted to sit down but there wasn't a chair.' She held her hand to her mouth and swallowed convulsively. 'And then Mrs Clarke started banging on the kitchen window. She kept screaming that God would never forgive my wickedness, and there was dribble coming out of her mouth.' A shudder ran through the big shoulders. 'I knew I had to shut her up because she was making it all so much worse. So I picked up the rolling pin and ran across to the back door.' She sighed. 'But I fell over and she wasn't there any more anyway.'

'Is that when you called the police?'

'No.' The wet face worked horribly. 'I can't remember it all now. I went mad for a bit because I had their blood all over me and I kept scraping my hands to clean them. But everything I touched was bloody.' Her eyes widened at the memory. 'I've always been so clumsy and the floor was slippery. I kept stumbling over them and disturbing them and then I had to touch them to put them back again and there was more blood on me.' The sorrowful eyes flooded again. 'And I thought, this is all my fault. If I'd never been born this would never have happened. I sat down for a long time because I felt sick.'

Roz looked at the bowed head in bewilderment. 'But why didn't you tell the police all this?'

She raised drowned blue eyes to Roz's. 'I was going to, but nobody would talk to me. They all thought I'd done it, you see. And all the time I was thinking how it was all going to come out, about Edward and me, and Edward and my father, and the abortion, and Amber, and her baby, and I thought how much less embarrassing it would be for everyone if I said I did it.'

Roz kept her voice deliberately steady. 'Who did you think had done it?'

Olive looked miserable. 'I didn't think about that for ages.' She hunched her shoulders as if defending herself. 'And then I knew my father had done it and they'd find me guilty whatever happened because he was the only one who could save me.' She plucked at her lips. 'And after that, it was quite a relief just to say what everyone wanted me to say. I didn't want to go home, you see, not with Mum dead, and Edward next door and everyone knowing. I couldn't possibly have gone home.'

'How did you know your father had done it?'

A whimper of pure pain, like a wounded animal's, crooned from Olive's mouth. 'Because Mr Crew was so beastly to me.' Sorrow poured in floods down her cheeks. 'He used to come to our house sometimes and he'd pat me on the shoulder and say: "How's Olive?" But in the police station' – she buried her face in her hands – 'he held a handkerchief to his mouth to stop himself being sick and stood on the other side of the room and said: "Don't say anything to me or the police, or I won't be able to help you." I knew then.'

Roz frowned. 'How? I don't understand.'

'Because Dad was the only person who knew I wasn't there, but he never said a word to Mr Crew before, or to the police afterwards. Dad must have done it or he'd have tried to save me. He let me go to prison because he was a coward.' She sobbed loudly. 'And then he died and left his money to Amber's child when he could have left a letter, saying I was innocent.' She beat her hands against her knees. 'What did it matter once he was dead?'

Roz took the cigarette from Olive's fingers and stood it on the table. 'Why didn't you tell the police you thought it was your father who had done it? Sergeant Hawksley would have listened to you. He already suspected your father.'

The fat woman stared at the table. 'I don't want to tell you.'

'You must, Olive.'

'You'll laugh.'

'Tell me.'

'I was hungry.'

Roz shook her head in perplexity. 'I don't understand.'

'The sergeant brought me a sandwich and said I could have a proper dinner when we'd finished the statement.' Her eyes welled again. 'I hadn't eaten all day and I was so hungry,' she wailed. 'It was quicker when I said what they wanted me to say and then I got my dinner.' She wrung her hands. 'People will laugh, won't they?'

Roz wondered why it had never occurred to her that Olive's insatiable craving for food might have been a contributory factor in her confession. Mrs Hopwood had described her as a compulsive eater and stress would have piled on the agonies of the wretched girl's hunger. 'No,' she said firmly, 'no one will laugh. But why did you insist on pleading guilty at your trial? You could have made a fight of it then. You'd had time to think and get over the shock.'

Olive wiped her eyes. 'It was too late. I'd confessed. I had nothing to fight with except diminished responsibility and I wasn't going to let Mr Crew call me a psychopath. I hate Mr Crew.'

'But if you'd told someone the truth they might have believed you. You've told me and I've believed you.'

Olive shook her head. 'I've told you nothing,' she said simply. 'Everything you know you've found out for yourself. That's why you believe it.' Her eyes flooded again. 'I did try at the beginning, when I first came to prison. I told the Chaplain but he doesn't like me and thought I was telling lies. I'd confessed, you see, and only the guilty confess. The psychiatrists were the most frightening. I thought if I denied the crime and didn't show any remorse, they'd say I was sociopathic and send me to Broadmoor.'

Roz looked at the bent head with compassion. Olive had never really stood a chance. And who was to blame at the end of the day? Mr Crew? Robert Martin? The police? Poor Gwen even, whose dependence on her daughter had mapped Olive's life. Michael Jackson had said it all: 'She was one of those people you only think about when you want something done and then you remember them with relief because you know they'll do it.' It had never been Amber who set out to please, she thought, only Olive, and as a result she had grown completely dependent herself. With no one to tell her what to do she had taken the line of least resistance.

'You'll be hearing this officially in the next few days but I'm damned if you should have to wait for it. Mr Crew is on bail at the moment, charged with embezzlement of your father's money and conspiracy to defraud. He may also be charged with conspiracy to murder.' There was a long pause before Olive looked up.

The strange awareness was back in her eyes, a look of triumphant confirmation that made the hair prickle on the back of Roz's neck. She thought of Sister Bridget's simple assertion of *her* truth: *You were chosen, Roz, and I wasn't.* And Olive's truth? What was Olive's truth?

'I know already.' Idly Olive removed a pin from the front of her dress. 'Prison grapevine,' she explained. 'Mr Crew hired the Hayes brothers to do over Sergeant Hawksley's restaurant. You were there, and you and the Sergeant got beaten up. I'm sorry about that but I'm not sorry about anything else. I never liked Mr Hayes much. He always ignored me and talked to Amber.' She stuck the pin into the tabletop. Bits of dried clay and wax still clung to the head.

Roz arched an eyebrow at the pin. 'It's superstitious rubbish, Olive.'

'You said it works if you believe in it.'

Roz shrugged. 'I was joking.'

'*The Encyclopaedia Britannica* doesn't joke.' Olive chanted in a sing-song voice: 'Page 96, volume 25, general heading: Occultism.' She clapped her hands excitedly like an over-boisterous child and raised her voice to a shout. ' "*Witchcraft worked in Salem because the persons involved believed in it.*" ' She saw the frown of alarm on Roz's face. 'It's all nonsense,' she said calmly. 'Will Mr Crew be convicted?'

'I don't know. He's claiming that your father gave him the go-ahead, as executor, to invest the money while the searches were made for your nephew, and the bugger is' – she smiled grimly – 'if the property market takes off again, which it probably will, his investments look very healthy.' Of the other charges, only the conspiracy to defraud Hal of the Poacher had any chance of sticking, purely because Stewart Hayes's brother, a far weaker character than Stewart, had collapsed under police questioning. 'He's denying everything, but the police seem fairly optimistic they can pin assault charges on both him and the Hayes boys. I'd give anything to get him for negligence where your case was concerned. Was he one of the people you tried to tell the truth to?'

'No,' said Olive regretfully. 'There was no point.

He'd been Dad's solicitor for years. He'd never have believed Dad had done it.'

Roz started to gather her bits and pieces together. 'Your father didn't kill your mother and sister, Olive. He thought *you* did. Gwen and Amber were alive when he went to work the next morning. As far as he was concerned, your statement was completely true.'

'But he knew I wasn't there.'

Roz shook her head. 'I'll never be able to prove it but I don't suppose he even realized you'd gone. He slept downstairs, remember, and I'll bet a pound to a penny you slipped out quietly to avoid attracting attention to yourself. If you'd only agreed to see him, you'd have sorted it out.' She stood up. 'It's water under the bridge, but you shouldn't have punished him, Olive. He was no more guilty than you are. He loved you. He just wasn't very good at showing it. I suspect his only fault was to take too little notice of the clothes women wore.'

Olive shook her head. 'I don't understand.'

'He told the police your mother owned a nylon overall.'

'Why would he do that?'

Roz sighed. 'I suppose because he didn't want to admit he never looked at her. He wasn't a bad man, Olive. He couldn't help his sexuality any more than you or I can help ours. The tragedy for you all was that none of you could talk about it.' She took the pin from the tabletop and wiped the head clean. 'And

I don't believe for one moment that he would ever have blamed you for what happened. Only himself. That's why he went on living in the house. It was his atonement.'

A large tear rolled down Olive's cheek. 'He always said the game wasn't worth the candle.' She held out her hand for the pin. 'If I'd loved him less I'd have hated him less, and it wouldn't be too late now, would it?'

Twenty

HAL WAS DOZING in the car outside, arms crossed, an old cap pulled over his eyes to block out the sun. He raised his head and surveyed Roz lazily from under the brim as she tugged open the driver's door. 'Well?'

She dumped her briefcase on the back seat and slipped in behind the wheel. 'She shot my version down in flames.' She gunned the engine into life and reversed out of the parking slot.

Hal eyed her thoughtfully. 'So where are we going?'

'To tear strips off Edward,' she told him. 'He's had nothing like the punishment he deserves.'

'Is that wise? I thought he was a psychopath.' Hal pulled the cap over his eyes again and settled down for another snooze. 'Still, I'm sure you know what you're doing.' His faith in Roz was unshakeable. She had more bottle than most of the men he knew.

'I do.' She inserted the tape she had just made into the deck and rewound it. 'But you don't, Sergeant, so cock an ear to this. I'm inclined to think it's you I should be tearing strips off. The wretched child – because let's face it, that's all she really is, even now – was starving, and you promised her a "proper dinner" when she'd finished her statement. No wonder she couldn't confess fast enough. If she'd told you she *hadn't* done it you'd have kept her waiting for her food.' She turned the volume up full blast.

It took several rings of the doorbell before Edward Clarke finally opened the door to them on the burglar chain. He gestured angrily for them to go away. 'You have no business here,' he hissed at Roz. 'I shall call the police if you persist in harassing us.'

Hal moved into his line of sight, smiling pleasantly. 'Detective Sergeant Hawksley, Mr Clarke. Dawlington CID. The Olive Martin case. I'm sure you remember me.'

A look of dejected recognition crossed Edward's face. 'I thought we'd done with all that.'

'I'm afraid not. May we come in?'

The man hesitated briefly and Roz wondered if he was going to call Hal's bluff and demand identification. Apparently not. The ingrained British respect for authority ran deep with him. He rattled the chain and opened the door, his shoulders slumped in weary defeat. 'I knew Olive would talk eventually,' he said. 'She wouldn't be human if she didn't.' He showed them into the sitting room. 'But on my word I knew nothing about the murders. If I'd had any idea what she was like, do you really think I'd have befriended her?'

Roz took the chair she had sat in before and surreptitiously switched on the tape-recorder in her handbag. Hal walked to the window and looked out. Mrs Clarke was sitting on the small patio at the back of the house, her face, vacant of expression, turned towards the sun. 'You and Olive were rather more than friends,' he said without hostility, turning back into the room.

'We didn't harm anyone,' said Mr Clarke, unconsciously echoing Olive. Roz wondered how old he was. Seventy? He looked more, worn out by care of his wife perhaps. The rough wig she had painted on cellophane over his photograph had been a revelation. It was quite true that hair made a man look younger. He squeezed his hands between his knees as if unsure what to do with them. 'Or should I say we did not set out with the intention to harm anyone. What Olive did was incomprehensible to me.'

'But you felt no responsibility for it?'

He stared at the carpet, unable to look at either of them. 'I assumed she had always been unstable,' he said.

'Why?'

'Her sister was. I thought it was a genetic thing.'

'So she behaved oddly before the murders?'

'No,' he admitted. 'As I say, I wouldn't have

pursued' – he paused – 'the – relationship – if I had known the kind of person she was.'

Hal changed tack. 'What exactly was your relationship with Olive's father?'

He clamped his knees tighter about his hands. 'Friendly.'

'How friendly?'

Mr Clarke sighed. 'Does it matter now? It was a long time ago and Robert is dead.' His eyes drifted towards the window.

'It matters,' said Hal brusquely.

'We were very friendly.'

'Did you have a sexual relationship?'

'Briefly.' His hands struggled from between his knees and he buried his face in them. 'It sounds so sordid now, but it really wasn't. You have to understand how lonely I was. God knows it's not her fault, but my wife has never been much in the way of a companion. We married late, no children, and her mind has never been strong. I became her nurse and keeper before we'd been married five years, imprisoned in my own house with someone I could barely communicate with.' He swallowed painfully. 'Robert's friendship was all I had and he, as you obviously know, was homosexual. His marriage was as much a prison as mine, though for different reasons.' He pressed the bridge of his nose with a finger and thumb. 'The sexual nature of the relationship was simply a by-product of our dependence on each other. It mattered a great deal to Robert and very much less to me, though I admit that at the time – a period of three or four months only – I genuinely believed myself to be a homosexual.'

'Then you fell in love with Olive?'

'Yes,' said Mr Clarke simply. 'She was very like her father, of course, intelligent, sensitive, really quite charming when she wanted to be, and extraordinarily sympathetic. She made so few demands, unlike my wife.' He sighed. 'It seems strange to say it, in view of what happened later, but she was a very comfortable person to be with.'

'Did Olive know about your relationship with her father?'

'Not from me. She was very naïve in many respects.'

'And Robert didn't know about you and Olive.'

'No.'

'You were playing with fire, Mr Clarke.'

'I didn't plan it, Sergeant. It happened. All I can say in my defence is that I ceased being' – he sought for the right word – 'intimate with Robert the minute I recognized my feelings for Olive. We did not stop being friends, however. That would have been cruel.'

'Bullshit!' said Hal with calculated anger. 'You didn't want to be found out. My guess is you were shafting both of them at the same time and loving every exciting minute of it. And you have the bloody gall to say you don't feel responsible!'

'Why should I?' Clarke said with a flash of spirit. 'My name was never mentioned by either of them. Do you imagine it wouldn't have been if I had unwittingly precipitated the tragedy?'

Roz smiled contemptuously. 'Did you never wonder why Robert Martin wouldn't speak to you after the murders?'

'I assumed he was too distressed.'

'I think you feel a little more than simple distress when you discover that your lover has seduced your daughter,' she said ironically. 'Of course you precipitated it, Mr Clarke, and you knew it. But, by God, you weren't going to say anything. You'd rather see the entire Martin family destroy itself than prejudice your own position.'

'Was that so unreasonable?' he protested. 'They were free to name me. They didn't. How would it have helped if I had spoken out? Gwen and Amber would still have been dead. Olive would still have gone to prison.' He turned to Hal. 'I regret intensely my involvement with the family but I really can't be held responsible if my connection with them led to tragedy. There was nothing illegal about what I did.'

Hal looked out of the window again. 'Tell us why you moved, Mr Clarke. Was it your decision or your wife's?'

He clamped his hands between his knees again. 'It was a joint decision. Life there became unbearable for both of us. We saw ghosts everywhere. A change of environment seemed the only sensible course.'

'Why were you so keen to keep your forwarding address secret?'

Clarke raised haunted eyes. 'To avoid the past catching up with me. I've lived in constant dread of this.' He looked at Roz. 'It's almost a relief to have it out in the open at last. You probably won't believe that.'

She gave a tight smile. 'The police took a statement from your wife on the day of the murders, saying that she saw Gwen and Amber on the doorstep that morning after you and Robert left for work. But when I came here the other day, she said she had lied about it.'

'I can only repeat what I said to you then,' he answered wearily. 'Dorothy's senile. You can't put any reliance on anything she says. She doesn't even know what day it is most of the time.'

'Was she telling the truth five years ago?'

He nodded. 'In so far as saying they were alive when I left for work, yes, she was. Amber was at the window, watching. I saw her myself. She ducked behind the curtain when I waved at her. I remember thinking how odd that was.' He paused. 'As to whether Dorothy saw Robert leave,' he resumed after a moment, 'I don't know. She said she did and I've always understood that Robert had a cast-iron alibi.'

'Has your wife ever mentioned seeing the bodies, Mr Clarke?' asked Hal casually.

'Good God, no.' He sounded genuinely shocked.

'I just wondered why she saw ghosts. She wasn't particularly friendly with Gwen or Amber, was she? Rather the reverse, I'd have thought, in view of the amount of time you spent at the Martins' house.'

'Everyone in that road saw ghosts,' he said bleakly. 'We all knew what Olive had done to those wretched women. It would have required a very dull imagination not to see ghosts.'

'Can you remember what your wife was wearing the morning of the murders?'

He stared at Hal, surprised by the sudden switch. 'Why do you ask?'

'We've had a report that a woman was seen walking down past the Martins' garage.' The lie rolled glibly off his tongue. 'From the description it was too small for Olive but whoever it was was dressed in what looked like a smart black suit. We'd like to trace her. Could it have been your wife?'

The man's relief was palpable. 'No. She never had a black suit.'

'Was she wearing anything black that morning?'

'No. She wore a floral overall.'

'You're very certain.'

'She always wore it, every morning, to do the housework. She used to get dressed after she'd finished. Except Sundays. She didn't do housework on Sundays.'

Hal nodded. 'The same overall every morning? What happened when it got dirty?'

Clarke frowned, puzzled by the line of questioning. 'She had another one, a plain blue one. But she was definitely wearing the floral one on the day of the murders.'

'Which one was she wearing the day after the murders?'

He licked his lips nervously. 'I can't remember.'

'It was the blue one, wasn't it? And she went on wearing the blue one, I suspect, until you or she bought a spare.'

'I can't remember.'

Hal smiled unpleasantly. 'Does she still have her floral overall, Mr Clarke?'

'No,' he whispered. 'It's a long time since she did any housework.'

'What happened to it?'

'I can't remember. We threw out a lot of things before we moved.'

'How did you find the time to do that?' asked Roz. 'Mr Hayes said you upped and left one morning and a removal company turned up three days later to pack your stuff for you.'

'Perhaps I sorted through everything when it came here,' he said rather wildly. 'I can't remember the precise order of things so long afterwards.'

Hal scratched his jaw. 'Did you know,' he murmured evenly, 'that your wife identified some charred remains of a floral overall, found in the incinerator in the Martins' garden, as being part of the clothing that Gwen was wearing the day she was murdered?'

Colour drained from Clarke's face, leaving it an unhealthy grey. 'No, I didn't.' The words were barely audible.

'And those remains were carefully photographed and carefully stored, ready to be produced at a future date if there was ever any dispute over their ownership. Mr Hayes, I'm sure, will be able to tell us whether it was your wife's overall or Gwen's.'

Clarke raised his hands in helpless surrender. 'She told me she'd thrown it away,' he pleaded, 'because the iron had scorched a hole through the front. I believed her. She often did things like that.'

Hal hardly seemed to hear him but went on in the same unemotional voice. 'I very much hope, Mr Clarke, that we will find a way of proving that you knew all along that it was your wife who killed Gwen and Amber. I should like to see you tried and convicted of allowing an innocent girl to go to prison for a crime you knew she hadn't committed, particularly a girl whom you used and abused so shamelessly.'

They could never prove it, of course, but he drew considerable satisfaction from the fear that set Clarke's face working convulsively.

'How could I know? I wondered' – his voice rose

– 'of course I wondered, but Olive confessed.' His eyes strayed beseechingly to Roz. 'Why did Olive confess?'

'Because she was in deep shock, because she was frightened, because she didn't know what else to do, because her mother was dead, and because she had been brought up to keep secrets. She thought her father would save her, but he didn't, because he thought she had done it. *You* could have saved her, but you didn't, because you were afraid of what people would say. The woman at Wells-Fargo could have saved her, but she didn't, because she didn't want to be involved. Her solicitor could have saved her if he had been a kinder man.' She flicked a glance at Hal. 'The police could have saved her if they'd questioned, just once, the value of confession evidence. But it was six years ago, and six years ago, confessions' – she made a ring with her thumb and forefinger – 'were A-OK. But I don't blame them, Mr Clarke. I blame you. For everything. You played at being a homosexual because you were bored with your wife and then you seduced your lover's daughter to prove you weren't the pervert you thought he was.' She stared at him with disdain. 'And that's how I'm going to portray you in the book that will get Olive out of prison. I really despise people like you.'

'You'll destroy me.'

'Yes.'

'Is that what Olive wants? My destruction?'

'I don't know what Olive wants. I only know what I want, which is to get her released. If it means your destruction, then so be it.'

He sat for some moments in silence, his fingers plucking shakily at the creases in his trousers. Then, as if reaching a sudden decision, he looked at Roz. 'I would have spoken if Olive hadn't confessed. But she did, and I assumed like everyone else that she was telling the truth. Presumably you have no desire to prolong her stay in prison? Her release in advance of your book's publication would improve your sales considerably, wouldn't it?'

'Maybe. What are you suggesting?'

His eyes narrowed. 'If I give you the evidence now that will hasten her release, will you in return promise not to divulge my real name or address in the book? You could refer to me by the name Olive called me, Mr Lewis. Do you agree?'

She smiled faintly. What an unbelievable shit he was. He could never hold her to it, of course, but he didn't seem to realize that. And the police would release his name, anyway, if only as Mrs Clarke's husband. 'I agree. As long as it gets Olive out.'

He stood up, taking some keys out of his pocket, and walked over to an ornate Chinese box on the sideboard. He unlocked it and raised the lid, removing something wrapped in tissue paper and handing it to Hal. 'I found it when we moved,' he said. 'She'd hidden it at the bottom of one of her drawers. I swear

I never knew how she got it, but I've always been afraid that Amber must have taunted her with it. She talks about Amber a lot.' He washed his hands in mimicry of Pontius Pilate. 'She calls her the Devil.'

Hal peeled away the tissue paper and looked at what was revealed. A silver bracelet with a tiny silver-chair charm and a tag on which U.R.N.A.R.N.I.A. was barely discernible through a welter of deep angry scratches.

It was almost Christmas before the scales of justice had tipped enough in Olive's favour to allow her to leave the confines of her prison. There would always be doubters, of course, people who would call her the Sculptress till the day she died. After six years the evidence in support of her story was desperately thin. A silver bracelet where it shouldn't have been. Tiny fragments of a burnt floral overall, identified by a senile woman's bitter husband. And, finally, the painstaking reappraisal of the photographic evidence, using sophisticated computer enhancement, which had revealed a smaller, daintier shoe print in the blood beneath a huge ribbed rubber sole mark left by Olive's trainer.

No one would ever know what really happened that day because the truth was locked inside a brain that no longer functioned, and Edward Clarke could not, or would not, shed any light from statements his wife had made in the past. He maintained his complete ignorance of the whole affair, saying that any qualms he might have had had been put to rest by Olive's confession and that the onus for mistakes must lie with her and with the police. The most probable scenario, and the one generally accepted, was that Amber waited until Edward and Robert had left for work and then invited Mrs Clarke into the house to taunt her with the bracelet and the abortion. What happened then was a matter for guesswork but Roz, at least, believed that Mrs Clarke had set about the murders in cold blood and with a clear mind. There was something very calculating about the way she must have donned gloves to perform her butchery and her careful stepping around the blood to avoid leaving too many traces. But most calculating of all was the clever burning of her blood-stained overall amidst Gwen and Amber's clothes and her cool identification of the pieces afterwards as being the overall worn by Gwen that morning. Roz even wondered sometimes if the intention all along had been to implicate Olive. There was no telling now why Mrs Clarke had drawn attention to herself outside the kitchen window, but Roz couldn't help feeling that, had she not done so, Olive might have had enough presence of mind to phone the police immediately before she ran amok in the kitchen and obliterated the evidence that might have exonerated her.

There were to be no disciplinary charges against the police team involved. The chief constable issued a press release, pointing to the recent tightening of police procedure, particularly in relation to confession evidence, but he stressed that as far as Olive's case was concerned the police had taken all available steps to ensure her rights were fully protected. In the circumstances it had been reasonable to assume that her confession was genuine. He took the opportunity to reiterate forcefully the duty imperative on the public never to disturb evidence at the scene of a crime.

Peter Crew's association with the case, particularly in view of his subsequent mishandling of Robert Martin's estate, had attracted considerable and unwelcome interest. At worst he was accused of deliberately engineering Olive's conviction in order to gain access to unlimited funds, and, at best, of bullying an emotionally disturbed young woman at a time when he had a responsibility to safeguard her interests. He denied both accusations strenuously, arguing that he could not have foreseen Robert Martin's success on the stock exchange nor his early death; and claiming that because Olive's story had been remarkably consistent with the forensic evidence he, in the absence of any denials on her part, had, like the police, accepted it as a true statement of fact. He had advised her to say nothing and could not be held liable for her confession. Meanwhile, he remained at liberty on bail, facing the sort of charges that for most of his clients would have resulted in a remand to prison, bullishly declaring his innocence on all counts.

Roz, when she heard what he was saying, was angry enough to waylay him in the street with a local journalist in tow. 'We could argue about liability for ever, Mr Crew, but just explain this to me. If Olive's statement was as consistent with the forensic evidence as you maintain, then why did she claim there was no mist on the mirror at a time when Gwen and Amber were still alive?' She caught his arm as he tried to walk away. 'Why didn't she mention that the axe was too blunt to cut off Amber's head? Why didn't she say she had struck her four times before resorting to the carving knife? Why didn't she describe her fight with her mother and the stabbing incisions she'd made in her mother's throat before cutting it? Why didn't she mention burning the clothes? In fact, try quoting me one detail from Olive's statement that does accord fully with the forensic evidence.'

He shook her off angrily. 'She said she used the axe and the carving knife,' he snapped.

'Neither of which had her fingerprints on them. The forensic evidence did not support her statement.'

'She had their blood all over her.'

'All over is right, Mr Crew. But where does it say in her statement that she rolled in it?'

He tried to walk away but found the journalist blocking his path. 'Footprints,' he said. 'At the time, there were only her footprints.'

'Yes,' said Roz. 'And on that one piece of evidence, which was at odds with all the rest, you made up your mind she was a psychopath and prepared a defence on the grounds of diminished responsibility. Why did you never brief Graham Deedes on the lifelines her poor father was trying to throw her? Why didn't you question your own judgement when she was pronounced fit to plead guilty? Why the hell didn't you treat her like a human being, Mr Crew, instead of a monster?'

He stared at her with dislike. 'Because, Miss Leigh,' he said, 'she *is* a monster. Worse, she's a clever monster. Doesn't it worry you that this wretched woman you've set up to take Olive's place is the only one who's not mentally fit to fight the accusation? And doesn't it worry you that Olive waited till her father died before she would talk to anyone? Mark my words, *he* was the one she intended to smear with her guilt – because he was easy. He was dead. But you gave her Mrs Clarke instead.' He thrust his face angrily into hers. 'The evidence you've unearthed raises doubts, but no more. Computer-enhanced photography is as open to interpretation as the nature of psychopathy.' He shook his head. 'Olive will get out because of it, of course. The law has become very flabby in the last few years. But I was there when she told her story and, as I made clear to you at the start, Olive Martin is a dangerous woman. She's after her father's money. You've been led by the nose, Miss Leigh.'

'She's not half as dangerous as you, Mr Crew. At least she's never paid to have people's businesses destroyed and their lives threatened. You're a cheap crook.'

Crew shrugged. 'If that appears in print, Miss Leigh, I shall sue you for defamation, and it will cost you considerably more in legal fees than it will cost me. I suggest you remember that.'

The journalist watched him walk away. 'He's doing a Robert Maxwell on you.'

'That's the law for you,' said Roz in disgust. 'It's nothing but a big stick if you know how to use it or you're rich enough to employ someone else to use it for you.'

'You don't think he's right about Olive, do you?'

'Of course not,' said Roz angrily, sensing his doubt. 'But at least you know now what she was up against. This country is mad if it assumes that the presence of a solicitor during an interview will automatically protect a prisoner's rights. They are just as fallible, just as lazy, and just as crooked as the rest of us. It cost the Law Society millions last year to compensate clients for their solicitors' misdeeds.'

*

The book was scheduled to come out within a month of Olive's release. Roz had finished it in record time amidst the peace and seclusion of Bayview, which she bought on impulse when she discovered it was impossible to work above the continuous noise of people enjoying their food in the restaurant downstairs. The Poacher had been relaunched in a whirl of somewhat exaggerated publicity featuring Hal as the heroic underdog fighting the evil of organized crime. His association with the Olive Martin case, particularly his latter efforts to help in securing her release, had only added to the hype. He applauded Roz's decision to buy Bayview. Making love against the back-drop of the ocean was a vast improvement on the metal bars at the Poacher.

And she was safer there.

Hal had discovered within himself a capacity for caring that he hadn't known existed. It went deeper than love, encompassing every emotion from admiration to lust, and, while he would never have described himself as an obsessive man, the stress of worrying about Stewart Hayes, free on bail, slowly became intolerable to him. He was prompted finally to make Hayes a surprise visit at home one day. He found him playing in the garden with his ten-year-old daughter and it was there that he made Hayes an offer Hayes couldn't refuse. A life for a life, a maiming for a maiming, should anything happen to Roz. Hayes recognized such compelling purpose in the dark eyes, perhaps because it's what he would have done himself, that he agreed to an indefinite truce. His love for his daughter, it seemed, was matched only by Hal's love for Roz.

Iris, claiming almost more credit for the book than Roz – 'if it hadn't been for me it would never have been written' – was busy selling it around the world as the latest example of British justice reeling under the body blows of its own inflexibility. A small, rather ironic footnote to the story was that the boy Crew's firm had located in Australia proved not, after all, to be Amber's lost child and the search for him was promptly abandoned. The time limit, set in Robert Martin's will, had run out and his money, swollen by Crew's investments – which were now out of his reach – continued in limbo while Olive sought leave to contest her right to it.

Epilogue

AT 5.30 ON a dark and frosty winter morning the Sculptress walked free from the gates of her prison, two hours earlier than the time announced to the press. She had sought and obtained permission to slip back into society well away from the glare of publicity that had surrounded the release of other celebrated cases of wrongful imprisonment. Roz and Sister Bridget, alerted by telephone, stood outside in the lamplight, stamping their feet and blowing on their hands. They smiled in welcome as the Judas door opened.

Only Hal, sheltering ten yards away in the warmth of the car, saw the look of gloating triumph that swept briefly over Olive's face as she put her arms around the two women and lifted them bodily into the air. He recalled some words that he'd had stencilled on his desk when he was still a policeman. '*Truth lies within a little and certain compass, but error is immense.*'

For no apparent reason, he shivered.